Characters and Plots in the Fiction of Ring Lardner

Also by Robert L. Gale

Characters and Plots in the Fiction of Graham Greene
(McFarland, 2006)

An Edwin Arlington Robinson Encyclopedia
(McFarland, 2006)

Characters and Plots in the Fiction of Ring Lardner

Robert L. Gale

McFarland & Company, Inc., Publishers
Jefferson, North Carolina, and London

Selected words are reprinted with the permission of Scribner, an imprint of Simon & Schuster Adult Publishing Group, from *The Ring Lardner Reader* by Ring Lardner, Jr., edited by Maxwell Geismar. Copyright © 1963 by Charles Scribner's Sons. All rights reserved. Quotations under copyright are from "Absent-Minded Beggar," "Anniversary," "Bob's Birthday," "Claude Diphthong, Student of Crime," "Contract," "Cured!," "A Day with Conrad Greene," "Dinner," "Ex Parte," "Freedom of the Press," "Great Blessings," "Haircut," "High-rollers," "Holycaust," "How Are You?," "Hurry Kane," "I Can't Breathe," "The Ides of June," "'In Conference,'" "Insomnia," "The Jade Necklace," "Liberty Hall," "Lose with a Smile," "The Love Nest," "Mamma," "Man Not Overboard," "Mr. Frisbie," "The Maysville Minstrel," "Meet Me in St. Louie," "Mr. and Mrs. Fixit," "Nora," "Now and Then," "Old Folks' Christmas," "One Hit, One Error, One Left," "Pity Is Akin —," "Poodle," "Reunion," "Rhythm," "Second-Act Curtain," "The Spinning Wheel," "Stop Me — If You've Heard This One," "Sun Cured," "Take a Walk," "That Old Sweetheart of Mine," "There Are Smiles," "Travelogue," "The Venomous Viper of the Volga," "Wedding Day," "What of It?," "When the Moon Comes Over the Mountain," "Who Dealt?," "Widow," "Women," "Words and Music," "Zone of Quiet."

LIBRARY OF CONGRESS CATALOGUING-IN-PUBLICATION DATA

Gale, Robert L., 1919–
Characters and plots in the fiction of
Ring Lardner / Robert L. Gale.
p. cm.
Includes bibliographical references and index.

ISBN 978-0-7864-3688-0
softcover : 50# alkaline paper ∞

1. Lardner, Ring, 1885–1933 — Encyclopedias. 2. Lardner, Ring, 1885–1933 — Characters — Encyclopedias. 3. Lardner, Ring, 1885–1933 — Stories, plots, etc. — Encyclopedias. 4. Baseball stories, American — Encyclopedias. I. Title.
PS3523.A7Z67 2009 813'.52 — dc22 2008038142

British Library cataloguing data are available

Front cover by TG Design

Manufactured in the United States of America

McFarland & Company, Inc., Publishers
Box 611, Jefferson, North Carolina 28640
www.mcfarlandpub.com

Remembering my beloved Maureen
and now for our family

Acknowledgments

Grateful acknowledgment is made as follows:

To Ariane de Pree, of Stanford University Press, for permission to quote from *The Annotated Baseball Stories of Ring Lardner, 1914–1919* (1995).

To James E. Elfers, for permission to quote from *The Tour to End All Tours* (2003).

To Susan Lardner, gracious spokesperson for the Lardner family, for permission to quote from her grandfather Ring Lardner's copyrighted fiction.

To Roger Lathbury, editor of Orchises Press, for permission to quote from *Letters of Ring Lardner* (1995).

To Jeff Silverman, for permission to quote from his introduction to *Lardner on War* (2003).

To Simon & Schuster, Inc., for permission to quote from 55 copyrighted stories.

Table of Contents

List of Abbreviations

After the title and first-publication data of each of Lardner's 96 reprinted short stories is included an acronym to indicate important books containing a reprint or reprints of it:

ABS	*Annotated Baseball Stories of Ring Lardner*
BT	*The Big Town*
GT	*Gullible's Travels*
HTW	*How to Write Short Stories*
LN	*The Love Nest*
LOB	*Lardner on Baseball*
LOW	*Lardner on War*
LWS	*Lose with a Smile*
OYH	*Own Your Own Home*
PRL	*The Portable Ring Lardner*
RAB	*Ring Around the Bases*
RD	*The Real Dope*
RLR	*The Ring Lardner Reader*
RU	*Round Up*
SC	*Some Champions*
TER	*Treat 'Em Rough*
WOI	*What of It?*
YI	*The Young Immigrunts*
YKM	*You Know Me Al*

Preface

Dear Reader: Do be persuaded that Ringgold Wilber Lardner was a genius. Do agree that Ring Lardner was a successful author despite parlous odds. And do be sympathetic toward Ring. He was brought up comfortably by indulgent parents, but they then fell on hard times and needed his help. He was curiously educated, even ill-educated by most standards, whether politically correct or not. He flailed through tedious jobs until he found his groove. He worked hard at the writing game, scribbling and typing, meeting deadlines, traveling, observing, and especially listening. His pay was minimal in the years between the Spanish American War and World War I. When he entered into an old-fashioned marriage, he supported a pampered, rest-at-home, conservative, faithfully adored wife and four loved and loving sons. Ring made, delighted, and treasured innumerable friends. He was a Roaring Twenties product, exemplar, and victim. His engaging, self-abandoned, self-destructive roar was far too soon muffled by a deadly combination of alcoholism, tuberculosis, and careless indifference. Through it all, he made his readers laugh. And like — Oh, who was that rascal?— the fellow that also used a gift of laughter, since he too sensed that the world is increasingly mad.

To picture the living Ring, let me quote Grant Overton (1887–1930), who interviewed our subject and published the following word portrait:

> He stands high [at 6'2"] but can generally enter elevators without stooping and he has a handsome brown skin with red tones in it. That skin does its best to make him a handsome looker. He has black, heavy, extra-size eyebrows and this shiny black straight hair in an up-to-date haircut, and his head is ovoid. But the truly monumental thing about him is his repose. He has as much repose as a piece of granite. The strong modeling of his face suggests granite just as the skin makes you think of satin. He speaks in a low tone. He is unhurried. Practically ... the only quiet person in New York, Ring Lardner is the only noticeable and audible person in New York. The city ought to hire him to come to town oftener [Overton, 44–45].

This reference book is intended to acquaint and reacquaint readers new and old with the brilliance of Lardner's short stories. Lardner was the first and remains the best of a now-chronic type of baseball writer — accurate, colloquial, funny. The characters, real and fictional, in, and plots of, some 35 stories devoted to baseball are handled here. But Lardner was more versatile than many readers think. His 92 non-baseball stories are sometimes hard to categorize; in addition, some categories overlap. But here's a try. A scary number of characters in upwards of 30 stories are caught in tragi-comic, or starkly tragic, domestic situations, often bad marriages, odd family situations, and much other trouble. A dozen or so stories involve people in boxing, football, gambling, and golf. A dozen more, all perennially fresh, are devoted to writers and theatrical and musically inclined performers. War and travel stories number nine each. A few stories are in unique classes; for example "I Can't Breathe,"

"Haircut," and "There Are Smiles." Some 34 Lardner stories have never been reprinted in book form. This is surprising, since they have continuing appeal, notably "The Busher Abroad," "How Are You?," "The Last Night," and "Oh, You Bonehead!"

I hope that when readers find this book crammed with both data and fun, they will rush to reread, or read for the first time, Lardner's stories, many of which not only still inspire impulsive, out-loud laughter but also cast light on his troubled era — a time like ours — oh so horribly in need of both sober information and the saving grace of humor. Ring Lardner should be as much an eponym as his friend F. Scott Fitzgerald* still is. Simultaneously, the modernity of Lardner's uncounted fictive situations and often down-and-sleezy lingo comes through right here, despite my inevitable paucity of quotations. Lardner grew big in the nineteenth century, planted his footprint in the twentieth, and its vibrations echo into our twenty-first.

Without access to the incredibly thorough *Ring W. Lardner: A Descriptive Bibliography* (1976) by Matthew J. Bruccoli and Richard Layman, I would have started this reference book only to stumble, fall, and stop. I am also grateful to Donald Elder's *Ring Lardner: A Biography* (1956), to Ring Lardner Jr.'s *The Lardners: My Family Remembered* (1976), and to Jonathan Yardley's *Ring: A Biography of Ring Lardner* (1977). Walton R. Patrick's *Ring Lardner* (1963) remains usefully insightful. Valuable has been the editorial and annotative work of Clifford M. Caruthers' *Ring Around Max: The Correspondence of Ring Lardner & Max Perkins* (1973) and Caruthers' *Letters of Ring Lardner* (1995). Donald Phelps's "Shut Up, He Explained" is the most insightful brief treatment of Lardner's fiction that I've encountered. Robert J. Higgs's *Laurel & Thorn: The Athlete in American Literature* offers the best treatment of Lardner's athletes. Douglas Robinson's puzzler, *Ring Lardner and the Other* (1992), seems valuable mainly for encouraging Lardnerites (and Lardner followers) to think for themselves. I include too many dates but hope they prove useful to some readers; most are in parentheses, to encourage skimmers. Note that asterisks signal cross-referencing — from Frank Parker Abbot Sr.* to Florenz Ziegfeld.*

I thank several correspondents for various kindnesses. They include Matthew J. Bruccoli, Clifford M. Caruthers, James E. Elfers, Samuel J. Rogal, and Jeff Silverman. Academic colleagues, computer experts, librarians, and bibliophiles are often unheralded coworkers for the likes of me. I should name more but list the following here: H. David Brumble, Patricia Duff, Frank N. Kremm, and Thomas M. Twiss (all of the University of Pittsburgh), Alicia Carberry, Taira Marecic, Don Wentworth, and Sylvia J. Wilson (all of the Carnegie Public Library, Pittsburgh), Ronald Emerick (Indiana University of Pennsylvania) and Janet McCann (Texas A&M University), and Jay Dantry and John Schulman (ingenious bookfinders). Last and always, I give my love to my family — Maureen, John, Jim, Christine, Diana, Caroline, Stephanie, Bill, Lisette, Marjie, and Helen.

Chronology

1885	Ringgold Wilmer Lardner born March 6, in Niles, Michigan, to Henry Lardner Sr.* (1839–1914) and Lena Phillips Lardner* (1843–1918).
1890	Is taught at home by mother.
1897–1901	Attends high school in Niles, plays football, sings in quartet, writes class poem, graduates at 16.
1901	Becomes office boy in Chicago for McCormick Harvester Company, then for real-estate firm; home again, is freight handler for Michigan Central Railroad.
1902	At father's urging, attends Chicago's Armour Institute (now Illinois Institute of Technology) in January, with brother Rex Lardner*; both flunk out when spring term ends.
1903	Is idle in Niles.
1904–1905	Is employed by Niles Gas Company as bookkeeper, bill collector, meter-reader; joins Niles minstrels, writes music and some lyrics in *Zanzibar*, musical comedy, and acts therein.
1905–1907	Is reporter for South Bend, Indiana, *Times* (fall 1905 to November 1907); covers Central League baseball (1906–1907).
1907–1908	Is sports writer, with his first byline as "R. W. Lardner," for Chicago *Inter-Ocean* (February–November).
1908	Is baseball reporter (as "James Clarkson") for Chicago *Examiner* (February–November), traveling with Chicago White Sox and covering their games.
1909–1910	Is baseball reporter for Chicago *Tribune* (to December 1910).
1910–1911	Works at St. Louis *Sporting News* as editor and feature writer (December–February).
1911	Covers Boston Braves baseball team for Boston *American* (February–October); marries Ellis Abbott (June 28).
1911–1912	Works at copy desk for Chicago *American* (November-February).
1912	Son John Abbott Lardner* born May 4.
1912–1913	Lardner is baseball correspondent for Chicago *Examiner* (February 1912–May 1913).

1913–1919	Writes "In the Wake of the News" column for Chicago *Tribune* (June 3, 1913 to June 20, 1919).
1914	Publishes first Jack Keefe baseball story, in *Saturday Evening Post*, March 7. Son James Phillips Lardner* born May 18.
1915	Lardner publishes first story of Fred A. Gross, Chicago detective, in *Red Book*, January. Son Ringgold Wilber Lardner Jr.* born August 19.
1916	Publishes first Joe Gullible story, in *Saturday Evening Post*, February 19. *You Know Me Al.*
1917	Is war correspondent in France for *Collier's*, August. *Gullible's Travels.*
1918	*Treat 'Em Rough.*
1919	Son David Lardner* born March 11. *Own Your Own Home*; *The Real Dope.*
1919–1927	Writes "Ring Lardner's Weekly Letter" for Bell Syndicate.
1920	*The Young Immigrunts.*
1921	*The Big Town.*
1922–1925	Provides continuity for *You Know Me Al* comic strip.
1924	*How to Write Short Stories [With Samples].*
1926	Begins to suffer from tuberculosis. *The Love Nest and Other Stories.*
1929	*Round Up.*
1930–1933	Remains productive in declining health.
1932	*Lose with a Smile.*
1933	Dies of heart attack, East Hampton, Long Island, New York, September 25.
1963	Is posthumously granted the J. G. Taylor Spink Award for excellence in baseball writing.
1965	Ring Lardner Middle School is built, dedicated, and opened in Niles, Michigan.
1988	Lardner is depicted by John Sayles in the movie *Eight Men Out*, about the 1919 "Black Sox" World Series scandal.

THE ENCYCLOPEDIA

ABBOTT, DOROTHY *see* **KITCHELL, DOROTHY ABBOTT**

ABBOTT, ELLIS *see* **LARDNER, ELLIS ABBOTT**

ABBOTT, FLORENCE *see* **TORRENCE, FLORENCE**

ABBOTT, FRANK ("Haircut"). He drove Whitey in his flivver to John Scott's home and later drove Doc Ralph Stair there to examine Jim Kendall's body.

The name of Lardner's father-in-law was Frank Parker Abbott Sr.*; that of his brother-in-law, Frank Abbott Jr.*

ABBOTT, FRANK PARKER (1858–1912). Lardner's father-in-law. He was the husband of Jeannette Hascall Abbott.* Their children were Ruby Abbott Hendry,* Dorothy Abbott Kitchell,* Ellis Abbott Lardner,* Florence Abbott Torrence,* Frank Abbott, Jr.,* John Abbott Kitchell, Jane Abbott,* and William C. Abbott.* The Abbotts lived in their big, comfortable house in Goshen, Indiana. Abbott was a successful lumber merchant, specializing in the wholesale manufacturing of walnut, and was later a bank president. The family owned a cottage at Lake Wawasee, 15 miles southeast of Goshen. After Ellis and Lardner planned to marry, Lardner wrote Abbott a formal letter (July 5, [1910]) requesting permission. Abbott's ignoring the letter was embarrassing. He didn't want any of his daughters to marry and leave the nest; he also disliked Lardner's association with professional sports figures. Lardner was finally entertained by the family and met Abbott (October 25, 1910), by which time the engagement and wedding plans had been made public. Abbott's wedding present to the Lardners was $300. When Abbott died, his family inherited from his large life insurance policy. Ellis's modest share enabled the Lardners to build a house in Riverside, a suburb west of Chicago. Lardner's *Own Your Own Home* reflects aspects of this windfall. (Sources: Caruthers [1973], 1; Elder, 77–78; Lardner, Jr., 27–28, 56, 86; Caruthers [1995], 54, 59–61, 123; Yardley, 68, 104–106, 112–113, 129)

ABBOTT, JANE *see* **KITCHELL, JANE ABBOTT**

ABBOTT, JANE (*The Big Town*). She is a chorus girl and a friend of Katie's. She praises Jimmy Ralson to Katie.

Lardner derived Jane Abbott's name from the maiden name of his sister-in-law Jane Abbott Kitchell.*

ABBOTT, JEANNETTE HASCALL (1853–1926). Lardner's mother-in-law. She was the wife of Frank Parker Abbott.* Their three sons and five daughters, in order of birth, were Ruby Abbott Hendry,* Dorothy Abbott Kitchell,* Ellis Abbott Lardner,* Florence Abbott Torrence,* Frank Abbott, Jr.,* John Abbott Kitchell,* Jane Abbott,* and William C. Abbott.* Her husband's resistance to Lardner's desire to marry Ellis embarrassed her mother, who invited Lardner to visit and meet the family and promoted his suit. After the wedding, Lardner wrote a sweet letter (July 4 [1911]) to Mrs. Abbott, whom he began addressing as "Dear Mother II." In it he expressed love and gratitude for his "everlasting happiness." Ring Lardner Jr. describes Jeannette Abbott as "a cultured woman" of Presbyterian faith, who enjoyed her family with "serenity," was partially deaf from young womanhood, and wrote poetry. (Sources: Lardner, Jr., 25 28, 29; Caruthers [1995], 58, 59, 95; Yardley, 104–105)

ABBOTT, JOHNNY ("Hurry Kane"). He is on the St. Louis baseball team. He attended Cornell University for two years. He rooms with Hurry Kane on the road, kids him, helps him, and marries Helen Kerslake.

**Throughout the text an asterisk denotes an entry in the encyclopedia.*

ABBOTT, WILLIAM C. Lardner's brother-in-law. A letter survives (November 29 [1920]) which Lardner wrote William when he was a senior at the University of Michigan. Lardner amiably declines an invitation to give a speech there, saying "if you'd ever heard me make one, you wouldn't have asked me." (Source: Caruthers [1995], 128)

ABRAMS ("Meet me in St. Louie"). He was Irving Berlin's manager in New York. Danny Warner and Casey Stengel* visited him to discuss Danny's baseball song. Abrams and Stengel needled each other.

"ABSENT-MINDED BEGGAR" (*Cosmopolitan*, March 1929). (Characters: Beth Beasley, J. L. Beasley, Wallie Blair, H. N. Comerford, Irene Comerford, Miss Davenport, De Setto, Sam Drake, Edward, Francis Elliott, Butch Harper, Fred Howard, Mrs. Howard, Knowles, Charlotte Knowles, John Knowles, Mrs. Knowles, J. M. McInerney, Maynard, Murray, Nora, Ellen Parrish, Mrs. Prendergast, Doctor Stetson, Deems Taylor, Tuttle.)

Charlotte Knowles, nine, is surprised when her widowed mother tells her friend Mrs. Prendergast that Charlotte's brother John Knowles, 12, is a wool-gatherer just like their father. Could gathering wool enable him to leave his family fairly well provided for? And how can John gather any wool? He goes to school, does well in English, Greek, and Latin, dislikes mathematics, history, and physics, is absent-minded at recitation, passes examinations only by memorizing textbooks just in time, and writes poetry in his room at home. For his high-school commencement he absent-mindedly appears in dinner shirt, pants, brown coat. Beth Beasley, who loves the unresponsive fellow, tells him to go home for a black coat. Nora the maid finds his black coat, but he puts the brown one back on, strays off mumbling poetry, realizes it's late, and returns home to await his mother and sister. They return from the event, upset. Charlotte calls him crazy. Mrs. Knowles says she doesn't know what to do with him. John asks her to describe what occurred. Charlotte says Beth is "wild about you" and probably retrieved his diploma to bring it to him. John reads part of a libretto he's composing for a grand opera about De Setto and a "Getto" princess, plans to seek a composer in New York, but his mother persuades him to accede to his father's wish, attend college first, and maybe take literature courses and work on his libretto.

September: Mrs. Knowles is ill. Charlotte has a tennis date with Wallie Blair. Alone, John, aiming for "his state university, Michigan," boards the west-bound train, is advised to catch the east one at Niles, does, but leaves his luggage heading for Chicago. He gets to Ann Arbor, scrapes through freshman year, manages Christmas and spring break at home somehow, and remains careless about clothes. June: John hastens home, to avoid seeing a next-door co-ed who, among other girls, was "strong on him." July: John reads about a composer "we will call Deems Taylor" planning to hide in Europe to write a libretto. John gets his mother to let him go abroad. He goes to New York, has trouble obtaining a passport, is driven by a surly, drunk taximan to one of Cunard's piers, and boards the wrong ship — bound not for France but Naples. He seeks Taylor in Paris but learns Taylor was in Naples.

John remains in Paris four years. He drinks wine, writes French libretti, sees two of them flop at the Opéra Comique, and "grew better looking and more absent-minded every day." His mother writes that her diminished investments prevent his remaining abroad. Returning home somehow, he is greeted by busy Charlotte and adoring Beth. He "feel[s] silly." Charlotte has spent much of "bedridden" Mrs. Knowles's money on cars, clothes, entertainment for boyfriends, mainly Wallie. Beth drives John and Charlotte home. Beth's father is J. L. Beasley, who recently formed an opulent brokerage firm with newly arrived H. N. Comerford, whose daughter is Irene. Charlotte tells John he'd love to meet Irene, whereupon Beth warns him that Irene is engaged to Sam Drake, whom Beth calls "a regular Ed Wynn." After John has visited with his mother upstairs, Beth, waiting patiently, corrals him, asks him about French girls, parries questions about Taylor's opera, wonders what John will do next, and when he says family finances are low tells him he can work in Daddy's brokerage and attract female customers with his good looks. Beth leaves. Charlotte, learning of Beth's plan for John: John should take the job, earn money for their mother's care; Charlotte got some gin from Butch Harper for a party here; Irene and Sam may attend it; John must laugh at Sam's jokes, also take any phone call from Wallie. Alone, John absent-mindedly lights two cigarettes. Irene and Sam enter. While Sam jokes about two-cigarette "fiend[s]," John is staring at Irene's eyes. His empty responses inspire the other two to hint at his absent-mindedness. Irene takes Wallie's phone message to Charlotte that he'll be late. John doesn't hear this. Sam says that since John is just back from "gay Paree" he hasn't heard recent "parlor jokes" and starts one about "two colored caddies at Palm Beach." John laughs before the punch line, stares at Irene, starts reciting poetic lines about being sad "Till you are mine, my loved one, sweetheart, wife." Questioned by Irene, he says the lines, which he just composed, will be part of his libretto. Sam doubts all this and says Irene is his "inspiration," not John's. John: Does Irene visit her father's office often? Sam: When she's broke. John departs upstairs before his guests leave. Charlotte returns, irate after two flat tires, and asks about Wallie, who John reports didn't call. Wallie arrives, and John "saves Irene" by admitting Wallie must have spoken to her. He "pacifies" Charlotte by agreeing to accept any offer from Beasley.

Beasley hires John next day for $200 a week and assigns him a private office, which Beth immediately makes "a second home." On his fourth day there, Beth: Like me for getting you this job? John: I liked you before that but must make "good here" before thinking "of— of other things." Beth: I'll be patient.

Thursday, John's fifth day: Comerford goes to Chicago, Beasley goes fishing, their chief clerk Fred Howard breaks a leg, can't work. John must take market orders while dictating the daily market report to the office's pretty airhead secretary Miss Davenport. Wallie phones to tell John to come to the Maynard lake cottage Saturday. J. M. McInerny orders shares in the Murray Corporation. Irene phones for John to mail her a telegram from Daddy care of the Parrish lake cottage. Francis Elliott orders Linseed shares — John thinks it was preferred, not common. John dictates jibberish about investing in Ice, General Motors, U.S. Steel, rails, automobiles.

Friday: Beasley returns, fortunately doesn't read yesterday's market report. Elliott enters, reminds John that he ordered Linseed common, which is down; John says he erroneously made it preferred, which is up. Mustached Elliott nearly kisses John, promises not to reveal John's error, will sell off and tip John $100.

Saturday: John drives to the lake, remembers the names Maynard and Parrish but mistakenly seeks Wallie at the Parrishes. Ellen (Mrs. Charles) Parrish calls Irene, who is irate at John's seeming "freshness," but quickly admires his candid explanation, orders him to dump plans regarding Wallie. John, lacking evening clothes, firmly rejects her invitation to a post-dinner party with her, Mrs. Parrish, and Sam. Countering, Irene tells him to continue writing his libretto, which she'll be happy to say she inspired, and they'll be dining right here. He proceeds to his assigned room, uniquely in love and unable "to resist Irene's voice and eyes." Summoned to dinner, he encounters pleasant Mrs. Parrish, well-dressed Irene, and surly, cocktail-guzzling Sam. Sam: John is uninvited. Irene: I want him to remain. John: You can't want both Sam and me; I should go see Wallie. Irene: Stay; I won't go to the party with drunk Sam. Mrs. Parrish: I must attend the party at the oft-ignored Tuttles. Sam: Irene must prefer John, this snake, gutter-snipe. John: Sam, if we meet sans women, I'll flatten you. John, alone now with Irene: I love you. Irene: Beth says she's engaged to you. John: I know better, must go "square" things with Wallie, will be back soon.

John finds Wallie at the Maynard cottage, nearby. On the way back, John sits absent-mindedly on a strange dock, with moonlight striking the lake, and works a new scene into his libretto.

Next morning, John to Irene, cool at breakfast: I was working on my libretto; I'm not engaged to Beth; you're not engaged to Sam; we should get engaged. Irene: You're engaged to your libretto. John: I'll destroy it. Irene: No, I'll sit watching whenever you write. John: I'll be distracted but will try; I may lose my job with Beasley. Irene: My Daddy has more stock than he does.

"Absent-minded Beggar" is an inept story, full of weaknesses beginning with the title. Lardner salts it with references to contemporary persons of note, including Deems Taylor* and Ed Wynn (1886–1966), American comedian, lyricist, and composer. Sam Drake downgrades John Knowles's poetry by likening it to that of "Eddie Guest," Edward Guest (1881–1959) being a syndicated newspaper poet whose offerings were saccharine but popular. Knowles warns Clark that if they fight, Clark will end up resembling "the late Tom Heeney." Not truly "late," Tom Heeney (1898–1984) was a New Zealand–born boxer, who after fighting elsewhere began boxing in the United States (1927), won several matches, was knocked out by Gene Tunney (1928), went professionally downhill (by 1933), but became an American citizen and was in the navy during World War II. (Source: Carpenter, 74)

ADA ("Mr. and Mrs. Fix-It"). She is the narrator's tolerant wife. Both suffer from well-meaning meddlers' unwelcome intrusions.

ADAMS, MR. ("Ball-A-Hole"). He is mentioned as having played golf a few times with Mr. Perkins.

ADAMS, MRS. ANTHONY ("Ex Parte"). She was Mildred Dwan's great-grandmother. Mildred displays a quilt Mrs. Adams made in 1859, at Lowell, Massachusetts.

ADAMS, WALLIE ("Champion"). He is Midge Kelly's manager in New York. He feeds *News* reporter Joe Morgan attractive lies about Midge. To make sure he is understood, he repeatedly says, "Get what I mean?"

AGNEW ("Take a Walk"). He is a major-league third baseman playing for the city in which the narrator and Bleat, both umpires, occasionally work. Agnew makes excuses for misplays, argues with Bleat's decisions, spikes his feet, and insults him. Bleat finally slugs him, after which Bleat is banned from future work.

AINSLEE ("A One-Man Team"). He is one of Coach Belden's football players. During the game against Doane, Belden sends him in to substitute for Hayes and signal a new strategy. Ainslee arrives too late to help.

AL (*You Know Me Al*, etc.) *see* **BLANCHARD, AL**

ALCOCK ("A New Busher Breaks In"). Jack Keefe reports that in a game with Detroit, Alcock of the White Sox bunted well against pitcher Joe Hill.

John Forbes Alcock (1885–1973) played for the Chicago White Sox (1914). (Sources: *Baseball Encyclopedia*, 727; Hilton, 136)

ALCOCK, JOHNNY (*The Real Dope*). He is a member of Keefe's army company in France. When Keefe receives a phony letter from General Pershing, Alcock, who may have written it, kids Keefe into believing that he can join Pershing's staff in Paris. Alcock gets even with Keefe for an April Fool prank by making Jack think fellow-soldier George Shaffer is a German spy and by encouraging Jack to report him. Alcock helps those encouraging Keefe to write to the fictitious Miss Marie Antoinette in Cologne. Alcock and Jack Brady sell Simple Simon fake German souvenirs and persuade him to seek more in "Nobody's Land." Keefe crawls in darkness to look for the missing Simon, encounters Alcock, thinks he is a German, and is hurt beating him up.

George W. Hilton believes that Lardner named Johnny Alcock after John J. Alcock (1890–1944), whom Lardner knew when both were Chicago *Tribune* sports reporters. The two probably continued their friendship when Alcock was the New York *Daily News* sports editor (1919–1936). (Source: Hilton, 28)

ALCOHOLISM AND LARDNER Numberless people resort to alcohol in an attempt, often futile, to find relief from their problems or for stimulation. Many writers do so for these reasons and allegedly for inspiration. Tom Dardis lists five American Nobel laureates in literature as alcoholics — William Faulkner, Ernest Hemingway, Sinclair Lewis, Eugene O'Neill, and John Steinbeck — along with 23 other American writers, including Ring Lardner and his close friends F. Scott Fitzgerald* and Dorothy Parker.* Dardis says "alcoholism is the American writer's disease."

Ringgold Wilber Lardner Jr.* often touches on his father's alcoholism, most cogently when applying to it his belief that alcoholism, which he calls a disease, "is more likely to be the cause of depression than the result of it," and when he adds that alcoholism caused "Ring's ... loss of self-respect." He notes that two of his father's brothers, William Lardner* and Henry Lardner, Jr.,* "had drinking problems." It is significant that John Abbott Lardner,* one of Lardner's four sons, wrote seven chapters of a book to be entitled *Drinking in America*, a short time before his death.

Jonathan Yardley discusses Lardner's alcoholism, often building on information from Lardner Jr. Lardner began drinking in Niles, Michigan, his home town, no later than when he was 16, could successfully fib to an obliging bartender that he was "ein und zwanzig Jahre alt," and soon preferred bourbon to twenty-cent beer. When Lardner was hired by the Chicago *American* (1908) to write sports headlines fast, he found relief from boredom in South Side saloons. When he received a letter (1910) from Ellis Abbott, to whom he was engaged, stating her uncertainty about their projected marriage, Lardner dropped off the wagon with a drinking buddy; his resistance was hardly strengthened when naive Ellis wrote him to keep his promise of abstaining or not, because doing as he wished would do no harm. When he especially disliking work on the St. Louis *Sporting News* (1911), he again wrote about drinking to Ellis, who became less sympathetic; he averred that when they were married he'd be too happy ever to drink. Traveling with the Boston *American*, he wrote her about his inability to be practical and confident concerning money while on the wagon, which may be regarded as his unconscious confession of alcohol dependence (1911). Recovering from a boozing party with some singing Chicago Cubs buddies, he wrote of their curing his thirst forever. On his voyage to France, during his time there, and while returning home, Lardner drank excessively (1917) and wrote about it in *My Four Weeks in France* (1918). He morosely lamented the ratification of the Eighteenth Amendment by writing the music and lyrics of "Prohibition Blues" (April 1919); he memorialized its legal enforcement by Ohio (as of July 1) by boozing with Ohio friends (June 30, 1919), by writing "Toledo Blues," and by playing hangover golf next morning. On his voyage home after a European vacation with Ellis, Lardner was in what he labeled a drinking fog and, feeling physically endangered, vowed to quit (November 11, 1924). Intermittent, embarrassing, and personality-twisting failures followed. He wrote fellow-boozer Fitzgerald (December 1927) that he was off liquor since August. Ring Lardner Jr. states that his father's and Fitzgerald's "joint dependence on alcohol was ... a factor" reinforcing their friendship; but then, perhaps with familial pride, he asserts that his father could drink more and stay in shape better than Fitzgerald. Lardner celebrated his successful play *June Moon* (written with George S. Kaufman*) by going on a three-month bender, according to another letter to Fitzgerald (February 1930). During a stay ordered by his physician in a sanatorium in Tucson, Arizona (March–April 1931), Lardner sneaked out, found a Chicago friend in Phoenix, and got drunk again. Without a doubt, alcoholism, especially when combined with tuberculosis, hastened Lardner's early death.

Martin Seymour-Smith curtly, and with 50 percent accuracy, diagnoses Lardner: "Unfortunately he spent much of his last decade in states of alternating alcoholism (of a type specific to TV sufferers) and suicidal depression." Douglas Robinson opines that Lardner "dealt extensively with his alcoholism in his stories, both incidentally, in the inclination of almost every Lardner character to cope ... by taking a drink, and explicitly, in stories like 'Sun Cured' ... and 'Cured!'...: as befits Lardner's doubly bound alcoholic ascesis, the former denies and the latter asserts the possibility of a cure." Robinson also seeks to define the psychological causes of Lardner's affliction by dragging in both his mother and his wife. (Sources: Dardis, 3; Elder, 224–229; Lardner, Jr., 21, 160, 163, 164, 194, 195, 350; Robinson, 88 and *passim*; Seymour-Smith, 203; Yardley, 58, 83–84, 97–99, 110, 118, 122, 201, 208–211, 281–284, 319, 339, 349)

ALEXANDER In "Sick 'Em," he pitched well for the Philadelphia Phillies, had arm trouble for a while, recovered, and tried again. In "Back to Baltimore," when pitching for Philadelphia, Alexander beans William Baker, Jr., batting ineptly for the Boston Braves. Alexander is mentioned in "The Hold-Out."

Grover Cleveland Alexander (1887–1950) pitched for the Phillies (1911–1917), the Cubs (1918–1925), the Cubs and the Cardinals (1926), the Cardinals (1927–1929), and the Phillies again (1930). He was elected to the Baseball Fame of Fame (1938). George W. Hilton notes that publicizing Alexander's alcoholism rendered his post-baseball career "little short of tragic." (Sources: *Baseball Encyclopedia*, 1788; Hilton, 367)

ALEXIS, GREEK ("Greek Tragedy"). He is a wrestler. He lets Big Bill Buell win a match in the mistaken hope that Buell will then defeat Legs Lamont and share the purse with him.

ALIBI IKE ("Alibi Ike") *see* **FARRELL, FRANK X.**

"ALIBI IKE" (*Saturday Evening Post*, July 31, 1915; ABS, HTW, LOB, PRL, RAB, RLR, RU). Characters: Red Ames, Big Rube Benton, Carey, Diamond Joe, Dolly, Doyle, Frank X. Farrell, Kid Gleason, Hayes, Joe, Kane, McDonald, Jack Mack, Big Rube Marquard, Meyers, Sallee, Sam, Smitty.)

I. Frank X. Farrell earns a position on the baseball team the semi-literate narrator plays for, fields and bats excellently, defeats everyone at billiards, but apologizes so stupidly for not doing better that he is dubbed Alibi Ike. He replaces Kane.

II. During a Cincinnati rainout, Smitty, Carey, and others organize a poker game. Ike plays, apologetically discards a full house and then four tens, speaks about his "old man" in Yuma, Idaho, and his uncle in various places, wins $65, but departs without it.

III. Against Big Rube Marquard's pitching in New York, Ike hits foul homers, strikes out, and alibis that the scoreboard said 3–1. Caught trying to steal second, he alibis about the batter Smitty's wrong sign. Ordered to bunt, he hits a homer, and alibis that he swung to miss and planned to bunt thereafter. Cap fines him $100 but relents when Ike hits superbly later. In Philadelphia, he gives the narrator a different alibi about that homer against Marquard.

IV. During five games in St. Louis, Ike meets Dolly, Cap's pretty wife's prettier sister, from "St. Joe." He hits and fields magnificently. She mistakes his apologies for modesty. At a three-week home "serious," Ike gets daily letters from Dolly but pretends they're from a friend of his from college, then adds he didn't really attend. His friend plays baseball for the Texas league in Fort Wayne. Confused talk follows. The girlish handwriting is owing to his friend's sister's having written for him, since an accident severed the friend's hand. His pals can't tempt him to date another girl and go to Joe's spaghetti joint.

V. The narrator and Carey pull a dreadful "boner" on Ike. In Boston they see he's given Dolly a ring and plans to take her to "the theayter." He fibs until they force him to confess about Dolly, whom he then fibs he kind of felt sorry for. Overhearing, Dolly returns the ring, with a note. She and Cap's wife leave town.

VI. Disconsolate, Ike whiffs in Brooklyn and fails to alibi. The team falls in four weeks from first to fifth. In Pittsburgh, Cap demands action; so "I and Carey" write Dolly a careful letter explaining Ike's modesty and his awareness of her beauty. Cap's wife writes that Dolly will give Ike another chance. Cap will send Ike from Cincinnati to St. Joe. After Ike, rejuiced, helps defeat Cincinnati, he fibs he's "goin' scoutin.'" His pals offer him a drink, which he says might help a cold.

Lardner wrote Max Perkins* (February 3, 1933) claiming he wrote "Alibi Ike" in nine hours. George W. Hilton explains that "Alibi Ike" the first of Lardner's baseball stories in which he "forsook his practice of setting the scene on actual teams with genuine players as teammates of the fictional characters." Hilton adds that since opponents of the team in this story are all the National League teams, this team is the Chicago Cubs. The story was so popular that "Alibi Ike" became for decades a catch phrase in the English language. A movie entitled *Alibi Ike* was produced (1934) starring the versatile comic Joe E. Brown (1892–1973), whom Jack Spears describes as playing "the cornfed rookie with a good excuse for everything, and the humor revolved around his preposterous alibies and explanations." In applying to "Alibi Ike" the theory of the Other as enunciated by Jacques Lacan (1901–1981), Douglas Robinson writes seven pages explicating Ike's "obedience and disobedience" in ignoring (or did he?) Cap's order to bunt and then hitting a home run deliberately (or was it?); this insight includes Robinson's partial identification of himself as Ike. (Sources: Caruthers [1995], 270; Hilton, 448; Robinson, 133; Spears, 265)

ALICE ("Wedding Day"). She is Ed's wife. They live in New York. When Alice has the flu, Ruth Richards, Alice's unmarried sister visiting from Detroit, becomes her substitute guest at the wedding in New York of musical-comedy stars Jimmy Shane and Brownie Burt.

ALLAH (*The Big Town*). He and Omar are Trumbull's twin-like servants. Allah serves cocktails to Finch, Ella Finch, and her sister Katie when Trumbull entertains them.

ALLEN In "A Busher's Letters Home," he is a Coast League pitcher, rooms with Keefe, tries out for the White Sox, but is released. Keefe plays cards with Allen and his wife. In "The Busher Comes Back," Keefe complains that Allen pitched badly against Cleveland. When he plays cards again with Allen and his wife, Keefe meets her sister Florence and will marry her. In "The Busher's Honeymoon," Allen and his wife Marie get Keefe and his bride Florence to rent a flat in their apartment building. When the Allens move in on the Keefes, Keefe feels they're spongers. Trouble erupts. When Allen goes to Paso Robles for spring training, Marie accompanies him, and he gives Florrie money to abandon Keefe and go to Texas. In "A New Busher Breaks In," Keefe still dislikes Allen, who tries to mediate between Keefe and Florrie. Keefe hopes the White Sox will trade Allen. When Florrie has Keefe's baby, she names it Allen. In "The Busher's Kid," Allen pitches ineffectively for the White Sox, argues with Keefe, drinks excessively, and is happy when Marie disputes with Florrie and demands that she take the baby and get out. In "The Busher Beats It Hence," Keefe continues to dislike Allen; but when Callahan threatens to hire Allen for the world tour, Keefe decides to go. In "The Busher Abroad," Keefe mentions his dislike of Allen. In "The Busher's Welcome Home," Allen and his wife take Florrie and little Al to California.

ALLEN, LOUISE ("Reunion") *see* **MARSHALL, LOUISE**

ALLEN, MARIE ("A Busher's Letters Home," etc.) *see* **ALLEN, MRS.**

ALLEN, MRS. In "A Busher's Letters Home," Keefe plays cards at the home of Allen and his wife. In "The Busher Comes Back," he meets Mrs. Allen's sister Florence and will marry her. In "The Busher's Honeymoon," Mrs. Allen, named Marie, induces Florence Keefe to remain in Chicago. Keefe regards Marie and her husband as freeloaders. The Allens leave for Paso Robles. Keefe says Marie says she is 22, but if so "Kid Gleason is 30." In "A New Busher Breaks In," Marie travels with the White Sox, including Allen. She is presumably happy to become Allen Keefe's aunt. In "The Busher's Kid," Marie and Florrie deceive Keefe by hiring a baby sitter so they can go watch the White Sox play the Cubs in "the city serious." Keefe finds out, argues, and the result is that the three Keefes quit living with the Allens. In "The Busher Beats It Hence," Florrie continues to live and associate with her sister Marie. In "The Busher Abroad," Marie Allen is mentioned. In "The Busher's Welcome Home," the Allens take Florrie and little Al to California. In *Treat 'Em Rough*, Florrie plans to visit her sister in Beaumont, Texas, and during that time pays Keefe a surprise visit in Houston. In *The Real Dope*," Marie evidently helped Florrie after she gave birth to her daughter.

ALLEN, TOM ("Reunion"). He lives in Buchanan, Michigan. Bob Mason gossips to his sister Rita Johnston ad nauseum about Tom and his daughter Louise Marshall.

ALLISON, JIM ("Sun Cured"). He and Jess Andrew live at the Beach in Miami. Ernie Fretts tells C. L. Walters that after he met Jess and Jim, the three of them "hit up the old barber shop harmony."

"ALONG CAME RUTH" (*Saturday Evening Post*, July 26, 1919; ABS, LOB, RAB, SC). (Characters: Jakey Atz, Bagby, Barry, Al Blanchard, Bertha Blanchard, Bush, Eddie Cicotte, Ty Cobb, Collins, Danforth, Davenport, Drew, Ellison, Felsch, Flagstaff, Francis, Bert Gallia, Larry Gardner, Gleason, Hooper, Jackson, Joe Jenkins, Al Keefe, Florrie Keefe, Florrie Keefe, Jack Keefe, Kramer, Lynn, Mays, Babe Ruth, Schang, Schalk, Scott, Sisler, Sothoron, Speaker, Strunk, the Swede, Tobin, Veach, Williams.)

Keefe writes 10 letters to Al Blanchard. (See also *You Know Me Al.*)

"St. Louis, April 26 [1919]." Keefe's White Sox have won two games and lost one to St. Louis, and he wanted to pitch tomorrow to avoid having "the serious" only even. But Gleason wants to hold him for the Detroit opener Sunday [April 27]—unless he's afraid of Detroit? Keefe replied that "they can't no club beat me the way I am going." Florrie, having visited him in St. Louis, returned home to Chicago to run her beauty parlor. Gleason kidded Keefe that she was making more money than Keefe, who griped that his $2,400 pay was too little. Gleason promised him a new, better contract if he continues pitching well. Their catcher Joe Jenkins is back from France. Veterans going around to Verdun, Flanders, Nice, and "the Oregon forest" must be faster than when they run bases.

"Detroit, April 28." Keefe didn't have his best stuff but "enough to make a monkey out of Cobb and Veach" and humiliate Detroit's "new outfielder ... name Flagstaff or something." Keefe will beat "Chi Thursday" and tell Gleason he wants more "jack or trade me." Florrie wrote Keefe a letter, puzzling as usual, this time saying she has a surprise for when he returns home. "Detroit, April 30." Rain caused Keefe to get so cold sitting on the bench yesterday that later when a Detroit pal was waiting in the hotel to see him the two went to Keefe's room. The pal said they could get bourbon even in this dry town, ordered a bottle from "a bell hop," and stalled so Keefe paid $15—but no tip. The pal guzzled some; but before Keefe could drink any, Gleason entered wondering why Keefe missed dinner, took the bottle, told Keefe what was left was worth $11.50, and called it the value of his fine "for haveing liquor in your room." Keefe told his pal he would have hit Gleason but "didn't want to make no seen before a outsider." Gleason knows Keefe won't tolerate interference in his private life; so Gleason must apologize or "be shy of a pitcher tomorrow."

"Chi., May 3." Keefe boasts of winning his last three games. Two were recent shutouts, and today he held St. Louis to one run, undeserved because Felsch misplayed Tobin's fly ball. Rain delayed the opener in Chicago. Gleason had Williams pitch, not Keefe, which annoyed the crowd. Gallia defeated the White Sox. Keefe asked why Gleason confiscated his bottle. Gleason said Keefe could be a great pitcher, earn higher pay, but must "lay off the old burb," and would start today's game. When Keefe walked on the field, the crowd roared. His bad start was owing to Felsch's again misplaying Tobin and by Sisler's getting a hit by swinging "at a ball he couldn't hardly reach." When Keefe came to bat, the crowd gave him some luggage—so small they'll "give it to 1 of Florrie's friends next xmas." Florrie's surprise? She's thinking of selling her interest in her beauty parlor in south Chicago, buying a one-third interest for $3,000 on payments in a downtown parlor owned by "some partys" she recently met, and receiving "a salery of $300.00 per mo." She wanted to consult with Keefe, but she'll do whatever she pleases despite his advising her to stay "where she was makeing so good." No matter. He will soon get "real jack," undoubtedly play "in the world serious," and Florrie can stay home. As is, "the Swede nurse" will soon have the kids saying "I ban this and I ban that."

"Chi., May 6." Keefe boasts that he has beaten Detroit twice, including today's 7–2. He struck out Ty Cobb and later forced him to hit to Weaver for a double play. Cobb shouted an insult. Keefe shouted back at "Ty," and "the boys give him the laugh." When Keefe "eased up on acct. of the lead we had," Cobb hit a triple to score their two runs. It's "God help" Speaker when Keefe gets to Cleveland.

"Cleveland, May 9." Gleason will pitch Keefe Sunday. The cold weather is awful, especially for "Southren league" players. Sothoron was pitching for St. Louis against Cleveland, when their rookie catcher Drew was at bat with two men on. St. Louis infielders yelled that he would hit into a double play; so he took three strikes to avoid doing so. When Francis, "a busher" pitching in a Cleveland-St. Louis game, was at bat against St. Louis pitcher Davenport with a 3–1 count, he tripled off a wild pitch and lamented that "if he had of left that ball go by" he'd have walked. Florrie wrote that she has sold and invested saved cash with those "pardners in that place down town." Keefe fears she's pulled "a boner," but he can't manage for her any more than he can for Gleason.

"Chi, May 12." Keefe beat Cleveland yesterday [Sunday, May 11], returned to Chicago today, and learned from the Swede that Florrie was at work in her new beauty parlor. Florrie phoned and said she hadn't read in the papers about his fifth straight win. He "got kind of sore." They abruptly agreed to talk at supper. After the game, Keefe returned home at 6:30 P.M. The Swede said Florrie phoned she was having supper with business friends. His lonely supper tasted bad; so he had some beer at Kramer's. Home again. The phone rang, and some man asked if Florrie got home all right and hung up without identifying himself. In came Florrie, and they argued over phone calls each answered when the other was being sought by unknowns. Florrie then "went to her rm. and shut the door." Keefe will get answers tomorrow — or else. He tells Al he's lucky his wife, maybe not "the best looker," anyway "isn't flighty" and "has got something under her hat besides marcel wavers."

"Chi, May 14." Gleason told Keefe to choose whether to pitch today against Mays pitching for Boston, or pitch tomorrow against Ruth; further, if Keefe wins, he gets a new contract "for a $600.00 raise or $3000.00 per annum." Keefe decided to rest "my old souper" until tomorrow. Keefe describes how their pitcher Eddie Cicotte defeated Mays 1–0, by getting Mays to fly to Jackson, Hooper to pop to Collins, Barry to foul to Schalkie, by striking Ruth out twice; and then Jackson doubled Collins home. Florrie admitted that "the bird that called her up" is the husband of a girl she had supper with; said she teased Keefe because "she liked to see me jealous." Keefe's advice regarding women? "Make them come to you Al is the way to get along with them." He hasn't explained to Florrie the importance of tomorrow's game — to surprise her.

"Chi, May 16." Keefe says he's through with baseball and home life both. This morning Florrie left word she'd try to bring "her pardners" to the game. While Keefe took batting practice, he saw Florrie in the stand with "a man ... if that's what you want to call him." Keefe sent an usher to fetch her. She explained the stranger was her "pardner," is two-thirds owner of their beauty parlor, is good "fixing lady's hair." Upset, Keefe warmed up crazily, and in the game Hooper doubled, Barry advanced him, and Keefe wild-pitched him home. Gleason ordered Keefe to stay in. He walked Strunk, and Ruth homered. Keefe left the park dazed and remembers nothing before awakening in a hotel still dressed. He concludes that "a man can't have the kind of home life I have got and pitch baseball." He wonders what will happen if "they don't ward them ['his kiddies'] to me."

"Chi, May 20." Keefe phoned the Swede to pack his things. She said Gleason tried to get hold of him. He phoned Gleason, who came to the hotel. He told Keefe he should reconcile with Florrie, who was a better parent than he was, "sported your kids" steadily, had a business partner whose wife also worked in their shop, and if Keefe pitched well on the 19th against Philadelphia — "a club that even you should ought to beat" — he'll have his new contract. He agreed, pitched a two-hitter, drove in two winning runs, and showed Gleason "a money pitcher."

"Along Came Ruth" is considered one of Lardner's premier baseball yarns. It combines nine fictional characters, 42 real-life baseball persons, and a domestic drama, narrated by a self-absorbed and deceived pitcher, jealous husband, and careless father.

ALTROCK In "The Busher Comes Back," he is a fun-loving Washington coach whose antics Keefe witnesses before pitching against Johnson. In "The Busher Pulls a Mays," Keefe and "handsome" Nick Altrock exchange remarks.

Nicholas Altrock (1876–1965) pitched for the Boston Red Sox (1902), the Red Sox and the Chicago White Sox (1903), the White Sox (1904–1908), the White Sox and the Washington Senators (1909), and the Senators (1912–1924). George W. Hilton reports that Altrock gained more memorable fame as a Senators clowning coach in the 1920s. In annotating the passage in which Altrock and Keefe banter, Hilton advises his readers to "[s]ee the accompanying photograph of Altrock." It depicts a somber-looking man with middle-parted graying hair, a slit-eyed stare, jug ears, and wide, drooping mouth, all above bow tie and black suit. (Sources: *Baseball Encyclopedia*, 1790; Hilton, 88, 318)

AMES, RED ("Alibi Ike"). He and Rube Benton play for the Cincinnati baseball team. Alibi Ike, hearing that Dolly forgives him, rallies to help defeat Cincinnati.

AMOS ("My Roomy"). He is the proprietor of the Boston hotel where the narrator and his teammates stay.

George W. Hilton identifies Amos as Amos H. Whipple (1856–1916), proprietor of Boston's Copley Square Hotel, where the Chicago Cubs and other National League players stayed during games with the Braves. (Hilton, 353)

"AND MANY A STORMY WIND SHALL BLOW" (*Saturday Evening Post*, July 6, 1918; RD).

ANDERSON, GOAT (*The Big Town*). He is a friend Finch knows from South Bend days. Living in Buffalo, Goat wires Finch to meet him at the Belmont but doesn't appear.

This non-appearance is a weak plot device, enabling Finch to bump into Sid Mercer at a speakeasy later.

ANDRELL, DR. ("How Are You?"). He is a New York dental diagnostician recommended to Bob Dayton.

ANDREW, JESS ("Sun Cured"). He and Jim Allison live at the Beach in Miami. Ernie Fretts tells C. L. Walters he met the two and sang some barber-shop songs with them.

ANDREWS, JACK ("A Caddy's Diary"). He is the golf pro at the club where the diarist caddies. Jack won't play with the diarist, who is a better golfer. Jack plays less than his best, to tempt members to continue playing and betting with him, lose slightly, and continue paying.

ANDREWS, JACK ("The Poor Simp"). The narrator remembers him as a baseball player who spikes Bill Garwood, when Bill, who bats ahead of him, gets on base and can be run into.

ANDY ("Carmen"). He is at a place where Gullible goes and gambles for relief from family talk.

ANNIE ("How Are You?"). She is Bob Dayton's secretary. When she is attending her brother-in-law Frank Russell's funeral, a substitute secretary, Mrs. Gurnsey, helps out; Bob and Mrs. Gurnsey discuss physical ailments and physicians.

ANNIE (*Own Your Own Home*). She is a baby-sitter or a friend of Fred Gross, who says she will watch their children while he and his wife Grace look over "the subburbs."

"ANNIVERSARY" (*Cosmopolitan*, January 1928; RLR, RU). (Characters: Berger, Cobb, Ed, Mrs. Frayne, Walter Frayne, Grace, Eva Grayson, Florence Hammond, Perce Hammond, Lindsay, Mrs. Lindsay, Helen Morse, Thomas Parvis, Riker, Harry Riker, Jim Satterly, Mrs. Satterly, Bess Taylor, Louis Taylor, Charlie Thomas, Tommy, Marjorie Trumbull, Walter Trumbull.)

Bess Taylor, 33, has been a wife for nine childless years as of today, November 12th. She married Louis Taylor instead of Walter Frayne or Jim Satterly. Louis quit remembering their wedding anniversary three years ago. Once called charming and beautiful in Milton's newspapers, Bess appears "cool, indifferent," as she plays solitaire, wins by harmless cheating, and is bored by Louis's reading newspaper items aloud. His often-repeated anecdotes are even more boring. Louis, regarded as "industrious and 'solid,'" is rich Thomas Parvis's well-paid secretary, at $4,000 a year. Louis is stingy, won't buy a car, avoids vacations with Bess. He intones about car production in the U.S.A., car trouble in Chile, then tells again how Walter Trumbull, one of his Wednesday evening bowling pals, and Walter's wife Marjorie ran out of gas driving toward Harper City to see the movie *Seventh Heaven*.

While Louis reads about unemployment abroad and poverty in America's South, which he recalls seeing when he and Purvis drove once to Daytona, Bess shuffles her cards and interrupts with sometimes unheard and usually unrecognized sarcasm. Bess's friend Florence Hammond rings the door bell, is admitted, tells Louis she and her husband Perce have a flat tire and need a flashlight. Criticizing cars, Louis goes to help, while Florence unloads some gossip on Bess. Florence's sister Grace is married to Ed, in a town called Clyde. Ed gives Grace expensive gifts and plenty of money for her needs, but sometimes goes on benders starting Saturday nights at his Yacht Club and lasting for days. One night he returned home, punched Grace in the eye, went to bed, noticed her shiner next morning, apologized, saying he thought Grace was Eva Grayson, a girlfriend he had been with. Grace forgave him. Florence tells Bess they should be happy being married to stable gentlemen. Florence and Perce leave to go play bridge. Bess reminds Louis of their anniversary. He suggests giving her flowers tomorrow. She asks instead for a punch in the eye. He says she's funny, maybe sampled Florence's homemade gin? No, she says, and goes up to bed before he can define sisel for her. He's reading about Haitian sisel.

One moral of Bess's biography must be that regardless of her choice in men, she would be doomed to unhappiness. Would she be any happier married to Frayne or Satterly? Lardner renders life around poor Bess undistinguished by including three Thomases, two Walters, and a Grace and a Grayson. Donald Elder says the "sorry picture" of Bess's "hopeless marriage is accentuated by the very flatness of the manner in which it is presented." *Seventh Heaven* (1927), the movie the Trumbulls wanted to see, starred lovely Janet Gaynor, was immensely popular, and won several Academy Awards. (Source: Elder, 310)

THE ANNOTATED BASEBALL STORIES OF RING W. LARDNER, 1914–1919 edited by George W. Hilton (Stanford, CA: Stanford University Press, 1995). This collection contains 24 short stories.

ANTOINETTE, MISS MARIE (*The Real Dope*). She is a fictitious person created by Keefe's buddies, who get him to write letters to her suggesting that they meet in Cologne, her French city.

ARCHBOLD, CHIEF ("Holycaust"). He is the Centralia fire chief, who will investigate the cause of the "holycaust."

ARCHER ("My Roomy"). He is one of several Chicago players who refuse to accept Buster Elliott as a roommate. Called Jim Archer in "Horseshoes," he is the Cubs catcher. Speed Parker, playing third, mistakenly throws home but luckily saves face by tagging the errant runner sliding and casually missing the plate. In "The Busher Reënlists," Jim Archer, Joe Benz, Artie Hofman, and Charley O'Leary are baseball players who offend Keefe by not asking about his war experiences.

James Peter Archer (1883–1958) played for the Pirates (1904), the Tigers (1907), the Cubs (1909–1917), and the Pirates and the Dodgers and the Cincinnati Reds (1918). George W. Hilton notes that Archer would be credibly seeking more baseball work in Chicago when Keefe was there chatting with "the boys," and that Archer, failing to do so, was in reality hired as hog buyer by Armour & Co. (Sources: *Baseball Encyclopedia*, 742; Hilton, 222)

ARCHIE ("Widow"). He was Mrs. Milburn's first husband, deceased and replaced by Fred Milburn.

ARDEN, VICTOR (1893–1962). Popular musician (real name: John Fuiks). Trained in music at the University of Chicago, Arden played music in silent-movie theaters in New York, wrote compositions, worked for the QRS Piano Roll Company, and met Phil Ohman.* The two became partners, conducted the pit orchestra for the musical *Lady Be Good* (George Gershwin,* 1924), worked on other Gershwin musicals, and co-recorded innumerable songs and spectacular piano rolls (until 1934). After "Ohman and Arden," as they were called, split up, Arden formed a dance band and conducted orchestras for radio shows and as background for recording artists.

Records produced by Ohman and Arden are mentioned in "Lose With a Smile" and "There Are Smiles." Lardner closes "Crooner," a section of "An Infant Industry" (radio review, *The New Yorker* [February 25, 1933]), thus: "Good night, Ohman and Arden dear."

ARLEN, MICHAEL (1895–1956). Fiction writer, born Dikran Kouyoumdjian in Ruse, Bulgaria. He studied and wrote in England, and changed his name to Michael Arlen (1920), after that of a character in his *The London Venture* (1919). Arlen gained popularity with his titillating high-society novel *The Green Hat* (1925), which was translated into Dutch, German, and Swedish (1926) and later other languages, and was dramatized in London, New York, and Los Angeles. Arlen visited New York and Hollywood (1925–1926). *The Green Hat* was made into *A Woman of Affairs*, a movie starring Greta Garbo (1928). Arlen married and lived in France (1926), England (1939–1941), Hollywood (1941–1945), and New York (1945–1956). His many titles include the popular fantasy-novel *May Fair* (1925) and the futuristic political novel *Man's Morality* (1933), his most serious work. Innumerable friends and readers include Noël Coward (1899–1973), F. Scott Fitzgerald,* and Ernest Hemingway. A born charmer, Arlen described himself as "every other inch a gentleman."

Ring Lardner Jr. mentions Arlen's surprise visit (1925) to Lardner, who was "intrigued" by Arlen's "abrupt leap to fame." In "Reunion," Rita Johnston boasts to Bob and Jennie Mason about meeting Michael Arlen, who she says wrote *The Green Hat* and *May Fair*. In "Rhythm," Peggy Leech's salon guests include Michael Arlen and Noël Coward. In "Contract" Shelton likes Mrs. French until she says it's really nice that he edited a magazine and can thereby meet Michael Arlen. (Sources: Elder, 198; Lardner, Jr., 172; Caruthers [1995], 176, 187)

ARNOLD ("The Crook"). He is a St. Louis catcher. He tries but fails to upset Bull, when Bull first begins umpiring.

ARNOLD (*Own Your Own Home*). The Arnolds were Chicago neighbors missed by Fred and Grace, now living in Allison.

ARNOLD ("There Are Smiles"). He and his wife Mary Arnold play cards occasionally with Ben Collins and his wife Grace Arnold.

ARNOLD, AMY ("Insomnia") *see* **SPEARS, EDITH**

ARNOLD, JAY ("The Last Night"). He is an alcoholic, 37, in Chicago. His love of liquor is costing him his life until, thinking prohibition is starting next day, he drinks almost enough to kill him but is then sobered up, and even made patriotic, by Walter Crowell's story.

ARNOLD, LESLIE ("Insomnia") *see* **SPEARS, ALLAN**

ARNOLD, MARY ("There Are Smiles"). She and Grace Collins have been playing cards when Mary's husband Ben Collins arrives home one rainy afternoon.

ARNOLD, MRS. (*Own Your Own Home*). Fred says he misses the Arnolds, whom he and his wife knew in Chicago.

ASHTON ("Oh, You Bonehead!"). He was a fullback on the Coach's Leighton football team. He was earnest but not very reliable.

ATZ, JAKEY. In "Along Came Ruth," Keefe mentions Jakey Atz. Keefe says he can no more manage his wife Florrie than he could order Gleason, White Sox manager, to "send for Jakey Atz" to replace Collins at second. In "The Yellow Kid," Jake Atz recommended Lefty Crosby, an excellent Dallas pitcher, to the narrator Bill's team.

Jake Atz (1879–1949) played for the Washington Senators (1902) and the Chicago White Sox (1907–1909). George W. Hilton adds that Atz became a good minor-league manager, especially with the Texas League's Fort Worth, that he grew tired of being last in alphabetical order and changed his name to Jake Atz from Jacob Henry "Jake" Zimmerman, and his lack of ability and his sense of humor "could only have endeared him to Lardner." See also Jake ("Sick 'Em"). (Sources: *Baseball Encyclopedia*, 747; Hilton, 267)

AVERY, SARGENT (*The Real Dope*). He is part of Keefe's army "Co." in France. Ruth Palmer gave him Jack's valentine poem, which he read aloud to the troops.

BABCOCK ("Travelogue"). Hazel Dignan tells Dan Chapman she met the lovely Babcocks in Tampa last winter.

"BACK TO BALTIMORE" (*Red Book Magazine*, November 1914; ABS, RAB). (Characters: Alexander, Mrs. William Baker, William Baker, William Baker, Jr., Byrne, Cheney, Cravath, Devore, Dixon, Doc, Red Dooin, Dunnie, Bill Fox, Hayes, Mrs. Hayes, Otto Hess, Higgins, Hub, Kelly, Knabe, Luderus, McGraw, Connie Mack, Magee, Maranville, Pat Moran, O'Day, Rigler, Rixey, Rucker, Smith, Red Smith, Sullivan, Tony, Tyler, Whalin, Williams, Young.)

Dixon, the narrator, is a baseball player traveling (apparently with the Cubs heading east in 1914) to Pittsburgh. He tells this story to a Cub player:

I'm not going with the Cubs or the Pirates but am jumping "to the Baltimore Feds." Knabe (their manager) is free to use me in any way. My trouble was Mrs. Hayes. When she took "hold o' the ball club, *good night.*" If "a skirt [is ever] elected President o' the United States, I'll move to Paris ... if I have to walk." Mrs. Hayes has bossed the club (Boston Braves) since "the old bird croaked." Otherwise, I'd have stayed and the team would have the best record "since Frank Selee [Boston Braves successful manager, 1890–1901] had 'em." So I'm back to play in the minors and Baltimore. Good-looking Mrs. Hayes married "Old Man Hayes" knowing he'd die soon and she'd have the club. Soon, she'll marry William Baker, Jr., a ball player but no manager; he'll quit playing and their co-managing will be "comedy enough."

Hayes fired Bill Fox and hired me as manager, which I agreed to only because I needed money. Hayes was too optimistic when the season started. We defeated (John J.) McGraw (Giants manager), who lacked good pitchers, played even with the Phillies, and licked Brooklyn; but then Philly and "you guys" went ahead of us, distressing Hayes. In the West, we played even with "Cincy," but our four-straight losses to Higgins (Cardinals manager) caused Hayes to sicken and die on the train going home. The papers reported that Mrs. Hayes would manage the team.

Back home (in Boston) Mrs. Hayes told me that she and Williams, the vice president, were sending Sullivan "to spend some dough for new players" from college teams. I warned her that doing so was illegal, but she planned "to make this here club a team of gentlemen," which colleges are full of. I felt the need of brandy.

We continued playing so-so ball. Sullivan returned without bringing any "collegers," who he said couldn't even "carry bats in the Japanese League." One day when Brooklyn was ahead of us in the eighth, we had two on, with me up next. Mrs. Hayes ordered me to homer. I struck out. When we lost 12–0 against Cheney pitching for the Cubs, Mrs. Hayes told me to tell O'Day, Cubs manager, not to pitch Cheney against us again because his "spitball ain't sanitary." She objected to our pitcher Hub's wad of tobacco and didn't believe me when I said he pretended to have ulcerated teeth to make batters pity him. She told me to have our players quit sliding because it dirtied their uniforms. One day Mrs. Hayes went to a party at Yale and signed Baker for the team. He preferred studying to sports; she didn't know what position he'd play; she was paying him $5,000. When I griped that $5,000 equaled my salary, she replied that he was worth it, being "off'n a good family."

In New York I met "the colleger." He was "William Baker Junior," big, hair plastered, rainbow-like shirt and tie. He said he couldn't play today because of an engagement. I offered to excuse him forever, but no, he wanted to earn his pay. Next day he hailed a taxi to go to the park, and explained this mode of transportation was in his contract. Doc gave him a uniform. He objected "because they wasn't no feet in the stockin's"; so he kept his purple socks on too, got kidded, and Hub called him "Gertie"; but "he never wised up."

During warm-up, Baker, capless, complained that practice pitches stung his hands, the bat was too heavy, and balls pitched at him were scary. I let him get dressed and watch from the stand, wired Williams to avoid paying Baker, but was rebuked by a letter "from the skirt" for criticizing Baker after only one day. I wired William about resigning, but he persuaded me "to stick." The boys would hit well-dressed, idle Baker with stray balls, spike his feet, bow, and apologize. On travel-day trains, he avoided poker games, saying he played only "bridge w'ist." He read magazines and summarized a short story about a pitcher who won a game despite having to pitch with a sore arm [*see* "Sick 'Em"]. When Baker praised that pitcher's courage, Hub told everyone about how a nervy Nashville teammate of his named Smith won in a game against New Orleans in the 21st inning by hopping over the catcher's head to score despite having earlier been deliberately horribly spiked on one foot. Two toes dropped off when he was dressing, and infection caused him to have a leg amputated. Baker praised Smith's nerve.

Hub relished feeding Baker more tall tales on the road. But when back for home games, I had to lie to Mrs. Hayes that Baker needed more bench time to become sufficiently experienced to play. I hoped the team's directors would buy "the doll" out and I could "can" Baker. Mrs. Hayes brought her brother and his pals from Yale to Boston, to see Baker play against Philadelphia. I put him in my position (first base). He fielded "a perfect hop" but threw to an empty second base when Pat Moran, Phillies first-base coach, told him to. Hit by a pitched ball when bunting, Baker questioned the umpire's order to take first. He was out trying to steal second on the suggestion by Luderus, Phillies firstbaseman.

The rest of the Phillies-Braves game featured Baker's avoiding grounders, wrongly stepping on a bag instead of tagging a runner, chasing another runner instead of throwing him out, thus allowing 12 runs in one innning. To end the game, the umpires "pulled a couple o' raw ones," which included ejecting Baker for language. Mrs. Hayes defended Baker, said he was out of practice, and warned me to play him daily.

I ordered our pitcher Young to hit Baker during practice batting, but Young kept missing. During another Phillies game, I told Baker to stand closer to the plate when batting; their pitcher Alexander beaned him. "I felt like a murderer." Baker dropped, staggered, got help, soon was better but with "a mean lookin' bump."

Baker accompanied the team to Pittsburgh. His saying he'd show Hub his own nerve meant he was "thinkin' about that one-legged guy." I wired Mrs. Hayes I benched Baker because of his head bump. In St. Louis I asked Doc to take him to Tony's and get him drunk so I could suspend him. When I entered, I found him "lappin' up lemonade." Coaxed, Baker admitted that if he proved to his father he could earn $5,000 in one year after college his $100-a-month allowance would be doubled; he said his mother worried about his associating with "tough" athletes. Inspired, I asked him for his mother's address.

I wrote Mrs. Baker anonymously that we ball players were foul-mouthed, womanizing drunks, her son "was stuck on a burlesque queen" costing him "all his dough," and our manager killed his wife and was dangerous. In "Chi," Baker showed me a letter from his mother saying his father would double his allowance but he must immediately quit baseball — or else. He left. I played excellently against Cincinnati, New York, St. Louis, and Pittsburgh, and hoped we were scaring you Cubs. We returned to Boston. Mrs. Hayes appeared annoyed when I explained that Baker's mother ordered him home. After a game, Mrs. Hayes ordered me to her office, where two cops were present — to protect her, she said. She had read my letter to Baker's mother, was happy Baker had escaped immoral ball players, but accused me of killing my wife. I said that I was unmarried and that somebody "gave the old lady a bum steer." Why? Because something had to be done to release Baker. She fired me as manager but had to let me continue playing if I could cooperate with the new manager. Who is he? Never mind. After criticizing Baker and calling him a "seamstress" who must have graduated from Wellesley not Yale, "I turns and beats it for the door."

Just outside, I saw "Gertrude" Baker, all smiles. I kicked him in the shin, squashed his shiny shoes, and wired Knabe. He told me to meet him in Pittsburgh and begin managing Baltimore. If "she" files an "injunction ... agin' me," I'll happily "tell my story to a judge," if male. Everyone knows who'll both manage and be president of Mrs. Hayes's failing club.

George W. Hilton dismisses "Back to Baltimore" as "an implausible account of a woman's mismanagement of the Boston Braves." Incidentally, it is tempting to wonder whether Lardner ever saw *One Touch of Nature* (1917), an early baseball movie in which a Yale College baseball player is disinherited by his wealthy father for getting married, but he gets a job with the New York Giants and is forgiven when he helps the Giants win the World Series. Plot parallels, admittedly, are minimal. (Source: Hilton, 20)

BAER, ARTHUR ("BUGS") (1886–1969). Journalist, humorist, and cartoonist. Baer was born in Philadelphia into a large Alsace-Lorraine immigrant family. He quit school at 14, worked, attended art school, was an artillery officer (1918), and was an ardent golfer. His professional employment was on newspapers in Philadelphia, Washington, D.C., and New York. In Washington, he drew a popular cartoon of an insect with the body of a baseball and the name "Bugs," which Baer adopted and insisted on being called.

Lardner knew Baer and admired his humor. The narrators of many Lardner baseball call fans "bugs." An early Lardner baseball item is "Oddities of Bleacher 'Bugs'" (*Boston American*, July 23, 1911). Lardner wrote a poem entitled "Bugs Baer's Comeback" (*Columbia Jester* [February 1922]). Jonathan Yardley reports that when Lardner was covering the 1924 Democratic National Convention in New York and the balloting dragged on, he offered to nominate himself— if Calvin Coolidge* would withdraw — and then offered to nominate Baer. (On the 103rd ballot, John W. Davis was nominated. He lost to Coolidge, a Republican.) Like Lardner, Baer was attracted to contract bridge when in the mid–1920s it began successfully challenging auction bridge. Many humorists, Baer among them, made fun of this new form of the old card game. Charles Goren writes that "Arthur 'Bugs' Baer established several systems — one in which the dummy is permitted to point out cards in the enemies' hands; another is 'the leaping finesse,' allowing the declarer to reach over and play cards from his opponents' hands."

In "Zone of Quiet," Eleanor Lyons tells her patient that she heard humorist Bugs Baer on the radio talking about a woman so fat she wore her wrist watch on her thumb. This is an early, especially egregious example of Lardner's frequent poking of fun at fat people. Earlier, Lardner wrote "Ring Favors Segregation of Fats and Leans — Misery Loves Company Basic Rule of New Social Theory Invented by Great Neck Sage" (Bell Syndicate, February 24, 1924; republished as "Segregate the Fats," in *What of It*, 1925). In it he opines that "Of the people that ain't right in one way another [*sic*], the big majority belongs to the class that is overweight." (If alive today, Lardner would see that America's obesity problem has grown larger.) In an interview with Grant Overton, Lardner said that "[h]is choice among humorists is Bugs Baer." (Sources: Goren, 16; Overton, 46; *Some Champions*, 62–66; Yardley, 227)

BAGLEY ("Along Came Ruth"). He pitched well for Cleveland against St. Louis until he developed a sore finger and was relieved.

James Charles Jacob Bagley Sr. (1887–1954) played for the Cincinnati Reds (1912), the Cleveland Indians (1916–1922), and the Pittsburgh Pirates (1923). (Source: Hilton, 266)

BAILEY ("Three Without, Doubled"). This is the name of the couple whose vacationing in California creates a vacancy in the San Susie bridge group which the Gullibles fill.

BAKER In "A Busher's Letters Home," Callahan told Keefe that he and other White Sox pitchers didn't "pitch right to Baker." In "The Busher Comes Back," Keefe boasts he pitched well against Baker. In "Horseshoes," Baker plays for the Athletics. In their World Series against the Giants, Baker hits a homer in the first game and hits in the second. In "The Busher Pulls a Mays," Baker hit a pitch by Keefe past Liebold, the White Sox rightfielder. In "Back to Baltimore," Dixon sarcastically says that this Baker and William Baker, Jr., on the Boston Braves team that Dixon manages, are alike only by both having ears. In "The Crook," Larry, of the White Sox, tries unsuccessfully to encourage Martin Gregory by saying he can make Baker and Tyrus Cobb "look like a rummy." In "Women," Frank Baker was a third baseman for New York. His "slipping" performance caused Mike Healy to think Huggins would hire him to replace Baker.

John Franklin Baker (1886–1963) was a Philadelphia Athletics third baseman and slugger (1908–1914), was a hold-out (1915), then played for the New York Yankees (1916–1922). He was elected to the Baseball Hall of Fame (1955). (Sources: *Baseball Encyclopedia*, 754–755; Hilton, 55)

BAKER, GERTIE ("Who Dealt?"). She and her husband Ken Baker bumped into Tom Cannon and his wife, who knows them both well, when the Cannons were honeymooning in Chicago.

BAKER, KEN ("Who Dealt?"). When he and his wife Gertie Baker chanced to meet Tom Cannon and his wife during the Cannons' honeymoon, he tried ineffectively to get Tom to have cocktails before they all have dinner.

BAKER, MRS. WILLIAM ("Back to Baltimore"). She is a rich man's wife and William Baker Jr.'s indulgent mother. Dixon writes her an anonymous letter to frighten her into ordering her son to quit playing baseball with those immoral Boston Braves.

BAKER, PROF. ("Tour No. 2"). He is a teacher from Ohio. Larry and Minnie Burns meet him on their trip to Europe. He kids Larry but is of help when Larry gets into trouble with German army officers in "Belljum."

BAKER, WILLIAM ("Back to Baltimore"). He is William Baker Jr.'s wealthy father. He challenges his son to make $5,000 in one year; if he does, his $100 monthly allowance will be doubled.

BAKER, WILLIAM, JR. ("Back to Baltimore"). He is a family-petted Yale graduate, hired by Mrs. Hayes to play baseball for the Boston Braves, for $5,000. He agrees, though uncoordinated and untrainable, to please his father and have his $100 monthly allowance of $100. Dixon, Boston's manager-player, finally gets rid of Baker by writing a scary letter to his mother. Mrs. Hayes, after becoming a widow, will marry Baker. Because of his non-athletic ways, his teammates nickname him "Gertie" and "Gertrude."

BALCH, GEORGE ("The Maysville Minstrel"). He is a friend of Charley Roberts, writes a column for the New York *Standard*, and at Roberts's suggestion publishes "To Stella," Stephen Gale's wretched poem, obviously as a joke.

"BALL-A-HOLE" (*Saturday Evening Post*, May 12, 1917). (Characters: Mr. Adams, Mr. Conklin, Mr. Davis, Mr. Harper, Jake, Mr. Joyce, Mac, Mr. McNally, Mr. Perkins, Davy Schultz.)

The narrator, 16, caddies at a nine-hole golf course at a Riverside club. Mac, the pro, is crabby and uncooperative. The narrator's friend Jake is "the second oldest kid that's caddying here." The two boys practice when the course is empty and are about even when the narrator, usually shooting 48 or 49, spots Jake "three strokes on the nine." They caddy for 25 cents per nine holes, plus occasional tips from nice players like Mr. Joyce and Mr. Davis. The boys "make the best clean-up"when Mr. McNally and Mr. Harper play with Mr. Joyce and Mr. Davis, for $1 to $5 a hole. Some men are tight. One man last year kept saying he had only a $20 bill until the narrator "copped" the twenty once, made change, and kept his back debts. Other men blame caddies for their own misplays and also when the caddies report correct scores whereas "you're supposed to ... lie" so the men needn't.

When Davy Schultz, another caddy, griped about getting no tips, the narrator bet Davy a week's take that he could squeeze tips out of tightwads like rich banker Mr. Perkins and rich church warder Mr. Conklin. Perkins rarely shoots 59; Conklin averages 63.

A week later Jake praised a Conklin practice putt and said Perkins would need to watch out. Why? Because Jake said Perkins said Conklin had some "bad [golf] habits" and Perkins could "trim you three up on nine holes." Learning Conklin averages 60, Perkins agreed to meet and play him. Next, Jake praised one of Perkins's approaches and lured him into challenging Conklin, by saying he heard Conklin tell Mac that Perkins's stance could benefit from professional help. Perkins waited until one Thursday Conklin drove up. The narrator got Mac to assign Jake and him to caddy for.the two men. Perkins challenged Conklin, who learned Perkins shoots about 60. Conklin bet "a ball-a-hole." The narrator, Conklin's caddy, scrubbed one of Conklin's three misshapen Whizz golf balls, while Jake's Perkins drove first, for 20 yards. Conklin smiled but, with kneecaps kissing, drove his Whizz six feet. Perkins said he teed too high, should try again. But Conklin preferred to slice with his brassy into a mudhole. Dropping his second Whizz and ignoring Perkins's suggestion to use his mashie safely, Conklin brassied his day's best shot near the green. Perkins after two more divot-launching strokes was just behind Conklin's ball. Perkins's cleek topped his ball into a ditch. Conklin's mashie likewise. Conklin illegally put his half-buried ball atop weeds. Conklin pitched 10 feet from the hole; Perkins, eight. Conklin's putter drove the ball "acrost the green," then he putted short. Perkins putted six inches short and picked up his ball. Picking his up, Conklin said "we halved." They argued. Saying he won, Perkins asked the caddies. Jake said Perkins won; the narrator said they tied. More arguing, until Conklin agreed he lost 6–7. After lying about second-hole strokes, the men agreed they tied 8–8. Next, Conklin lost his Whizz in some rough and said his "boy" should have spotted it. Everyone searched. Jake stepped on "a Major, Number 28" ball, which Conklin lied and called his. Perkins "mowed" so much rough that he gave Conklin the hole, 6 to a fibbed 7. Fourth hole. Both men topped into a bunker, pitched into mud near railroad tracks, eventually got to the green. Perkins said he was ahead 6–7. The narrator said they were even. Perkins holed after two more strokes. Conklin's putt hit a pebble and bounced in. He went "one up." They played holes five and six in an hour, halving by separate fibs. The narrator told Jake his "fella" must win two and split one of holes six, seven, and eight, so the boys could "blackmail them" on the ninth. On seven, a short, narrow par 3, Conklin hooked his Major 28 into the water. Perkins sliced into rough but got a 6 — "his count" — to Conklin's 11. Eighth hole: Perkins, into the water, shot another ball so badly he uttered several unchurchly words. Conklin, losing his remaining ball in "the forest preserves," couldn't borrow one from Perkins. The narrator offered one of his for twenty cents. It brought him luck until he refused the narrator's suggestion to run up to the green and instead brassied into the watery "Canyon." Conklin dribbled toward the green. Perkins "accidentally" pitched four feet from the hole. The narrator "thought we were gone." After two putts, Conklin was still out. Perkins could win by three-putting but bobbed, shook, and got stymied by Conklin's ball. Conklin offered to putt, but Perkins picked up both balls and called the hole 7–7 — "seven" seemingly "his favorite number." The ninth hole was "funny," with a hill eclipsing the green. So the caddies gave their men their drivers and climbed ahead to spot their tee shots, both in rough close together, ready for mashies. Jake planned to jar Perkins by reminding him of his whiffs in the woods on the eighth. The narrator worried Conklin by urging him not to miss the ball, which he did. Conklin changed from mashie to niblick, got mad at the narrator's needling, and paid him a "two-spot" to avoid dealing with him later. Soon Jake was yelling at Perkins to kick his bad lie free of weeds, as he did. Perkins coughed, got irate, paid Jake early, cut weeds fiercely with his mashie, and putted onto the green. Conklin's shot was off the green, ending the narrator's fear for his man. Conklin approached well. Perkins in anguish started to put with his spoon, smiled at Jake's query, confessed to Conklin he tried "too hard," suggested they call the game "square." Agreeing, Perkins recorded halving "in fives," thus totalling each at a medal-class 54.

Afterwards, Jake said he got $1.50. The narrator suggested showing Davy Schultz their winnings, calling off the bet, and caddying for the two men again, especially since Jake revealed that Perkins promised him $10 if he could save $25 by Christmas. Both boys decided to bank more of "these geezers' money." The narrator agreed but not use a Conklin bank.

Lardner appeals to his immediate readers by having his narrator mention that Francis Ouimet "started as a caddy" and learned to play golf by practice not instruction, and by having Schultz say that if Chick Evans cheated like Conklin and Perkins, "he could play this [9-hole] course four times in thirty-six." Francis DeSales Ouimet (1893–1967) and Chick Evans (1890–1979) were champion amateur golfers. Each won the U.S. Open (Ouimet, 1913; Evans, 1914, 1916). "Ball-A-Hole" is a rehearsal for "A Caddy's Diary" (1922), which is a more compelling story. (Source: Sommers, 320)

BAN ("The Crook") *see* **JOHNSON, BYRON BANCROFT**

BANCROFT In "Lose with a Smile." Danny Warner, playing for Brooklyn, calls him the Giants coach. The two engage in banter and antics. In "Holycaust," (Casey) Stengel* calls Bancroft "Banny" and kids him. In "The Ides of June," it is said that Bancroft left active work with the Giants and will be the secretary of [John J.] McGraw.

David James Bancroft (1891–1972) played for the Philadelphia Phillies (1915–1919), the Phillies and the New York Giants (1920), the Giants (1921–1923), the Boston Braves (1924–1927), the Brooklyn Dodgers (1928–1929), and the Giants (1930). He managed the Braves (1924–1927). Bancroft entered the Baseball Hall of Fame (1971). This Bancroft wasn't a Giant when "Lose with a Smile" takes place. (Source: *Baseball Encyclopedia*, 686, 757)

BARNES ("A Chip of the Old Block"). He was Evan Barnes's father, killed during the Spanish American War.

BARNES, BOB (*Own Your Own Home*). He is the sheriff of Cook County, Illinois. Fred gets him to send Parker, his deputy, to Mrs. Hamilton's home to pretend to raid her bridge party for gambling.

BARNES, CAPTAIN EVAN ("A Chip of the Old Block"). Barnes, 21, of Weedsburg, writes letters to his Grandfather. In them, Barnes unconsciously reveals that total self-absorption misguides him into thinking he's doing important detective work for the war-time Sleuth Department in Washington, D.C. He is to marry Kathyn Stark, whose fiancé is wounded in France and hence unavailable. This news causes his Grandfather to rebuke him.

BARNES, HARRY R. ("A Chip of the Old Block"). He is Captain Evan Barnes's grandfather, a Civil War veteran living in Sandusky, Ohio. He endures so many vain letters from Evan that he finally answers that he will bequeath Evan nothing and to stop bothering him.

BARNES, JOE ("Battle of the Century"). He was "a big horse" of a boxer. Larry Moon arranged for Jim Dugan to fight Barnes for $100,000. Dugan won in the 12th round but looked so weak that people thought Goulet, Dugan's next opponent, had a chance.

BARNES, JOE ("Haircut"). He is the marshal of narrator Whitey's town.

BARNES, MRS. ("A Chip of the Old Block"). She is the widowed mother of Captain Evan Barnes, who is commissioned after she wrote Congressman Shultz. She rooms with Evan in the Shoreham in Washington, D.C.

BARNES, MRS. ("Haircut"). She is the town marshal's wife. He probably told her about Jim Kendall's joke on Julia Gregg. If so, that's how the town learned about it.

BARNETT, JACK ("Sick 'Em"). He plays baseball for Evansville in the Central League. Barnett knows the narrator well and tells him Smitty and Fogarty pitch excellently but only when they are rivals on the same team. This tip is so vital to the Phillies' success that the narrator gathers a purse of $150 to send to Barnett in gratitude.

George W. Hilton says that Barnett is fictional, that Lardner could easily have assigned a real-life baseball player to his role in "Sick 'Em," and that the narrator's friendship with Barnett is vital to the plot. (Source: Hilton, 26–27, 373–374)

BARROWS ("A One-Man Team"). He is a member of Coach Belden's football team. Barrows promises to tackle Davis, star of the Doane team, but doesn't. Barrows also drops a Doane kick.

Lardner writes charmingly that when Belden asks Barrows a question, the reply comes from "a picture of health." Lardner calls the dropped kick "a square muff." In baseball slang, a "muff" is a fumble of a ball resulting in a spoiled play. But, linguists, what is "square" about a fumble? (Sources: Dickson, 332; McBride, 68)

BARRY In "The Busher Comes Back," Keefe of the White Sox gripes that when he pitched to Barry, an Athletics player, he was awarded a hit the reporters should have called an error. In "Horseshoes," Barry plays for the Athletics. In the second game during the World Series against the Giants, Barry is robbed of two hits when thirdbaseman Speed Parker fields with pure luck. In "Along Came Ruth," Keefe says Barry fouled out to Keefe's catcher "Schalkie." In *The Real Dope*, Keefe, soldiering in France, remembers pitching against Barry's Boston team. In "Holycaust," when Danny Warner mentioned "holycaust," Jack Quinn said he thought Danny "ment the college wear Jack Barry coaches." Quinn was thinking about the College of Holy Cross, not any "holycaust."

John Joseph Barry (1887–1961) played for the Philadelphia Athletics (1908–1914), the Athletics and the Boston Red Sox (1915), and the Red Sox (1916–1919), managed the Red Sox (1917), and finally coached baseball for the College of the Holy Cross, from which he had graduated. (Sources: *Baseball Encyclopedia*, 686, 763–764; Hilton, 78)

BARRY, GEN. (*Treat 'Em Rough*). He commanded and praised Jack Keefe's army unit.

BARRYMORE FAMILY Lionel Barrymore (1878–1954), Ethel Barrymore (1879–1959), and John Barrymore (1882–1942) were children of an acting family. Lionel was a leading Broadway actor (1900), studied painting in Paris (1903–1907), starred in Biograph films (1911), was directed by D. W. Griffith (1875–1948) in early movies (1912–1914), quit Broadway (1925) for Hollywood and MGM (1926–1954). Ethel Barrymore starred on Broadway (1900), acted in films (1914–1919), preferred the theater, but later returned to Hollywood. John Barrymore debuted on the New York stage (1903), appeared in silent movies (from 1913), was outstanding in William Shakespeare's *Richard III* (1920) and *Hamlet* (1922), and starred in many movies. Although he continued acting (to 1941), he might have been even more towering but for alcoholism, womanizing, and four marriages. (Sources: Ephraim Katz, 95–87; Spears, 205–06, 294–95)

Barrymore names arise in "I Can't Breathe" and "The Love Nest." Jonathan Yardley quotes a letter by Lardner's wife to her family saying that after having dinner at the home of Damon Runyon (famous Broadway writer, 1880–1946) and his wife, the four attended a play starring Ethel Barrymore. (Source: Yardley, 229)

BARTLETT ("The Love Nest"). He is a magazine journalist. He accompanies movie mogul Lou Gregg for an overnight stay in his mansion north of New York. He is to interview Gregg. During the evening, Gregg leaves briefly to go to Tarrytown on business. His wife Celia Gregg gets drunk and explains to "Barker," as she calls their guest, that her homey "love nest" is hellishly frustrating and boring.

BARTLETT, GALE ("Contract"). He writes for Shelton's magazine and recommends E. M. Pardee and his wife as pleasant bridge-playing neighbors for Shelton and his wife, unlike Cameron and his wife, and Robert French and his wife.

BARTLETT, MRS. ("Contract"). She is Gale Bartlett's wife. Gale tells Shelton she knew the sisters of E. M. Pardee and his wife.

BARTON, HARRY ("Dinner"). This eligible bachelor, 33, who works in Manhattan, is invited by Grace Halpern to a dinner, for gender balance among guests, and to meet Miss Coakley and Miss Rell. He endures their inane monologues as long as he can. Miss Coakley calls him "Burton" and "Buckley."

Donald Elder believes that Lardner probably enjoyed identifying himself with Barton, who, Elder notes, kids the "two rattlebrained, garrulous girls," laps up drinks, and "escapes the party with a triumphant sense of relief." (Source: Elder, 308)

BASEBALL TEAMS *see* **MAJOR-LEAGUE BASEBALL TEAMS IN LARDNER'S TIME**

BATEMAN, HARLEY ("Travelogue"). Hazel Dignan tells Dan Chapman about this man's friends, including Bess Eldridge, and about his drinking, not playing football, etc. Hazel adds that she wouldn't marry him.

"THE BATTLE OF LONG ISLAND" (*Saturday Evening Post*, November 27, 1920; BT).

"THE BATTLE OF TEXAS" (*Saturday Evening Post*, May 24, 1919; ABS, LOB, RAB). (Characters: Belden, Al Blanchard, Joe Cantillon, Ed Collins, Shano Collins, Comiskey, Red Faber, Felsch, Gedeon, Kid Gleason, Jackson, Joe Jenkins, Johnson, Al Keefe, Florrie Keefe, Florrie Keefe, Jack Keefe, Miss Krug, Liebold, Schalk, Sisler, Buck Weaver, Lefty Williams, Wolfgang, Cy Young.)

Jack Keefe writes 11 letters to Al Blanchard.

"On the Rattler, March 22 [1919]." Keefe is on the train for pre-season practice in Texas. Some teammates are playing cards, which seems childish to "a real man" who has been "over to France." Keefe prefers writing letters, reading newspapers, and lowering the shades to avoid seeing "Kas." scenery. Kid Gleason warned them against carrying liquor "in to dry territory." Ex-servicemen Joe Jenkins, Red Faber, and Ed Collins are aboard. Others said that Keefe's war stories differed from newspaper accounts; so Keefe criticized "these here reporters" who might as well have used "opera glasses looking west" from Pikes Peak before writing their war articles. Gleason told Keefe to pitch well or get traded to Joe Cantillon "up to Minneapolis." Keefe regards the pitching recruits on the train as no competition.

"Mineral Wells [Texas], March 24." Rain caused everyone to "lay around the hotel." Keefe said "shut your mouth" when Buck Weaver complained about his comparing Texas railroads with roads in France. Gleason said "tomorrow rain or shine" they'd practice after breakfast, which he hoped Keefe wouldn't break the door down to get to first. Lots of "gals" here like ball players. Keefe is untempted, despite Miss Krug's "goggly eyes on me." She's supposedly "a swell heiress" from St. Louis and "driveing" about in "a big car," "the wile her mother is takeing the [mineral-water] treatment."

"Mineral Wells, March 26." A right-handed pitcher named Belden, recommended to Comiskey, is with the team, which Gleason ordered to practice. Passing muddy roads and a cemetery reminded Belden about his military service in France. Weaver got sarcastic, and Belden shut up. During practice, Eddie Cicotte said Belden would cause hits so often that no catcher would be needed. Miss Krug's "machine come hunking up." She asked who wanted a ride. Keefe smiled at her, but Belden intervened and off they went.

"Mineral Wells, March 29." Gleason praised Keefe's four innings of pitching in a game "between the 1st. and 2d. clubs" and told him to practice with two recruits and not eat too much, while Gleason would be taking most of the team to play in "Ft. Worth and Dallas" Saturday and Sunday. Keefe hopes for more "jack." Saturday morning Keefe pitched four innings, got tired running, and left early. Miss Krug appeared. Keefe waved, and they drove to the hotel. She said Belden said Keefe was in France. They "kidded back and 4th." She broke a date with her mother to attend a movie that night with Keefe. Keefe will "play around with her" and then "work in ernest" when the team returns on Monday.

"Mineral Wells, March 31." The team returned. Gleason got critical and "give us a long work out." A young catcher "name Cosgrove" misjudged a high foul, discarded his mask, and was conked by the ball. Gleason said he might as well be "laying there as standing up." Keefe let Miss Krug drive him to the hotel. Gleason said Keefe could surely "run the car" by now, and ordered the whole team to get to and from the park "on your own dogs" and to use the hotel stairs, not the elevator. Keefe just let Gleason talk and hopes he didn't hear how Keefe spent Sunday with Miss Krug, who is "smart as a whip." Belden, single, might be better for her, but talks about himself, and "his looks is against him." Anyway, "in a burg like this" everyone must "amuse themself" or "the crazy [mineral] wells" wouldn't help.

"Mineral Wells, April 3." Keefe pitched five innings "for the 1st. club" today, was scored on five times because Weaver and Collins made errors and Shano Collins got a hit the wind helped. The team'll play in Houston, Austin, Georgetown, and Dallas, then head north. Gleason told Keefe to start his farewells soon, to avoid missing the train, and said "next time" they should practice "in a man's convent where they's no gals." Keefe wonders what Gleason would think if he knew Miss Krug is driving to Dallas — "she hates me eh Al?" During practice, Belden suggested using French words instead of hand hit-and-run signals. Cicotte countered by saying that when opposing players caught on they could substitute Russian words. Some fellows went to "a picture show" that screened old scenes in France. Belden, overseas "4 mos," he said, recognized so many places that Cicotte jeered that "its no wonder you wasn't shot as you never stood still a minute."

"Georgetown, April 8." Keefe boasts of pitching excellently against Houston on Saturday [April

5] and in Georgetown today, with Williams pitching relief fairly well. Gleason was pleased. In Austin, Keefe made "these scollege boys" [the University of Texas players] look weak until he relented. Gleason compared Keefe to Johnson, said he'd be in the four-pitcher rotation if he forgot "some millionaire janitor's daughter with rheumatism on the mother's side," and promised Keefe "some dough that is some dough." Keefe feels it won't hurt Gleason to know Keefe simply can't impolitely ignore Miss Krug when she visits Dallas.

"Fort Worth, April 13." Miss Krug phoned him at the hotel. He was paged, answered, and made a date for "a picture show or somewheres ... that night." Gleason heard and asked if "the bell of St. Louis was folling me." Keefe said no, then lied that he was going to a show with teammates. Gleason offered to go along. Keefe admitted the truth. Gleason insisted on taking Keefe and Miss Krug to the movies and for sodas afterwards, and mentioned Keefe's wife and kids. Back at the hotel, Gleason curtly ordered Keefe to pitch next day, which he did, excellently. Although he "was just going to tell" Miss Krug about his family, he can't stand Gleason's interference and when home again will ask Comiskey to trade him. Maybe he'll go into business and not have anyone "noseing around in to your private affairs."

"Louisville, April 18." Keefe pitched well in Nashville, will pitch at "Cincy," rest, and likely pitch the season opener at St. Louis. He has generously forgiven Gleason for "the stuff he pulls." Keefe overheard that Belden, the "2d. club" pitcher gabbling about France, might have "beat Germany" but couldn't "last 2 innings vs. Boston and Cleveland." Keefe laughed until Gleason kicked him, playfully.

"Cincy, April 20." Keefe writes that "I and Lefty Williams will pitch 5 and 4 innings today." Therefore, he's sure he'll open Wednesday [April 23] in St. Louis. He says he told Gleason about Miss Krug, then got a letter from her saying she'll be in St. Louis for his opener and could she see him. Gleason said Keefe's "rosy cheeks" signaled who sent the letter. Keefe sassed Gleason, who said he was asking every player his home address and phone number. Keefe gave him his before heading "to the pk."

"St. Louis, April 24." Keefe pitched a two-hitter yesterday, striking Sisler out twice. Gleason and "the boys" praised him. But the best part? That morning before breakfast, "Florrie, all dolled up," was in the lobby. "Gleason had wrote her ... from Cincy ... to come down here at the club's expense." Her being in the stand made him pitch even better. Gleason bought a bottle of wine to share with them "in the dinning rm." afterwards and was "never ... so tickled over winning 1 ball game." He'll need pitchers like Keefe, who wonders if Miss Krug also saw the game.

"THE BATTLE OF THE CENTURY" (*Saturday Evening Post*, Oct. 29, 1921; SC). (Characters: Joe Barnes, Bradford, Robert Crawley, Doc, Jim Dugan, Tommy Fogel, Goulet, Bill Guthrie, La Chance, Senior Lopez, Larry Moon, Senior Pancho, Pinkie, Charley Riggs, Big Wheeler.)

I. Pinkie, the narrator, explains that two years ago in Omaha he saw Larry Moon and Jim Dugan. Larry manages Jim Dugan, the heavyweight champion boxer who defeated Big Wheeler. Larry and Dugan were unhappy because Dugan was starring in a circus troupe, wanted only to box, but no contenders were available. Larry said their only hope was to publicize "some young fella" to defeat some so-called "contenders" and hence qualify against Jim — for big money.

II. Later, Pinkie saw Larry and Dugan in New York. Larry read in the newspapers that Goulet had defeated Bradford, the British champ. Goulet, handsome war hero, was champion of Europe. Larry decided that proper publicity could result in Dugan's fighting Goulet.

III. Larry told Pinkie that the British press laud Goulet. Larry planted a news story that Dugan was afraid a Frenchman might take the title away from "the old U.S.A." La Chance, Goulet's manager, brought him to America to make a movie, since there wasn't much money "in France even for a champion." La Chance agreed to let Larry pick an American pushover for Goulet to knock out and then return with Goulet to France and await developments. "Oui, oui."

IV. During the next months Dugan "has to eat." So he easily knocked out a set-up in Michigan, then defeated "old Tommy Fogel" in Jersey, but had trouble beating tough Joe Barnes in "the Big Town" in the 12th round. Gossip began to favor Goulet.

V. Steamship partners Robert Crawley and Bill Guthrie agreed to back Goulet and guarantee "a suitable purse." Pinkie accompanied Larry to a Spanish restaurant in lower Broadway, whisked the head waiter and a "greasy" waiter away, fitted them with handsome clothes, and gave them strict orders. The following afternoon Crawley and Guthrie visited Larry and offered to promote a fight, with $100,000 for Dugan and $50,000 for Goulet. Scoffing, Larry let his butler introduce "Senior Lopez and Senior Pancho, from Havana," garbed "for a wedding," waving an envelope, and talking gibberish. The bluff worked: Guthrie and Crawley offered $300,000 for Larry's Dugan and $200,000 for La Chance's Goulet, with the patriotic fight to be held in America not fever-laden Cuba. Larry later explained to Pinkie that he'd get Charley Riggs, a big promoter, to up the ante to a million and thus shake out Crawley and Guthrie. This happened.

VI. Next spring Pinkie "run acrost Larry," who hired Pinkie to talk sense into Dugan at his Jersey training camp. Dugan foolishly figured his bulk would easily outmatch Goulet's speed and therefore required "the toughest kind of work" to win.

VII. Pinkie reported as asked. Dugan brooded about the fight: He was an aggressive boxer; he expected to take hits on the chin while boring in; the American public might hope he'd lose; he hoped the mat was padded to keep a knockout from resulting in tragedy.

VIII. Over some Prohibition drinks, Pinkie listened to chatter about the upcoming "big fight." Opinions were divided: Big guy would beat little guy; romantic war hero with "superhuman stren'th" would mysteriously win; La Chance and Goulet mysteriously smiled before the fight, whether because of sure victory or "the two hundred thousand fish." After the fight, Pinkie, drinking again, declined to tell "somebody something they don't want to believe." Certain reporters made enemies by writing that "Goulet didn't have a chance." Did Dugan do it "quick ... or ... [hold] back a w'ile"? Regardless, the result was profit for Riggs and control of future "big fights." A fellow drinker theorized to Pinkie that the Frenchman just "wasn't big enough." Pinkie praised his insight.

Clifford M. Caruthers reports that the *Saturday Evening Post* editors feared that "The Battle of the Century" was such "a thinly disguised narrative of the Dempsey versus Carpentier heavyweight title mismatch of 2 July 1921" that a libel suit might result. Lardner replied in a letter (August 4, 1921) identifying models for Cochran, Crawley, Moon, and Riggs, avowing that there was nothing "remotely libellous," but offering to consider alterations. He did alter Cochran slightly. Caruthers also produces evidence that "the deception practiced through the Cuban waiters was connected with the Dempsey-Willard fight of July 4, 1919." (Source: Caruthers (1995), 134, 135)

Lardner made "The Battle of the Century" more au courant for his first readers by having Larry outfit his Spanish waiters with, among other haberdashery items, "collars like Senator Smoot's," and by having Pinkie opine that "many American fight writers ... knows more about fights and fighters than Bernard Shaw." The references are to Reed Smoot (1862–1941), who served in the U.S. Senate (1903–1933), and to George Bernard Shaw (1856–1950), Irish-born man of letters popular in the United States for many plays but no sports acumen. Lardner also has Pinkie mention pugilists of "twenty or thirty years ago ... like Fitz, Corbett and McCoy, and Choynski, Sharkey, Ruhlin, big Jeff, and all that gang." The references are to Joseph Bartlett Choynski (1868–1943), James John Corbett (1866–1933), Robert James Fitzsimmons (1863–1917), James Jackson Jeffries (1875–1953), Gus Ruhlin (1872–1912), and Thomas J. Sharkey (1873–1953), and to either Alexander Rudolph McCoy (1894–1966) or (less likely) Charles ("Kid") McCoy (1872–1940). Pinkie rightly says "any one of them [is] liable to knock each other's block off," since several of them fought each other.

BAUER, L. N. ("The Jade Necklace"). He runs Colossal Films Incorporated. He buys the film rights to *Harridan*, a novel by David Wallace, learns that "a harridan" is a vixen or a jade, and supervises his writers' conversion of the novel about a woman wrongly regarded as a harridan into a movie entitled *The Jade Necklace* and — without Bauer's awareness, surely — paralleling *Madame Butterfly*.

BAUMGARDNER ("A Busher's Letters Home") *see* **BUMGARDNER**

BEAN, JOE ("A Caddy's Diary"). He is a fellow caddy with the diarist. Joe is a quick, bright smarty; so lady golfers prefer the diarist.

Donald Elder regards Joe as a "thankless" wit, whose "character ... as a humorist and moralist is so carefully ... built up that his [final] comment [for Dick to shut up] becomes the point of the story." (Source: Elder, 215–16).

BEARDSLEY ("Three Without, Doubled"). This is the name of a couple in whose home Bertha Hatch boasts to Mrs. Gullible that she and her husband Jim Hatch recently played bridge, with the San Susie bridge club.

BEARDSLEY, ALEXANDER ("ALEC") ("Freedom of the Press"). He was the late Robert

J. Warner's secretary. Alec reports to Warner's shy daughter Constance Warner to help clear up business matters but soon falls in love with her. They marry but have their honeymoon disrupted by Hunter, a *Ferret* reporter.

BEASLEY, BETH ("Absent-minded Beggar"). She is John Knowles's friend from high-school days and thinks they will love one another. When John returns from Paris, he falls in love with Irene Comerford.

BEASLEY, J. L. ("Absent-minded Beggar"). He is Beth Beasley's father. He establishes a brokerage firm with H. N. Comerford and hires John Knowles in an effort to help his daughter, who loves John.

BEATTY, KEN ("Haircut"). He was the coroner of the town where Whitey lives. When Beatty died, Doc Ralph Stair replaced him.

"BEAUTIFUL KATIE" (*Saturday Evening Post*, July 10, 1920; BT).

BEISTLE, DR. ("How Are You?"). He is a New York physician recommended to Bob Dayton.

BELDEN ("The Battle of Texas"). He is a recently recruited pitcher, who seems to be a challenge to Keefe, but only briefly.

The only major-league baseball player named Belden was Ira Allison Belden (1874–1916), who was a one-season outfielder for the Cleveland Indians (1897). Was Keefe's brief challenger Ira's son or nephew, perhaps? (*Baseball Encyclopedia*, 775)

BELDEN ("Widow"). He and his wife Flora, from Frankfort, Kentucky, happened to meet Archie's widow, their friend, in Miami. They took her to a party at the Casino, where she met Fred Milburn, who became her second husband.

BELDEN, COACH ("A One-Man Team"). He is a school football coach. He figures his defense can defeat the "one-man" Doane team by having a strong defense concentrate on Davis, their only outstanding player. Belden is outwitted by Smith, Doane's coach.

BELDEN, FLORA ("Widow"). She and her husband chanced to meet their friend, Archie's widow, in Miami and were indirectly responsible for her meeting Fred Milburn, whom she married.

BELDEN, HENRY J. ("Zone of Quiet"). He was Miss Eleanor Lyons's patient in Great Neck. She tells her present patient that Belden died.

BELDEN, MR. ("Bob's Birthday"). He owns Belden's Orchestra and employs Bob as an all-around musician.

BELLOWS, CAPTAIN JARVIS ("A Chip of the Old Block"). He is identified by Tracy in conversation with Captain Evan Barnes as belonging to the Toy Balloons army unit. Bellows has a Rolls-Royce.

BEN ("Gullible's Travels"). He is a friend of the Gullibles, who plan to go dancing with him until they feel too conceited to do so.

BEN ("The Last Night"). He serves Jay Arnold drinks at a Chicago saloon called Carney's.

BEN ("What of It?"). He is Ben Lacey's sister Bertha's two-year-old son, about whom Ben talks to Dexter Cosset.

BENHAM, DR. ("How Are You?"). He is a New York tooth extractor recommended to Bob Dayton.

BENHAM, EARL ("Ex Parte"). He runs the store where the narrator buys a new suit.

BENHAM, EARL ("The Jade Necklace"). He is the scenarist whom L. N. Bauer hires to convert Wallace's novel *Harridan* into a movie. In doing so, Benham writes a plot paralleling *Madame Butterfly*.

BENJAMIN ("A One-Man Team"). He is an outstanding football player for the team of a school called Monroe. Coach Belden is pleased to remember that his team defeated the "one-man team" of Monroe by concentrating his defense on Benjamin.

BENNETT ("Words and Music"). He is the secretary of Roman Starr, the popular singer.

BENNETT, AMY ("The Spinning Wheel"). She is a pretty but dumb lady, 22 or 23, who pretends to like Jess Dorsey, a roulette dealer, thinking he can cheat and enable her and her boyfriend, who she tells Jess is her brother, to win. They lose.

BENSON ("Oh, You Bonehead!"). He is a member of the Coach's unnamed football team.

BENTLEY ("Oh, You Bonehead"). He was the coach of the Pelham football team when, owing to Joe Draper's "bonehead" play for the Leighton team, Pelham won.

BENTON ("My Roomy"). He is a left-handed pitcher for "Cincy." Buster Elliott hits a double off him. In "Horseshoes," Benton is a Cincinnati pitcher when Dick Grimes and Speed Parker are playing for the Cubs against Cincinnati.

John Clebon "Rube" Benton (1887–1937) played for the Cincinnati Reds (1910–1915, 1923–1925) and the New York Giants (1915–1921). (Source: Hilton, 342)

BENTON, RUBE ("Alibi Ike"). Rube Benton and Red Ames play on the Cincinnati baseball team defeated by Alibi Ike and his teammates.

BENZ In "A Busher's Letters Home," Keefe says Callahan, White Sox manager, pitched him in Los Angeles more often than he did Benz. In "The Busher Comes Back," Keefe says Benz is in poor shape in Chicago. "A New Busher Breaks In," Keefe says Joe Benz got married, and "must of got a good wife" because he shut out Cleveland in the season opener. In "The Busher's Kid," Keefe praises Benz for winning a "city serious" game, and easily since "the club made 6 runs for him." In "The Busher Reënlists," Keefe is bothered when Joe Benz, Jim Archer, Artie Hofman, and Charley O'Leary, all Chicago players, don't ask about his war experiences. In "The Busher Abroad," Benz is on the world tour. In "The Busher's Welcome Home," Benz and Keefe pitch against each other in a game in London. Keefe mentions Benz in *The Real Dope*.

Joseph Lewis ("Blitzen") Benz (1886–1957) spent his career (1911–1919) pitching for the White Sox. James E. Elfers reports that during the world tour Benz appeared in 33 games (1913) and that his "fireballing" speed caused the Benz racing car to be named after him. Nicholas Dawidoff reports that "Butcher Boy Joe Benz ... [was] a notable unsophisticate who once pitched an exhibition game for the White Sox while dressed in hip boots" and that he was one model for Lardner's immortal Jack Keefe. (Sources: *Baseball Encyclopedia*, 1823; Dawidoff, 81; Elfers, 28; Hilton, 55)

BERGER ("Anniversary"). He is one of Louis Taylor's bowling pals. Berger was recently too drunk to play, according to Louis's report to his bored wife Bess Taylor.

BERGER ("The Busher Comes Back"). Keefe gripes that Berger's fumble cost the White Sox a run in a game against Cleveland.

Joseph August Berger (1886–1956) was a Chicago White Sox utility infielder (1913–1914). (Source: Hilton, 82)

BERGER ("Great Blessings"). He runs a "cash market," where Clara Stewart can't shop any more.

BERGERT ("Lose with a Smile"). He played outfield for the Boston Braves in a game against Danny, who hit a Seibold pitch that Bergert and Maranville misplayed. Danny razzed Maranville afterwards.

Walter Antone Bergert (1905–1988) played for the Boston Braves (1930–1936), the Braves and the New York Giants (1937), the Giants and the Cincinnati Reds (1938), the Reds (1939), and the Philadelphia Phillies (1940). (Source: *Baseball Encyclopedia*, 784)

BERLIN, IRVING (1888–1989). Songwriter and composer. Russian-born Isadore Baline migrated to New York City with his family (1893) and was eight when his father, a cantor, died. To help support his family, Berlin sold newspapers on the streets, sang on street corners, and was a singing waiter. He published his first song (1907), published upwards of 20 more songs (1909), sang in vaudeville (1910), and became famous with "Alexander's Ragtime Band" (1911). Berlin wrote for several *Follies* of Florenz Ziegfeld* (from 1911), and built his own Broadway theater (1921). He composed music and wrote lyrics for musical comedies, and scored movies and Broadway shows. Some authorities say Berlin wrote upwards of 1,500 songs; others, about 3,000. "God Bless America" (1918, rev. 1938) and "White Christmas" (1940) are the most beloved.

Irving Berlin is mentioned in "Facts," "Meet Me In St. Louie," "Rhythm," and "Stop Me — If You've Heard This One." (See also Igoe, Battling.) (Sources: Elder, 257; Farnsworth, 81, 126; Streissguth, 363–364)

BERNARD ("High-rollers"). Bernard and Craig are "Publicity Engineers" in New York. Walter Finch quits working for Ripley to get high pay from Bernard and Craig.

BERNER ("The Hold-Out"). He was a competent shortstop on the team Mr. Edwards owned. Berner laughed at Lahey's poor playing.

BERT ("My Roomy"). He is a Chicago baseball player. He is almost hit by a ball Buster Elliott smashes during batting practice.

Albert Humphries (1880–1945) pitched for the Phillies (1910), the Phillies and Cincinnati (1911), and the Cubs (1912–1915). (Sources: *Baseball Encyclopedia*, 2088; Hilton, 336).

BERT ("Widow"). According to Mrs. Gordon, Bert was her sister Julia's wealthy husband, lived with her in Minnesota, and died leaving Julia financially comfortable.

BERTHA ("The Busher Comes Back," etc.) *see* **BLANCHARD, BERTHA**

BERTHA ("What of It?"). She is Ben Lacey's sister, about whom Ben jabbers to Dexter Cosset.

BESCHER ("Horseshoes"). He is an outfielder for the Giants during their World Series against the Athletics. He walks in the third game and can't possibly catch Dick Grimes's fierce homer in the sixth game.

Robert Henry Bescher (1884–1942) was an outfielder for the Cincinnati Reds (1908–1913), the New York Giants (1914), the St. Louis Cardinals (1915–1917), and the Cleveland Indians (1918). (Sources: *Baseball Encyclopedia*, 788; Hilton, 412–413)

BESS (*Gullible's Travels, Etc.*) *see* **GORTON, BESS**

BETH ("The Facts"). She was a girlfriend of Walter McDonald, who dumps her for Kathryn.

BETTY ("Mamma"). She is Mamma's daughter.

BETTY ("That Old Sweetheart of Mine"). She is Will's utility girlfriend. When Stella Crane seems available, he breaks a date with Betty. When Stella demurs, he phones Betty and continues their affair.

B.F. ("Zone of Quiet"). He was a boyfriend of Miss Eleanor Lyons, in Washington, D.C.

B.F. ("Zone of Quiet"). One of Roy Stewart's friends, he knows Marian.

BIG JEFF ("My Roomy") *see* **TESREAU, JEFF**

THE BIG TOWN: HOW I AND THE MRS. GO TO NEW YORK TO SEE LIFE AND GET KATIE A HUSBAND (1921). Five novel-like short stories: "Quick Returns" (*Saturday Evening Post*, March 27, 1920), "Ritchey" (originally entitled "Beautiful Katie" [*Saturday Evening Post*, July 10, 1920]), "Lady Perkins" (originally entitled "The Battle of Long Island" [*Saturday Evening Post*, November 27, 1920]), "Only One" (*Saturday Evening Post*, February 12, 1921), and "Katie Wins a Home" (originally entitled "The Comic" [*Saturday Evening Post*, May 14, 1921]).

"Quick Returns" (Characters: Eckhart, Mrs. Eckhart, Finch, Ella Finch, Francis Griffin, Hector, George Hull, Katie, H. L. Krause.)

Finch, the narrator sells cigars in South Bend, Indiana, for $1,800 a year, has been married five years. He declines his wife Ella's step-father's invitation to work in his leather factory in Niles, Michigan, for $900, live with him, Ella and her sister Katie, 20, and later maybe become factory manager. During the war the father-in-law gets rich on government contracts. When peace comes he "died of grief," leaving Ella and Katie $75,000 each. The daughters sell "the odor factory," grab $5,000 each "for pin money," invest the rest in bonds, and Katie moves in with the Finches and goes husband-hunting. Ignored by friends because of news concerning their sudden wealth, the girls "hired a cater" and an orchestra and throw a dismal party. Finch dances with stiff Mrs. Eckhart, lubricates her husband with bourbon in the kitchen, but his wife encourages all the guests to leave.

Friendless all winter, Finch, Ella, and Katie summer at a Lake Wawasee hotel, where Katie innocently likes a cheap gambler until his wife appears. Ellen persuades Finch to sell some bonds to augment their $8,000-a-year interest, try New York, which he says he's heard of, and find Katie a rich husband there. Katie "squealed and kissed us both." They sell their furniture and "set forth to see Life."

On the train, Finch gives "the fish eye and the non-stop signal" to traveling salesmen who like Katie's looks and would take advantage. The three are seated in the diner with a guy named Francis Griffin, who boasts of adoring his native New York City, especially Broadway. The girls giggle when he says he's "an old bachelor." He recommends the Baldwin Hotel in central New York, at $12 a day, within walking distance to theaters and shops. He and Finch needle each other about Prohibition, which Griffin says real New Yorkers ignore. Getting "dirty looks" from the girls, Finch makes peace with Griffin by producing some bourbon.

Next morning Finch is hung-over. Griffin treats the girls to breakfast in the diner and says he makes $20,000 a year on Wall Street. After Katie and Griffin sit alone and chat, the four resume discussing money. Griffin says $20,000 is just enough for him to enjoy alone but adds that two can live as cheaply as one. The girls giggle. Finch treats everyone for dinner. Griffin promises dinner on him some time, but when they deboard at Grand Central Station he lacks time to show them to the Baldwin. The "oil-haired clerk" tells Finch they lack room. Ella lies that they wired for reservations; so the clerk finds them a double at $15 daily. At dinner Katie wears "the riskiest dress she'd bought in Chi." Ella praises other diners' skimpier ones. Their slight meal cost $20. Katie wants to go shopping tomorrow, with Ella but not with Finch.

Wednesday: Ella phones Griffin, who cashes a check for her. She and Katie buy evening gowns for $1,600, as an investment, Ella says, to lure "Mister Wall Street to-night." She also reserves theater tickets to *Ups and Downs*, to follow Griffin's treating them to dinner. He arrives. They dine. He dazes Finch with a hip-flask drink. Finch pays $13.20 for the tickets to *Ups and Downs*, which features stale jokes. Ella browbeats Finch into escorting the party to the Castle Roof, promising "quick returns" for Katie. At their $20 table, Griffin tells Finch to get real drinks through Hector, his head-waiter friend there. So it's chicken, Scotch, and a "dinge orchestra ... jazz." Griffin dances, first, with Ella. Katie admits to Finch that Griffin is "shy" and almost wordless. Finch turns "practic'lly unconscious" after his Scotch until the $40 check awakens him. Although Finch regards Griffin as "gun-shy" near Katie, Griffin does take the girls to the Palace on Friday. Finch has "scotch influenza" and is excluded.

Saturday: Ella meets Griffin to inspect "a little furnished apartment" he wants to surprise "Sis" with. She soon returns, furious, saying he kissed her in the taxi first thing. "'Quick returns,' I says." Finch spends Sunday "training" on a bell hop's $15 rye while Katie, to whom Ella explained matters, moans "like a prune-fed calf." Finch visits Wall Street's H. L. Krause company, locates Griffin, and creates records resembling those of several famous college and professional athletes by using Griffin as boxing opponent, football, and baseball.

"Quick Returns" opens and closes with references to a New York newspaper report that a "Hoosier" cleaned up on Wall Street, that his name is known only to an H. L. Krause company employee named Francis Griffin, that Griffin can't "recall" the Hoosier's name. The cleaning, which refers to Hoosier Finch's beating of Griffin, makes sense only at the end. "Quick Returns" opens *The Big Town* with some of the most uproariously funny writing, in and out of dialogue, in all of Lardner.

"Ritchey." (Characters: Allah, Doyle, Ella Finch, Tom Finch, George, Katie, Kitchell, Kathleen Mavourneen. Omar, Ritchey, Trumbull, Wilmot.)

Soon after Finch gets accustomed to life at the Baldwin, Ella announces her intention to find a six-room apartment in which to welcome Katie's suitors. Despite his grumbling, they rent one in the Lucius on Riverside Drive for $4,000 a year. Finch complains that $4,000 is about half the girls' income. They'll economize, says Ella. Yeah, counters Finch, by a few servants, a car, and several evening gowns. Yes, buy us a car, says Katie. The sixth-floor apartment has a good view, is over-loaded with furniture; being Drive residents, the girls mustn't cook. They advertise for a cook for $8 a week, interview "a colleen" Finch calls Kathleen Mavourneen, who demands $90 a month and "No washin.'" Finch persuades outraged Ella to try her for a month.

Katie shops for a car but finds all possibilities "too expensive" or looking "like they wasn't." One day after shopping, Ella is stopped by Trumbull, a tall, handsome, but old Lucius neighbor in a limousine, and is given a lift home. Saying he thinks Ella's sister is "a beautiful girl," he invites both plus Finch to dinner the next night. Questioned by Finch, Ella says that Trumbull is "not old ... not even that old" and adds that he says he keeps "bachelor quarters."

They dress for dinner. Finch finds Trumbull so old he nicknames him Methuselah (and later Old Noah). His identical servants Finch dubs Omar and Allah. Dinner features "hootch" after every course. They dance to a "steam piano." The guests have a tour of the apartment. Trumbull says this chair cost $200, that dining-room suit $1,800, a "rag carpet" $2,000, "Marie Antoinette's bed" $1,000, his "Rose D. Barry" bathrobe $200. The girls get drowsy. Trumbull flourishes "a pair of African golf balls," invites happy Finch to shoot craps with him, $25 limit, and genially loses to him. Going home, Katie tells Finch to shut up when he asks if she likes Trumbull.

Next night Trumbull orders Ritchey, his chauffeur, to drive the four of them to "up the river to a place I know." Katie says liveried Ritchey looks "stunning" standing by the "Rools-Royce." Finch hears "mine host" call Ritchey a trustworthy "boy." They enter the Indian Inn. Trumbull buys two $20 bootlegged bottles. The four dine near a cornet-blaring orchestra to. Kate orders $4.50 guinea hen. They all dance. Soon Katie begs to go home, confiding in Finch that old Trumbull was "fresh," squeezed her hand, and she doesn't like him. Home they go, with Ella separately urging Trumbull to be patient with the "kid," and Katie to be sensible. Katie says she "wouldn't care" if Trumbull "was fresh ... if he was fresh." Trumbull offers the "limmie" plus Ritchey for the shopping-addicted girls any time.

Next day Ritchey drives Katie to shop. Trumbull, tolerant and generous with car and hootch, visits the Finches about 5:00 pm. Katie returns two hours later. All dine, play rummy until they're "blear-eyed," and, with Trumbull gone until a promised drive tomorrow, Ella advises Katie to encourage the oldster.

Next morning Trumbull says he's called to Washington for a few days but they can use the car. When Finch suggests driving to Bridgeport to visit his cousins the Wilmots, Katie, ever "so calm" at news of Trumbull's departure, says she'll be busy being driven by Ritchey to dressmakers. Trumbull returns in a week, pops in for dinner, and happens to praise Ritchey for caring well for his wife and two children. Katie "kind of fell into a swoon." The trio sublet their Drive apartment, after two weeks there, at a $1,000 a year loss, and return to the Baldwin.

"Lady Perkins." (Characters: Gene Buck, Bob Codd, Decker, Finch, Ella Finch, George Henkel, Katie, Martha, Perkins, Lady Perkins, Doctor Platt, Snell, Mrs. Snell, Tracy, Williams, Palmer Williams, Ed Wurz.)

In May, Katie complains about New York's hot weather. A diner named Gene Buck, to whom Katie and Ella talk about their money, suggests that the two and Finch summer at Long Island's exclusive Hotel Decker, where there's golfing and dancing. The girls take a train, follow Buck's directions, find the place, and rent two rooms with baths at $200 weekly, meals included, and plan on 20 weeks. Finch gripes uselessly about depleting their income.

Next day Finch wrestles the luggage, while the girls carry their parasols and wrist watches. The Decker is a family place, meaning many of "the cay-nine family." Couples who "can't afford dogs has got children." Night noises come from "the dogs' dormitories" and the bachelor "souses." The hotel features ballroom, card rooms, parlor, tiny orchestra. The men commute to New York "on Business." Some women walk dogs in the yard. Benches are over-occupied during days by other women and nurses reading "to the dogs or kids," and later by tired waitresses. After "a four-course breakfast," porch-sitting women discuss recent murders, pets, the stock market. Late lunches include soup, duckling "caught fresh," salad, pie à la mode, and coffee. Then naps until "Dear" reappears after "Business." Saturday night evening clothes fail to make anything happen. Sunday mornings the men arise early for "real business, ... golf"; following is evening conversation, about golden wedding anniversaries, careless caddies, chiropodist appointments, etc., then bridge games and "song hit[s]" from *The Bohemian Girl* [1839].

Hotel conveniences include light bulbs and bathtub stoppers, and a barber doubling as a valet. Finch plays solitaire a lot. By week's end, Ella and Katie try chatting with other "squatters," but talk regularly becomes "a short monologue." They make friends with the head waiter, their waitress, clerks, "telephone gals." Katie cries nightly. Finch suggests returning to New York; so they don't. Ella describes one nice guest — Lady Perkins, 35, English, husband on business in Texas, uses cane, has German police dog and small chow. Finch's saying he'll go meet Lady Perkins results in Ella's warning him to stop looking so untidy that guests think "we was leopards ... out of a pest-house."

Next morning Finch spots Lady Perkins and watches her "nurse" escort her two dogs away for food. Ed Wurz, the hotel manager, invites him to play golf. No, my dogs hurt, is Finch's reply. Lady Perkins asks about his health. Wickedly engaging her in conversation, he pretends his injured dogs are Dakota yaphounds, here earlier but hospitalized in Haverton for "blanny," a contagious, rash-producing Peruvian disease. Her dogs might be exposed too. He'll buy them some medicine. Lady Perkins leaves to check on her dogs. Finch's "girls" appear. When Lady Perkins returns to talk with him, the girls regard him with awe.

Before dinner, Finch fills an empty bottle with soapy water. At dinner, Lady Perkins asks him about his dogs. Better. The girls, whom he introduces, "stagger ... pop-eyed." He says he'll give Perk anti-rash medicine. In the "card room," she gratefully requests, departing. He tells the open-mouthed girls that he confessed to sore feet, she said she was similarly afflicted, and they discussed medicine. The girls rush dinner but aren't allowed to accompany Finch when he takes the "medicine" to Perkie. Ella says if he flirts with that "old hag," she and Katie will encourage some men in retaliation. Relenting, Finch tells Ella everything, is permitted to meet with the woman alone, and warns Ella to brief Katie. The three will ambush the lady on the porch tomorrow. He interrupts Perk, a Mrs. Snell, a Doctor Platt, and some dude at "bridge w'ist." Platt voices his suspicions about blanny and yaphounds; so Finch sneeringly leaves and finds Ella and Katie, the latter agog over Bob Codd, who is here to demonstrate his newly invented "aeroplane" at the nearby "flying field" of the Williams Company. He could sell it for a million. Learning about the bridge players, Ella gushes: Mrs. Snell is that bridge champion; her husband, "the sugar man"; her father, banker George Henkel. Ella wants to meet Mrs. Snell, though not to gamble at bridge with her. Codd promises to take Katie for a flight after he tests his "machine."

Finch, Ella, and Katie meet Perkie on the porch next morning. He advises her to tell Martha, the dog nurse, to let the medicinal lather dry on the dogs to kill the blanny germs. Ella mentions bridge, which she'd like to learn; but Perk complains that it takes a while, Doctor Platt talks endlessly during play, and last night cost her $370. Ella wants to watch them play. All right, but not tonight, counters Perkie, owing to a rare hotel dance, which Mr. Snell is "mad" for. That evening, Finch pleads a "corn" and therefore attends the ball without dancing. Attendance at the "knock-out" event includes the Finches, Katie, Codd, the Snells, Platt with "a gal" in childish clothes, and "a pair of shimmy shakers." The Snells tire and leave. Platt freezes Finch with a look. Codd alternates dancing with Katie and Ella. Everything ends about ten o'clock.

Next night Codd takes Ella for a drive. Ella wheedles Finch into watching the bridge game. Perk hopes their watching will bring her and her "anonymous dude" partner victory over Platt and Mrs. Snell. With phenomenal cards, Perkie and her dude are "seven hundred berries" ahead. Next morning Perk thanks her "mascots" for bringing her good fortune, says she's still behind overall, but with more luck she'll win and thereafter gratefully "treat" her mascots. After her late breakfast, Katie reveals this: Codd seems "stuck on her"; his "machine" is perfected; the Williams brothers like it; Codd is giving Katie a plane ride tomorrow; tonight she's free to watch the bridge players because Codd is partying "in Town" with some college buddies. That evening Perkie admits the trio with a smile. The game goes badly for her, improves to about even, but then "the blow-off come." During a crucial deal, Perk holds four aces but her bidding is interrupted. Katie exclaims that Perkie holds "Four aces!" Perk calls Katie a meddlesome fool and expresses the hope that her "aeroplane falls a million feet."

Katie weeps all night and therefore doesn't fly with "poor" Codd, whose machine does an "involuntary nose dive" next day and he "was spilled all over Long Island." Urging Finch not to worry, Ella says that Katie said that Codd's invention "couldn't of been" worth "a plugged dime." Reading on the porch, Lady Perkins speaks but once to Finch. When he tells her "the veter'nary" had to shoot his sick dogs, "'That's good,' said Perk, and went on reading."

"Only One." (Characters: Goat Anderson, Bradley, Captain Alcock, Carney, Cleopatra, Herbert Daley, Ernest, Finch, Ella Finch, Fly-by-Night, Great Scott, Haynes, Honor Bright, Katie, Sid Mercer, Joe Meyer, Only One, On Watch, Sammy Pass, Lady Perkins, Sap, Sea Mint, Sena Day, Streak of Lightning, Sweet and Easy, Tamarisk, Wurz.)

Lady Perkins's husband telegraphs her to join him in Texas. Finch's "two gals pretty themselves ... for dinner" nightly. Katie attracts Herbert Daley's attention with a "'Welcome' embroidered on her pan." Wurz, the hotel manager, tells Finch that "Daley the horseman" has a stable of racehorses at Jamaica, aims to "clean up round New York" by racing his uniquely fast "Only One," will give Wurz some betting tips, is single, and asked about "Miss Kate." Finch relays this thrilling news to the girls, reassures modest Katie that Daley has been staring at her, and can't discourage the girls from planning to go bet at some races. At dinner, Daley seats himself with the trio, says he's shipped 30 horses for racing, goes most afternoons to Jamaica events, invested $200,000 in Liberty Bonds, and happily spends plenty at the Decker because he meets "young ladies like the present company." Finch escapes when "the orchestra begin to drool" and later is informed that the three are accompanying Daley tomorrow "in his small car."

Before entering Daley's huge automobile, Finch packs some illegal hooch, which occasions Daley's comments on his jockey, Sid Mercer. Sid got fired by one horse owner after arguing with his girlfriend and getting drunk; Daley demanded sobriety, hired Sid at "$20,000 for first call," and lets him "make all he can on the side." Daley treats for lunch at his reserved track table and tells naive Katie about betting, bookmakers, and how they both could bet on one horse he'd recommend. While Daley visits the paddock "to see what's new," Finch scans the crowd and sees numerous "former wifes" with too much makeup betting and surrounded by fat "guys with chins that runs into five and six figures," "ham actors" and "losers'-end boxers," and shouting enthusiasts with binoculars. Daley returns, having bet $1,000 on Sweet and Pretty to "place and show" in the first race. Once he explains all that, the girls each bet $10 to show. Daley places their bets. He explains jockeys' colors, including his. Second race: Daley bets $1,000 4 to 1 on Sena Day to place and makes the girls do so with $20 each. Finch accompanies Daley, meets bookie Joe Meyer, but doesn't bet. Sena Day wins. Winners are the girls, with $160 minus the lost $20, and $2,000 for Daley, who buys "sarsaparilla" for three. Finch "poured my own." Daley advises avoiding the third race. Fourth race: Daley wins $800 on Tamarisk, and the girls win $8 each. Fifth race: Daley stoically watches his Fly-by-Night, ridden by Sid, lose. Final race: Daley and the girls win. In all, he's ahead $4,000; the girls, $160 together. Before driving everyone to the hotel, Daley introduces tiny Sid. He and Katie "give each other a smile with a future in it."

Time passes. Daley and the trio eat together. The girls go shopping "in Town." Daley likes Katie, who, despite Ella's advice, "kept him at arm's len'th," preferring dates with a New York "golf champion" she calls Goldberg. Daley sulks. Katie charms him again. He says he'd like to include Sid at a hotel get-together. Katie declines. Daley takes her for a walk and proposes. She says she needs a "wile to think." As "a novelty, I suppose," Finch retorts.

Next day, Only One will run at the Belmont. Finch reminisces about whispered tips concerning horses he remembers from days past. Daley advises restrained betting, puts $2,000 for himself on Only One's nose, $20 for each girl, and Finch, who's been betting and winning, risks $200, all at 3 to 1. Breaking the track record, Only One wins ahead of Streak of Lightning "by a flea's jaw." Katie: "O you Sid!"

Daley, ahead by $14,000, is called briefly to Kentucky. He orders his driver, Ernest, to chauffeur the trio around. Katie and Ella bet successfully on tips from Goldberg, whom Katie has a date with one night in town. Finch and Ella go see a show, are driven to Manhattan by Ernest, decide to pick up Katie at the Pennsylvania Station, but see her with "Goldberg," really Sid. He ducks off. Ernest spots the well-paid jockey. The girls don't. Finch does, but keeps quiet "for fear of spoiling the show." Ella urges Katie to accept Daley. Katie says Sid is well paid, dances great, but she may marry neither.

The girls keep winning on tips from Sid, who takes the trio via train to a New York party. Daley returns on Wednesday and has Ernest drive him alone to the track. Undoubtedly Ernest "squealed." Daley acts the same that evening, however, and he and Katie become engaged. On Thursday Finch and Ella hear Katie tell Sid on the phone that her "note" said "why" and then "Not with no jail-bird." Katie, looking glum, says Ella should be satisfied with her engagement.

Friday Finch receives a wire from Goat Anderson, a South Bend friend, to meet him at the Belmont, goes there, but, when Goat doesn't appear, returns to the Pennsylvania Station, has a drink nearby, and is hailed by Sid. Drunk and belligerent, Sid asks if Ella "told Daley about your sister-in-law and I?" When Finch says no and Ernest must have, Sid vows he'll fix Daley and "smiled ... silly." Anxious to see Sid safely back to their hotel, Finch waits and drinks, and they talk. Finch says Daley has been "a good friend," upon which Sid unloads the following: Daley told Mercer he'll marry Katie and then instantly say "good-by, family-in-law!" because Finch is a "smart Aleck ... wise cracker ... clown" and Ella is herself "fishing for a sucker with her sister as bait"; Daley recognized that Katie liked Sid and therefore told her about Sid's shooting at a love-rival in Louisville resulting in 11-months' jail time; Katie wrote Sid farewell; Daley pays Sid $10,000 not $20,000; Sid plans to quit starving himself to make his weight, quit jockeying, take tomorrow's winnings, and work with his successful brother in Oklahoma oil. Rambling on, Sid tells Finch that tomorrow's handicap race will involve only three horses; he's betting on Sap, not Only One, on whom Daley is betting "his right eye"; Finch should bet his, Ella's, and Katie's money on Sap too. Sid still admires Katie. Finch happily anticipates a financial break for Katie and getting even with bad-mouth Daley.

Saturday at the Belmont. Fourth race, a handicap, with Only One (1 to 3), Sap (6 to 1), and heavy Honor Bright (20 to 1), all others scratched. Daley bets $15,000 on Only One. Finch pretends to bet the girls' $1,200 on Only One but doesn't, and has bookie Haynes put $1,000 for him on Sap, who wins "three len'ths" ahead of Honor Bright. Crushed are the girls and Daley, who drinks from Finch's flask while getting called a cheating thief by Katie. "Romance was knocked" dead.

Monday's mail brings Katie a farewell note from Sid, heading for Oklahoma, and Haynes's $8,000 check for Finch, who confesses to the girls that he got "rattled" at the track, bet his money on Sap, but forgot to bet the girls' money on Only One. The girls' $1,200 is safe. They kiss Finch, who dares them to lay hands on his check.

Lardner's knowledge of racing, bookies, and horseracing odds, and his colorful names for horses, combine to indicate considerable track expertise.

"Katie Wins a Home." (Characters: Jane Abbott, Bridget, Finch, Ella Finch, Bunny Granville, Gussie, Katie, Jimmy Ralston, Bobbie Shaw, Captain Francis Shaw, Mrs. Shaw, Thornton, Ziggy Ziegfeld.)

Finch, Ella, and Katie move into New York's Graham Hotel. He is content, having won "close to $10,000 on the ponies." But the girls dislike other residents — "tune thieves," female reporters, and defeated boxers — until handsome Jimmy Ralston, the Follies "comic," checks in and attracts Katie's attention. She heard he had been "a scream ... on a party" when drunk just right, denies wanting Ralston "as a possible suitor," but longs to tell him she liked the Follies, and to talk with a man that "doesn't bore a person to death." The trio taxi to the Spencer, buy Follies tickets, dine minimally for "eleven smackers," and see the Follies. Ralston is featured between "the big gal numbers." His gags are old, but his "fool make-up and that voice" are richly comic.

Two days later the trio force themselves on Ralston during their breakfast and his lunch. Katie and Ella gush about his Follies. He replies that he moved from the Ritz to the Graham's "best suite" to avoid autograph seekers, demanded $1,500 instead of $1,000 weekly from Ziggy Ziegfeld, doesn't care about money, and wants to play Shakespearean roles. Invited by Ella for refreshments tonight, Ralston leaves, without paying his check. Finch agrees: Ralston doesn't care about money. Ralston comes to the Finches' room, gorges on Finch's "yearling rye," gazes in the room mirror, breaks a nearby vase, finds and enjoys Finch's hidden McAllister scotch, consumes Finch's delicatessen chicken and olives, and litters the carpet with bones, stones, cigarette butts. Ralston reminisces about his smallpox-killed father, train-killed mother, jaundiced-killed sister, about comics' stealing his gags, about giving them to Eddie Wynn and other joke-poor strugglers — without pay, since "They're all brothers to me." Two McAllister bottles later, Ralston confides that he's quitting cheap Ziegfeld, will star in his own play with his own "troupe," and seeks an investor. Katie offers "some money." Ralston heads for his room to show her his script and but falls unconscious "in the chili sauce." Finch and a "bellhop" get him to his "dinky little room."

Next noon Katie says she phoned Ralston and he apologized for getting sick. Finch himself turns feverish, is hospitalized with the flu, and two weeks later learns the news, from Ella: Katie, in love with Ralston, has sold her bonds, put $50,000 in a checking account, advanced $10,000 to Ralston, and has a role in his play, "Bridget Sees a Ghost." After secret rehearsals, it opens in the costly Olney theater. The play is about Captain Francis Shaw, his wife Maizie, and their baby Bobbie. Francis goes to France in 1917, is reported dead; Maizie weds Thornton after the Armistice; while the two are out, Francis returns, on crutches; Bobbie doesn't want another "papa"; the Shaws' maid Bridget sees him, regards him as a ghost, promises not to talk about him; he disappears forever. The play is jeered by audience and reviewers alike. Ralston "canned" Katie, who weeps, confesses to Finch that she gave Ralston $25,000 in all, but soon brightens. She and Ralston get married and head for Boston, where he rejoins the Follies at his original weekly salary, $400, Katie says. Finch and Ella return by train to South Bend. Finch feels that Katie probably likes "to just set and listen" when her comedian-husband talks.

Lardner has big-mouth Ralston drop several stage performers' names, including but not limited to Leon Errol, Al Jolson, Bert Williams,* and Ed Wynn. Australian-born comic Leon Errol (1881–1951) began in vaudeville (Sydney, 1896), moved to the United States (1906), was popular as "Rubber Legs" in the *Follies* (1911–1915) of Florenz Ziegfeld* as a wobbly-legged drunk, and produced and starred in *The Century Girl* (1916), music by Irving Berlin.* Errol became an American citizen (1923), made movies (from 1924), and was on television with Ed Wynn. Lardner sent Zelda Fitzgerald, wife of F. Scott Fitzgerald,* a letter with a Christmas poem (1922), one line being "I worship Leon Errol." Lardner includes a clever pun on "Leon" and "herculean" in "Claude Diphthong, Student of Crime." Al Jolson (1888–1950), born Asa Yoelson and raised in Washington, D.C., was famous as a blackface singer, and produced and starred in his autobiographical movie *The Jazz Singer* (1927), the first talking film. Ed Wynn (1886–1966), born Isaiah Edwin Leopold in Philadelphia, starred in vaudeville and developed a lisping act in Ziegfeld's *Follies* (1915). Blackballed for supporting an actors' strike

(1919), he became a Broadway producer-entertainer, appeared in movies (from 1927), radio shows (from 1932), and on television performances, even after being slowed by illness and tax problems. Wynn was the Lardners' much-admired Long Island neighbor. (Sources: Elder, 200; Farnsworth, 39–41; Caruthers [1995], 129, 146; Yardley, 239, 240)

Walton R. Patrick contends that *The Big Town* not only "presents a revelatory picture of American society in the immediate postwar years of 1920 and 1921" but also while doing so "represents his [Lardner's] literary talent near its peak." Jonathan Yardley says that "[n]o other book of Ring's, *You Know Me Al* included, has the coherence of vision *and* structure that *The Big Town* has." Clifford M. Caruthers regards the book as "superior to any of the fiction Lardner previously had written, except *You Know Me Al*," partly because "the social satire is ... sharply depicted" and "the low-brow narrator's language is perfect." Grant Overton says that "'The Big Town' ... so closely resembles a novel that I think Lardner perjures himself when he says he can't write one." Agreeing, Donald Phelps says that *The Big Town*, though "novella-length, ... displays much of a novel's copiousness and reflective march." He also regards it as Lardner's "most ambitiously amplified and ... strongest achievement." John V. A. Weaver says that after he read *The Big Town* he thought he should caution readers to revise the common slogan "Laugh with Lardner" to "Laugh — and sigh — with Lardner," since Lardner here is "a serious artist, a realist of the first rank, and a master of pathos as well as of bathos." Carl Van Doren defines the narrator of *The Big Town* "as a provincial Mid-Western who nevertheless feels as much at home in New York as Benjamin Franklin felt in Paris or Mark Twain in Jerusalem. ... He is that perennially popular figure in American fiction, the Yankee unabashed." (Sources: Caruthers [1995], 130, 131; Overton, 48; Patrick, 72; Phelps, 87, 96; Van Doren, 474; Weaver, 587; Yardley, 234)

BILL ("Dinner"). He, Frank, and Lester Graham decline Grace Halpern's dinner invitation. Harry Barton accepts reluctantly, goes, and is bored.

BILL ("Sick 'Em"). He is the Phillies catcher and admires Smitty's fast ball.

William Lavier Killefer (1887–1960) played for the St. Louis Browns (1909–1910), the Philadelphia Phillies (1911–1917), and the Chicago Cubs (1918–1921), and managed the Cubs (1921–1925) and the Browns (1930–1933). (Sources: *Baseball Encyclopedia*, 698, 1222; Hilton, 370)

BILL ("The Yellow Kid"). He is the narrator. He played for the team [the White Sox] that hired Lefty Crosby, a fine pitcher but a fellow irrationally afraid of girls and guns. Bill condoned practical jokes perpetrated on Crosby, mainly by Harry Childs, but finally helped Crosby win the affections of Mary Lloyd.

BILL (*The Young Immigrunts*). He is the uncle of Bill, the narrator. The narrator and his parents visit Bill, who lives in Ann Arbor, Michigan, on their way to "Grenitch Conn."

BILL (*The Young Immigrunts*). He is the four-year-old narrator, naming himself "Ring W. Lardner, Jr." His family includes father, mother, older brothers John and Jimmie, younger brother David, and nurse. Bill accompanies his parents on the trip to their new house in "Grenitch Conn."

Donald Elder reports that in the real-life drive by Lardner and his wife Ellis Lardner* to Greenwich, Connecticut, "John [Lardner*] ... accompanied his parents, but Ring [Lardner*],, Jr., was substituted ... because of his name." Ring Lardner Jr. provides details of the switch. (Sources: Elder, 166; Lardner, Jr., 102)

BISHOP ("Freedom of the Press"). He is a *Dispatch* reporter hounding Constance Warner for news.

BISHOP (*Own Your Own Home*). He and his wife attend Fred and Grace's bridge party, along with Farrell and his wife, Grimes, his wife, Carry, his wife, and Curtis and his wife.

BISHOP In *Treat 'Em Rough*, he is a soldier whom Keefe asks to phone Florrie, Keefe's wife, to say Keefe looked for her unsuccessfully. Bishop says he forgot. In *The Real Dope*, Sargent Bishop is aboard Keefe's troop ship and says privates should take to the lifeboats ahead of corporals and sergeants.

BISHOP ("Where Do You Get That Noise?"). He is a Cub player on first when Carey, batting after him, signals hit-and-run but lines into a double play — three times in three days.

BISHOP, DOC ("Greek Tragedy"). He is involved in the wrestling business and knows reporter Jack Wells, whose judgment and information are trusted by Ike Morris, wrestler Big Bill Buell's manager.

BISHOP, ELMER In "Three Kings and a Pair," Bishop meets Bessie Gorton on a train to Chicago, says he writes movie plays, is entertained by the Gullibles at dinner and at the opera *L'Amore dei Tre Re*, which he pretends to know and understand. Mrs. Gullible hopes he'll marry Bessie, her sister. Bishop is a tight-wad. (Does Lardner have Gullible call Bishop "Mr. Smartenstein" to indicate a touch of anti-Semitism in this early fictional character?) In "Gullible's Travels," Gullible remembers going to *The Three Kings* with his wife, Bishop, and Bess. In "The Water Cure," Gullible outwits Bishop, now called Elmer Bishop and continuing his policy of sponging and lying. Gullible makes Bishop so well acquainted with Bess during a weekend vacation on a boat and at a hotel that he disappears.

BISHOP, MR. ("Bob's Birthday"). He is a magazine editor and advises Miss Tyler to write a family story, not a mystery story.

BISHOP, MRS. (*Own Your Own Home*). She and her husband attend the bridge party given by Fred and Grace.

BISHOP, MRS. ("Widow"). She knows Margaret Winslow, visits to comfort her after her husband John Winslow dies, breaks down herself, and must be consoled by Alice Winslow, Margaret's sister-in-law.

BITTING ("The Golden Honeymoon"). This Detroit Rotarian gives a talk about quitting storytelling at a church social Charley and Mother attend in Florida.

BIXBY ("BIX") ("Oh, You Bonehead!"). He was a football player on the Coach's Leighton team. He tackled well in their game against Pelham.

BLACK, JAKE ("Gullible's Travels"). He, his wife, and their mothers are at the Alcazar hotel in St. Augustine. He orders for all of them when dining.

BLACK, MRS. ("Gullible's Travels"). She and her husband and their mothers are vacationing in St. Augustine. When Mrs. Gullible says that she and her husband are going on to Palm Beach, either Mrs. Black's mother or mother-in-law replies that people prefer Palm Beach to St. Augustine because "It ain't so expensive there, I guess."

BLACKBURNE ("A New Busher Breaks In"). Keefe complains that in a game against Detroit Blackburne and Weaver of the White Sox "looked like a couple of rums."

Russell Aubrey Blackburne (1886–1968) played for the Chicago White Sox (1910–1915), the Boston Braves and the Philadelphia Phillies (1919), and the White Sox again (1927, 1929). He managed the White Sox (1928–1929). (Sources: *Baseball Encyclopedia*, 686, 793; Hilton, 137)

BLADES, JERRY ("Stop Me — if you've heard This One"). He is a playwright and a friend of fellow playwright Luke Garner. In "raconteur" Henry Wild Osborne's presence, Garner mentions an event in his life which Osborne later appropriates, alters, and tells as though it happened to him. Blades and Garner joke about it afterwards.

BLAIR, ROBERT ("A Day with Conrad Green"). He is a writer who stole an idea and presents it as his to Conrad Green, who rejects it, so that he can try to steal it.

BLAIR, WALLIE ("Absent-minded Beggar"). He is Charlotte Knowles's boyfriend.

BLAKE ("Freedom of the Press"). He was the late Robert J. Warner's butler in the Warner mansion. Blake remains to help Warner's daughter Constance Warner. Blake and Lena Goetz are witnesses when Constance marries Alexander Beardsley, Warner's former secretary.

BLAKE, MR. ("A Caddy's Diary"). He is a golfer and is a business partner of Dunham. Blake plays Thomas $10 a hole, spots him a stroke a hole, and neither gains much.

BLANCHARD, AL He is the friend of Jack Keefe, lives in Bedford, Indiana. Al receives Jack's numerous letters. A subheading of "A Busher's Letters Home," originally published in the *Saturday Evening Post*, March 7, 1914, identifies Al's last name as Blanchard. Keefe in his letter to Al dated October 17 [1913] in "The Busher's Honeymoon," first says Al's last name is Blanchard.

You Know Me Al comprises six sets of letters, 94 in number, from Jack Keefe to Al.

In "A Busher's Letters Home," Al was to see Keefe pitch in Chicago but failed to make the trip. In "The Busher Comes Back," Keefe asks Al to rent him a house in Bedford because he is marrying Hazel Carney, then not Hazel but Florence. Al and his wife Bertha will like her. In "The Busher's Honeymoon," Al is probably sad when Keefe and Florrie decide not to visit Bedford over Christmas, and evidently can be sympathetic with Keefe and help him with money. In "A New Busher Breaks In," he lends Keefe $75, eventually repaid. In "The Busher's Kid," Keefe asks Al to get Cutting to renew the house lease in Bedford, instead accepts his invitation to stay with him and Bertha in Bedford, tells him when the train will arrive from Chicago, and suggests the supper menu Bertha should prepare. In "The Busher Beats It Hence," Keefe writes Al that he's not going on the world tour, is going, isn't, etc. When he decides to go, Keefe asks Al to help Florrie, and if he drowns to see that she gets his insurance and savings.

In 10 later works, Keefe writes more letters to Al. In "The Busher Abroad" Blanchard receives 32 letters, about Keefe's sightseeing and being fooled by teammates on their tour around the world. In "The Busher's Welcome Home," Keefe treats Blanchard to eight more letters written toward the end of the tour. In "Call for Mr. Keefe!," Al endures boasts and complaints from Keefe about his pitching, an unconscious insult to Al's wife Bertha, and both Keefe's fears of the military draft and his phony pride about his patriotism. In "The Busher Reënlists," Keefe boasts, fibs, and rationalizes. In "The Battle of Texas," Keefe writes Al about temptress Miss Krug. In "Along Came Ruth," Keefe describes his pitching wins and losses, and his unfound suspicions concerning Florrie. In "The Courtship of T. Dorgan," Keefe advises Al to bet on Jess Willard* against Jack Dempsey,* then writes he's glad he didn't so advise him. In "The Busher Pulls a Mays," Keefe rationalizes to Al and invites him to come watch him pitch in Cincinnati; afterwards, "we could go somewheres and hist a few." In *Treat 'Em Rough*, "Friend Al" receives 30 more letters from Keefe, boasting, rationalizing, and mentioning Blanchard's not being in the army. In *The Real Dope*, Keefe sends 54 letters to Al, some written aboard the troop ship taking his regiment to France, then others from France. In these letters, Keefe boasts and rationalizes.

BLANCHARD, BERTHA In "The Busher Comes Back," she is Al's wife. Jack Keefe writes Al that Bertha will like Florence, Keefe's wife-to-be. In "The Busher's Honeymoon," Keefe without intending harm relays to Al some demeaning, snide remarks Florence Keefe uttered about Bertha. In "A New Busher Breaks In," Keefe says Bertha will be glad about Keefe's baby boy. In "The Busher's Kid," Keefe suggests "spair ribs and crout" for supper when he, Florrie, and their baby will arrive to begin staying with the Blanchards. In "The Busher Beats It Hence," Keefe figures Bertha will be happy to greet and help Florrie. In "The Busher Abroad," Keefe says he'll send Bertha some "Salome iland" tea. In "The Busher's Welcome Home," Keefe, back in Chicago, promises to send the tea. In "Call for Mr. Keefe!," Keefe tells Al that Bertha can be helped to better looks at Florrie's beauty shop, at no charge. In "The Busher Reënlists," Keefe sends regards to Bertha. In "Along Came Ruth," Keefe writes that Bertha may not be pretty but she's sensible. In "The Courtship of T. Dorgan," Keefe says he "wouldn't never accuse her [Bertha] from being a spend drift." In "The Busher Pulls a Mays," Keefe invites Al to watch him pitch in Cincinnati but to "leave Bertha home." In *Treat 'Em Rough*, Keefe writes Al in one letter that Bertha is lucky Al didn't enlist in the army. In *The Real Dope*, Keefe writes Al that Florrie feels superior to Bertha but did compliment both Blanchards as "homely," dependable people, and also that he shouldn't tell Bertha about Keefe's flirting with French women. In one letter, Keefe says that the Blanchards should adopt a Belgian orphan.

BLEAT ("Take a Walk"). He is a major-league umpire, as is the narrator, his close friend. When working in what becomes his favorite town, Bleat rooms with Edith's pleasant mother. Bleat and Edith fall in love; he is 30, she, 17. Trouble occurs when Bleat's honest calls inflame Agnew, the town's popular third baseman. Agnew spikes Bleat; the crowd attacks Bleat; Agnew's lies are believed. In a later game, Agnew insults Bleat about Edith; Bleat slugs him and gets banned from umpiring. He becomes a garage mechanic in Texas. Bleat's nickname was derived from the fact that, despite his enormous bulk, he has a high, thin voice.

BLISS, JACK ("The Busher Abroad"). He is a baseball catcher mentioned by Keefe as on the tour around the world and wearing his mask to ward off birds.

John Joseph Bliss (1885–1943) played for the New York Giants (1908), the St. Louis Cardinals (1909–1913), and for minor-league teams (1914–1915). James E. Elfers reports that Bliss was "the last world circler to join the tour." (Sources: *Baseball Encyclopedia,* 797; Elfers, 81)

BLOOM, IKE ("Hurry Kane"). He is a friend of baseball-player Topping. At Ike's "place," Topping sees gambler Sam Morris and his girl Evelyn Corey.

BLYTHE, MARIE ("The Love Nest"). Bartlett courteously recalls to Lou Gregg, movie-mogul, that Gregg's wife played the young sister in *The Cad*. Gregg says yes, with Marie Blythe and Harold Hodgson.

BOB ("Now and Then"). He is long-suffering Irma's insufferable husband Bob, who is sugary-solicitous during their delayed honeymoon, and three years later is hypocritically neglectful. She adores him at first and makes excuses for him later.

Jonathan Yardley avers that Bob is "clearly headed for unfaithfulness." (Source: Yardley, 332)

BOBBY ("Where Do You Get That Noise?"). Dode, playing for the Phillies, tells the narrator that "I and Bobby" concluded that Pat Moran, their manager, got tired of hearing Hawley talk and therefore traded him.

"BOB'S BIRTHDAY" (*The Red Book Magazine*, November 1933; SC). (Characters: Mr. Belden, Mr. Bishop, Kathleen Dennis, Mr. Dennis, Mr. Gaines, Mrs. Hackley, Kemp, Lavelle, Mrs. Lavelle, George Marshall, Lucille Marshall, Olga, Silvers, Sterrett, Tyler, Bob Tyler, Grandfather Tyler, Miss Tyler, Mrs. Tyler, Warren.)

Miss Taylor is the daughter of an unemployed man and his wife, and is Bob Taylor's sister. She wants to write a mystery story for money, to help Bob. But Mr. Bishop, his friend who edits a magazine, said she should write about something that happened in her family. This is her story:

I am 14. My brother Bob, 17, is a skillful musician. He wanted to finish high school, form an orchestra like Rudy Vallée* to enable him to attend Yale and "learn some profession like medicine or a lawyer." He might then marry his girlfriend Kathleen Dennis, daughter of Mr. Dennis, president of Dennis & Co. and a Stock Exchange Market member. Kathleen might not wait "8 or 9 years for Bob to carry out this idea." When Dad lost his job with Kemp and Warren two years ago, Bob left high school, held various jobs as a musician, and now works with Belden's Orchestra playing saxophone and clarinet, arranging new music, and making $150 a week — to support us. Bob complains that Dad can't find work because he plays contract bridge all afternoon and goes to the club evenings with Mother and George Marshall, her unemployed brother, and Lucille Marshall, George's wife. Father and Uncle George argue about who got fired first, as though Congress would vote the winner "the Legend of Honor."

Mother had "good news" for Bob a few months ago. Uncle George and Aunt Lucille were moving in with us and would pay $25 a week. Bob didn't mind having to sleep on the couch; his work prevented his sleeping much anyway. Uncle George began to eat a light noon-hour breakfast and then dine at the club with Aunt Lucille, Dad, and Mother — especially after they'd been drinking. The trouble was that, like Dad, Uncle George, evicted for not paying his rent, regularly borrowed "gin money and taxi money from Bob." After three months, Uncle George owed Bob more than "he owed us for board and lodging."

Two weeks ago Mr. Belden gave the orchestra a rare week's vacation before changing to a new hotel engagement. Bob had rehearsals and arrangements to make that week but hoped to have some dinners with us, since Mother promised that she and Dad would stay home "so we could get acquainted again," just like some old times I recalled. I hoped Uncle George and Aunt Lucille would keep going out. Even on one drink Uncle George wouldn't "add to the gayety," because he'd then ask Bob for $10, boast about being unemployed, or say "real musicians" play violins, not saxophones or clarinets. Biting his tongue, Bob would agree the saxophone was "a mongrel instrument." Still, he played the clarinet better than anyone "just greasing their hair like Rudy Vallée."

Mother and Dad broke their promise to dine with Bob and me at home. Monday they had to go to the club to meet Mr. Gaines, who, though unemployed, might offer Dad work. Tuesday Mr. Sterrett hosted them there and might give Uncle George a job. Wednesday Bob had to be out for a radio broadcast. Thursday Mother, forgetting "Bob and me," agreed to meet the Lavelles at the club. I made Mother promise to stay home Friday, which was Bob's birthday, and even spend a dime, from his loans to them, for a present.

I had saved money for clothes I needed to go with Kathleen, who had invited me to spend a weekend at Southampton. Instead, I bought Bob a biography of Richard Wagner, "a great German composer," and also had Olga bake a cake. Oh, I forgot: Bob and Kathleen were still in love, though her father wouldn't permit them even to say they were engaged. Anyway, how could Bob support a wife, plus Mother, Dad, Uncle George, Aunt Lucille, "and myself"? Oh, about Grandfather. He was a bookkeeper with Silvers & Co., roomed and boarded with Mrs. Hackley, and saved a bit weekly toward his retirement.

My story now gets "kind of embarrassing." Thursday's party lasted until Friday morning for Dad, Mother, Uncle George, and Aunt Lucille. That afternoon, Dad borrowed $10 from Bob and disappeared with Uncle George. Mother and Aunt Lucille appeared for Bob's birthday celebration in kimonos. Dinner was ruined. At 8 o'clock Dad and Uncle George surprisingly reappeared, with two presents for Bob—"a bottle of gin and Grandfather." What "a 'happy birthday'": Lucille in kimono, Uncle George unshaven, my parents—"welcome heaven knows," but looking and feeling odd—and now Grandfather, dirty with coal dust, drinking gin, and repeatedly saying "Hotcha!" Only Bob and I could stand looking at food. Olga presented the cake, which caused everyone to recall Bob's birthday and congratulate him. Grandfather said "Hotcha!" Dad announced that Grandfather had been unemployed three months and had used up his savings and his credit with his landlady. Dad also said he was giving Grandfather to Bob for a present—not for long, he added, because he was 62 and Tylers rarely reach "much beyond eighty."

Mr. Dennis suddenly arrived with Kathleen, who brought Bob some homemade birthday fudge. Mr. Dennis praised Dad for having a fine son. Dad replied that Mr. Dennis would also have a fine son-in-law. Mr. Dennis, however, said Bob had enough financial responsibilities without including "Kathie." Dad blasted him for refusing to employ Dad and Dad's brother-in-law George, which would reduce Bob's burdens; said that men like Mr. Dennis "are to blame for present conditions in this country"; and concluded by saying he wouldn't allow Bob to wed Kathleen. Uncle George: "That's talking!" Grandfather: "Hotcha!" Mr. Dennis told Kathleen "we have stayed at least long enough." They left. I wept on the couch. Bob patted me. I asked where Bob could sleep, with Grandfather here. Bob said he wasn't sleepy and would read about "Old Man Wagner." I could write about our new sleeping arrangements, but our story already "is 'at least long enough.'"

Present-day readers might blister Bob for not shucking worthless parents and leech-like relatives, and instead nurturing only sweet little sister. Many older readers, however, remember the Great Depression or recall family anecdotes about it. At the very month that Bob was especially burdened—let us say March 1933—the U.S. Index of Industrial Production was at bottom, over 5,500 banks closed, 24 states declared bank holidays or other restrictions; unemployment of civilian labor peaked at 24.9 percent. President Franklin D. Roosevelt took action with respect to banking and allied financial activities, embargoes, and precious metals and currencies, and initiated the New Deal. Many struggling families were taking in indigent relatives, alcoholic or otherwise, because alternatives were limited to non-existent. Nowadays, would-be familial parasites are often treated differently.

BODIE In "A Busher's Letters Home," Keefe says he dined at the same table with Bodie at Paso Robles. In "The Busher Comes Back," Keefe, pitching for the White Sox, complains that Bodie "ought to of eat up" a fly ball Barry of the "Athaletics" hit. In "A New Busher Breaks In," Kid Gleason says Bodie resembles "a broom straw" compared to obese Keefe. Later, Keefe praises Bodie for getting a hit off Joe Hill, Detroit's pitcher. In "The Busher's Kid," Keefe criticizes Bodie's fielding during "the city serious."

Frank Stephan Bodie (1887–1961), born Francesco Stephano Pezzolo, played for the Chicago White Sox (1911–1914), the Philadelphia Athletics (1917), and the New York Yankees (1918–1921). Bodie had a weight problem, at 5' 8", 195. James E. Elfers reports thus: Bodie was nicknamed "Ping" because, even before aluminum bats, when he hit a baseball the sound had a ring to it; he was "Lardner's favorite player"; and Jack Keefe has enough of Bodie's characteristics to be partly based on Bodie. (Sources: *Baseball Encyclopedia*, 800; Elfers, 86, 87; Hilton, 47)

BOEHLING In "Sick 'Em," Boehling pitches successfully for Washington against the Phillies in a (fictional) World Series game. In "Horseshoes," he is a Washington pitcher, said to be a "nasty lefthander" when Dick Grimes of the Athletics is hitless against him. In "A New Busher Breaks In," Keefe says he saved a game for the White Sox pitching against "this left-handed stiff Boehling," who pitched for Washington.

John Joseph Boehling (1891–1941) was a left-handed pitcher for the Washington Senators (1912–1916) and the Cleveland Indians (1916–1920). (Source: Hilton, 141)

BOLAND ("Poodle"). Jack Ingram works as a chemist for the Boland Drug Company until he is released.

BOLER ("Tour Y-10"). He owns a barber shop. Kate Hayes says that if Coles and Lester are college graduates, their school was probably "Boler's Barber College."

BOLES, HI ("Good for the Soul"). He was a former baseball player whom Buck Warner knew from Association days and who played for A.T. Grant's minor-league team with Buck and others.

BOLTON, GUY ("Rhythm"). He has written a book for a musical that Conrad Green wants Harry Hart to write tunes for.

BOND, FELIX ("The Facts"). He is an elevator operator in Billy Bowen's office building. Bowen's secretary quits to marry Felix.

BONHAM, DAVE ("Great Blessings"). He was a boyfriend of Clara, then 23, until she married Tod Stewart. Tod is a lousy, alcoholic husband. Dave, never marrying, is successful in Detroit real estate. He called on Clara last October. After another disastrous Thanksgiving Day dinner with her mother-in-law and father-in-law, Clara remembers Dave fondly.

BONHAM, JOE ("Hurry Kane"). He plays on the St. Louis baseball team, rooms at first with Hurry Kane, and reveals Kane's secret eating habits.

BONNER ("Hurry Kane"). He is a White Sox starting pitcher.

BONNIE BLUE ("A Day with Conrad Green"). She is a theatrical performer signed by Conrad Green for next season.

BOONE ("One Hit, One Error, One Left"). Danny mentions Boone and Odoul as Brooklyn outfielders he occasionally replaces.

Isaac Morgan Boone (1897–1958) played for the New York Giants (1922), the Boston Red Sox (1922–1925), the Chicago White Sox (1927), and the Brooklyn Dodgers (1930–1932). (Source: *Baseball Encyclopedia*, 806)

BOONE, BILL ("Women"). He played for Springfield against Dayton, Mike Healy's team. Mike, at third base, tagged Boone so hard "they had to take stitches," but Baldy Pierce, umpire, said Mike missed the tag.

BOOTH ("Second-Act Curtain"). He and Chambers have written a play. Mr. Rose, the manager, wants a second-act curtain. Booth goes to his hotel room, which he has engaged to avoid his fun-loving Long Island neighbors. He gets drunk, peeps across the court into a nice girl's room, imagines aspects of her life, starts to write a second-act curtain by matching words to a tune that pops into his head, phones Youmans only to be told that the tune came from Youmans' *Great Day* [1929], is interrupted by phone calls from Rose, sleeps, and awakens half-strangled with his phone cord.

Did poor Booth phone Vincent Youmans* only in his alcohol-fired imagination? Booth is surely Lardner's autobiographical figure. Lardner lived on Long Island, occasionally rented a hotel room in New York to write uninterruptedly, and, like Booth, was an alcoholic, and had trouble working on *June Moon* (1929), a play with collaborator George S. Kaufman.* Jonathan Yardley relates these facts to "Second-Act Curtain" and also notes that Lardner in "Large Coffee" (*New Yorker* [September 28, 1929]) describes his summer efforts to write in a hotel and having trouble ordering coffee by room service. (Source: Yardley, 340).

BOSTON BRAVES A National League baseball team. It was established in 1876 and was active through 1952, after which it moved to Milwaukee. (Source: Light, 104–106)

BOSTON RED SOX An American League baseball team (1901–). (Sources: Light, 106–108; Streissguth, 41)

BOWEN (*Treat 'Em Rough*). He is a soldier in Keefe's army unit.

BOWEN, BILLY ("The Facts"). William Bowen is a successful but alcoholic Chicago businessman, 28. When he meets Ellen McDonald, he goes on the wagon, becomes engaged to her, and modifies his hilarity when associating with numerous members of her family. Tommy Richards, a college "pal," entices Billy to drink again — with results ruinous to his marriage plans.

BOWEN, JACK ("High-rollers"). He summers with his wife Peggy Bowen and their little son Jack at Hampton Dunes, Long Island, and encourages his friend Walter Finch to play bridge and golf with his millionaire friends Kenneth Hart and Dick Parker. Bowen explains that losers don't pay up but are "good for it."

BOWEN, JACK ("High-rollers"). He is the son of Peggy and Jack Bowen. The boy plays on the beach with Anne Finch and Junior Finch, the young children of Bowen's friend Walter Finch and his wife Marion.

BOWEN, PEGGY ("High-rollers"). She is the wife of Jack Bowen, Walter Finch's friend. She and Walter's wife Marion play bridge at Hampton Dunes, Long Island.

BOWEN, THELMA ("The Jade Necklace"). She is the actress who plays the naval lieutenant's wife in *The Jade Necklace.*

BOYER ("That Old Sweetheart of Mine"). He is the employer that Will boasts to Stella Crane he has returned to work for, at higher pay.

BOYLES, JIMMY ("JIM") ("Good for the Soul"). He was an old friend of Buck Warner's. The two broke into baseball in Des Moines together and met again when both were recruited by A.T. Grant for his major-league team. The two players ridiculed and took advantage of Grant. Billy Carmody, whom Grant hired as manager, switched Boyles, mainly a catcher, to other positions to try for winning combinations.

BRADFORD ("The Battle of the Century"). He was a boxer whose loss in London to Goulet in the first round caused headlines helpful to building Goulet's reputation.

BRADLEY (*The Big Town*). He owns racehorses, fired his jockey Sid Mercer for drinking and brawling, and hired Carney to replace Sid and ride Great Scott, who lost.

BRADY, JACK (*The Real Dope*). He is a soldier in Keefe's unit in France. He encourages Keefe to ask for leave to visit "O. D. Cologne," supposedly a rest billet. Then Brady and his bunch create a fictitious resident of Cologne named Miss Marie Antoinette and encourage Keefe to write her. Brady and Johnny Alcock also sell Simple Simon phony souvenirs supposedly connected to the German army.

BRAINARD ("A Day with Conrad Green"). He is an international polo star. Conrad Green likes Brainard's wife Joyce Brainard.

BRAINARD, BENJAMIN ("BEN") ("Man Not Overboard"). He is the author, 30, of two popular novels but has become so disaffected by lack of publishers' interest in his third novel and also by his girlfriend Pauline Lannin's heartlessness that he contemplates suicide aboard the *Gargantua.* Meeting Fred Lemp causes Ben to change his mind and consider writing a novel based on Lemp's tales of woe, which, unknown to Ben, are fictitious. Brainard was a survivor of the battle of Château-Tierry [June 3–4, 1918].

BRAINARD, EDDIE ("Hurry Kane"). He is the White Sox best starting pitcher.

BRAINARD, JOYCE ("A Day with Conrad Green"). She wants Conrad Green to discuss a stage career with her. Though lusting for her, he won't talk shop with her as long as her polo-playing husband is alive.

Elizabeth Evans writes, perhaps too darkly, that the Green's and Joyce's "impasse [will continue] until ... Brainard is disposed of." (Source: Evans, 70)

BRANT ("When the Moon Comes over the Mountain"). He was a left-handed pitcher for Boston. Brooklyn's Danny Warner calls him "there star man," hopes to bat against him, but doesn't.

Edward Arthur Brandt (1905–1944) pitched for the Boston Braves (1928–1935), the Brooklyn Dodgers (1936), and the Pittsburgh Pirates (1937–1938). (Source: *Baseball Encyclopedia*, 1846).

BRENNAN, BILL ("A Frame-Up"). He is a boxer who trains in Kid Howard's gymnasium in Chicago.

BRENT, MISS ("Widow"). She rents rooms. Alice Winslow says she will see if Margaret Winslow, her widowed sister-in-law, can be accommodated by Miss Brent. Margaret has other plans.

BRID ("My Roomy"). He is a Chicago baseball player, on base during a game against "Cincy."

Albert Henry Bridwell (1884–1969) played for the Cincinnati Reds (1905), the Boston Braves (1906–1907), the New York Giants (1908–1910), the Giants and the Braves (1911), the Braves (1912), the Chicago Cubs (1913), and the Federal League's St. Louis team (1914–1915). (Sources: *Baseball Encyclopedia*, 824; Hilton, 343)

BRIDGET (*The Big Town*). She is the maid in "Bridget Sees a Ghost," the play by Jimmy Ralston. Katie plays Bridget.

BROCK, EDDIE ("The Venomous Viper of the Volga"). He is a boxer pitted against Mike Moran.

BROCK, LOUIE ("Nora"). He is a successful producer of musicals. He introduces Hazlett, playwright, to Frank Moon, successful lyricist, and Jerry Morris, successful tunesmith. The three revise Hazlett's play "Nora" to their liking, mangling its plot the while.

Clifford M. Caruthers calls Brock "a philistinic producer." It would have pleased Lardner to live to see Lou Brock (b. 1939), stellar left-fielder for the Chicago Cubs (1961–1964) and the St. Louis Cardinals (1964–1979). He was inducted in the Baseball Hall of Fame (1985). (Sources: *Baseball Encyclopedia*, 826; Caruthers [1995], 217)

BROCK, MRS. ("Nora"). She is Louie Brock's wife, described as someone he must have "married ... in a dense fog."

BRODIE ("The Crook"). He struck out pitch-hitting for Cleveland. When he criticized the call, Bull, the witty umpire, out-talked him.

BROOKLYN DODGERS A National League baseball team. It was established in 1890, was active through 1957, then moved to Los Angeles. (Source: Light, 119–123)

BROOKS, JACK ("Who Dealt?"). Mrs. Cannon remembers that a comedian — "Jack Brooks or Ned Frawley or something" — humorously said "apple sauce" in a Portland vaudeville show that she and her husband Tom Cannon recently saw.

BROTHER ("Mamma"). This is the name by which Mamma refers to her son.

BROUN, HEYWOOD (1888–1939). Brooklyn-born New York journalist and critic. His articles appeared in the New York *Tribune*, the New York *World*, and *The New Republic*. *The A.E.F.* (1918) concerns his experiences as a war correspondent. Other books collect his theater criticism and newspaper columns. Broun also wrote fiction, a biography of Anthony Comstock (1927), and an attack on anti–Semitism (1931).

Lardner and Broun knew and admired each other greatly. They often traded witticisms at the Algonquin Round Table, in New York's Algonquin hotel. (Sources: Elder, 226; Lardner, Jr., 193; Yardley, 243–244)

BROWN ("Great Blessings"). He and his wife are friends of Grace Stewart in Detroit. When Grace's mother-in-law becomes too hostile, Grace escapes to the Browns to play bridge.

BROWN ("Insomnia"). He is a baseball player the sleepless author remembers.

BROWN, MRS. ("Great Blessings"). She is a friend of Grace Stewart in Detroit. When Grace's mother-in-law is too bothersome, Grace goes for a bridge game with the Browns.

BRUNNER, FAT ("A Caddy's Diary"). He caddies at the club where the diarist also caddies. He and another caddy, Lou Crowell, fight over the honor to be remembered as having caddied last for bank-embezzler Charley Crane.

BRYANT-WALKER ("A Day with Conrad Green"). He is evidently an aristocrat in New York. He and his wife entertain Conrad Green, among others more notable.

BRYANT-WALKER, MRS. ("A Day with Conrad Green"). She and her husband are socially prominent in New York. At a party they give, Conrad Green meets and is attracted to Joyce Brainard. Mrs. Bryant-Walker wants him to provide entertainment at a bazaar she gives, and he reluctantly agrees.

BUCK ("Harmony"). He is the trainer of the baseball team. At one point he tells Bill Cole that Waldron wants him.

BUCK ("Rhythm"). He and his wife host a party at their Long Island home where Harry Hart is a guest.

These hospitable Long Island Bucks are patterned after Lardner's friends and drinking buddies Gene Buck* and his wife, of Great Neck, Long Island. (Sources: Caruthers [1973], 35; Yardley, 239 and *passim*).

BUCK, GENE (1885–1957). Detroit-born Eugene Edward Buck was artist, song writer, and director. After attending Detroit University and the Detroit Art Academy, he designed sheet-music covers, moved to New York (1907), became chief writer and chief production assistant for musical-impresario Florenz Ziegfeld* (1912–1926). When several songwriters and publishers formed ASCAP (American Society of Composers, Authors and Publishers, 1914), Buck was a charter member; later he served as director (1920–1957) and president (1924–1941). He wrote innumerable songs and stage scores, and often collaborated with the most popular composers of his time.

Buck married Helen Falconer (1919), and they had two sons. The Bucks lived in Great Neck, Long Island. The Lardners were their neighbors (1922–1924) and were the Bucks' close friends for many years. The two men tried abortively to convert *Gullible's Travels* into a musical comedy for Ziegfeld (1925). Lardner occasionally makes fictional use of Gene Buck and Helen Buck. In *The Big Town*, Gene Buck tells the Finches where they should vacation on Long Island. Both Buck and Ziegfeld humorously figure in "Liberty Hall." The horrid marriage depicted in "The Love Nest" may possibly be based on Lardner's notion of the Bucks' marriage. In "Rhythm," Buck and his wife give a party at their Long Island home. In "Women," Helen Buck dates umpire Baldy Pierce. The movie *The Great Ziegfeld* (1936), which Lardner did not live to see, features William Demarest playing Buck.

BUCK, GENE (*The Big Town*). He is a New Yorker who suggests that Finch, his wife Ella, and her sister Katie should vacation during the hot summer at a hotel owned by Decker on Long Island.

Lardner names this man after his Long Island friend Gene Buck* and relishes having Finch say that this Buck "knowed New York like a book, only he hadn't never read a book."

BUCK, HELEN ("Women"). She was a girl from Hamilton, Ohio, and had a date with Baldy Pierce, who umpired a game between Mike Healy's Dayton team and Springfield. Pierce made bad calls against Dayton to enable him to keep a date with Helen next day. (See Buck, Gene.)

BUCK, MRS. ("Rhythm"). She and her husband invite Harry Hart to a party where he is asked to play the piano.

BUCKLEY ("Liberty Hall"). He is a New York businessman who is transferred to Albany. When Ben Drake and his wife, both of whom knew Buckley and his wife in New York, visit them in Albany, the Drakes respond unfavorably to the Buckleys' hospitality.

BUCKLEY, MRS. ("Liberty Hall"). She is businessman Buckley's wife.

BUELL, BIG BILL ("Greek Tragedy"). He is a wrestler, is managed by Ike Morris, defeats his friend Greek Alexis in a staged match, but will probably not share any future winnings with him.

BULL ("The Crook"). He is an honest umpire who defuses vociferous batters by witty comebacks. When Cahill, of the White Sox, accuses him of being dishonest and calls him a crook, Bull batters him and is fired. Larry, the narrator, recognizes Bull's deep despondency, gets him to explain why he was jilted by his girlfriend Maggie Gregory, goes to Ban Johnson and explains, and gets Bull reinstated.

BULLARD ("Hurry Kane"). He, Robinson, and Roy Smith are traded from the St. Louis baseball team to the Boston baseball team for Frank Miller and Lefty Glaze. All five are ineffective players.

BUMBLE, OLD MAN ("A Frame-Up"). He is the grandfather of Honey Hives and is "the bee man" with a "country place on Ellis Island," according to Jack Grace's silly talk, which Burke believes.

BUMGARDNER ("A Busher's Letters Home"). Keefe says that during a game with the Boston Browns "a righthander named Bumgardner" was pitching against Keefe's White Sox and was winning despite mediocre pitching.

George Washington Bumgardner (1891–1970) pitched moderately well when the St. Louis Browns were mediocre (1912–1916). (Sources: *Baseball Encyclopedia*, 1813; Hilton, 62)

BURKE ("A Frame-Up"). He is the boxer Burke's father, a well-to-do peach farmer in Benton Harbor. When young Burke ignores Charley Porter's girlfriend, his father disinherits him.

BURKE ("BURKEY") ("Claude Diphthong, Student of Crime"). He and McMahon are New York Murder Squad detectives investigating Gardner Lyle's murder.

BURKE ("BURKEY") ("A Frame-Up"). He is a natural-born boxer from Benton Harbor. He defeats Charley Porter to impress Porter's girlfriend, whom Burke drops in pursuit of richer ladies, only to be frustrated in seeking Esther Fester (really Mary Holt) because of the machinations of Nate, his manager, and of Jack Grace, Nate's jokester friend. To a New York audience, Joe Humphreys introduces Burke as "the Michigan Flash."

BURKE, JACK In "Sick 'Em," Burke is said by Jack Barnett to be the manager of their Evansville baseball team. Barnett tells the narrator that Burke negotiated the trade giving their team Smitty and Fogarty. In "The Courtship of T. Dorgan," Jimmy Burke manages the St. Louis Browns. Keefe says that Burke "maybe ... could get somewheres" if he had more pitchers like Keefe. In "The Busher Pulls a Mays," Keefe while in Philadelphia declines to accompany Cicotte to go see Philadelphia play Burke's St. Louis team.

James Timothy Burke (1874–1942) played for the Cleveland Indians (1898), the St. Louis Cardinals (1899), the Chicago White Sox and the Pittsburgh Pirates (1901), the Pirates (1902), and the Cardinals (1903–1905). He managed the Cardinals (1905) and the St. Louis Browns (1918–

1920), and later coached for the Chicago Cubs and the New York Yankees. George W. Hilton says Lardner may have confused this James Burke and John Patrick Burke (1877–1950), a minor-league manager. (Sources: *Baseball Encyclopedia*, 687, 843; Hilton, 297, 376, 398)

BURKE, JIMMY ("The Courtship of T. Dorgan") *see* **BURKE, JACK**

BURKE, RED ("The Venomous Viper of the Volga"). He is a boxer who defeats Barney Williams.

BURLEIGH, CONGRESSMAN ("Dinner"). He is a politician whom Miss Rell repeatedly tells Harry Barton her father knows. The Burleighs, she explains, are "the paint people in South Chicago."

BURNETT, CLARA In "One Hit, One Error, One Left," Jessie writes her boyfriend Danny that her friends Clara and Dave have just had their first baby. Jessie probably writes thus to encourage Danny to firm up his half-hearted proposal. In "When the Moon Comes over the Mountain," Jessie writes that Clara's baby "is cuter than ever." In "Meet Me in St. Louie," Jessie decides not to ask Clara to accompany her to visit Danny in St. Louis. In "Holycaust" Clara is mentioned. In "The Ides of June," Jessie visited Fritz and Grace Nymeyer with Clara and Dave and watched the four play whist. Jessie said she disliked the men's strong language.

BURNETT, DAVE In "One Hit, One Error, One Left," Jessie writes her boyfriend Danny that her friends Clara and Dave just had their first baby. Dave relays baseball news to Jessie. In "When the Moon Comes over the Mountain," Dave continues to inform Jessie about baseball news. Dave tells Jessie to write Danny that he knows Schofield Gross but not Gross, the (fictional) friend of Casey Stengel.* In "Meet Me in St. Louie," Dave's being on the road would have made it hard for Clara to go to St. Louis with Jessie. In "Holycaust," Dave is mentioned. In "The Ides of June," Jessie heard Dave and Fritz Nymeyer talk improperly while playing whist game with Grace Nymeyer and Clara.

BURNS, ED ("EDDY") ("Tour No. 2"). He is Larry's brother, is married to Kate Burns, lives in Detroit, is a bartender there, and receives Larry's letters about his tour to "europe."

BURNS, KATE ("Tour No 2"). She is Ed's wife and Larry's sister-in-law.

BURNS, LARRY ("Tour No. 2"). Lawrence Martin Burns lives with his wife Minnie in Chicago, has a garden business, is interested in politics, and is persuaded by Minnie to tour "europe." They encounter trouble in "Belljum."

Lardner with remarkable subtlety has Larry unconsciously reveal himself to be a complex combination of stupidity, conceit, hypocrisy, self-absorption, and likeability.

BURNS, MINNIE ("Tour No. 2"). She is Larry's wife, from Milwaukee and evidently fluent in what Larry calls "dutch." She insists on a vacation in Europe, which because of the outbreak of war causes difficulties in Germany and Belgium. She is a domineering, demanding, long-suffering, and pretty dumb woman.

BURNS, RED In "The Poor Simp," the narrator remembers Red Burns as a stupid baseball player now doing well in Cleveland contracting work. In *Treat 'Em Rough*, Jack Keefe remembers replacing an outfielder named Burns in Terre Haute.

BURNS, SAMMY ("Cured!"). He draws alcoholic Dick Streeter's cartoons for him, for bribes of $200 a week.

BURT, BROWNIE (Wedding Day"). She is a beautiful, successful, insecure, spendthrift musical comedy star. She and Jimmy Shane, popular comedian and long-time lover, get married because she has threatened to sue him otherwise.

BURTON ("Harmony"). He sang tenor well but played second base worse than Cragin, then outfield so poorly that he was bruised by missed flies and got released.

BURTON, BEAU ("The Venomous Viper of the Volga"). He is a handsome boxer, nicknamed "the Student Prince," who has defeated Jack Ryan to become champion.

BUSH In "A Busher's Letters Home," Keefe, pitching for the White Sox against the Detroit Tigers, complains that Bush stole bases on him. In "The Busher Comes Back," Keefe complains that Bush is so little "you can't pitch to him" and walked him twice. In "Along Came Ruth," Keefe admits that when he was pitching against Detroit Bush and Ellison got on base twice. Still, Keefe won the game. In "The Busher Pulls a Mays,"

Keefe notes that Jennings, Detroit's manager, said Gleason when talking trades wanted only Bush or Cobb, impossibly. Bush is mentioned in "The Busher Abroad" and "The Hold-Out."

Owen Joseph Bush (1886 or 1887–1972) played for the Detroit Tigers (1908–1920), the Tigers and the Washington Senators (1921), and the Senators (1922–1923). He managed the Senators (1923), the Pittsburgh Pirates (1927–1929), the Chicago White Sox (1930–1931), and the Cincinnati Reds (1933). George W. Hilton reports that Lardner tried unsuccessfully "to interest the White Sox in Bush while the young infielder was playing in the Central League in 1906 and 1907." (Sources: *Baseball Encyclopedia*, 688, 848; Hilton, 66)

BUSH In "Horseshoes," he pitches badly for the Athletics in the third game of their World Series against the Giants, but he pitches well in the sixth game. In "The Crook," Bush and Coveleskie of the Phillies, pitching against the narrator Larry's White Sox, "was havin' a whale of a battle" when Bull, the honest umpire, called a third strike, perfectly thrown by Bush, on Martin Gregory. Martin became dishonest in his subsequent complaints.

Leslie Ambrose Bush (1892–1974) pitched for the Philadelphia Athletics (1912–1917), the Boston Red Sox (1918–1921), the New York Yankees (1922–1924), the St. Louis Browns (1925), the Washington Senators and the Pittsburgh Pirates (1926), the Pirates and the New York Giants (1927), and the Athletics (1928). Bush pitched in World Series games for the Athletics (1913, 1914), the Red Sox (1918), and the Yankees (1922, 1923). (Sources: *Baseball Encyclopedia*, 848; Hilton, 412)

"THE BUSHER ABROAD" (*Saturday Evening Post*, March 20, April 10, May 8, and May 17, 1915). (Characters: Allen, Marie Allen, Benz, Al Blanchard, Bertha Blanchard, Jack Bliss, Callahan, Comiskey, Sam Crawford, Donlin, Doolin, Larry Doyle, Dr., Egan, Steve Evans, Falkenberg, Hill, Al Keefe, Florrie Keefe, Jack Keefe, Leverenz, Sir Thomas Lipton, Honest Lobert, Mcgraw, Maggie, Mare of Vanila, Herman Dutch Schaefer, Jim Scott, Slight, Speaker, Stewart, Stewart, Indian Thorpe, Buck Weaver, Wiltse, Wingo.)

Jack Keefe, Chicago White Sox pitcher, writes his friend Al Blanchard 32 letters while on the world tour with the White Sox and the New York Giants. The first eight letters are written from "On the Ship bord."

Nov. 22. Keefe will write Al often and "male" letters from Yokohama. He had bad food in Seattle and feels sick. He asks to be remembered to Bertha Blanchard. He mentions pitcher Walter Johnson.

Nov. 23. Keefe explains "shovvle bord," a game they play. He mentions fellow passengers Callahan, Sam Crawford, "steve" Evans, Mcgraw, Dutch Schaefer. Evans admires Keefe's "evening cloths," but Keefe doesn't want to impress "the wommen" by dressing like Bert Williams.*

Nov. 26. Evans says dates changed when the ship crossed "the line on the ocean." Keefe mentions passengers Cobb, Russell, Herman Schaefer, "jim" Thorpe.

Nov. 27. Keefe wrote a poem mentioning Callahan, Comiskey, and Mcgraw.

Dec. 1. Keefe mentions his son "little Al," baseball player Larry Doyle, and umpire Bill Klem. Evans explained that schools of sharks would attack the ship except that he rang the recess bell.

Dec. 2. Keefe won't write his wife Florrie for $24 to be sent "special the Livery."

Dec. 4. Keefe mentions players Joe Benz, Bunny Hern, George Wiltse, Buck Weaver. Keefe might return straight home from Yokohama. Schaefer tricked Keefe by saying his fast ball wouldn't hurt Schaefer's bare hand. Keefe pitched one; Schaefer ducked and won $1.

Dec. 5. Florrie and their son must be sick, since she's not writing. Evans told Keefe he must tip the "Stewart" and other ship workers; so Keefe gave $1.10.

"Yokohama, Dec. 6." Keefe mails all his letters. He'll continue the trip. Japanese doctors boarded the ship. The team enjoyed dinner at "the Councils place" in "Tokio." Keefe pitched for the Giants against the White Sox at "the Tokio Collige ball park," but his "super" was in poor shape and didn't know the Giants' "sines." Callahan phoned home and reported to Keefe that Florrie and little Al are all right, as are Florrie's sister Marie Allen and her husband Allen, and that Florrie says Keefe needn't "hurry home."

The next nine letters are from "On the ship bord." Dec. 8. Keefe pitched at a "colllige" field yesterday, winning 16 to 3. The "peopl" watched, sitting on their feet on mats "like a taylor." Some Americans in Japan hosted a dinner last night. Keefe read his "pone," which "brot down the Hotel where the banquit was at." Keefe bought "2 Kumonnas" for Florrie.

Dec. 10. The ship took on "cole" at "Naggasak." Schaefer warned about rats cooked in

Chinese "chop suye." Evans is "lerning" some Chinese words; for example, "Lie Hung Schang" isn't referring to the "Athaletics" Schang. Evans suggested changing money in "Honk Honk" not in "the Philip Beans ilands." On to Vanila.

Dec. 17. Schaefer was sick from eating rat poison. Dr. gave him "anicdotes" to prevent "hiderofobeya," which is so "contajus" Keefe won't scare "the wommen" by talking. Keefe longs for "Berthas pan Cakes."

Dec. 19. Mcgraw should have pitched Faber, Wiltse, or Hern in Vanila. Keefe's curve couldn't work in the "muggy" weather there. Also playing were Benz, Larry Doyle, Slight, Merkle, Crawford (who hit against Keefe), Indian Thorpe (who booted a play), and Doolan. Evans pointed out a vanilla-bottling factory. The "colored" natives are so small they couldn't box like Jack Johnson or "lengferd." Evans gets Keefe to buy winter clothes for when they're in Australia in December. Keefe meets the "Mare of Vanila" and Stewart, the prison manager. Keefe names their ship: "The Umpires of Japan."

Dec. 21. They passed "some vol Canos,' then crossed the "Eqater." Although Schaefer said to hang over "the rale" to see, the ship didn't even "jar" on crossing.

Dec. 24. The men are planning "a xmas tree" for Callahan's children aboard and have promised Keefe a gift for a "pome."

Dec. 25. Keefe reads his "pome," which expressed thanks for his yet-unopened gift, "in ribons and tissu paper." Opened, as ordered, in his "birth room," it is one of his own dirty shirts. Evans said he didn't know about the mean joke. Except for "ladys" around, Keefe would've made trouble. He'll return home from Australia.

Dec. 27. Keefe told Evans he might become a sports writer or open "a billard rm. in Chicago." The ship passed the "thursday ilands," so named, Keefe learned, because an Australia ship is "do there thursday." He might borrow from Comiskey or Callahan and go home.

Dec. 30. Mcgraw assured Keefe he didn't know about the dirty shirt, needed him to pitch at "Brizz Bay," and promised him a decent gift.

Jan. 2 [1915]. Pitching against Jim Scott, Keefe won 2 to 1 for Mcgraw, even though "Weaver and Egan kicked a couple." On to Sidney, the last name of which Keefe doesn't know. He received a letter from Florrie; she wants $250 by check and is "jellus" he might hold hands with foreign "qeens and princes." Keefe sent the check. Mcgraw gave him a silk-like shirt.

"Sidney, Jan. 4." Mcgraw rested Keefe yesterday. After watching a Sidney "crickit" game, he boasted he could win by swinging a plank and hitting that little "boleing" ball near some planted sticks, and bet "2 lbs.," about $10.

"Sidney, Jan. 5." Keefe was robbed. While playing "crickit," he swung at the ball bouncing on rough ground, hit some sticks, and was ruled out. He borrowed $10 from Mcgraw, paid up, and won't "monky with no crickit game" again with anyone making "rules to sute themself."

"Melbourne, Jan. 7." Keefe pitched another winner. Schaefer explained that the ship's Stewart kept the nice shirt the men bought for Keefe and wrapped Keefe's dirty shirt in its place. Schafer wants Keefe to write a "pone" to read at "the Melbourne saviges club." Governor Dennis was there with his wife. Dennis admired and felt Keefe's arm and "caff." His poem, "the hit of the entertanemunt," praised Australia as the second-best country, after America. Schaefer warned Keefe about the Australia "Bite," an eagle-like bird that bites men's heads, but not small-eared women; so men must wear "catchers masts" as protection.

"Fremantle, Jan. 13." Keefe avoided the Bite by remaining inside their ship. While sailing in "the indian Ocean," Schaefer warned Keefe that "wild indians liveing on the ilands" are dangerous, but worse are their "Thomas Hawks" that bite heads and cause sores. Keefe remained off even the ship's "porch," thus escaping.

Six letters from shipboard follow. Jan. 16. By roasting inside "like a Pnut," Keefe avoided "Thomas Hawks." Evans tutored him to use "africa" language by saying "Ahm done lost." Florrie will regard him as "a collige school teacher," outdoing "willy boys" from "Yale and Harlem."

Jan. 19. Going "acrost the eqater" was bumpier heading north. Schaefer said if Keefe broke his right arm getting hurled about in his "birth room," he "could lern" to pitch left-handed.

Jan. 21. Cobb, Mcgraw, and "indian Thorpe" warned everyone to avoid the Hawks. Bliss, Wingo, and Slight wore their catchers' "masts." Keefe helped several fellows pull a rope to hoist the ship over the "eqater," making the crossing "the smoothist ... ever," said the captain. They are invited "by a wirelest telegram" to meet "sir Thomas Lipton," the "boat racer," at "Salome iland." Schaefer wants Keefe to write "poultry" about tea for the occasion. Since telegrams are "on all the boats," Keefe could send Florrie a $10 wire if he were sick or killed.

Jan. 24. Schaefer forgot to let Keefe "speak my pone" at Columbus, but here is "a coppy," which Callahan read and liked. Leverenz pitched a game for the White Sox. They're now "on the Ray Bean Ocean."

Jan. 28. Schaefer fibbed. Moses couldn't "wade ... acrost" this so-called "red Sea," which Schaefer read "in the bibble" is "red" not "brown."

Jan. 31. Evans says they'll land safely in "africa" because the animals head south in the winter. Therefore, no "Polo bares" or "lepers." They'll stop at "Sue S," a place with a girl's name.

The last three letters are from "Cairo. Africa." Feb. 1. Even though little Al can't read, Keefe sent him, as well as Florrie, post cards from "Hellopolis Hotel." They saw "Pyrmids of Geezer and ... Spinix." Evans said skulls in the "Pyrmids" would make a baseball team. The "Spinix" is a "homily mans head build from concreet." People "rode on them campbells." Keefe and Benz pitched a 3–3 game in "sand up to your neck," with "K. Dive the king of africa" and others watching. Keefe, tutored by Evans, asked one spectator "How you all like dat ole game[?]" He replied in "englich."

Feb. 2. "Mohammed Ali ... rents the musk from L. A. Baster." Keefe was urged to pray in a "musk" by lying on his "stomick" and pretending to be "swiming" just like "1 of the sex" in there. Speaker bought Keefe a "fezz" at one of the "buzzards."

Feb. 3. Evans permits Keefe to buy "a scarab from Cops tume." It's a special $50 dead bug that brings constant good luck. Evan doesn't need luck; so he took Keefe to a man who sold him a $10 stolen scarab for $7.50, which Keefe borrowed from Callahan. Evans advised Keefe never to talk about his scarab, because it might be stolen. Keefe told only Doyle and Doolin. For their farewell party, Keefe read his "pone" beginning "Wear going to leave Cairo / and Boys we hate to leave," and ending "And we will all ways remember / Cairo and the boys of Council 8." On to Alexander. Keefe will try out his scarab. His pitching will cause Allen to "probily jump the league" unless Comiskey fires him first.

This world tour was fascinating. Charles A. Comiskey,* White Sox owner and president, and John J. McGraw,* Giants manager, took major-league players representing their teams on a 1913–1914 around-the-world tour. Upwards of 60 people went along. They included a couple dozen players, and also managers, administrators, family members, two umpires, camera personnel, a few paying fellow travelers, a doctor, and a minister. After playing 31 games in nine states (October–November 1913), they started overseas from Victoria, British Columbia (November 19, aboard the R.M.S. *Empress of Japan*). They went to Japan, China, and Hong Kong (December), the Philippines (aboard the S.S. *St. Albans*, December), Australia (January 1914), Australia and Ceylon (aboard the R.M.S. *Orontes*, January), Egypt (February), Italy (aboard the S.S. *Prinz Heinrich*, February), France and Monte Carlo (February), England (February), and New York (from Liverpool aboard the *Lusitania*, arriving March 7, 1914).

A supreme spelling à la Keene is his naming their first steamship *The Umpires of Japan*. In *The Home Coming* are photographs of "S.S. Empress of Japan" and its captain, W. Dixon Hoperaft, photographs and lists of managers (2), players (24), umpires (2), and mascot (1), and a list of non-participating "tourists" (40). Keefe indicates his knowledge of recent and contemporary figures of importance by mentioning boxers Jack Johnson and "this here langferd," and naval hero "Ad. Dooley." John A. ("Jack") Johnson (1878–1946) was an African-American heavyweight boxer who won the championship (1908) and lost it to Jess Willard* (1915). Johnson is mentioned in "Stop Me—if you've heard This One." Keefe's "this here langferd" was Sam E. Langford (1883–1956), a ranking heavyweight (early 1900s). Admiral George Dewey (1837–1917) was the hero of the Battle of Manila [not Vanila] Bay (May 1, 1898). Walton R. Patrick downgrades "The Busher Abroad," noting that "Lardner deprived himself of some of the resources which gave pungency to *You Know Me Al*"—such as Keefe's having no "domestic relationships" relating to Florrie and "playing in [baseball] games where nothing is really at stake." Still, Patrick admits that "*The Busher Abroad* is not totally lacking in interest and appeal," and even contends that "[a]t its best, the quality of humor in *The Busher Abroad* approaches that of Mark Twain's *Innocents Abroad*." (Sources: Elder, 126–128; Elfers, [xvii]–xxiii; *Home Coming*, 13, 28–29; Patrick, 49, 50)

"THE BUSHER BEATS IT HENCE" (*Saturday Evening Post*, November 7, 1914; YKM).

"THE BUSHER COMES BACK" (*Saturday Evening Post*, May 23, 1914; YKM).

"THE BUSHER PULLS A MAYS" (*Saturday Evening Post*, October 18, 1919; ABS, LOB, RAB). (Characters: Nick Altrock, Baker, Al Blanchard, Bertha Blanchard, Burke, Bush, Eddie Cicotte, Ty Cobb, Cocky Collins, Comiskey, Dumont, Mrs. Dumont, Erickson, Faber, Felsch, Gandil, Gleason, Groh, Huggins, Jennings, Ban Johnson, Judge, Al Keefe, Florrie Keefe, Florrie Keefe, Jack Keefe, Kerr, Liebold, Lowdermilk, Connie Mack, Mayer, Carl Mays, Moran, Joe O'Neill, Page, Peck, Ragan, Roush, Cracker Schalk, the Swede, Geo. Van Haltren, Veach, Vick, Williams.)

Jack Keefe writes Al Blanchard 11 letters.

"N.Y., July 29 [1919]." Keefe, White Sox pitcher, writes from "the gay white way" but is unhappy about his teammates' troubles. Gandil is "in a hospital with appendix," Felsch is limping, Cracker Schalk is playing badly, and Keefe himself has stomach problems. Jennings's Detroit team "is comeing like a house on fire." Cicotte pitched well but lost because Felsch fielded badly. The big news is that Carl Mays of the Boston Red Sox quit pitching against the White Sox because of poor team support, and Huggins paid "4 or 5 ball players and the liberty loan" for his "N.Y. club" to get Mays. This gives Keefe the idea that if Gleason, his manager, "looks X eyed at me I will Mays him," since "wouldn't some clubs jump ... to get a hold of me," particularly Detroit. New York is so dry Keefe had to pay $2.40 for "6 high balls" to repair his "freting" stomach.

"Boston, Aug. 2." The White Sox have "clumb in to 1st place" despite Gleason's depending only on pitchers Cicotte and Williams and not using "the rest of us." Still, Kerr, Faber, and Lowdermilk pitched badly. So did Keefe, losing "in Chi" to St. Louis and New York because of his stomach. Jennings works his pitchers "like a mgr. should." Gleason should've signed "some pitcher like Page with the Phila. club." Instead, he got Pat Regan. Ban Johnson "suspend it Mays." Johnson banned Ty Cobb too, but someone is playing centerfield for Detroit "called ... Ty" regardless. The $7 "qt." bottle of "refreshmunts" Keefe bought for "over the sabath" in Boston was so poisonous that he'll tip "the chamber horse" with it. "In the old days" in Boston hotels, you could get drinks on Sunday if "you ordered sandwichs with it."

"Phila., Aug. 4." Keefe says his club is in Boston, but Gleason sent him and Cicotte ahead here. Gleason urged Keefe to quit "that liquid diet," and if he doesn't, then pitches badly in Philadelphia ,"it won't be nobody's fault only your own." Cicotte couldn't get Keefe to accompany him to the Philadelphia-St. Louis game, "study Mack's batters," watch "Connie waggle his score card," and maybe steal his signals. A hotel waiter says it's easy to buy liquor here, but Keefe plans to "be in shape"; still, "3 or 4 wouldn't hurt," and Gleason wouldn't know.

"Phila., Aug. 6." Keefe writes Al he'd "pull a Mays," leave the White Sox, and join a square-deal club, except his teammates need him. He told Cicotte the more a pitcher "seen of Mack's club why the lest he would know about how to pitch to them." Instead of going to the game, Keefe called a friend, "histed a few" with him, went to Atlantic City, resisted when "all the queens was giveing us the double O," bought "a qt.," rested on the beach, missed the train, and returned next morning to Philadelphia. Gleason pitched Keefe, but he "walked the 1st. 2 men" and was taken out. Gleason said he knew Keefe went to Atlantic City, and didn't take a dip but a dipper. Cicotte won "1 to o" over Philadelphia's Page. Gleason has signed old Mayer, of the National League. Keefe would leave the team except some pals "has got their heart set on winning."

"Washington, Aug. 9." Keefe says that when his team played Philly yesterday, the Washington team, having finished hosting Detroit, had free time, came over, and watched. Keefe hinted to their manager, Jennings, that he might desert Gleason "like Mays done on Boston" and pitch for Jennings. Keefe interprets Jennings's obscure words about trading with Gleason, as well as Jennings's smiles and winks, as encouragement. Keefe even confided in "Bush of the Detroit club," who said "go ahead and pull a Mays and see what happened." A reporter on the train to Washington told Keefe not only that Gleason unsuccessfully dickered with Mack for Page, but also that, no, Gleason said nothing about Keefe "that could be printed." Encouraged, Keefe hinted he might "pull a Mays" and be treated better elsewhere. The reporter warned him about how stories spread. Keefe doesn't care if Gleason hears, but doesn't want him to though, but hasn't told anybody, but has told some teammates trustworthy "enough to keep their mouth shut."

"On Train, Aug. 12." Keefe says Washington was happy, even though "we took 2 out of 3 from them," because they made a lot of "jack out of our serious." Keefe "put the brakes on them" when Gleason substituted him for "wilt[ing] Lefty Williams." Gleason "give me the old oil but I just ... pertended like I fell for it." Keefe expects "world serious dough," maybe beating Moran's Cincinnati team "in 4 days" or "N.Y." in "probably ... 5," counting travel time. Keefe anticipates pitching against Reds hitters Groh and Roush.

"Chi, Aug. 15." Keefe gripes to Gleason that

he politely took Ed Cicotte out when he was losing to Boston yesterday but "barked like a dog" while yanking Keefe in Philly. Keefe tells Al he should come see him pitch for the White Sox "if the big show comes off in Cincinnati." Keefe would sell Al one of his tickets; afterwards, they could "hist a few." Leave Bertha at home; "ladys is a nuisance." Meanwhile, Florrie isn't getting along with her beauty-parlor partners the Dumonts and may sell out to them. Anyway, "a womans place is home."

"Chi, Aug. 20." Keefe reports that when they were playing Washington here, Keefe shouted to Nick Altrock and called him "handsome." Altrock called him "Carl." Gleason explained that this was a reference to Keefe's talk about imitating Carl Mays and going to another team. Keefe demanded to be pitched more. Gleason countered that Keefe pitched only "2 good innings in a month." Keefe says Cicotte beat Washington against Erickson's pitching because the White Sox "got 10 runs for Eddie," unlike when Keefe pitches. Florrie will sell her share but get back little more than her $250 investment.

"Chi, Aug. 25." Gleason, whose "brains has been A.W.O.L. for the last 2 mos.," hasn't pitched Keefe regularly; so Keefe wired Jennings "telling him what come off." Keefe will be "moveing" soon. It seems Gleason made him do nothing last "Sat. P.M." [August 23] but warm up, until "my old souper squeeked like a rat." Later that night Keefe threw a party to help Florrie, her friends, and their husbands celebrate. He "triped the life fantastic"; they found a place that "served us rat poison in tea cups"; Keefe "eat something that didn't set right." Next day, despite a fever, Keefe went to the park; Gleason pitched him against "the N.Y. club" instead of Williams, who said he was sick. Keefe felt "dizzy," beaned Vick, walked Peck, and Baker with a count of "2 and o" foolishly swung for a homer. Keefe quit, told Gleason he wouldn't pitch "for a mgr." who makes someone work who is "2 laps this side of a corps," and boasts he'll go to Detroit. Why would "cuckoo" Gleason make him pitch "64 innings in 3 days in the bull pen"? Keefe hopes both that Jennings will answer his telegram and that Gleason will "try and square things with me." Anyway, he can give Detroit "the kind of help they need."

"Chi, Aug. 29." Keefe is happy at home with Florrie and the kiddies while awaiting news from Jennings, who may be dickering with Gleason in a deal trading Keefe for some good Detroit players short of Cobb or Bush, perhaps for "Bob Veach and no money on the side." Keefe could help Detroit "Bring the old flag home."

"Chi, Aug. 31." Keefe repeats newspaper news to Al that he is "tickled to death" to be going to pitch for Connie Mack of "the Athaletics," to help that young team progress. The news "come to me in a funny way." Keefe, out late Friday [August 29], "overslept myself," and awoke to Florrie's "sobing" into the papers about Philadelphia getting "you and $5000.00 for Page." She and Keefe "was ... snuffleing" together a little, discarded the idea of dining out "and take in a picture" because they had "less than $200.00 to our name." After much discussion, they decided this: Philadelphia was ideal — near Atlantic City "for Florrie and the kids ... all summer"; Florrie might get a beauty-parlor job "to help out this winter"; Keefe will help the "young ball club" win "2 or 3 seasons in a row"; by then "Gleason's club and Jennings's to will be in the old folks home lapping up gruel." Keefe will ask "Connie" to pitch him twice in September, against Detroit and against the White Sox. He'll show everyone "old Jack Keefe" can pitch when well managed.

For the pun of it, Lardner might have entitled this story "The Busher Does a Mays." George W. Hilton notes that "Lardner correctly recognized that [Ban] Johnson lacked the power to implement his policy" of suspending players. (Source: Hilton, 306)

"THE BUSHER REËNLISTS" (*Saturday Evening Post*, April 19, 1919; ABS, LOW, RAB). (Characters: Jim Archer, Joe Benz, Al Blanchard, Bertha Blanchard, Callahan, Comiskey, Kid Gleason, Harry, Artie Hofman, Al Keefe, Florrie Keefe, Florrie Keefe, Jack Keefe, Kelly, Charlie O'Leary, Hy Pond, Bobby Roth, Rowland, Scott, the Swede, Walsh.)

Jack Keefe writes 10 letters to Al Blanchard.

"Chi, Dec. 2 [1918]." Keefe reports that the doctor says his left arm, which "the Dutchmens shot full of holes," is "as good as new." Fortunately, his right, pitching arm wasn't hurt. After what he "went through acrost the old pond," playing baseball again is "baby games." Hee doesn't want to leave his "wife and 2 kiddies" during away games. Instead, he'll enter the business world and soon "be drawing $15000.00 per annum or something." In the army, he could have been more than a corporal but preferred to "pal around" with his buddies and not "lord it over them." Business men ought to favor an ex-ballplayer who served "the stars and strips."

"Chi, Dec. 8." Profit-seeking, unpatriotic business men enrage Keefe. While "histing a few" with some White Sox fans, he heard about a department-store opening, applied, was told "they was shy of a floor man," but the manager then got insulting. Keefe also declined a job reading gas meters. He'll wait for employers to come to him. When Florrie heard this, she suggested his returning to baseball. Agreeing, he figures Comiskey will double his old $2,500, available before he "quit and enlisted"; with Florrie's "$250.00 per mo. clear profit," they'll have "$8000.00 per annum." He refused Florrie's suggestion that if he can't get $5,000 for pitching he could fire "the Swede" and babysit "little Al and "little Florrie" himself.

"Chi, Dec. 12." Outside the American League meeting at a downtown hotel, Keefe kidded with Bobby Roth, who played for Cleveland against the White Sox; announced he's aiming for a business career; was distressed that Artie Hofman, Charley O'Leary, Jim Archer, and Joe Benz all failed to ask about his war experiences; and figures he could be sent a $5,000 pitching contract by waiting but still prefers a future in big business. With Hy Pond, his old Central League pal, he "histed a couple beers," but beer is watered down now ever since "we was over there takeing the fight out of the Germans." He saw an ad for a Detroit job for "a young man of good appearances," but he won't move. Having "2 or 3 pretty good chances" so far, he'll let people bid for him.

"Chi, Dec. 23." Florrie told Keefe she was "lonesome ... wile I was away." Her Christmas present purchases, though, indicate she had many friends. When he complained about "the jack she was spending," she threatened to use her own money. She talked Keefe into their buying "little Florrie" a $47.50 gold chain with four pearls, with room for more pearls as she ages. Florrie has bought Keefe's present. Maybe a corset or false teeth for use later? Keefe is sorry sending Al and Bertha Blanchard only "xmas cards," but it's wrong to splurge when our soldiers are still in France and "another liberty loan [is] comeing along."

"Chi, Dec. 31." Keefe awaits his best chance among many. He might try "takeing up newspaper work and writeing articles about baseball or maybe army life." His baseball articles "would be different then some of these birds that's reporting the games." He'd laugh if offered insufficient pay. Today while Florrie was at "her looks garage" and the Swede was walking the kids, Keefe took a streetcar to "the ball pk." He talked with Harry in Comiskey's office about "what I seen over acrost the pond" but nothing about news of Keefe's possibly pitching again. They'll probably mail him a contract for $4000—"the lease I would sign up for." Anyway, he'll decline and mention his business ambitions.

"Chi, Jan. 16. [1919]." Good news: Kid Gleason has been named White Sox manager. Gleason likes Keefe because he kids him and Keefe kids back fast. So Keefe won't aim to rise in the business world but will pitch again. Good for the White Sox, too, because "I will come pretty near winning that old flag single handed." Cheering crowds will remember his service in France.

"Chi, Feb. 13." The newspapers report Gleason's conferring with Comiskey in Chicago. Keefe says he plans to let them offer him work. He wrote Comiskey "a couple wks. ago" suggesting he'd quit his business plans and pitch for "$3600.00 per annum." No answer means they want a face-to-face. So he left them his "phone No." Florrie said this: She could be either "glad or sorry" about his pitching again; if there's another war she isn't "a dependant husband" to be exempt; she might go fight like Russian women; they didn't retreat. Keefe said the Russian men retreated faster than the women. Keefe will laugh at Gleason and Comiskey if they don't meet his offer.

"Chi, Feb. 20." Gleason must not have gotten Keefe's "phone No." So he "went over to the pk." and waited until Gleason left Comiskey's office. They talked. Gleason: He wished Keefe had been shot by "them long distance guns." Keefe: He was wounded "in June and was invalid home." Gleason: As usual, Keefe was yanked "in the 5th. inning." Keefe: He'd accept $3,000 a year. Gleason: That's better than $30 a month army pay. Keefe: He has a Stock Yards offer. After more banter, Gleason promised to take him south to see how good he is and added that Comiskey would mail him a contract, which he should accept. Keefe is confident, "specially with the stuff I've got."

"Chi, March 8." Keefe is quitting baseball. The letter from Comiskey offered $2,400. Keefe went to see him. After a while, Harry admitted him. Keefe said that he wanted his old $2,500 and that Gleason wanted him. Comiskey said he told Gleason that, if so, he could make up that difference in pay, and added that he could trade Keefe to Griffith's Washington team. Refusing, Keefe said he was going into the business world. Keefe is happy to be able to stay in Chi "with Florrie and the kiddies." Gleason is so new as manager that he feared giving Keefe the $2,800 he demanded.

"Chi, March 20." Keefe boasts about letting "them come to me." The Swede told him someone phoned him; so he phoned "the ball pk." and learned Gleason was there. Gleason wondered if Keefe was "going along with us." Keefe agreed to go at $2,400, which he says was his former "salery." Gleason promised more if he could "earn more jack." His teammates rejoiced when they "seen me stride in." He'll miss Florrie and the babies, but "they's nobody on this ball club that lays awake all night crying for their bottle." So in Texas he can "get a little sleep."

"THE BUSHER'S HONEYMOON" (*Saturday Evening Post*, July 11, 1914; YKM).

"THE BUSHER'S KID" (*Saturday Evening Post*, October 3, 1914; YKM).

"THE BUSHER'S LETTERS HOME" (*Saturday Evening Post*, March 7, 1914; YKM).

"THE BUSHER'S WELCOME HOME" (*Saturday Evening Post*, June 5, 1915). (Characters: Allen, Marie Allen, Benz, Al Blanchard, Bertha Blanchard, Bush, Callahan, Comiskey, Daly, Dr., Dr., Mike Donlin, Steve Evans, Gilmore, Al Keefe, Florrie Keefe, Jack Keefe, Mcgraw, Demon Runyon, Schaefer, Schalk, Scott, Slight, Speaker, Joe Tinker, Weaver, Weegman.)

Jack Keefe writes Al Blanchard eight letters during the final weeks of the tour around the world taken by baseball players, mostly White Sox and Giants.

"On the Ship bord. Feb. 6." Keefe writes about sailing on "the Meadow Training ocean" heading for Naples "Itly." Schaefer showed Keefe 10 fake scarabs he bought for 5¢ each and tells him that real ones squeak like rats when bitten. Keefe bit his expensive lucky scarab, but it didn't squeak.

"Naples It. Feb. 8." Sunday. Keefe has received no "male." He is tired of Naples. Callahan urged the men to see "Pump A," and "a wop give us a couple of bronx statues."

"Rome. It. Feb. 13." Their old hotel lacks baths. Schaefer said the ancient Romans didn't need them, since they dressed like statues and could bathe by standing in the rain. While it was raining, Mcgraw explained baseball to Rome's "mare." Schaefer said this rain was the worst since "the rain of Nearo." Keefe has seen too many "runes." Steve Evans lied to "the pope" that Keefe was sick and couldn't see him. Lies are bad, especially to a pope. They head for "Niece" tonight.

"Niece. It. Feb. 16." Mcgraw kept Keefe from pitching today, saving him for Paris. The Giants lost. Keefe and some others went to "monte Carlo," where Keefe bet "5 liars" on red three straight times. His scarab enabled him to win $4. Though urged to play more, he quit ahead. Others lost, "trying to pick out Nos. insted of collers." He wouldn't sell his scarab to Scott. Girls flirted with Keefe at a parade of ballplayers.

"Paris. Feb. 21." Rain. Evans and Schaefer told Keefe that Lajoie and Jackson were jumping to the (Chicago) federal league and Keefe should too. A hotel worker paged Keefe and gave him a telegram. Since it was written "in France," Evans translated and said it was from Joe Tinker, federal manager, offering him $10,000 a year for a "3 yr. contrack." To celebrate, Keefe bought Evans two "ciggars" and Schaefer one. They persuaded Keefe to wire his acceptance to Tinker at 31¢ a word; it cost $3.72. Keefe will annoy Comiskey by telling him but won't tell Callahan. In Paris they visited the graves of "Lajoies grate granfathers." When a manufacturer of "champlain wine" hosted a party for the players, Keefe presented one of his "pones."

"London. Eng. Feb. 27." Keefe pitched in a game but lost when Daly, who plays in "the new Eng. league," got a lucky homer off him. Keefe's arm was lame, because of the "fogy" weather. Benz pitched poorly against Keefe, but Keefe's team mates couldn't get hits. According to "mike Donlin," the cricket-loving crowd foolishly praised Evans for catching an easy fly. Evans told Keefe the king was entering and he must remove his cap. The fellow didn't look like a king, because he had a beard. Sightseeing included "West Mr. Abie." Tomorrow "Liver pool."

"N. Y. city. March 7." Keefe told Comiskey about jumping to the federal. They won't tell Callahan. Keefe is excited about seeing Florrie and their little Al. He might have "a jaw full of teeth" and not know Keefe "from a rabbit." Inspectors entered their ship to "serch evry body to see if there smuggleing dimonds or purls." Evans got Keefe to hide his scarab in "a big chew" of tobacco. "Demon Runyon," with the team ever since Paris, said the inspector ought to "put on a brown sute of cloths before he ast me any qestions." Oh, Speaker got "sined" by "the Boston club." At a city "banquit" for the teams, Schaefer suggested that Keefe prepare some more "poultry." And "I wisht you could of herd them clap" when his reciting ended with praise of "the stars and strips." Mcgraw gave Keefe "a box of ciggars." Keefe sent Florrie a night wire about being home soon. If Callahan knew Keefe's plans, he'd try to sign him right on the train.

"Chicago. March 11." Keefe is home. No Florrie. A neighbor gave him a letter from her. Florrie, little Al, her sister Marie Allen, and Allen were all in California, since the Dr. told her little Al missed daddy so much that California would do him good. The apartment was messy, with one light on. Keefe tried to phone Tinker, but he and team-owner Weegman were south with the players. Keefe talked with team-president Gilmore. He knew nothing but would wire Tinker for an explanation. Tinker, in "Skreevport," replied that he got Keefe's wire, which meant nothing to him, and concluded that Keefe's friends were kidding him. Keefe explained everything to Comiskey, with Callahan listening. Comiskey, laughing, kept Keefe on the White Sox. Keefe concludes that he is glad he "dident fall for no federal league skin game." He wasn't fooled even when they pretended "Cobb and them [including Jackson and Walter Johnson] had sined so theyd get me to sine but I was to smart for them." Still, Keefe must pay Allen for money lent to Florrie to go with little Al and the Allens to California, and pay for Florrie and little Al to return to Chicago. With his scarab providing luck, Keefe figures his pitching will "go threw that american league this yr. like gravy threw a sift." That tea he bought in "Salome" he'll send to the Blanchards.

"The Busher's Welcome Home" adds little new about Keefe except for two cruelties he suffered. Evans and Schaefer tempt him to leave the safety of his position with the White Sox by "jumping to the league." Worse, perhaps, Florrie doesn't write Keefe and, instead, leaves their Chicago apartment filthy and goes to California. Some welcome home. When Keefe laments that little Al won't know him from a rabbit, Lardner is punning, as he often did in family letters, on Abbott, the maiden name of his wife Ellis.

BUSHMAN, FRANCIS X. (1883–1966). Handsome movie actor. Bushman quit school at 15 and became a handsome actor and a statuesque model. He appeared in silent films (1911–1917). He married, secretly, so as to continue appearing to gasping female audiences. But then he divorced, married his leading-lady, and fled briefly to Europe with her. Returning, he appeared in only three movies (1920–1925), divorced, and married again, and again. After more movies and some television spots, he appeared in one final film (1966). Jack Spears dismisses Bushman as a "once-great" film talent when he appeared in *Hollywood Boulevard* (1936). Will both Skull Scoville, of "The Poor Simp," and Lefty Crosby, of "The Yellow Kid," said to resemble beautiful Bushman, also fade in time? Bushman is also mentioned in *The Big Town*. (Source: Spears, 352)

BUTLER ("Great Blessings"). He is Frank Butler's brother, 12. The kid delivers a message to Tod Stewart, which takes Tod away from his parents, who are visiting for Thanksgiving Day.

BUTLER, FRANK ("Great Blessings"). He is a bootlegger who supplies Tod Stewart. Tod is also sweet on Mamie Butler, Frank's sister.

BUTLER, MAMIE ("Great Blessings"). She is Frank Butler's cute, loose sister, 25. Tod Stewart's wife Clara has seen Tod and Mamie flirting.

BYERS ("Who Dealt?"). Mrs. Cannon says that an editor maybe named Byers or Runkle didn't read her husband Tom Cannon's short story.

BYERS, PEEWEE ("Zone of Quiet"). He used to play for Paul Whiteman* and his orchestra, according to Miss Eleanor Lyons. She says Peewee now "has got the orchestra" at the place owned by Barney Gallant.* She went there after seeing *What Price Glory?* (1924) by Laurence Stallings (1894–1968).

BYRD ("Holycaust"). Jessie Graham writes that the Centralia fire involved the Byrd-Watson building.

BYRNE ("Back to Baltimore"). In a game against Boston, Byrne, batting for the Phillies, gets on base because of William Baker Jr.'s inept fielding.

Robert Mathew Byrne (1884–1964) played for the St. Louis Cardinals (1907–1908), the Cardinals and the Pittsburgh Pirates (1909), the Pirates (1910–1912), the Pirates and the Philadelphia Phillies (1913), the Phillies (1914–1916), and the Phillies and the Chicago White Sox (1917). (Sources: *Baseball Encyclopedia*, 851; Hilton, 440)

BYRNE, CAPTAIN ("Stop Me—if you've heard This One"). He is the Chicago police officer who, according to Henry Wild Osborne's fib, discovered with him the suicide in Chicago of the mysterious Scandinavian, identified as John Janssen, whom Osborne saw earlier on the train from New York to Chicago.

BYRNE, DENNIS ("The Jade Necklace"). He is a matinée idol called a "beautiful Mick" and starring in *Danny Darling*, a movie produced by "the Supreme people." L. N. Bauer, head of Colossal Films Incorporated, hires Maurice Kavanaugh, a handsome Irish actor, as a rival.

BYRON ("A One-Man Team"). He and Moxey are halfbacks for the Doane football team. Byron plays well, to the surprise of Coach Belden's team, coached entirely to defend against Davis, Doane's star. Moxey plays well also.

C., MR. ("Contract"). He is a bridge-playing friend of Lardner, who hopes in a postscript that C. won't take this story personally.

"A CADDY'S DIARY" (*Saturday Evening Post*, March 11, 1922; HTW, PRL, RU). (Characters: Jack Andrews, Joe Bean, Mr. Blake, Fat Brunner, Mr. Carter, Mrs. Carter, Clayton, Colby, Chas Crane, Lou Crowell, Dick, Mr. Doane, Mrs. Doane, Mr. Dunham, Heisman, Joyce, Klabor, Alex Laird, Mr. Langley, Harry Leer, Mr. Lewis, Mr. Perdue, Miss Rennie, Mr. Thomas, Mrs. Thomas.)

Dick, the diarist, 16, caddies at the Pleasant View Golf Club and wants to become a pro. When he "cadded" for Mr. Colby, a journalist, they discussed Alex Laird's golf columns. Colby said Laird didn't write them but "split 50–50" with the person who did. The caddy figures that as a pro he could write about golf and golfers and not split fees. He asks Colby how to learn to write and is told to practice by keeping a diary. He starts:

"*Friday, Apr. 14.*" Showers prevent my "cadding" a few days. I've caddied 5 years, quit school 3 years ago at father's, not mother's, insistence. I shoot around 75 now, better than most members and better than jealous Jack Andrews, the pro, who plays members, sometimes spotting them a stroke a hole, betting $5 a hole, and making plenty. Women prefer me, though I'm "no Othello," instead of my pal Joe Bean, about 16, another caddy. Women don't tip; but I'd caddy free anytime for Mrs. Doane, since she's very pretty.

"*Sat. Apr. 15.*" Today Joe caddied for Mr. Blake. I caddied for Mr. Thomas, who is a bank vice president and has 16 heavy clubs. Both cheat on their scores and have caddies, for example, confirm they reached green in 4 when it was over 6. Mr. Thomas asked Blake, a better golfer, what club he "better take" when he was still off a 3-par green after 3 dubs. Joe whispered "take my advice and quit."

"*Mon. Apr. 17.*" I "cadded 45 holes" yesterday, then today for "good looker" Miss Rennie, engaged to Chas Crane, who works in Mr. Thomas's bank and is the club's "best player." She played against Mrs. Thomas, who was "2 bits" ahead when darkness halted the game. Miss Rennie, whose 18th hole position would have meant victory, told me she would have tipped me but for Mrs. Thomas's "quarter she dont deserve."

"*Thurs. Apr. 20.*" Today was a best-ball match with Mr. Thomas and Mr. Crane, who was caddied by me, opposing Mr. Blake and Jack Andrews, who was caddied by Joe. After the match, really between Mr. Crane and Jack, Thomas lacked change and Crane paid me — exactly, no tip. Joe and I agree golfers shooting par can't cheat because everyone sees their good drives and customary 2 putts.

"*Wed. Apr. 26.*" Mrs. Doane, back from golfing "down south all winter," still played badly. She "is just to pretty to be a golf player." I carried for her and Mrs. Carter, "a ugly dame"; Joe, for Mr. Carter, who drinks and is "near always stood [stewed]." Mr. Doane is "dirty with money." Mrs. Doane shot badly on the 3rd hole. I agreed "winter rules was in force." She teed, patted my "sholder," and called me her "pal." I'd caddy for her free.

"*Sat. Apr. 29.*" This was the first monthly tournament of the year. A best-ball foursome was Mr. Dunham, handicap 50, and Mr. Carter, handicap 15, against Mr. Thomas, handicap 30, and Mr. Blake, handicap 15. Mr. Dunham on 1st tee drove 3 balls outside the grounds. Mr. Carter wanted to call them practice drives. No, said Mr. Thomas. On the 1st green, Mr. Dunham putted for a 13; Mr. Blake 2-putted for "a 8," winning. On the 2nd tee, Mr. Dunham whiffed; so did Mr. Thomas, who claimed Mr. Dunham's example "would spoil anybody's game." They messed up on No. 3 and let "a 2 some" through. Mr. Thomas blamed toothaches for shooting 7 on No. 3. On the 7th tee, Mr. Blake suggested Mr. Thomas try his wood, since "you cant do no worse." He "swang" and broke its head off. The witnesses "stood there in silents," while Mr. Thomas broke his remaining 4 woods against a tree and said "all right gentlemen that is over." For the "first 9," Mr. Thomas scored 60. He did well on the 2nd 9, and said breaking his woods "broke my hoodoo." By the 18th, he had 39 strokes, meaning 99 for 17 holes. Another golfer informed Mr. Thomas that Charley Crane shot 75, meaning Mr. Thomas would need 6 on 18. He took 5 to hit the green, but when asked I lied he took 4. His 2 putts let him tie, figuring his handicap. He and Mr. Crane split first prize, 12 balls, and second prize, 6 balls, getting "9 golf balls a piece."

"*Tues. May 2.*" On "the first ladies day," Joe and I carried "for the fair sex." Miss Rennie and Mrs. Thomas, against Mrs. Doane and Mrs. Carter, shot 1000 "if they had of kept their score right." Mrs. Doane praised Miss Rennie's $100 dress. Miss Rennie didn't like it and challenged Mrs. Doane to play golf for it. If Miss Rennie won, Mrs. Doane would buy it for $50. If Mrs. Doane won, she could have it "for nothing." On the 16th hole, Mrs. Doane drove out of sight left. Her lie was bad. She "give me one of her looks." Unseen, I "give the ball a shove with my toe." Mrs. Doane won and bought the dress.

"*Fri. May 5.*" Exciting news Wednesday: Mr. Crane stole $8,000 from Mr. Thomas's bank, "went south," and a bank stenographer "elloped with him." Fat Brunner and Lou Crowell fought over who "cadded for" Mr. Crane last. Thursday Mr. Thomas played with Mr. Blake and expressed sorrow that "young" Crane had wrecked his "carreer" for "a doll face girl." Today I "cadded for Mrs Thomas and Mrs. Doane." They gossiped about Mr. Crane. Mrs. Thomas said he "was geting $4000 a yr" and would "sell his soul for $8000 and a pretty face." Later, I asked Joe what selling your soul meant. He said if you do "something dishonest" for money or "a gal" or a reward, you sell your soul. I said I wanted to go warn Mr. Thomas about lying about his score, Mrs. Thomas about placing her ball better, Mrs. Doane about making me kick her ball from "a rut" for a dress. Joe told me I sold my soul too when I lied about Mr. Thomas's score for a tip and improved Mrs. Doane's position for a smile. We both decided to keep our mouths shut.

The diary begins on Friday, April 14th. Such Fridays fell in 1916 (too early) and again in 1922, the year "A Caddy's Diary" was published, in March. Therefore, tardy *Saturday Evening Post* readers could imagine that as time moved on for them, the diarist's educative adventures kept pace. (Or maybe Lardner was careless.) Donald Elder defines " A Caddy's Diary" as "a devastating revelation of the pettiness and dishonesty of a group of golfers at a fashionable club." Elizabeth Evans says the story "explores the price for which people will sell their honest nature." It may be added that the diarist's mangling of language, perhaps not surprising in a 16-year-old forced to quit school at 13, partly eclipses the dreadful lessons in morality he is gaining from adults whose burdens he carries. No adult is his role model, except his mother, whose hope for his education her husband squelched. Clifton Fadiman says that "A Caddy's Diary" is "a scathing exposure of the moral bankruptcy of the millionaire sportsman," and, he adds, so is the later "Mr. Frisbie." (Sources: Elder, 213; Evans, 87; Fadiman, 316)

CADY ("The Crook"). He was the Red Sox catcher who tagged Larry, of the White Sox, out at home. Bull, the umpire, silently endured Larry's complaint.

Although Cady and Cahill are fictional characters, their names may have been suggested to Lardner by those of the early minor-league player Charles B. Cady (1885–1909) and John Patrick Parnell Cahill (1865–1901), who played for the St. Louis Cardinals (1886). (Source: *Baseball Encyclopedia*, 1871)

CAHILL In "The Crook," he played for the narrator Larry's White Sox, against the Red Sox. Cahill objected when Bull, umpiring behind the plate, refused to overrule a call by Tommy, umpiring at third base. Cahill called Bull "crooked," and Bull slugged him. In "The Yellow Kid," Cahill was manager of the narrator Bill's team, warned Harry Childs and others to ease up on kidding their fine pitcher, Lefty Crosby, and benched him when continued kidding upset him. (See also Cady.)

CAHILL, DAN ("Three Without, Doubled"). He is an "elevator starter," presumably in the office building where Gullible works. Gullible says you can't kid with him.

CALDWELL ("The Ides of June"). He is a Brooklyn baseball player whom manager Max Carey says he is sending to Hartford.

Bruce Caldwell (1906–1959) played for the Cleveland Indians (1928) and the Brooklyn Dodgers (1932). (Source: *Baseball Encyclopedia*, 854)

"CALL FOR MR. KEEFE!" (*Saturday Evening Post*, March 9, 1918; ABS, LOB, RAB, SC). (Characters: Al Blanchard, Bertha Blanchard, Chapman, Cicotte, Collins, Comiskey, Bill Evans, Gandil, Kid Gleason, Griffith, Graney, Jackson, Hughey Jennings, Johnson, Ban Johnson, Al Keefe, Florrie Keefe, Jack Keefe, McMullin, Milan, Miss Nevins, Silk O'Loughlin, Roth, Rowland, Schalk, Speaker.)

Jack Keefe writes 12 letters to Al Blanchard.

"St. Louis, April 10 [1917]." Training trips are finished, and if Rowland, manager of the White

Sox, for which Keefe pitches, handles the players right, they should be far ahead by July. Keefe feels war should have been declared right after the Germans sank the "Louisiana." Keefe said he'd volunteer but for his wife Florrie and their "little Al" "depending on me for sport." Gleason jeered that the army wouldn't accept Keefe. Maybe Rowland is saving Keefe for Detroit's opener.

"Chicago, April 15." Rowland may be saving Keefe for the home opener against St. Louis. Little Al, now three, greeted Keefe with "Who are you?," which Keefe found cute. Florrie is wasteful, "has boughten" too many clothes, even hired a girl for $8 a week to cook, clean, and watch little Al. Keefe said they don't need "no help from Norway." Florrie replied that Keefe loses enough at poker and that she might get a job, maybe "go in business."

"Chicago, May 19." Keefe hears about the draft. Gleason said left-hander Keefe wouldn't qualify, since guns are made for right-handers, and said they don't send draftees straight to France without teaching them German first. Keefer said he'd like to be an aviator. Gleason said Keefe was already "up in the air all last Tuesday afternoon," pitching against "the Phila. club." Florrie asked for half Keefe's $200 pay, cried when he refused, then accepted it. When women cry, "you can't do nothing with them."

"Chicago, May 24." Florrie and a Miss Nevins started a beauty parlor at "43th St. right off of Michigan," catering to women without time to go downtown. Keefe says since there aren't beauty parlors in Bedford, where Al lives, he'll explain: If Al and Bertha came to Chicago to a show, she would have "grime [washed] out of her hair," have it fluffed, "clean up her complexion with buttermilk," paint or "get rid of the moles," put eyebrows on, redden her lips, and "polish her teeth and pair her fnger nails." Florrie's "joint" smells rich enough to cost the whole $100. Umpire Silk O'Loughlin called a low Johnson pitched strike three on Gandill. Gleason said Silk would be rejected by the army for poor eyesight. Silk ejected him. Keefe, sassing Silk, also got tossed. Keefe boasts that this season they will "cop that old flag and play the Giants for the big dough," unless the Cubs continue winning.

"Chicago, June 6." Rowland took the White Sox east and left Keefe home with a sore "souper." Anyway, he had to register at the draft board. They asked questions, some foolish, like are you "a natural born citizen?" (he replied he didn't fall from a tree), are you missing an arm? (he said his was only sore), what race are you? (he wanted to say "pennant"). Why register at all, once he said he was "married with dependents" and could "claim exemption"? They could prove he was married by phoning Florrie. Maybe the hired girl would answer and shout "Swede talk." She is so loud she should be a ball-park announcer. Oh, Florrie is becoming such a success that she might have you, Al, "white washing some dames nose or levelling off their face with a steam roller." Only "jokeing."

"Chicago, June 21." Keefe explains his actions in yesterday's game against Cleveland. His fly ball would have been a hit between Speaker and Graney but for Speaker's playing out of position and catching it. Evans, the umpire living in Cleveland, called Keefe's pitched strike a ball and walked Chapman. Keefe told Evans he'd flunk the army eye test. Schalk, Keefe's catcher, called for wrong pitches; Speaker got a hit; he and Chapman "pulled a double steal"; Roth hit one that Jackson "could of caught in his hip pocket" but didn't. Rowland yanked Keefe, who threatened to join the army, at which Rowland said if Keefe had a grenade to throw he'd "wind up and loose a hand." But for his family, Keefe would go to Fort Sheridan and "try for a captain."

"Chicago, July 5." Florrie and Miss Nevins cleared $400 in June. Florrie may want to hire more help and also a nurse for little Al. Rowland kept Keefe in Chicago when the White Sox played Detroit. The Sox may face the Giants in the "worlds serious," which would mean "about $4500.00 a peace per man" for the winners.

"Chicago, July 20." Keefe says his draft number, 3403, was "the 5th number drawed at Washington." Wipe "Washington off of the map," because Johnson pitched for Washington and won 3–2 over Keefe, the White Sox pitcher. Keefe explains he'd eagerly enter the army, except for his family and for "the people" needing baseball for amusement and for his own making more money than friend Al, who unless he has flat feet might go, especially since he has no kids and Bertha could live with Al's mother and "pick up a few dollars sowing." Keefe bought a $50 Liberty Bond, at interest so low it "couldn't sport a flee."

"Chicago, Aug. 6." Keefe reported to the draft board. He told the doctor he didn't feel good after meals and his arm was sore. The doctor admired his "shoulders and chest," recorded him "at 194 and 6 ft. 1 and a half," and checked his eyesight "like I didn't know the alphabet or something," Keefe said he had a wife and child and wouldn't want to desert Comiskey. The doctor gave him a form for Florrie to complete and notarize, and said to forget Comiskey.

"Chicago, Aug. 8." When Keefe returned to the draft board with Florrie's affidavit, a stranger told him a certain unsigned letter had been received informing him that Florrie made $250 a month, could support "she and your boy," and so if Keefe presented her affidavit he could be imprisoned. He said Keefe should "just lay quiet and take a chance," or leave the affidavit and appeal if necessary. Keefe presented the affidavit, returned home, told Florrie she should sell out to Miss Nevins, and they could take the profit, plus his earnings, and buy a house in the south. Florrie decided to wait until the board drafted him, then sell and he'd be exempt. "Al it looks like a cinch."

"Chicago, Aug. 22." "The Dist. board won't let me off." When interviewed, Keefe admitted Florrie averaged $250 a month but spent it on clothes, was asked how she kept warm in August, was told shoes worn a second time would prove more comfortable, and replied "She don't never have no trouble with her feet." When Keefe told Florrie "see what your dam beauty parlor has done for us," she cried, after which he "couldn't find no more fault with her." He phoned the club he was sick. Tomorrow he wants to pitch against Washington.

"Chicago, Aug. 23." At the club house, Keefe was about to tell Rowland and Gleason his news, but first off they said he was sold to Washington. Keefe had the last laugh, though, telling them he had "signed ... with Uncle Sam." Both men praised him, especially Gleason, who said little Al would be proud "because you went while a lot of other kids dads stayed home." Rowland let Keefe pitch, and he managed a three-run shut-out, one hit being a bunt wrongly called safe.

"Chicago, Sept. 18." Florrie packs Keefe's things. He'll train in a camp "to learn to talk German and shoot and etc." When told, little Al asked if he could "go to daddy?" He'll be proud. Keefe "won't be in the serious against New York" but in "the real worlds serious."

"Call for Mr. Keefe!" has 20 real-life characters. All but three — Gandil, Graney, and Rowland — were introduced in *You Know Me Al.* Ring Lardner Jr. calls this story "as good as the best of *You Know Me Al.*" Jeff Silverman notes that although Lardner in his non-fictional dispatches as a war correspondent (1917) "never quite found his traction on French soil," he was "on much more secure footing in the series of stories ... that sent his Busher meal ticket through basic training and then off to France." Silverman concludes that in the "11 war-themed Busher stories in all," beginning with "Call for Mr. Keefe!," the Busher is "the same stunningly wrought boor in khakis that he was in baseball flannels." (Sources: Lardner, Jr., 94; Silverman, xi, xii)

CALLAHAN ("CAL") In "A Busher's Letters Home," he is the White Sox coach. Keefe complains that Callahan criticizes his pitching but rarely understands Cal's witty sarcasm. In "The Busher Comes Back," Cal inserts him in important games, and razzes but occasionally praises him. In "The Busher's Honeymoon," Keefe hopes Callahan will pitch him every third day when the new season starts. In "A New Busher Breaks In," Callahan continues to manage, criticize, and praise Keefe. In "The Busher's Kid," Callahan, Kid Gleason, and others tried unsuccessful bribes to Florrie to stay home and babysit. In "The Busher Beats It Hence," Callahan kids Keefe but apparently wants him to go on the world tour. Callahan even says President Wilson wrote Comiskey urging him to get Keefe to participate, in order to avoid trouble with the Japanese government. In "The Busher Abroad," Callahan tolerates Keefe on the tour. Keefe mentions him in one of his poems. In "The Busher's Welcome Home," Cal is aware that Keefe was fooled into trying to leave the White Sox. In "The Busher Reënlists," Keefe remembers when Callahan managed the White Sox.

James Joseph Callahan (1874–1934) played for the Philadelphia Phillies (1894),the Chicago Cubs (1897–1900), the Chicago White Sox (1901–1913), and managed the White Sox (1903–1914), and the Pittsburgh Pirates (1916–1917). James E. Elfers reports that Comiskey wanted Callahan to go on the world tour "as a third bankroll" since he was known to be generous in "spending his own money for the benefit of his ball players"; that Callahan's wife and their two children also took the trip; and that, as Keefe says in "The Busher Abroad," the children received Christmas presents aboard. (Sources: *Baseball Encyclopedia*, 688, 855; Elfers, xvii, 12, 148; Hilton, 43, 94–95)

CALLIGHAN ("Tour No. 2"). This is a saloon in Detroit where Ed Burns tends bar.

CAMERON ("Contract"). He and his wife play bridge very seriously with Carl Dittmar and his wife and Robert French and his wife. Shelton, who is a newcomer in the bridge-playing circle, as is Mrs. Shelton, gets criticized. When Shelton's friend Gale Bartlett comments unfavorably on both Cameron and French, Shelton turns critical.

CAMERON, MRS. ("Contract"). She is regarded as a statuesque blonde, but she has disfiguringly wide nostrils. She and her husband, and Carl and Mrs. Dittmar, and Robert and Mrs. French all play bridge with Shelton and his wife — but not for long.

CAMPION, FLOSSIE ("Claude Diphthong, Student of Crime") *see* **LAWLOW, FLOSSIE**

CANNON, MRS. ("Who Dealt?"). She is the babbling speaker of this story, which takes place at the Gratz home. She is playing bridge with Tom Cannon, whom she married three months ago, and with his old friend Helen Gratz and her husband Arthur Gratz. Mrs. Cannon ignorantly and unconsciously reveals Tom's unforgotten love for Helen, before Helen married Arthur, and that Tom wrote a short story detailing events and including a personal poem expressing sorrow at his loss.

Mrs. Cannon blurts that she is "wild about books," but complains that if she mentions a good novel, "like, say, 'Black Oxen,'" friends "think you're trying to put on the Ritz." *Black Oxen* (1923), the bestseller by popular-novelist Gertrude Atherton (1857–1948), might appeal to her. Its heroine is a 58-year-old woman who after glandular surgery looks a vibrant 28. Would Mrs. Cannon miss its message, which is that the heroine prefers power not love? One might say that Lardner's "heroine" here is another loose cannon.

CANNON, THOMAS ("Who Dealt?"). He went to Yale, failed at football, and was in love with Helen Bird Strong, who promised to marry him but instead married Arthur Gratz four years ago. Tom, now a successful businessman in Portland (Oregon), married elsewhere three months ago. His wife meets Helen and Arthur, with embarrassingly revealing results. Mrs. Cannon calls him Tom and Tommie.

CANTILLON, JOE. In "Harmony," he evidently plays for the Minneapolis baseball team. Mike McCann's pitching is so poor that he says soon he'll be exchanging Civil War stories with Cantillon, i.e., will be traded down. In "The Battle of Texas," Keefe is afraid that if he doesn't improve early in the White Sox practice time in Texas, he could be sent to Joe Cantillon of Minneapolis.

Joseph D. Cantillon (1861–1930) was manager and also part owner of the Minnesota Millers, American Association (1910–1923). He also umpired in the American League (1901–1903) and in the American Association (1929), managed the Washington Senators (1907–1909), and scouted for the White Sox (mid–1920s). (Source: Hilton, 238).

CAP In "Alibi Ike," he manages the baseball team that the narrator, Alibi Ike, and others play on. Cap's wife is pretty, but her sister Dolly is even prettier. In "The Poor Simp," Cap manages the team the narrator plays for. Cap was initially pleased with Skull Scoville's pitching but was kept in the dark concerning practical jokes Carey pulls on Skull, with the narrator's acquiescence. In "Where Do You Get That Noise?," Cap manages the team tortured by Hawley's idiotic, unceasing talk. When Carey gets Hawley to praise brunettes over blondes, Cap, whose wife is an attractive blonde, puts Hawley on waivers.

George W. Hilton adduces evidence to show that Cap's club is the Chicago Cubs. (Source: Hilton, 486, 504)

CAP ("Harmony") *see* **RYAN, CAP**

CAPONE, AL ("Holycaust"). Danny Warner says that when a Cub player talked with "Cigar face Al Capone" in the stands, owners feared a possible bribe offer and stopped allowing players to talk with fans. Danny also misspells Capone's nickname a different way, as "Sigar face."

Alphonse Capone (1899–1947), born in Naples, Italy, migrated to Brooklyn, turned to crime, moved to Chicago, and made a fortune during Prohibition by selling illegal beer and whiskey, bribing officials, and murdering rivals. He was imprisoned in Atlanta for income-tax evasion (1931–1939) and died in Florida. He was called "Scarface"" because of a facial knife wound. (Streissguth, 365)

CAPTAIN ALCOCK (*The Big Town*). This is a race horse at the Belmont.

Lardner has fun giving this horse the last name of his friends John J. Alcock, sports reporter, and John Forbes Alcock, White Sox baseball player.

CAREY In "Alibi Ike," he plays on the team with the narrator. The two pull a mean trick on Alibi Ike, causing his fiancée Dolly to dump him, temporarily. In "The Poor Simp," Carey is a member of the team the narrator is on. Carey plays vicious practical jokes on Skull Scoville, a naive pitcher recently acquired. In "Where Do You Get That Noise?," Carey, playing center field and twice called "old," finds that Hawley's unremittingly inane conversation trumps his joking so much that he engineers Hawley's being put on waivers. Carey thinks his batting will improve thereafter, but it doesn't.

Carey's verbal lances at Skull border on the sadistic. George W. Hilton notes that Lardner's introducing Carey in "The Poor Simp" "identifies the team as the fictional version of the Chicago Cubs introduced in 'Alibi Ike.'" It should be added that Lardner doesn't otherwise identify Carey's team. (Source: Hilton, 486)

CAREY ("Oh, You Bonehead!"). He was a big guard on the Coach's Leighton football team. Carey played well against Pelham until he was piled on and knocked unconscious.

CAREY, MARY ("The Facts"). She is Ellen McDonald's mother's sister. She lives with the McDonalds in Chicago, goes to church with Ellen's father Sam McDonald, and does "settlement work" with Sam's nearby sister Louise McDonald and Aunt Harriet. Tommy Richards, acting on Billy Bowen's behalf, sends her a Catholic prayer book in Latin.

CAREY, MAX In "One Hit, One Error, One Left," he is the Brooklyn baseball team's manager when Danny Warner is a rookie on trial. Carey and his coach Casey Stengel* discuss, encourage, and razz Danny, who writes his girlfriend Jessie Graham that Carey once studied to become a priest. In "When the Moon Comes over the Mountain" and "Lose with a Smile," Max Carey continues to manage Danny, often kids him, and occasionally orders him to pinch hit. In "Meet Me in St. Louie," Max Carey decides to keep Danny. Jessie expresses unwillingness to meet "Mr. Carey" because of her shabby dresses. In "Holycaust," Carey continues to manage Danny. Stengel keeps Carey in ignorance about Danny's misbehavior. In "The Ides of June," Max Carey tolerated Danny only so long and then offered to send him to Hartford for seasoning.

Maximilian Carnarius Carey (1890–1976) played for the Pittsburgh Pirates (1910–1925), the Pirates and the Brooklyn Dodgers (1926), and Brooklyn (1927–1929), then managed Brooklyn (1932–1933). Carey was elected to the Baseball Hall of Fame (1961). (Source: *Baseball Encyclopedia*, 688, 863)

CARLISLE, J. H. ("'In Conference'"). He and others work for Kramer & Company. They converse vacantly "in conference." J. H. C., as he is called, is president and tries, with little success, to steer talk back to the subject of an unstamped letter addressed to the company which is being held by the post office until a 2¢ stamp is provided.

CARLOTTA ("What of It?"). She is Dexter Cosset's girlfriend. Both clerk "in Ellsworth's," in South Bend. Carlotta would dump Dexter for Orville Pleat if she learned that *Ghosts*, Dexter's play, is revised and retitled *Carlotta's Corns*, because she doesn't have corns.

CARLOTTA ("What of It?"). This is the name of the heroine of *Ghosts*, Dexter Cosset's play.

CARLTON, MR. ("Fore!"). He is president of Allison, Illinois, a member of the golf club, and said to be a better player than Mr. Thomas.

"CARMEN" (*Saturday Evening Post*, February 19, 1916; GT, PRL).

CARMODY ("There Are Smiles"). He is a Forty-eighth Street traffic cop. He whistles at Edith Dole when she drives past him going too fast down Fifth Avenue.

CARMODY, BILLY ("Good for the Soul"). He was an experienced baseball player hired by A.T. Grant to manage his minor-league team. When Grant also hired Buck Warner, both players took advantage of Grant, to their financial benefit. Warner's wife Ethel persuaded Buck to confess the truth in a recorded deposition and include Carmody in his revelations.

CARNEGIE, LIZZIE ("The Poor Simp") *see* Conahan, Mary

CARNEY (*The Big Town*). He was a jockey whom Bradley, Herbert Daley's friend, hired to replace Sid Mercer, whom Bradley fired for drunken brawling. Carney, riding Great Scott, Bradley's racehorse, then lost.

CARNEY ("The Crook"). He played baseball for Detroit. When Walsh, pitching for narrator Larry's White Sox, caught Carney off third base, he "begin to whine" until umpire Bull's gentle sarcasm silenced him.

CARNEY ("Hurry Kane"). He pitches for the St. Louis team, teaches Hurry Kane to throw slow balls, and worries with the narrator about Kane.

CARNEY ("The Last Night"). He owns or owned the Chicago saloon where Ben serves Jay Arnold some drinks.

CARNEY, HAZEL ("The Busher Comes Back") *see* **LEVY, HAZEL**

CARPENTER (*Own Your Own Home*). He and his wife are unsociable neighbors of Fred and Grace in Allison. They took pleasure in embarrassing Grace. Fred seeks revenge on the Carpenters when Mrs. Carpenter snubs Grace. In "Fore!," when "Mr. Carpenter" is in briefly Chicago and can't play against Fred in the golf tournament, Fred won't reschedule, wins by default, and causes Carpenter, with Mr. Thomas's help, to get revenge on Fred.

CARPENTER, MRS. (*Own Your Own Home*). She and her husband fail to be kind to Grace Gross when she visits them. They also are unpleasant at the dance to which Fred wrongly thinks he and Grace have been invited. Fred tries to get even when Mrs. Carpenter snubs Grace.

CARRY (*Own Your Own Home*). He and his wife are Fred and Grace's neighbors in Allison. Carry runs a "grosery store." The four become friendly. Fred and Grace invite the Carrys to their big party.

CARRY, MRS. (*Own Your Own Home*). She proves to be an amiable neighbor in Allison when Grace asks her to babysit. The two couples overcome a dispute over invitations to a dance. The Carrys attend Fred and Grace's party.

CARSON, FRANK (*The Real Dope*). He is Keefe's army friend in France who takes Jack to "the Red X canteen." They meet a worker whom Keefe hears Carson introducing as "Madam Moselle."

CARTER ("My Roomy"). He is a Georgia "bush pitcher" who starts a fight with Buster Elliott and nearly gets himself killed.

Paul Warren Carter (1894–1984) pitched for the Cleveland Indians (1914–1915) and the Chicago Cubs (1916–1920). George W. Hilton says that Paul Carter was not at the Cubs' Tampa training camp (1913) and that "My Roomy" was published in 1914, whereas the Cubs didn't acquire him until 1916. (Source: Hilton, 339)

CARTER ("What of It?") *see* **SMYTHE-CARTER**

CARTER, CAROLINE ("Old Folks' Christmas"). She is the selfish, thoughtless daughter, 17, of Tom and Grace Carter, and is Ted Carter's sister. Originally christened Grace, Caroline changed her name. She returns home from boarding school for Christmas vacation and parties with her friends.

Elizabeth Evans brilliantly hints that Caroline, whose original name was Grace, may have "fallen" from grace. (Source: Evans, 71)

CARTER, GRACE ("Old Folks' Christmas"). She is Tom Carter's considerate wife and the gently resigned mother of Ted and Caroline Carter. When the children callously treat their parents, the seniors still have each other.

CARTER, MR. ("A Caddy's Diary"). He is an alcoholic member of the golf club where the diarist caddies.

CARTER, MRS. ("A Caddy's Diary"). The diarist says this wife of the golfer is ugly, with a bad complexion.

CARTER, TED ("Old Folks' Christmas"). He is the inconsiderate drinking son, 19, of Tom and Grace Carter, and is Caroline Carter's brother. He changed his name from Tom Junior. A freshman at the university, he comes home for Christmas vacation and carouses with his classmates.

CARTER, TOM ("Old Folks' Christmas"). He is Grace Carter's well-to-do husband and Ted's and Caroline's father. His and Grace's lavish Christmas presents for their children aren't quite acceptable and must be replaced. Still, Tom and Grace have each other.

CASEY, JACK ("The Courtship of T. Dorgan"). He is a friend of Keefe's in St. Louis. He advises Keefe to bet on Jess Willard* to defeat [Jack] Dempsey.* He does, losing $600.

CASTLE, HERB ("Old Folks' Christmas"). He and Bernard King are university classmates of Ted Carter, who carouses with them during Christmas vacation back home.

CASTLE, TOM BOWEN (*Treat 'Em Rough*). He is a harmless soldier in Jack Keefe's unit. Jack's buddies kid him that Castle, whom they nickname "Tom the Trigger," is "a gun man."

CASWELL, FRANK ("I Can't Breathe"). He is from "Darthmouth" College, age 24, comes from a wealthy family, and is ambitious to write. The breathless diarist, 18, becomes engaged to him (probably briefly).

The diarist suggests Friday, December 10th, as

the day to marry Frank. Friday fell on that day in 1925, the year before Lardner published her July effusions.

CHAMBERS ("Second-Act Curtain"). He and Booth, having written a play, are asked by the manager Mr. Rose to write a second-act curtain for it. Chambers suggests that he and Booth try to do so separately. Chambers returns to his Manhattan mansion. Booth phones him that he is trying to create a song for the second-act curtain. Chambers hopes it can be a good one.

Since Booth resembles Lardner, Chambers may be likened to the better-established playright George S. Kaufman,* with whom Lardner co-authored *June Moon*.

CHAMBERS ("Tour No. 2"). He and his wife, from the South, take the tour with Larry and Minnie Burns. They strike Larry as uppity.

CHAMBERS (*Treat 'Em Rough*). He is a soldier in a company near Jack Keefe's army unit, said to be "a bum" reluctant to take showers until practically bayoneted into doing so. Then he became proud of himself.

CHAMBERS, MRS. ("Tour No. 2"). She and her husband go on the tour to Europe with Larry and Minnie Burns, neither of whom care much for them.

"CHAMPION" (*Metropolitan*, October 1916; HTW, PRL, RLR, RU). (Characters: Wallie Adams, Happy Collins, Bud Cross, Demon Dempsey, Mrs. Margaret Dorgan, Duane, Faulkner, Young Goetz, Goldberg, Grace, Holyoke Dan Haley, Tommy Haley, Doc Hammond, Jerome Harris, Mrs. Harris, Lou Hersch, Mrs. Hersch, Kelly, Connie Kelly, Ellen F. Kelly, Emma Kelly, Michael Kelly, McCann, Young Milton, Joe Morgan, Niemann, Dr. Ryan, Smiley Sayer, Stein, Young Tracy, Wall, Freddie Welsh.)

Michael ("Midge") Kelly, 17, sees his brother Connie, 14, hiding a coin. A cripple with a crutch, Connie received a fifty-cent piece from a lady whose "electric" almost hit him. Midge demands the money, is refused, and slugs Connie in the mouth, kicks him, takes the money, and leaves. Ellen F. Kelly, their mother, works at Faulkner's Steam Laundry, finds Connie and summons Dr. Ryan, who later tells a neighbor near (Chicago's) Halstead Street that Michael undoubtedly caused Connie's injuries. Midge, returning, answers his mother's complaints by knocking her down. He browbeats his friend Happy Collins out of "six bits," lies that Connie stole money from him and that he and their mother both attacked him; so he's "leavin' town for a w'ile." He hops a freight for Milwaukee.

Six months later Midge viciously defeats Demon Dempsey in his first preliminary bout at the Star Boxing Club. While drinking at Duane's saloon, Midge accepts praise and drinks from Lou Hersch, in his early 20s. The two become friends. One night Hersch double dates with his "prettiest little thing," and his sister Emma Hersch, "no bum for looks herself," and Midge. Doc Hamilton, Star matchmaker, books Midge against Young Tracy — $20 if he wins. Tracy's manager pays Midge $80 to throw the fight. Unpopular for four months thereafter, Midge is about to depart for Chicago when a sinister-looking heavy tells him Emma's mother wants him to marry Emma — or else. Though blustering, he does so but, when alone with her, slugs "the bride's pale cheek," then leaves town, by freight.

Two years pass. Tommy Daley, boxing manager, got Midge out of the gutter in Philadelphia, staked him, made him quit drinking, and watched him defeat Smiley once, Tracy three times, and Bud Cross twice. In Boston with Midge, Tommy tells his brother Holyoke Dan Daley that he needs no contract with Midge, who has $7,000 in the bank, is grateful, wants more action, but is gaining weight. Midge enters, overdressed, borrows $20 from Tommy, and has a drinking date with a woman sporting gold and silver teeth.

New Orleans, five months later. Having defeated Cross again, Midge is well trained by Tommy for a welter-weight match with Goetz. Midge receives three letters — one from Emma, who would like money for their sick baby girl; one from his mother, also needing money but mainly hoping he'd write her and Connie, bedridden; and one from Grace, wanting "more money," say, $200. Midge complains they all want money, tells reluctant Tommy to wire Grace in New York $200, and discusses matches Goldberg will arrange with Tommy if— of course, when — he wins tonight.

Grace is with Midge, her "hon," in Chicago. She mentions "the deed" he's to do before she returns from shopping. Having defeated Goetz, Midge is a vaudeville star, doing gymnastics stunts and reciting self-praising monologues. Tommy wants a contract for 25 percent, would settle for less, mentions favors done Midge, is told he's fired, curses Grace, and when threatened leaves. Grace returns, gloating that with the deed is done she controls Midge 100 percent.

Jerome Harris talks Midge's vaudeville people into increased pay, impresses Grace, and on tour in Detroit signs Midge to a contract for a 25 percent share. Harris takes Midge's show to Milwaukee, where he presents Mrs. Harris to Midge and Grace. Midge lusts for the "doll." Grace says the doll's brains are sawdust. Lou Hersch seeks Midge in his hotel, demands money, but a right in his "narrow chest" encourages him to depart. After Milwaukee performances, Midge, in submissive Harris's presence, dances so much with Mrs. Harris that Grace gets suspicious and demands marriage tomorrow. Midge gives her Emma Kelly's Milwaukee address to prove he's already married, tells her to behave, or he'll put her in the hospital. When Grace returns, Midge has left with Mrs. Harris, without Harris.

Before Midge fights Young Milton in New York City, Wallie Adams, Midge's manager, preps New York *News* sports writer Joe Morgan thus: Midge is reluctant to injure Milton, is a clean, modest husband and father, generous son, and generous brother of a lad who'll be a teen-aged champion. Morgan's two columns are read by unprintably voluble Grace, Tommy, and Harris, but remain unread by Midge's mother and his wife, since the *News* copies costs a nickel. If Morgan interviewed those who knew Midge, their comments wouldn't pass his editor. Readers don't want to see a champion criticized.

George W. Hilton reports that Lardner was paid $600 for "Champion." For verisimilitude, Lardner has Midge and Tommy Haley mention real-life boxers (Jess) Willard,* who was white, and (Jack) Johnson, black (1878–1946), whom Willard defeated for the world's heavyweight championship (1915). Johnson made a deal to throw the fight (Havana, 1915) to avoid a prison sentence but was jailed anyway. Lardner probably didn't know all this. In his preface to *How to Write Short Stories*, Lardner quips that "'Champion' is ... an example of the mystery story. The mystery is how it came to get printed." Tom Quirk comments that "The life of Midge Kelly in 'Champions' is a very unfunny restatement of [Mark] Twain's 'Story of the Bad Little Boy.'" Thomas Boyd admires most of Lardner's early fiction and says "Champion" "is veracious enough, but that very honesty results in a lack of verisimilitude at the close." John Berryman calls "Champion" "simple-minded and incredible," undeserving of "its fame." Other critics find it worthy of discussion. Clifford M. Caruthers calls it "a scathing denunciation of the glorification of the sports hero." (Glorification, true then, true today.) Leverett T. Smith Jr. agrees, defining "Champion" as "a polemic on the subject of the moral nature of public figures in sports, and the moral nature of the community which demands them." Caruthers reports that in 1926 Lardner's editors negotiated the sale of "Champion" in a German translation to three papers, in Germany and Austria, and that Lardner receive 90 marks. Elder observes that, "impressive and memorable" though it is, "'Champion' ... is far too melodramatic to be entirely believable." Elizabeth Evans notes that "[a] catalogue of Midge Kelly's exploits ... sounds like exaggerated melodrama, but like the adventures in *Candide* where the rapid cumulative effect creates a sense of unreality, no one doubts the truth of the individual deed." Clifton Fadiman compares "Champion" and "Fifty Grand" (1927) by Ernest Hemingway, saying that both "are equally effective, but one feels that Lardner is far closer to the facts of American sport than is Hemingway." Au contraire, Hemingway, writing a year after Fadiman demeaned Lardner, uses "Champion" as proof that Lardner squeamishly declined to have his boxers, Midge implicitly included, talk like boxers, instead "distorting the language that they speak into a very comic diction, so there's no tragedy ever, because there is no truth." (Sources: Berryman, 421; Boyd, 602; Caruthers [1973], 5, 95; Elder, 208; Fadiman, 317; Hemingway, 158B; Hilton, 19; Quirk, 121; Smith, 148)

CHANCE ("Insomnia"). He is a baseball player the sleepless author remembers.

CHANDLER ("Oh, You Bonehead!"). He was the successor of the Coach of the Leighton football team, after Leighton lost to Pelham.

CHAPLIN, CHARLIE (1889–1977). London-born Charles Spencer Chaplin was a comedic genius. He was a child actor in England, toured the United States with a vaudeville troupe (1910), and starred in silent films featuring a little tramp (1914–1918), with bowler, outsize moustache, baggy trousers, cane, and unique walk. Chaplin and Mary Pickford* founded United Artists Films(1919). His major movies (1920–1952) are classics. Although his private life, political opinions, and income-tax evasions caused him to move to Switzerland (1952), he was later honored in America and knighted in England.

Chaplin is mentioned in *Gullible's Travels*,

"Harmony," "The Hold-out," "Rhythm," and "Where Do You Get That Noise?" Two letters by Lardner to F. Scott Fitzgerald* indicate his friendship with Chaplin. In one (August 8, 1925), Lardner mentions that Chaplin's movie *The Gold Rush* (1924) opens in a week and "we are going to a party in his honor at Nast's." Wealthy New Yorker Condé Nast (1874–1942) published *Vogue, Vanity Fair,* and *House and Garden.* In another letter (May 10, 1926), Lardner says that when he and his wife were in Hollywood "Charlie Chaplin had us out to dinner and was more or less amusing and we met all the nuts." Jonathan Yardley adds that at this time the Lardners also watched Chaplin's filming of *The Circus* (1928). (Sources: Caruthers [1995], 183, 200;Yardley, 300)

CHAPMAN In "The Busher Comes Back," Keefe says he walked Chapman during the White Sox game with Cleveland. In "Call for Mr. Keefe!," Keefe, pitching after the war, says a bad call from umpire Bill Evans enabled Chapman to walk.

Raymond John Chapman (1891–1920) played for Cleveland (1912–1920) until he was killed in New York when he was hit in the head by a submarine ball from Yankee pitcher Carl William Mays. (Sources: *Baseball Encyclopedia,* 879; Hilton, 82)

CHAPMAN, DAN ("Travelogue"). He is purportedly a well-traveled war veteran. He meets Hazel Dignan and Mildred Orr on a train going from Chicago to San Francisco. He is often prevented by Hazel's rambling chatter from talking, even about a tooth extraction and the resulting vacancy in his mouth that he wants the girls to finger. Hazel regards herself as attractive, but Chapman prefers Mildred.

CHARLEY ("A Busher's Letters Home"). He is a billiard-hall manager back home. Keefe says that when he fails with the White Sox he'll work for Charley.

CHARLEY ("The Facts"). He is the aproned Chicago bartender where Tommy Richards is in the process of helping his good friend Billy Bowen fall off the wagon.

CHARLEY ("The Golden Honeymoon"). He and Lucy Frost were married 50 years ago. Charley and "Mother," as he calls her, go on their golden honeymoon to Florida and have a predictably routine but perhaps heartwarmingly memorable time.

H. L. Mencken* opines that "the old man in 'The Golden Honeymoon' is not merely well done; he is perfect." Donald Elder says that Charley "recites the entire timetable of the journey and all the irrelevant details that are the stock topics of the empty-minded." Brian T. Cowlishaw suggests that Charley is "partly inferior and partly likable," being not only "deeply banal," lacking in sportsmanship, vapid, and petty, but also "affectionate, supportive"; therefore the "implied reader" should react to him with "both affection and disdain." Clifton Fadiman sees nothing good about Charley, or his wife either, averring that the rickety honeymooners are a "quarrelsome, vain, literal old couple who for fifty years have disliked life and each other without ever having had the courage or the imagination to face the reality of their own meanness." Fadiman is even meaner for saying all this. (Sources: Cowlishaw, 213, 214; Elder, 210; Fadiman, 316; Mencken [1924], 377)

CHASE In "A Busher's Letters Home," Keefe says Kid Gleason said he pitched all right but let Chase take too great a lead on second, in a White Sox two-team practice game in Paso Robles. Keefe criticized Chase's fielding in Los Angeles. In "The Busher Comes Back," Keefe praises and criticizes Chase's fielding. In "A New Busher Breaks In," Keefe incomprehensibly gripes thus in a game against San Francisco: "Fournier would of eat it up [a liner] if it had of been Chase playing first base instead of Fournier." In "The Hold-Out," Lahey is favorably compared to Chase.

Harold Harris "Hal" Chase (1883–1947) was an excellent first baseman for the New York Yankees (1905–1912), the Yankees and the Chicago White Sox (1913), the White Sox and the Federal League's Buffalo team (1914), Buffalo (1915), the Chicago Cubs (1916–1918), and the New York Giants (1919). He managed the Yankees (1910–1911). George W. Hilton reports that Chase, while playing for the Giants, heard of the upcoming Black Sox scandal, attempted to profit from his knowledge, was indicted (1920), but escaped being banned from baseball by retiring. It was already being alleged that he had been involved in throwing games. For these reasons, he never became a Baseball Hall of Famer. Hilton notes an error in "A Busher's Letters Home": Chase did not join the White Sox until after Keefe was in Paso Robles. (Sources: *Baseball Encyclopedia,* 688, 880; Hilton, 48)

CHASE, MISS LUCY (*Treat 'Em Rough*). She is a "girlie" from Texas whom Jack Keefe dishonestly encourages to write him. When they meet in Houston, he ignores her, not least when his wife Florrie Keefe appears, to surprise him over Christmas.

CHENEY In "The Busher Comes Back," Keefe mentions Cheney as a Cub pitcher. In "The Busher's Kid," Keefe says Cheney's manager didn't have him pitch after Keefe was warming up because "he seen my smoke" and knew Cheney would be wasted in a certain loss. In "Back to Baltimore," Cheney pitches so well against the Boston Braves that Dixon says "we didn't never have a look-in." Mrs. Hayes objects that Cheney's spitball is unsanitary.

Laurence Russell Cheney (1886–1969) was a right-handed ace spit- and knuckle-baller for the Chicago Cubs (1911–1914), the Cubs and the Brooklyn Dodgers (1915), the Dodgers (1915–1918), and the Dodgers, the Boston Braves, and the Phillies (1919). See also Larry. (Sources: *Baseball Encyclopedia*, 1889; Hilton, 95)

CHICAGO CUBS A National League baseball team (1876–). (Source: Light, 149–155)

CHICAGO WHITE SOX. An American League baseball team (1901–). (Sources: Light, 154–156; Streissguth, 14, 43, 232)

CHIEF, THE ("Horseshoes"). He pitches victoriously for the Athletics in the first game of their World Series against the Giants, unsuccessfully in relief during the third game, and also unsuccessfully in the fourth.

Charles Albert ("Chief") Bender (1883 or 1884–1954) played for the Philadelphia Athletics (1903–1914), the Philadelphia Phillies (1916–1917), and the Chicago White Sox (1925). George W. Hilton says the Chief was of "part Chippewa ancestry." He was inducted into the Baseball Hall of Fame (1953). (Sources: *Baseball Encyclopedia*, 779; Hilton, 77, 410)

CHIEF, THE ("My Roomy") He is the Giants catcher in a game during which Elliott, of the Cubs, deliberately strikes out hoping thus to curry favor with McGraw, manager of the Giants.

John Tortes ("Chief") Meyers (1880–1971), a Native American from the Mission Indians of Southern California, played for the New York Giants (1909–1915), the Brooklyn Dodgers (1916), and the Dodgers and the Boston Braves (1917). George W. Hilton reports that Meyers attended Dartmouth College but didn't graduate. (Sources: *Baseball Encyclopedia*, 1363; Hilton, 357–358)

CHILDS, HARRY ("The Yellow Kid"). He played outfield for the narrator Bill's team, and kidded their pitcher Lefty Crosby because of his fear of women. When Childs showed off his gun at a card game, he noticed that guns also terrified Crosby. Childs' razzing often rendered Crosby incapable of pitching; but Childs got his comeuppance when Bill and Joe Martin persuaded Crosby to cozy up to Mary Lloyd, whom Childs planned to propose to but who preferred Crosby.

The name Harry Childs, when attached to a major-league baseball player, suggests an unattractive mental midget. It is a coincidence that long after Lardner wrote "The Yellow Kid," a real-life Harry Child — Harry Stephen Patrick Child (1905–1972) — pitched for the Washington Senators (1930). (Source: *Baseball Encyclopedia*, 1890)

"A CHIP OF THE OLD BLOCK" (*Red Book*, September 1918). (Characters: Barnes, Captain Evan Barnes, Harry R. Barnes, Mrs. Barnes, Captain Jarvis Bellows, Major G. Willis Faulkner, J. Hammond, Mr. Leslie, General Robert, Congressman Shultz, Kathryn Stark, Captain F. Conklin Stone, Tracy.)

Evan Barnes writes nine letters to his grandfather, Henry R. Barnes. The first and second are from Weedsburg; the rest, from Washington, D.C.

May 16. Evan thanks "Dear Grandfather" for sending him a check on his 21st birthday. He won't spend it but will bank it or buy a Liberty Bond, because "a person ought to do all they can for the Government at a time like this." Mother shuddered at his idea of joining the navy or "the aviation." Mr. Leslie, Evan's father's friend from their Spanish American War days, said to "wait until the next draft." But what if the draft overlooked Evan. Mother is writing Congressman Shultz for advice. To "avenge his death," Evan wishes a German not a Spaniard had killed Dad.

May 30. Congressman Shultz may arrange for Evan to get a commission for duty in Washington. Maybe "the secret service." Mother is sad, but Evan says these times call for bravery. She'll rent their home and keep house for him in Washington. They saw G.A.R. graves today. He won't fail his Civil War grandfather and his war-hero father.

Washington, D.C., June 2. The city is no longer "staid," as when Evan and Mother saw it in 1915, but is bustling and with "no room for a slacker." On the train Evan met a newspaper man — Tracy from Cincinnati — who tried to "jolly me" by saying Washington has 200,000 men and 300,000 officers, by which he means N.C.O.'s, that is, "noncombatant officers." Evan said he was staying at the Shoreham. Tracy said he'd like to interview Evan, who agreed, though regarding Tracy as "breezy" and "tedious."

June 2. Grandfather may "salute your grandson." Congressman Shultz got Evan commissioned captain this morning, assigned to the Sleuth Department, and ordered to seek out "German propagandists and spies." Dangerous but worth it. Evan wishes his father could've seen him "make good." If Grandfather had had Evan's education, he could've been more than a sergeant after all those years of service. Mother wired congratulations but warned him to be careful. What are risks, though, in wartime? Evan is to report at 10:00 A.M. and mostly check for suspicious behavior in cafés. He hopes to make his grandfather proud of him "by doing 'something big,'" maybe getting promoted.

June 11. Last Sunday Evan heard two men talking at the Willard Hotel. One pronounced General Foch's last name gutterally. Yesterday Evan heard someone near the White House say he'd not trade jobs with "W.W." He clearly meant Woodrow Wilson. He reported both tips to his Department, with careful descriptions of the talkers. He has met some nice girls. One, however, is engaged. Did Grandfather also lose a girl he liked? Evans enjoys his work, except for "the military discipline."

June 17. Mother arrived, and the two plan to room indefinitely at the Shoreham, "in the midst of things," among "the best of the young officers," here in "the social center." Evan especially likes Kathryn Stark, the one who's engaged — to a fellow who's a corporal in France. Tracy, that Cincinnati newsman, didn't follow up and interview Evan; so, not wishing to seem snobbish, Evan invited him to lunch. Evan declined to answer "impertinent questions" about his work; so Tracy asked if he knew Major G. Willis Faulkner of the Cushion Department or Capt. F. Conklin Stone of the Monument Department. Tracy explained that Faulkner tracked "lost or injured" baseballs at the park, until a vendor shell-shocked him by hitting him with a bag of peanuts. Tracy added that Stone, rejected from joining "the regulars" for having long eyelashes, risks a stiff neck by having to check thrice weekly that the Monument top is still on. Pointing to Captain Jarvis Bellows at a window table, Tracy said that he was kept out of the Marines by a hangnail, was "of the Toy Balloons," must inflate balloons for children here, and risks injury should any explode.

June 24. Tracy gave Evan a tip about a Florida Avenue shoe-shine place run by a German. Workers at such parlors are usually "either black or tan." Tracy said subversives in such parlors polished soldiers' shoes with poison giving them fallen arches that rendered them militarily useless. Evan and Mother taxied to Florida Avenue, which was so disreputable that he sent Mother by their taxi back to their hotel. Evan couldn't find the place. Tracy later said maybe he gave Evan the address incorrectly and suggested that he find "the shoe-stand ... not conducted by negroes." He couldn't try, because he had a dance date; so "this morning" he gave a Department man a written report on Tracy's tip. Sadly, Miss Stark missed the dance; "it seems" she just heard that her fiancé was wounded and is hospitalized in France. The news upset her. So "I had a rather tedious evening."

July 1. Today Captain Bellows introduced Evan to General Robert, a big man around here. When Evan revealed his branch of service, the general was interested, asked about his physical condition, was told he had morning nervousness, and wondered Bellows why "some of you boys don't try to get to France." Bellows said "most of us" had visited there with families and planned to return when the war ended and "the country would be rebuilt to look something like its old self." Pleading nausea, the general asked the two to leave him. Evan thinks General Robert is probably too old to be of further service to the country. Evan expresses discontent with his Department. The "four or five clues" he has reported have gone unpursued. He feels like "chucking" everything and returning home with Mother, but duty still calls. Miss Stark is "pretty blue" because she's learned her fiancé can't be shipped home yet. Still, that's part of "the game."

July 8. Evan is marrying Kathryn Stark this fall. She is related to J. F. Hammond and his family in Sandusky, near Grandfather, who probably doesn't know the Hammonds because "you don't get around much any more." Evan and Kathryn can live on his salary. He'll bring Kathryn to meet Grandfather. Her "poor sucker" of a fiancé "is through as a soldier" because of his bad wound; therefore "we don't want any big splurge." Sorry it's troubling for Grandfather to write congratulations, but "I will see you" soon.

Grandfather Harry R. Barnes replies from "Sandusky, O., July 11." He'll trouble to write a couple of times before "my pen and I are too hopelessly rusted." Glad Evan's income is sufficient. He'll "dispose of my modest means" elsewhere. If Evan should be killed by "poisoned shoe-blacking" or something else risky, the government will provide for his widow unless "other weighty matters" make the authorities neglectful. Three requests: Don't bring "your lady" here, because his doctor says "any excitement" would kill him; send him the name and address of that wounded "sucker" who earned only corporal stripes after a year of combat; let Evan's letter including the corporal's address be the last from Evan, since it's troublesome to write but more so to read.

Although Lardner satirically focuses on World War I slackers, he would agree that wars earlier and later have also had their pompous, self-deceiving goldbricks.

CICOTTE In "A Busher's Letters Home," Keefe says that in the White Sox game against the St. Louis Browns Callahan replaced him as pitcher with Cicotte. In "The Busher Comes Back," Keefe says Callahan was saving Cicotte for a later game. In "A New Busher Breaks In," Keefe boasts saving a game in the ninth for Cicotte against New York. In "Call for Mr. Keefe!," Keefe says Cicotte shut out Washington. In *Treat 'Em Rough*, Keefe reports that "Cicotte trimmed them yesterday." (This is a reference to the real White Sox victory over the New York Giants in the October 6, 1917 World Series game.) In *The Real Dope*, Keefe says that in one game against Detroit "Eddie Cicotte didn't have nothing." In "The Battle of Texas," Eddie Cicotte kids Belden about his military service in France. In "Along Came Ruth," Keefe praises Eddie Cicotte. In "The Busher Pulls a Mays," Keefe praises Ed Cicotte with a tinge of envy, because Gleason relies on Cicotte excessively.

Edward Victor Cicotte (1884–1969) was an ace pitcher for the Boston Red Sox (1908–1912) and the Chicago White Sox (1912–1919). He was banned from baseball for his part in the 1919 Black Sox Scandal. Donald Gropman says that "first baseman Chick Gandil and pitcher Eddie Cicotte were leaders among the conspiring players." Donald Elder and Jonathan Yardley write extensively about Cicotte's participation in the scandal and about Lardner's discussion with Cicotte about it. In many non-fictional pieces, Lardner wrote affectionately about Cicotte. David L. Fleitz summarizes Cicotte's remorse, confession, and fears. (Sources: *Baseball Encyclopedia*, 1892; Elder, 159–193; Fleitz, 223–224; Gropman, 160; Hilton, 65; Lardner, Jr., 146; Yardley, 212–216)

CINCINNATI REDS A National League baseball team (1890–). (Sources: Light, 159–162; Streissguth, 14, 232)

CLAGUE, DR. ("How Are You?"). He is a New York pyorrhea expert recommended to Bob Dayton.

CLANCY, MISS ("Sun Cured"). She is Ernie Fretts's secretary in his Brooklyn insurance agency. Miss Clancy, 53 and unattractively large, urges him to vacation in Florida. While he is doing so, she evidently handles the office well.

CLARA ("One Hit, One Error, One Left") *see* Burnett, Clara

CLARK ("The Busher Comes Back"). Keefe says he will buy furniture at Clark's store on Cottage Grove Avenue, in Chicago, for when he and Florence are married.

CLARK In "One Hit, One Error, One Left," He is a left-handed pitcher for the Brooklyn team Danny Warner is trying out for. When Danny attempts to bat left-handed against him in practice, he does badly. In "Lose with a Smile," Danny pinch hit for Clark in a game against the Boston Braves. In "Meet Me in St. Louie," Clark is mentioned. In "Holycaust," he pitched well against Cincinnati. In "The Ides of June," when Danny pinch hit for Clark in a "game again phila," Elliot walked him.

William Watson Clark (1902–1972) pitched for the Cleveland Indians (1924), the Brooklyn Dodgers (1927–1932), Brooklyn and the New York Giants (1933–1934), and Brooklyn (1935–1937). (Source: *Baseball Encyclopedia*, 1894)

CLARKE In "Horseshoes." he is a Cincinnati catcher. When Dick Grimes and Speed Parker are playing for the Cubs, Clarke throws wild over second enabling Speed to score. In "Where Do You Get That Noise?," Hawley theorizes that if Clarke, with a non–German name, won Cincinnati, it would distress everyone with German names.

Thomas Aloysius Clarke (1888–1945) played for the Cincinnati Reds as catcher (1909–1917) and one game for the Cubs (1918). (Source: Hilton, 402)

"CLAUDE DIPHTHONG, STUDENT OF CRIME" (*Ellery Queen's Mystery Magazine*, August 1954). (Characters: Detective Burke, Claude

Diphthong, Verne Diphthong, Gabriel Downey, Face towels, Leonard K. Failing, Flossie Lawlow, Sir Albert Lawlow, Gardner Lyle, Detective McMahon, Piccolini, Telwell, Margalo Trawley.)

One blustery January day Gardner Lyle was seen murdered in New York's exclusive Hotel Baldwin. House detective Lincoln H. Martingale found him at 2:00 A.M. under his bed, bullet hole in head, feet shoeless. Martingale phoned authorities. Burke and McMahon, illiterate but diligent Murder Squad detectives, arrived.

The three discuss Lyle, bank official, polo and football star, Yale crew captain, recently divorced husband of beautiful Follies' girl Margalo Trawley. Burke says he often saw Lyle enjoying night life. McMahon says a woman killed Lyle. Martingale reveals this: Lyle, when divorced, took young women, usually theatrical ones, to night clubs; last November began dating a beauty just back from Europe; two weeks later, started regretting he was so handsome that this beauty, of whom he had "grown tired," vowed to shoot him if he didn't marry her; wished he were ugly like Martingale, ex-boxer with "broken nose" and "mushroom ears." Martingale offered unprevailingly to rearrange Lyle's face for protection. Two nights ago, Martingale saw that beauty tiptoeing outside Lyle's hotel room. To McMahon's query, Martingale names her: Flossie Campion, known as "Dental Floss" for having trouble with her teeth.

The two detectives are about to go find Flossie, but police reporter Gabriel Downey and a dapper fellow enter. Downey introduces him: Claude Diphthong, 30, wealthy son of Verne Diphthong, Wall Street investor. Diphthong is carrying a bugle, having studied it in Florence. He also "dabbled in criminology" throughout Europe. When the detectives name Flossie Campion as their suspect, Diphthong states that Lyle was shot by "a tall, left-handed man with a walrus mustache, who spoke with a southern drool," that Miss Campion days ago married Sir Albert Lawlow, and that they're honeymooning midway across the Atlantic now. The detectives exit, to check on Flossie for themselves.

Martingale tells Dithphong he entered Lyle's room at 2:00 A.M. "to change the bedding" and collect mail for himself from Leonard K. Failing, in the partridge business in Lancaster, Pennsylvania. Martingale's mail was probably mixed with popular Lyle's. Martingale exits. Diphthong practices 20 minutes on his bugle, then tells impatient, admiring Downey about an almost "exact duplicate" case he solved of a poor woman who was conned into investing in Pennsylvania partridges, starved to death in Texas, and was found without shoes under her bed. Diphthong adds that Lyle was in his evening clothes when shot, therefore wasn't asleep, and that Lyle read, tore, and discarded a letter in the wastebasket. Diphthong blows "the fragments ... together with his bugle." The letter, concerning Lyle's generously helping innumerable troublesome school children, proves, says Diphthong, Lyle's desire to have "a large family," which his ex-wife refused. When, garbed in evening clothes for dinner, he got this letter, he felt depressed by remembering children, removed his shoes, lay under his bed, and in comes the murderer — almost six feet, with megaphone, with goateed chins, wearing useless bicycle clips, his initials being "L.K.F." Diphthong smilingly declines to tell Downey his deductive methods and says he hears Burke and McMahon outside, "without their quarry."

The two detectives enter with a beautiful, weeping, handcuffed woman, say they found Miss Campion's address in the phone book, and arrested her in her apartment. Unchagrined, Diphthong tells "Miss Campion" not to worry and explains how she was nicknamed "Dental Floss": Swedish woman, new in America, asked for any mail for her at the post office, said her name was "Face towels." "Miss Campion" flashes beautiful teeth in a smile; voila, isn't Dental Floss. Uncuffed by the sheepish detectives, she suggests playing some games. Downey proposes announcing a word which someone must put in a sentence "in a novel way." Downey: Use "homicidal." Miss Campion: I have ineffective partner in tennis doubles, "and I don't see homicidal win." Downey: Use "vertigo." Burke: On my night off, "I can't make up my mind vertigo." McMahon: Use "herculean." Downey: Leon Errol during a stage show wondered why Anastasia Reilly, acting with him, didn't follow up on his lines and was answered "That's not herculean."

Diphthong interrupts by saying Lyle's killer will soon appear, phones downstairs, and summons Martingale. He arrives. Diphthong trips him and deafens him with his bugle. The detectives restrain him. Downey observes that he identically resembles the man Diphthong described as having robbed the Mineral Springs woman. Diphthong says he is Leonard K. Failing, the Pennsylvania partridge crook. Failing says he'd never be exposed except Diphthong intervened in the Lyle case. Burke asks Failing to confess to the murder, either at headquarters or immediately. "What murder?" Failing asks. Everyone looks for Lyle's body. Gone. Failing explains: Diphthong figured Lyle sent his shoes outside to be shined, lay down to rest; everyone was distracted by that word game; the boy returned the shoes and left; Lyle left, unnoticed, for dinner. Downey asks about Lyle's bullet hole. A birthmark, says Diphthong, proposes breakfast, and exits with Burke and McMahon. Downey, lingering, suggests breakfast with the beauty. She murmurs "Yes," senses "that here was the story's love interest," and grows "livid."

Lardner gives some timeliness in "Claude Diphthong, Student of Crime," by naming George Ade, Leon Errol, and Anastasia Reilly. Lardner knew and admired George Ade (1844–1944), versatile Indiana-born author. In *The Big Town* Lardner mentions Leon Errol (1881–1951), comic actor. Anastasia Reilly (d. 1961) was a Florenz Ziegfeld* Follies' dancer.

Ellery Queen's Mystery Magazine editors report that Lardner sold "Claude Diphthong, Student of Crime" to *Cosmopolitan* for $5,000, that it was shuffled to *Good Housekeeping*, and that *Ellery Queen's Mystery Magazine* bought it. Lardner devotees relished it in 1954, and new devotees should seek it out now — despite obvious flaws. Need Lardner have said Diphthong collected bicycle handlebars? Why would Martingale change Lyle's bedding? Why say the crook played a bugle in Texas? Was his victim a widow, as stated only later? How is the Swedish woman germaine? Was her name "Face towels"? Undeveloped is a connection between face towels and the fact that Sir Albert Lawlow heads the Pullman Company towel department. A clever touch is the early identification of the bad guy as "L.K.F." (which some readers won't connect with Failing). Critics have ignored the untidily funny "Claude Diphthong." Its puns are among Lardner's best. (Source: Farnsworth, 160)

CLAYMORE ("Hurry Kane"). He plays on the White Sox baseball team.

CLAYTON, MIKE ("Cured!"). He owns a speakeasy near Grand Central Station, frequented by Dick Streeter and Joe Gale, Rudy Miller, and Paul Stroud, Dick's fellow alcoholics.

CLAYTON, MR. ("A Caddy's Diary"). He and Mr. Joyce are golfers. Slow-playing Mr. Blake, Mr. Carter, Mr. Dunham, and Mr. Thomas let the twosome play through their foursome.

CLAYTON, ROY ("Greek Tragedy"). He is a man from Arizona who knows that the wrestler Greek Alexis is really Tom Meyers. During their match, Big Bill Buell scares Alexis into believing that Clayton is in the crowd and will expose him. Though Clayton probably isn't there, Alexis throws the fight and hopes Buell will reward him later.

CLEOPATRA ("CLEO") (*The Big Town*). This is a horse scratched at the Belmont.

CLEVELAND INDIANS An American League baseball team (1901–). (Sources: Light, 163–166; Streissguth, 43)

"THE CLUBBY ROADSTER" (*Red Book*, February 1918). (Characters: Harry Cross, Nan Cross, Jack, the Missus, Aunt Myrtle.)

The unnamed narrator works in a Chicago office. One day Harry Cross, a fellow worker, announces that his wife Nan Cross's Aunt Myrtle died in May and left Nan $2,500. The Crosses decide they won't buy a Liberty Bond at 3.50 percent. Instead they'll quit living with her folks, get an apartment, furnish it for $600, and with $1,500 of the remaining money buy a Champion model called "the Clubby Roadster." It seats two in front and two behind. Cross will easily learn to drive with "half nerve and half good judgment." The narrator says Cross will be 50 percent efficient.

Cross picks up the narrator and his Missus one Saturday morning in June for an overnight trip. Crawling through town, Cross explains he knows he's going 15 m.p.h. because of "this thing on the dashboard" he calls a "speedometer." The narrator says he thought it was "a kind of germicide." They return to pick up Nan, slow getting ready and weeping because her brother Jack was just turned down at Fort Sheridan for the Officers' Reserve. The narrator remarks that if the regular army had vacancies Jack "might horn in there as a private." The Crosses show off their ultra-tiny flat. Nan fusses about what kind of pajamas Cross should pack, then whether they locked the door. Cross says their destination is to be a secret. The narrator agrees, since Cross is driving and Nan is navigating by "the Blue Book." Two hours later and after several wrong turns they approach the Auto Inn in South Chicago. Saying accidents are caused "by liquor," Nan vetoes the narrator's suggestion that they stop for "a couple of quick ones." Cross suggests some drinks after they've proceeded 60 miles to Michigan City. Near Hammond,

Cross races at 16 m.p.h. Nan cautions him to slow down. He turns into an intersection, is stopped by a traffic cop, but is released when he says they must get the narrator's sick wife to the hospital in Gary. They cross numerous railroad tracks, then some rough gorges in Gary. The bumping awakens the narrator's wife. A sentry lets them pass a soldiers' camp east of Gary. Cross makes his three passengers walk while he drives across a bridge posting a 3,000-pound limit. Nan directs the party three miles wrong. Six miles shy of Michigan City, she tearfully says it's 1:00 P.M. and she's hungry. A front tire hisses flat. The men change it in 35 minutes, which Nan says took too long. Cross refuses to have the tire repaired at once, because they "could never have two punctures on one trip." The narrator admits he's "forgotten that rule." Cross stops in Michigan City only for water and gas, not a meal. The narrator gives his wife 50¢ for doughnuts, downs five drinks nearby, and is rebuked for delaying. Cross kills his engine on railroad tracks beyond New Buffalo, forgets to "shift into neuter," and jump-starts the car to safety. They speed at 19 m.p.h. into Three Oaks, at 4:00. The narrator tells his wife that the Crosses hate them, they hate the Crosses, the two Crosses hate each other, and soon he and she will hate each other. He persuades her to return with him to Chicago without the Crosses. Hearing this, Nan says not to, but coldly. Cross tells them to go ahead. The narrator counts "all the acorns" in Three Oaks until 7:00. For 462 times, his wife "hope[s] there's a diner." For 462 times, he hopes the Crosses have another flat tire. "We made a mistake" going with them, she says. The narrator thanks her for saying "we" but admits he's to blame.

After two weeks of silence in the office, Cross suddenly approaches the narrator, apologizes, and — with sarcastic interruptions — explains that he and Nan got to Sawyer, had a rule-breaking second flat there, stayed overnight there, and while he drove back to Chicago she returned by train. The Crosses' ensuing argument resulted in his agreeing to sell the Clubby Roadster for a $200 loss, their buying a Liberty Bond with the remaining cash, and their loving each other even more for their "little misunderstanding." "'Shut up!' I said."

Since "The Clubby Roadster" was published during World War I, Lardner felt obliged to include such wartime touches as gratuitous references to America's Fort Sheridan, in Highwood, Illinois (which Lardner mentions later in "Call for Mr. Keefe!"], and to Germany's Kaiser Wilhelm (1859–1941), Theobald von Bethmann-Hollweg (1856–1921), Paul von Hindenburg (1847–1934), and Erich Friedrich Wilhelm Ludendorff (1865–1837). This story provides evidence favoring part of Clifton Fadimar's theory that Lardner's characters hate each other, but provides no evidence to support his belief that Lardner also hates his characters. The narrator's sarcasm makes him, not Lardner, a mini-Iago, who displays "motiveless malignancy" like Othello's torturer. (Source: Fadiman)

COACH, THE ("Oh, You Bonehead!"). He is an experienced football coach. His story, which he tells to two assistants, reveals how he tragically hurt Joe Draper, his Leighton school player, by calling him a "bonehead" two years ago, and why, for that reason, he doesn't rebuke Dickie, another player with another team he's now coaching, despite a similar "bonehead" play. The Coach, unnamed here, is named Belden in "A One-Man Team."

COAKLEY, MISS ("Dinner"). She is a "strikingly pretty ... pony brunette." Harry Barton is attracted to her at Grace Halpern's dinner party in New York, until she asks him questions, doesn't listen to his answers, and rattles interminably.

COBB ("Anniversary"). This is the name of the couple with whom Florence Hammond tells Bess Taylor that she and her husband Perce Hammond are going to play bridge.

COBB In "A Busher's Letters Home," Keefe, pitching for the White Sox against the Detroit Tigers, complains that Cobb stole four bases on him. In "The Busher Comes Back," Keefe says he isn't afraid of Cobb, a notorious base stealer, and gripes when Cobb beat out "a scratch single." In "A New Busher Breaks In," Keefe boasts about what he does against Ty Cobb. He hopes Cobb is in good shape because he doesn't want to take advantage of a cripple. Keefe says he suggested that the White Sox should buy Cobb and Crawford rather than investing in new pitchers. In "The Crook," Cobb's spikes scared Parker, catching for the narrator Larry's White Sox, so much that he backed off home plate "into an alley somewheres." In "Along Came Ruth," Keefe boasts that for the St. Louis opener he had enough stuff "to make a monkey out of Cobb and Veach." Pitching against Detroit later, Keefe got Cobb to fly out once, but Cobb also hit a triple. Keefe then traded insults with "Ty." In "The Busher Pulls a Mays," Keefe sarcastically notes that Cobb successfully countered a suspension by Ban Johnson and continued to play for Detroit. Keefe also says Jennings, Detroit's manager, complains that Gleason when talking trades wants only Cobb and Bush — impossibly. Cobb is mentioned in "Back to Baltimore," "The Busher Abroad," "Harmony," "The Hold-Out," "A One-Man Team," *The Real Dope*, "Where Do You Get That Noise?," and "The Yellow Kid."

Tyrus Raymond "Ty" Cobb (1886–1961) was the record-setting, ill-tempered centerfielder for the Detroit Tigers (1905–1926), managed the Tigers (1921–1926), and played for the Philadelphia Athletics (1927–1928). He was notable for speed, audacity, and spiking. Lardner admired Cobb inordinately, as Leverett T. Smith Jr. shows. Smith makes use of Lardner's "Tyrus: The Greatest of 'Em All" (*American Magazine*, June 1915). George W. Hilton explains that Cobb attacked a heckler in the New York stands (May 15, 1912), was suspended indefinitely by Byron Bancroft Johnson,* but when the Detroit players struck to support him, he was allowed to return to play (May 20). Cobb became a member of the Baseball Hall of Fame (1936). (Sources: *Baseball Encyclopedia*, 894, 1899; Hilton, 52, 307; Smith, 142, 144; Streissguth, 43)

CODD, BOB (*The Big Town*). He is a pilot whom Katie meets on Long Island and likes because he may sell his modified "aeroplane" to Palmer Williams and his brother for millions. She narrowly misses taking a flight with Bob which results in his fatal crash.

COHAN, GEORGE M. (1878–1942). He was a versatile showman, singer, dancer, playwright, and screenwriter. Many of his plays became movies, for example, his stage adaptation (1914) of *Seven Keys to Baldpate* by Earl Derr Biggers (1883–1933) was immensely popular on the big screen (1917, 1925, 1929, 1935, 1947). Still popular are many of his songs, especially "Yankee Doodle Boy [Dandy]" (1904), "You're a Good Old Flag [Rag]" (1906), and "Over There" (1917).

In "Stop Me — if you've heard This One," Luke Garner, playwright, goes to Chicago to show George Cohan his play, which he says "Cohan turned down." Cohan is mentioned in "The Poor Simp," when Carey, to kid Skull Scoville, said he thought George Cohan managed the Giants. In *The Big Town*, Finch and Francis Griffin mention "Georgie" Cohan sarcastically to each other. When the Lardners lived in Great Neck, Cohan was one of their glittering neighbors. Donald Elder discusses Lardner's reliance on Cohan for guidance in writing plays and mentions Cohan's sending Lardner his *Seven Keys to Baldpate* script for possible use as a example "in matters of action and stage business." Lardner's "Hurry Kane" appealed to Cohan so much that in October 1927 he got Lardner to sign a contract to collaborate with him and adapt it as a play, to be called *Elmer the Great*. Ring Lardner Jr. discusses his father's collaboration with Cohan on it. Jonathan Yardley explains why the result was miserable: "Ring saw it [the story] as a satire, Cohan as a melodrama." The play failed, running on Broadway for only 40 performances and costing Lardner $6,000, only partly recouped when it was sold to the movies. (Sources: Elder, 251; Ephraim Katz, 281; Lardner, Jr., 176–179; *Patriotic Cohan: A Medley* [(n.p.): Belwin-Mills Publishing Corp., 2004]; Yardley, 239, 318, 322–324)

COHEN ("Lose with a Smile"). Danny Warner explains that Cohen, a Brooklyn teammate, got a scratch double in a game against "Phila," but that Carey, Danny's manager, wouldn't let him bat next as a pinch hitter.

Alta Cohen (1908–2003) played for the Brooklyn Dodgers (1931–1932) and the Philadelphia Phillies (1933). (Source: *Baseball Encyclopedia*, 895)

COLBY, MR. ("A Caddy's Diary"). He is a member of the club where the diarist caddies. He caddies one Sunday morning for Colby. Colby writes newspaper articles. When the diarist expresses an interest in becoming a writer, Mr. Colby first tells him that Alex Laird pays someone to write golf articles ascribed to Laird and then advises the caddy to practice writing by keeping a diary.

COLE, BILL ("Harmony"). He is a pitcher for the team and sings bass in the team quartet. He tells him one version of how Waldron joined the team. Art Graham tells another version.

COLES, MR. ("Tour Y-10"). He travels with Violet Emerson and Kate Hayes to Yellowstone. Violet encourages his attention; but he proposes to Kate, who rejects him.

COLE, MRS. ("Harmony"). She is Bill Cole's wife. He wouldn't want to sing on vaudeville in the off season, because doing so would mean his being away from his "Missus" during otherwise free months.

THE COLLECTED SHORT STORIES OF RING LARDNER (New York: Modern Library [1941]). Republication of the 35 stories published in *Round Up.*

COLLIER, BUSTER (1902–1986). William C. Collier Jr. was a movie star, who appeared as a child actor with his father, debuted in films (1916), and became a leading man in silents. He continued in talkies but (1930), then became an agent. Buster Collier is mentioned in "I Can't Breathe." (Source: Ephraim Katz, 285)

COLLINS In "The Busher Comes Back," Keefe boasts that while pitching for the White Sox against "the Athaletics" he had "no trouble with Collins neither." In "Horseshoes," Eddie Collins is a member of the Athletics and hit successfully in the second game of their World Series against the Giants. George W. Hilton reports that this comment concerns the 1913 World Series between the New York Giants and the victorious Philadelphia Athletics. In *Treat 'Em Rough*, Keefe praises Collins. In "The Battle of Texas," Keefe notes that Ed Collins was a marine during the war. Keefe gripes that Collins and Weaver played badly behind him when he was pitching in an intra-team game. In "Along Came Ruth," Keefe praises Collins's hitting ability. In "The Courtship of T. Dorgan," Keefe complains again about Collins's and Weaver's play during a Washington game. "The Busher Pulls a Mays," Keefe mentions "Cocky Collins" and Schalk "or myself" as players Gleason won't trade to Boston. In *The Real Dope*, Keefe recalls games in which Collins played. Lardner admired Collins and wrote about him in non-fictional pieces as well as in fictional ones. Late in life and ill, Lardner wrote a letter (June 4, 1932) to John J. McGraw* (quoted by Donald Elder) praising McGraw, Gleason, and Collins as "among the few men left who personified what I enjoyed in the 'national pastime.'"

Edward Trowbridge Collins (1887–1951) played for the Philadelphia Athletics (1906–1914) and the Chicago White Sox (1915–1924), which he managed (1924–1926) before returning to the Athletics (1927–1930). Collins was elected to the Baseball Hall of Fame (1939). Much earlier, Collins, a good man, got wind of the conspiracy resulting in the 1919 Black Sox Scandal. David L. Fleitz comments that "Collins visited Charles Comiskey [owner of the White Sox] in early September to vent his suspicions, but Comiskey merely shrugged his shoulders." See Comiskey, Charles Albert. (Sources: *Baseball Encyclopedia*, 689, 900; Elder, 362; Fleitz, 283; Hilton, 77–78, 394)

COLLINS In "A Busher's Letters Home," Keefe boasts that in a two-team White Sox game in Paso Robles he struck out Collins, "one of the best batters of the bunch." Keefe later complains that Collins made an error in a Los Angeles game. In "A New Busher Breaks In," Keefe says that when pitching to Detroit's famous Cobb he "eased up" and Collins "took a fly off of the fence." In "The Busher's Kid," Keefe says he made "the Athaletics" hit so many flies that Collins' "tongue [was] hanging out from running back to the fence." (Would that indicate Keefe pitched well?) In "Call for Mr. Keefe!," Keefe says that Collins was on second when umpire Bill Evans made a bad call favoring Johnson, Washington's pitcher. In "The Battle of Texas," Keefe gripes that when he was pitching in an intra-team game Shano got a lucky hit. In "The Courtship of T. Dorgan," Keefe says that when Gleason has Jack Collins hit for him, Coumbe, pitching for Cleveland, "made a monkey out of him."

John Francis ("Jack," "Shano") Collins (1885–1955) played for the White Sox (1910–1920) and the Boston Red Sox (1921–1925), and managed the Red Sox (1931–1932). (Sources: *Baseball Encyclopedia*, 689, 902; Hilton, 46–47)

COLLINS ("Nora"). He is a crooked politician in Hazlett's play "Nora." In it, Crowley wants Collins to swing business his way, goes to jail, and leaves his son John Collins penniless.

COLLINS, ARTHUR ("Three Without, Doubled"). He and his wife are members of the San Susie bridge club. Gullible and his wife are invited to join.

COLLINS, BEN ("Poodle") *see* **POODLE**

COLLINS, BEN ("There Are Smiles"). He is a genial traffic policeman, 6' 4", 218 lbs., about 30. He handles traffic violations at Fifth Avenue and Forty-sixth Street by good-humored wisecracks. One day he stops a girl for reckless driving. Her radiant smile affects him profoundly. She gives him occasional lifts to his home in the Bronx, which he shares with his wife Grace. During a rainy afternoon drive toward his house, she tells him that her name is Edith Dole and that she's getting married. Next morning he reads in the newspaper that she was killed that same afternoon skidding into a street-car. Her death turns him into a snarling traffic cop that at least one driver formerly let off after a violation can't recognize.

COLLINS, GRACE ("There Are Smiles"). She is traffic-cop Ben Collins's staid, solicitous wife. She doesn't like his anecdotes about women drivers. He fibs to her harmlessly. Grace was playing cards with their friend Mary Arnold shortly before Edith Dole, a radiantly smiling, reckless driver by whom Ben has been platonically smitten, is killed in a skidding accident.

COLLINS, HAPPY ("HAP") ("Champion"). He is a Chicago friend of Midge Kelly, who gets money from Collins by his threatening manner.

COLLINS, JOHN ("Nora"). He is crooked old Collins' son, 23 or 24, in Hazlett's play "Nora." In it, John and Nora Crowley love each other.

COLLINS, MRS. ("Three Without, Doubled"). She and her husband Arthur Collins belong to the San Susie bridge club. Gullible and his wife are invited to join. Gullible's irrational play enables Mrs. Collins to defeat Mrs. Messenger and win the prize.

COLONEL, THE (*The Real Dope*). He is one of Keefe's superior officers. When they are aboard a troop ship heading for France, the Colonel rebukes Doran, Bob Lee, and Freddie Smith for kidding Keefe. When in France, the "Col." asks for volunteers to go on a patrol. Keefe doesn't volunteer. The patrol is lost.

COLTON ("Cured!"). He and his wife evidently live near Dick and Mary Streeter in Westchester, north of New York. They invite the Streeters to a dinner party. They accept, but Dick gets drunk in New York and spoils plans.

COLTON, MRS. ("Cured!"). She is Mary Streeter's "best friend" and invites her and Mary's husband Dick to a dinner party. Dick persuades Mary to accept but then gets drunk in New York too long. Mary must call to express their regrets.

COMERFORD, H. N. ("Absent-minded Beggar"). He is Irene Comerford's father and J. L. Beasley's wealthy brokerage-firm partner.

COMERFORD, IRENE ("Absent-minded Beggar"). She is H. N. Comerford's beautiful daughter. She is engaged to rowdy Sam Drake, until John Knowles enters the scene. She and John become engaged.

"THE COMIC" (*Saturday Evening Post*, May 14, 1921; BT) *see* ***THE BIG TOWN***

COMISKEY, CHARLES ALBERT (1859–1931). Comiskey was a baseball player, manager, cofounder of the American League, and owner and president of the Chicago White Sox. He was elected to the Baseball Hall of Fame (1939). From early in his sports-writing days, Lardner made it his business to know Comiskey and to write about him, sometimes humorously. Donald Elder and David L. Fleitz report on Comiskey's actions in connection with the 1919 Black Sox Scandal. Fleitz concludes that "Comiskey's stinginess ... contributed to the tragedy that destroyed the careers of Shoeless Jackson and seven of his teammates." James E. Elfers, in his account of the White Sox-Giants 1913–1914 world tour, often writes about Comiskey and memorably begins thus: "Comiskey [was] ... owner of the Chicago White Sox and the richest man in baseball ... overweight, florid faced, and sanctimonious ... [with] the miserly mind of one of the game's greatest benefactors and one of its cruelest tightwads." (Sources: Elder, 159–161; Elfers, 2–3; Fleitz, 284; Hilton, 35, 37; Yardley, *passim*)

In "A Busher's Letters Home," Keefe explains that Comiskey had Jack Doyle scout Keefe in Terre Haute, bought him as a White Sox pitcher, ridiculed him, paid him half what he wanted, and sold him to Frisco. In "The Busher Comes Back," Keefe says he did well, planned to demand $5,000 for next year, but settled when Comiskey offered $2,800. In "The Busher's Honeymoon," Keefe ruins his chances for the coming season by demanding more pay, losing his cool, and walking away. In "A New Busher Breaks In," Keefe tries to outface Comiskey, puts on his best face, and remains with the White Sox. In "The Busher's Kid," Keefe explains his hope that Comiskey will be impressed and increase his "salery next year." In "The Busher Beats It Hence," Callahan tells Keefe that Comiskey appealed to President Wilson to get Keefe to go on the world tour to avoid international trouble with the Japanese. In "The Busher Abroad," Keefe and Comiskey are on the world tour. Keefe mentions Comiskey in one of his poems. In "The Busher's Welcome Home," Comiskey, knowing Keefe is being fooled into trying to leave the White Sox, allows him to return to his old team. In "Call for Mr. Keefe!," Keefe tells the draft board that Comiskey will vouch for him. In "The Busher Reënlists," Comiskey, in the background, offers to sign Keefe for $2,400. In *Treat 'Em Rough*, Keefe mentions Comiskey. In "The Last Night," Comiskey is mentioned, as "Commy." In *The Real Dope*, Keefe mentions

Comiskey twice and calls him "the old Roman." In "The Battle of Texas," when Keefe gets upset with Kid Gleason, he abortively thinks he'll ask Comiskey to trade him. In "The Courtship of T. Dorgan," Keefe boasts that Gleason told him to take his old contract to the office; he did, and "the old man give me my new 1." In "The Busher Pulls a Mays," Keefe reports that Jenning, Washington's manager, said that "when a club offers money to Comiskey why it is like takeing coal to a castle." In *The Real Dope*, Keefe, when wounded in France, thinks Comiskey will hire him because of his popular appeal among patriotic fans.

James E. Elfers writes about Comiskey's activities in helping to organize the famous 1913–1914 White Sox-Giants tour around the world. Comiskey suffered "a frightening illness" in Rome but quickly recovered. (Source: Elfers, 203 and *passim*)

CONAHAN ("The Poor Simp"). He owns a brewery making Silver Tip beer. Skull Scoville has impressed Conahan's daughter Mary, and will marry her and work for Conahan, who is in failing health.

CONAHAN, MARY ("The Poor Simp"). She is a pretty blonde who happened to attend a baseball game with a friend. Carey saw their appearance as his opportunity to pull yet another practical joke on Skull Scoville, who was "shaggin' in the outfield." Carey told Skull that she was Lizzie Carnegie and admired Skull, and that her brunette companion was her sister-in-law. Fate provided Carey his comeuppance: Skull met and impressed her, will marry her, and will work for her ill father's lucrative brewery.

CONDON, LEFTY ("Hurry Kane"). He was the baseball player who, as Hurry Kane explains to Bull Wade, gave Kane his nickname. No, Kane explains, not because he hurries to the dining room but because "'Hurry' Kane ... is a kind of a storm."

CONKLIN, MR. ("Ball-A-Hole"). He is the director of several banks. He is inveigled by the narrator and Jake into playing golf with Mr. Perkins. The two men dispute but become friendly at last.

CONLEY, FRANK ("The Hold-Out"). He is the narrator and manages the baseball team Mr. Edwards bought. Frank advised his boss and mainly negotiated contracts. Frank planned to out-wait Bill Hagedorn, the team's capable first baseman who was holding out for a $6,000 contract instead of only $4,000. But when Bill told Frank that he was broke and that his wife just had a baby, Frank connived to get Mr. Edwards to pay the $6,000.

CONLEY, MRS. ("The Hold-Out"). She is Frank Conley's wife. He says that three people think he's "the greatest," one being his wife.

CONNOLLY In "Horseshoes," he is an umpire during the Athletics-Giants third World Series game. In "The Crook," Tommy (Connolly) umpired a dramatic baseball game. He denied an appeal at third base concerning Hooper, of the Red Sox. Cahill, of the White Sox, called Bull, another umpire, a "crook," which resulted in a fight leading to Bull's being fired. Afterwards, Larry reminisced with Tommy about Bull.

Thomas Henry Connolly (1870–1961) was an American League umpire (1901–1931), and League "supervising umpire until 1953." (Source: Hilton, 413, 551)

CONRAD ("Oh, You Bonehead!"). He played on the Coach's Leighton football team against Pelham.

"CONTRACT" (*Harper's Bazar*, March 1929; RLR, RU). (Characters: Gale Bartlett, Mrs. Bartlett, Mr. C., Cameron, Mrs. Cameron, Carl Dittmar, Mrs. Dittmar, Mrs. French, Robert French, E. M. Pardee, Mrs. Pardee, Peterson, Mrs. R., Shelton, Mrs. Shelton, Mr. T., Mrs. W., Wilson, Mrs. Wilson.)

Shelton works for a magazine publisher. He and his wife, married six years, live in the city. She wishes they had more friends; he doesn't. When he is promoted to associate editor and given a raise, they can afford to move to Linden, a suburb. Their neighbors Robert French and his wife visit. Mrs. French mentions contract bridge parties. Shelton, having card sense and wanting to please his wife, agrees to participate. His wife is delighted, but is just learning bridge and fears being rebuked for mistakes. Shelton says such criticism would be impolite. Wednesday at the Frenches' house. Mrs. Shelton is French's partner, against guests young Carl Dittmar and Mrs. Cameron, notable for nostrils so huge they could carry "two after dinner mints." Mrs. Shelton makes errors, is criticized, but doesn't mind. She notices, however, that at the other table, when ultra-courteous Shelton makes boo-boos, he apologetically requests lessons, which his partner Mrs. French, but especially Cameron and his aging partner Mrs. Dittmar, provide abundantly. After his table switches partners, Shelton happily watches Cameron blast his partner Mrs. French for not doubling Shelton's partner Mrs. Dittmer, who counterattacks their opponents' bad bidding. Partnering with Cameron, Shelton makes his bid by clever finessing. Cameron calls him foolishly lucky. The Sheltons win $6 and are invited next Wednesday to the Dittmars.' Shelton is so happy on their way home that his wife is suspicious, though glad they are developing unique gregariousness.

Shelton encounters Gale Bartlett, a writer for his magazine and back from Paris. He was the one who recommended that the Sheltons' move to Linden, where he already has a house. Shelton explains that they are playing bridge with Dittmar, Cameron, French, and their wives. Bartlett says that he doesn't know Dittmar but that Cameron and French are dirty "new rich," suggests his dumping all of them, and promises to introduce the Sheltons to some courteous bridge-playing Lindenites.

Shelton formulates some trickery at the Dittmars' next Wednesday. Shelton's wife has one of her inconvenient two-day headaches, phones him at work to go alone, and phones Mrs. Dittmar to get a substitute. She says fine, her brother will sub. Fortified with office rye, Shelton reports straight to the Dittmars. Mrs. Dittmar introduces her "B'udder," who mangles "Rhapsody in Blue" on the piano during cocktails. At dinner, Shelton launches his attacks. It was rude last week to criticize his bridge playing. They say they meant to improve him. Well, is creative criticism warranted beyond bridge? Yes. So he criticizes Cameron's manner of spooning soup, Mrs. Cameron's ungrammatical playful rejoinder, Mrs. Dittmar's baby-talk. When French starts a Scotchman-Jew golf story, Shelton says all present have heard it unless they've "been unconscious for years." Cameron tries to rationalize: Shelton was "a new beginner" at bridge. Shelton wonders if anyone is an "old beginner," and criticizes Mrs. French for forking in her fish left-handed, despite Mrs. Dittmar's supposed fish forks actually being salad forks. He corrects repetitious "enoughs" by Dittmar, who orders him away. Leaving, he tells "B'udder" he must be deaf because his sister said he played the piano by ear.

Home again, Shelton polishes his bender and tells his wife they won't be going to the Camerons. Wednesday they are invited to the Pardees, Gale Bartlett's recommended neighbors. But Mrs. Pardee pronto rebukes "Mr. Shelvin" for ignoring her discards and not leading her a club. In a postscript, Lardner says he expects his bridge-playing cronies won't take this story personally.

Howard W. Webb,, Jr., regards "Contract" as "an essentially trivial story, little more, in fact, than the pettish expression of a personal irritation." However, Webb also fits its implications neatly into his argument that the overarching theme of Lardner's writing is the inability of people to communicate. (Source: Webb, 439)

COOK, JEM ("The Venomous Viper of the Volga"). He is an African-American boxer once known as "the Black Bull of Biloxi," but now "middle-aged and slow." He is matched against Teddy Walsh in Buffalo, and will surely lose, because the scheduled referee is Larry Woltz, "born in the South."

Lardner has his narrator implicitly criticize the white referee for racial prejudice but then criticize the black boxer by gratuitously adding that Cook "never whipped anyone but his children."

COOLIDGE, CALVIN (1872–1933). Politician and president. Vermont-born Coolidge graduated from Amherst College (1895), practiced law (1897–1910), was governor of Massachusetts (1919–1920), and was vice president (1921–1923) in the Republican administration of President Warren Harding (1865–1923). When Harding died, Coolidge became president (1923–1925) and was reelected to a full term (1925–1929). His pro-business administration was popular because of good economic times. Choosing not to run again, he supported the successful campaign for president of Herbert Hoover (1874–1964), who had been his Secretary of Commerce.

For the Bell Syndicate, Lardner covered the uneventful 1924 Republican Convention in Cleveland in four dispatches (June 10–13). In 15 dispatches, he covered the 1924 Democratic Convention in New York, which took 103 ballots before John W. Davis was nominated. In one dispatch (June 24), Lardner offered himself as a candidate if Coolidge would withdraw; in another (June 25), he nominated his friend Arthur Baer. Coolidge is mentioned in "Hurry Kane," "Mr. Frisbie," and "What of It?" In "The Venomous Viper of the Volga," Louis Angel Firpo's punch is said to resemble "Mrs. Coolidge's gentlest handshake" compared to the Viper's slugging power. In "A Night Letter from Ring Lardner" for the Bell Syndicate (February 27, 1931), Lardner, gravely ill, apologetically rationalizes its being "too short" by comparing it to Coolidge's laudable "brevity." During an interview with Grant Overton, Lardner said, "Bell letters ... but bell me no *belles lettres*." (Sources: Overton, 44; Yardley, 226, 227, 347)

COOPER ("Horseshoes"). He is a Pittsburgh pitcher in a game when Dick Grimes and Speed Parker are playing for the Cubs against him. Speed scores on a muffed pop-up.

Arley Wilbur Cooper (1892–1973) was a superb left-handed pitcher for the Pirates (1912–1924), the Cubs (1925), and the Cubs and the Giants (1926). (Sources: *Baseball Encyclopedia*, 1909; Hilton, 400)

COOPER, BESS ("Ex Parte"). She is Jeff Cooper's wife. She will accompany Jeff when he goes to China on business.

COOPER, BESS ("That Old Sweetheart of Mine"). She is a friend with whom Stella Crane plays bridge.

COOPER, JEFF ("Ex Parte"). He accepts a job with Standard Oil in China. The narrator buys the Coopers' new, attractively furnished house, which Florence, the narrator's wife, then proceeds to dislike.

CORA ("Insomnia"). She was the family cow the sleepless author remembers chasing.

COREY, EVELYN ("Hurry Kane"). She is a former Broadway performer who flirts with Hurry Kane, the St. Louis pitcher, so he will throw the crucial game against the White Sox for Sam Morris, her gambler friend.

CORLISS, HYPE ("The Hold-Out"). He and Jack Moran were two poor pitchers traded by Frank Conley to get Johnny Gould.

CORNELL ("Holycaust") *see* **HAUSLER AND CORNELL**

"CORPORAL PUNISHMENT" (*Saturday Evening Post*, April 13, 1918; TER).

COSGROVE ("The Battle of Texas"). He is a young White Cox catcher who during practice in Texas foolishly discards his mask, goes after a high foul, and is knocked unconscious when the ball comes down.

COSSET, DEXTER ("What of It?"). He clerks at Ellsworth's in South Bend, has a girlfriend named Carlotta, and has written a play entitled *Ghosts* and accepted by New York producer Joe Martin. While on the train to New York to discuss his play with Martin, Cosset is bothered by a nonstop talker named Ben Lacey. Harrison Quolt silences Lacey by answering every comment with "What of It?" but then stops Cosset's response by saying "What did you say?"

COUMBE ("The Courtship of T. Dorgan"). He is a Cleveland pitcher who defeated the White Sox in a game pitched badly by Keefe and then Danforth. Keefe, who claims he can hit left-handers "as good as anybody on the club," is pleased that Coumbe "made a monkey" out of Jack Collins when Gleason ordered him bat for Keefe.

Frederick Nicholas Coumbe (1889–1978) pitched for the Boston Red Sox and the Cleveland Indians (1914), the Indians (1915–1919), and the Cincinnati Reds (1920–1921). (Sources: *Baseball Encyclopedia*, 1912; Hilton, 295)

"THE COURTSHIP OF T. DORGAN" (*Saturday Evening Post*, September 6, 1919; ABS, RAB). (Characters: Al Blanchard, Bertha Blanchard, Jimmy Burke, Jack Casey, Collins, Jack Collins, Comiskey, Coumbe, Danforth, Tom Dorgan, Dumont, Mrs. Dumont, Flagstead, Fohl, Chick Gandil, Gleason, Jack Graney, Griffith, Harper, Jennings, Al Keefe, Florrie Keefe, Florrie Keefe, Jack Keefe, Johnson, Liebold, Miss Josie Mulvihill, Pipp, Tex Ricketts, Babe Ruth, Ray Schalk, Shaw, Speaker, Dummy Taylor, Buck Weaver.)

Keefe sends nine letters to Al Blanchard.

"Chi, May 22." Keefe has pitched for the White Sox so well that Gleason recommended a $600 raise, which "the old man" (Comiskey) approved. Gleason warned Keefe to tell nobody; so he told only Tom Dorgan, his on-the-road roommate and the team's "3th string catcher." Tom is single and lonely; so Keefe will try to find him a girl. When Keefe told his wife Florrie about the raise, she wanted to buy a car. The Dumonts, "her new pardners" in the downtown beauty parlor, got a second-hand one for $700. Keefe sees no need for a car, which Florrie would drive up a building anyway. The Washington team is coming to town, and Gleason is saving Keefe to go against Walter (Johnson).

"Chi, May 27." Keefe says Gleason started "big Lowdermilk" to pitch against Griffith's pitcher Jim Shaw and then Johnson. Johnson was winning until Keefe took over and "we knocked his can off" and won. Florrie, the Dumonts, and their friend, a "sweet looking doll ... named Miss Mulvihill or something," attended the game. Afterwards they picked up Dorgan at Dumont's suggestion for Miss Mulvihill to have a date. Dorgan's eyes popped out when he saw "the Mulvihill trick." All six crowded into the Dumonts' small car, with Dorgan on Keefe's lap, and headed out of town "to eat and drink." While "on the porch of the joint," Keefe provided witty talk because Dorgan dummied up. Keefe got stuck with the check for "more drinks and a chicken dinner," told Miss Mulvihill he "was tickled to death to pay for being in her company," and she blushed. Well, "gals feels" like that with him, but not with "speechless" Dorgan. On the drive back, Miss Mulvihill said she'd sit on Keefe's lap if Florrie didn't object. Florrie let her, and Keefe Miss Mulvihill her to her door. Keefe asked her how she liked Dorgan. She puzzled Keefe by asking "Why don't you speak for yourself John?" Why would she call him John when he's always called Jack? At home, Florrie turned chilly. Next day Gleason made him pitch after pitching two innings yesterday. Collins and Weaver played badly for the White Sox, and Washington's Harper shut them out. When asked, Keefe admitted he'd been out last night, and Gleason fined him $50. Keefe, aware he's handsome, with "a wife and 2 kiddies," may quit baseball, where "the gals can look you over and make a fool of themself."

"Chi, June 1." The White Sox beat Cleveland three games, including one Keefe pitched. For yesterday's game, Gleason let Keefe sit in the stand with Florrie, the Dumonts, and Miss Mulvihill. He explained the game to her, which further bothered Florrie. During the game, Chick Gandil had Speaker of Cleveland out at first, but Speaker slid into him and the two started a fight and were tossed by "the umps." Keefe told Miss Mulvihill that if the fight had grown deadly he would have run down and broken it up. He added that he told Jack Graney earlier that if Speaker monkeyed with him that way, Fohl, the Cleveland manager, would have to replace Speaker. Miss Mulvihill praised his manliness. Her admiring smile bothered Florrie. The Dumonts invited the Keefes to have dinner downtown, and Mrs. Dumont got Keefe to bring Dorgan along, to Miss Mulvihill's displeasure. She and Dorgan danced. Keefe was glad, because "things might get to personal" if he and Miss Mulvihill sat and talked a lot. When she "managed to ask" where the team would be staying for the upcoming games with Detroit, he told her and she'll probably be sending him postcards he'll ignore. She'll "be better off" if he's away "a wile."

"N.Y., June 5." Keefe pitched badly in Detroit. While there, he "run across a bird that wants to sell ... a 1918 Blaine that hasn't only been drove 4000 miles." Keefe plans to get him down from the $1,200 he wants. Dorgan thinks about Miss Mulvihill constantly and wonders would "it do any harm him writeing her." Keefe says go ahead, but it won't help because she "has let her heart run away from her" to Keefe, already with "a wife and troubles of my own." He promised Dorgan to try to help him. Keefe hopes to pitch well against "the N.Y. club."

"Boston, June 11." Keefe feels he ought to be running "a matrimony burro." Dorgan is "nuts over" Josie Mulvihill, "that little queen out in Chi," but she looks only at Keefe when the three are together. Dorgan confessed he's "a busher in the lady league" and asked Keefe to write her and mention him favorably. Keefe did and sends Al a copy. In it Keefe wrote her that an unnamed "pal of mine" that she knows through the Dumonts likes her but hasn't much chance catching backup behind Ray Schalk, "has a fair arm" but must improve his stance to throw better, must quit being "spike shy"; that "he don't draw no star salery" but may "make good in the big league or at lease in Class A"; that Keefe is happy to buy the beers when they drink; that "the more you see of him he is just the same all the wile"; that "looks is not everything or money neither one"; and that Josie should be "just good friends" with Keefe "like I am with other girlies." Keefe tells Al that his motives were to set Josie straight with him and also for her to give Dorgan a chance quickly "or else ... the sooner he gets the bad news he will get over it that much sooner." Yesterday, Keefe had Babe Ruth, who's well named, swinging like a baby and fouling twice. Ruth would have struck out once, but Keefe couldn't curve the ball since it was "bran new." Regards to Bertha.

Detroit, June 22. Gleason didn't pitch Keefe today against Detroit, probably wanting to hold him for the home game tomorrow against Cleveland. The man with the Blaine car said another man is offering him the full $1,200; so he won't go lower, but likes Keefe so much that he'll hold it for him for a $100 option, and he can discuss the deal with Florrie. Keefe gave him the $100, hopes "Florrie will go in with me 50 50," and he'll wire the man and get Gleason to let him "run over here from Chi," and drive the car back fast. He plans to "burn up Michigan Ave." with it but not let Florrie drive "the car neither wile I am in Chi or on the road." You can't trust women. The owner demonstrated the car, which "run like a watch charm," but couldn't persuade him "to try and run it a wile." Keefe can "learn how to run it ... like childs play" later. Josie wrote Keefe simply to tell him to tell Dorgan what she told Keefe, which was "why don't he speak for himself." When Keefe "showed him the message," his face fell.

Chi, June 24. When Keefe wouldn't agree to let Florrie drive the car, she refused to share the cost. Keefe helped the White Sox lose to Cleveland, partly because Gleason relieved him, had Jack Collins bat for him, and their pitcher Coumbe "made a monkey out of him." Worse, before the game started, Speaker accused Keefe of telling Graney that Speaker better not fight Keefe or Fohl would have to replace Speaker. To avoid trouble, Keefe said he'd rather discuss the incident at their hotel later. Keefe almost beaned Graney, was warned, tried again to bean him, but grooved the pitch and Graney got a double. Up next, Speaker sarcastically asked to be beaned. Keefe tried, but the pitch slipped outside and Speaker doubled Graney home. Keefe avoided both of them when they jeered him, because they wanted him to fight and get suspended. That night Keefe would've gone to their hotel and battered them, except little Florrie was "kind of croopy." Dorgan told Keefe he has a date with Josie, who'll probably tell him in person that "they wasn't no chance for him" and probably "let him down easy." The White Sox will go to St. Louis in two days.

"St. Louis, June 28." Keefe tells Al he wired the Detroit salesman that "Florrie or no Florrie" he'll buy the car, because he is going to have the needed $1,200. He has a buddy in St. Louis named Jack Casey who knows the fight business "A to Z." While "we was all over St. Louis lapping them up," they "run in to ... boys that is interested in the fight game." When talk turned "to the Willard Demspey fight in Toledo on the 4 of July," it was suggested that Tex Ricketts, who built the expensive arena there, would arrange for Willard to "get the decision" so a rematch could follow and Ricketts could "clean up a bunch of jack." Casey told Keefe to "bet my head off on the big fellow." A man there would take Keefe's check, but he decided to wait to get to Cleveland for the odds to get still better. Back at the hotel, he told Buck Weaver and two other players what he knew. They doubted his inside information and acted like "smart Alex"; so he bet $200 on Willard with each of the three. He'll own the car without Florrie and won't let her "get a hold of it and try to clime trees." Keefe is going to Cleveland to "play a postpone game Monday [June 30]." Gleason left Dorgan "in old Chi," where on June 30 he can drink a lot even though "the ladys don't go nuts over him." Keefe advises Al to bet "your jack on the big fellow."

Chi, July 5. Keefe writes Al it's goodbye car. He's glad he didn't advise Al to bet on Willard. Casey wouldn't steer Keefe wrong. Probably "Dempsey double crossed the big fellow." But for what Keefe was told in St. Louis he would have bet on Dempsey. "Jess wasn't in no shape to fight" and was "pretty near 40." If the White Sox "win the world serious," Keefe will have money enough to buy a good car and "not no broke down 2d hand Blaine" that is "he — ll on tires and the cylinders keeps getting gumed up." Keefe told Florrie nothing about his bet. If the Detroit "bird" doesn't return his $100 option, he "will knock him for a gool." Keefe was so upset that in Chicago yesterday that Detroit pitcher Flagstead got "to me for 3 hits." After the game Dorgan led Keefe out to see Miss Mulvihill. They are getting married and thanked him "for kind of helping them fix it up." Dorgan is welcome to her. Keefe is married, and Miss Mulvihill is not "a young gal" any more. Dorgan told Keefe "on the quite" that he bought the "big diamond solitary stone" she now wears "with some of the jack he win on the fight down to Toledo." The boys call Keefe "Jess" now. He might "Jess them in the jaw" if they keep kidding him.

Lardner intends the title "The Courtship of T. Dorgan" to echo that of Henry Wadsworth Longfellow's immortal *The Courtship of Miles Standish*, as is made plain when Miss Josie Mulvihill asks Keefe, "Why don't you speak for yourself John?" and later tells him to get Dorgan to do the same. George W. Hilton points out Lardner has Keefe use the expression "knock him for a gool" 14 times, beginning in "The Battle of Texas" and continuing in "The Courtship of T. Dorgan," discusses several possible meanings "of this obscure expression," and concludes that Keefe intends it to mean "the delivery of a blow." It may be added that Danny Warner in "Holycaust" says that when a doctor said it was not "schrimps" but "gin sauce" that sickened him, he was tempted to "knock him for a Gould." (Source: Hilton, 237)

COVELESKIE ("The Crook"). He pitched for the Phillies against the White Sox. When he threw a perfect strike and Bull, the umpire, called Martin Gregory out, trouble began for Bull. Bull was in love with Martin's sister and lost her — until Larry, of the White Sox, intervened and explained matters.

Harry Coveleski (1886–1950) pitched for the Philadelphia Phillies (1907–1909), the Cincinnati Reds (1910), and the Detroit Tigers (1914–1918). Charles F. Faber and Richard B. Faber report that Harry Coveleski was "called the 'Giant Killer' for his success against John McGraw[*]'s team," and prove by statistics that his brother Stanley Anthony Coveleski was a splendid spitball hurler. Stan Coveleski (1889–1984), a Hall of Famer (1969), pitched for the Philadelphia Athletics (1912), the Cleveland Indians (1916–1924), the Washington Senators (1925–1927), and the New York Yankees (1928). (Sources: *Baseball Encyclopedia*, 1913; Faber and Faber, 78, 187; Hilton, 569)

COX, DOCTOR ("Zone of Quiet"). He is the physician of the patient who endures nurse Miss Eleanor Lyons's chatter.

CRAGIN ("Harmony"). He plays second base so much better than Burton that, though Burton sang well, he was cut.

CRAGIN ("What of It?"). He was a "picture director" murdered in Los Angeles, or so Ben Lacey tells Dexter Cosset.

CRAIG ("High-rollers"). Bernard and Craig are New York "Publicity Engineers" and hire Walter Finch away from Ripley at twice his old salary.

CRAIG ("Liberty Hall"). He and his wife are friends of Ben Drake and his wife. The Craigs live in Stamford. When the Drakes visit the Craigs, they so dislike their brand of hospitality that Ben devises an "emergency exit" to enable them to leave such hosts expeditiously.

CRAIG, FLORENCE ("Mr. Frisbie"). She is the daughter of Allen Frisbie, who told her to marry Junior Holt. Instead, she married Henry Craig, of whom Frisbie disapproved, correctly.

CRAIG, HENRY ("Mr. Frisbie"). He becomes Florence Frisbie's husband, over the objections of her father. Craig turns out to be an alcoholic "tramp," as Frisbie feared.

CRAIG, MRS. ("Liberty Hall"). She and her husband live in Stamford and know Ben Drake and his wife.

CRANDALL ("Mr. and Mrs. Fix-It"). He is the husband of the narrator's wife Ada's friend. The narrator doesn't like Crandall's boasting about his war experiences.

CRANDALL ("Who Dealt?"). Crandall and Nelson's is a dress shop. When asked by Mrs. Cannon, Helen Gratz says that's where she bought the dress she's wearing.

CRANDALL, MRS. ("Mr. and Mrs. Fix-It"). She is the friend of Ada, the narrator's wife. The two women are from the same home town. When Mrs. Crandall happened to be filmed in Atlantic City by a movie crew, her friends think that if she went into film work she could outdo Gloria Swanson.*

CRANE (*Treat 'Em Rough*). He is the husband of a friend of Florrie Keefe. Mrs. Crane tells Jack Keefe that her husband's bad teeth prevented his enlisting in the army.

CRANE, CHARLEY ("CHAS") ("A Caddy's Diary"). He is a golfer, works in Mr. Thomas's bank, steals $8000 and a stenographer from it, and leaves town with her.

CRANE, MRS. (*Treat 'Em Rough*). She is a friend of Florrie Keefe. Her appearance in the Keefes' apartment bothers Jack during his short leave time with Florrie.

CRANE, RALPH ("That Old Sweetheart of Mine"). He is Stella Crane's boring husband. A patent lawyer in New York, he is in Washington on business when Will happens to phone Stella. The two manage an afternoon date, which proves unsatisfactory.

CRANE, SARGENT (*The Real Dope*). He is a non-com in Keefe's unit in France. Crane orders Keefe to go to the listening post with Ted Phillips.

CRANE, STELLA ("That Old Sweetheart of Mine"). She has been married to New York attorney Ralph Crane for 15 years. Stella, now 39, is bored and lonely. So when Will, a former boyfriend, phones, she agrees to have lunch with him and attend a play. The afternoon frustrates both.

CRAVATH ("GAVVY"). In "Sick 'Em," the narrator praises Cravath, Magee, and Luderus for being good and reliable hitters for the Phillies when the season began. The narrator says that in a game against St. Louis, "Gavvy" dropped a fly with a man on, which cost Smitty, pitching for Philadelphia, a shutout. (The narrator knows that Gavvy is Cravath, but how would the ordinary reader?) In "Back to Baltimore," Cravath hits a hopper to William Smith, Jr., who fields the ball well at first base but throws it into the outfield.

Clifford Carlton Cravath (1881–1963) played for the Boston Red Sox (1908), the Chicago White Sox and the Washington Senators (1909), and the Philadelphia Phillies (1912–1920). Cravath managed the Phillies unsatisfactorily (1919–1920). George W. Hilton provides Cravath's nicknames, "Gavvy" and "Cactus." (Sources: *Baseball Encyclopedia*, 690, 920; Hilton, 368)

CRAWFORD, SAM In "A Busher's Letters Home," Keefe, pitching for the White Sox against the Tigers, complains that Crawford stole bases on him. In "The Busher Comes Back," Keefe boasts he "whiffed" Crawford twice. In "A New Busher Breaks In," Keefe boasts of showing up Crawford last year and later suggested the White Sox buy Ty Cobb and Sam Crawford instead of new pitchers. In "The Busher Beats It Hence," Keefe says the world-touring baseball teams include Crawford, even though he fears Keefe's pitching. In "The Busher Abroad," Sam Crawford tolerates Keefe on the world tour. In "The Crook," Crawford drove Tyrus Cobb home from third. When Parker, the White Sox catcher, objected, Bull, the umpire, silenced him with a pleasantry. Crawford is mentioned in "Where Do You Get That Noise?" In "Harmony," a baseball player named Sam Crawford is such a poor hitter that Bill Cole gets sarcastic about it.

Samuel Earl Crawford (1880–1968) played for the Cincinnati Reds (1899–1902) and the Detroit Tigers (1903–1917), and later played and umpired in the Pacific Coast League. He was elected to the Baseball Hall of Fame (1957). James E. Elfers reports that Crawford remembered his audience with Pope Pius X (February 11, 1914) as "the most impressive event of the tour." (Sources: *Baseball Encyclopedia*, 921; Elfers, 208; Hilton, 67)

CRAWLEY, ROBERT ("The Battle of the Century"). He was "a big steamship man." He and his partner Bill Guthrie negotiated with Larry Moon to promote the Dugan-Goulet boxing match for $500,000. Larry gulled them out of "a forfeit of $100,000" by getting Charley Riggs to put up twice their offer.

Crawley is based on Charles B. Cochran, as Lardner explains in a letter (August 4, 1921) to a *Saturday Evening Post* editor. Clifford M. Caruthers identifies Cochran as "a British theatrical producer and sports promoter." (Source: Caruthers [1995], 135)

CROFT, L. M. ("'In Conference'"). He and others work for Kramer & Company. While "in conference" they talk vacantly. He is a vice president, shares talk about a 2¢ stamp, and mentions his sister Minnie Wilcox.

"THE CROOK" (*Saturday Evening Post*, June 24, 1916; ABS, LOB, RAB). (Characters: Arnold, Baker, Ban, Brodie, Bull, Bush, Cady, Cahill, Carney, Tyrus Cobb, Coveleskie, Crawford, Doran, Douglas, Gregory, Maggie Gregory, Martin Gregory, Mrs. Gregory, Griffith, Hooper, Jack, Jennin's, Walter Johnson, Kennedy, Larry, Lawton, Duff Lewis, Connie Mack, Matty, Milan, Parker, Ted Pierce, Sawyer, Shano, Stanage, Tommy, Walsh, Weber.)

The narrator is Larry, first baseman (for the White Sox), He says that tomorrow's newspapers will explain that Bull was not discharged because he was "pickled on the field," that he was "took back on the staff," but not that a "dandy little fixer" was responsible. Larry, who knew the secret, told Ban, saved Bull, and "got him his girl back." Here is Larry's story:

Usually Bull, an "ump," made jokes when players hollered at his calls — until two days ago. I saw he didn't behave normally when Jack signaled me to try for home and Duff Lewis threw to home plate and Bull called me out and I complained. Bull said nothing. But suddenly when Hooper scored on a sacrifice fly and Cahill said he left third too soon and Tommy the ump at third ruled otherwise and Cahill asked Bull to overrule and Bull wouldn't, Cahill called Bull a "crook." Bull charged Cahill, hit him repeatedly, and was arrested and jailed. Ban, who witnessed everything from the stands, conducted quick hearings, concluded that Bull must have been drunk on duty, and fired him.

Tommy got Bull back to their hotel, told Bull "he was canned," but Bull revealed nothing. I sought Bull at "the umps' beanery." Not there. When I queried Tommy, he said Bull "was grouchin'" about something but swore he'd drunk nothing but coffee before the game. "I and Tommy" began reminiscing about Bull's sense of humor:

Bull's first umpiring in our League was on opening day "in Chi," four or five years earlier. About 26, he looked younger. Arnold, the Browns catcher, called him a kid. Despite some insulting jibes, Bull merely joked back. A few days ago, the Detroit team visited us, and Crawford hit into a possible double play. Tyrus Cobb made it home because Parker, our catcher, was "spike-shy" and retreated. Parker objected to the call, but Bull merely joked. He umped when we visited Cleveland, kidded a griping Cleveland fielder who pretended the sun bothered him, and kidded a Cleveland pinch hitter who objected to a called strike. When Kennedy, batting for us in a game in Washington, struck out three times and threw dirt at Bull, he tossed him but with gentle jokes. Next day Bull, umping "the bases," asked Walter Johnson to walk Kennedy so the two could chat. Back home, Johnson pitched against us and kept striking out little Weber, who jibed but got outjoked. Bull kidded Jennin's' rookie pitcher Sawyer and a player named Carney opposing Walsh, our pitcher. By season's end, Bull had scared "the boys" into silence. But for season after season, the same pattern resumed. Until this season. By July Bull harmlessly outjibed everyone so much that "they're tired o' bein' laughed at ... so they lay off." "Not me, though." I remembered kidding Bull regularly and wish now I'd "wrote down even half" the "pippins" he yelled back. We razzed each other at the end of the 1912 season, when we played Boston and with a hangover I made errors at first base. I overslid second base against St. Louis in 1914, got called out, and we yelled at each other. Last year [1915] in Boston I got caught off first, sassed Bull, and he told me to play in my "pyjamas." In New York we griped at each other again. And in "Washin'ton." No matter how clever you thought your shouts at Bull were, his surprising answers would embarrass you.

After "I and Tommy set there talkin' ... to midnight" and Bull didn't appear, I started for a walk, but spotted Bull drunk and heading for the hotel bar. He said since he was fired for drinking when he was sober, he might as well get drunk. Said he didn't want to live. I sensed something besides umpiring was troubling him. After we two quietly "h'isted three or four," Bull wept and revealed his story:

When his parents died in Buffalo, Bull was already umpiring, lacked any family, and started wintering in the South, where he'd been born. He tried costly New Orleans two winters, then Montgomery, where he boarded with a family named Gregory. The husband worked in a hardware store. His wife was a great cook and fed Bull copiously. The Gregorys had twins, 18. They were Martin, lazy and pampered, and Maggie, "learnin' the milliner trade." Bull liked her immensely but was shy. Maggie quickly "had him on her reserve list." Bull took the family to entertainments. When the Montgomery baseball franchise began practicing in March, Bull went to watch with Martin, who could rattle off baseball statistics, "peeled down to his shirtsleeves," practiced with the team, and revealed natural talent at fielding, throwing, and batting. After Bull and some others trained him, Martin signed with Montgomery and became a South League sensation by June, when Bull was umpiring up North again and enjoying postcards from Maggie. Next winter Bull boarded with the Gregorys again. Last fall, with extra World Series pay, Bull returned to Maggie and proposed. She said she'd think about it and persuaded him to wait. Devoted to her twin brother Martin, she asked Bull to recommend him to a manager in Bull's league. He said it wasn't legal. She pouted. So he promised to try. Martin by then was a conceited, well-dressed dude still sponging off his doting family. In December Bull heard that Ted Pierce, Montgomery's manager, was in town. Bull conferred with him. Pierce said Martin was too cocky, batted .329, fielded and batted well when his team was ahead, but always froze when it was time to bat in a winning run. Hesitating when Bull wondered if Martin were "yellow," Pierce said only that he wouldn't recommend him to any manager he liked simply so that Bull could then legally endorse him if "I was ast about him." Bull told Maggie about Pierce, who, she retorted, was "jealous" of Martin. She gave Bull an ultimatum: Martin must get "his chance this spring" or she'd dump Bull. Bull had an Irishman write Connie Mack, whose team needed improvement, to give a good prospect named Martin a try, and if Connie wanted an endorsement he could ask Bull. When Connie questioned Bull by letter, he recommended Martin as having potential. Bull flattered Martin and urged him to become confident. Pierce released Martin. Grumbling, he tried out with the Athletics in Jacksonville. Maggie hinted that Bull must "help" Martin, otherwise he obviously didn't love her. Bull umpired the Detroit-Philadelphia season-opening series, asked Connie about Martin, and was told he "looked like a find" in practice but always "faded away ... in a pinch," and would be released unless as a pinch hitter he came through immediately. Second game, ninth inning. Detroit ahead 1–0, two out. Philly on third. Martin pinch hitting, count 3–2. Jennings from the Tiger bench taunted Martin: "He's too scared to swing!" Coveleskie "pitched as perfect a strike as was ever pitched." Though seeing Maggie's face before him, Bull called him out. Connie "canned" Martin, saying he would have done so regardless of Bull's call, and lauded Bull for his honesty. Martin, however, wrote Maggie that Bull called a low pitch a strike because he hated Martin, and Maggie wrote Bull to call off her engagement. That letter, two days ago, was what made him cry. No wonder Bull pommeled Cahill for calling him a crook. We drank some more. I got Bull to bed. Next morning I confidentially told Ban "the romance." He reinstated Bull, calling his behavior a "first offense."

Yesterday by chance I saw a fellow who introduced himself as Martin Gregory. He said he wanted a try-out with our White Sox. I agreed but only if he wired his sister that Bull's strikeout call was honest, that Connie would have released him regardless, and that his sister must wire Bull care of me to reconsider Bull. Otherwise I promised Martin not a job opportunity but his "worst lickin' ... ever." I have Maggie's nice telegram "in my pocket," will show it to Bull when I find him, and Martin should hit well for us because I'll scare him worse than pitchers could.

The umpire Tommy's last name is Connolly (*which see*). "The Crook" is in two distinct halves. The first half is a virtual anthology of one witty umpire's cracks gently deflating ball players. The second half is in large part an awkwardly related flashback by a drunk. Both halves are neatly bookended by a self-confessedly clever player-narrator. George W. Hilton calls this story "an excellent study of the consequences of honorable behavior among umpires." (Source: Hilton, 21)

CROSBY, LEFTY ("The Yellow Kid"). He was a pitcher, 20, drafted from Dallas of the Texas League by the boss of the narrator Bill's baseball team. Crosby was praised for his speed, but it was said he ought to be wilder to scare batters more. He was effective on and off the field but went to pieces emotionally when girls or guns were near him. Harry Childs, an outfielder, led a few other players in cruelly razzing Crosby. Crosby got even when, helped by his friend Joe Martin and by Bill, he won the affections of lovely Mary Lloyd, the object of Childs' marital ambitions. Ironically, Crosby proposed only after Childs told him unmarried men 19 and 20 would be drafted.

Crosby is so handsome that he is compared to the popular movie actor Francis X. Bushman.*

CROSS, BUD ("Champion"). He is a boxer, from Baltimore, whom Midge Kelly defeats in Boston.

CROSS, HARRY ("The Clubby Roadster"). He is Nan Cross's husband and is the narrator's fellow office-worker. Cross buys a Champion "Clubby Roadster," takes the narrator, his "Missus," and Nan for a drive, which he manages ineptly. Arguments result.

CROSS, HARRY ("Ex Parte"). He is a friend of the narrator. The two sample some "early American rye" bootlegged to Cross by Mike Farrell.

CROSS, NAN ("The Clubby Roadster"). She is Harry Cross's wife. She inherits $2,500 when her Aunt Myrtle dies. With part of the money, Harry buys a car. The two take the narrator and his wife for a drive, during which unpleasant disagreements ensue.

CROWELL, LOU ("A Caddy's Diary"). He caddies at the club where the diarist also caddies. He hits Fat Brunner in the nose during a dispute over who caddied last for bank-embezzler Charley Crane. Lou did that caddying.

CROWELL, MRS. ("The Last Night"). She is Walter Crowell's wife. She disapproves of Walter's urging Jay Arnold to have more drinks when he interrupts the couple's evening of dancing at the Red Duck.

CROWELL, WALTER ("The Last Night"). He is an alcoholic who is dancing with his wife at the Red Duck until Jay Arnold interrupts them. Walter encourages Arnold's drinking so much that it bothers her. He sends her home by taxi and remains. Next day he delights her by vowing to go on the wagon. He plans to enlist if his poor vision will later permit him to do so. His lecture on patriotism inspires Arnold.

CROWLEY ("Nora"). He is an old Irish builder in Hazlett's play "Nora." He wants crooked politician Collins to throw business his way. Collins gambles, goes to prison, leaves his son John Collins penniless. John loves Crowley's niece Nora Crowley.

CROWLEY, NORA ("Nora"). She is Crowley's niece in Hazlett's play "Nora." She falls in love with John Collins.

CUCKOO ("Poodle") *see* **HUGHES, PHIL**

CUNNINGHAM, GEORGE ("Holycaust"). Jessie writes Danny that George Cunningham was rescued by Marion Sligar from the Byrd-Watson building during the Centralia fire.

"CURED!" (*The Red Book*, March 1931; SC). (Characters: Sammy Burns, Mike Clayton, Colton, Mrs. Colton, Duane, Myrna Evick, Joe Gale, Rudy Miller, Olga, Dick Streeter, Mary Streeter, Paul Stroud, Watson, Dr. Wendell.)

Dick and Mary Streeter live in Westchester County, 30 miles from New York. He has a "great job" in New York as a comic-strip artist for the Duane Syndicate. He thirsts for all alcoholic drinks except "light wines and beer." If he drinks, he drinks too much to be able to recover, have breakfast, and go to work. They dine at friends' homes, but he's tedious when he drinks excessively, bored when he doesn't, and grows "party-shy." Mary makes excuses for Dick when they get more invitations, and he sometimes persuades her to accept and go alone. He stays home alone and reads a little. Sammy Burns, his understudy, for "a paltry two hundred dollars a week" draws cartoons exactly like Dick's. Dick often goes to New York alone and drinks at Mike Clayton's upstairs speakeasy with buddies Joe Gale, Rudy Miller, and Paul Stroud. They aren't "woman-crazy"; they like their wives well enough; if occasionally they get home a day or more late "it was ... because the trip was ... an effort"; taxis are costly, and train passengers talk excessively.

For two months Dick, staying sober, has "golfed himself into ... uncomfortable healthiness." So when Mary's close friend Mrs. Colton invites Mary and Dick to a dinner party tomorrow night for eight, including the Coltons, Mary says Dick might be working on his Sunday layout. Dick says let's accept. Mary reminds him he has to sign his new contract tomorrow morning. He promises to do so, catch the 2:35 train back home, and be in time for the party. She says he often misses trains. Not to worry, he replies. So Mary phones Mrs. Colton they're "tickled to accept." Next morning Dick signs again for Mr. Watson, Duane Syndicate owner, who praises his appearance and asks how long he'll be on the wagon. Dick says he probably won't ever drink again. After a haircut, shave, and shine, he chances to walk toward Grand Central Station near Clayton's, has his shiny shoe stept on by a mounted cop's horse, and limps into Clayton's, where Joe, Rudy, and Paul easily persuade him to drink and joke, catch a later train, a still later train, and still attend the party.

After six drinks Dick phones Mary at 4:40 P.M., aware that the Coltons and their guests would see he'd "fallen from grace," and asks her to "get me out of going." She says she'll get them both out of going and asks what day he'll be home. Dick rejoins his pals, has two more drinks, and they sing for three hours. After 40 hours, Dick returns home.

When Dick awakens next afternoon, Mary explains that her friend Myrna Evick has recommended Dr. Wendell, a "psychologist and psychiatrist" who thoroughly cured Myrna's brother of drinking, and that Dr. Wendell is coming now. Gruff and walrus-mustached, the doctor quizzes Dick about his parents and family. He answers, "nearly perfect." Interrogated further, Dick says he likes to drink, it provides "a kind of mental release," he isn't depressed, and the drive to drink "comes ... suddenly." When Mary says Dick claims drinking is "a disease," not "a bad habit," Dr. Wendell says Dick is "perfectly right." Mary is sorry she spoke.

Dick agrees to hole up in a hotel a while, and Mary will go visit her aunt in Maine. For two-plus weeks, Dr. Wendell checks on Dick at 4:00–5:00 every afternoon. He regularly finds Dick abed, "thin and sober." Because every 5:00 P.M. to the next 4:00 A.M. Dick has been drinking and singing with his cronies at Claytons, then "a bath and a barber," and bedding down breakfastless. When the third week starts, Dick finds "Mary's absence" unbearable, tells Dr. Wendell on Tuesday he wants her back Thursday, tells him to give him one powerful sleeping pill, pronounce him cured, and accept full credit. Dick wires Mary to return. She wires she'll arrive Thursday at 9:00 A.M.

Dick avoids Clayton's Tuesday night, sleeps until Thursday morning, catches a shave and clam broth, and greets Mary so warmly that witnesses smile "a little wistfully." While they breakfast before catching the 9:58 A.M. for home, Dick "choked down some wheatcakes" and praises the doctor. Mary says she "had the right hunch." Dick wonders if they should invite the Coltons for dinner and bridge tonight. Mary suggests staying "home together, alone." For a month all's well. "So the cure is beginning to look permanent."

The height of irony is reached, along with bubbling high notes, when Dick, Jim, Rudy, and Paul strike up the song that goes "I want a girl just like the girl that married dear old Dad." Jonathan Yardley, locating autobiographical touches in "Cured!," observes not only that "Ring is clearly on the side of Dick Streeter, ... [with] obvious memories of Ring's periods on the wagon in the story," but also that "there is the pleasure Streeter finds in the company of his buddies at Mike Clayton's speakeasy." Douglas Robinson believes that while Lardner's earlier story about alcoholism, "Sun Cured" (1927), "denies" the possibility of a cure," "Cured!" "asserts the possibility of a cure." Such optimism is unwarranted. Mary dislikes hearing that alcoholism is a disease and may therefore lapse into an enabler role again. She has been deceived into believing Dick is cured. When she becomes less magnetic to Dick, he may lapse all by himself. Donald Elder regards the exclamation point in the title "Cured!" as "significant." Will it cause some readers to muse, then say, "Yeah? What cure?" (Sources: Elder, 228; Robinson, 88; Yardley, 374)

CURTIS (*Own Your Own Home*). He is in the business of selling wood and coal in Allison. He and his wife thrill Fred and Grace by visiting them. The four play cards with Carry and his wife. The Curtises entertain Fred and Grace, who then include them in Fred and Grace's big party. When Curtis drinks too much and makes too much noise, the night watchman breaks up the party.

CURTIS, MRS. (*Own Your Own Home*). She and her husband delight Fred and Grace by paying them a surprise visit. Fred and Grace remain friendly with the Curtises, are entertained by them, and invite them to their party.

CUTSHAW ("Where Do You Get That Noise?"). In a game against the narrator's team, Brooklyn's Cutshaw hits a fly into center field. Carey throws home wild, and Wheat scores from third. Hawley outrages Carey by phony words of sympathy.

George William Cutshaw (1887–1973) played for the Brooklyn Dodgers (1912–1917), the Pittsburgh Pirates (1918–1921), and the Detroit Tigers (1922–1923). (Sources: *Baseball Encyclopedia*, 933; Hilton, 519)

CUTTING In "The Busher Comes Back," Keefe gets Al to rent Cutting's "yellow house" in Bedford for him, because he is marrying Hazel Carney, then says he is not to do so because the marriage is off, then says to do so because he is marrying Florence. In "The Busher's Kid," when Keefe plans to move for the winter to Bedford, he asks Al to get Cutting to renew the house lease.

CUTTS, MISS ("Now and Then"). She is Mrs. Griffin's sister. Bob meets Miss Cutts, as well as both Griffins, during his and his wife Irma's second trip to the Bahamas. Bob neglects Irma to have fun with Miss Cutts.

D. (*The Real Dope*). He is a friend back home of George Shaffer, a fellow soldier with Keefe in France. Keefe reads part of a letter in which Shaffer asks his addressee to tell D. that he's on the wagon except for some "Vin Blank."

DAD ("Mamma"). This is the affectionate way Mamma refers to her husband.

DALE ("Where Do You Get That Noise?"). Hawley theorizes that if Dale, with a non–German name, should pitch well for Cincinnati, it would distress citizens with German names.

Emmett Eugene Dale (1889–1958) pitched for the St. Louis Cardinals (1911–1912) and the Cincinnati Reds (1915–1916), after which he was suspended and quit playing baseball. (Sources: *Baseball Encyclopedia*, 1924; Hilton, 514)

DALEY ("A Frame-Up"). He has a place in or near New York where boxers train. Burke prepares there for his fight with Willie Kemp.

DALEY, HERBERT (*The Big Town*). He is a wealthy, loud-mouthed, but generous and basically good owner of a stable of racehorses. He meets Finch, Ella Finch, and her sister Katie at the Decker Hotel on Long Island. He befriends and successfully proposes marriage to Katie, but then learns Katie is dating his dishonest jockey Sid Mercer, who throws a big race. Finch could have warned Daley but was bad-mouthed by him and therefore didn't.

When Finch reminisces about former horse races, he mentions a blow-hard gambler who boasts of knowing Madden. John Edward Madden (1856–1929) was a Pennsylvania-born horse breeder and trainer, who raced his own stable of horses, and was eventually a self-made millionaire. He sold one horse to millionaire mine-owner Marcus Daly (1841–1900). Though unlikely, Lardner may have known about Daly and named Herbert Daley after him.

DALY ("The Busher's Welcome Home"). Daly hits a winning homer against Keefe, who is pitching in a game in London, played during the world tour of White Sox and Giants baseball players.

Thomas Daniel Daly (1891–1946) played for the Chicago White Sox (1913–1915), the Cleveland Indians (1916), and the Chicago Cubs (1918–1921). James E. Elfers reports that Daly did indeed hit that game-winning home run in London, on February 26, 1914, against Urban ("Red") Faber. (Sources: *Baseball Encyclopedia*, 937; Elfers, xvii, 235)

DALY, CORPORAL (*Treat 'Em Rough*). He is a non-com in Jack Keefe's army unit. Daly forced Nick Sebastian to take a shower.

DANA ("Oh, You Bonehead!"). He is an assistant working under the Coach of an unnamed football team. He and Bert Harris, another assistant, listen as the Coach explains why he didn't criticize Dickie after he made a costly"bonehead" play.

DANA ("A One-Man Team"). He is an assistant football coach under Coach Belden. He believes that having defeated Monroe's "one-man team" does not mean that Belden's defensive strategy against Doane will automatically mean victory.

DANFORTH In "Along Came Ruth," to warm up, Keefe took batting practice with Danforth, a White Sox pitcher, then pitched badly against the Boston Red Sox. In "The Courtship of T. Dorgan," Danforth relieved Keefe in a game against Cleveland; they both pitched poorly.

David Charles Danforth (1890–1970) pitched for the Philadelphia Athletics (1911–1912), the Chicago White Sox (1916–1919), and the St. Louis Browns (1922–1925). George W. Hilton reports that Danforth had chronic arm trouble. (Sources: *Baseball Encyclopedia*, 1925; Hilton, 175, 325)

DANFORTH, HARRY ("How Are You?"). He is an acquaintance of Bob Dayton and lends Dayton his secretary Mrs. Gurnsey to help out.

DANIELS, JOSEPHUS (1862–1948). North Carolina–born American journalist, publisher, and statesman. He attended the University of North Carolina law school, edited the *State Chronicle* (1885–1894) in Raleigh, North Carolina, founded Raleigh's *News and Observer* (1894) and edited it carefully (1894–1913, then nominally until 1948). Daniels was President Woodrow Wilson's secretary of the navy (1913–1921). President Franklin D. Roosevelt, formerly Daniels' undersecretary of the navy, appointed Daniels ambassador to Mexico (1933–1941). His written works include *Our Navy at War* (1922) and *Life of Woodrow Wilson* (1924).

When Mrs. Gullible in "Three Without, Doubled" breathlessly asks Gullible to guess who telephoned her, he suggests Josephus Daniels or Henry Ford. In *Treat 'Em Rough*, Keefe thinks "Secty. Daniels" is in charge of the American army.

DANIELS, S. P. ("'In Conference'"). He and others work for Kramer & Company. They talk vacantly "in conference." He is a vice president and discusses Scotch with Paul Sickles.

DANVERS, LEFTY (*Treat 'Em Rough*). He was a teammate Keefe recalls playing with in Terre Haute.

DAVE ("Hurry Kane"). He manages the St. Louis baseball team and worries about Hurry Kane.

DAVE ("One Hit, One Error, One Left") *see* **BURNETT, DAVE**

DAVENPORT ("Along Came Ruth"). Keefe mentions that Davenport was wild when he was pitching for St. Louis against the White Sox.

David W. Davenport (1890–1954) pitched for the Cincinnati Reds (1914) and St. Louis in the Federal League (1914–1915), and remained with the St. Louis Browns (1916–1919). (Sources: *Baseball Encyclopedia*, 1927; Hilton, 267)

DAVENPORT, MISS ("Absent-minded Beggar"). She is the pretty but addle-pated secretary in the brokerage firm of J. L. Beaseley and H. N. Comerford. She tries ineffectively to help John Knowles, their new employee.

DAVID (*The Young Immigrunts*). He is the narrator's baby brother, in age "almost nothing." He goes with his brothers John and Jimmie and their nurse by train to "Grenitch Conn."

DAVIES, MARION (1897–1961). Movie actress. Born Marion Cecilia Douras, she was a Broadway chorus girl (1913), a 1916 Follies star of Florenz Ziegfeld,* began a movie career (1917), and became the mistress of William Randolph Hearst (1863–1951). Hearst often bankrolled her lavish, inartistic work. Their affair flourished in lush palaces (to the mid–1930s). Lardner published four articles and three parodies in *Hearst's International* (1923–1924), then 28 stories and two articles in *Hearst's International Cosmopolitan* (1925–1931), including "I Can't Breathe," in which Marion Davies is tactfully mentioned. In a letter (about December 10, 1925) to F. Scott Fitzgerald,* Lardner hints at shenanigans involving Davies, Hearst, Charlie Chaplin,* and Ziegfeld. Jonathan Yardley comments that Lardner "published only six stories between September, 1926 and July, 1927," but that since those six appeared in Hearst's well-heeled *Cosmopolitan*, they earned him $27,000. (Sources: Katz, 347; Caruthers

[1995], 207–208; Farnsworth, 131, 154; Spears, 181, 208. 216, 239; Yardley, 312)

DAVIS ("Freedom of the Press"). He is a *Bulletin* reporter hounding Constance Warner for news.

DAVIS ("Great Blessings"). He is the married son of Mrs. Davis, who is the landlady of Tod Stewart's mother and father. Mrs. Davis tells the Stewarts that her son and his wife need their rooms and therefore they must leave.

DAVIS ("Horseshoes"). He is a coach for the Athletics and chats with Dick Grimes on the bench during the fifth game of their World Series against the Giants.

Harry H. Davis (1873–1947) played for the New York Giants (1895), the Giants and the Pittsburgh Pirates (1896), the Pirates (1897), the Pirates and the Washington Senators (1898), the Senators (1899), the Athletics (1901–1911), the Cleveland Indians (1912), and the Athletics (1913–1917). George W. Hilton says Davis also managed the Cleveland Naps (1912) and coached for the Athletics (1913). (Sources: *Baseball Encyclopedia*, 944–945; Hilton, 415)

DAVIS ("A One-Man Team"). He is Doane's outstanding football player, passes and runs well, and hence is Doane's "one-man team." Coach Belden trains his opposing team to concentrate defensively on Davis and thus win. Belden is surprised and disappointed.

DAVIS ("Sick 'Em"). He is a tough little infielder obtained by Red, Phillies manager of the Phillies, from the New England League. Davis married a beautiful girl. He resents it when Smitty and Fogarty flirt with his innocent bride, who is happily sitting in the stand. So he grabs a bat and hits Smitty in his pitching hand and Fogarty on his pitching arm. When "big Honus" warned Davis to back off to avoid being hurt, Davis challenged him by calling him a "big slob." (Davis is fictional. The reference is to John Peter "Honus" Wagner. See Honus.)

DAVIS, MR. ("Ball-A-Hole"). He is mentioned as a golfer who always tips the narrator, his caddy. He and Mr. Joyce play against Mr. Harper and Mr. McNally for $1 to $5 a hole.

DAVIS, MRS. ("Great Blessings"). She rents rooms to Tod Stewart's old parents. She tells them that her son and his wife need their rooms and they must leave. She undoubtedly manufactured this story to evict the couple, who aren't paying their rent.

DAVIS, MRS. ("Great Blessings"). She is the daughter-in-law of the landlady of Tod Stewart's parents, who are behind in their rent.

DAVIS, MRS. ("Sick 'Em"). She is the bride of Davis, who was acquired by the Phillies. When she waves at Davis, on the bench, Smitty and Fogarty think she is flirting, flirt back, and are injured by Davis, who takes umbrage and a bat.

DAWES, GENERAL CHARLES ("Stop Me — if you've heard This One"). He supposedly wired Henry Wild Osborne to come from New York to Chicago to discuss something important. This is part of Osborne's fib. In reality, Charles Gates Dawes (1865–1951) was a brigadier general with the A.E.F. in France (1917–1919), and a distinguished statesman both before and after serving as vice president during the second term (1925–1929) of President Calvin Coolidge.* (Source: Streissguth, 367)

DAY, CLYDE ("One Hit, One Error, One Left"). He is a Brooklyn pitcher. Danny writes Jessie that Day is nicknamed "Pea ridge Day because he come from a town name Pea ridge"; that Day, a "hog coller from Arkansaw," bothered fans for a while by hog-calling after every pitch; that Day once won a $10 bet by jumping "in a fish pond with his close on," and his big suit "schrink to just the right size." Day has to be fictional.

"A DAY WITH CONRAD GREEN" (*Liberty*, October 3, 1925; LN, PRL, RLR, RU). (Characters: Robert Blair, Bonnie Blue, Brainard, Joyce Brainard, Bryant-Walker, Mrs. Bryant-Walker, Casper Ettelson, Fraser, Conrad Green, Marjorie Green, Harry, Hawley, Miss Jackson, Bert Kalmar, Kate, Lewis, Joe Martin, Ezra Peebles, Herman Plant, Rose, Harry Ruby, Schuyler, Mrs. Schuyler, Sam Stein, Sutton, Mrs. Sutton, Vanderbeck, Mrs. Vanderbeck.)

Conrad Green, a successful theatrical producer, was a guest at the aristocratic Bryant-Walkers last night with Green's wife Marjorie, a former Vanities chorus girl. Conrad let her drive home alone to Long Island, remained, and later went to his rooms in the Ambassador.

Awakening at 10 A.M., Green wonders why he's sad. Oh, yes, his long-time secretary Herman Plant, at $45 a week, just died. Bathed, breakfasted, and barbered, Green goes to his Broadway office. He orders his secretary Miss Jackson to fetch the newspapers. Plant's replacement, Lewis ($60 a week), brings the mail, is rebuked for opening private correspondence, says he was told to do so, talks back, and humbles Green, who checks the society pages, irate that he isn't mentioned in coverage of the Bryant-Walker party. Mrs. Bryant-Walker's secretary phones to request help at her charitable bazaar. He hangs up on her. Miss Jackson reports that she sent a $45 bouquet to Plant's funeral. Green gripes. Robert Blair enters, to summarize a scene he's planning for Green. Green disapproves, ejects him, sends for his chief librettist Joe Martin, and checks his safe for a rope of pearls, just arrived from Philadelphia. Miss Jackson shows *Gay New York* reporter Hawley in. He persuades Green to place a $1,500 *Gay* advertisement because his colleague might otherwise disclose a gambling debt Green is welshing on. Lewis asks what to do with Plant's final $45 check. Green says destroy it, he'll send Mrs. Plant more, but he doesn't.

Green lunches large at the Astor, happy to hear his name whispered by admirers. Back at work, he summarizes Blair's plot to Martin, who retorts it's something already staged. Miss Jackson reminds Green it's time to attend Plant's funeral. Green tells Lewis that lunch upset him and orders Lewis to represent him at the funeral. Green's wife Marjorie enters, griping that their names were omitted from the Bryant-Walker write-up. Green lies that he hasn't seen the newspapers. Marjorie asks him if he's forgotten something. To prove he knows it's her birthday today (which he had forgotten), he extracts the pearls from the safe. She is thrilled. They'll celebrate at dinner: Ambassador, 6:30 P.M. She leaves. Rose enters, demands the pearls he promised if she'd leave Harry, doesn't believe his lie that they haven't arrived yet from Philadelphia, says Harry will be her lover for now, and storms out. Green calls Mrs. Bryant-Walker and promises help at her bazar. Lewis returns from Plant's funeral and says that Mrs. Plant wishes Green had been there. Green wishes so too.

The plot contortions in "A Day with Conrad Green" are so transparent that they amount to little more than dialogical slapstick. Jonathan Yardley finds the story lacking in the "vigor and bite" of earlier stories. He adds that Green "is etched not in acid but in sour milk," with "devices" betraying him "as a cad ... embarrassingly obvious"—the "cad" bearing many resemblances to Florenz Ziegfeld.* Earlier, Josephine Herbst noted—too generously?—that Lardner "scorches [Ziegfeld] as a slippery heel with the geniality peculiar to people who have done something disgraceful." (Sources: Elder, 268; Herbst, vii; Yardley, 292)

DAYTON, BETH ("How Are You?"). She is Bob Dayton's wife, dislikes his paying attention to Hilda Pratt, and is indifferent to his hypochondria. She insists on going with him on a vacation.

DAYTON, BOB ("How Are You?"). He is a non-productive New York businessman, eats too much candy, is persuaded that he has a variety of physical ailments, and after expensive, often useless examinations learns he has badly infected teeth. He and his wife Beth then vacation in the South.

DAZZY ("Lose with a Smile") *see* **VANCE**

DEAL, ELINOR ("Rhythm"). She is probably Spencer Deal's wife. Harry Hart enjoys "hobnobbing" with her.

DEAL, SPENCER ("Rhythm"). He is a musicologist who "discovers" Harry Hart, puffs his "new American jazz" rhythms in a pretentious article, introduces him to salonist Peggy Leech, and makes Hart think he's an important composer not a tune thief. Hart's collaboration with Deal, a would-be lyricist, displeases Frank Tours, Conrad Green's musical consultant.

DEAN ("Reunion"). This is the name of a family in Buchanan, Michigan. While Bob Mason is gossiping to his sister Rita Johnston about Tom Allen and his sister Louise Allen, he says that the Allens lived near door to the Dean family.

DEAN, DIZZY ("Meet Me in St. Louie"). Danny Warner, who plays for Brooklyn, says that his manager Max Carey wants to schedule "[Dazzy] Vance to pitch again Dean so as it will be Dazzy again Dizzy."

Jay Hanna Dean (1910–1974) pitched for the St. Louis Cardinals (1930–1937), the Chicago Cubs (1938–1941), and the St. Louis Browns (1947), and was elected to the Baseball Hall of Fame (1953). (Source: *Baseball Encyclopedia*, 1953)

DEAN, GIFFORD ("The Jade Necklace"). He plays the naval lieutenant in *The Jade Necklace*, the movie L. N. Bauer produces.

DECKER (*The Big Town*). He owns the Hotel Decker on Long Island. Finch's acquaintance Gene Buck recommends this hotel for Finch, his wife Ella, and her sister Katie to spend the summer in, to avoid New York's hot weather.

"DECORATED" (*Saturday Evening Post*, October 26, 1918; RD).

DEMAREE ("Horseshoes"). He is a competent Giant relief pitcher during the fifth game of their World Series against the Athletics.

Albert Wentworth Demaree (1884 or 1886–1962) pitched for the New York Giants (1912–1914), the Philadelphia Phillies (1915–1916), the Chicago Cubs and the Giants (1917), the Giants (1918), and the Boston Braves (1919). George W. Hilton notes that Demaree later became a successful sports cartoonist. (Sources: *Baseball Encyclopedia*, 1934; Hilton, 415)

DEMPSEY, DEMON ("Champion"). He is a boxer whom Midge Kelly defeats in Milwaukee.

DEMPSEY, JACK (1895–1983). Champion prize-fighter. William Harrison "Jack" Dempsey was born in Manassa, Colorado, and was a hard-rock miner and a brawler in Western saloon yards. In his boxing career he defeated Jess Willard* (Toledo, July 4, 1919) to win the world heavyweight title, and held it against Billy Miske (1920), Georges Carpentier (1921), and Luis Angel Firpo (1923). Dempsey lost to Gene Tunney (1926) and in "The Battle of the Long Count" (1927). In 69 bouts, Dempsey won 47 by knockouts. He fought only in profitable exhibition matches thereafter (1931–1932) and became a popular New York restaurant owner.

For the Bell Syndicate, Lardner wrote 13 columns on the Dempsey-Willard fight (June 22-July 5, 1919), 15 columns about the Dempsey-Carpentier fight (June 19–July 3, 1921), 14 about the Dempsey-Firpo fight (September 3–15, 1923), and two on the 1926 Dempsey-Tunney fight (September 24, 1926). "Carpenteer," Dempsey, and Firpo are mentioned in "The Venomous Viper of the Folga." Lardner evidently wrote the column on the Dempsey-Tunney fight published as by Grantland Rice* in the *New York Herald Tribune* (September 24, 1926). In a letter (October 13, 1926) to F. Scott Fitzgerald,* Lardner called the Dempsey-Tunney fight "a very well done fake." Donald Elder and Jonathan Yardley discuss Lardner's admiration for Dempsey, especially in connection with Lardner's reporting on the Dempsey-Willard match. Dempsey is mentioned in *The Big Town*, "Champion," The Courtship of T. Dorgan," "High-rollers," "The Jade Necklace," "When the Moon Comes over the Mountain," and *The Young Immigrunts*. (Sources: Bruccoli and Layman, 374; Elder, 158–159 and *passim*; Caruthers [1995], 205; Streissguth, 13, 43, 112, 216, 231–232, 241, 368; Yardley, 210–211 and *passim*)

DENNIS, KATHLEEN ("KATHIE") ("Bob's Birthday"). She is Bob Tyler's young girlfriend. They are in love, but Bob must support his parasitic family, of whom her father disapproves.

DENNIS, MR. ("Bob's Birthday"). He is evidently a wealthy executive. He disapproves of his daughter Kathleen's relationship with Bob Tyler, a fine teenage musician who is burdened by having to support a selfish family.

DENTAL FLOSS ("Claude Diphthong, Student of Crime") *see* **LAWLOW, FLOSSIE**

DE SETTO ("Absent-minded Beggar"). He is a character in the early version of John Knowles's libretto.

DETROIT TIGERS An American League baseball team (1901–). (Sources: Light, 206–209; Streissguth, 43)

DEVORE ("Back to Baltimore"). In a game against the Phillies, Devore, playing for Boston, walks. When William Baker, Jr., is hit by a pitch, he is too dumb to go to first, because he says Dixon, Boston's manager, ordered him to bunt.

Joshua Devore (1887–1954) played for the New York Giants (1908–1912), the Giants and the Cincinnati Reds and the Philadelphia Phillies (1913), and the Phillies and the Boston Braves (1914). George W. Hilton reports that Devore was obtained from the Phillies by the Braves (July 3, 1914) in time for the action of "Back to Baltimore." Hilton also notes an anachronism in the story: Devore went to the Braves "four days after Perdue was dealt to the Cardinals." (Sources: *Baseball Encyclopedia*, 960; Hilton, 438)

DEWEY, K. M. ("'In Conference'"). He and others work for Kramer & Company. While "in conference" they talk vacantly. He is a vice president, and mentions a letter he and his wife received that wasn't addressed to them.

DEWEY, MRS. ("'In Conference'"). Her husband tells his associates when they are "in conference" that after he and his wife got a letter not addressed to them she figured it "don't belong to us at all."

DIAMOND JOE ("Alibi Ike"). He works in New York and sells Alibi Ike the engagement ring he gives Dolly.

DICK ("A Caddy's Diary"). He is the diarist, 16. To keep his caddying job and get tips, he must lie and cheat to help various golfers improve their scores. Joe Bean, a wise young caddy, advises him to shut up about it all.

DICK ("Haircut") *see* **WHITEY**

DICKIE ("Oh, You Bonehead!"). He is a football player whom the Coach resists calling a "bonehead" when he makes a poor play costing the team a victory, and instead praises him gently. When the Coach's assistants, Dana and Bert Harris, wonder why, the Coach explains.

DICKIE ("A One-Man Team"). He is a member of Coach Belden's football team. Belden tells him not to miss practice even if it means cutting a class.

DICKSON, PAUL ("Haircut"). He is the mentally challenged butt of Jim Kendall's cruel humor, which costs Jim his life.

DIGMAN ("Hurry Kane"). He plays short stop for St. Louis. Sam Morris bribes him and Stout to throw the crucial St. Louis-White Sox game. They try but fail. (Digman's name is also given as Dignan.)

DIGNAN, HAZEL ("Travelogue"). She and her friend Mildred Orr meet Dan Chapman while all three are traveling by train from Chicago to San Francisco. Hazel monopolizes the conversation with boasting and gossip to such an extent that Chapman ultimately prefers Mildred.

DIGNAN, MISS ("Freedom of the Press"). She is a *Mail* reporter hounding Constance Warner for news.

DIMITRI ("How Are You?"). He is Wallie Pratt's wolfhound. Bob Dayton, who admires Wallie's wife Hilda, wonders why Willie prefers Dmitri to her.

DINNEEN, BILL (*The Real Dope*). While in the army in France, Keefe remembers umpire Bill Dinneen's bad calls during a game Keefe pitched for the Chicago White Sox against "Phila."

"DINNER" (*Harper's Bazar*, September 1928; RLR, RU). (Characters: Harry Barton, Bill, Congressman Burleigh, Miss Coakley, Frank, Lester Graham, Halpern, Grace Halpern, Rosa Raisa, Rell, Lou Rell, Miss Rell, Rimini, Lee Roberts, Mrs. Roberts, Ruffo, Dave Wallace.)

Harry Barton, a good-looking bachelor, 33, reluctantly accepts an invitation from his friend Grace Halpern, when she and her husband can't get a second bachelor to balance genders for a dinner party. Miss Coakley and Miss Rell, Grace's friends from boarding-school days, are visiting New York from Chicago, and the two "peaches" are "free" for bachelors to pursue. Miss Rell asks Barton questions and interrupts his answers with stringy talk. Miss Coakley cannot finish her uninterruptible sentences. Miss Rell disbelieves "Mr. Burton" when he denies working in Wall Street—which earlier triggered her comments on bears and bulls, bullfights, the opera *Carmen*—and wants a tip on General Motors to share with her father. Barton tells her his college was the Electoral College, which makes her say he's an engineer and ask if he plays bridge. She tried auction bridge but then along came contract bridge, for which she lacks nerve to bid slams. She told him earlier she flew with Lindbergh and can swim and dive; so he asks if she flew with Lindbergh and can dive. She says she "read[s] the funny pages ... religiously." To her re-query as to his college, he says "War College," which she knows means West Point, which reminds her of "the Annapolis Navy" and Chicago's "Soldiers' Field." Miss Coakley blurts ocean-liners' names; so Burton says he crossed only on the Santa Maria. Miss Rell wonders if her golfing father could shoot 120. Burton says, "Easily." After Burton and Dave Wallace, the other bachelor guest, compare notes, Burton tells Grace the bootleg scotch she served gave him a headache, he must depart, and her girl guests are "still free."

Lardner gives "Dinner" timely touches by having Miss Rell name (Sidney S.) Lenz (b. 1873), Works, and Whitehall as bridge experts, make mangled mention of Charles Lindbergh (1902–1974) and his Atlantic flight (1927), and Gertrude Ederle (1906–2003) and her English Channel swim (1926), and by having Grace Halpern's brother mangle "Rhapsody in Blue" by George Gershwin.* (Lardner also mentions Lenz in "High-rollers.")

The inane chatter of Miss Rell and Miss Coakley makes for priceless reading. Inattentive Miss Rell is typical of self-absorbed "listeners" alive today. Miss Coakley is gauche in another still-relevant mode. Lardner marks pauses in her verbal associational misfirings with dashes. If alive today, Lardner would be listening but would fill the blanks with what many contemporary American speakers, especially youngsters, adolescents, coeds, athletes both amateur and professional, and cell phone misusers punctuate their dangling sentence fragments with—i.e., "wow," "like," "I mean," and "you know." Douglas Robinson seems too kind to Miss Coakley when he says "it is a safe guess that she was systematically interrupted in her childhood by a talkative parent who urged her to join the conversation, *and* by a taciturn parent who silenced her with a disapproving look." Why not theorize that this airhead's boarding-school was run by Catholic nuns who whacked her for talking, not talking, talking out of turn? Donald Elder lumps "Dinner" and the earlier "Contract" together as "funny if not very deep depictions of social behavior into which Ring put all the weariness and irritation he suffered from rude and boring people." (Sources: Elder, 307; Robinson, 135)

DIPHTHONG, CLAUDE ("Claude Diphthong, Student of Crime"). He is the foppish, dilettante detective who solves the mystery surrounding Gardner Lyle.

DIPHTHONG, VERNE ("Claude Diphthong, Student of Crime"). He is Claude Diphthong's wealthy father. Verne danced so vigorously when he made New York Stock Exchange killings that he was nicknamed "Shake Yo' Feet."

DITTMAR, CARL ("Contract"). He and his wife play serious bridge with Cameron and his wife and Robert French and his wife, until Shelton, a newcomer in the circle, as is his wife, is rebuked for poor play, and turns critical himself.

DITTMAR, MRS. ("Contract"). She and her husband are members of a bridge-playing circle including the Camerons and the Frenches. Shelton, a newcomer with his wife in the group, is tolerant of criticism but soon turns the tables. Among other objects of his targets is Mrs. Dittmar's penchant for baby-talk. Aging, she calls her young husband "Daddy" and feebly tries to rebuke Shelton for being "a mean, bad man ... [who will] make us cwy." Shelton suggests that she pronounce "cry" properly.

DIXON ("Back to Baltimore"). Dixon, the narrator, is the manager and first baseman of the Boston Braves. He gets into unacceptable difficulties with Mrs. Hayes, president of the Braves. She wants him to play William Baker, Jr., an inept athlete but her pet. By a ruse, Dixon rids the team of Baker, but gets fired as manager and will join the Baltimore Feds.

DOANE, MR. ("A Caddy's Diary"). He is a rich member of the golf club where the diarist caddies.

DOANE, MRS. ("A Caddy's Diary"). She is a golfer where she and her rich husband play. The diarist says he would gladly caddy free for her, since "she looks like Lillian Gish[*] and it is a pleasure to just look at her." She smiles at him and also calls him "pal." His helping her cheat enables her to win Miss Rennie's unwanted $100 dress for $50.

DOC ("Back to Baltimore"). He is a Boston Braves trainer, helpful to Dixon, the manager. Doc tries unsuccessfully to get William Baker, Jr., drunk so that Dixon can fire him.

George W. Hilton discovered that Doc was James B. Neary (1878–1944), a competent runner who trained Braves in sprinting techniques (1909–1941) and also worked elsewhere. (Source: Hilton, 433)

DOC ("The Battle of the Century"). He was the physician at the New York hotel where La Chance, the French boxer Goulet's promotor, was staying. When Larry Moon mentioned $200,000 as Goulet's purse, La Chance "swooned." Doc was summoned and concluded that La Chance hadn't had a heart attack but was merely shocked.

DR. ("The Busher Abroad"). He is aboard the ship taking the baseball players around the world. He allegedly treats Herman Dutch Schaefer with "anicdotes" when he allegedly swallows rat poison.

James E. Elfers identifies the doctor as Dr. Frank Finley, who accompanied the players as John J. McGraw's personal physician. (Source: Elfers, xviii)

DR. ("The Busher's Welcome Home"). He is a physician who examines the baseball players in Naples.

DR. ("The Busher's Welcome Home"). He is a Chicago physician who, according to a letter Florrie Keefe wrote Keefe, advised her to take their little Al to California for a change of scenery because he missed daddy so much.

DOCTOR ("Mamma"). Mamma refers to the physician who cared for her husband, son, and daughter, during their attack of the flu, as simply Doctor.

DODE ("Where Do You Get That Noise"?) *see* **PASKERT**

DOLE, EDITH ("There Are Smiles"). She speeds in her Cadillac roadster. Ben Collins, a humor-loving traffic policeman, stops her for speeding down Fifth Avenue. While kidding her, he is captivated by her "impudent, ill-timed, irresistible smile." One rainy afternoon while giving Collins a lift to his home, she tells him her name, says she's getting married somewhat reluctantly, but after leaving him is killed by carelessly skidding into a street-car.

Surely Edith's radiant smile in this 1928 story owes something to that of Jay Gatsby, of *The Great Gatsby* (1925), by F. Scott Fitzgerald,* one of Lardner's closest friends. Flashy yellow cars also figure in both works. And surely Maxwell Geismar is simplistic when he says that "Edith Dole of 'There Are Smiles' believes she is far too adorable to perish in the automobile crash caused by her reckless driving." (Source: Geismar, 10)

DOLLY ("Alibi Ike"). She is Cap's wife's beautiful sister, lives in St. Joe, falls in love with Alibi Ike, accepts his diamond ring, overhears his harmless talk demeaning her, but soon forgives him.

DONAHUE, JERRY ("The Swift Six"). He is a friend of Fred A. Gross. Jerry, who may be a Chicago policeman, warns Fred he's driving his new car without a license.

DONALDSON, WALTER ("Rhythm"). He is praised by Harry Hart for composing "Yes, Sir! That's My Baby!" Willis Merwin, theatrical producer, is contracting with Donaldson and another composer named Gus Kahn to provide melodies for a new show.

Walter Donaldson (1893–1947), Brooklyn-born, was a popular composer, lyricist, and publisher. He and lyricist Gus Kahn created many popular songs, including "Yes, Sir, That's My Baby" (1925).

DONLIN, MIKE ("The Busher Comes Back"). Keefe says Violet's breaking their engagement and planning to marry Joe Hill made him so depressed he considered going to Australia with Mike Donlin. In "The Busher Beats It Hence," Keefe says that Dutch Schaefer ribbed him that he was "hog fat" compared to Mike Donlin and Wiltse. In "The Busher Abroad," Keefe mentions Donlin.

Michael Joseph Donlin (1878–1933) played for the St. Louis Cardinals (1899–1900), the Cincinnati Reds (1902–1903), the Reds and the New York Giants (1904), the Giants (1905–1908), the Giants and the Boston Braves (1911), the Pittsburgh Pirates (1912), and the Giants (1914). George W. Hilton says that Donlin was a vaudeville performer and participated in the White Sox-Giants world tour. James E. Elfers reports this: Donlin was a "[h]ard-drinking actor/baseball player with a vicious, violent temper"; he "once served jail time for assaulting a woman"; and he was "especially awed," as were other "former jailbirds," when the baseball players all visited the well-managed Bilibid Prison in the Philippines. (Sources: *Baseball Encyclopedia*, 969; Elfers, [xvii]–xviii, 31, 143; Hilton, 94)

DONOHUE, JIMMY ("The Venomous Viper of the Volga"). He is a boxer. Fight promoters Luke Lewis and Sandy King are aware that he "can hit" but is too small to be matched against Jack Ryan.

DOOIN, RED In "Back to Baltimore," he plays for the Phillies. In a game against the Boston Braves, he grounded toward William Baker, Jr., who was playing first base and jumped to avoid the ball. Baker then chased him instead of trying to throw him out. (See also Red ["Sick 'Em"].) In "The Busher Abroad," Keefe mentions Dooin.

Charles Sebastian Dooin (1879–1952) played for the Philadelphia Phillies (1902–1914), managed the Phillies (1910–1914), and played for the Cincinnati Reds and the New York Giants (1915) and the Giants (1916). (Sources: *Baseball Encyclopedia*, 691, 971; Hilton, 362)

DORAN ("The Crook"). He was pitching for Larry's White Sox in a baseball game against Washington when a play at first base confused them. Larry criticized Bull, the umpire, for calling the batter safe. Bull joshed Larry right back.

George W. Hilton believes that although Doran is a fictional character here, "the name is an adaptation of George H. Doran, publisher of the first book edition of *You Know Me Al*." It may be added that Thomas J. Doran (1880–1910) and William James Doran (1900–1978) were both major-league baseball players. (Sources: *Baseball Encyclopedia*, 971, 972; Hilton, 558)

DORAN (*The Real Dope*). He is a sailor aboard Keefe's troop ship. He and others kid Keefe.

DORGAN, MRS. MARGARET ("Champion"). She is a sympathetic neighbor of Ellen F. Kelly, Midge Kelly's mother.

DORGAN, TOM ("The Courtship of T. Dorgan"). He is, according to Keefe, the White Sox "3th string catcher." He rooms with Keefe during away games. Dorgan likes Miss Josie Mulvihill, who Keefe fancies prefers him. When shy Dorgan asks Keefe to commend him in a letter to

Josie, Keefe thinks he is doing so but really is critical. Even so, Tom and Josie decide to get married.

George W. Hilton notes that the fictional character Dorgan is named after Thomas Aloysius "Tad" Dorgan (1877–1929), sports cartoonist and Lardner's friendly Great Neck, Long Island, neighbor. Donald Elder and Jonathan Yardley discuss the real Dorgan. (Sources: Elder, 158, 176–177; Hilton, 28, 280; Yardley, 210)

DORSEY, JESS ("The Spinning Wheel"). He is a handsome, widowered roulette dealer. Amy Bennett encourages his advances in the hope that he'll cheat and enable her and her "brother" (really a stupid fellow conspirator) to win at the wheel. They lose, but so does Jess, who trusted and fell in love with her.

DOUGLAS, HANK ("The Crook"). He played for the St. Louis Browns in a game against Larry's White Sox. When Bull, the home-plate umpire, called Douglas out, he said Bull favored the home team and was "yellow." Bull mildly replied by calling Douglas "Brown."

DOUTHIT ("Holycaust"). He is a Cincinnati outfielder. Danny, playing for Brooklyn, boasts that he hit a ball so far that while Douthit was chasing it Danny scored a homer.

Taylor Douthit (1901–1986) played outfield for the St. Louis Cardinal (1923–1930), the Cardinals and the Cincinnati Reds (1931), the Reds (1932), and the Reds and the Chicago Cubs (1933). (Source: *Baseball Encyclopedia*, 973)

DOWNEY, GABRIEL ("Claude Diphthong, Student of Crime"). He is the *Morning Light* police reporter who brings Claude Diphthong to the murder scene.

Lardner undoubtedly concocted the name Gabriel Downey with the Rio San Gabriel Park in Downey, California, in mind.

DOYLE ("Alibi Ike"). He plays for the New York baseball team. Alibi Ike makes excuses after brilliantly catching Doyle's fly ball. Doyle is probably Larry Doyle (*which see*).

DOYLE (*The Big Town*). He runs a New York establishment where Finch plays "intercollegiate kelly pool" and at one point wins $75.

DOYLE, BILL ("The Hold-Out"). He was evidently a scout who saw Lahey playing first base for Davenport and persuaded Mr. Edwards to buy him.

DOYLE, JACK ("A Busher's Letters Home"). Keefe says Jack Doyle, White Sox scout, observed him in Terre Haute and "wired Comiskey to buy me," which he did.

John Joseph Doyle (1869–1958), born in Killorglin, Ireland, played for the Cleveland Indians (1891), the Indians and the New York Giants (1892), the Giants (1893–1895), the Washington Senators and the Giants (1898), the Giants (1899–1900), the Chicago Cubs (1901), the Giants and the Senators (1902), the Brooklyn Dodgers (1903), the Dodgers and the Philadelphia Phillies (1904), and the New York Yankees (1905), and then was the chief scout for the White Sox in the Central League. George W. Hilton reports that when Lardner was a reporter for the South Bend *Times* (1906–1907), he became friendly with Doyle. (Sources: *Baseball Encyclopedia*, 691, 975–976; Hilton, 35)

DOYLE, LARRY In "Horseshoes," he is an infielder for the Giants during their World Series against the Athletics. In the second game, he puts Plank out. In the third game, Doyle pops up trying to bunt, which enables Bush to remain pitching for the Athletics. In "The Busher Beats It Hence," Keefe mentions Doyle as one "of them ... real stars" on the world tour. Later, Keefe complains that when he was pitching in San Francisco, Doyle got three lucky pop hits that the wind blew into the stands. Keefe mentions "larry Doyle" in "The Busher Abroad" as playing well and as being the Giants captain during the famous 1913–1914 around-the-world tour.

Lawrence Joseph Doyle (1886–1974) played for the New York Giants (1907–1915), the Giants and the Chicago Cubs (1916, the Cubs (1917), and the Giants 1918–1920). James E. Elfers reports that Doyle got married shortly before the world tour began; that therefore "he and his wife, Edith, had an around-the-world honeymoon"; and, for good measure, that he won "two hats full of Francs" gambling in Monte Carlo on an off-day during the tour (February 14, 1914). Sources: *Baseball Encyclopedia*, 976; Elfers, xviii, 217; Hilton, 179)

DRAKE, BEN ("Liberty Hall"). He is a talented New York composer for musical comedies. He hates to go visit friends, makes his wife stop doing so, and ultimately leaves her alone often. His scheme to escape unpleasant hosts and hostesses backfires at the posh residence of Hilda and Ralph Thayer.

Clifford M. Caruthers says that "Lardner himself identified, one suspects, with Ben Drake." (Source: Caruthers [1973], 118)

DRAKE, MRS. ("Liberty Hall"). She is the narrator and recounts her talented husband Ben Drake's difficulties in trying to avoid being treated to too much hospitality.

DRAKE, SAM ("Absent-minded Beggar"). He is the ill-tempered fiancé of Irene Comerford, until she falls in love with John Knowles.

DRAPER, JOE ("Oh, You Bonehead!"). He was a star runner and kicker on the Coach's Leighton football team. Earlier, he was a winning member of Murphy's Leighton track team. In the last moments of the Coach's game against Pelham, Joe misunderstood the Coach's sent-in order, drop-kicked for three points, and lost the game 7–6. The Coach called Joe a bonehead and rebuked him so severely that Joe lost his girlfriend and quit school. Murphy lectured the Coach helpfully for his vicious egotism.

Quite rightly, Lardner doesn't dignify and particularize Joe's feckless girlfriend by assigning her a name. She remains an unpleasant type.

DREW ("Along Came Ruth"). He is a rookie Cleveland catcher. When batting against Sothoron, the St. Louis pitcher, he is kidded by St. Louis infielders that he will hit into a double play. So he deliberately strikes out and boasts about it.

DREW ("Sun Cured"). He is Ben Drew's brother. The two are partners in a Brooklyn furniture business. His illness delays but doesn't prevent Ben's vacationing with Fretts in Florida.

DREW, BEN ("Sun Cured"). He and his brother own a furniture–business partnership in Brooklyn. Delayed by his brother's illness, Ben arrives late, with Stevens, his girlfriend, to vacation in Florida with his friend Ernie Fretts. Once there, Ben and Stevens party strenuously to make up for lost time.

DREW, DOROTHY (Wedding Day"). She plays "soubrette" roles in New York musical comedies. She attends the wedding of her colleagues Brownie Burt and Jimmy Shane and jibes at Jimmy later, perhaps through jealousy.

DRISCOLL ("How Are You?"). He and his wife are new friends of Bob and Beth Dayton. When they call on the Daytons, Driscoll and Beth discuss "old houses."

DRISCOLL ("The Jade Necklace"). He is the Hollywood director of *The Jade Necklace*, the movie scripted by Earl Benham for L. N. Bauer, the head of Colossal Films Incorporated. Driscoll must know, though Bauer doesn't, that Benham's plot parallels that of *Madame Butterfly.*

DRISCOLL, DAVE ("When the Moon Comes over the Mountain"). Danny says that Dave Driscoll is "the secy" of the Brooklyn baseball team.

DRISCOLL, MRS. ("How Are You?"). She and her husband are new acquaintances of Bob and Beth Dayton. When the Driscolls visit the Daytons, Mrs. Driscoll tells Bob that Dr. George Phelon is New York's best diagnostician.

DRURY ("How Are You?"). He was fortunately a patient of pyorrhea-expert Dr. Clague, according to information Mrs. Gurnsey shares with Bob Dayton.

DUANE ("Champion"). He owns a bar in Milwaukee where Midge Kelly drinks, runs up a bill, and doesn't pay.

DUANE ("Cured!"). The Duane Syndicate has Dick Streeter, an alcoholic cartoonist, under contract.

DUANE, VIVIAN In "One Hit, One Error, One Left," she is the pretty phone operator in the Clearwater hotel where Danny and fellow Brooklyn baseball players stay. Danny writes his girlfriend Jessie that he likes Vivian, she wants him to find her a job up in Brooklyn, she plays the piano well, and he is having her mail two sponges to Jessie for him. Jessie replies sarcastically about "Miss Duane." Danny is too dumb to realize he's playing with fire behaving as he does. In "When the Moon Comes over the Mountain," Danny writes Jessie about Vivian's wanting a job in Brooklyn. He adds that she sent him a photo of herself in a "batheing suit." In "Lose with a Smile," Danny writes Jessie about Vivian's piano-playing and her desire to work in Brooklyn. In "Holycaust," Vivian came to Brooklyn and got in touch with Danny, who entertained her in New York and thus derailed his friendship with Jessie. In "The Ides of June," Danny keeps on writing Jessie about seeing Vivian. He wished she'd return to Florida, but when he took her to "n y" she advised him to try a crooning career.

One can suppose that Lardner saw the baseball movie *One Touch of Nature* (1917), in which actress Viola Cain marries a Yale College baseball player, whose wealthy father disapproves. The name Viola Cain, however, closely resembles Vivian Duane. Anyway, Danny didn't distance himself from Vivian Duane because her initials are "V.D." (Source: Spears, 256. 260)

DUBUQUE ("The Busher Comes Back"). Keefe boasts that his White Sox team "made a monkey out of Dubuque, or whatever his name is."

Jean Arthur Dubuc (1888–1958) pitched for the Cincinnati Reds (1908–1909), the Detroit Tigers (1912–1916), the Boston Braves (1918), and the New York Giants (1919). He was banned from baseball in connection with the 1919 Black Sox Scandal. (Sources: *Baseball Encyclopedia*, 978; Hilton, 80)

DUFFY, MR. (*The Young Immigrunts*). He is a friend of the narrator's father. While driving part of his family to "Grenitch Conn.," the father stops in Syracuse, where Mr. Duffy lives. He tries unsuccessfully to persuade the father to accompany him to a boxing match.

DUGAN, JIM ("The Battle of the Century"). He was a big professional boxer. His manager, Larry Moon, promoted several fights for him. He won them all. Owing to Larry's connivance, Dugan next boxed Goulet for an enormous purse. One wonders how much Larry kept.

DUGAN, JOE ("Women"). He played third base for Huggins's New York team. Mike Healy says Huggins would have hired him to replace Dugan except that a girlfriend fibbed to Huggins that Mike wasn't in his hotel room to see him.

DUMONT In "The Courtship of T. Dorgan," he is a hair-dresser partner of Florrie Keefe, as is Mrs. Dumont. The two have a car and drive Florrie and Keefe around, often with Tom Dorgan and Miss Josie Mulvihill along. In "The Busher Pulls a Mays," Florrie "don't get along very good with the Dumonts," who buy her out.

DUMONT, MRS. ("The Courtship of T. Dorgan"). She and her husband are partners in the beauty parlor in which Florrie Keefe invests and works. The Dumonts and the Keefes are friendly with Tom Dorgan and Miss Josie Mulvihill. In "The Busher Pulls a Mays," the Dumonts buy back Forrie's share in the business.

DUNHAM, MR. ("A Caddy's Diary"). He and his business partner Mr. Blake play golf at the club where the diarist caddies. The caddy calls Mr. Dunham the "worst man player" there.

DUNNIE In "Horseshoes," he manages the Baltimore team, likes Dick Grimes when he plays there, and reluctantly releases him to the Athletics. In "Back to Baltimore," Dixon, manager of the Boston Braves, recalls that when he played for Dunnie "Them Baltimore people used to like me O.K."

George W. Hilton identifies "Dunnie" as John Joseph Dunn (1872–1928), successful owner-manager of the International League Baltimore Orioles (1907–1925). (Source: Hilton, 405)

DUTCHMAN, THE ("Champion") *see* Goetz, Young

DUTTON, MRS. ("The Swift Six"). She is Grace Gross's friend. They see a piano for sale in Chicago. Grace buys even though no one in the Gross family can play it.

DWAN, JIM ("Ex Parte"). He and his wife Mildred entertain the narrator and his wife Florence in their home, which is a "reorganized barn." The two women spend so much time admiring the renovated place and the awkward old furniture in it that Jim doesn't have time to serve cocktails.

The name Dwan surely came to Lardner from that of Allan Dwan (1885–1981), who enjoyed a long career as a movie director (from the 1910s). Among the stars he directed were Mary Pickford* and Gloria Swanson.* (Source: Spears, 33, 154)

DWAN, MILDRED ("Ex Parte"). She is Jim Dwan's wife. She and the narrator's wife are friends from schooldays together. They gush over their preference of old houses with old furniture in them.

EARL, FRANK In "Lose with a Smile," he is a Brooklyn rookie pitcher. Glenn Wright, team captain, praises his deceptive delivery. Danny, who feels that Frank will be cut from the team, visits the home of Frank and his wife for meals. In "Holycaust," Danny writes Jessie that Earl has been sent to Hartford.

EARL, MRS. In "Lose with a Smile," she is Brooklyn pitcher Frank Earl's wife. Danny, also a Brooklyn player, visits the Earls and is encouraged to "groon [croon]" when Mrs. Earl plays the piano. In a letter to Jessie, Danny calls Mrs. Earl "dum." In "Holycaust," Danny blames her because her "sister and law" Miss Fleming has caused trouble between Danny and Jessie.

EARLY, DOC ("Insomnia"). He told the sleepless author "the other night" about Allan and

Edith Spears. The author hopes to convert their activities into a short story.

EASTERLY ("A Busher's Letters Home"). Keefe says Callahan stupidly had Easterly pinch hit for him when Keefe was pitching for the White Sox against the St. Louis Browns.

Theodore Harrison Easterly (1885 or 1886–1951) played for the Cleveland Indians (1909–1911), the Indians and the Chicago White Sox (1912), and the White Sox (1913). (Sources: *Baseball Encyclopedia*, 988; Hilton, 64–65)

EATON ("Oh, You Bonehad!"). He was Pelham's quarterback "plunger" whom Carey, Leighton's guard, stopped in their game.

ECKHART (*The Big Town*). He is a South Bend friend of Finch, who at the Finches' party invites Eckhart to have some Prohibition bourbon in the kitchen. When he offers to dance with Ella Finch, Eckhart's wife makes him take her home.

ECKHART, MRS. (*The Big Town*). She and her husband attend the Finches' party in South Bend. It doesn't go well. Finch's attempt to dance with her ends in a "stalemate," and the party ends.

ED ("Anniversary"). He is Florence Hammond's sister Grace's husband. Ed is an alcoholic philanderer. Grace keeps forgiving his abusive treatment.

ED ("Wedding Day"). He is Ruth Richards' brother-in-law. Ed is a New York "publicity man for the Shuberts." When his wife Alice gets the flu, he takes Ruth as a substitute guest to the wedding of show-business stars Brownie Burt and Jimmy Shane.

EDDIE ("The Last Night"). He is a bartender at one of Jay Arnold's watering holes. He is surprised when Arnold, drunk there the day before, tells him he is going on the wagon.

EDDY (*Treat 'Em Rough*). He is a soldier in Jack Keefe's unit. Capt. Whiting recruits Eddy, a Princeton man, to play football.

EDGAR ("Gullible's Travels"). He is a person to whom Gullible confidentially tells his story.

EDITH ("Some Like Them Cold"). She is Mabelle Gillespie's apartment roommate. Mabelle likes but demeans "Edie" in letters to Chas. F. Lewis.

EDITH ("Take a Walk"). She is the daughter of the woman from whom Bleat, a major-league umpire, rents a room when he is working in their town. Edith and Bleat fall in love despite her being 13 years younger. When Bleat makes honest calls against third-baseman Agnew, Edith's home-town hero, she spurns him in favor of Parvis, who plays the ukulele in a local radio program.

EDMISTON-NICHOLS ("Holycaust"). Jessie writes that the Centralia fire involved the Edmiston-Nichols shoe store.

EDNA ("Meet Me in St. Louie"). She is named as Danny Warner's sister in his song about his father.

EDWARD ("Absent-minded Beggar"). He is Ellen Parrish's servant at her lake cottage. He handles the baggage of John Knowles when he is a guest there.

EDWARDS, MR. ("The Hold-Out"). He is the financially troubled owner of the baseball team managed by Frank Conley, the narrator. Last season's loss was $18,000. Frank out-maneuvered him, in part ignorantly, finally even getting him to pay Bill Hagedorn, the clever "hold-out" first baseman, his asking price of $6,000, not the $4,000 that both Mr. Edwards and Frank originally planned on.

EGAN ("The Busher Abroad"). He is a baseball player on the trip around the world. Keefe says he made an error in one game.

Richard Joseph Egan (1884–1947) played for the Cincinnati Reds (1908–1913), the Brooklyn Dodgers (1914), the Dodgers and the Boston Braves (1915), and the Braves (1916). James E. Elfers reports that Dick Evans and Steve Egan were "the only active National Leaguers to tour the world as members of the White Sox," and that they were the shuffleboard champions as the ship left Australia. (Source: Elfers, 27, 172; *Baseball Encyclopedia*, 991)

ELDRIDGE, BESS ("Travelogue"). She is a friend of Hazel Dignan, who yammers to Dan Chapman about her travels with Bess; about Harley Bateman, Bess's former fiancé Harley Bateman; about Wannop, Bess's husband; about Bess's fingernail biting; etc.

ELLIOT, JIM In "Lose with a Smile," he is a left-handed pitcher "for Phila," as Danny explains, against Danny's Brooklyn team. Danny hoped to pinch hit but wasn't inserted. He explains that "on account of he being so big is why they call him jumbo." In "The Ides of June," Jumbo Elliot walked Danny, when he pinch hit for Clark.

James Thomas ("Jumbo") Elliot (1900–1970) pitched for the St. Louis Browns (1923), the Brooklyn Dodgers (1925–1930), the Philadelphia Phillies (1931–1933), and the Phillies and the Boston Braves (1934). (Source: *Baseball Encyclopedia*, 1963)

ELLIOTT, BUSTER ("My Roomy"). He is with the Chicago baseball team and the narrator's roommate. Elliott is a big, strong young man and a phenomenal left-handed batter, refuses to learn to play outfield or infield, and is used to pinch-hit. After being tolerated despite displays of eccentricity, including wild singing, he is released, goes berserk, attacks his former girlfriend from Muskegon and her brand-new husband with a baseball bat, is defined as criminally insane, and is put in a Kalamazoo asylum.

George W. Hilton says that although Elliott is fictional, "the syndrome of psychiatric symptoms attributed to him is so consistent that scholars and psychologists have always presumed Lardner observed it in an actual player." Hilton adds that Lardner as a reporter roomed with a similarly unbalanced left-handed baseball player who ultimately failed to be hired.

Donald Phelps says that Elliott's "manic-depressive convulsions ... [in the] self-service elevator" dramatize "possibly the most ominously ambiguous scene Lardner ever wrote." Elliott's model was Curtis Elston (1879–1950). Elston was in the minor leagues (1903–1913), trained with the Chicago Cubs (1908), but wasn't hired. Elston was reportedly predisposed to violence but rarely, could sing, was happily married to Winifred Laurie Little (from 1914 until she died [1947]), and was gainfully employed (until 1949). And finally, "My Roomy" is "impressive for its remarkable foreshadowing of the psychiatric problems of the American League batting champion of 1970, Alex Johnson."

It may be added that Alexander Johnson (b. 1942) played for the Philadelphia Phillies (1964–1965), the St. Louis Cardinals (1966–1967), the Cincinnati Reds (1968–1969), the Cleveland Indians (1972), the New York Yankees (1974–1975), and the Detroit Tigers (1976).

Donald Elder says that "Elliott is an intolerable character in every way, yet throughout ... is entirely sympathetic," and concludes that he "is just another eccentric busher — until the macabre finish, when he becomes a towering grotesque." Howard W. Webb Jr. contends that "Elliott's bizarre behavior is never explained, but clearly it is a twisted cry for recognition." Robert J. Higgs reductively says that "Elliott is simply a maniac and an exception to the bushers in the other stories." Douglas Robinson invokes the Other-as-minority concept espoused by Jacques Lacan (1901–1981), to lament the fact that Elliott, clearly not a member of any "majority" (quantitative or qualitative), cannot be accepted, cannot be "both crazy *and* loved, ... let loose, go wild, be as deviant as you feel, and still be not only tolerated but pampered, protected." Robinson asks whether Elliott's "deviant behavior" shouldn't be "perceived as the necessary by-product of ... [his] brilliance, and therefore ... cherished along with the talents that make ... [him] a success?" In truth, though, ordinary baseball players, to survive, can't be expected to tolerate any compadre's lights and noises at night, waving razors, unearthly singing, hurling water pitchers, and deliberate misplays jeopardizing team success. (Sources: *Baseball Encyclopedia*, 1187; Elder, 208; Hilton, 20, 332, 333, 339, 345, 361; Phelps, 87; Robinson, 129–130; Yardley, 129, 129–130)

ELLIOTT, FRANCIS ("Absent-minded Beggar"). He is a customer at the brokerage firm which is owned by J. L. Beasley and H. N. Comerford, and in which John Knowles works. By mistake, Knowles buys some preferred not common stock Elliott orders, but the preferred makes money. Elliott is thrilled.

ELLISON ("Along Came Ruth"). Keefe says that when he was pitching for the White Sox against Detroit, Ellison and Bush were on base, he "eased up" on Ty Cobb because the White Sox were ahead, and Cobb hit a triple.

Herbert Spencer Ellison (1895 or 1896–1955) was a Detroit Tiger utility player (1916–1920). (Sources: *Baseball Encyclopedia*, 994; Hilton, 265)

ELLSWORTH ("What of It?"). This is the name of a South Bend dry-goods store, where Dexter Cosset and his girlfriend clerk.

EMERSON, MRS. ("Tour Y-10"). She is Violet Emerson's mother, living in Chicago. When she goes to the movies, Violet phones Don Kellogg for a book. He comes right over.

EMERSON, VIOLET ("Tour Y-10"). She lives in Chicago. She keeps a diary of her vacation with her friend Kate Hayes to Yellowstone. Miss Emerson misunderstands everyone on the trip, thinks Mr. Coles and Mr. Garrett fall in love with her, and can't forgive Kate for rejecting Coles and accepting Garrett's proposal of marriage. She turns her attention back home to Don Kellogg.

Among other things, Violet is a stupid traveler. She contents herself with describing every beautiful view as "different than anything."

ENGLISH, MR. ("Pity is Akin —"). He is Marian Moore's defense attorney in her trial for violation liquor laws in the Prohibition era.

ENRIQUETA ("Nora"). She is an expensive actress whom musical-producer Louie Brock has under contract. She is to play the heroine in the mangled version of Hazlett's play "Nora."

EPH ("Gullible's Travels"). Gullible uses this name to refer occasionally to hotel employees in Florida.

ERICKSON "The Busher Pulls a Mays," Keefe reports that the Washington Senators obtained "a Swede named Erickson," a pitcher, from Detroit, and sarcastically says that the only White Sox batters "that could hit him were those that batted against him."

George Adolph Erickson (1892 or 1895–1965), born in Goteburg, Sweden, pitched for the New York Giants (1914), for the Detroit Tigers (1916–1917, 1919), and the Washington Senators (July 5, 1919–1922). (Source: *Baseball Encyclopedia*, 1966; Hilton, 319)

ERNEST (*The Big Town*). He is Herbert Daley's chauffeur. He resents his low pay compared to that of Daley's jockey Sid Mercer. When Ernest learns that Sid is dating Daley's fiancée Katie, he evidently informs Daley.

ERNESTINE (*The Real Dope*). She is a French girl in the estaminet whom Keefe meets. He agrees to teach English to her and learn French from her. When he ventures to kiss her, her father enters, turns irate, but accepts a bribe of "20 franks" and lets Keefe leave.

ESTHER ("Now and Then"). She is the recipient of eight letters from Irma, seven of which were written from Nassau, Bahamas, and the eighth from Miami.

ETTELSON, CASPER ("A Day with Conrad Green"). He is a composer whose "imaginative, whimsical music" is praised by Deems Taylor* in his *World* column. Taylor adds that an Ettleson score, a Barrie libretto, and a Conrad Green production would be a hit. When Green asks who "this Barrie" is, Green's confidential secretary Lewis replies that he is James M. Barrie, author of *Peter Pan.*

Yes, Barrie (1860–1937) wrote *Peter Pan* (1904). Lardner takes other digs at semi-literate Green.

EULALIE ("Rhythm"). She is the title figure in "Yes, Yes, Eulalie," with music by tune-thief Harry Hart and lyrics by Sam Rose.

EVANS In "The Busher Comes Back," Keefe comments adversely on Evans's umpiring a game between his White Sox and Washington. In "A New Busher Breaks In," Keefe criticizes Evans's inaccurate calls. In "Call for Mr. Keefe!," Keefe reports that Bill Evans favored Johnson, Washington's famous pitcher.

William George Evans (1884–1956) was a sports writer in Youngstown, then an American League umpire (1906–1927), and afterwards held managerial jobs in baseball and football (until 1951). He was elected to the Baseball Hall of Fame (1973). (Source: Hilton, 89)

EVANS ("Haircut"). He runs a traveling circus. Jim Kendall played a cruel joke on Jim's wife and two children. He told them he had circus tickets and to wait for him at the tent, then didn't show up.

EVANS, CORP (*The Real Dope*). He is a noncom serving with Keefe in France. He tells Keefe that Simple Simon is missing in action.

EVANS, STEVE In "The Busher Beats It Hence," Keefe says McGraw was happy that Steve Evans and Dutch Schaefer were part of the world tour because "they is both of them funny." In "The Busher Abroad," Evans is friendly with Keefe but fools him with clever practical jokes. Keefe says Evans is "comical when you get to know him." In "The Busher's Welcome Home," Evans tells Keefe that Hal Cane wrote almost as many books as in the Bible. Evans and Schaefer persuade Keefe to believe that he should quit the White Sox and jump to the Federal League.

Louis Richard ("Steve") Evans (1885–1943) played for the Giants (1908), the St. Louis Cardinals (1909–1913), and in the Federal League (1914–1915). George W. Hilton says that McGraw so disliked Evans's "antics" when the two were members of the 1913–1914 world tour that he quickly traded him to the Cardinals. James E. Elfers reports that Evans and Dick Egan were the only two active National League players, as White

Sox, on the tour and that they were the champion shuffleboard players aboard. Elfers also reports that one of the "bronx statues" to which Keefe refers while the players are in Rome was a copy of *The Discus Thrower* and that Hall Caine provided an inscription for the bronze. Sir Hall Caine (1853–1931) was a British novelist, devout biographer, and Isle of Mann politician. (Sources: *Baseball Encyclopedia*, 1002–1003; Elfers, 27, 172, 201; Hilton, 176).

EVERS ("Insomnia"). He is a baseball player the sleepless author remembers.

EVICK, MYRNA ("Cured!"). She is a friend who tells Mary Streeter that Dr. Wendell cured Myrna's brother's alcoholism. Mary then requires her husband Dick to consult Dr. Wendell.

EWING, MR. ("Fore!"). He is a coal merchant in Allison, Illinois, and is the president of the Allison golf club. The president's prize for the winner of the tournament is a silver cup.

"EX PARTE" (*Cosmopolitan*, November 1928; RLR, RU). (Characters: Mrs. Anthony Adams, Earl Benham, Bess Cooper, Jeff Cooper, Harry Cross, Jim Dwan, Mildred Dwan, Mike Farrell, Florence, Ken Garrett, Helga, Kane, Ed Osbourne, Mrs. Osbourne, Joe Paxton, Marjorie Paxton, Taylor, Wolfe, Jake Wolfe.)

The narrator explains that when man leaves wife, it's man's fault, and man gets ostracized. When woman leaves husband, it's also husband's fault, and nobody listens to "his side of the case." So the narrator writes his explanation of trouble with his wife Florence and leaves this document in his will, for his friend Ed Osbourne to reveal:

I went on business (from the West coast) to New York a year ago last May. My friends Joe and Marjorie Paxton invited me to dinner, where I met Florence, Marjorie's friend from school days. We fell in love and planned to marry this April. We decided to room into my place at the Belden while house-hunting. My friend Jeff Cooper, about to work in China with Standard Oil, offered me his and his wife Bess's house, including furniture, for $40,000—a loss of $5,000. I inspected the place, admired everything, especially the attractive new furniture, and bought it—to surprise Florence. We wed in Chicago, where her parents lived, honeymooned zestfully in Yellowstone, and moved into the new house. Florence cried, but not through homesickness, and stayed gloomy. Her friend Mildred Dwan phoned in May; she and her husband Jim Dwan visited us; Mildred cried mysteriously with Florence; Mildred invited us to Sunday dinner at their place alongside the Turnpike. It was a barn the Dwans bought from the Taylors after their own house burned and they moved. The Dwans hired wreckers to remove the barn stalls and sheds, and a Seattle contractor to install pine walls, floor, and plastered ceiling, and to convert the hay-loft into rooms. The rotten-beamed main room was furnished in what I called ugly "Early American" maple, and also with hooked rugs but no pictures. Upstairs—all maple. The maid Helga's announcement that dinner was ready precluded cocktails. Florence admired the sawbuck, nailed-plank dining table with its slat-back chairs, all shipped from Pennsylvania by Mildred's antique-hunting mother. After a dismal dinner, rain precluded an immediate escape; so we played some imperfectly lighted bridge hands, around an oddly non-period card table. Florence and I won $12, unpaid, and soon departed.

Home again, I asked Florence how she could pretend "to admire all that junk." She called everything beautiful and chilled me for the next "six nights and five days." During Saturday lunch, I broke silence by asking Florence what was wrong. She said she hated our shiny home and its "new things" and adored Mildred's taste. I offered to sell our place, buy Ken Garrett's livery stable, which new owners had been turning into a garage, and convert it into a Mildred-style "dump." Mildred escaped upstairs. I went out, bought a new suit, sampled some "Early American rye" with my friend Harry Cross, then bought shears, a blow torch, and an axe. I returned home, scissored my suit, muddied my hat, and surprised Florence by my appearance—which I called "not too new." Wanting to "antique this place," I added, I aged the dining table with torch and axe. When it was looking "pretty Early," Florence packed and left. So did the maid, who smelled fire.

"Eddie," this is my version of events, and I recommend Cross's bootlegger, Mike Farrell, available Tuesdays at the Belden.

The narrator is evidently a successful song writer. He tells Florence he could buy that garage by simply writing an introduction to a song or "maybe just the vamp" (i.e., a musical composition based on older material).

The Latin legalese phrase *ex parte* means "from the other side," said usually of legal matters or proceedings; Here it suggests that the narrator will explain his "side" of the dispute with Florence. Imbedded in Lardner's slapstick parable are the narrator's sharp verbal digs. Two examples: He says that rats must have used the Paxtons' "dirty old rotten [ceiling] beams for gnawing practise"; after the Dwan dinner he "was all ready to go home and get something to eat." James M. Cox finds evidence in "Ex Parte" and a few other Lardner stories that his satirical prowess "is extremely heavy-handed, depending as it does upon melodramatic structure." Cox concludes that Lardner "lacked the *mind* for satire and therefore could not displace ... anger and indignation with ... wit and analysis." (Source: Cox, 322)

FABER In "The Busher's Kid," Keefe says that during the White Sox "city serious" game the Cubs "give this here Faber a good beating." In "The Busher Beats It Hence," Keefe says that when his arm hurt in the San Francisco game, "Faber went in to finnish it up." In *Treat 'Em Rough*, Keefe mentions Faber. In "The Battle of Texas," Keefe heard that Red Faber served "in the navy up to Great Lakes" during the war. Later Kid Gleason has Keefe "work out" with Faber and Wolfgang. In "The Busher Pulls a Mays," Keefe complains that batters get hits when "Kerr and Faber and Lowdermilk" are pitching for the White Sox. In *The Real Dope*, Faber is mentioned.

Urban Clarence "Red" Faber (1888–1976) pitched for the Chicago White Sox (1914–1933) and was elected to the Baseball Hall of Fame (1964). George W. Hilton reports that Faber's early ineffectiveness encouraged certain disgruntled players "to conceive the [1919] Black Sox plot." Earlier, Faber participated in the 1913–1914 White Sox-Giants world tour; he sails unmentioned, however, by Keefe in "The Busher Abroad." Charles F. Faber and Richard B. Faber prove by elaborate statistics that Faber was the greatest spitball pitcher in the history of baseball. (Sources: *Baseball Encyclopedia*, 1970; Elfers, xviii; Faber and Faber, 187; Hilton, 163)

FACE TOWELS ("Claude Diphthong, Student of Crime"). This may be the nickname of a Swedish woman, in an anecdote told by Claude Diphthong.

"THE FACTS" (*Metropolitan*, January 1917; HTW, RLR, RU). (Characters: Beth, Felix Bond, Billy Bowen, Mary Carey, Charley, Allie French, Dr. Gish, Aunt Harriet, Anna Henderson, Kathryn, Bob McDonald, Edith McDonald, Ellen McDonald, Florence McDonald, Louise McDonald, Mrs. McDonald, Sam McDonald, Walter McDonald, Wilma McDonald, Marsh, Violet Moore, Leslie Painter, Paul Potter, Pratt, Tommy Richards, Tonio.)

I. Billy Bowen, 28, is a businessman from Chicago's South Side; Ellen McDonald, 21, is from the North Side. At Tonio's in New York, Billy is with one business friend; Ellen, with several friends. A male among them knows Billy and hails him over. Billy, somewhere between his 14th and 21st drink, spellbinds everyone with witty dialogue and ravishing dancing. Everyone, that is, but his business friend, who is handed the checks.

II. Next day at the Army-Navy game, "by accident or ... fate," Ellen's party's box adjoins Bowen's. Ellen sits beside him, plans to be "amused" again, but instead is "conquered." Aiming at her heart, he appears to speak thoughtfully, indifferent to the mere sport of football. She promises to write him after her eastern travels and when she returns to Chicago.

III. December 6, Monday. Ellen, having truncated her trip east, returns home, writes Bowen briefly, skips attending the opera with her parents, breaks a date with Paul Potter, and awaits Bowen.

December 8. Billy Bowen appears on the wagon now and clear-brained; he listens as she discusses war, shows, books, college, cars, the stock market. He mentions his family, a married sister in South Bend and two gad-about married cousins, and, hypocritically, his love of stay-at-home reading. She gushes about her bridge-playing parents, sleepy Aunt Mary, sisters Northampton-students Edith and Wilma, next-block Aunt Louise and Aunt Harriet, married brother Bob in Evanston, and brother Walter, a schoolboy wastrel. When Ellen demeans herself, Billy smilingly doubts such modesty. Walter fumbles in, speaks of the late hour. Soon, after goodnights all around, Walter is dreaming of a new girlfriend named Kathryn; Ellen is dreaming of Billy, and Billy of Ellen.

IV. December 10. Billy and Ellen attend "The Follies" but are too interested in each other to enjoy it, then go dancing. She is too much in love to note that his "trotting" is clumsy; he wants her; she is happy. Next morning, Ellen confides about Billy to her mother and her mother's live-in sister Mary Carey, writes her own sisters, and phones brother Bob's wife. Walter learns everything in confidence and promptly tells Kathryn.

December 12. Sunday dinner at the McDonalds. Billy meets Ellen's father Sam McDonald, who, combining pomposity and prevarication, lectures him on collegians' foolish conduct fortunately outgrown in maturity, the beneficence of cigars, and the evils inherent in cigarettes, gambling, and drinking. When Sam and Mary go to evening church service, Mrs. McDonald remains, to lecture Bill on her bridge-playing expertise. Home again, Aunt Mary describes church doings. When Walter, who briefly appeared in church with Kathryn, returns, Sam orders him to bed. Billy taxies home, smoking furiously.

December 20. After a week's business trip, Billy on the Buffalo train doesn't know that bright Wilma and athletic Edith are also aboard. At the Chicago station, Sam and Ellen greet everyone; the disclosed coincidence triggers light-veined hysterics. Going to his office, Billy finds the card of Miss Violet Moore, an applicant seeking to replace his secretary, who is leaving to get married. A note on Miss Moore's card requests that he phone her any evening.

December 22. Billy attends the McDonalds' family dinner. Aunt Harriet, Aunt Louise, Bob, and his wife Florence are guests. Billy's courteous talk with "Flo" arouses Bob's sense of proprietary jealousy, momentarily. At table, Billy meets Walter's giggling Kathryn, observes Wilma consume many large oysters and Louise's avenue-wide hair part. Billy makes small talk with others. He tells Ellen he must spend Christmas Day with his married sister in South Bend and will see her the day after, and leaves sadly sober to catch a night train to St. Louis on business. Her family "unanimously" like him, although Bob and Edith decry his lack of a sense of humor, to which Ellen responds that when he's "in a funny mood ... [they'll] die laughing!"

V. December 23. Tommy Richards, Billy's college pal, is returning by train from a long western business trip, stops in Chicago, on his way home to Minneapolis, to see Billy, learns at his office that Billy will return next day, stays overnight, and then finds him.

December 24. Learning of Billy's engagement to Ellen, Tommy suggests some drinks. No. He bets a lunch that Billy will fall off the wagon. Billy loses that bet by 9:30 A.M. and offers to pay fast, since he must buy Christmas presents for the McDonalds. Instead, they drink until 2:50 P.M., then hilariously start shopping together for Billy's gifts, at Marsh's, where Billy has a charge account. Billy confusedly describes his future in-laws to Tommy. Out of drinking condition, Billy rests in Marsh's waiting room. Promising to shop for him, Tommy takes Billy's business cards, and charges gift cigarettes for Samuel, and other ironically apt items for the rest — poker set for Walter, diet book for Wilma, hair piece for Louise, etc. He orders everything sent to the McDonald household. Billy must rush to his train. Only Ellen remains to shop for. Tommy has no more cards identifying Billy, who mutters "Pocketbook," from which Tommy extracts Violet Moore's card. Billy taxies to the station but mistakenly boards the train for St. Joe, Missouri. Tommy happens to enclose Violet's card in a package gifting Ellen a wrist watch, then catches his Minneapolis train. When everything arrives, Ellen takes to her bed, Sam burns the present aimed at Walter, and Walter praises Billy's "nerve."

The narrator frames "The Facts" with a terse introduction, that "[t]he engagement was broken off before it was announced," and with a terse conclusion, that "it was quite a job to dig ... up" the facts. The Christmas season in question was that of 1915. Lardner more generally grounds "The Facts" in time by saying drunk Billy's dancing at Tonio's resembles "Frank Kinney doubling as Vernon Castle," and by having Ellen supposedly study at her piano the "harmony" of Irving Berlin,* Jerome Kern, and Egbert Anson Van Alstyne. Frank Tinney (1878–1940) performed in musical comedies, including the 1913 "Follies" of Florenz Ziegfeld.* Vernon Castle (1887–1918) and his wife Irene Castle (1893–1969) were ragtime ball-room dancers, invented the foxtrot (1914), and starred in Berlin's *Watch Your Step* (1914), his first musical comedy. The Castles are also mentioned in "Gullible's Travels." Kern (1885–1945), musical-comedy composer, achieved his greatest successes with "Look for the Silver Lining" (in *Sally*, 1920), *Showboat* (1927), and "Smoke Gets in Your Eyes" (in *Roberta*, 1933). Van Alstyne (1878–1951) collaborated in New York with lyricist Harry H. Williams to create popular and ragtime songs, including "Navajo" (1903) and "In the Shade of the Old Apple Tree" (1905); they moved to Chicago (1907), where Van Alstyne died. Brian T. Cowlishaw finds "The Facts" a uniquely challenging fictional narration, because, as he explains, "the implied author, implied reader, and narratee are actually *friends*"; therefore, Lardner's audience is especially urged to "perceive his ironies and enjoy them." (Source: Cowlishaw, 215)

FAILING, LEONARD K. ("Claude Diphthong, Student of Crime"). He was a boxer and a criminal who bilked a woman in Texas, ran a partridge farm in Lancaster, Pennsylvania, changed his name to Lincoln H. Martingale, and is now the house detective in New York's Hotel Baldwin. Claude Diphthong exposes him.

FALKENBERG In "Horseshoes," Dick Grimes says that for the seventh Athletics-Giants World Series game, the stands were so packed that Falkenberg could not find a place to sit down. In "The Busher Abroad," Keefe mentions that Falkenberg, though tall, couldn't walk through the "red Sea" even when it was parted for Moses.

Frederick Peter Falkenberg (1880–1961) pitched for the Pittsburgh Pirates (1903), the Washington Senators (1905–1907), the Senators and the Cleveland Indians (1908), and the Indians (1909–1913). Lardner's comment about Falkenberg's inability to find a place to sit was humorous for readers who knew that Falkenberg was 6'5" and a skinny 180 lbs. (Sources: *Baseball Encyclopedia*, 1971; Hilton, 419)

FARRELL (*Own Your Own Home*). He and his wife are invited to attend Fred and Grace's bridge party, along with Bishop and his wife, Grimes and his wife, Carry and his wife, and Curtis and his wife.

FARRELL, FRANCIS X. ("Alibi Ike"). He is a baseball player, notable for two attributes. He plays excellently, but also makes excuses for every play, good or less so. Hence the nickname "Alibi Ike." His full name must be Francis Xavier Farrell. But the narrator says that the "X" must stand for "excuse." Ike even apologizes for playing billiards excellently, although, the narrator says sarcastically, "not quite" like Willie Hoppe. William F. Hoppe (1887–1959) was the world's best billiard player for decades. H. L. Mencken* verbalizes to the effect that "the idiotic Frank X. Farrell ... [is] an extravagant grotesque and yet quite real from glabella to calcenous." George W. Hilton calls Farrell "one of his [Lardner's] most sympathetically drawn heroes." Donald Phelps says that Alibi Ike and the later Hurry Kane both have "stoically sarcastic, sun-parched midwestern voices." Tom Quirk puzzlingly avers that "Alibi Ike ... belongs in the company of Scotty Briggs and Jim Blaine [from Mark Twain's *Roughing It*] as someone comically aware of his hilarious effects upon both his companions and his readers." (Sources: Hilton, 21; Mencken [1924], 377; Phelps, 84; Quirk, 121)

FARRELL, KID ("Hurry Kane"). He plays on the St. Louis baseball team, trains Hurry Kane to field better, kids him, and worries when he threatens to quit the team.

FARRELL, MIKE ("Ex Parte"). He is Harry Cross's bootlegger and supplies him with "Early American rye."

FARRELL, MRS. (*Own Your Own Home*). She and her husband attend the bridge party given by Fred and Grace.

FATHER (*The Young Immigrunts*). He is the young narrator's father, a sports reporter. He writes the Preface to the narrator's travelogue. The father gets the family to "Grenitch Conn.," and on the way is grouchy, opinionated, and rude.

FAULKNER ("Champion"). Ellen F. Kelly works at Faulkner's Steam Laundry in Chicago.

FAULKNER ("Insomnia"). He, his wife, and their daughter Lucy lived in Clayton, Michigan. The sleepless author remembers chasing his family cow Cora into the Faulkners' yard one day and also bothering the Faulkners by serenading Lucy one night.

FAULKNER, LUCY ("Insomnia"). She is a pretty girl the sleepless author remembers admiring when they were young in Clayton, Michigan. He and three beer-drinking pals serenaded her one night and bothered the family. He disliked the name Lucy until this Lucy came along, after which "it was music."

FAULKNER, MAJOR G. WILLIS ("A Chip of the Old Block"). He is identified by Tracy in conversation with Captain Evan Barnes as an officer in the Cushion Corps.

FAULKNER, MRS. ("Insomnia"). She was the mother of Lucy Faulkner. The sleepless author remembers bothering the Faulkner family when he serenaded Lucy one night.

FAUST, CHARLIE ("My Roomy"). He is a New York baseball player. McGraw refuses to accept Buster Elliott from the Chicago team, saying he already has Faust, which was "enough for him."

George W. Hilton identifies Faust as Charles Victor Faust (1880–1915), a psychotic mascot for the Giants (1911–1912), who warmed up regularly, pitched twice but in relief only, and was declared insane (1914–1915). McGraw's statement is an obscure allusion to Faust's weird behavior. (Source: Hilton, 358–359)

FELSCH In *Treat 'Em Rough*, Jack Keefe says that Felsch hit a pitch by Sallee "out of the park." This concerns the October 6, 1917 World Series game between the Chicago White Sox and the

New York Giants. In "The Battle of Texas," Felsch is a White Sox player. While Kid Gleason and Keefe are discussing the rookie pitcher Belden, Felsch joins in and asks "how Belden is comeing along." In "Along Came Ruth," Keefe complains that when he was pitching against St. Louis, Felsch misplayed a ball hit by Tobin. In "The Busher Pulls a Mays," Keefe complains that Hap Felsch's limp keeps him from fielding well. Felsch is mentioned in "The Last Night."

George W. Hilton reports that Oscar Emil ("Happy") Felsch (1891–1964) was a good-hitting White Sox centerfielder (1915–1920) but being "[a] sixth-grade dropout from Milwaukee" was easily persuaded by Arnold Gandil to join the conspiracy resulting in the 1919 Black Sox Scandal. As a consequence, Felsch and seven others were banned from baseball. (Sources: *Baseball Encyclopedia*, 1009; Hilton, 251)

FELTON ("Poodle"). Felton's Restaurant, on 42nd Street in New York, is the place where the narrator is about to go for the unappetizing "Fifty-Cent Blue Plate Lunch" when he decides to go see a movie instead.

FERGUSON, MRS. ("Meet Me in St. Louie"). She is a friend of Jessie's and could stay with Jessie's mother if Jessie went to St. Louis to see Danny. She finally doesn't go.

FERRELL, MRS. ("How Are You?"). She recommends "x-ray man" Dr. Julius to Bob Dayton.

FESTER, ESTHER ("A Frame-Up"). This is the name Jack Grace makes up as that of a beautiful girl Burke sees in New York and determines to marry. Grace writes letters as from Esther to Burke, fending him off temporarily and encouraging him to box well to impress her. Burke eventually meets this girl, who is Mary Holt.

FESTER, LESTER ("A Frame-Up"). This is the name Jack Grace concocts as that of Esther Fester's father. Grace tells Burke, who wants to marry Esther, that Lester made billions selling waffle irons to Belgians during the war.

FIELDS ("That Old Sweetheart of Mine"). He and his wife have been friends of Stella and Ralph Crane. The four used to dine together but, Stella laments, not recently.

FIELDS, LILLIAN ("That Old Sweetheart of Mine"). She is a friend of Stella Crane. Stella and her husband Ralph used to dine with the Fieldses but not recently. Stella remembers that Lillian cried when the two saw the play *Journey's End* together.

Journey's End (1928) by R. C. Sherriff (1896–1975) was a realistic play about World War I trench warfare.

FINCH (*The Big Town*). He is the narrator. His wife Ella, living in South Bend, Indiana, and her unmarried sister Katie inherit considerable money. They try in South Bend to help Katie catch a husband, fail, and go to New York to try harder. When Francis Griffin, working in Wall Street, goes after Ella instead of Katie, Finch goes to Griffin's office, identifies himself as Sam Hall, and beats up Griffin. Finch has to move with Ella and Katie to an expensive Riverside Drive apartment, where their neighbor is rich old Trumbull. Finch enjoys Trumbull's hospitality, which includes "hootch," losing at craps, and a "Rools-Royce." When Katie dislikes Trumbull and can't have his married chauffeur Ritchey, she and the Finches try summering at a Long Island hotel. Finch amuses himself by pretending to Lady Perkins he can help cure her pet dogs with an anti-rash medicine. Finch relishes "horseman" Herbert Daley's courtship of Katie, her cheating on him with Daley's jockey Sid Mercer, being driven in Daley's big car by his chauffeur Ernest, drinking with Sid and getting a racing tip, and betting against Daley at the Belmont because Daley bad-mouthed Finch to Sid. Finch returns with the girls to New York, where Katie meets and admires Jimmy Ralston, a Follies comedian. Finch sees through the phony actor but is pleased when he and Katie get married, whereupon Finch and Ella return to South Ben, sadder, wiser, and poorer.

FINCH, ANNE ("High-rollers"). She is Marion and Walter Finch's daughter. She and her little brother, called Junior, play with Jack, Peggy and Jack Bowen's son, at the beach by Hampton Dunes, Long Island.

FINCH, ELLA (*The Big Town*). She has been Tom Finch's wife for five years. They live in South Bend, Indiana. She and her unmarried sister Katie inherit money from their war-profiteering stepfather, who was a manufacturer of leather products and died shortly after the Armistice. Ella tries unsuccessfully to entertain and attract suitors for Katie, persuades Tom to join the girls in New York to try further. Ella fails when Francis Griffin, who she thinks likes Katie but is shy, has amorous intentions toward Ella. Ella demands that the three leave their hotel and rent a Riverside Drive apartment. Their neighbor is rich, generous old Trumbull. Ella wants Katie to marry him. Katie prefers Trumbull's chauffeur Ritchey, briefly. The Finches take Katie for the summer to a Long Island hotel, where Ella encourages her to go after Bob Codd, an aviator-inventor. Codd dies in an airplane crash. Ella encourages Katie to pursue wealthy "horseman" Herbert Daley. He proposes, is accepted, but learns Katie is seeing his jockey Sid Mercer, and dumps her. Back in New York, Ella encourages Katie to be appealing to comedian Jimmy Ralston. The two get married, after which the Finches return to South Bend.

FINCH, JUNIOR ("High-rollers"). She is the little son of Marion and Walter Finch. He and his sister Anne are beach companions of Jack, the son of Peggy and Jack Bowen, who are summering at Hampton Dunes, Long Island.

FINCH, MARION ("High-rollers"). She and Walter Finch, married 10 years, have a son and a daughter, and live in New York City. When Walter gets a job for better pay, Marion insists on renting a cottage for the summer at Hampton Dunes, Long Island. She gambles at bridge with Perry Bowen, Mrs. Hart, and Mrs. Parker, all of whom are married to rich gamblers. Marion wins, isn't paid, and tires of cards. She and Walter give a party at the Dunes to repay their gambling friends' hospitality.

FINCH, TOM (*The Big Town*). He is the husband of Ella Finch and the brother-in-law of her unmarried sister Katie. When the girls inherit money, the three move from South Bend to New York and then Long Island, always in unsuccessful search for a husband for Katie. Once she finds one in Jimmy Ralston, Tom and Ella return to South Bend.

FINCH, WALTER ("High-rollers"). He and his wife Marion have two children. He moves from employment with Ripley's in New York to "Bernard and Craig, Publicity Engineers," still in the sweaty, crowded city. Better pay enables the family to rent a summer cottage at Hampton Dunes, Long Island. Walter visits his family on weekends, joins a club, and plays golf for money with his friend Jack Bowen and also with Kenneth Hart and Dick Parker, two millionaire friends of Jack's. When Walter wins, he isn't paid. Once when he loses to Parker, he pays Parker. Walter learns that the millionaires don't settle their bets but keep mental tabs. So he loses at cards to Parker and tells Marion it's a kind of victory.

FISHER ("The Last Night"). He is a stranger Jay Arnold talks to on their way by street car to a Chicago baseball game. He shocks Arnold by suggesting that prohibition is coming, as an indirect means of assuring more food for the army.

FISHER, BUD ("A Frame-Up"). He is "the ukulele king" and Mildred Whiffletree's uncle, according to Jack Grace's silly talk, which Burke believes.

FITCHBURG'S FIGHTING FOOL ("The Venomous Viper of the Volga") *see* **FITZGERALD, FRANKIE**

FITZGERALD, F. SCOTT (1896–1940). Born in St. Paul, Minnesota, Fitzgerald attended Princeton (1913), served in the U.S. Army (1917–1919), and published *This Side of Paradise* (1920), a popular jazz-age novel. Early short stories followed, collected in *Flappers and Philosophers* (1920) and *Tales of the Jazz Age* (1922). He married (1920) Zelda Sayre (1900–1948) and lived in Westport, Connecticut, and abroad, then Great Neck, Long Island (1922–1924), then elsewhere. Fitzgerald's later works include *The Great Gatsby* (1925), *All the Sad Young Men* (1926), *Tender Is the Night* (1934, Abe North in it is based on Lardner), *Taps at Reveille* (1935), and *The Last Tycoon* (1941). Like Lardner though more successfully, Fitzgerald wrote for the movies. Unlike Lardner's marriage, Fitzgerald's, which produced one daughter, was more ruinously marked by Roaring Twenties excesses, including wasteful spending, alcoholic binges, and infidelity on both sides. Zelda Fitzgerald was hospitalized abroad and in the United States for exhaustion, schizophrenia, nervous instability, and psychiatric disorders, and when institutionized a final time burned to death.

The Lardners were the Fitzgeralds' Great Neck neighbors. The two men talked, cavorted, and drank together. While drunk one night they sought to serenade and meet the novelist Joseph Conrad, then staying at his American publisher's home in Oyster Bay, Long Island, but were kicked out for trespassing (1923). Fitzgerald persuaded Maxwell Perkins,* his editor at Scribner's, to collect and publish what became Lardner's *How to Write Short Stories* (1924). The Lardners visited the Fitzgeralds in France (also 1924). Jay Gatsby's hospitable house in *The Great Gatsby* is partly based on the Lardners' boozy Great Neck residence. Fitzgerald undoubtedly quizzed Lardner about the 1919 Black Sox Scandal when he set about to characterize Meyer Wolfsheim, Gatsby's shady pal. After Lardner's death, Fitzgerald published "Ring" (1933), a subjective, controversial interpretation of his friend's opinions and writings.

Clifford M. Caruthers concludes that "[t]he friendship between Fitzgerald and Lardner appears to have developed from a mutual recognition of the ways they complemented each other." He explains that Fitzgerald admired Lardner's humor, cynicism, judgment of human nature, and talent as an author, and that Lardner respected Fitzgerald's ideas, literary acumen, and precise literary style. Lardner's surviving letters to both Fitzgeralds are wise, knowledgeable, hilarious, and revealing. He addresses them as "Dears Scott and Zelda," "Gents," "Dear Wops," "Dear Scott and Darling Zelda," "Heap Big Zelda and Scott." He frequently signs himself idiotically — F. Farmer Fox, Gil Boag, I, Mrs. Nell, "Tallulah," etc. He often encloses cleverly goofy poems. Lardner proofread *The Great Gatsby* and in a letter (March 24 [1925]) tactfully listed errata. (Source: Caruthers [1995], 150–151, 175–176, and *passim*; Yardley, 261)

FITZGERALD, FRANKIE ("The Venomous Viper of the Volga"). He is a successful boxer, a Rumanian dubbed "Fitchburg's Fighting Fool." He defeats Mike Moran and, when the Viper backs down, is likely to fight Jack Ryan for the world championship.

Lardner had fun naming this able pugilist after his friend F. Scott Fitzgerald.*

FITZSIMMONS ("FITZ") ("A Frame-Up"). He manages boxer Charley Porter in Benton Harbor. He matches Porter against Burke, who breaks Porter's jaw and defeats him.

FITZSIMMONS ("Lose with a Smile"). Danny identifies Fitzsimmons as a right-handed Giants "nuggle ball" pitcher who beat Danny's Brooklyn team.

Frederick Landis Fitzsimmons (1901–1979) pitched for the Giants (1925–1936), the Giants and Brooklyn (1937), and Brooklyn (1938–1943). He managed the Philadelphia Phillies (1943–1945). (Source: *Baseball Encyclopedia*, 692, 1983)

FLAGSTAFF ("Along Came Ruth" and "The Courtship of T. Dorgan") *see* **FLAGSTEAD**

FLAGSTEAD In "Along Came Ruth," Keefe boasts that he pitched so well to "this new outfielder they [the Detroit Tigers] have got name Flagstaff or something" that he made him feel "about half mast." In "The Courtship of T. Dorgan," Keefe, spelling the name correctly, says Flagstead pitched for Detroit successfully against Keefe, who wasn't himself after losing his bet on the Willard[*]-Dempsey[*] fight.

Ira James Flagstead (1893–1940) played for the Detroit Tigers (1917–1922), Detroit and the Boston Red Sox (1923), the Red Sox (1924–1928), the Red Sox and the Washington Senators and the Pittsburgh Pirates (1929), and the Pirates (1930). (Sources: *Baseball Encyclopedia*, 1018; Hilton, 260)

FLEMING ("Widow"). He and his wife express their sympathy to their friend Margaret Winslow after her husband John's death. Thereafter, Fleming "sneaked" into another room to hear Margaret's brother-in-law Ed Winslow discuss John's financial situation with Somers.

FLEMING, MISS ("Holycaust"). She is Frank Earl's sister-in-law, evidently so pretty that she was given a screen test. She flirted with Danny, who took her to an expensive speakeasy in Brooklyn, only to be called cheap.

FLEMING, MRS. ("Widow"). She and her husband visit Margaret Winslow after her husband John's death. Mrs. Fleming says the news of his death "shocked her." Later, Margaret reminds Dick Randall that they attended a party two weeks earlier at the Flemings' home.

FLETCHER ("Horseshoes"). He plays infield for the Giants in the World Series against the Athletics. Early in the sixth game, his error puts Murphy on but Dick Grimes fails to advance him by a sacrifice fly.

Arthur Fletcher (1885–1950) played for the New York Giants (1909–1919), the Giants and the Philadelphia Phillies (1920), and the Phillies (1922). He managed the Phillies (1923–1926) and then the New York Yankees (1929), and also was their third-base coach (1927–1945). (Sources: *Baseball Encyclopedia*, 692, 1020; Hilton, 419)

FLICK, ELMER (*The Young Immigrunts*). The narrator's father mentions that Elmer Flick, "the old ball player," once lived in Goshen, Indiana.

Elmer Harrison Flick (1876–1971) played for the Philadelphia Phillies (1898–1901), the Philadelphia Athletics and the Cleveland Indians (1902), and the Indians (1903–1910). He was elected to the Baseball Hall of Fame (1963). (Source: *Baseball Encyclopedia*, 1021)

FLINT, GORDON ("I Can't Breathe"). He is a

young man, 21, whom the diarist, 18 and presumably engaged to him, can't help stringing along.

FLOOD, PEGGY ("Mr. and Mrs. Fix-It"). She is a friend of Ada, the narrator's wife. He finds her boring because she is happy only when going for surgery or recovering from surgery.

FLORENCE ("The Busher Comes Back") *see* **KEEFE, FLORENCE**

FLORENCE ("Ex Parte"). She is the narrator's wife. He surprises her by buying Jim and Bess Cooper's house, new and furnished in modern style. But she voices her displeasure and her preference for old stuff, like what is in her friend Mildred Paxton's barn-turned-house. When the narrator "antiques" their own home, with blow torch and axe, Florence leaves.

FLY-BY-NIGHT (*The Big Town*). He is one of Herbert Daley's racehorses, described as "a dog" at the Jamaica race-track.

FLYNN ("A Busher's Letters Home"). He was an outfielder when Jack Keefe pitched against Grand Rapids in the Central League. Keefe says Flynn misjudged a fly and spoiled a shutout when Jack Doyle was scouting him.

FLYNN ("A One-Man Team"). He was a kicker for Marshall's football team. Coach Belden recalls defeating Marshall one year because its "one-man team" was built on Flynn.

FLYNN ("Tour No. 2"). He and his wife, as well as Fogarty and his wife, are subjects of Larry's unamusing Irish jokes.

FLYNN, MRS. ("Tour No. 2"). She and her husband, and Fogarty and his wife also, are subjects of jokes Larry likes to tell.

FOGARTY ("Sick 'Em"). He is a handsome, vain pitcher. He and Smitty are Central League pitchers effective only when they are on the same team, because then they compete for success. When Smitty goes to the Phillies and Fogarty to the Cubs, each fails. The narrator, a Phillies man, learns of their rivalry from Jack Barnett, a former teammate, and persuades Red, the Phillies manager, to trade for Fogarty. Both men then pitch brilliantly. Trying to outdo Smitty, Fogarty even pitches well with a badly bruised throwing arm. The narrator calls Fogarty "the Turk."

FOGARTY ("Tour No. 2"). He and his wife, and Flynn and his wife are butts of Larry's unamusing jokes.

FOGARTY, MRS. ("Tour No. 2"). The Fogartys and the Flynn's are subjects of jokes Larry tells.

FOGEL, TOMMY ("The Battle of the Century"). He was an old boxer. Jim Dugan's manager, Larry Moon, arranged for a match with Dugan, who won in three easy rounds in Jersey.

FOHL ("The Courtship of T. Dorgan"). He is the manager of the Cleveland Indians. Keefe witnesses a fight between Cleveland's Speaker and Gandil of the White Sox and boasts that if Speaker tangled with him Fohl would need a new center fielder to replace Speaker.

Leo Alexander Fohl (1870–1965) played for the Pittsburgh Pirates (1902) and the Cincinnati Reds (1903), and managed the Cleveland Indians (1915–1919) until Speaker replaced (July 19, 1919). Fohl then managed the St. Louis Browns (1921–1923) and the Boston Red Sox (1924–1926). George W. Hilton reports that there was a real Speaker-Gandil fight (May 31, 1919). Hilton doesn't add that Lardner's readers in the 1920s might conclude he was hinting that Fohl's not breaking up the rhubarb caused his dismissal as manager a few weeks later. (Sources: *Baseball Encyclopedia*, 692, 1023; Hilton, 287)

FOOTE, DOC ("Haircut"). He and Doc Gamble are old, evidently ineffective physicians in Whitey's town. Whitey and Julie Gregg preferred newcomer Doc Ralph Stair.

"FORE!" (*Red Book*, May 1917). (Characters: Mr. Carlton, Mr. Carpenter, Mr. Ewing, Fredericks, Gross, Charley Gross, Ed Gross, Fred A. Gross, Grace Gross, Mary Gross, Mr. Thomas, Mrs. Thomas.)

Fred A. Gross writes his brother Charley nine final letters, from Allison, Ill.

May 1. Fred has joined the Allison country club, will take some time off work, and "take a whirl at golf." With his "powerful muscles and a strong physic," he should beat "the whey" out of "high brow" club members. Fred once played "shinny," and "golf is a hole lot like it." His playing will help Grace, "the Mrs.," "bust in to society out here." Mr. Carlton, village president, and Mr. Ewing, coal merchant, "ast me" to join, for $150 plus $50 a year dues. When Fred said golf was "for people that was weak physicly," Mr. Carlton said it would be harder than Fred thought. Fred joined, because "a mans 1st. duty is tords your wife." He'll play the "baby game" a little. Train commuters talk about golf and the stock market.

May 7. Fred "layed off yesterday P.M. ... and

hired a rig" to the club. The "stewart" introduced him to the "teacher." Fred said he didn't need a lesson to learn any game. The teacher provided Fred with "5 [clubs] to start with": "driver," "brassy," "click," "masher," "putter that the blade on it is like the masher and click only it dont turn up," "bag," and "3 balls and a boy to carry my bag and chase up the balls." Fred teamed with Fredericks, a garage owner Fred knows. Fredericks drove "about 150 yds." Fred put his ball on some mud, missed it, swung gently, hit behind it, "swang easy" and hit it "5 or 6 ft," used "the brass club" and it went "20 ft.," etc. When near "the short grass," Fred counted eight hits but was told to count the misses too; so "the man that gets the least strikes wins the game." They recorded Fredericks' "6 strikes" for "the 1st. hole" and Fred's "12 not counting the times I missed the ball." By the seventh hole Fred was out of balls and "1 of Frederick's besides." Fred lost some balls where "the coarse ... [had] long grass and weeds." During the last three holes Fredericks showed Fred some pointers. Fred agreed to buy the clubs at "the 1st. of the month"— maybe $2.50 for all five? He will take two lessons, at $1 an hour, and "learn all they is to know." Some mounds should be leveled. A nearby river distracted him.

May 18. Two lessons have taught Fred "a few little things." After all, "a man might play a yr. before he got on to them by yourself." Monday he hit the ball off "the tea ... to 1 side." The teacher said nothing was wrong, except back swing, left foot raised, eye off ball, head moved, "no aim," and vicious swing. Friday he learned about brassy, click, and masher. The teacher suggested more lessons. But Fred figured he "knowed the principals and ... would half to practice them up." He got "7 strikes" on that seventh hole, "and thats only 2 more strikes than the best of them." The Mrs. wants Fred to spend his "wk. off next month" with "the kids and she over to St. Joe."

June 14. Fred is playing golf daily at the Allison club during his free week. He played nine holes in "63 strikes." Balls cost "65 cents a peace and the clubs was $2.50 a peace." Expensive, they say, "on acct. of the war." When the Mrs. criticized how he spent his vacation, he said, "All your life is just 1 long vacation you and the kids both." They yelled a while, because otherwise "the neighbors would ... think we wasent married or something." Fred will please her by entering the golf tournament and trying for the president Mr. Ewing's prize, a "solid silver cup." Fred's "48 handicap" should make him a winner.

July 23. The tournament started a week ago, and "I played better than I ever did." His handicap put him "way up in the list." Mr. Carpenter was in "Chi." Fred, scheduled to play him, refused to wait and won by forfeit. Mr. Thomas, because of his handicap, "win his match" against Mr. Carlton, a better player. So Fred and Mr. Thomas are finalists for tomorrow. Grace and Mrs. Thomas will be watching and "can make friends between themselves" and all will "party ... who ever wins the cup." Fred won't be nervous before the crowd.

July 25. Mr. Thomas arrived without his wife. Fred introduced Grace, who walked with them. For the first hole, Fred drove well. Mr. Thomas sliced, recovered, and would have won; so Fred shouted and made him miss his putt. This bothered him. He would have won the next hole, but Fred pretended "like they was a snake or something behind him." He missed. Grace cheered. Fred was "2 holes advantage." They ended "the 1st. 9 holes," started the first again, and Fred sank a "50 ft." shot. Mr. Thomas quit. When Fred offered to play even, Mr. Thomas said, "I havent got no body along to lead the cheers for me," and added he didn't bring his wife because she "ain't nowheres near a match for yours." Fred reminded him "beauty isent only skin deep" and lectured him on improving his stance, swing, leg movement, and head movement. So Fred won the cup. Grace waited on the porch. Fred happened to say he needed a drink. The "stewart" brought him a high ball, said he needn't pay, but could sign that he got one. Fred was pleased.

July 29. There was a police "banquet" two nights ago. The chief assigned Fred to see "they wasent no dips" there trying to steal "women['s] ... rocks and etc." Fred and some friends went to the bar. Fred "had a hole lot to drink," called in sick next morning, and decided to go play golf. The "stewart" brought him "about a dozen" drinks. Hungry, he signed for lunch, which must have been "poisened because ... I was kind of dizzy." Mr. Carpenter and Mr. Thomas appeared. Fred invited them to prove they weren't sore by drinking with him. After looking "at each other ... they both excepted" and suggested wine. Fred signed for five bottles. Thomas asked about Fred's golf game. Fred answered by saying he would bet $100 he could beat him, with no handicap. Thomas would put up only $50 cash to Fred's $50 check, which Carpenter held. Fred felt ill but, not being "yellow," played anyway. Well, "they ain't no use telling you," Charley. Fred did badly;

Thomas lectured Fred that he "swang back too fast"; Carpenter cheated keeping score; Fred lost, then signed for six more bottles of wine. Fred says that the ham, the ketchup, or "them pickles" at lunch wrecked his game.

Aug. 3. Last night the Mrs. was crying over a bill mailed from the golf club: $150 entrance fee, $12.50 for "3 months dues," and "$65 for bar." Phoning "the treasure," Fred was referred to "the stewart," who explained about signing and then paying. He phoned "the treasure" again, said he wouldn't pay, was told that he'd be expelled from the club but it would be worth the $227.50 total "to have you quit." Fred couldn't stop that $50 check to Thomas. Those "preserved peaches ... poisoned me." Golf is a foolish "baby game."

Aug. 8. Fred took his clubs down to "Chi," was planning to sell them to "a hawk shop," but saw the chief first. He was surprised Fred played. Fred told him golf was "too easy for a groan man to monkey with it." The chief challenged him to play for drinks at a free public course at "Garfield Pk." He won because Fred was "out of practice." Fred will win tomorrow. Golf is "a swell game" and "grand exercise." In a P.S. Fred says Grace was crying tonight, confessed she left the door unlocked when she took "the babys out," and some one stole Fred's silver cup. He "scolded her," but only a little, and told her the cup wasn't worth very much. That's true too, Charley since "a hawk shop" gave him only $4.50 for it this morning.

FOSTER ("Gullible's Travels"). This is a travel agent Gullible is referred to in Palm Beach. He thinks Foster will be a man, but "Mr. Foster happened to be a girl." She promises to reserve the Gullibles a Fort Pierce hotel room with a bath but doesn't.

FOURNIER In "A Busher's Letters Home," Keefe says that at Paso Robles he ate at the same table with Fournier, among others. In "The Busher Comes Back," Keefe says he breakfasted with Fournier in Washington. In "A New Busher Breaks In," Keefe says that when he was pitching against San Francisco, Fournier could have fielded better than Chase.

John Frank Fournier (1889 or 1892–1973) played for the Chicago White Sox (1912–1917), the New York Yankees (1918), the St. Louis Cardinals (1920–1922), the Brooklyn Dodgers (1923–1926), and the Boston Braves (1927). Fournier then became a minor-league manager and scout, and finally a baseball coach for the University of California at Los Angeles. (Sources: *Baseball Encyclopedia*, 1028; Hilton, 47)

FOX ("What of It?"). He is Ben Lacey's friend, who talked with Ben about watches and Cragin's murder, or so Ben tells Dexter Cosset.

FOX, BILL ("Back to Baltimore"). He managed the Boston Braves last year, after which Dixon replaced him. Fox is a fictional character.

"A FRAME-UP" (*Saturday Evening Post*, June 18, 1921; HTW, RU). Characters: Bill Brennan, Old Man Bumble, Burke, Burke, Daley, Esther Fester, Lester Fester, Bud Fisher, Fitzsimmons, Jack Grace, Red Harris, Honey Hives, Mary Holt, Kid Howard, Joe Humphreys, Battling Igoe, Willie Kemp, Jimmie Mason, Min, Miss Morgan, Nate, Charley Porter, Rickard, Joe Rivers, Hap Stein, Gwendolyn Weasel, Mildred Whiffletree.)

I. The narrator is knowledgeable about boxing. He says Burke's fight with Jack Britton is being delayed until "another frame-up that may take a long w'ile to fix." Then he explains:

Kid Howard, a boxing instructor, has a gymnasium "in Chi," where Bill Brennan works out. An awkward-looking lad enters and says he'll pay $700 to be taught boxing. His name is Burke. His father, a peach farmer in Benton Harbor, Michigan, is wealthy. Burke wants to box Charley Porter, an experienced fighter also from Benton Harbor, and then retire. Howard says Burke can't fight Porter soon if ever. Burke says he'll tease Porter, who'll then meet Burke in a fight arranged by Fitzsimmons back home. He doesn't know Porter but has a reason for fighting him. Howard agrees to train Burke.

II. Appearing "stripped for action," "Burkey" is magnificently muscled. Howard has him train with Joe Rivers, whom he easily outclasses but won't knock down, since he "won't hurt nobody for nothing." Burke refuses to be matched with contending welterweights, seeks no prize money; and a month later Howard reads that Burke, back in Benton Harbor, defeated Porter in one round.

III. Burkey soon returns, can't find Howard, tells Nate, another trainer, he wants into "the fight game." Nate knows about Burke from Howard, is interested, and learns Burke liked Porter's girl, who said she'd go for him if he defeated Porter. Therefore he did, and they became engaged. He learned to dress well and dance, saw some "rich Chicago society dames," and ditched "this hick" girl. His doing so caused his father, who admired her, to disinherit him. To distract Burke, Nate tells him that after he wins some "bouts in Milwaukee or somewheres" he can help himself "to the cream" of women "in the Big Town." Burke defeats hard-hitting Red Harris in Milwaukee but without hurting him. Nate matches him against Hap Stein, Fitzsimmons's excellent Benton Harbor fighter. Later Nate takes Burke to Milwaukee to fight Stein, tells him Burke defeated Harris without slugging as he did in breaking Porter's jaw, and explains that Burke wanted to impress Porter's girl but now aims for "a millionaire society belle." Outdancing Stein, Burke wins, again without "cut[ting] loose and punch[ing]."

IV. Burke defeats Jimmie Mason in Milwaukee. Nate says he's got to stop "cuddling and really fight." Burke says he might fight differently if they go east. Nate schedules him against Battling Igoe in Boston. Burke wonders about Boston ladies. Nate counters that only "New York's the place," so don't "finance ... yourself to no bean counter." Nate terrifies squeamish Igoe, managed by Rickard, into taking a dive in the fourth. The crowd razzes Igoe. In New York, Nate gets Jack Grace, ex-boxer and inveterate kidder, to take Burke for a walk and point to beautiful women, unattainable until he smashes contender Willie Kemp's chin and gets invited to thereby impressed ladies' exclusive homes. If he wins, Rickard will schedule him against welterweight-champ Britton. But how to make Burke slug tough Kemp?

V. Grace does it. Nate takes Grace, Burke, and the narrator to a fashionable benefit for "devastated France," where Burke sees a gorgeous lady. He wants to marry her. Grace says she is "Esther Fester," is there with her billionaire father "Lester Fester," and has vowed to wed only a star athlete. Nate gets Burke to approach the ringmaster, who identifies Burke as Kemp's challenger, the winner slated to fight Britton. Burke grins at "Miss Fester," who automatically smiles back. Later, being unable to find her phone number, he won't fight Kemp unless he meets her. Grace plans to string Burke along with fake letters from her. This saddens Nate.

VI. Esther's first letter to "Dear Mr. Burke" apologizes for her forwardness, explains she admired him at the Garden; asks "was it me you was smiling at?"; says Pa will take her to his fight with Kemp, who may win and become champ. She continues, that he mustn't reply since "Pa don't approve" of her writing men she's not engaged to, but do smile again at her. Burke trains at Daley's but wastes so much time asking for mail there that Grace "spill[s] another note." In it Esther says they will attend the fight five days hence; she irresolutely admires both boxers, and "may the best man win"; Kemp probably will; he punches hard and you, "Mr. Burke," don't. On the fight day Esther writes that if he wins she'll phone him for a dance or a chat unless she's "too much a fool." Burke tells Grace and the narrator to bet "some ... crackers" he'll win in round one.

VII. They bet 3-to-1 on a knockout. Grace tells Burke "the little peach" and her father are there in a dark upper box. In the first round Burke wins by knockout in two minutes.

VIII. To "keep Esther alive till the Britton bout," Grace and the narrator send Burke an Esther letter explaining her instant departure for Europe with her demanding father. She'll return to see her champion defeat Britton. Nate gets $10,000 from Rickard for Burke to meet Britton. When Nate is taking Burke from New York for "Chi" by train, Burke chances to spot "Esther" seeing another beautiful woman off and grabs her. She denies being Esther or writing him. On the train, Nate observes Burke ask his "gal's pal a couple of cars back" about Esther Fester and is told her friend's unpoetical name is Mary Holt. Burke silently disembarks at Albany, later shows up in Chi, and asks Nate for money.

The narrator explains that's why "the Britton show had to be postponed."

When "A Frame-Up" first appeared, and perhaps later, Lardner's pugilistically addicted readers must have found it exciting. Four real-life boxers figure in it: Jack Britton (1885–1962) was welterweight champion, said by Lardner here to have fought his fictional Charley Porter. Britton was soon to lose his title to Mickey Walker (1922). Benny Leonard (1896–1947) was one of the greatest lightweight champions of all time, whose 6th-round knockout of Richard Harvey ("Richie") Mitchell (1895–1949) occurred in the Old Madison Square Garden (January 14, 1921)—witnessed by Jack Grace, Nate, and the narrator, if not Burke, who was busy ogling "Esther Fester." Britton fought Leonard, who knocked out Britton but lost when disqualified for flooring Britton and striking him when he was down (1922). (Lardner mentions Leonard in *The Big Town.*) Mitchell, long-time world-class lightweight (1912–1923) from Milwaukee, twice defeated by Leonard (1917 and later, just noted). The Lewis mentioned by Lardner as fighting Charley Porter twice may have been Ted "Kid" Lewis (1894–1970), welterweight champion and Britton's years-long rival (1915–1921).

Though fun as docudrama, "A Frame-Up" has its weaknesses: Lardner blurts the names of six separate characters, confusingly, in the first short paragraphs of section I; the narrator, who has to be told some of the action, jabs and feints bewilderingly along the time line. Donald Elder and Walton R. Patrick both call the story "inferior." Jonathan Yardley does believe that Lardner used the fake-letter plot trick better in "A Frame-Up" than he did later in "Hurry Kane." (Sources: Elder, 205; McCallum; Patrick, 96; Sugar; Yardley, 318, 331)

FRANCIS ("Along Came Ruth"). He is a rookie Cleveland pitcher who gets a lucky hit off Davenport, pitching for St. Louis. Francis is evidently a fictional character.

FRANK ("A Busher's Letters Home"). He is a home-town friend of Jack Keefe, who writes asking Al to give Frank his regards.

FRANK ("Dinner"). He, Bill, and Lester Graham decline Grace Halpern's invitation to dinner, which Harry Barton accepts and later regrets.

FRASER ("A Day with Conrad Green"). He is a comic actor whom Conrad Green might use in a show he tells his librettist Joe Martin about.

FRASER, MISS ("Mamma"). She is a nurse at New York's city hospital psychiatric ward. She tries unsuccessfully to question Mamma, an amnesiac. Miss Fraser later learns Mamma's family was wiped out by the flu

FRAWLEY, NED ("Who Dealt?"). According to Mrs. Cannon, "Jack Brooks or Ned Frawley or something" humorously shouted "apple sauce" in a vaudeville show she and her husband Tom Cannon saw in Portland.

FRAYNE, MRS. ("Anniversary"). She lived in Milton, inherited money when her parents died, and married Walter Frayne, who was on the rebound and became irresponsible.

FRAYNE, WALTER ("Anniversary"). He is someone Bess might have married in Milton but chose Louis Taylor instead. Walter flunked out of college, was wild, loved only Bess, married a rich "orphan" instead, ran through her money, and became chronically unemployed.

FRAZIER, JOE ("Liberty Hall"). He is a magazine editor. Mrs. Ben Drake tells him she'd like to write a short story. When she describes how she and her husband, a talented musical composer, were treated by Hilda and Ralph Thayer, Frazier thinks that experience would make a good story.

FRED ("Wedding Day"). He is Jimmy Shane's chauffeur and drives him to and from his wedding to Brownie Burt.

FRED, DOCTOR ("Great Blessings"). He treats Clara Stewart's daughter Myrtle when the child's grandfather feeds her too much candy. Doctor Fred warns Clara to regulate Myrtle's diet. Clara is embarrassed that he's unpaid.

FRED, DR. ("Meet Me in St. Louie"). Jessie remembers that when Ernie got scratches when he punched the door screen, "Dr. Fred ... painted them with iodine."

FREDA ("The Facts"). She clerks in Marsh's book department. Tommy Richards buys a Catholic prayer book in Latin and sends it to church-doing Mary Carey as Billy Bowen's Christmas present to her.

FREDERICK In "Lose with a Smile," he played for Brooklyn, hit "a fly ball so far out" in a game with the Boston Braves that Danny scored. In "Meet Me in St. Louie," Frederick is mentioned. In "The Ides of June," Johnny Frederick hit a fly in a game against Philadelphia; Danny, who had walked, thought it was a hit and became an easy out.

John Henry Frederick (1902–1977) was a Brooklyn outfielder (1929–1934), (Source: *Baseball Encyclopedia*, 1032)

FREDERICKS ("Fore!"). He owns the garage in Allison, Illinois. Fred plays a game of golf with him and gets lectured on his poor stance, swing, etc.

It seems uncreative for Lardner to give Fred A. Gross an associate named Fredericks. Since Fred feels superior, he doesn't refer to him as "Mr. Fredericks," whereas he calls other golfers "Mr. Carlton," etc.

"FREEDOM OF THE PRESS" (*Pictorial Review*, November 1935). (Characters: Alexander Beardsley, Bishop, Blake, Davis, Miss Dignan, Lena Goetz, Miss Horne, Hunter, Aunt Julia, Mr. Kingston, Klein, the Rev. Wallace Macomber, Stevens, Dr. Veley, Walsh, Constance Warner, Robert J. Warner.)

Robert J. Warner, a middle-aged multimillionaire, writes his 22-year-old daughter Constance Warner, who has been living with her Aunt Julia and her Gallic husband in France ever since Constance's mother died 11 years ago, to return home, incognito. He doesn't add that he has two months to live. Convent-bred and preferring France to her generous but unfeeling father, arrives at New York's dock to be told by Warner's lawyer Mr. Kingston that Warner has just died and all this secrecy is to protect her from family publicity, which Warner hated.

Diffident Constance, not imagining why newspapers would care to publicize her, moves into the Hempstead family mansion her father hoped she'd like and maintain. Mr. Kingston persuades her to invite her aunt and uncle to come live with her or at least pay her a long visit. Leaving town on business, Kingston says Alexander Beardsley, Warner's secretary, will handle Constance's business affairs. One of many servants tells her that a *Ferret* reporter is outside and wants to interview her. She says no. Hunter, supposedly "a tree surgeon" hired by Warner, is admitted. He is the "fresh" *Ferret* reporter.

Constance tells Hunter she won't be interviewed. He says that's why he will. He asks her age, is told 22, asks if he's in love with a count, is told no, learns she's partly covent-educated, wants the "low-down" on convent "inmates," wonders if that "frog" suitor "the count" wants her "jack," is told there's no count. Hunter is refused a drink, calls her less "dumb" than she acts, and departs. Constance is bewildered.

Alec Beardsley, also bewildered, reports to Constance next day. On the train to Hempstead he read a *Ferret* column about her. Alec had hoped she would be "reserved," "reticent," "shy," like Warner, and Alec too, and maybe even "nice." But the report said this: Constance was a Frenchified sophisticate, with "pithy" comments, Anna Held-like gestures; after escaping a "hot" convent she relished two wild years in Paris; she refused her strict father's repeated invitation to come home; the mansion, now hers, won't "be a hermitage"; she's engaged to a count — "don't print that yet," she said — who may follow her here; she plans to entertain men, doesn't "care so much for girls." An accompanying photo of Constance reminded shy Alec of a star in a movie he once saw. Alec is taxied to the mansion. Crowds of reporters and photographers are outside. An "astute journalist" shouts to Alec, "Hey, Count!" A "Warner lackey" lets Alec in. Constance approaches. Instantly smitten, he tells her she's nothing like the *Ferret* photo. He summarizes the write-up, which she says Hunter invented. Alec warns her the frustrated crowd will treat her as they did her reclusive father. Alec cleverly suggests that she answer their questions, permit photographs, and after a few weeks they'll quit "covering you ... and leave you to one man."

Constance: Such abuse would quickly cause a nervous breakdown. Alec: If you ignore the reporters, they'll concoct stories of your being ill, crazy, dying; you'll need guards to prevent their breaking in. Constance: I wish I were in France, where I was often alone but never lonely. Alec: Stay inside; I'll tell the reporters that the *Ferret* story is "wrong," that you never speak for publication; I'll visit every other day, but not to discuss "business matters"; really, "any kind of company is better than none." Constance, agreeably: "You're nice!" The two chat briefly. Alec tells the reporters this: The *Ferret* lies; he's Warner's secretary Beardsley, not a count; he's assisting Constance until Kingston's return. Alec counsels Blake, Warner's ex-butler, to keep newspapers from poor Constance. Reporters write that Constance was mysterious, retarded, crippled. Stevens, the *Blaze* reporter, steals through the mansion kitchen, enters Constance's room, takes Aunt Julia's picture, which the *Blaze* publishes retouched as "the Warner heiress." Alec, returning again, learns what's happening and wants to kill Stevens. Blake advises him "to forget the incident" and hire "uniformed cops" instead. Alec comforts Constance so pleasantly that she gets him to visit daily.

The *Star* reports that Beardsley, unemployed since Warner's death, is wooing this ugly, ill spinster heiress, almost as old as her father; that the "hard-boiled fortune hunter" figures she'll die soon or remain too demented to cope with this "adventurer." Alec rejects thoughts of killing the anonymous *Star* reporter or risking publicity by suing for libel. He has found Constance desirable simply for herself. This depiction of himself as money-mad so sickens him that he mustn't see her again. But wait. Should scandal-mongers "wreck his happiness, and perhaps hers?" Any vacillation is lost, however, when he sees adorable Constance again. Constance: I'm terrified, wish you could stay here always. Alec: That wouldn't "be wise ... unless —." Constance: "Unless what?" Alec: The *Star* made me out as unemployed; true, once Kingston returns; the *Star* said I sought to marry you for your fortune. Constance: I didn't know you were trying to marry me. Alec: I am. Constance: I believed you loved me but feared marrying me, not because of money but because of "my evident notoriety." Alec: I'll plan our secret marriage.

And Alec does. He confers with a license clerk, the Rev. Wallace Macomber, Dr. Veley, and a New York railroad official whom Warner chummed with. One bright day soon, Macomber, disguised as a plumber, drives past hordes of reporters, enters the mansion kitchen, and with Blake and a maid named Lena Goetz as witnesses marries Constance and Alec. The bridegroom then admits the reporters, offers drinks, promises a story, and says Miss Warner is coming downstairs and is his—. But the reporters fall into a two-hour sleep, doped by Dr. Veley's medicinal potions. Alec plans to switch with Constance from a Chicago-bound train's second section to its first section at Yonkers. A porter of Alec's section says Hunter of the *Ferret* was on the second section but was "left behind." Just beyond Cleveland, however, a voice "in Negro dialect" at the door of bride and groom intones thus: Telegram for Mrs. Beardsley. Constance: Is Blake reporting the wine killed someone? Hunter: "Hello."

Lardner includes a gratuitous reference to Anna Held (1873–1918), who was one of the attractive actress-wives of Florenz Ziegfeld,* Lardner's friend the theatrical impresario. (Farnsworth, 11–17 *passem*)

FRENCH ("Take a Walk"). He pitches for Pittsburgh against the team for which Agnew is playing.

Lawrence Herbert French (1907–1987) played for the Pittsburgh Pirates (1929–1934), the Chicago Cubs (1935–1940), the Cubs and the Brooklyn Dodgers (1941), and the Dodgers (1942). (Source: *Baseball Encyclopedia*, 1995)

FRENCH, ALLIE ("The Facts"). He or probably she is a friend of Mary Carey. Allie tells Mary about their pastor Dr. Gish's recovery from illness.

FRENCH, MRS. ("Contract"). She and her husband Robert French play bridge with Carl Dittmar and his wife and Carl Dittmar and his wife. Shelton and his wife are newcomers in their bridge-playing circle, and get criticized for faulty play. Shelton's friend Gale Bartlett comments unfavorably on both French and Cameron; so Shelton turns vengefully critical.

FRENCH, ROBERT ("Contract"). He and his wife play bridge to their satisfaction until newcomer Shelton, distressed by criticism, criticizes.

FRETTS, ERNIE ("Sun Cured"). He is a successful Brooklyn insurance agent whose secretary, Miss Clancy, makes him take a month's vacation in Florida to relax. Fretts, 38, alcoholic, and out of condition, intends to play golf and tennis, swim and fish, but instead he plays poker and roulette, drinks late, and skips meals. When Fretts gets Bonnie Werner, his girlfriend, to come down and join him, he dances and drinks with her, gambles with some men, and sleeps well into the afternoon. Fretts reveals all this in uninterruptible jabber to C. L. Walters, a fellow passenger both on the rain from New York to Florida and then, a month later, back again.

Walton R. Patrick calls Fretts a "self-obsessed character ... damaging nobody but himself," unlike the similarly self-indulgent son and daughter in "Old Folks' Christmas," who are cruel to their parents. Surely, however, Fretts's misleading treatment of Bonnie constitutes cruelty to dumb creatures? (Source: Patrick, 109)

FRIEND, HARRY (*The Real Dope*). He is a soldier with Keefe in France. Friend's supposed success with and writing to French women encourages Keefe to seek the companionship of Miss Marie Antoinette.

"A FRIENDLY GAME" (*Saturday Evening Post*, May 5, 1917). (Characters: Jim Hatch, Mrs. Hatch, The Missus, Harry Quinn, Marion Quinn, Joe Tuttle, Joe Tuttle, Millicent Tuttle, Mrs. Tuttle.)

I. The narrator plays poker, less enthusiastically than his wife does, "two or three times a week" at their house, the Hatches' house, and the Tuttles' house. Women don't know how to play poker. The narrator regards Mrs. Hatch as "The best female poker I know," because she doesn't "never come into a pot and she never antes without a court order." When "the Missus" gripes that Mrs. Hatch "sets there like a dummy," the narrator says he'd prefer a wife costing him only 40¢ every evening to "a female philanthropist." At the Tuttles, Mrs. Hatch suggests using 5¢ checks (i.e., chips) but agrees on 10¢ ones. The narrator complains ineffectively when his Missus wants deuces wild. Each six to eight weeks the narrator and Joe Tuttle win roughly what their wives lose, while Jim Hatch mostly wins and Mrs. Hatch doesn't bet. But then, usually, the Missus and Mrs. Tuttle order "everything's a jack pot with deuces loose," and Hatch wins everything. If host and hostess are losing, the game continues to 2:00 A.M.; if they're winning, it's sandwich time, and the losing couples go separately and argue separately until "the party of the second part" cries.

II. In February, Harry Quinn, 23 or 24, a clerk in the narrator's office, questions him about expenses once he marries his girlfriend Marion in April. The narrator kids him about buying beefsteak, potatoes, and shoes on his $16 weekly pay. Next, Quinn reports that when the two marry they'll room and board with her well-off parents for $4 per week. The narrator says those parents must either be "the best" or nutty or see qualities in Quinn unrevealed at work. Asked next about honeymoons, the narrator fibs that his father-in-law, a rich Wabash plumber, staked him and his wife to a trip via the Panama Canal to Honolulu and says Quinn might take Marion to Michigan City and back for $5.

III. Next, Quinn explains that he and Marion spent their honeymoon visiting car factories and ending in Kenosha because "dearie" worried about abandoning her parents and also got homesick. When Quinn says looking into Marion's eyes intoxicates him, the narrator says she probably has "regular bourbon eyeballs" and would like to gaze at her. Contrary to the narrator's expectations, Quinn continues to rave into June about his "best little wife a man ever had." Wondering how to rid himself of Quinn, the narrator gets a break. Quinn says he lost lunch money playing cards with his in-laws last night, doesn't play poker in that family foursome, but before marrying enjoyed "a little friendly game" of poker with "boys" he boarded with. The narrator wonders if Marion also plays. Quinn says she just knows poker-hand values but can learn "quick." When phoned, Marion agrees for the Quinns to visit the narrator's home and friends for poker, with "dime chips," tomorrow night.

IV. The narrator tells his Missus that Quinn, his office clerk, and his bride lack friends and would enjoy "a friendly game." Seven play: narrator, Missus, two Hatches, Joe Tuttle (his wife has to babysit, since the "maid went out"), and two Quinns. Trouble: Marion has a voice like a flagman's air whistle, her conversation is sickly sweet, and she has "giggleitis." The Quinns confess to limited knowledge but agree when the narrator, for the "wild" wives' sake, suggests deuces "amuck" and "nothin' but jack pots." Reluctant to risk much, Marion buys $2 in dime chips for herself and Quinn. Tuttle invests $2, Hatch and the narrator $4 "each for ourself and lady." First deal: All but Mrs. Hatch "decorate the mahogany" by anteing; Marion prematurely reveals five 10s counting wild cards, wins only eight chips, giggles. The narrator says she could've won more by holding. Quinn says they "didn't want to break nobody." Next deal: The Missus antes for neglectful Mrs. Hatch, Quinn wins by really bluffing with what he wrongly contends was a straight; Hatch explodes. Mrs. Hatch mistakenly deals the entire deck. Hatch rebukes her and snarls when the narrator defends her. Her correct deal is uneventful. Quinn deals: Marion opens, the narrator "tilts" her with 4-straight flush; she announces she'll keep only her two deuces and discards — face up! — what breaks up "a straight flush." The narrator "catched" into "a plain flush," raises Marion, who, advised by Quinn, raises, draws three clubs, and her straight flush wins. Dealing, Marion wrongly exposes Tuttle's draw, which reveals a heart and spoils his flush. He would keep the card, until Hatch rightly says he can't. They trade insults and almost fight. The narrator reminds Quinn this is "a friendly little game." Dealing, Mrs. Hatch wrecks the narrator's "four cold treys" by dealing him two cards instead of one. He "raved," is told off by Tuttle and Hatch, complains about Mrs. Hatch's never anteing, and the Missus rebukes him. Marion laughs, and the Quinns suggests quitting. Hatch calls them "pikers" for quitting while ahead. Hatch delays the Missus's proffered refreshments by raising the game limit to 50¢. Last deal: The Missus has three queens but tosses them, and "the sweet young bride" calls and wins over Hatch's discarded "two bullets." Everyone loses to the giggling Quinns' $21 victory. Afterwards, the three losing couples variously abuse each — to tears and sleep.

V. In the office next day, Quinn proves he's the exception to the rule that if men ever saw their girlfriends playing poker they'd never marry. He tells the narrator that Marion never played before, won nicely, and is "The best little wife a man ever had!" The narrator, biting his bed sheets that night, figures he must replace "grand old" poker with "somethin' swift, sure, fatal!"

FRISBIE, ALLEN ("Mr. Frisbie"). He is a wealthy man, a duffer of a golfer, and a domineering husband and father. The narrator, who is his chauffeur and caddy, cheats to improve Frisbie's scores, and uses other subterfuges to help Frisbie's wife to get a player piano, Frisbie's son Robert Frisbie to learn to drive a car, and — unfortunately — Frisbie's daughter Florence to marry worthless Henry Craig.

FRISBIE, FLORENCE ("Mr. Frisbie") *see* Craig, Florence

FROST, LUCY ("The Golden Honeymoon") *see* **MOTHER**

FUCHS ("When the Moon Comes over the Mountain"). He is mentioned as "judge Fuchs," an unsatisfactory Boston pitcher. He appears to be fictional.

FULTON, RED ("Good for the Soul"). He was a former Philly baseball player whom A.T. Grant hires for his minor-league team. Billy Carmody, hired as manager, switched Fulton, a catcher, to other positions in a vain effort to win.

GAINES, MR. ("Bob's Birthday"). He is a member of the club which Bob Tyler's parents frequent.

GAINOR ("A Busher's Letters Home"). Keefe gripes that when Gainor, playing for the Detroit Tigers against the White Sox, "lifts a fly," Lord, who was Keefe's teammate, "drops it," causing two scores against the Sox.

Delos Charles Gainor (1886–1947) played as the Detroit Tigers excellent first baseman (1909–1913), then for the Tigers and the Boston Red Sox (1914), the Boston Red Sox (1915–1919), and the St. Louis Cardinals (1922). (Sources: *Baseball Encyclopedia*, 1041; Hilton, 68).

GALE, JOE ("Cured!"). He and his buddies Rudy Miller and Paul Stroud are Dick Streeter's drinking companions. They meet in Mike Clayton's saloon, and drink and sing so long that Dick misses a dinner date with his wife Mary.

GALE, MRS. ("The Maysville Minstrel"). She was Stephen Gale's mother, deceased. After becoming a widow, she was an ill-paid dressmaker and needed financial help from Stephen, who quit school at 12 to work.

GALE, STELLA NICHOLS ("The Maysville Minstrel"). She is Stephen Gale's wife and the mother of their two children. When she learns he's writing poetry, she encourages him, in the impossible hope of their becoming rich.

GALE, STEPHEN ("The Maysville Minstrel"). He is 31, married to Stella, and the father of their two children. He has worked for eight years for Old Man Townsend, owner of the Maysville gas company. Charley Roberts cruelly encourages Stephen to write poetry, although his verses are wretched, if sincere, doggerel. For example, he rhymes "mellow" and "Stella," "Lackawanna," and ""honor," etc. He resigns from the company and is lucky to be rehired by Townsend, who lords it over him.

Earlier, after his father's death, Stephen left school at 12 to work for Western Union, then as a grocery-truck driver, a drugstore soda clerk, and a Lackawanna depot freight handler. This all parallels Lardner's varied employment until he broke into the writing game.

GALLANT, BARNEY (1884–1968). New York restaurateur. Bernard Gallant was born in Riga, Latvia, came to the United States (1903), learned English, was a cub reporter In St. Louis, a freelance reporter in New York, and press agent for Venustiano Carranza (later president of Mexico). In New York, Gallant owned a club and restaurant, and then banker- and racketeer-crowded speakeasies during Prohibition. When he ran the Greenwich Village Inn in Sheridan Square, he became famous as the first man convicted and imprisoned under federal Prohibition laws. He knew the celebrities of his day, including Peter Arno, Tallulah Bankhead, Robert Benchley, Heywood Broun,* William Randolph Hearst, Mark and Gladys Hellinger, Sinclair Lewis, and Eugene O'Neill. Bachelor Gallant was courtly to many female friends, felt all men should be single and all woman should be married, died in Miami, and willed most of his $15,000 estate to New York writers and journalists he knew. (Source: *New York Times* obituary, June 24, 1968)

The diarist in "I Can't Breathe" says she told Frank Caswell that she once sat next to "Jack Barrymore" (*see* Barrymore Family) at Barney Gallant's. In "Zone of Quiet," Miss Eleanor Lyons goes to Barney Gallant's place after seeing *What Price Glory?* (1924) by Laurence Stallings (1894–1968).

GALLANT FOX ("Widow"). He was a race horse at Saratoga, remembered by Frank Hastings.

GALLIA, BERT ("Along Came Ruth"). Keefe says Bert Gallia pitched excellently for St. Louis, defeating the White Sox twice.

Melvin Allys Gallia (1891–1976) pitched for the Washington Senators (1912–1917), the St. Louis Browns (1918–1919), and the Browns and the Philadelphia Phillies (1920). (Sources: *Baseball Encyclopedia*, 2000; Hilton, 257)

GALT ("'In Conference'"). While in conference with his associates, K. M. Dewey says he mistakenly received a letter addressed to "some name like Jennings or Galt or something like that."

GAMBLE, DOC ("Haircut"). He and Doc Foote, old-timers in Whitey's town, are seemingly too old to be effective physicians. Whitey and Julie Gregg preferred young Doc Ralph Stair.

GANDIL In "Sick 'Em" the narrator says that when Smitty pitched for the Phillies against Washington in the World Series, neither Gandil nor Milan could get hits. In "Call for Mr. Keefe!," Keefe says that when Johnson, pitching for Washington against Gandil, batting for the White Sox, threw a ball "down by his corns," umpire Bill Evans called it a third strike. Later, Keefe gripes that during a game he pitched against Cleveland Gandil gloved Speaker's drive but then "messed it all up." In *The Real Dope*, Keefe reminisces about a game in which Gandil figures against "Phila." In "The Courtship of T. Dorgan," during a White Sox game against Cleveland, a fight broke out between Chick Gandil and Cleveland's Speaker. In a later game, against the Boston Red Sox, Keefe pitched to Babe Ruth, and "Gandil speered that line drive off in him." In "The Busher Pulls a Mays," Keefe makes genuine excuses for Gandil's ineffective playing because of appendicitis.

Arnold ("Chick") Gandil (1887–1970) played for the Chicago White Sox (1910), the Washington Senators (1912–1915), the Cleveland Indians (1916), and the White Sox (1917–1919). George W. Hilton notes that Gandil had an appendectomy after the World Series (1919), helped organize the 1919 Black Sox Scandal, and was banned from organized baseball. David L. Fleitz brands Gandil as "an experienced fixer" of the Scandal, who "not only cheated the public but swindled his own teammates as well," through "greed." Donald Gropman calls "first baseman Chick Gandil and pitcher Eddie Cicotte ... leaders among the conspiring players." (Sources: *Baseball Encyclopedia*, 1044–1045; Fleitz, 279, 282, 284; Gropman, 160; Hilton, 199, 302, and *passim*)

GARDNER (*Treat 'Em Rough*). He is a soldier in Jack Keefe's army unit.

GARDNER, LARRY ("Along Came Ruth"). Keefe says that Larry Gardner, of the Cleveland Indians, overheard Francis, a rookie on his team, lament hitting a triple instead of walking.

William Lawrence Gardner (1886–1976) played for the Boston Red Sox (1908–1917), the Philadelphia Athletics (1918), and the Cleveland Indians (1919–1924). George W. Hilton adds that Gardner later worked as coach and still later manager of the University of Vermont baseball team. (Sources: *Baseball Encyclopedia*, 1049; Hilton, 267)

GARNER, LUKE ("Stop Me — if you've heard This One"). He is a New York playwright, as is his friend Jerry Blades. In Henry Wild Osborne's presence, Garner tells about going to Chicago to confer with George Cohan about a play Garner had written. On the train, he helped a beautiful girl who was mysteriously involved with a handsome, Spanish-looking man. The girl got off in Toledo, and the man was arrested in Chicago. Osborne appropriates the story and morphs it into an anecdote about himself.

GARRETT ("Three Without, Doubled"). He and his wife entertain the San Susie bridge club when Gullible and his wife are among the guests. Gullible, who is deliberately discourteous, asks Garrett how much rent they pay to Robert Messenger, owner of the apartment building in which they live.

GARRETT ("Tour Y-10"). He is in charge of the vacation tour from Chicago to Yellowstone and back. Although Violet Emerson fancies he's falling in love with her, he proposes to and is accepted by Violet's companion Kate Hayes.

GARRETT, KEN ("Ex Parte"). This old man sold his garage to people who converted it into a garage. The narrator sarcastically tells his wife Florence, who loves antiques, that they can buy it and make a house out of it.

GARRETT, MRS. ("The Jade Necklace"). She is the woman that the widowered hero marries in *Harridan*, the novel by David Wallace. Though never "a nun by any means," neither was she a harridan.

GARRETT, MRS. ("Three Without, Doubled"). She is the hostess when the San Susie bridge meets on the evening Gullible and his wife play. Mrs. Gullible tells Gullible that Mrs. Garrett is the best player and is also "one o' the smartest women in Chicago." Gullible's irrational bridge playing enables his "pardner" Mrs. Collins to defeat Mrs. Garrett.

GARVEY ("Sun Cured"). He lost to Ernie Fretts during an alcoholic poker game in Brooklyn, according to Fretts's story as told to C. L. Walters. Fretts says that with deuces wild, he had the five and nine of clubs and three deuces.

GARWOOD, BILL ("The Poor Simp"). He is remembered by the narrator as a catcher on their baseball team. Cap was pleased to see Bill handle Skull Scoville's wild pitching well. Bill bats ahead of Jack Andrews. Jack viciously spikes Bill when he bats after him and both get on base and have occasion to advance.

"GAS, OIL AND AIR" (*Milestones*, June 1917). Searched for, unsuccessfully.

GATES ("Reunion"). He is Rita Johnston's chauffeur. He drives her brother Bob Mason and his wife Jennie Mason from New York to the Long Island residence she and her husband Stuart own.

GEDEON ("The Battle of Texas"). When Keefe is pitching for the White Sox against St. Louis, Gedeon fouls out to bring victory to Keefe.

Elmer Joseph Gedeon (1893 or 1894–1941) played for the Washington Senators (1913–1914), the New York Yankees (1916–1917), and the St. Louis Browns (1918–1920). George W. Hilton notes that Gedeon participated in a minor way in the 1919 Black Sox Scandal and was banned from baseball. (Sources: *Baseball Encyclopedia*, 1053; Hilton, 253–254)

GEORGE (*The Big Town*). He is "a colored boy in uniform" at the door of the Riverside Drive apartment the Finches and Katie rent. Finch nicknames and describes the lad thus.

GEORGE ("Gullible's Travels"). He is a valet in the Alcazar hotel in St. Augustine. He presses Gullible's pants for $1.

GEORGE ("Gullible's Travels"). He is a waiter in the dining room at St. Augustine's Alcazar, or at least Gullible refers to him thus.

GEORGE ("The Last Night"). He is a waiter at the Red Duck. When Jay Arnold demands a drink he's never tried before, George suggests absinthe.

Arnold's rudeness prompts George to have him try brain-rotting absinthe.

GEORGE ("What of It?"). He is a Pullman porter to whom Dexter Cosset appeals for a place to sit, smoke, and think. George leads Cosset to a washroom, where he encounters super-loquacious Ben Lacey.

Lardner makes a Roaring Twenties stereotype out of "George something," with his "laughable darky dialect," especially when he addresses Cosset as "massa," rolls "those big eyes," and does a "double shuffle."

GEPHART ("Women"). He is "a spare catcher" on Mike Healy's team, has often heard Mike's boastful stories about women, tries to interrupt them, but can't.

GERARD, MRS. WALLACE EULALIE ("Rhythm"). She is a patroness of young composers. Harry Hart misunderstands her interest in him, tries "petting," and is no longer welcome.

GERSHWIN, GEORGE (1898–1937). Brooklyn-born Gershwin wrote popular songs and orchestral pieces combining jazz and pop-music incredients. His works include *Rhapsody in Blue* (1923), *Piano Concerto in F* (1925), *An American in Paris* (1928), and *Porgy and Bess* (1935). His music graced movies and Broadway shows. Bandleader Paul Whiteman* invited Gershwin to showcase his piano technique. Gershwin's *Of Thee I Sing* (1931) was the first musical comedy to be awarded a Pulitzer prize.

In Lardner's "Dinner" and "Poodle," Gershwin and his *Rhapsody in Blue* figure. In "Rhythm," Harry Hart suggests that Gershwin's "ultra rhythms and near dissonants sound like the doxology." Donald Elder says that Lardner "had reservations about Gershwin" and regarded *Rhapsody in Blue* as "high-brow." Jonathan Yardley reports that Lardner grew impatient with Gershwin's "quasi-'classical' compositions, saying he preferred him when he wasn't so Gershwinesque." (Sources: Elder, 290; Streissguth, 371; Yardley, 268)

G.F. ("Zone of Quiet"). She was Miss Eleanor Lyons's girl friend in Baltimore. Miss Lyons said G.F. lied about her to Charley Pierce.

GIBSON ("Horseshoes"). He is a Pittsburgh infielder. His collision with Mowrey enabled Speed Parker, a Cub, to get a two-run double.

George C. Gibson (1880–1967) played for the Pittsburgh Pirates (1905–1916) and the New York Giants (1917–1918), then managed the Pirates (1920–1922, 1932–1934) and the Chicago Cubs (1925). (Sources: *Baseball Encyclopedia*, 693, 1059; Hilton, 401)

GIFFORD, DR. ELSTON ("How Are You?"). He is recommended to Bob Dayton as New York's best diagnostician.

GILBERT ("Meet Me in St. Louie"). He was a Brooklyn baseball player. Abrams, a manager for Irving Berlin,* told Danny and Casey Stengel that only "Gilbert was good enough to write the lyrics 1st [before Sullivan composed the music]." Stengel replied that Danny couldn't write a song with

Gilbert, "as we trade it him to Cincinnati." The allusion is obviously to the famous Gilbert & Sullivan musical team.

Walter John Gilbert (1900–1958) played for the Brooklyn Dodgers (1928–1931) and the Cincinnati Reds (1932). (Source: *Baseball Encyclopedia*, 1061)

GILBERT ("GIL") ("The Yellow Kid"). He played on the narrator Bill's baseball team. Bill carelessly told Gil that their new pitcher, Lefty Crosby, was afraid of women. Although Bill asked him to keep it a secret, Gil told Harry Childs, who then kidded Crosby relentlessly.

GILBERT, MRS. INA ("Travelogue"). Hazel Dignan tells Dan Chapman that she knows this woman, who owned a launch, had lovely hair ruined by typhoid, and played Mah Jongg.

GILLESPIE ("That Old Sweetheart of Mine"). Stella Crane habitually answers the phone because her maid allegedly confuses the names Gillespie and Hammond.

This forced humor enables Lardner to show that the Cranes are well enough off to afford a maid, and to have Stella respond immediately when Will, her former boyfriend, phones.

GILLESPIE, MABELLE ("MIBS") ("Some Like Them Cold"). She, in Chicago, and Chas. F. Lewis, in New York, write insincere letters to each other. Mabelle presents herself as a modest, attractive potential homemaker, and clearly wants to marry him, until he writes of his engagement to Betsy Sears. Mabelle writes that her apartment mate Edith calls her "Sunny."

Donald Elder lauds Lardner for showing "compassion for the shallowness and ineptitude" of both Mabelle and Chas without any accompanying "scorn or hatred." (Source: Elder, 213)

GILLESPIE, MRS. ("Some Like Them Cold"). She is Mabelle Gillespie's widowed mother, living in Toledo, and, according to Mabelle, in ill health and willing to bequeath Mabelle and her sister some nice things.

GILLESPIE, SIS ("Some Like Them Cold"). She is Mabelle Gillespie's sister, who from Toledo visits Mabelle, living in Chicago.

GILMORE ("The Busher's Welcome Home"). Keefe names Gilmore as the president of the federal league, which Keefe tries unsuccessfully to joins.

James E. Elfers explains that James A. Gilmore and Charles Weeghman sought to develop the Chicago Whales in the Federal League in 1914, that Gilman received a death threat in the process, and that Charles A. Comiskey* and Byron Bancroft Johnson* tried to frustrate their efforts. (Source: Elfers, 170, 203, 237–238)

GISH, DR. ("The Facts"). He is the pastor of the church attended by Sam McDonald, Mary Carey, and others. Allie French tells Mary that Dr. Gish, who has been sick, will be able to preach next Sunday.

The name Gish is so unusual that Lardner undoubtedly took it from that of Lillian Gish.*

GISH, LILLIAN (1896–1993). Actress. She appeared as the delicate heroine in *The Birth of a Nation* (1915), directed by D. W. Griffith, *The Scarlet Letter* (1926), and many other films. Lardner probably named Dr. Gish in "The Facts" as he did because of Lillian Gish's immense popularity. Lillian Gish is mentioned in "A Caddy's Diary," the diarist of which could have seen her in *The Scarlet Letter*. In a letter (Mach 25 [1925]) to F. Scott Fitzgerald,* Lardner reports that Lillian Gish and drama critic Jean George Nathan (1882–1958) are an attractive pair often seen together. (Source: Caruthers [1995], 177)

GLAZE, LEFTY ("Hurry Kane"). He and Frank Miller are traded to the St. Louis baseball team from the Boston baseball team for Bullard, Robinson, and Roy Smith. All five are ineffective players.

GLEASON, WILLIAM J. ("KID") (1866–1933). Kid Gleason, born in Camden, New Jersey, was a baseball coach in the National League, for Philadelphia, St. Louis, Baltimore, New York, and Detroit (1888–1912), and a manager in the American League, for Chicago (1919–1923). George W. Hilton says that in 1914 Gleason was 5' 7" and weighed 158 pounds. Lardner knew and admired Gleason. During the 1919 World Series Scandal, Gleason was managing the Chicago White Sox against the Cincinnati Reds. David L. Fleitz and Jonathan Yardley report details of the scandal. Fleitz says "Gleason ... told [Charles Arlbert] Comiskey[*, owner of the White Sox] what he suspected and got nowhere." Yardley also discusses innocent Gleason's dismay and Lardner's awareness of "the Black Sox Series." F. Scott Fitzgerald,* Lardner's friend, touches on the scandal in *The Great Gatsby* (1925). (Sources: Fleitz, 285; Hilton, 42–43, 148; Yardley, 213–218)

In "A Busher's Letters Home," Keefe says Kid

Gleason "is a kind of asst. manager" of the White Sox and comments on Gleason's sarcasm concerning Keefe's excessive weight. In "The Busher Comes Back," Keefe writes about Gleason's continued kidding but also his words and acts of encouragement and kindness. In "The Busher's Honeymoon," Keefe, in trouble with Comiskey, says Gleason "would of fixed me all up" but was out of town. In "A New Busher Breaks In," Keefe dislikes but forgives Gleason for kidding about his weight. In "The Busher's Kid," Keefe repeats Gleason's jokes about Keefe's baby, calls Gleason "a little runt," and suffers when Gleason and Callahan secretly bribe Florrie $50 to stay home and babysit. In "Call for Mr. Keefe!," Keefe thinks he's clever calling Gleason mentally slow because he is 60. When Keefe boasts of joining the army, Gleason praises him. In "Alibi Ike," Ike, after fielding superbly, complains that his glove is insufficiently broken in. Carey replies that the glove "could easy of been Kid Gleason's gran'father." In "The Busher Reënlists," Gleason kids Keefe about his alleged war experiences but likes him and is happy Comiskey rehires him. In *Treat 'Em Rough*, Keefe, in the army at Camp Grant, says Gleason will be happy to see him watch the White Sox play the Giants in the "world serious"; however, Keefe doesn't get to attend the game in Chicago (October 6, 1917). In "The Battle of Texas," Gleason urges Keefe to develop, praises his increasing skill, warns him about dating Miss Krug, and assists in saving Keefe's marriage by bringing Florrie to watch him pitch in St. Louis. In "Along Came Ruth," Gleason manages, encourages, and criticizes Keefe, and advises him to avoid liquor. When Keefe defeats "the Philadelphia club," Gleason increases his salary from $2,400 to $3,000. In "The Courtship of T. Dorgan," Gleason helps engineer Keefe's improved contract, cancels the $50 fine imposed for bad pitching earlier, and treats him better. In "The Busher Pulls a Mays," Gleason humors Keefe even while razzing him. After one more of Keefe's rationalized benders, Gleason deals Keefe plus $5,000 to Connie Mack for Page, the Philadelphia pitcher. "Kid" Gleason is mentioned in "Stop Me — If You've Heard This One."

GLOOM, SIDNEY ("Good for the Soul") *see* **WARNER, BUCK**

GLORE ("Holycaust"). Jessie writes that the Cincinnati fire was more devastating than "the holycaust of 1909" that destroyed the Clore Lumber Company.

GOEBEL ("Some Like Them Cold"). Levy's and Goebel's are song publishers in New York, according to Chas. F. Lewis. Lewis writes Mabelle Gillespie that the two are crazy about his music, and later writes that a Goebel agent said his work might be better in the Follies.

GOETZ, GUS (*Own Your Own Home*). He owns a place where liquor is served. Fred frequents it. When Goetz sent Fred a case of whisky "for xmas," Fred offers one bottle as "Gents prizes" at his and Grace's bridge party.

GOETZ, HENRY ("The Venomous Viper of the Volga"). He is a huge, thick, 24-year-old assistant to a ventriloquist named Prentiss. Sandy King converts Goetz into the would-be boxer Ivan Ivanovich, "the VenomousViper of the Volga." The Viper defeats Manuel Martinez, in fact kills him with a fierce punch, and would next fight Frankie Fitzgerald except that the Viper and King's girlfriend Mabel Ives fall in love and King beats him up.

GOETZ, LENA ("Freedom of the Press"). She is a maid for the Warner family. She and Blake, the butler, are witnesses at the wedding ceremony of Constance Warner and Alexander Beardsley.

GOETZ, YOUNG ("Champion"). He is "the welter champ" but is described as "broken down." Midge Kelly defeats him in New Orleans.

GOLDBERG (*The Big Town*) *see* **MERCER, SID**

GOLDBERG ("Champion"). He is mentioned by Midge Kelly to Tommy Haley as the man handling their weekly pay, with prospects in New York and Milwaukee.

"THE GOLDEN HONEYMOON" (*Cosmopolitan*, July 1922; HYW, PLR, RLR, RU). (Characters: Bitting, Charley, Hartsell, Frank Hartsell, Mrs. Hartsell, Kendall, Mrs. Kendall, Edie Kramer, John H. Kramer, Judge Lane, Mrs. Morse, Lucy, Mrs. Newell, Mrs. Oxford, Pat, Mrs. Ryan, Pence, Mrs. Pence, Royal Tin Can Opener of the World, Weaver.)

Charley, the narrator, has been married to Lucy, whom he calls "Mother," for 50 years now, in New Jersey. Their daughter Edie and her husband, John H. Kramer, persuade them to take a golden anniversary vacation to St. Petersburg, Florida. They go by train via Trenton, Philadelphia, Baltimore, Washington, D.C., Virginia, North Carolina, South Carolina, and Georgia, to

St. Petersburg. They rent a room for $12 a week, near a place frequented by "bona fide auto campers" called "Tin Can Tourists." They register with the Chamber of Commerce, observe visitors from many states, and scout out restaurants. Williams Park features concerts and games such as roque, checkers, and horseshoes. Charley defeats a fellow named Weaver at checkers. At a concert Mother sees Frank M. Hartsell's wife. Frank was engaged to Mother 52 years ago, until Charley "stepped in and cut him out." When Frank spots Mother — Ah, Lucy Frost! — he quits a horseshoe game in delight. The four have dinner at a cafeteria Frank suggests. Charley laments paying 10¢ more for their two dinners than at their own place. Next day Charley and Mrs. Hartsell oppose the other two at "five hundred," and lose, because Mrs. Hartsell was "a miserable card player." They attend some church socials featuring a singer, a ventriloquist, and a bird-song imitator. Hartsell challenges Charley to checkers, loses, and gets heckled by bystanders. Another social offers a lecture about "business conditions" and another bird mimic. Charley tells jokes and is applauded as "quite a speechifier." Mother and Mrs. Hartsell play roque with ladies met at the chiropodist's. Frank challenges Charley to play horseshoes and beats him — through sheer luck and because Charley suffers a rubbed-raw thumb. Charley spitefully insults Frank about losing Lucy and about Ms. Hartsell's poor card playing. Mother gets Charley mad defending the Hartsells. She and Charley viciously blurt a wish they hadn't married each other, soon reconcile, and "we got kind of spoony." They play cards with the Kendalls, a new couple regularly wintering there. If Charley and Mother return next year, the four might meet again. They go home again, pretty much along the same train route, after "having been gone just one month and a day."

Long before writing "The Golden Honeymoon," Lardner wrote a letter (November 9, 1911) to Jeannette Hascall Abbott,* his mother-in-law, in which he said his parents "celebrated their golden wedding anniversary last Monday [November 6], the celebration consisting of staying at home and entertaining their grandson ... and his mother." Lardner replied by letter (May 13, 1932) to an inquiring correspondent that "I believe I like 'Golden Honeymoon' best of my immortal works." Genius that he was at capturing ordinary Americans' thought and talk processes, Lardner, aware of Charley's intellectual limitations, gently fills the sweet old man's narrative with clichés, repetitions, grammatical manglings, and trivia about train schedules and room and board expenses. Thomas Boyd declares that the story "would be barren if written in any other way" and also that "a lifetime is summed up in those few pages." Ring Lardner Jr. reports that after the *Saturday Evening Post* rejected "The Golden Honeymoon," *Cosmopolitan* bought it for $1,500. Ernest Hemingway didn't care much for Lardner's fiction but liked "The Golden Honeymoon," because in it "he wrote about people that he truly admired." John Berryman praises it as "a beautifully modulated thing about the persistence of rivalry and pettiness into an area where everything ought to be solved." Donald Phelps describes the story as "a miniature history, impeccable and mum as a fossilized maple leaf." It is now regarded as one of Lardner's finest stories. Not so, however, by some early critics. Clifton Fadiman labeled it "one of the most smashing indictments of a 'happy marriage' ever written, composed with a fury so gelid as to hide completely the bitter passion seething beneath every line." Ludwig Lewisohn, agreeing, calls the old couple "poor clods in human form." Maxwell Geismar regards the theme of "The Golden Honeymoon" as "the sterile old age which results from the narcissistic passion." In a letter (June 5 [1924]) to F. Scott Fitzgerald,* Lardner says that John Golden (1874–1955), New York-born theatrical producer, playwright, and songwriter, asked him to dramatize "The Golden Honeymoon" but said he couldn't without introducing a couple of young lovers. (Sources: Berryman, 421; Boyd, 602; Fadiman, 316; Geismar, 9; Hemingway, 158B; Lardner, Jr., 153; Caruthers [1995], 98, 159, 257; Lewisohn, 515; Phelps, 90)

GOOD In "Horseshoes," Good is a Cub outfielder when Dick Grimes joins the team in a utility capacity. In "The Busher's Kid," Keefe boasts that in the first inning of a "city serious" game he retired "them good hitters Leach and Good and this here Saier."

Wilbur David Good (1885–1963) played for the New York Yankees (1905), the Cleveland Indians (1908–1909), the Boston Braves (1910), the Braves and the Chicago Cubs (1911), the Cubs (1912–1915), the Philadelphia Phillies (1916) and the Chicago White Sox (1918). (Sources: *Baseball Encyclopedia*, 1073; Hilton, 159)

"GOOD FOR THE SOUL" (*Saturday Evening Post*, March 25, 1916; ABS, LOB, RAB). (Characters: Hi Boles, Jimmy Boyle, Billy Carmody, Red Fulton, A.T. Grant, Griffin, Aunt Julia, Mac, Paul, Steele, Charley Wade, Ethel Warner, Buck Warner, Whiskers.)

Robert Frederick ("Buck") Warner volunteered to appear before a member of the prestigious Baseball Writers' Association of America on February 1, 1916, and dictate a confession. Once a major-league baseball player, he is now part-owner of an automobile garage in Hopsboro, a Cincinnati suburb. This is his story:

I. My wife Ethel threatened to go live with her Aunt Julia, outside Dayton, if I didn't stop "grouchin' round the house." I promised, but Ethel said my conscience would make me break my promise. She showed me a newspaper article about a man who relieved a bad conscience by writing his minister a confession of a long-ago theft. She told me to find someone to listen to my "horrible crime" and not shield others, not even Carmody.

For six years I played shortstop well in the National League, shouldn't have played other positions, but got into trouble by shooting bad billiards in Brooklyn until I owed $4,000 to gamblers. In Pittsburgh I met Ethel when she was visiting friends I also knew. We got engaged. I told her about my debt. She said we must wait until it was paid. I said I'd be clear next fall, not this. But while playing in Chicago I fell rounding first base and crippled my knee. Two doctors said I could walk well but never run or even stoop again. Mac, my manager, agreed to keep silent until I could "find somethin' to do."

Ethel suddenly wrote me this: Aunt Julia promised a $2,500 gift when we married; Ethel's brother Paul, "a swell mechanic," would match that sum; we could buy the only garage in Hopsboro, up for sale; I could quit baseball, manage the garage, and live at home. Though worried, I wrote Ethel with false cheerfulness. Suddenly I was approached by A.T. Grant, who had purchased "a club [Indianapolis, 1915] in the new [Federal] league." Grant wanted me to play baseball for him. Doing "some tall thinkin'" and questioning, I learned that Grant's manager was Billy Carmody, whom I'd heard of but never met, and also that my salary would be $5,000. I thought maybe I could play, demanded right field to avoid infield running and stooping, and we shook hands. Back in Dayton I told Ethel everything, and we became hopeful.

II. Winter papers didn't waste space covering "our club," which I joined in Dixie Springs in March. I walked from the deserted hotel to the field, talked my way past a bewhiskered guard and saw Mr. Grant, who didn't remember me at first. I recognized four players among two dozen out practicing: Jimmy Boyle, a catcher I'd started with in Des Moines nine years ago; Billy Carmody, whose pictures I'd seen; Hi Boles, from "the Association"; Charley Wade, a catcher with Boston's team "for w'ile"; and Red Fulton, a former Philly catcher. Wanting me to rest today, Grant walked to the hotel with me, commented on his recruits' handsomeness, said he had a rule against their drinking or cavorting at night, and planned to "perjure baseball of its evils" and win the pennant.

Jimmy Boyle got the hotel clerk to have me room with him — to have someone to laugh with, he said, explaining thus: Grant wanted to hide the team to assure winning the first game and therefore the pennant; his pitching staff included a splendid fellow named Steele, three weak righties, and three weak "cockeyes [left-handers]"; and Grant and Carmody planned to switch players around. I said right field was mine by contract, then told Jimmy about my knee and my marriage plans. Jimmy said the players, especially Griffin, who played third base by planting his foot there, were best at devouring hotel meals lavishly provided by pallbearer-like waiters. Grant also sent huge lunches to the practice field. Hi, Jimmy, Red, and I sat aside, joking. Hi said those feeders should be "heavy hitters," while Jimmy called dinner "The Royal Gorge."

During practice sessions, Carmody and I failed in efforts to train our teammates. Anyway, with my bad leg, I couldn't "frolic round" much. During one practice game, my side had the bases full, mostly on errors, and I went to bat. Carmody regularly ordered everyone to take two strikes, but with Steele pitching nothing but smooth strikes I belted a home run. Carmoday bawled me out; so I criticized his two-strike orders and told him he managed so badly he shouldn't be paid. He countered that I lacked good legs and shouldn't be paid either. He said we didn't deserve Grant's money; so we agreed to keep quiet. When we headed north to start the season, I was to play outfield with two half-promising kids, Jimmy first base, Hi third, Red second, Carmody shortstop, and Wade catch. Grant rhapsodized about winning the pennant and a trip to Europe, if the war ended.

III. We played at home against Buffalo. In Grant's pretty stands, the 800 fans resembled "fleas on a flat car." But Steele pitched a shutout, and I hit a two-run homer. Next day Steele didn't pitch; therefore Wade, behind the plate, was busy "shaggin'" wild pitches and we lost 14 to nothing. Steele then lost one, won one; a lefty won, because an ex–Association umpire had poor vision; May went into June, and Jimmy made numerous errors. Home fans liked our "low comedy" and attended until mid–June, when we went west to poor gates. The next home game attracted only 37 spectators. So Grant dropped bleacher prices to 10¢ and hired a band. By August I was hitting .420, mostly on home runs because I ran so carefully that "Mr. Leggo ... wabble[d]" only twice.

Trouble came when we were playing at home in Indianapolis mid–August: Wade broke his ankle, Carmody's "right arm went dead," and Aunt Julia argued with Ethel, who wired to me to come to Dayton immediately. Carmody said I could visit her if I returned tomorrow and played shortstop, because he was moving to first and planned to avoid throwing by dropping every ball he had to field. I objected until he told me Grant gave him a contract at $1,800 a month but only if he played all season. He confessed that, in order to switch to first base, he told Grant that Boyle played first badly, he would replace Boyle there, and I'd have to play shortstop because Grant said he would order it. I said I'd play only right field and left in a huff for Dayton, knowing Carmody was upset but we could blackmail each other into silence. Ethel, weeping, told me that Aunt Julia had fallen in love with an old "G[rand]. A[rmy of the]. R[epublic]." veteran and was retaining her promised $2,500. Ethel got mad, criticized Julia for "tyin' up with a bird twenty years older than herself," and "a riot" ended Ethel's money hopes. When she repeated she'd not marry me until I was out of debt, I almost cried too. Then I had an idea. I told her I'd wire her good news or bad tomorrow night from Indiana.

Next morning back with the team, I told Carmody I'd play shortstop but would "coax" Grant first. When I located Grant, he said Carmody was planning some changes "that would leave shortstop open." I suggested that he "get a hold o' some semi-pro shortstop." He insisted he wanted me so his team, with six weeks to go, would finish in seventh place, not eighth. I asked for a new contract, since I'd signed for a mere $5,000 at right field, and, though I was a "born" shortstop, playing that position shortened anyone's playing life. I demanded a $9,000 contract but settled for a $2,500 bonus.

I wired the good news to Ethel. Her return wire suggested I'd robbed somebody. Maybe so. During our last six weeks we won only five games. I felt awful about Steele's having pitched "two to four games a week," and for $400 a month. But he's with "a real team this year" and is worth watching.

"Good for the Soul" is a light-hearted but subversive amorality play. Its dramatis personae include, but are not limited to, dishonest narrator (Buck) and long-suffering soul mate (Ethel), conniving friend (Carmody), self-absorbed guffawers, gluttons, naive spendthrift (Grant), and promise-breaker (Julia). The morals of the show are that clever dishonesty pays and that an honest confession is a joke. Lardner pinpoints the time of action as 1915 and suggests a general 1910s time frame by mentioning Mary Pickford* and "Pawnee Bill," the latter being identified by George W. Hilton as "Major Gordon William Lillie [1860–1942], proprietor of one of the principal Wild West shows of the day." (Source: Hilton, 535)

GORDON, JOE ("Widow"). He and his wife call on Margaret Winslow to express sympathy after her husband John died.

GORDON, MRS. ("Widow"). She and her husband Joe visit Margaret Winslow when her husband John died. Mrs. Gordon repeatedly offers to help in any way they can.

GORE, WALLACE ("Stop Me—if you've heard This One"). He is a New York publisher who hosts a dinner party attended by Jerry Blades, Luke Garner, and Henry Wild Osborne, among others. During the event, Osborne fibs and relates as truth a variation of a real story Garner told him earlier.

How often does a harmless, forgotten little American short story contain a character whose two names coincide with the last names of two decades-later vice presidents? Do recall Henry Wallace (1888–1965), vice president (1941–1945); Al Gore (b. 1948), vice president (1993–2001).

GORTON, BESSIE ("BESS") In "Three Kings and a Pair," she comes from Wabash to visit her sister Mrs. Gullible. She meets "Mr. Bishop" on the train, and both she and her sister would like her to marry him. In "Gullible's Travels," Gullible recalls taking Bess to *The Three Kings* opera, with Mrs. Gullible and Bishop. In "The Water Cure," Gullible torpedoes Bess's impossible love affair with Elmer Bishop by throwing them together during a weekend vacation with the Gullibles. The outcome is that Bishop, a lying welcher, disappears.

Jonathan Yardley calls Bess a "quintessential Lardner character, the unmarried sister-in-law." (Source: Yardley, 285)

GOULD ("Gullible's Travels"). He is a businessman from St. Louis. Gullible talks with him on the train during his trip to Florida with Mrs. Gullible. Gould is offensively boastful.

GOULD, COL. *(Treat 'Em Rough)*. He is a "Co. B" officer whom Jack Keefe says his buddy Red Sampson overheard discussing General Pershing's orders.

GOULD, HETTY ("Tour Y-10"). She is a friend whom Violet Emerson and Kate Hayes know. Violet says they're not as wealthy as Hetty, who could better afford the Yellowstone vacation Violet and Kate are about to take.

GOULD, JOHNNY ("The Hold-Out"). He was a splendid baseball player whom Frank Conley, manager of Mr. Edwards's team, neatly traded to obtain. Gould regularly laughed at Lahey's inept fielding.

GOULET ("The Battle of the Century"). He was a French war hero and a trim, handsome boxer, the champion of Europe. He was managed by La Chance in a match in New York against Jim Dugan, who won despite rigged publicity puffing Goulet.

GRABINER, HARRY ("The Busher Reënlists"). Harry, as Keefe calls him, is the White Sox secretary, in Chicago. He chats with Keefe before Comiskey lets Keene in to discuss his contract.

George W. Hilton reports that Harry Grabiner (1891–1948) began working for the White Sox at age 13 when he happened to wander into the ball park after a heavy rain and helped Comiskey clean the place. Harry sold scorecards, became assistant secretary (1912), then secretary (1916), then to high administrative positions (to 1945), after which he was vice president of the Cleveland Indians (1946–1948). (Source: Hilton, 40, 122, 226)

GRACE ("Anniversary"). She is Florence Hammond's sister, married to Ed, abused by him, but always forgiving him.

GRACE ("Champion"). She is one of Midge Kelly's paid and greedy girlfriends. Midge dumps her, threatens her, and prefers Mrs. Harris.

Elizabeth Evans notes that "[w]hat becomes of Grace is another story. Midge discards her as he does other people when he finishes with their usefulness." (Source: Evans, 69)

GRACE, JACK ("A Frame-Up"). He is an ex-boxer and a friend of Nate, who manages boxer Burke. To get Burke to train vigorously, Grace writes fictitious letters to him as from Esther Fester, pretending she'll adore him if he defeats Willie Kemp.

GRAHAM In "One Hit, More Error, One Left," he is Jessie Graham's father and has a store in Centralia, Illinois. In "When the Moon Comes over the Mountain," Jessie writes Danny that "Papa" said hanging your tongue out like a dog while in a subway doesn't relieve the air pressure. In "Meet Me in St. Louie," Graham was willing to escort Jessie to St. Louis to visit Danny, until, that is, Jessie properly cancelled her travel plans. In "Holycaust," Graham observed that when the Centralia fire spared his store, he thought he could rent it. In "The Ides of June," Jessie's father finances her trip to meet Danny in New York and go with him to Jersey City, where Graham has a step-brother.

GRAHAM, ART ("Harmony"). He plays center field, often warms the bench, sings tenor in the team quartet, and tells the narrator one version of how the team acquired Waldron. Bill Cole tells another version.

GRAHAM, ERNIE In "Meet Me in St. Louie," he may have been Jessie Graham's brother. She writes Danny that Ernie, when little, cut his hand on a door screen. In "When the Moon Comes over the Mountain," Danny writes Jessie that he told Carey, manager of the Brooklyn baseball team, that she had a brother who died in 1928.

GRAHAM, JESSIE In "One Hit, One Error, One Left," Jessie receives letters from and writes to her boyfriend Danny Warner, who is trying out as an outfielder for the Brooklyn baseball team. She lives with her parents in Centralia, Illinois. Her father runs a store. Her mother is ill. Jessie coyly encourages Danny to remember his promise of marriage but, golly, not to feel bound by it. She demeans herself by saying she's a poor letter writer and a poor piano player. She shows some spunk when Danny begins playing up his friendship with Vivian Duane, of Clearwater, Florida, where his team is practicing. In "When the Moon Comes over the Mountain," Jessie writes Danny encouragingly but retains her negative attitude toward "Miss Duane." In "Meet Me in St. Louie," Jessie was to visit Danny in St. Louis until he wrote that the two of them would be lunching with Mrs. Earl and her "kid sister." In "Holycaust," Jessie finally rebukes Danny for writing about his friendships with Vivian Duane and Miss Fleming. In "The Ides of June," Jessie remains upset by Danny's immaturity but goes to New York to meet him. Will he be at Penn Station? Howard W. Webb, Jr., for one, has his doubts, saying that "it is just as likely that while the girl [Jessie] waits forlornly at the station Danny will be wandering about New York, as lost in his way as Mamma [*see* Mamma in "Mamma"] is in hers." (Source: Webb, 444)

GRAHAM, LESTER ("Dinner"). He, Bill, and Frank decline Grace Halpern's dinner invitation, which Harry Barton reluctantly accepts.

GRAHAM, MRS. In "One Hit, One Error, One Left." She is Jessie Graham's ailing mother. In "When the Moon Comes over the Mountain," Jessie writes Danny that she will stay with her parents "till they are gone." In "Meet Me in St. Louie," Jessie uses her mother's continuing illness as one excuse for not visiting Danny in St. Louis. In "Holycaust," Jessie curtly writes Danny that her mother is all right.

GRANEY In "Call for Mr. Keefe!," Keefe of the White Sox complains that when he hit the ball into the outfield in a game against Cleveland, it would have gone between Graney and Speaker, except that Speaker caught it while out of proper position. In "The Courtship of T. Dorgan," Keefe witnesses a fight between Speaker and Chick Gandil, of the White Sox, and boasts to Graney that Speaker had better not fight him. Speaker later challenges Keefe, who backs down.

John Gladstone Graney (1886–1978) played for the Cleveland Indians (1908–1922). George W. Hilton adds that Graney was later the first baseball player to become a full-time radio broadcaster (for the Indians, 1932–1953). (Sources: *Baseball Encyclopedia*, 1079–1080, 2020; Hilton, 203)

GRANT, A.T. ("Good for the Soul"). He was the inexperienced, naive purchaser of a minor-league team. He recruited Billy Carmody as manager, and as players Buck Warner and other major-leaguers, but also inexperienced athletes, because they were handsome and he wanted to improve baseball's image. Grant fed his team lavishly, hoped to win the pennant, and planned to take his players to Europe if the war ended. Warner, Carmody, and others took advantage of Grant. Warner called Grant "the Old Boy."

GRANT, LEFTY ("The Hold-Out"). He is team-owner Mr. Edwards's left-handed pitcher, whose last-year's 3–11 record Mr. Edwards deplored. Grant "after a little crabbin'" agreed to a salary cut from $7,000 to $5,000.

GRANVILLE ("Now and Then"). He is from Chicago. Bob, Irma's husband, snubs Granville during their first visit to the Bahamas; but when Bob and Irma return to the Bahamas he urges Irma to spend time with Granville, so that Bob can cavort elsewhere.

GRANVILLE, BUNNY In *The Big Town*, he is a singing character in a Follies show attended by Finch, Ella Finch, and Katie. Jimmy Ralston plays the part. In "Insomnia," the sleepless author remembers Bunny Granville.

GRATZ, ARTHUR ("Who Dealt?"). He is a Princeton man, and a handsome ex-athlete as well. He and Thomas Cannon both loved Helen Bird Strong, but Arthur married her. Four years later, Cannon and his talkative wife and the Gratzes are playing bridge when Mrs. Cannon reveals that Cannon wrote a short story detailing his sorrow at losing Helen.

Donald Elder says that Arthur Jacks, whose family owned a paper mill in Niles, Michigan, was Lardner's childhood friend and "remained Ring's closest friend for many years," and that Jacks and his wife Helen became the Lardners' neighbors in Great Neck, Long Island. Jonathan Yardley presents evidence that Lardner and his wife Ellis Lardner* enjoyed playing bridge with Arthur and Helen Jacks, and explains that they provided the first names of the Gratzes because "Ring loved to drop the names of his friends into his stories." (Sources: Elder, 18, 180; Yardley, 229, 293)

GRATZ, HELEN ("Who Dealt?"). She is the former Helen Bird Strong and is now Arthur Gratz's wife. Both Arthur and Thomas Cannon loved her. Helen promised to marry Thomas, grew impatient, and accepted Arthur. Helen and Arthur have been married four years. Cannon married an air-head three months ago. While the four are playing bridge, Mrs. Cannon recites her husband's poem expressing sorrow over the loss of his faithless beloved. (See also Gratz, Arthur.)

GRAVES ("Poodle"). Grave's Hospital is the unpleasantly named place where the man calling himself Phil Hughes is being treated by a physician calling himself Dr. Gregory.

GRAYSON, EVA ("Anniversary"). She is a girl that Ed, Grace's husband, horsed around with one night. Ed came home late drunk and slugged Grace, thinking she was Eva.

"GREAT BLESSINGS" (*Cosmopolitan*, December 1929). (Characters: Berger, Dave Bonham, Brown, Mrs. Brown, Butler, Frank Butler, Mamie Butler, Davis, Mrs. Davis, Mrs. Davis, Doctor Fred, Kendall, Kendall, Sloan, Clara Stewart, Father Stewart, Grace Stewart, Harry Stewart, Mother Stewart, Myrtle Stewart, Tod Stewart.)

The President proclaims Thursday, November 28th, as Thanksgiving Day, a time to thank "the Giver of All Good and Perfect Gifts" for productive fields, industries, and commerce, and for "increased wages" resulting from "honest toil."

Mother Stewart and Father Stewart have two sons, Tod and Harry, both of whom drink excessively. Tod's wife is Clara. They have a daughter, Myrtle. Harry's wife is Grace. They are childless. For six years after Tod and Clara were married, Harry and Grace had the family Thanksgiving dinner at their home, which was bigger than Tod's and Clara's. Mother disapproved of Grace, who drank a little, smoked a lot, and was a poor hostess. Myrtle's birth inspired Mother to prefer Clara as a daughter-in-law. Harry and Grace moved five years ago to Detroit. Harry began managing a hotel with a liquor license. His annual income, $15,000, exceeded his salary. He sent $100 "home" every Christmas, and Mother voiced approval of Grace. For five years, Father and Mother have enjoyed Thanksgiving dinner at Clara and Tod's.

Action begins on this fifth Thanksgiving Day. Myrtle, 10, demands more cranberry sauce. Grace says it'll make her sick. Mother tells Grace to obey Myrtle, explaining that she refused Tod and Harry nothing when they were little and they're none the worse for it. Grace obeys, wishes she could sneak some gin later to recover, "but one small shot made her sick." Besides, she'll have to tend to Tod and Myrtle, both always sick after "the old people" visit.

Worse, Clara's two in-laws swoop down on her several times a month, just before dinner, and Father always brings Myrtle a "brutal brand of candy." Last July, Tod and Clara went to a show one night, left Myrtle alone, the in-laws paid a surprise visit, and their voices awakened her.

Mother pontificates thus today: Myrtle isn't made sick and nervous by sweets; she's been nervous ever since awakening that July night, abandoned in a dark house; a hungry "tramp" might have entered the house then and "stopped at nothing." Tod: Oh, Myrtle would scare tramps. Mother: I hate that talk; Myrtle should live with me and be appreciated. Clara: I appreciate her. Mother: You're too strict. Father, slipping Myrtle candy under the table: Tod, you've been at your new job two weeks; how's everything? Tod: They disliked me, released me last Saturday. Mother: Don't speak thus before Myrtle; children misunderstand and repeat "nonsense"; "Old Kendall" doesn't appreciate you; maybe his son is jealous; their office was filthy anyway; don't worry. Tod: I don't worry but can't blame Clara for worrying. Clara: I didn't mention worrying. Mother: Clara should be proud of Tod and see to his "proper food and rest."

This reminds Tod to go for his secret medicine bottle, jocosely "labeled Gordon." While Myrtle stuffs herself, Clara tells Mother that Tod may have an opening to sell 20-volume encyclopedias, by door-to-door presentations of a Chicago firm's prospectus. Mother tells Clara to have potential customers come to Tod's home, serve them sandwiches and soft drinks, and thus prevent Tod's recallousing his tender feet.

Tod's reappearance makes further job talk unseemly. Clara: Myrtle, get grandfather some water? Mother: Making the child a servant hurts her digestion; Tod, eat more. Tod: I'm full. Mother: Clara, you're becoming a better cook. Father: Harry and Grace served wine; I don't get wine now. Tod: I remember when Grace got "pie-eyed." Mother: Myrtle, ignore your daddy's "silly jokes," eat, grow strong; I'll help with the dishes. Clara: You're "nice ... to offer," but "amuse Myrtle" instead.

Later, Clara finds Father dozing, Tod hunting "more medicine," Mother petting Myrtle, asleep and "get[ting] over that fright." Mother lectures Clara on how Grace and Harry can't entertain Mother and Father just now because the hotel is full and noisy, how Grace is getting better at ministering to her husband's needs just the way Mother has always done for Father. Clara checks on Tod, napping until Frank Butler's kid brother rings the bell. Tod is given a quiet message from Frank, who supplies Tod's "medicine," is going to a football game this afternoon, and has a sister, Mamie Butler, 25, cute and loose, and observed by Clara to like Tod. Father breaks some news. He and Mother are being evicted by their landlady Mrs. Davis, whose son and his wife are arriving and need their "rooms." Tod suggests that his parents come live with him and Clara. He'll discuss it with her later, since he must go see Frank now about a job prospect. Mother and Father also leave. Clara summons Doctor Fred. He treats Myrtle's cramps and tells Clara to regulate Myrtle's diet or she'll never be healthy.

Tod returns late, so drunk that Clara has to help him undress for bed, after which she lies awake, pondering. Father owes Mrs. Davis back rent. Clara worries about money for food, needed clothes, Doctor Fred's bills, gas, phone, etc. Now 35, Clara remembers Dave Bonham, who liked her when she was 23 and married Tod, who after college dreamed of becoming a writer in Chicago or New York. She remembers Dave worked in his father's garage, inherited it, ran it, sold it profitably, and went into highly successful real-estate work in Detroit. Clara remembers that Dave, never marrying, visited Clara briefly last month, "romped with Myrtle," and though he gave her no candy she cried when he left suddenly. Dave "was an orphan," Clara also remembers.

GREAT SCOT (*The Big Town*). He was a fine racehorse owned by Herbert Daley. When Sid Mercer, Daley's jockey, got drunk and couldn't ride Great Scot, Daley hired Carney, who rode but lost.

"GREEK TRAGEDY" (*Esquire*, February 1934). (Characters: Greek Alexis, Doc Bishop, Big Bill Buell, Roy Clayton, Fred Hoffmann, Legs Lamont, Chesty Leach, Harry Marsh, Bull Montana, Ike Morris, Old Man Richards, Lou Schwartz, Jack Wells.)

Two wrestlers, Greek Alexis and Big Bill Buell, are friends from Arizona. In different parts of the United States, each is recognized as world champion. A publicized grudge match will enable the winner to fight Legs Lamont and Chesty Leach, both of whom are also called world champions, for the title. Alexis is managed by Lou Schwartz; Buell, by Ike Morris. Jack Wells, the *Record* sports reporter, increases the fighters' supposed animosity by having each describe the other's ugliness. The two converse so much during their fake falls that referee Fred Hoffmann urges them to hasten. Buell whispers to Alexis that Roy Clayton, a Phoenix reporter in the crowd, will expose him as Tom Meyers, his real name. He throws the fight, hopes Buell will defeat Lamont and share the purse with him, and quits the wrestling game. But in truth, Wells learned the Arizona background of both wrestlers and offered information to Morris about Clayton, who probably wasn't even in the crowd that night.

"Greek Tragedy" was evidently the last story Lardner wrote.

GREEN, CONRAD In "A Day with Conrad Green," he is a conceited, unprincipled Broadway theater producer. He is unfaithful to his wife Marjorie Green, lies to and tries to browbeat his employees and associates, and loses his mistress Rose, at least briefly. His librettist Joe Martin calls him "Connie." Conrad Green figures in "Rhythm," as a producer who obtained tune-thief Harry Hart's services in the popular "Upsy Daisy," and seeks him again, to provide music for a book by Jack Prendergast and then another by Guy Bolton.

In a letter (July 27, 1925) to F. Scott Fitzgerald,* Lardner says that "Flo is the hero" of "A Day with Conrad Green." Donald Elder and Jonathan Yardley confirm that Conrad Green is to be recognized as an unpleasant portrait of Florenz Ziegfeld.* H. L. Mencken* says that Green "is a successful theatrical producer [but] ... turns out to have the professional competence of a chiropractor and the honor of a Prohibition agent." Donald Douglas comprehensively defines Green as "a tyrant and a seducer and a liar and a pompous fool." (Sources: Douglas, 585; Elder, 268; Caruthers [1995], 182–183; Mencken [1926], 255; Yardley, 292, 303)

GREEN, MARJORIE ("A Day with Conrad Green"). She is the wife of Conrad Green, who is unfaithful to her. When she surprises him by coming into his Broadway office on her birthday, he reluctantly gives her a rope of pearls he bought for his mistress Rose. Marjorie was Marjorie Manning, a Varieties chorus girl.

GREGG ("Haircut"). He was Julie Gregg's father, was in the lumber business, drank too much, and died. He left Julie and her mother with so little insurance that they had to "skimp along."

GREGG ("The Love Nest"). She is a youngest daughter, 1½ of Lou and Celia Gregg.

GREGG, CELIA ("The Love Nest"). She is the unhappy wife of movie-mogul Lou Gregg. Former starlet, she married at 20, had three daughters, is now 27 and a secret alcoholic. When Bartlett arrives to interview Lou, the "great" man must leave briefly, and Celia drinks copiously and tells Bartlett she hates her husband, hopes her daughters can escape her fate, and calls her "love nest" a horrid "baby ranch." She calls Lou "sweetheart" mechanically. Her professional name was Celia Sayles.

H. L. Mencken* too harshly says that "on the surface she [Celia] seems to be nothing but a noodle, but underneath there is simply a sewer: the woman is such a pig that she makes one shudder." Donald Phelps calls Celia's gabble a "highly and impeccably theatrical aria." John Berryman finds Celia unrealistically portrayed, because "if she is so afraid of her husband, as she says she is, she would never dare confide in Bartlett, especially Bartlett, a writer." (Sources: Berryman, 421; Mencken [1926], 255; Phelps, 84)

GREGG, GRACE ("The Love Nest"). She is the pretty daughter, 4, of Lou and Celia Gregg.

GREGG, JULIE ("Haircut"). She is a pretty girl in Whitey's town. Though regarded as aging, being almost 30, she remained too nice for the roughnecks there. She was kidded cruelly by Jim Kendall for passively preferring Doc Ralph Stair to Jim. Jim's joke was his last one.

Ludwig Lewisohn opines that "Haircut" is uniquely splendid in Lardner's oeuvre because "in it alone are two human beings not fiercely stupid and vulgar to the bone." The happy two are presumably Julie and Ralph. (Source: Lewisohn, 514)

GREGG, LOU ("The Love Nest"). He is the rich, powerful, essentially stupid president of Modern Pictures, Inc., of New York. He takes Bartlett to his mansion to stay overnight and be entertained, interview him, and meet his wife Celia and their "kiddies." He has to be away part of the evening, during which Celia reveals to Bartlett the truth about her life. Lou's favorite conversational fill-in is "I mean," which he uses 56 times. Today he would add "you know" and "like." He calls Celia "sweetheart" often.

John Berryman dislikes the way Lardner presents Gregg, feeling that "his stupidity ought to be more impressively conveyed." Elizabeth Evans summarizes tersely: "Lou Gregg has successfully transformed his talented wife into drunken chattel without ever letting the public suspect the slightest flaw in his happy home." (Sources: Berryman, 420; Evans, 66)

GREGG, MRS. ("Haircut"). She is Julie Gregg's widowed mother. Her asking Doc Ralph Stair to treat her mother's ailing foot was the indirect cause of Jim Kendall's undoing.

GREGG, NORMA ("The Love Nest"). She is the pretty daughter, 6, of Lou and Celia Gregg. Her first name might reflect Lardner's admiration for stunningly beautiful actresses Norma Shearer* and Norma Talmadge.*

GREGORY ("The Crook"). He works in a hardware store in Montgomery, is married, and is the father of Maggie Gregory and Martin Gregory.

GREGORY, DR. ("Poodle"). For private gain, he treats the demented man calling himself Phil Hughes. Dr. Gregory tells the narrator that he is really Dr. Tyson.

GREGORY, MAGGIE ("The Crook"). She is Martin Gregory's pretty twin sister, 18, studies "the milliner trade" in Montgomery, and is the object of the affections of Bull, an umpire who boards with the Gregorys in winter seasons. Maggie selfishly uses his love for her to tempt him to favor Martin, at times an ineffective hitter. Bull indirectly did so, but Martin played unacceptably. Larry, Bull's friend, gets Maggie to accept Bull.

GREGORY, MARTIN ("The Crook"). He is Maggie Gregory's twin brother, 18. He was arrogant and lazy, and sponged off his family in Montgomery. He was a natural-born athlete but in clutch situations froze at the bat when playing for Connie Mack's Phillies. Bull, an umpire who loved Maggie, properly called Martin out on strikes in a game and Martin spread lies about him. Larry, Bull's friend, threatened Martin to do the right thing — or else.

When Maggie told Bull that Martin was "delicate," Bull thought the lout was "delicate lookin,' like Frank Gotch." George W. Hilton identifies Frank Alvin Gotch (1878–1917) as a heavyweight professional wrestler, and long-time world champion (1905–1913). (Source: Hilton, 561)

GREGORY, MRS. ("The Crook"). She is Maggie's and Martin's mother. She lavished good food on Bull, the umpire who boarded with the Gregorys in Montgomery during winters.

GREINER, HAROLD ("Three Without, Doubled"). He is a bookkeeper "down to the office" where Gullible also works. Gullible feels that you can't kid with him.

GRIFFIN ("Good for the Soul"). He was an inexperienced baseball player recruited by A.T. Grant for his new team. Typical of the many inept athletes Grant assembled, Griffin's main accomplishment was overeating.

GRIFFIN ("Harmony"). He is or was a baseball

player or manager involved, according to Bill Cole, in a trade bringing Art Graham to the team Cole plays for.

GRIFFIN ("The Jade Necklace"). This is the name of the "people" the narrator quits working for, to become secretary-valet for L. N. Bauer, head of Colossal Films Incorporated.

GRIFFIN ("Now and Then"). He, his wife, and his wife's sister Miss Cutts are aboard the ship taking Bob and Bob's wife Irma to the Bahamas again. Bob prefers the company of the three to that of Irma.

GRIFFIN, FRANCIS (*The Big Town*). He works for H. L. Krause & Co., Wall Street brokers. On the train from Chicago to New York, he meets Finch, his wife Ellen, and her sister Katie, impresses the two women, and Katie hopes to marry him. Griffin is a pretentious sponge who makes Ellen his amorous target and gets beaten up by Finch.

GRIFFIN, MRS. ("Now and Then"). She, her husband, and her sister Miss Cutts meet Bob on their way to the Bahamas. When spending time with Bob, the three neglect Bob's wife Irma.

GRIFFITH In "The Busher Comes Back," Keefe mentions Griffith as the Washington Senators manager. In "Where Do You Get That Noise," Carey jokes to Hawley that Griffith should cut shade trees in Washington, D.C., so his players can become accustomed to bright sunlight. In "The Crook," he was managing the Senators when Larry, playing first base against them, was involved in a disputed play. In "Call for Mr. Keefe!," Keefe's being sold to Washington is negated by his being drafted for military service. Keefe tells Griffith, who shakes his hand and praises him. In *The Real Dope* and "The Courtship of T. Dorgan," Keefe mentions that Griffith managed the Washington team.

Clark Calvin Griffith (1869–1953) played for the Chicago Cubs (1894–1999) and managed the Chicago White Sox (1901–1902), the New York Yankees (1903–1908), the Cincinnati Reds (1909–1911), and the Washington Senators (1912–1920), and was part owner of the Senators. He became a member of the Baseball Hall of Fame (1946). (Sources: *Baseball Encyclopedia*, 694, 1087–1088, 2025; Hilton, 88)

GRIFFITH, MISS ("Tour No. 2"). She, Miss Hendricks, and Miss Lamont, all from What Cheer, Iowa, and each about 25, are on the tour with Larry and Minnie Burns. Larry regards them as pretty but uppity. They see through his witlessness.

GRIMES ("One Hit, One Error, One Left"). He was a baseball player that Danny says was involved in a St. Louis-Brooklyn trade.

Ed Grimes (1905–1974) played for the St. Louis Browns (1931–1932). (Source: *Baseball Encyclopedia*, 1088)

GRIMES (*Own Your Own Home*). He and his wife are invited to attend Fred and Grace's bridge party, along with Bishop and his wife, Farrell and his wife, Carry and his wife, and Curtis and his wife.

GRIMES, DICK ("Horseshoes"). He is a mediocre baseball player, for the Ishpeming semipro team, the Battle Creek Club in the Northern Peninsula League, and for the Cubs, Indianapolis, Baltimore, and finally the Athletics. During the Athletics-Giants World Series, he plays left field in the sixth game, gets even with his enemy Speed Parker of the Giants by making a miraculous catch of Speed's almost sure homer, by hitting a victorious fluke homer himself, by slugging Speed for insulting him, and finally by marrying the girl that both love.

Grimes's ability to recall all key plays of innumerable games is typical of many professional athletes, who may simultaneously be blissfully ignorant of unnecessary niceties of correct grammar. "If him and I woulda went," for one example among more, is common over contemporary radio and TV air waves. George W. Hilton says that Grimes's "phenomenal run of misfortunes would challenge the probability theory taught in elementary statistics courses." Hilton adds that Grimes, Joyce, and Parker are "fictional characters." When Lardner named Grimes, he may have had another busy Grimes in mind. Burleigh Arland Grimes (1893–1985) pitched for the Pittsburgh Pirates (1916–1917), the Brooklyn Dodgers (1918–1926), the New York Giants (1917), the Pirates (1928–1929), the Boston Braves and the St. Louis Cardinals (1930), the Cardinals (1931), the Chicago Cubs (1932), the Cubs and the Cardinals (1933), and the Cardinals and the Pirates and the New York Yankees (1934); managed the Dodgers (1937–1938); and was elected to the Baseball Hall of Fame (1964). According to Charles F. Faber and Richard B. Faber, Grimes was a premier spitballer. (Sources: *Baseball Encyclopedia*, 694, 2026; Faber and Faber, 187; Hilton, 20, 395)

GRIMES, MRS. (*Own Your Own Home*). She and her husband attend the bridge party given by Fred and Grace.

GRINER ("My Roomy"). He is a St. Louis pitcher. Buster Elliott takes a perfect third strike from him and explains he did so because he feared he'd "kill somebody" if he smashed it.

Donald Dexter Griner (1888–1950) pitched for the Cardinals (1912–1916) and the Dodgers (1918). (Sources: *Baseball Encyclopedia*, 2027; Hilton, 343)

GROH In "Horseshoes," he is the Cincinnati short stop or second baseman when Dick Grimes and Speed Parker play for the Cubs. His error gives Speed a lucky break. In "Where Do You Get That Noise?" Carey, a Cub, says so many Cincinnati players, including Groh, have German names that fans of German background ought to be pleased. Hawley retorts that if Groh plays badly, those fans will be upset. In "The Busher Pulls a Mays," Keefe, pitching for the White Sox, says that "we will see if Roush and Groh is such wales when they get up vs. real pitching" in a possible "world serious" against the White Sox.

Henry Knight Groh (1889–1968) played for the New York Giants (1912), the Giants and the Cincinnati Reds (1913), the Chicago Cubs (1914–1921), the Giants (1922–1926), and the Pittsburgh Pirates (1927), and managed the Reds (1918). (Sources: *Baseball Encyclopedia*, 694, 1090; Hilton, 316)

GROSS (*Own Your Own Home*). This is the last name of Fred and Grace's younger child. She and her brother Ed wake up when there is too much party noise, caused once by Martin and later by Curtis. In "The Swift Six," she and the other Grosses have one ride in Fred's new car. In "Fore!," Grace is often at home with her.

GROSS ("When the Moon Comes over the Mountain"). To kid Danny, Casey Stengel says he knows a man named Gross who owned an orchard, and asks Danny to ask Dave Burnett if he knows this Gross.

GROSS, CHARLEY In *Own Your Own Home*, he is Fred A. Gross's brother, lives in New York, and receives letters from Fred. Charley and Mary have a daughter named May. When Fred and his wife Grace have difficulties in building a home in suburban Chicago and moving in, Fred alternately recommends that Charley and Mary do the same and that they avoid doing the same. Fred frequently demeans both Charley and Mary. In "War Bribes," Fred writes him about his family's bout with "whopping cough" and about his dabbling in the stock market. In "The Swift Six," Fred tells Charley how he bought a new car, called a Swift Six, learned to drive it, and took the family on a drive in the rain, during which the car was stolen. In "Fore!," Fred writes Charley about his golfing prowess.

GROSS, ED In *Own Your Own Home*, he is the son of Fred A. Gross and Grace Gross. Fred is glad that Ed and his infant sister are safer now that they've all moved to Allison. Neighborhood noise occasionally awakens both kids. Grace tells Mrs. Martin that Ed was born three years ago. In "War Bribes," he is still their son but now called "little Fred." Both children have "whopping cough." In "The Swift Six," the children accompany Fred when he takes the family for one ride in his new car. In "Fore!," Grace still watches over her children.

GROSS, FRED (*Own Your Own Home*) *see* Gross, Ed

GROSS, FRED A. In *Own Your Own Home*, he and his wife Grace decide to leave their Chicago flat and move to "the subburbs." They buy a lot in Allison, Illinois, hire an "archateck," have trouble with bankers and builders, but are happy when they move in. Fred is a policeman. Fred and Grace are rebuffed by the unneighborly Hamiltons and Carpenters. Fred reluctantly attends a dance to which he and Grace are actually not invited and get rebuffed again. Eventually, they become friendly with their neighbors the Carrys and the Curtises. Fred tries to get revenge on his neighbors the Hamiltons and the Carpenters by throwing a party and excluding them. On his party "invatations" he identifies himself "asst. Chief of Detectives Chicago Police dept." Fred continues to entertain and be entertained, suspects Hamilton and then Martin are playing jokes on him, but believes Hamilton when he says that Martin called the fire department to come and hose down Fred. In "War Bribes," Fred tells Charley about his family's suffering from "whopping cough." He gives Charley a running account of his investing in the stock market on margins, losing, borrowing from his chief, being bailed out by Grace's father, and planning to return to the market and shorting. In "The Swift Six," Fred lets Grace buy a piano with her money, then buys a car called a Swift Six mostly with her money, drives it badly, and is caught in the rain driving Grace and their two children. When they seek shelter in a saloon, the car is stolen. In "Fore!," Fred plays golf and takes advantage of opposing players; Mr. Carpenter and Mr. Thomas get even by stiffing him for a big wine bill. Fred is fired for not paying when he is billed for dues, food, and the wine. He plays golf with his "chief," hocks his victory silver cup, and lets Grace think it was stolen when she left the door open to take the kids out for a walk. Fred calls one of his golf clubs his "click." The first meaning of the noun *cleek* (from Scottish "cleek," a walking stick with a hook, from Old Scottish "cleke," "cleik," "cleek," a metal hook [spelled "click" sometimes in the nineteenth century], probably because of the sound of a club hitting a ball) is a narrow-bladed golf club made of iron. The second meaning of *cleek* is the No. 1 golf iron. (Source: Davies)

Gross is selfish, hypocritical, self-deceiving, and dishonest. To boot, Elizabeth Evans deplores his writing ability and specifically criticizes his "pronunciation," "heavy use of numbers, fractions, and abbreviations," "ignorance of convention," "[d]ouble negatives," and "[m]alapropisms." George W. Hilton regards Gross as "aptly named." It might be added that politically correct persons nowadays would object to Fred's three initials. (Sources: Evans, 36–37; Hilton, 19)

GROSS, GRACE In *Own Your Own Home*, she is Fred A. Gross's wife. They have two children, Ed and a baby. The Grosses build and move into a home in Allison, a Chicago suburb. Their financial troubles are mitigated because Grace gets money from her father, often as birthday presents. Grace is unhappy when their neighbors the Hamiltons and the Carpenters are rude. She makes friends with Mrs. Carry, another neighbor, lets her babysit, argues briefly with her over dance invitations, but soon becomes amiable with the Carrys and also the Curtises. Grace acquiesces when Fred decides to give a big party and exclude the Hamiltons and Carpenters. She prepares the "refreshmunts," but Fred starts serving high balls too early. Grace continues to seek entrance into Allison society, entertains the Martins, accepts Mrs. Martin's sarcastic comments about her "close" as praise, and evidently doesn't notice when Mrs. Martin flirts with Fred. In "War Bribes," Grace wants new "close," loses at "auction bridge," and is kept ignorant of Fred's dabbling in the stock market. She is delighted when her father gives them $3,000. In "The Swift Six," Fred lets Grace buy a piano with her own money. He then buys a car and takes his family for a drive. Caught in the rain, they seek shelter in a saloon, and the car is stolen. In "Fore!," Fred calls Grace "the Mrs.," lets her watch him play golf against Mr. Thomas, and by lying to her lets her think she was responsible for a theft of his prize silver cup after he had hocked it.

GROSS, MARY In *Own Your Own Home*, she is Fred Gross's brother Charley Gross's wife and the mother of May, their daughter. Fred writes Charley that Fred's wife Grace is touchy and adds that "you know how wommen feels & probly Marys the same way." Fred informs Charley that the "Ladys prize" offered at Fred's bridge party will be the two corsets Mary sent Grace as "xmas" presents some years ago, since they didn't fit. Fred sends Mary his "Rgds." and also comments that her clothes are all right but inferior to Mrs. Martin's. In "War Bribes," "The Swift Six," and "Fore!," Fred sends best wishes to Mary.

GROSS, MAY (*Own Your Own Home*). She is the little daughter of Charley and Mary Gross.

GROSS, SCHOFIELD ("When the Moon Comes over the Mountain"). Dave Burnett tells Jessie to write Danny that he doesn't know Gross, a friend of Casey Stengel, but does know Schofield Gross. Stengel is joking with gullible Danny.

GULLIBLE, JOE (*Gullible's Travels, Etc.*) He is the narrator of the five stories in the collection. Most readers are surely more tolerant of Gullible than Walton R. Patrick is. He excoriates him "as a kind of common denominator of the flatness, barrenness, and vulgarity of middle-class American life, not so crude as the drunk in the barroom — or so vile-tempered as Gullible's 'elite' bridge hostess, but a nameless, average, white-collar citizen." On the other hand, Edward A. Martin regards Gullible's "verbal dexterity" as a function of "his lower-class midwestern vernacular" and finds energy in it. (Sources: Martin, 162; Patrick, 71)

In "Carmen," Gullible and his wife attend a performance of *Carmen* as guests of Jim Hatch and his wife. Gullible reads "the liberetto" of the opera by "Busy," follows and often objects to the plot, and summarizes it. Gullible razzes Hatch, his gruff friend, in funny dialogue. Gullible reveals what today would be called ethnic insensitivity when he avers that *Carmen* is unlike a "regular musical show where a couple o' Yids comes out and pulls a few lines o' dialogue."

In "Three Kings and a Pair," Gullible, whom his wife calls Joe, reluctantly both welcomes Bessie Gorton, his wife's sister, as house guest, and participates in entertaining Bishop, Bessie's friend at home and at the opera *L'Amore dei Tre Re*.

In "Gullible's Travels," Gullible and his wife get uppity. He is talked into going to Palm Beach with his wife . They try to enjoy their stay at the Alcazar in St. Augustine and at the Poinciana in Palm Beach, but really don't. When Mrs. Gullible is mistaken for a hotel maid in Palm Beach, they leave via Fort Pierce, Rockledge, Daytona, and Jacksonville, return to Chicago, and also return to more familiar activities.

In "The Water Cure," Gullible fears that if Bess marries Bishop, now called Elmer Bishop, she will be marrying a welching liar and the Gullibles will have to support them. So he arranges for the four to have a weekend vacation by Lake Michigan boat and St. Joe hotel. This forces the youngsters to dislike one another through becoming too well "acquainted."

In "Three Without, Doubled," the Gullibles join the San Susie bridge club. They attend a dinner meeting at the apartment of the fancy Garretts, where Gullible bad-mouths the food and his fellow guests, plays cards badly, but irrationally bids in such a way that by chance his final "pardner," Mrs. Collins, defeats Mrs. Garrett and wins the prize. Elizabeth Evans properly notes that Gullible "not only does not know the rules [of bridge], he remains flippant and rude toward those who take the game seriously." (Source: Evans, 85)

GULLIBLE, MRS. (*Gullible's Travels, Etc.*). In "Carmen," she and Mrs. Hatch sulk until Jim Hatch agrees to treat the Gullibles to a performance of *Carmen*. Mrs. Gullible dresses better than dowdy Mrs. Hatch. Gullible refers to his wife as "the Frau," "the Missus," and "the Wife."

In "Three Kings and a Pair," Mrs. Gullible welcomes her sister Bessie Gorton as a guest and encourages Bishop, Bessie's friend, to want to marry her.

In "Gullible's Travels," the Gullibles tire of their old ways in Chicago. She talks him into an expensive Florida vacation. They try to enjoy various activities there, until she is mistaken for a Palm Beach hotel maid by Mrs. Potter of Chicago, whom Mrs. Gullible recognizes and wants to meet. Gullible then does all he can to make their return home more pleasant.

In "The Water Cure," Gullible fools his wife into going on the vacation that spells doom to the Bess-Bishop romance through over-familiarity. When Mrs. Gullible thinks she's perceptive, Gullible calls her "Clara Voyant."

In "Three Without, Doubled," she is thrilled to join the San Susie bridge club, lords it over Bertha Hatch, and goes with Gullible to a party for dinner and bridge at the Garrett apartment. Gullible plays so irrationally that they aren't invited again. Bertha Hatch gets her revenge when she and her husband Jim Hatch become the Gullibles' replacements in the club.

"GULLIBLE'S TRAVELS" (*Saturday Evening Post*, August 19, 1916; GT, PRL, RLR).

***GULLIBLE'S TRAVELS*, ETC.** (1917). Collection of five connected short stories, all narrated in mangled English by Gullible. Jonathan Yardley says that in them "Ring truly established himself as a satirist of middle-class suburban life," and displays "subtlety, satiric skill and sylistic sureness." (Source: Yardley, 184)

"Carmen" (*Saturday Evening Post*, February 19, 1916). (Characters: Gullible, Mrs. Gullible, Jim Hatch, Kenneth Hatch, Mrs. Hatch, Katz.)

Gullible and his "Missus" lose $7.50 playing rummy at the Hatches. Gullible gripes so much at Jim Hatch's luck that Mrs. Hatch suggests treating all four to a show. Despite Hatch's complaints, his wife opts for "Grand op'ra" at the Auditorium. Gullible thinks the women should go to it while he and Jim go "see Charlie Chaplin," but notices Mrs. Gullible sulking and therefore also votes for an operatic evening. The ladies see by the newspaper that "a musical show called *Carmen*" will be presented Friday. Mrs. Hatch blubbers so much when Jim mentioned his Friday lodge meeting that he too succumbs. Going home, the Gullibles criticizes each other's card playing until they are "without no more dialogue."

On Friday Mrs. Gullible makes her husband put on his dress suit and she also dolls up. The Hatches call for them, not dressed fancy. Riding the streetcar downtown, they are all glum. Their theater seats, at $1.50 each according to Hatch, are high up. The music starts fine, but the actors, "smuggled in from Europe," sing in foreign languages. Hatch finds "a liberetto" a lady mislaid, gives it to Gullible, and departs for a drink. Gullible reads enough to understand the plot. He watches and later comments on "Don Joss," Carmen sung by "Genevieve Farr'r," "Michaels girl" from "Janesville," a "Chink," Lily and Pat, etc.

Hatch returns during the third act, slumps asleep, snores "a new aria," and is poked by his wife.

On leaving, Hatch says the plot was easy. Mrs. Hatch says she understood the singing in French. Hatch says he "thought it was Wop or ostrich." He commandeers the one empty streetcar seat. The other three "clubbed together on the straps" and discuss the costumes, singing, acting, and the heroine's on-stage death.

The morning newspapers list only the people in the boxes at the opera, which disappoints "my Missus." Gullible asks her what boxes cost. She says $6 or $7. He suggests that the Hatches come play cards "the followin' night." He will try to win money enough to buy cheap tickets for the Hatches, say they bought four tickets but couldn't get them together, seat the Hatches, and sneak into box seats. But Hatch wins because Mrs. Gullible starts "collectin' pitcher cards again." Gullible asks Hatch to buy theater tickets again. Hatch won't "go to the same show twict." Despite learning it would be a new show, he declines. His "welshin'" won't discourage the Gullibles. He gets tickets for the Gullibles to see the first performance of *Armour's Do Re Me*, next Tuesday. Gullible thinks that opera was "prob'ly named after some soap."

Gullible as narrator mangles opera news. He mentions "Alda," *Armour's Do Re Me*, "Genevieve Farr'r," "Busy," and two puzzlers, "Daddy" and "Mooratory." New Zealand–born Frances Alda (1883–1952) and Massachusetts-born Geraldine Farrar (1882–1967) were opera sopranos. *Armour's Do Re Me*, as clarified in "Three Kings and a Pair," is *L'Amore dei Tre Re* (1913), the opera by Italo Montemezzi (1875–1952). "Busy" was opera-composer Georges Bizet (1838–1875). How did Gullible learn to pronounce Bizet's name demi-correctly? And is Lardner's having fun with the name *Armour* because he attended Chicago's Armour Institute of Technology? Lardner is prescient in associating conflating "soap" and "opera," since the term "soap opera" didn't come into vogue until the 1930s, when Procter & Gamble began advertising their soap products on daytime television serials, soon known as soap operas.

"Three Kings and a Pair" (*Saturday Evening Post*, March 11, 1916). (Characters: Andy, Bishop, Bessie Gorton, Joe Gullible, Mrs. Gullible.)

Gullible feels it's better if one's in-laws are dead. Proof? Gullible and his wife live in "Chi." Her sister Bessie Gorton, tired of Wabash society, writes that she will visit them in two weeks, then arrives sooner. She says she met nicely mustached Mr. Bishop on the train, and he said he makes $10,000 a year writing "motion-pitcher plays." Mrs. Gullible wants him to come to dinner and tells Gullible he can exchange their two opera tickets for four to attend. Gullible resists until Bessie pouts. The Missus tells Gullible that Bessie might find Bishop a splendid catch and makes Gullible agree that four $5 box seats would be more acceptable than four $3 balcony seats. The two women soon "was all smiles and pep"; so Gullible "blowed down to Andy's" to gamble.

On Sunday Bishop arrives three hours before 1:00 P.M. dinner. The women are still dressing. Gullible finds Bishop skinny but garbed with "class." Gullible mentions opera. Bishop reveals knowledge of opera, speaking of *Madame Buttermilk*, *La Bohemian Girl*, and *Ill Toreador*. Gullible says he likes *Carmen* but not *Armour's Dee Tree Re*. Bishop says *L. Armour's Day Trey Ray* is sung in Latin, *Day* meaning "God," *Trey* "three," *Ray* "Kings." Gullible says it's a poker game. Bishop, disagreeing, says he saw and disliked it. Gullible figures he'll save money Tuesday because Bishop won't accompany them — until, that is, the women are informed, Bessie starts "chokin' up," and Bishop agrees to attend. At dinner, Bishop eats so voraciously that Gullible says "writin' them scenarios" must leave him "No time to eat or nothin.'" Bishop praises Mrs. Gullible's cooking. Bessie says he should "taste my cookin.'" Mrs. Gullible advances Bessie's cause by telling Gullible to accompany her to visit Mrs. Hatch. They know the Hatches are away. The Gullibles spend hours walking and talking in the cold. She: Bishop would fit into the family. He: Or into a flute. She: He'd be a match for Bessie. He: He resembles a match. She: They're a pair. He: A pair of deuces. Meanwhile, Bishop remains for supper and beyond. Mrs. Gullible vetoes Gullible's suggestion for a card game. He follows her into the kitchen and watches her wash the dishes.

At noon Monday, Gullible exchanges his two cheap tickets for four at $10 more, "down-stairs ... seventh row." On Tuesday he misses lunch to rush home to dress, only to find his room occupied by the two women, getting dressed. Mrs. Gullible says they can't eat until after the show. Gullible says he has a dollar left. She thinks dinner may be hosted by Bishop, who arrives to praise Bessie, dressed in Mrs. Gullible's one fine dress. Mrs. Gullible stops Gullible's gripes by saying she wants "sis" to look pretty. They get to the streetcar. Bishop lacks change. They get to the Auditorium. Gullible buys a libretto. Bishop says he doesn't need one. Their seats are "down amongst the high polloi." The show starts late. Gullible reads the libretto and sees why the title "*The Love of Three Kings*" rightly doesn't have "no 'of god' to it." Bessie hints to Bishop she'd like to see many operas but wouldn't want "you throwin' all your money away on me." Asked his favorites, Bishop mentions and discusses the plots of "*Polly Archer* and *Cavalier Rusticana*," translating the latter as "Rural Free Delivery." Gullible recalls the *Three Kings* plot thus: Archibald [really King Archibaldo], his son Fred [Manfredo[, Fred's wife Flora [Fiora], and her lover Veto [Vito]; Archibald "stays on the stage quarrelin' with the conductor"; in a love duet, Flora "can't resist his [Veto's] high notes"; Archie returns, "looses his temper and wrings her neck"; Fred laments, "She was the best cook we ever had;" Veto dies kissing dead Flora, whose lips "Old Fox Archibald" smeared with "rat poison and garlic"; Fred enters, "helps himself to the garlic," and also dies.

Gullible tells his three guests that the old king was crazed by hunger. Gullible hopes this hint will encourage Bishop to take them to dinner. But when the Gullibles board a streetcar heading for a Loop restaurant he names, Bishop and Bessie stay off and wave. Mrs. Gullible says the pair want to be alone and suggests "The Ideal" for their own "little supper," but Gullible pleads lack of money and home they go to some crackers. Mrs. Gullible awakens her husband "Joe!" at 1:30 A.M. with the news that they've "won" because she just "happened" to see Bishop kissing Bessie. Gullible wishes Archibald had "fix[ed] up her lips."

Gullible says that one of his ideas "worked out every bit as successful as the Peace Ship." This allusion makes sense to readers familiar with a plan of Henry Ford (1863–1947), Michigan-born automobile maker, industrialist, and philanthropist, to end World War I. He chartered an American vessel (1915), proceeded to Christiana, Norway, soon recognized the futility of his pacifist efforts, and returned home.

"Gullible's Travels" (*Saturday Evening Post*, August 19, 1916). (Characters: Ben, Bishop, Jake Black, Mrs. Black, Edgar, Eph, Foster, George, George, Bess Gorton, Gould, Gullible, Mrs. Gullible, Hatch, Mrs. Hatch, Mrs. Potter, Maggie Rockefeller, So-and-So, Pat Vanderbilt, Vandeventer, Mrs. Vandeventer, Vincent.)

I. The Gullibles attend operas, visit friends, but gradually feel superior, ignore the Hatches, don't dance at Ben's place, and start "pretendin' we really was somebody." They have weekly hotel dinners, view "the high polloi," but feel out of it. They read newspaper columns about "the E-light" and doings "on the Lake Shore Drive." They squabble about vacations until she remembers their "dinky" honeymoon and wants to be taken to Palm Springs.

"Last fall" Gullible made $600 "dabblin' in Crucial Steel"; so he agrees. She explains about special "round-trip rates" on trains, how though "pretty steep" the hotels "throwed in" fancy meals, and how they could be "fox-trottin'" with the Vanderbilts and the Goulds. They check with "the railroad bandits," can get transportation to Palm Beach and back for $147.70, learn "the Florida East Coast" agency's quotations for rooms with or without bath, and decide on the Poincinia at $14 a day "without no bath" starting February 15th. He cashes his steel stock. She wants to go past Jacksonville to St. Augustine to see some of the "Four Hundred." They purchase lavish wardrobes, which she calls "an investment ... to get us in right with people worth w'ile." When Mrs. Hatch phones to invite them "for a little rummy," Mrs. Gullible boasts they're leaving for Florida.

II. Sights from the train, in which they have "an apartment," are varied: Cairo, Illinois, river-flooded; crossing a rickety bridge; missionaries, monopolizing the glassed-in "sun parlor" and tossing tracts to "the southern heathen"; fuzzy pines and yellow mud; small towns featuring busy women and idle men in overalls. While the Missus naps, Gullible goes to "the readin-room," but is bothered by an experienced traveler, "fat guy" named Gould from St. Louis. Gullible says that for six years they've been going to Palm Beach, which Gould says has gotten common. They mention the war. Gould says he'd fight, defensively. Gullible says he'd go to Brazil. When Gould says he could advise [President] Wilson but won't, Gullible says he should. Mrs. Gullible has been made ill by the train's swaying around curves. Gullible eats well. They arrive late in Jacksonville. Mrs. Gullible writes Chicago friends while Gullible buys a shave and several "rickeys," notices it's February 12th, is told it's Lincoln's birthday, and asks how old he is.

III. Once they get to the Alcazar in St. Augustine, Gullible begins toting up $9 in payouts thus far — lunch, shave, "refreshments," bus ride, bell hops, "clo'es pressed." Mrs. Gullible says their hotel is all-inclusive and to stop crabbing, and "she begin sobbin.'" During their 6:30 dinner, they see a woman veto her husband's desires, and instead order chicken, mashed potatoes, beans, toast, and coffee for him. The Gullibles feel they must see an art exhibit at the Ponce, named after a guy seeking water to make him feel young. The art "pitchers" had titles but all should be called "Lady Who Had Mislaid Her Clo'es." For Sunday breakfast they avoid sick people, tour weak Fort Marion, sail to Anastasia Island with familiar-looking tourists, and enjoy a good, cheap lunch at the bayside pavilion. Jake Black, his wife, and their mothers, all grubbily dressed, join the Gullibles at the hotel dinner table. Jake orders massive amounts of food. Mrs. Gullible says they're going on to Palm Beach tomorrow. Mrs. Black says it must be cheaper there. Jake, though feeling "kind o' heavy," says he'll avoid the European plan because of the war. Next day the Gullibles tour various streets and on each are shown America's oldest house. Their carriage is pulled by the oldest horse, whose driver tells "some ... oldest jokes." Their night train to Palm Beach is slow. The outstretched hands of the Poinciana luggage porters make Gullible realize why the place is called Palm Beach.

IV. A "pacemaker" leads the Gullibles through the vast hotel to their room, which by mistake includes a bath. Mrs. Gullible pouts until Gullible agrees to keep the $17 room. The dining room is so extensive and crowded that it's hard to find "trough space." Breakfast service is slow, and fellow-guests are offish.

The two, dress in sporty clothes, are carted to the beach—"somewheres near the ocean"—by something "part bicycle, part go-cart and part African." Gullible calls the bath-house porch near the Breakers "a ringer for the *Follies*," with eye-turning bathing beauties. Mrs. Gullible engages two bath-house rooms—$5 per week, each—to change in for sunbathing. They sit in the sand rather than on 10¢ chairs. Gullible resists those "man-eatin' waves." He surveys one bathing beauty, age "fourteen or twenty-four." At the Breakers porch, the Missus gets orange juice for 40¢ but beer for him would be impossibly slow. Back by "Afromobile" to their hotel. She has lunch while he registers via "the liquor locker law" for bourbon, gin, and "Vermouth brothers" for his highballs and her "bronix." After naps, they follow the program and attend the Cocoanut Grove tea and dinner. He wrestles into his Tuxedo. They find a table with honeymooners who keep "smilin' at each other or gigglin' at nothin.'" Gullible's joke at them gets "a Mexican look" in return. They sit in the lobby to eye the after-dinner crowd's evening suits and revealing dresses. They dance in the Palm Garden enough to make sleep in the "old hay-pile" really "grand."

Next day, swimming. Waves throw Gullible. His wife's hair soon looks "like spinach with French dressin.'" They turn in their beach-room keys, without a refund. The next few days are filled with observing bathers, "foxy trottin,'" being pedaled around, window shopping, and teas. The Missus discovers the Beach Club, which he tries to join but can't. She soon prefers "garden grill" dinners, enjoyable except for the $6 check. She gossips with a "ladies maid" about "who was who." They become confused "rubbin' elbows with all them celeb's," especially during "The Washington's Birthday Ball."

V. The first week's bill of $146.50 makes Gullible moan to the Missus that they see but can't speak to celebrities, don't play golf or tennis, can't swim, and gotta dance with each other, which they could do at home. She cries, knows he's right, but requires their staying three more days—for $60 more, he says. For 2½ days she tries but fails to ingratiate herself with some women "o' the E-light o' Chicago." Their last afternoon, as Gullible confidentially explains to Edgar, his wife happily sees "*the* Mrs. Potter from Chicago!" She approaches the Missus, who is trembling "like a leaf." Mrs. Potter asks her to be sure "they's some towels put in 559."

VI. Gullible most gently suggests to his wife that they take "a pretty river trip," proceed to Fort Pierce and Daytona, and "catch a north-bound train" there. "All right, I don't care," is her response. Next day they don't enjoy the river trip or their lunch aboard. He suggests a quick train to Jacksonville and hence home. When she would prefer delaying to avoid returning to Chicago embarrassingly early, he agrees to stall, gently saying "you're goin' to have your own way from now on." They reach Fort Pierce, have inadequate facilities and worse food, and the Missus, with a happy laugh, suggests renaming the place "Port Fierce." Quickly off to Jacksonville.

VII. Chicago, though cold and windy, is ever so welcome. The Missus says they both learned a lesson. He says yes but for "seven hundred bucks." She says they'll win it back, at rummy with the Hatches.

Helping to date "Gullible's Travels" dates are references to operatic basso Antonio Scotti (1866–1936) and to ballroom dancers Vernon Castle (1887–1918) and his wife Irene Castle (1893–1969). The Castles are also mentioned in "The

Facts." Martin Seymour-Smith names "Gullible's Travels" when he writes of Lardner that "in some of his stories one can sense a feeling of real pity for a situation in which each sucker ... believes that life, and the other suckers, will really give him a break." Seymour-Smith adds that Lardner "is on the whole a better short story writer ... than even Hemingway ..., who learned much from him." Jonathan Yardley says that in this "long title story ... Ring's talents as a social satirist bloomed." It combines satirical criticism of chronically disappointing Florida vacations, vacationers of various sorts out of their element, funny comments thereon by a wise boob, and — best of all — one epiphanic moment of heartbreaking poignancy when husband tells grieving wife she can have whatever she wants. Yardley calls this scene "one of the funniest, saddest and most devastating passages in Lardner's fiction." True, one may suppose. But the humor, the satire, and even the sadness are forever trumped for sensitive readers by Gullible's unique revelation of tenderness. Ernest Hemingway complained that Lardner never used dirty words. True enough. Lardner felt daring enough when he had Gullible say of self and wife that "we done a little spoonin,'" after which she says "We ain't swelled on ourself" and suggests a Palm Beach vacation. Robert J. Higgs rightly notes that "Lardner ... abhorred smutty tales." (Sources: Hemingway; Higgs, 26; Seymour-Smith, 203; Yardley, 185, 186)

"The Water Cure" (*Saturday Evening Post*, October 14, 1916). (Characters: Elmer Bishop, Bess Gorton, Gullible, Mrs. Gullible, Jennie, Swanson, Tim.)

On Tuesday June 13 [1916], not on Friday the 13th, Gullible has bad news. His wife's sister Bess arrives from Wabash, "makin' us a surprise visit." He remembers that Bess likes Bishop, that "loafer" who says he writes for the movies, who sponged for dinners, whom Gullible took to the opera *The Love o' Three Kings* with Bess and the Missus, and who promised to host the group to the opera *Ada* but let Gullible pay and even "frisked" him for $20. Well, Elmer Bishop is back, encouraged both by Bess's laugh that shows "real pretty" teeth with "lips ajar," and also by her "curves" reminiscent of pitches by Matty [Christopher Mathewson]. Mrs. Gullible hopes they'll marry. Gullible would have liked dependent kids but not grown-up ones. At supper he gets Bishop to boast he writes for the Criterion film company, then kids him until the Missus "sunk my shin with a patent-leather torpedo." By phoning the Criterion he learns Bishop is a $5-a-day extra actor. Gullible realizes that he must entertain Bishop, that strong-arming him will only cause Bess to defend him, and that he can't even mention Bishop's cheating when they all play rummy. Bess fondly remembers that Bishop hosted them to *Ada*, her favorite and only opera now.

Gullible summarize Gus Verdi's *Ada*: It took place between Memphis and Cairo; the mayor's jilted daughter punishes the tenor and Ada by locking them up; before they die, she should have released them because by then "they'd of been sick o' one another" and she could have the tenor herself. Gullible plots to make Bess and Bishop get similarly acquainted with and hence similarly sick of each other.

Gullible will host the two and his wife on a weekend "boat trip to St. Joe!" He springs the "party" idea, insisting the details must be his secret. Thrilled, Bess persuades Bishop that he can get away from work from Saturday afternoon through Monday morning. To the suspicious Missus at night, Gullible says they'll delight the youngsters by allowing them to be alone, but he won't disclose their destination.

The four take a boat onto Lake Michigan heading for St. Joe. Bess says, "Goody!," but Gullible's comments about past shipwrecks distress Bishop. Gullible encourages the Missus to socialize with "squalls of all nationalities," including Jennies with babies, thus leaving "Bess and Bishop to themself." The Gullibles look into the engine-room and then the bar filled with dancers, find Bess and Bishop on deck, but leave them again. After landing at St. Joe, Gullible has to take the foursome to dinner at the hotel. Bishop insists on going to his room at 8:00 P.M., and the Gullibles have to "entertain the Belle of Wabash."

Sunday they taxi to the Edgewater Club. Bishop, refusing to swim in cold water, simply watches Bess, in a swim suit resembling an inverted "Y." Back at the hotel, Gullible tells Bishop, "I was in love once myself," and forces Bishop to be alone with Bess, suggesting go "watch the interurbans come in from South Bend or Niles," sail, fish, "set on the beach and spoon," find a Greta Green–like town and "get a marriage license in any delicatessen." When Gullible drags the Missus off, she says that the youngsters "act like they was mad at each other" and adds that she overheard "Elmer" ask a waiter for "whiskey or poison." They see exhausted picnickers sticky with crackerjack and syrup, endure a 35¢ restaurant meal, and visit a combination "amusement park ... and ... religious sex" meeting of "Holy Roller Skaters." The Missus, bored, seeks conversation with men having "flourishin' beards." They return to the hotel and find Bess, upset. Gullible: Lovers' quarrel? No, "because they ain't no lovers," says Bess, adding that Bishop cares only for himself and they're not engaged.

Gullible locates Bishop in his room, drunk, learns that he and Bess were nothing "more'n friends," and that he wants — and is given — his return ticket, together with advice to avoid an enclosed stateroom since the ship may roll this "bad night." The return voyage was sick-making, all right; but Bishop wasn't aboard, and happily "I've never saw him from that day to this." Monday night the Missus gets around to asking what happened. "I says ... 'They got acquainted.'"

Lardner has Gullible demonstrate disfiguring chauvinism, induced by European-war jitters, when he tells a Greek immigrant on the Lake Michigan ship to "go back to your home over the sea" if he doesn't "like your Uncle Sammy."

"Three Without, Doubled" (*Saturday Evening Post,* January 13, 1917). (Characters: Bailey, Beardsley, Dan Cahill, Arthur Collins, Mrs. Collins, Garrett, Mrs. Garrett, Harold Greiner, Gullible, Mrs. Gullible, Bertha Hatch, Jim Hatch, Mrs. Kramer, Mrs. Messenger, Robert Messenger, Mike, Old Slumber, Pearson, Mrs. Pearson, Mrs. Phillips or Mrs. Rowley, Mr. Sleeper, Sparks, Mrs. Sparks.)

I. Gullible theorizes that some people don't mind certain jocose remarks while others do. His experience is that it is dangerous to say to his wife "San Susie!" The words "transferred over from the Latin" mean "Without no cares." It's all connected with the Gullibles' "latest plunge in the cesspools o' Society."

II. Friday evening the Missus asks Gullible to guess who phoned her. He wonders if Henry Ford or Josephus Daniels did. No. Mrs. Messenger, wife of Robert Messenger, owner of apartment buildings including the one they live in, phoned to "ast ... did I play bridge." She answered that both Gullibles do, despite her playing only "twice over to the Hatches." He complains he's never played. She says they can join the big 20-person neighborhood San Susie club, often mentioned in the newspapers. Arthur Collins and his wife belong. The Gullibles replace the Baileys, now wintering in California. Tuesday will be the Gullibles' first evening to play. Each guest contributes $2, used for purchasing prizes. Mrs. Gullible tries to teach Gullible, gets confused, and they decide to ask the Hatches over to play with them so they can learn better. This seems unfair because the Hatches, though also in the neighborhood, are too common for the club, according to Mrs. Gullible. Gullible buys a book called *Auction Bridge*, reads it on the streetcar, but finds it useless and leaves it behind. On Monday the Hatches come, they play, but the Gullibles hardly progress. When Mrs. Hatch suggests practicing on Tuesday, Mrs. Gullible fibs to her to avoid seeing Chaplin in *The Street Sweeper* with the Hatches then also. Gullible later says she made "a perjure out o' yourself."

III. The Gullibles report early to the Garretts' large apartment on Tuesday evening, await Mrs. Garrett's appearance, and bet on the Garretts' rent they pay to apartment-owner Robert Messenger. The Missus says $70; Gullible, $55. Guests are the Collinses, the Messengers, the Sparkses, and others. Dinner Gullible finds sparse, with "half sandwiches," "BB shot" on toast, checker-sized "little slices o' beef," etc. Queried, Garrett sarcastically tells Gullible that Mrs. Gullible wins the bet on rent. Mrs. Garrett seats the players, explains rules about deals and "pardner" changes, and answers Gullible's complaints about scoring and prizes. His first "pardner" is a woman named Phillips or Rowley, against Messenger and Mrs. Garrett. Gullible mishandles the cards, misunderstands her opening bid of "One without" until she explains it means "One no trump." He bids "one heart," is corrected, and is told to stop talking across the board. Messenger: Two spades. Mrs. Garrett: Two "without." Gullible leads a useless spade. Mrs. Garrett finesses, loses the trick, grows "sore as a boil," and gripes that his sneak lead cost her a little slam. Next hand, Gullible bids a heart, Messenger doubles, Gullible tries to redouble and is outbid by Mrs. Garrett, who makes a little slam. Gullible and his "pardner" leave the table 0–900. Next table, Gullible and a sleepy woman, whom he dubs Old Slumber, oppose his former "pardner," playing with Collins, and suffer another "trimmin.'" Next, it's Gullibles against Old Slumber and her husband. The Gullibles lose and criticize each other. Next, "I and Mrs. Messenger" oppose Garrett and the Missus, who win because Garrett overbid her so as to keep her from playing the hand. Next, "I and Mrs. Collins" oppose Collins and Old Slumber. Gullible and Mrs. Collins win and move to the final table. Mrs. Garrett and Messenger, "the two leaders" thus far, are there; so it's Mrs. Garrett and Gullible against Messenger and Mrs. Collins. Gullible wants Mrs. Collins to defeat Mrs. Garrett but feels one should play fair despite "where your sympathies lays." Mrs. Garrett wins two no trump; their opponents win the next two games; Mrs. Garrett then gets set on a five-club bid. Last deal: Mrs. Garrett bids "One without"; Gullible outbids Mrs. Collins's three spades with "Three without"; she doubles him; his laid-down hand has no spades; Mrs. Garrett furiously slams her hand down. Garrett comes over, umpires the play; Mrs. Collins sets Mrs. Garrett three tricks, wins ladies' prize; Messenger wins men's; Mrs. Garrett, smiling, presents prizes. Messenger, who doesn't travel, gets a leather money case. Mrs. Collins gets "a chafin' dish," which Gullible says is necessary immediately for the hungry guests here and suggests "welsh rabbit" when she entertains next. Everyone departs. Gullible asks the Collinses and the Messengers to come around the corner for drinks. No.

The Missus, "pleasant ... like a bloodhound" regarding Gullible that night, recovers by morning, admits they both play bridge badly, and suggests practicing with the Hatches before next Tuesday's club meeting. When Gullible returns from work, his wife tells him Mrs. Messenger phoned her that "San Susies is busted up," at least briefly, mainly because the Collinses plan to attend Tuesday night operas. To Gullible's idea that the Hatches might replace the Collinses, the Missus says the Hatches talk and dress too badly to be invited. Gullible is relieved, but the Missus said "It'd of been nice, though, ... to make friends with them people."

IV. One Tuesday night later the Gullible are about to enter the Acme to enjoy "a new Chaplin show' when they see the Hatches and invite them to come along. Bertha Hatch's rejoinder: Mrs. Messenger tonight is hosting the San Susie club, which the Hatches have joined; they like the Beardsleys; Bertha recently won a silver pitcher at the Collinses; Mrs. Collins served steak dinners and also "welsh rabbits in her chafin-dish." Gullible closes with criticism of Chaplin's *The Fly Cop*, which he says had no laughs.

Lardner's humor comes through with the names of the well-known Henry Ford, of the less well-known Josephus Daniels,* and of two movies that no one — certainly not Charlie Chaplin* — ever appeared in.

GURNSEY, MRS. ("How Are You?"). She is the secretary of Harry Danforth, who lends her briefly to Bob Dayton. She tells Bob that New York's best tooth extractor is Dr. Benham.

GUSSIE (*The Big Town*). This is a name in "Gussie's School for Manicures" in a song Jimmy Ralston sings in the Follies show attended by Finch, Ella Finch, and her sister Katie.

GUTHRIE, A. L. ("Who Dealt?"). He is a well-to-do lumberman in Portland, where Thomas Cannon and his wife live. Mrs. Cannon tells Arthur and Helen Gratz that when the Cannons were playing bridge with Guthrie and his wife some time ago, mention was made that Thomas was asked to run for mayor. Mrs. Cannon gratuitously adds that Guthrie plays bridge badly.

GUTHRIE, BILL ("The Battle of the Century"). He and Robert Crawley were "big steamship" men. Larry Moon gulls them into offering to put up $500,000 to promote a Jim Dugan-Goulet boxing match. When Larry gets Charley Riggs to offer a million, Guthrie and Crawley folded, forfeiting their $100,000 guarantee to Larry.

Guthrie is based on William A. Brady (1863–1950), as Lardner explains in a letter (August 4, 1921) to a *Saturday Evening Post* editor. Clifford M. Caruthers identifies Brady as "a New York theatrical impresario" and former manager of boxers James Jackson Jeffries (1875–1953) and James John Corbett (1866–1933), both mentioned in the story. Jeffries is also named in "Stop Me — if you've heard This One." (Source: Caruthers [1995], 135)

GUTHRIE, MAIDA ("The Jade Necklace"). She is the presumably stunning actress playing the part of the naval lieutenant's Japanese wife in *The Jade Necklace*, the movie L. N. Bauer is producing.

GUTHRIE, MRS. ("Who Dealt?"). She is lumberman A. L. Guthrie's wife. Mrs. Cannon tells Arthur and Helen Gratz that Mrs. Gratz was from an old Philadelphia family, graduated from Bryn Mawr, "was the first woman in Portland that called on me," has little in common with her husband, "plays a dandy game of bridge," dresses badly, and has unattractive hair.

HACKLEY, MRS. ("Bob's Birthday"). She lets Grandfather Tyler room and board with her, until he can't pay. Then he descends upon young Bob Tyler's parents.

HAGEDORN, BILL ("The Hold-Out"). He is a capable first baseman, able to bat right-handed helpfully, on the team Mr. Edwards owns. Bill became a hold-out when Mr. Edwards and

Frank Conley, his manager, wanted to reduce his pay from $6,000 to $4,000. Frank got Bill to agree to $4,000, but, on learning that the Hagedorns just had a baby, maneuvered Mr. Edwards into paying the higher figure. In gratitude, Bill promised to name his baby "Frankie."

HAGEDORN, MRS. ("The Hold-Out"). She is the wife, from Kentucky, of hold-out Bill Hagedorn. She wrote Frank Conley, manager of the baseball team her husband wanted to rejoin except for a salary dispute, that Bill was broke and growing desperate. Frank got team-owner Mr. Edwards to pay Bill the $6,000 he wanted.

HAINES ("Meet Me in St. Louie"). He pitches for the St. Louis Cardinals. Danny, playing for Brooklyn, says "I look worst" when trying to hit Haines's "nothing ball."

"HAIRCUT" (*Liberty*, March 28, 1925; LN, PRL, RLR, RU). (Characters: Frank Abbott, Joe Barnes, Mrs. Barnes, Ken Beatty, Paul Dickson, Evans, Doc Foote, Doc Gamble, Gregg, Julie Gregg, Mrs. Gregg, Jim Kendall, Mrs. Kendall, Hod Meyers, Purdy, Schrader, John Scott, Mrs. Scott, Milt Sheppard, Henry Smith, Mrs. Smith, Doc Ralph Stair, Charles M. Vail, Whitey, Wright.)

Whitey, the narrator, is the barber in a village near Carterville, not far from Detroit. He and his friends have good times in his shop, but less good since local-joker Jim Kendall got killed. Jim and Hod Meyers were great wisecrackers. They kidded Milt Sheppard, who had an Adam's apple as big as a mushmelon. Hod would warn Whitey not to cut it open while shaving Milt. Jim sold canned goods out of Carterville, was fired for wasting time joking, moved to Whitey's village, and said he sold canned goods until he was canned. The narrator emphasizes the pun involved. Jim took to drinking, razzed his dressmaker wife, and gave her little money earned when he took odd jobs. Once, he told her he bought tickets for Evan's Circus, said to wait with their children at the tent entrance, deliberately stayed drinking in Wright's pool room, and stood them up — for a joke, you see. He got mad when Doc Ralph Stair, new in town, heard about it and took the mother and her kids to the show. When coroner Ken Beatty died, the townspeople talked Stair into replacing him.

Now, about Paul Dickson. When Paul was about 10 he fell from a tree onto his head and was "silly" afterwards. Jim said he was "cuckoo" because he hurt his "bean." Jim once sent Paul to a garage to fetch a left-handed monkey wrench; once asked him to get a key from Schrader's hardware store for the baseball pitcher's box. For laughs, you understand. Paul stayed close to his mother, to Doc Stair, who treated him gently, and to Julie Gregg, an aging girl almost 30, educated good, too good for the young town roughs. Paul liked to trot after Julie when she shopped. She "treated him mighty nice." Her father drank too much and died. Once, when Whitey was taking his "old lady" to consult Stair, because the two older town doctors hadn't improved her health, he happened to see Julie enter to ask Stair to treat her widowed mother's ailing foot. Whitey could tell: Julie fell instantly in love with handsome Stair, who, though, wasn't much aware of her, and just said sure, he'd go see her mother.

Jim wasn't only a joker and drinker but also "quite a lady-killer." He lusted for Julie, even saying in Whitey's shop he'd trade his wife and kids for her. She ignored him, once even phoning marshal Joe Barnes when Jim tried "the rough stuff" on her. Word got out, though not to Stair. Hod kidded Jim in Whitey's shop. Jim vowed revenge. Townspeople could see how poor Julie was stuck, discreetly, on unknowing Stair. Jim could imitate other people's voices. Once, he phoned Whitey, pretended he was John Scott's wife, said John was dead and would Whitey come seven miles to his lakeside house and shave him before burial. Whitey went. John opened the door! Jim sure was "a card." One night when Jim knew Stair was at Carterville, he phoned Julie, pretended he was Stair, wanted to tell her something special, would she come to his office. "Well, poor Julie" did. Jim and some rough men hid, heard Julie knock on Stair's door, and made some noise. When she whispered, "Is that you, Ralph?" they imitated her until she was ashamed to be seen. No one told Stair. But when Jim gloated about it once, Paul Dickson happened to hear, understood somewhat, and rushed to tell Stair, who would've beat up Jim but for embarrassment to Julie that would obviously ensue.

A few days later Jim sought Hod in Whitey's shop, to go duck hunting. Hod was out of town, but Paul, there, offered to go. Jim asked Paul if he could shoot. No, never did. So Jim agreed, probably figuring he'd have fun kidding him in the boat. Next morning Stair entered, said he heard about Jim's taking Paul shooting, admitted he told Paul that anyone kidding Julie as Jim had "ought not to be let live." Well, Stair, as coroner, located Jim — shot dead by the Scotts' lake. Stair ruled Jim's "case ... accidental shootin.'" Whitey regarded Jim as a sucker to let "a new beginner have his gun, let alone a half-wit," adding that Jim'll be missed hereabouts and sure "was a card."

Maxwell Perkins* ecstatically praised "Haircut" in a letter to Lardner (March 16, 1925): "I can't shake it out of my mind. ... There's not a man alive who could have done better, that's certain. ... [I]t is a most biting and revealing story." Twice calling "Haircut" Lardner's "most famous story," Yardley lists its virtues: "conciseness," sustained "tone," skillful construction, verbal economy, "the barber's mindless laughter as he recalls Kendall's jokes" and his "unemotional reaction" thereto, and "the small town's life-must-go-on indifference to what has happened." Yardley feels he must undercut his praise and agree with criticism of "Haircut" by F. Scott Fitzgerald,* that yes, "[t]he use of the village idiot to take revenge on Jim Kendall is indeed a cliché, and the story as a whole is just a little bit too pat." Pat, hell. It's a classic. V. S. Pritchett says it "contains the essence of Lardner's ear for vivid illiteracy and shows the strength of the [talky vernacular] tradition he represents"; then Pritchett quotes a long, rambling passage and calls it "pure [Mark] Twain." Tom Quirk says that, in "Haircut," "Lardner reveals, through the barber narrator's recitation and headshaking and amused assent to the cruel adventures of Jim Kendall, a survival of the Bricksville crew in modern American life," Bricksville being that lazy Arkansas town in Mark Twain's *Adventures of Huckleberry Finn.* James Phelan discusses "the ideology of technique and the ideology of character while also doing justice to the way in which these analytically separable parts function within the whole system of a narrative"; analyzes "Whitey's 'unseductive unreliable narration'"; and considers "the ideological consequences of a reading experience in which we are apparently flattered for our superiority to the obtuse narrator." Elizabeth Evans says that "Haircut" is "one of Lardner's bitterest condemnations of small town meanness." Charles E. May, however, inflating such "meanness," feels that every reader slavers over violence, like Lardner's redneck villagers: "The reader [May continues] becomes as morally implicated in the death [of Jim Kendall] as the barber and the townspeople by accepting what was obviously their use of the idiot Paul to rid themselves of a troublemaker and prankster that they hated and feared," so that at last "the reader ... becomes an accomplice to the most evil act of all." Douglas Robinson applies the theory of the double bind, advanced by critic Gregory Bateson (1904–1980), to Kendall and Paul, who, "[t]ogether ... act out the son's maternal double bind, at once hating and loving the Julie-mother, deidealizing and idealizing her, inflicting harm on her and protecting her from harm." Robinson swims too far beyond the critic's deep end, however, by suggesting in his "reading beyond the end" of the story that Kendall has not been murdered after all but "merely kidnapped and held prisoner somewhere outside of town." Just perhaps, Robinson continues, "Jim Kendall is rescued from Doc Stair [kidnapper and private jailer] ... and discovers that he is gay, that he loves Whitey ...; he and Whitey leave town together, leave behind the scene of their repression by and as straights and set out on the road of shared self-discovery." Would all this have mystified Ring? Tony Hillerman and Otto Penzler do regard "Haircut" as a mystery story; they include it as one of the 46 stories (dated 1903–1999) in their edition of *The Best Mystery Stories of the Century* (Boston and New York: Houghton Mifflin, 2000). (Sources: Evans, 62; Caruthers [1995], 174; May; Robinson, 103, 186, 190; Pritchett, 580, 581; Quirk, 121; Yardley, 180, 287, 288)

HALEY, HOLYOKE DAN ("Champion"). He is from Holyoke, visits his brother Tommy Haley in Boston, and joyfully meets Midge Kelly there.

HALEY, TOMMY ("TOM") ("Champion"). He is Holyoke Dan Haley's brother and Midge Kelly's manager in Philadelphia and Boston, but is dumped and threatened by Midge in New Orleans for requesting adequate pay.

HALL, SAM (*The Real Dope*). He is a troopship stateroom mate of Keefe, who dislikes Hall's smoking.

HALL, SAM *see* ***THE BIG TOWN***

HALLAHAN In "Meet Me in St. Louie," Danny, playing for Brooklyn, says he hopes manager Max Carey will let him bat against Hallahan, a St. Louis Cardinal "left hand it" pitcher. In "The Ides of June," Danny hit an inside-the-park homer off Bill Hallahan to get the winning RBIs.

William Anthony Hallahan (1902–1981) pitched for the St. Louis Cardinals (1925–1935), the Cardinals and the Cincinnati Reds (1936), Cincinnati (1937), and the Philadelphia Phillies (1938). (Source: *Baseball Encyclopedia*, 2039)

HALPERN ("Dinner"). He is Grace Halpern's husband. When at the dinner his wife gives he speaks to Miss Rell, Harry Barton is obliged to begin conversation with Miss Coakley.

HALPERN, GRACE ("Dinner"). She is the well-meaning hostess of a dinner party in New York to which she invites Harry Barton and Dave Wallace, who as bachelors will provide gender balance for unmarried young Miss Coakley and Miss Rell.

HALSEY, MISS HELEN ("Zone of Quiet"). She is the patient's night nurse. Miss Eleanor Lyons tells him that Helen mourned the death of her Tufts College fiancé too long.

HAMILTON (*Own Your Own Home*). He and his wife live in a big house next to the new home Fred and Grace occupy. When Grace calls on the Hamiltons and presents a card saying "F. A. Gross," Hamilton pretends she is detective Gross and begins ridiculing her in the neighborhood. Hamilton foils Fred's attempt at revenge by using his clout with Bob Barnes, the Cook County sheriff. Fred blames the Hamiltons when their cat supposedly upsets Fred's garbage can but becomes friendly with Hamilton when Hamilton gets him to believe that Martin is the neighborhood villain. It seems more likely that Hamilton and Martin together conspire to trick naive Fred.

HAMILTON, MRS. (*Own Your Own Home*). She is one of Fred and Grace's neighbors. She takes every occasion to lord it over Grace and make her feel inferior. Fred tries to get even by getting Bob Barnes, the Cook County sheriff, to send Parker, a deputy, to Mrs. Hamilton's bridge party and arrest everyone for gambling. The ruse fails. Fred is upset with Hamilton at one point but decides not to make an impoverished widow out of Mrs. Hamilton by shooting him.

HAMLIN ("Widow"). This is the name of a couple or a family who invited Margaret and John Winslow, for the first time, to their annual costume party. Margaret silently wishes John had died after rather than before the party. Now she can't attend it.

HAMMOND ("That Old Sweetheart of Mine"). Stella Crane believes that her maid is so dumb that she confuses the names Gillespie and Hammond. Therefore, Stella fortunately answers the phone when Will, her old boyfriend, calls.

This mechanically inserted humor enables the reader to infer that the Cranes can afford a maid.

HAMMOND ("Who Dealt?"). During her flow of talk at the bridge table, Mrs. Cannon says she and her husband Thomas Cannon met at Hammond's home a writer named Hastings who said he knows editors often don't read submissions to them.

HAMMOND, DOC ("Champion"). He is the Star Boxing Club manager in Milwaukee. He arranges a bout with Young Tracey for Midge Kelly, who is then bribed to throw the fight.

HAMMOND, FLORENCE ("Anniversary"). She is Bess Taylor's friend. One night, Florence tells Bess about her brother-in-law Ed's abuse of her sister Grace.

In real life, Florence Hammond was the wife of Percy Hammond. The Lardners knew both Hammonds well, since Percy Hammond was a drama reviewer for the Chicago *Tribune* (from 1908) and the New York *Tribune* (1920s). (Sources: Elder, 47, 60, 156; Lardner, Jr., 139, 198; Yardley, 84, 243, 327)

HAMMOND, J. ("A Chip of the Old Block"). He is the head of an important family in Sandusky, Ohio, according to Captain Evan Barnes.

HAMMOND, JOE ("Sick 'Em"). Jack Barnett tells the narrator that Central Leaguers Joe Hammond, Bill Peck, and Bull Harper were involved in recent trades.

George W. Hilton annotates the three players as "presumed fictional." (Source: Hilton, 375)

HAMMOND, PERCE ("Anniversary"). He and his wife Florence ask Louis Taylor for help to repair a flat tire so they can drive to the Cobbs to play bridge.

According to Donald Elder and Clifford M. Caruthers, among Lardner's neighbors in East Hampton, Long Island, in the 1920s, were Percy Hammond and his wife Florence. (Sources: Caruthers [1973], 122; Elder, 306)

HAMPTON, MIRA ("Rhythm"). She is a pretty actress whom Harry Hart meets at a party given by Peggy Leech. He objects when Mira wants him to play the piano there.

HANEY, CORP. EDDY (*Treat 'Em Rough*). He is a member of Jack Keefe's army unit. They discuss money allotments to army wives.

HANK ("Sick 'Em" and "Horseshoes") *see* **O'DAY, HENRY**

HARDING, JOE ("Tour No. 2"). He is a friend of Larry's, also working in Chicago. When Larry returns from Europe, Joe tells him that Louis

Shaffer, supposedly looking after Larry's gardening business, "hadent been a round" for a while.

HARGER, DICK ("War Bribes"). He is a friend of Fred A. Gross's, "hangs a round up on LaSalle st.," and sells Fred stock-market information for $2. Fred follows Dick's suggestions and loses.

HARGRAVE, LEO ("Sun Cured"). He taxied with Ernie Fretts from the railroad station to their Miami hotel. According to Fretts's account to C. L. Walters, Fretts and Hargrave drank up two bottles of gin that were accidentally left in Fretts's room by the previous occupant.

"HARMONY" (*McClure's Magazine*, August 1915; ABS, HTW, LOB, RAB, RU). (Characters: Buck, Burton, Joe Cantillon, Bill Cole, Mrs. Cole, Cragin, Sam Crawford, Art Graham, Griffin, Dick Hodges, Jack, Lenke, Mike McCann, Jake Martin, Lefty Parks, "Cap" Ryan, Waldron.)

The narrator, a baseball journalist, is traveling by train to Springfield with "Cap" Ryan and his team. Art Graham, Bill Cole, Lefty Parks, and Waldron are practicing their "tonsorial treatment" of "Sweet Adeline." Lacking material, the narrator asks Ryan to give him something to write up. Ryan offers this story about acquiring Waldron, their superb hitter:

Ryan gave Art Graham, with a day off at Detroit, permission to visit relatives in Jackson and while there to try to spot a pitcher. He returned to report he'd found Waldron, who was a natural hitter — this in spite of the fact that Dick Hodges, manager of the Jackson team, kept Waldron under wraps for more money later, played him little, and he popped out the one time he batted in Graham's presence. Ryan bought him immediately, on Art's seemingly foolish recommendation. While the narrator composes his 700-word report about this, he hears Waldron directing his quartet — Cole bass, Lefty baritone, Art tenor, and Waldron himself the lead.

The narrator files his report in Springfield, returns to the train, and finds Graham. When the narrator says his report features Graham's finding "a second Cobb" after seeing him fly out, Art mainly smiles. So the narrator sits beside Cole in the diner and says his report concerned Ryan's account of Graham's picking Waldron. Cole replies that he'll tell the narrator what Ryan never knew, if the narrator promises not to report it until Art, Cole's closest friend and "roomy" since 1911, is finally released. OK. Cole explains:

Art visited his uncle in Springfield all right, met Waldron there, but never scouted him at all. Something happened earlier. A former teammate was Mike McCann, with "the swellest tenor voice." Cole, Mike, and Lefty used to sing together, with Mike often breaking into solo. Then Art came from "Washin'ton" to the team, made a quartet, but insisted on so much musical practice that Ryan got sore. Then Lefty, unmarried, fell for a girl and during June home games deserted the quartet to be with her. Art missed Lefty's singing; so he teased him "till he give up the girl." The quartet continued for three years, almost going on vaudeville one off-season. In 1911 Mike pitched so well, but so hard, that next year he was weak, and the following spring training — two years ago — was in jeopardy. Art says they'll lose their lead tenor. The season started. Ryan pitched Mike against St. Louis, to judge him. He played routinely, but his teammates fielded and scored well, and they might have won but Art, daydreaming about harmonizing, dropped a fly. Ryan let Mike stay in. He lost. Art wept. Mike went to Minneapolis. The team did badly. When Lefty tried tenor, "you think you're in the stockyards." Also, Art dropped too many flies.

During spring training a year ago, Art seemed better, was cheered by a team newcomer named Burton because he sang tenor well, and Cole and Lefty joined the two in harmonious music. But Burton played too badly to replace steady Cragin at second base, was cut, and Art turned grumpy again. By August Art was worse and asked Ryan to trade to obtain Harper, a good tenor. On that trip to Jackson, Art met Waldron, who was after Art's "swell doll" cousin but whose piano-playing and singing persuaded Art to get Ryan to hire him. He reported this spring. Now Waldron, as natural a player as Cobb, has replaced benched Art, and the team has a tenor "for nine years."

The narrator notices that the train is nearing Worcester. Cole is called away to rehearse some more with Art, Lefty, and Waldron, who quickly directs Cole to go up F to A, Lefty half-tone higher, Art "just like always," while he drops down a tone.

It's two years since Cole confided in the narrator, who, when he sees Ryan again, just after he finally released Art, tries to reveal Cole's version. Ryan replies thus: Cole is a big liar; Ryan didn't believe Art about seeing Waldron pop out; a Jackson player could explain the truth but wouldn't, through fear of Hodges' wrath; Art wouldn't "tout ball players" just for their singing. Still, the narrator believes Cole and ends by saying the team lacks on-the-field harmony — despite Waldron's excellence — since Art, Cole, and Lefty left.

George W. Hilton identifies the apparent source of "Harmony" as "Lardner's observation of a vocal quartet managed by Lew[is A.] Richie [1883–1936] of the Cubs in 1910." Hilton concludes that the team is "a fictional version of the White Sox," because the narrator mentions railroads to Minneapolis and because Detroit is one of his team's opponents. "Harmony" is best read without trying to keep the sinuous time line straight. Lardner peppers the story with such contemporaneous names as ballplayers Ty Cobb, Walter Johnson, and Tris Speaker, movie stars Charlie Chaplin* and Mary Pickford,* evangelist and ex–National League outfielder Billy Sunday (1863–1935), tenors Enrico Caruso (1873–1921), and John McCormack (1884–1945), and soprano Joanne Gadski (called a tenor by Cole) (1872–1932). (Fred A. Gross mentions "Crusoe" in "The Swift Six.") John Berryman opines that "Harmony" is Lardner's "only really fine baseball story." Did Berryman, given his thorough dislike of Lardner, read all of Lardner's baseball stories? Berryman adds that "Harmony" is "one of his few and affecting and well constructed stories, the kind of dramatic depthwork he only two or three times attempted." (Sources: Berryman, 421; Hilton, 21–22, 345, 466, 483)

HARMS ("Liberty Hall"). This is the name of Ben Drake's publisher. Harms's secretary is Irene.

HARPER ("The Courtship of T. Dorgan"). Keefe mentions that "the Washington club went mad" in one game against the White Sox, scored frequently, and Harper, their pitcher, shut them out.

Harry Clayton Harper (1895–1963) pitched for the Washington Senators (1913–1919), the Boston Red Sox (1920), the New York Yankees (1921), and the Brooklyn Dodgers (1923). George W. Hilton comments that Harper was a generally "futile" left-hander but became "a successful industrialist." (Sources: *Baseball Encyclopedia*, 1046; Hilton, 285)

HARPER, BULL ("Sick 'Em"). While talking to the narrator, Jack Barnett says that Bull Harper, Bill Peck, and Joe Hammond, all Central League players, were involved in recent trades.

George W. Hilton says that the three are "presumed fictional." (Source: Hilton, 375)

HARPER, BUTCH ("Absent-minded Beggar"). He is Charlotte Knowles's bootlegger, from whom she buys gin for a party.

HARPER, HILDA ("Words and Music"). She is a stenographer for "Lincke Brothers," lives with Margaret, and is enamored of Roman Starr, the popular stage and screen tenor. She pretends to be a reporter, wangles an appointment to interview Starr in his apartment, but is disillusioned when she discovers he is married to a raucous woman and is uncouth himself.

HARPER, MR. ("Ball-A-Hole"). He is mentioned as a golfer who plays with Mr. McNally against Mr. Davis and Mr. Joyce for $1 to $5 a hole.

HARPER, MRS. ("The Maysville Minstrel"). She is a customer of the Maysville gas company. Her pilot-light sometimes fails. She also doesn't pay her gas bill promptly.

HARRIET, AUNT ("The Facts"). She lives with the McDonald family in Chicago. She does "settlement work" with Louise McDonald and Mary Carey. Walter McDonald tells Billy Bowen that Harriet isn't their real aunt. She was Walter's father's housekeeper. Sam McDonald and his sister Louise McDonald stayed on after Sam married. Since Billy and Walter are aware of Harriet's poor grammar, Tommy Richards sends her a book on English grammar as Billy's Christmas present.

HARRIS ("Oh, You Bonehead!"). He is an assistant and a scout working under the Coach of an unnamed football team. The Coach explains to Harris and Dana, another assistant, why, when their player Dickie pulled a "bonehead" play, he didn't rebuke him.

HARRIS ("A One-Man Team"). He is an assistant under football Coach Belden. He scouted Doane, a team that Belden plans to defeat, reported only on Doane's star player Davis, and was therefore partly responsible for Belden's embarrassing defeat by Doane.

HARRIS, JEROME ("Champion"). He becomes Midge Kelly's manager in Detroit, replacing Tommy Haley. Harris does well by Midge financially in Milwaukee, but must be sad when Midge leaves him for New York with Mrs. Harris.

HARRIS, MRS. ("Champion"). She is Jerome Harris's wife but leaves him for Midge Kelly.

HARRIS, RED ("A Frame-Up"). He is a boxer Burke defeats in Milwaukee.

HARRISON ("The Jade Necklace"). He is the head of Supreme, the movie company against which L. N. Bauer competes.

HARRY ("The Busher Reënlists") *see* **GRABINER, HARRY**

HARRY ("A Day with Conrad Green"). He is Conrad Green's mistress Rose's boyfriend. When Green cannot produce pearls he promised Rose so she would dump Harry, she returns to Harry, perhaps only briefly.

HARRY ("Nora"). He is the bootlegger helpful to Hazlett, the frustrated author of the play "Nora."

HARRY ("The Spinning Wheel"). He is a roulette dealer where the narrator works. At Harry's wheel, Macomber plays by doubling after each loss until he wins $300.

HART, HARRY ("Rhythm"). He is a self-confessed tune thief, popular and financially successful in providing melodies for musical comedies, including one produced by Conrad Green. Hart is almost ruined when Spencer Deal, among others, takes him so seriously that he tries to compose high-class music. When he and lyric-thief Benny Kane resume their shady collaboration, all will probably be well again. Hart's girlfriend Rita Marlowe is even willing to take him back.

The name Harry Hart sounds like a cardiologist's nightmare. It is possible that Lardner derived the name Hart from that of Moss Hart (1904–1961), the playwright whose work was yet to come but who attended a performance of *June Moon* (1929), the play based on Lardner's "Some Like Them Cold" and written by Lardner and George S. Kaufman.* Kaufman knew Hart by 1926 (the date of "Rhythm") and may have introduced him to Lardner by then. Hart later approached Kaufman to ask him to collaborate on a comedy he had drafted spoofing the panic in Hollywood following the introduction of sound in movies. The two created *Once in a Lifetime* (1930), a hit that made Hart famous. Kaufman and Hart collaborated on other fine plays. Moss also wrote the libretto for *Face the Music* (1930) by Irving Berlin.*

Hart's conversation reveals unconscious disrespect for grammatical correctness. Walton R. Patrick's half-admiration of Hart, and of Benny Kane too, is indicated when he says that "although both characters are guilty of a type of dishonesty, they are at least honest about their dishonesty." (Sources: Patrick, 109; Yardley, 337)

HART, KENNETH ("KEN") ("High-rollers"). He graduated from Yale, is wealthy, and plays golf and cards at a Hampton Dunes club on Long Island for money with Dick Parker, Alex Spears, Jack Bowen, and Jack's friend Walter Finch. Walter, not wealthy like his competitors, learns that these fellows gamble, win and lose, but don't settle up.

HART, MRS. ("High-rollers"). She is wealthy Kenneth Hart's wife. She and Mrs. Parker play bridge with Peggy Bowen. Peggy gets Marion Finch to join their parties as a replacement for Mrs. Spears.

HARTSELL ("The Golden Honeymoon"). He is the son of Frank M. Hartsell and his wife. They brag about him. He lives in Grand Rapids, Michigan.

HARTSELL, FRANK M. ("The Golden Honeymoon"). He was engaged to Lucy Frost 52 years ago. But Lucy married Charley. By chance, she and Charley meet Hartsell and his wife in Florida. Frank became a veterinarian in Hillsdale, Michigan, and married there. Charley defeats Frank in checkers, is defeated at horseshoes, and vengefully calls him a "cow doctor."

HARTSELL, MRS. ("The Golden Honeymoon"). She is Frank M. Hartsell's wife. The two meet Charley and his wife in Florida. Charley calls Mrs. Hartsell "an old chatter-box."

HASTINGS ("Who Dealt?"). During her gushy talk, Mrs. Cannon says that a writer named Hastings, whom he and her husband Thomas Cannon met at Hammond's home, says he knows that editors often don't read submissions to them.

HASTINGS, DR. ("How Are You?"). He is a physician who, according to Beth Dayton, told her that her husband Bob Dayton shouldn't be alone. The Daytons therefore take a vacation together.

HASTINGS, FRANK ("Widow"). He and his wife call on Margaret Winslow after her husband John died. Frank retells fellow male mourners about his not betting on Jim Dandy, a Saratoga horse-race winner last summer.

HASTINGS, MRS. ("Widow"). She and her husband Frank offer condolences to Margaret Winslow after her husband's death.

HATCH, BERTHA ("A Friendly Game") *see* Hatch, Mrs.

HATCH, JIM In "A Friendly Game," he plays poker at the home of the narrator and his wife, as do fellow guests Mrs. Hatch, Harry Quinn and his wife Marion Quinn, and Joe Tuttle. An argument disrupts the friendly game. Hatch and his wife are reintroduced in *Gullible's Travels, Etc.* In "Carmen," he and his wife play rummy and socialize with Gullible and his wife. When Hatch wins at cards, the four attend *Carmen* at Jim's expense. Hatch leaves at intermission, returns drunk, and sleeps in his seat until his wife pokes him. In "Three Kings and a Pair," Mrs. Gullible gets Gullible out of the house — to free it for Bessie and Bishop — by pretending to visit the Hatches, who are away at Benton Harbor. In "Gullible's Travels," the Gullibles snub Hatch and his wife but after their unpleasant Florida vacation will socialize with them again. In "Three Without, Doubled," Mrs. Gullible acts superior to the Hatches when they are invited to join the San Susie bridge club. However, the Hatches eventually replace the Gullibles as club members.

HATCH, KENNETH ("Carmen"). He is the son of the Hatches. Gullible recalls that Hatch christened the baby Kenneth because "he got mad" at him.

HATCH, MRS. In "A Friendly Game," she is the inept, cheating poker player at the home of the narrator and his wife. Other guests are her husband Jim Hatch, Harry Quinn and Marion Quinn, and Joe Tuttle. Mrs. Hatch, whose first name is given as Bertha, is reintroduced in *Gullible's Travels, Etc.* In "Carmen," she and Jim are friends of Gullible and his wife. The four attend a performance of *Carmen*, despite the men's reluctance. In "Three Kings and a Pair," she and her husband are out of town, but Mrs. Gullible makes Gullible pretend to visit them with her. In "Gullible's Travels," Mrs. Gullible lords it over Mrs. Hatch by boasting of her planned Florida vacation with Gullible. When it proves less than expected, Mrs. Gullible says they'll play rummy with the Hatches again. In "Three Without, Doubled," Mrs. Hatch, whose first name is given as Bertha, gets snubbed by Mrs. Gullible when the Gullibles are invited to join the San Susie bridge club. Mrs. Hatch gets revenge when the Gullibles aren't invited to attend further club meetings and the Hatches become their replacements.

HAUSER ("Horseshoes"). He is a St. Louis infielder who misses a grounder hit by Speed Parker of the Cubs.

Arnold George Hauser (1888–1966) played for the St. Louis Cardinals (1910–1913). George W. Hilton notes that Hauser suffered from mental illness briefly (1914), after which he played for the Chicago Whales (1915). (Sources: *Baseball Encyclopedia*, 1121; Hilton, 400)

HAUSLER AND CORNELL ("Holycaust"). Jessie writes that the Centralia fire involved the Hausler and Cornell Building.

HAVERS, T. W. ("'In Conference'"). He and others work for Kramer & Company. Havers is a vice president. While "in conference" they talk vacantly. He reveals that he has three brothers: G. K. Havers, "pharmaceutical dispenser," N. D. Havers, "mortuary artisan," and V. F. Havers, "garbage practitioner."

HAWKS, HELEN She was an early girlfriend of Lardner's. She lived in Goshen, Indiana, knew Ruby Abbott Hendry* well, and liked Lardner very much. (Sources: Lardner, Jr., 33; Caruthers [1995], 4)

HAWLEY ("A Day with Conrad Green"). He is a reporter with *Gay New York*. He courteously, and successfully, persuades Conrad Green to buy a $1,500 ad in the *Gay*, to avoid being exposed as being "mixed up in a gambling story."

Nothing in Lardner's writings indicates awareness of homosexual connotations in the word "gay."

HAWLEY ("Where Do You Get That Noise?"). He is Hawley's father. Young Hawley, 27, foolishly says he can remember that his father let him go to ball games alone 19 years ago.

HAWLEY ("Where Do You Get That Noise?"). He is a good Philly baseball player traded to the narrator's team because his manager Pat Moran could no longer stand his constant chatter. Hawley tops everyone's comments, professional, informational, or personal, until Carey, the narrator's friend, inveigles Hawley into voicing his preference of brunettes over blonde; Cap, Carey's manager, whose wife is a gorgeous blonde, is so outraged that he puts Hawley on waivers. Pittsburgh takes him.

HAWLEY, MRS. ("Where Do You Get That Noise?") Hawley idiotically says that "my old lady" wouldn't let her husband take a raft, during a uniquely bad flood, from New York, where he was trapped, to Cleveland, where the Hawleys lived.

HAWLEY, ZEKE ("Where Do You Get That Noise?"). He is supposedly Hawley's uncle, a senator in Washington, and a friend of "Woodruff Wilson," whom Hawley met when Wilson was visiting Uncle Zeke.

George W. Hilton notes that Willis Chatman Hawley (1864–1941) was a real senator, from Oregon, and that he co-sponsored the Smoot-Hawley Tariff Act (1930). (Source: Hilton, 509)

HAYES ("Alibi Ike"). He plays on the narrator's baseball team.

HAYES ("Back to Baltimore"). He was the husband of Mrs. Hayes and was the principal owner of the Boston Braves. His wife took a great interest in the team also. He became ill after witnessing Boston losses in St. Louis, and died on a train taking him back home to Boston.

HAYES ("A One-Man Team"). He plays football for Coach Belden, who in the game against Doane has Ainslee substitute for Hayes.

HAYES, KATE ("Tour Y-10"). She and her friend Violet Emerson go on a vacation to Yellowstone. Violet, blond and petite, fancies she is more attractive than Kate, tall and dark, is; but it is Kate who attracts Coles and Garrett, and accepts Garrett's proposal of marriage.

HAYES, MRS. ("Back to Baltimore"). She is president and principal owner of the Boston Braves. She knows nothing about baseball but over-manages the team, once by insisting that manager Dixon hire William Baker, Jr., her pet from Yale. Next, Mrs. Hayes's husband died. Dixon ingeniously got Baker's parents to order him home. Mrs. Hayes replaced Dixon as manager with Baker, whom Dixon figures she will make president of the team and marry. Dixon alludes to Mrs. Hayes as "the skirt" and "the doll."

HAYNES (*The Big Town*). He is a bookie and a friend of Finch, who places a winning bet at the Belmont on the racehorse Sap. Sap defeats Only One, Herbert Daley's favorite racehorse.

HAZLETT ("Nora"). He is a playwright. When he timidly offers his "Nora" to Louie Brock, this domineering producer orders his lyricist Frank Moon and his tunesmith Jerry Morris to redo the plot to suit the three of them. This leaves Hazlett helpless and in need of Harry, his bootlegger.

Clifford M. Caruthers suggests that Brook, Moon, and Morris are "damning caricatures [that] probably reflect Lardner's frustations in theater ventures with Florenz Ziegfeld[*] and George M. Cohan[*]." (Source: Caruthers [1995], 217)

HEALY, MIKE ("Women"). He is a utility catcher on a baseball team. He warns Young Jake and others to avoid women, explains how his success with women has cost him professional advancement, but promptly says "yes" to "a mash note" sent him from the stand by a "cute" girl in "a tan suit."

HECHT, DAVE ("Holycaust"). Jessie writes that the Centralia fire involved the Dave Hecht Building.

HECTOR (*The Real Dope*). He is a head waiter at the Castle Roof. At Francis Griffin's recommendation, Finch and his guests are served Scotch highballs by Hector.

HEINIE ("My Roomy") *see* **ZIMMERMAN**

HEISMAN ("A Caddy's Diary"). He owns a store in the village. The diarist explains that during the winters he works there.

HELGA ("Ex Parte"). She is Marjorie and Joe Paxton's maid. She announces dinner too quickly to leave Joe enough time to serve cocktails to the narrator and his wife Florence.

HELGA ("I Can't Breathe"). She is evidently a servant at the diarist's home in New York. When Gordon Flint phones, Helga gives him the diarist's vacation address.

HENDERSON, ANNA ("The Facts"). She clerks in the book department at Marsh's store and sells Tommy Richards a book entitled *The Green-Eyed Monster*, which he sends as a Christmas present from Billy Bowen to Bob McDonald and his wife Flo McDonald. The gift is deliberately inappropriate, since Bob automatically grows jealous when any man talks to Flo.

HENDRICKS, MISS ("Tour No. 2"). She, Miss Griffith, and Miss Lamont, each about 25, are from What Cheer, Iowa, and are touring with Larry and Minnie Burns. Larry deems them pretty but conceited. They tolerate his stupidity.

HENDRY, JAMES R. He was the husband of Lardner's sister-in-law Ruby Abbott Hendry.* He was known as J. Robin Hendry.

HENDRY, RUBY ABBOTT Lardner's sister-in-law and the wife of James R. Hendry. Clifford M. Caruthers notes that Lardner was "especially close to Ruby, ... whose interest in music he found especially congenial." Ruby and Lardner's wife enjoyed playing bridge — interesting in light of Lardner's stories about bridge players. When Ruth was still single, Lardner was delighted when she came to live with him and his wife for a time (1912). The two young women played bridge. However, he wrote her later (April 18, 1913), addressed her as "Dearest Lillian," and objected that she wanted Lardner and his family to move to Goshen. In funny letters, he calls her "Dear Rubina C." and "Dear Rube" (August 22, 1910; October 4 [1926]; July 7 [1932]). Ring Lardner Jr. reports that in 1975 Ruby was 90 years old. (Sources: Elder, 79, 349; Lardner, Jr., 33; Caruthers [1995], 54, 98, 99, 102–103, 203; Yardley, 140)

HENKEL, GEORGE (*The Big Town*). He is a banker and Mrs. Snell's father, according to Ella Finch, who says she is "wild" to meet Mrs. Snell, because she's "a wonderful bridge player."

HENRY ("Horseshoes"). He is the Washington catcher, in the Johnson-Henry battery, playing against the Athletics before the Athletics get into the World Series against the Giants.

John Park Henry (1888–1941) played for the Washington Senators (1910–1917) and the Boston Braves (1918). George W. Hilton reports that Henry, a poor hitter, could catch the blazing pitches of Walter Perry Johnson. (Sources: *Baseball Encyclopedia*, 1135–1136; Hilton, 46, 407)

HENRY ("Old Folks' Christmas"), Lloyd and Henry's is a fur store. Grace Carter purchased a sealskin coat there as a Christmas present for Caroline Carter, her daughter. Caroline wants to exchange the coat for another one.

HERMAN, BABE In "One Hit, One Error, One Left." he was an outfielder for Brooklyn. Danny explains that Herman has a wife and two kids, was a "hole out," and was "trade it ... to Cincinnati." In "When the Moon Comes over the Mountain," Casey Stengel persuades Danny that Babe used to sleep in a tent in right field. In "Holycaust," Danny writes that Babe Herman and Lombardi were traded by Brooklyn to Cincinnati, whereupon they hit homers against Brooklyn. In "The Ides of June," Danny mentions Babe Herman's doing "a nose dive" when a fly ball goes beyond him.

Floyd Caves "Babe" Herman (1903–1987) played for the Brooklyn Dodgers (1926–1931), the Cincinnati Reds (1932), the Chicago Cubs (1933–1934), the Cubs and the Pittsburgh Pirates (1935), the Cubs (1936), the Detroit Tigers (1937), and Brooklyn (1945). (Source: *Baseball Encyclopedia*, 1136).

HERMANN, GARRY ("Where Do You Get That Noise?"). The narrator jocosely suggests to Hawley that Garry Hermann should "trade off all his Alleys for Dutch," that is, fill the Cincinnati team with players having German names in place of those with names indicating pro-Allied sentiments during the war. Hawley's automatic objection is that such trades would enhance only home-game attendance. ("Where Do You Get That Noise?" takes place in 1915.)

August Hermann (1850–1931) was the owner of the Cincinnati Reds (1902–1927). (Source: Hilton, 515)

HERN, BUNNY In "The Busher Beats It Hence," Keefe says McGraw needs him to pitch because he has only "Hern," who "is a young man and not got no experiense," and Wiltse, who "is a left hander." In "The Busher Abroad," Keefe says "bunny Hearn" is a baseball player on the world tour.

Bunn "Bunny" Hern played for the St. Louis Cardinals (1910–1911), the New York Giants (1913), and the Boston Braves (1918, 1920). George W. Hilton says that Hearn "was, indeed, short of experience" and that after his career in the major leagues ended he coached baseball at the University of North Carolina. (Sources: *Baseball Encyclopedia*, 2054, Hilton, 177)

HERSCH, EMMA ("Champion") *see* **KELLY, EMMA**

HERSCH, LOU ("Champion"). He meets Midge Kelly in Milwaukee, becomes his brother-in-law when Midge marries Lou's sister Emma, later tries to get money from Midge until he is punched and threatened.

HERSCH, MRS. ("Champion"). She is the mother of Emma Hersch and Lou Hersch. When she discovers Midge Kelly has taken advantage of Emma, she sends a goon to force Midge to marry Emma.

HERZOG ("Where Do You Get That Noise?"). Herzog, Heine Groh, Fritz Mollwitz, Count Von Kolnitz, Wagner, and Schneider play for the Reds. Carey, of the Cubs, says their names are enough for the Reds to break attendance records in

Cincinnati, which is full of citizens of German background. Hawley wonders what about away games.

Charles Lincoln Herzog (1885–1953) played for the New York Giants (1908–1909), the Boston Braves (1910), the Braves and the Giants (1911), the Giants (1912–1913), the Cincinnati Reds (1914–1915), the Reds and the Giants (1916), the Giants (1917), the Braves (1918), the Braves and the Chicago Cubs (1919), and the Cubs (1920), and managed the Reds (1914–1916). George W. Hilton reports that Herzog graduated from the University of Maryland and that after leaving baseball he became the Baltimore & Ohio Railroad athlete-passenger agent. (Sources: *Baseball Encyclopedia*, 696, 1140; Hilton, 513–514).

HESS (*Treat 'Em Rough*). He is "a big stropper" in Jack Keefe's army unit.

HESS, OTTO ("Back to Baltimore"). He is a Boston Braves pitcher. During batting practice, he frightened William Baker Jr. by throwing him a fast ball. When Baker asked Dixon, manager, for free passes to a game, Dixon gave him ten fake ones and signed them as by Hess.

George W. Hilton identifies Hess as "Otto C. Hess (1878–1926), erratic left-handed pitcher nearing the end of his career." Hess played for the Cleveland Indians (then called the Naps, 1902–1908) and the Boston Braves (1912–1915). Otto was born in Berne, Switzerland. (Sources: *Baseball Encyclopedia*, 1141, 2064; Hilton, 432)

HESTER, HARVEY ("'In Conference'"). He waits in the outer office of Kramer & Company, to tell A. T. Lansing, who works there and is Hester's friend from school days, that Lansing's wife is eloping. Lansing and his associates, "in conference," cannot be interrupted.

HEYWOOD, DR. (*The Young Immigrunts*). He treated the narrator for "obesity," when he and his wife lived in Riverside. So says the narrator's mother.

HEYWOOD, MRS. (*The Young Immigrunts*). She is a friend of the narrator's mother. When the narrator's father is driving the family to "Grenitch Conn.," and they are in Utica, Mrs. Heywood drives past them in the rain, stops, and they chat.

HIGGINS ("Back to Baltimore"). Boston Braves manager Dixon comments that "Higgins trimmed us four straight" in St. Louis. See Huggins, Miller James.

HIGGINS, GENE ("Horseshoes"). He manages the Battle Creek Club, a baseball team, when Dick Grimes and Speed Parker play for him.

George W. Hilton notes that "Battle Creek had a club in the Southern Michigan Association in 1911" and that Gene Higgins is probably fictional. (Source: Hilton, 398)

"HIGH-ROLLERS" (*Cosmopolitan*, June 1929). (Characters: Bernard, Jack Bowen, Jack Bowen, Peggy Bowen, Craig, Anne Finch, Junior Finch, Marion Finch, Walter Finch, Kenneth Hart, Mrs. Hart, Bob Morton, Dick Parker, Mrs. Parker, Ripley, Alex Spears, Mrs. Spears.)

Walter Finch leaves his job at Ripley's to work at $30,000, twice his old salary, for "Bernard and Craig, Publicity Engineers." His wife Marion insists on getting a summer place at Hampton Dunes, three hours from New York on Long Island, where Jack and Peggy Bowen live. Marion says that the two couples are friendly and that their children, Anne and Junior Finch, will like Jack, the Bowens' boy. Walter, aware that the four adults go to the theater and play bridge occasionally in town but that Jack's makes $150,000, is uneasy. The Bowens move in with too "wealthy and ... fast" a bunch, and Hampton is too far for a daily train commute. Regardless, in June Marion rents a furnished cottage for $4,000, and Walter joins a Hampton swimming and golf club for $500, and buys a $800 used "sedan." He stays in town Mondays through Fridays and has weekends with the family. Thus, his wife and children avoid "megrims and doldrums."

Marion begins sending Junior and Anne with an "inexpensive nurse" for fun at the Bowens' beach, and plays "contract bridge" with Mrs. Dick Parker and Mrs. Kenneth Hart, whose husbands parleyed inherited wealth into stock-market riches. Marion is substituting for Mrs. Spears, abroad with her husband Alex. The women gamble at 5¢–10¢ a point. Marion doesn't tell Walter. By July she's ahead by $800 but isn't paid. She handles food bills by checks, which astounds local merchants, used to being paid each April. Meanwhile, Walter sweats in his office until Friday dinner with his family, and golfs alone, swims, and lolls at the beach. Bowen persuades Walter to join him, Dick Parker, and Kenneth Hart at "a regular set game" of golf lasting "all through Saturday and Sunday." Walter substitutes for Alex Spears. The four couples start playing bridge Friday, Saturday, and Sunday nights — men at one table, women at another. Walter refuses to play at more than 5¢ a point, which is OK by the other men, who play at 10 a point. One night at the Bowens,' Walter asks, 10¢? No, $10, and Hart owes Parker $30,000 tonight. The two deal a "cold hand" of poker for each, double or nothing. Parker wins $60,000. Walter and Marion lag behind, and Bowen says these millionaires relish high stakes, he was inveigled by "Old Spears" into joining, was scared at first, but is now "pretty well ahead." This evening, Walter won $300, owed him by Hart, who doesn't pay.

The four men usually shoot golf in the 80s. Walter feels daring to be betting $10 on a Nassau. The three millionaires do constant side betting. One day Hart and Parker play a $1,000-a-hole plus a $5,000 Nassau; tied on the 18th, Parker bets $5,000 on a four-putt, misses, and loses $16,000 in all. One day Walter gets cocky, bets a Nassau $100, loses $300 to Parker, and mails him a check, which is quickly cashed. Walter says nothing about this to Bowen, because Bowen owes Walter $200-plus, unpaid.

Despite being college educated — Hart at Yale, his wife, Vasser; Parker at Harvard, his wife, Smith — their conversation concerns only stocks, golf, bridge, and booze. Bowen confides in Walter: Hart and Parker aren't "intellectual" but gamble daringly, win or lose; last summer he saw Hart win $200,000 from Spears; the players never pay but can be trusted; Parker called Jack "queer" for sending that check; Bowen in three years is ahead $70,000, unpaid; the debtors are all "good for it."

Walter and Marion should "repay some of their playmates' hospitality" by throwing a party at the club but can't afford to since they "haven't saved a dime all summer." Walter admits being ahead about $2,000 in golf winnings. Marion admits she's won about $800 at bridge, which she's tired of. They go ahead, give the party, charge it, figure they'll be paid what's owed before the dinner bill comes due. Sudden trouble erupts. Rather "squiffed" on Walter's cheap gin, Hart and Parker say they have only tonight, tomorrow, and next day to settle accounts. Does Hart owe Parker $180,000 or only $135,000 "this season"? They agree to "split the difference." When Marion wonders if Hart and Parker keep records, Mrs. Hart explains, "Just in their heads." Suddenly Hart and Parker remember unpaid wins and losses on old Harvard and Yale crew races and football games, the 1911 World Series, 1920 politics, the "Tooney"-Dempsey fight, "the Argentines," etc. Therefore, Parker owes Hart $240,000 or Hart owes Parker $200.000. They quit worrying. Bowen quietly tells Walter that Hart and Parker have bet 17 years without money being exchanged. At 3:00 A.M., Walter and Marion get home. Marion says she lost $2. Walter puzzles her by saying he wound up $8,400 ahead. How so? He volunteered to plunge at $5 a point, lost $2,800, bet it against Parker 2 to 1 on cutting a spade, lost, bet again, lost, losing $8,400 — which is by all this logic "clear profit." Marion is "too sleepy" to understand.

"High-rollers" is an Orwellian version of converting manifest losses to imagined victories. It is also a mighty silly story; so don't bet on it.

HILDEBRAND ("Hurry Kane"). He is evidently a member of the St. Louis baseball management. When Bull Wade is slow coming to bat against the White Sox, Hildebrand almost forfeits the game.

HILL, JOE In "The Busher Comes Back," Keefe complains that Violet, his girlfriend, is marrying Joe Hill, a left-hander procured by Jennings, Detroit manager, from Providence. Keefe gripes that Jennings' team beats the White Sox "bushers." In "The Busher's Honeymoon," Keefe notices that "Joe Hill the busher that Detroit has got that Violet is hooked up to was round the hotel" in Chicago.

Joe Hill is probably not Clifford Joseph Hill (1893–1938), a left-hander who pitched for the Philadelphia Athletics (1917). (Source: *Baseball Encyclopedia*, 2068)

HILL, VIOLET In "A Busher's Letters Home," Keefe says he hears "right along" from Violet, a cute little blonde. They would have dated except that before the White Sox played the Tigers in Detroit Keefe was sold to Frisco. In "The Busher Comes Back," Keefe boasts that this Detroit girl, "some queen," likes him. Suddenly, she calls him "a busher"; so he feels "well rid of her," because "Good riddance is rubbish." After he pitches well, she phones him and they renew their friendship, even though he's also going after Hazel Carney. Suddenly Violet writes Keefe she's marrying Joe Hill. In "The Busher's Honeymoon," Keefe foolishly tells his wife Florence about both Violet and Hazel Levy. In "The Busher Abroad," Keefe misses Violet when he goes dancing in the Philippines while on the world tour.

HOBBY ("My Roomy") *see* **HOBLITZEL**

HOBLITZEL In "My Roomy," Hobby plays baseball for "Cincy." Chicago's Buster Elliott hits a double over Hobby. In "Horseshoes." Hobby is the Cincinnati first baseman when Dick Grimes and Speed Parker play for the Cubs against them. In *The Real Dope*, Keefe while soldiering in France remembers when he was pitching for the Chicago White Sox against "the Boston club" and walked Hoblitzel to get at weak-hitting Scott, up next.

Richard Carleton Hoblitzell (1888–1962) played for the Cincinnati Reds (1908–1913), the Reds and the Boston Red Sox (1914), and the Red Sox (1915–1918). George W. Hilton notes that Hoblitzell later became a dentist, a baseball manager, and a minor-league umpire. (Sources: *Baseball Encyclopedia*, 1148–1149; Hilton, 342)

HODGES, DICK ("Harmony"). He managed the Jackson baseball team when "Cap" Ryan's team got Waldron away from Hodges, to his great annoyance.

HODGSON, HAROLD ("The Love Nest"). Bartlett remembers that movie-mogul Lou Gregg's wife played the young sister in *The Cad.* Gregg says yes, with Harold Hodgson and Marie Blythe.

HOFFMANN, FRED ("Greek Tragedy"). He is the referee during the fake match between Big Bill Buell and Greek Alexis.

HOFMAN In "My Roomy," the narrator recalls Hofman, Sheckard, and Richie as former Chicago baseball players whose combined "harmonizin'" was less noisy than Buster Elliott's solos. In "The Busher Reënlists," Keefe is offended when Artie Hofman, Jim Archer, Joe Benz, and Charley O'Leary, all Chicago baseball players, don't ask him about his war experiences. In *The Young Immigrunts*, the narrator says his father bought "pretty shirts" from an "old ball player Artie Hofman." In "Insomnia," the sleepless author remembers Hofman.

Arthur Frederick Hofman (1881 or 1882–1956) played for the Pittsburgh Pirates (1903), the Chicago Cubs (1904–1911), the Cubs and the Pirates (1912), the Pirates (1913), and the Yankees and the Cubs (1916). Jonathan Yardley quotes a dispatch by Lardner in the *Chicago Tribune* (June 16, 1910) showing that Lardner knew Hofman, Sheckard, and Richie, and traveled with them on trains between games. (Sources: *Baseball Encyclopedia*, 1152; Hilton, 222; Yardley, 102)

HOFMANN (*Own Your Own Home*). He owns a garden evidently in Chicago or Allison. Fred says the "bow" of his "irish girl" servant saves money by sitting with her when she babysits for Fred and Grace, instead of taking her to "Hofmanns garden."

HOGAN In "Lose with a Smile," Danny identifies "a big horse name Hogan who catchs" for the Giants in a game against Danny's Brooklyn team. The two sassed each other, after which Danny bunted Lopez home from third base. In "Holycaust," Hogan, "the big catcher" for the Giants, kids Thompson, a Brooklyn player at bat.

James Francis Hogan (1906–1967) played for the Boston Braves (1925–1927), the New York Giants (1918–1932), the Braves (1933–1935), and the Washington Senators (1936–1937). (Source: *Baseball Encyclopedia*, 1152–1153)

"THE HOLD-OUT" (*Saturday Evening Post*, March 24, 1917; ABS, LOB, RAB). (Characters: Berner, Frank Conley, Mrs. Conley, Hype Corliss, Bill Doyle, Mr. Edwards, Johnny Gould, Lefty Grant, Bill Hagedorn, Mrs. Hagedorn, Lahey, Bones McChesney, Joe Marsh, Jack Moran, Sheppard, Stremmle.)

Narrator Frank Conley says three people think he's "the greatest": his wife, his boss Mr. Edwards, and Bill Hagedorn. But Mr. Edwards would despise Frank if he knew "the truth o' the Hagedorn business." Bill deserved no consideration. He was "yellow" when demanding more money. But he was a peppy first baseman. Here is Frank's account:

As Mr. Edwards' manager, I worked all year, helping with contracts "and so forth." Last fall he told me our season's loss was $18,000 and we gotta cut salaries. I agreed, because our players were mostly inadequate. We discussed lowering their pay, now that their old Federal League contracts had "all run out." Bill Hagedorn hit .220 and fielded poorly; Mr. Edwards planned to cut his pay from $6,000 to $4,000. Bill agreed some players should be penalized but he shouldn't. He complained that reporters scored him unfairly, his legs hurt, his "missus" was sick, and his Louisville in-laws "kept botherin' us." When he refused to accept $4,000, I told him I hoped "the Kentucky climate agreed with your legs."

Mr. Edwards and I signed Joe Marsh and our weak pitcher Lefty Grant for lower pay. Bones McChesney wouldn't sign and Toronto bought him. I picked up "young Stremmle" from Indianapolis and Dayton's shortstop Berner, and traded our bull-pen occupants Hype Corliss and Jack Moran for St. Louis's good Johnny Gould. We bought Davenport's "young Lahey" as Bill's first-base backup, figuring Bill would see "we were in earnest" and would sign for $4,000. He announced, though, that he had $2,000 in savings after playing seven years and was quitting. I retorted that $2,000 at 6 percent would bring him $10 a month.

Bill reappeared around Christmas. Mr. Edwards had "more relatives than a perch"; he had spent a lot on Christmas gifts for them and was broke. Anyway, Bill said he was about to sign with the semi-pro Acmes. He'd play Sundays for $50 per game and perhaps also "sell automobiles or somethin.'" In January Mr. Edwards went to New Orleans scouting for players and left me in charge. Bill kept reappearing — looking for Marsh's address, asking for a postage stamp, etc. I "entertained him" by over-praising Lahey — until Bill a few days later returned and rattled off the "real facts" about Lahey; in Davenport he bat .260 and committed lots of errors. I made excuses for Lahey. Bill added that Lahey, Gould, and Berner all bat left-handed; so we would need a first baseman who could bat right-handed, like Bill, and he'd sign if "you'd meet my price." I said Mr. Edwards couldn't pay him $6,000 and then stand pat on his other players. Bill griped that no one would play for Mr. Edwards because "The fraternity's give orders that nobody's to sign till you hear from them" and there'll be silence until team owners meet the demands of a players' group close to being affiliated with "the Federation o' Labor." To my boast that Mr. Edwards had signed up the whole team, Bill replied that, signed or not, they'd obey fraternity orders. I asked if he were "draggin' down" $16,000, like Ty Cobb, would he choose the money or the fraternity. He said he'd be "a traitor" unless he went with the fraternity. But when I asked if he'd sign for $16,000 right now, he said he'd always sign for his price but planned to go into the garage business and fix cars, which he could quickly learn to do from his partner. I said there's bad-conscience money in repairing cars badly, as there is in "smugglin' or counterfeitin' or snatchin' purses," or "nap[ping] on the old ball field."

Back again, Mr. Edwards wondered what could be done about Bill. I said that his talk of "goin' into business" was "junk," that his frequent visit to the office meant he'd probably accept lower pay soon, but also that since Lahey was "a busher" first baseman we ought to pay Bill his $6,000, but still that he'd undoubtedly come around and sign before spring training. I joked at Mr. Edwards's suggesting that we could trade for a better first baseman, but I added that we had too many left-handed batters and that Bill "can murder" left-handed pitchers. We agreed to wait.

When he were taking the train south to the Springs, Bill tearfully shook hands to "see us off," wouldn't sign for $4,000, but volunteered to accompany us unsigned. I told him "this ain't no charity excursion." He said he'd rather freeze and starve than for "old Edwards to bull me out o' what's comin' to me." He predicted left-handed pitchers would give our left-handed batters trouble. Only ignorant reporters went down with us, since experienced ones were covering "the Americans" because of their publicized "fight for the pennant last year." I lied to those "kid" reporters about Lahey, since I knew Bill would read their trumped-up dispatches. Unfortunately, Mr. Edwards also believed the phony news and when he joined us was optimistic — until I told him I was only trying to worry Bill and we'd be in trouble for a first baseman if Bill "don't give in." I described Lahey's wretched play at first base during practice. He couldn't locate the base, stumbled regularly, spiked himself, was hit in the face by throws and bouncing grounders, but admittedly was brave. Gould nicknamed awkward Lahey "Charley" after "Charley" Chaplin.* To encourage Mr. Edwards, I praised Gould, Berner, Stremmle, Marsh, and "young Sheppard." I assured him Bill would probably sign soon at the lower figure. Then Bill's wife wrote me: Lahey's being praised in the newspapers "took all the zip" out of him; he felt hopeless and unwanted; he was broke and couldn't pay their bills; she feared "he'd do somethin' desperate." She asked us to wire him that "we'd carry him as an extra man."

While Mr. Edwards was in Dallas, I offered Bill by a telegram to assign him to first base for $4,000. He accepted, reported to me in person, and told me his wife had given birth to a baby boy last Sunday, and admitted he fibbed about having saved $2,000. I told him to go hide in Silver Creek, 20 miles north of Springs, and await my word. Though puzzled, he agreed. When Mr. Edwards returned, I told him we needed Bill and should pay him $6,000. Mr. Edwards reluctantly agreed. I phoned Bill to "blow into camp on Sunday." He did and got hired at $6,000. Bill and I agreed that I would let his wife think he bluffed his way to financial success and he wouldn't tell "certain people" what I had done. Bill promised to name his son "Frankie" after me.

The title "The Hold-out" is clever. Bill Hagedorn is an unsuccessful hold-out against Frank

Conley and Mr. Edwards; but then his holding out wins. Additionally, in the end Frank Conley, an early opponent of the hold-out technique, becomes a successful hold-out himself against Mr. Edwards. George W. Hilton explains how "the fraternity" was a reference to the players' frequent but unavailing efforts to unionize in opposition to "the monopsony held by the owners." (Source: Hilton, 581)

HOLDEN ("Insomnia"). He is Edith Holden's father in the story Doc Early told the sleepless author. Holden and his wife were opposed to and angered by Edith's marriage to Allan Spears.

HOLDEN, EDITH ("Insomnia") *see* **SPEARS, EDITH**

HOLDEN, MRS. ("Insomnia"). She and her husband opposed their daughter Edith's marriage to Allan Spears, according to Doc Early.

HOLLAND, DOCTOR ("Zone of Quiet"). He was Miss Eleanor Lyons's supervisor once. She says he treated her "like I was a Mormon or something." She said that when she told him she wasn't as dumb as she looked, he replied that he hoped not.

HOLLIS, KATE ("The Jade Necklace"). She is an actress whom both movie-magnate L. N. Bauer and his friend Quinn Martin are or once were aware of.

HOLT ("Mr. Frisbie"). He was Junior Holt's father and Allen Frisbie's former business partner.

HOLT, JUNIOR ("Mr. Frisbie"). He is the son of the former partner of Allen Frisbie, who wants his daughter Florence to marry Junior. Florence, unattracted to Junior, who is spongy and sneering, prefers and lands worthless Henry Craig instead.

HOLT, MARY ("A Frame-Up"). She is the beautiful young lady that Burke the boxer sees and falls in love with. Jack Grace tells Burke that she is Esther Fester, and he writes phony letters supposedly from her to Burke encouraging him to defeat Willie Kemp and thus win her affections. Burke is disabused upon accidentally meeting her.

HOLT, Z. N. ("'In Conference'"). He and others work for Kramer & Company. While "in conference" they talk vacantly. He mentions that he reads at night and that he knew a man named S. W. Kline in Marengo, Illinois.

"HOLYCAUST" (*Saturday Evening Post*, July 20, 1932; RAB).

HOMAN, DAVE ("Travelogue"). Hazel Dignan tells Dan Chapman that Dave Homan showed her and Bess Eldridge around New York and also proposed to Hazel. She refused because he's too fat and too funny.

THE HOME COMING (1914). *The Home Coming of Charles A. Comiskey, James C. Callahan, and John J. McGraw* was compiled by Lardner and fellow-sportswriter Edward G. Heeman, and was published in Chicago by Heeman. It describes the return of the White Sox and the Giants after their 1913–1914 world tour. Lardner draws on it in "The Busher Abroad" and "The Busher's Welcome Home." Ironically, *The Home Coming*, though Lardner's first book, is virtually ignored by Lardner critics and bibliographers. (Sources: Elder, 126; Elfers)

HONEY HIVES ("A Frame-Up"). She is Old Man Bumble's granddaughter, according to Jack Grace's silly talk, which Burke believes.

HONOR BRIGHT (*The Big Town*). He is a racehorse, described as "a ten-ton truck." At the Belmont he comes second to Sap and ahead of Only One, owned by Herbert Daley and ridden to lose by Sid Mercer, Daley's corrupt jockey.

HONUS ("Sick 'Em"). It was said that "big Honus," playing for Pittsburgh, warned Davis, an infielder newly acquired by the Phillies, to stay out of his way to avoid injury. Davis bravely sassed him back.

John Peter ("Honus") Wagner (1874–1955) was the Pittsburgh Pirates' record-setting shortstop (1900–1917), managed the Pirates (1900–1917), and became a charter member of the Baseball Hall of Fame (1936). Wagner is mentioned in "Where Do You Get That Noise?" (Sources: *Baseball Encyclopedia*, 711, 1703; Hilton, 388)

HOOPER In "The Crook," he played for the Red Sox in a game against Larry's White Sox. Hooper scored on what Cahill of the White Sox regarded as a questionable call. Cahill's shouting to Bull, an honest umpire, that he was a "crook" inspired the rest of the action. In "Along Came Ruth," Keefe joyfully reports that Eddie Cicotte, White Sox pitcher, forced Hooper to pop up to Collins.

Harry Bartholomew Hooper (1887–1974) played for the Boston Red Sox (1909–1920) and the Chicago White Sox (1921–1925), and was elected to the Baseball Hall of Fame (1971). George W. Hilton reports that Hooper had a degree in civil engineering from St. Marys College, and coached baseball for Princeton University (1931–1932). (Sources: *Baseball Encyclopedia*, 1156–1157; Hilton, 272)

HORNE, MISS ("Freedom of the Press"). She is a *Chronicle* reporter hounding Constance Warner for news.

HORNER ("Take a Walk"). He is a left-handed pitcher for the team on which Agnew plays third base during the game against Pittsburgh.

"HORSESHOES" (*Saturday Evening Post*, September 15, 1914; ABS, HTW, RAB). (Characters: Jim Archer, Baker, Barry, Benton, Bescher, Boehling, Bush, the Chief, Clarke, Eddie Collins, Connolly, Cooper, Davis, Demaree, Larry Doyle, Dunnie, Falkenberg, Fletcher, Gibson, Good, Dick Grimes, Groh, Hank, Hauser, Henry, Gene Higgins, Hobby, Johnson, Joyce, Klem, Leach, McBride, Connie Mack, McGraw, Jack McInnes, Magee, Marsans, Matty, Merkle, Meyers, Milan, Mowrey, Murphy, Murray, Oakes, Rube Oldring, Speed Parker, Plank, Rube, Saier, Schange, Schulte, Shafer, Stewart, Strunk, Jeff Tesreau, Tyler, Tyrus, Williams, Zimmerman.)

The narrator is a sports reporter traveling with the Athletics. They defeated the Giants for the World's Championship (October). They won because Connie Mack replaced injured Joyce by utility-outfielder Dick Grimes, and Grimes robbed McGraw's third baseman Speed Parker of a home run by a "miraculous catch" and hit a "fluky" homer. On the Chicago-bound train, the narrator meets Grimes and reads him the news that Parker, "stellar" Giant, is hospitalized "with nervous prostration" owing to Grimes's "lucky catch." Objecting, Grimes says he's unlucky, gets no praise, Parker was lucky, Parker is hospitalized to show off, Grimes slugged him because he called Grimes "Horseshoes." Grimes explains to the narrator over drinks:

Grimes and Speed came from Ishpeming, Michigan. Speed threw a rotten egg at the teacher; Grimes was blamed and expelled; Speed stayed in school; Grimes took menial jobs. Both fellows played semi-pro locally. On payday Grimes lost his money; Speed probably took it. They played in the Northern Peninsula League; their team lacked money, paid Speed, not Grimes. Two years ago they played for Battle Creek, were "bought" by the Chicago Cubs, who had many outfielders and for third base had Zimmerman, who broke his leg, whereupon Speed got his chance. Luck continued to aid Speed. Against St. Louis, Speed was on base, ran thinking there were two outs not one, scored on an outfield error; next day Speed's double-play grounder hopped, two scored, he got a triple. Against Pittsburgh, Speed popped up, two infielders bumped, he got two RBIs and a double, was safe at third when the catcher overthrew. In Cincinnati, Speed and Grimes missed midnight bed-check; Grimes was caught, fined; Speed hid safely all night, was too tired next day to play well, but it rained; next game Speed on first broke to second during the hidden-ball trick, first baseman dropped the ball then threw errantly; Speed stole third on an errant pitchout; later, Speed tagged a runner out at home when he slid missing the plate. Grimes subbed in the outfield against Boston, missed several flies in dreadful wind, was released to Indianapolis. He learned Speed got away with bad plays, Zimmerman's leg mended in June, and Speed played first, where "things kept on breakin' for him," earned "big [pennant] dough," then more in "the World Serious."

Speed and Grimes, wintering in Ishpeming, liked the same girl, who promised last February to marry Grimes. Speed called him "Horseshoes," meaning dumb-lucky. Speed was traded to play third base with McGraw's successful Giants; Grimes went to Connie's Philadelphia "Ath-a-letics." last August. Grimes, substituting when the pennant was clinched, did badly. Still, he wrote his girl, who predicted a Giants win, and set October 20th for their wedding.

Speed's Giants opposed Grimes's Athletics for the "Serious." Connie demanded fast victories, because he had only three good pitchers to the Giants' five. Grimes's team won Game 1, home, and game 2, away, despite Speed's luck, including a carom off a foot for an out at second. Game 3, home, 9–7 in the ninth, with Speed scoring on an error; but our Collins tripled with three on base to win. Grimes still feared Speed's luck. Game 4, away, the Athletics had Murphy on third, Baker on second, two outs, scoreless eighth inning; McInnes's scorcher hit third base, stopped, Speed threw him out. In Giants' eighth, Speed ducked a bean ball that hit his bat for a single, got to third on a dropped fly, scored, and the Giants won when the Athletics didn't score. Game 5, home, the Athletics ahead 4–2 in the ninth, bases full, two outs, Speed hit a curling grounder toward first, catcher Schang threw the ball and hit Speed on the head, the ball bounced wildly; three scored to win. Game 6, away, scoreless through eight. The Athletics scored one in the ninth when Joyce was beaned but remained playing. In the Giants' half, two outs and one on, Speed at bat hit an easy fly to left field, where Joyce was playing but fainted, costing 2–0 loss. Game 7, home by a coin toss. New York papers, touting Speed, added that he was marrying an unnamed girl. Scalpers got $7 per ticket in Philadelphia. With Joyce hospitalized, Grimes played left field, but fielded and hit badly until the scoreless eleventh. A sudden telegram to Grimes from his girl told him to forgive her and Speed also. Grimes turned savage and saved a run by miraculously catching Speed's fly before hitting the concrete wall headfirst. Bleacherites threw money at him. At bat, Grimes aimed ferociously, insanely, for a triple so as to spike Speed, but his ball bounced into a homer. Grimes slid into third, in savage hope, but Speed had left and heroic Grimes was urged to score. When Speed sarcastically called him "Horseshoes" again, Grimes slugged him until "his nose ... [was] over shakin' hands with his ear."

Grimes buys a drink for the narrator, who asks about the wedding. Grimes says he's substituting at it for Parker, and next year with "the Ath-a-letics" he'll hire someone to anger him helpfully before each game by calling him "Horseshoes."

HORTENSE ("The Love Nest"). She is a servant in the home of Lou and Celia Gregg.

HOSTELLER ("A One-Man Team"). He was a "plunger" for Pelham's football team. Coach Belden recalls defeating Pelham because its "one-man team" was built on Hosteller.

HOUDINI, HARRY (1874–1926), Born Ehrich Weiss in Budapest, Houdine came with his parents to America as an infant, took his professional name from that of French magician Jean Eugène Robert-Houdin, and soon became a world-famous magician, notable as an escape artist. Lardner compares too many of his slippery characters to Houdini to warrant their being listed.

HOUSE, COL. (*Treat 'Em Rough*). At one point rumor has it, says Jack Keefe, that his army unit "would be in Col. House's regt." Edward Mandell House (1858–1938) was a powerful Texas-born American politician and diplomat. During World War I he was a confidant of President Woodrow Wilson and represented him at inter-allied military and naval conferences (1917). He was known as Colonel House through having been a colonel on the staff of Charles Allen Culberson (1855–1925), when Culberson was Governor of Texas (1895–1899).

"HOW ARE YOU?" (*Red Book*, December 1935). (Characters: Dr. Andrell, Annie, Dr. Beistle, Dr. Benham, Dr. Clague, Harry Danforth, Beth Dayton, Bob Dayton, Dmitri, Driscoll, Mrs. Driscoll, Drury, Mrs. Ferrell, Dr. Elston Gifford, Mrs. Gurnsey, Dr. Hastings, Joey, Dr. Julius, Aunt Laura, Mark, Dr. George Phelon, Phyllis, Hilda Pratt, Wallie Pratt, Frank Russell, Mrs. L. S. Stacey, Louie Stacey.)

Bob's and Beth Dayton's bridge party breaks up so late that they persuade the last lingering guests, Wallie and Hilda Pratt, not to drive 60 miles home in the rain but to sleep over, tomorrow being Sunday. Wallie grumbles that it's already Sunday but acquiesces. Bob, happy that Beth is staying overnight, suggests a late brunch. Beth loudly commends this idea but silently hates Bob for it. Hilda says Sunday is Wallie's free time with their wolfhound Dmitri but agrees. Bob silently wonders why anyone would prefer a dog to Beth.

Bedtime. Hilda says to Wallie: The Daytons aren't a happy couple. Wallie: What couples are? Hilda: Bob isn't well. Wallie: He couldn't be, idle daily at his desk, then stuffing himself with food; at bridge tonight, he had chocolates in both hands, sorted his cards with his nose. Hilda: Candy is harmless. Wallie: Even eggs are harmful eaten by the crate.

Sunday brunch. Bob to Hilda: I'm ill, have vertigo, am dizzy. Hilda to Beth: Bob should consult a doctor. Beth: I've told him so for years. Bob: My ailments are minor; I don't know any doctors. Hilda: My cousin knows busy Dr. Elston Gifford, New York's best diagnostician, could get you an appointment. Bob: He's probably expensive. Hilda: It sounds like ulcers; think so, Wallie? Wallie: I rarely listen to ulcers. Hilda: Don't joke; Dr. Gifford said my brother Mark had a brain tumor; the surgeon found one. Wallie: Mark died. Hilda: The operation killed him. Wallie: Another doctor might have said Mark had indigestion and he'd still be alive. Hilda: Let me know if you want to consult Dr. Gifford. Soon the Pratts leave.

Bob commends Hilda's friendliness to dour Beth, wonders if he should see Dr. Gifford. Beth says doing so might stop him from being "miserable all the time." Bob fears it might cost $100, doubts he has a brain tumor, and wouldn't agree to surgery if he did have. The Driscolls, new friends, drop by. Bob, sharing marshmallow-like candies with him, mentions Hilda's recommending Dr. Gifford, to which Driscoll says Gifford is terrible; Dr. George Phelon is the best diagnostician, but busy; he could "engineer" an appointment and asks whether Bob's ankles are swollen. Bob says they're always big but no bigger than usual.

On Monday Bob, a businessman, sees a client named Mrs. L.S. Stacey. She declines proffered candy, and says her Dr. Troutman said she should avoid sweets, says he is New York's best diagnostician, and says her "Louie ... had gallstones." When Bob commends Gifford and Phelon, Mrs. Stacey sniffs, offers to get Bob an appointment with Dr. Troutman, who uses X-rays exclusively, and says she didn't know Bob was ailing. Probably only "minor symptoms," Bob replies. She boasts of being a bit of a diagnostician herself, adds that Dr. Troutman deplored her being a housewife not a physician. So Bob mentions his minor vertigo, dizziness, and swollen ankles. Mrs. Stacey asks if he has a temperature too. He's not sure. She makes him let her get him an appointment with Dr. Troutman. Back home, Bob asks Beth to feel his forehead. She says naturally it's hot because their house resembles "a bake-oven." Bob says he suspects he has gallstones. Beth tells him to "have them appraised."

On Tuesday Bob's secretary Annie is absent, attending her brother-in-law Frank Russell's funeral. Bob politely accepts the unneeded help of Harry Danforth's nearby secretary Mrs. Gurnsey. To fill their idle time, Mrs. Gurnsey gossips: Anne may have to support her sister since Russell died in debt, maybe of gallstones but more likely because he didn't have his poisonous teeth extracted. Bob: I wouldn't want my teeth out. Mrs. Gurnsey: Under gas there's no agony; the best New York extractor is Dr Benham — costly but "worth it." Bob: What were Russell's symptoms? Mrs. Gurnsey: Like my brother Joey's, who had headaches, vertigo, swollen ankles; Dr. Benham removed Joey's teeth and he's "a new man"; Joey learned about Dr. Benham when Joey's office associate Mr. Drury sent him to pyorrhea specialist Dr. Clague, who sent him to New York's finest dental diagnostician Dr. Andrell, who examined Joey's mouth and referred him to Dr. Benham; just think, Joey thought it was gallstones and ulcers. Bob, chewing "a hard chocolate": How long did Joey lack teeth? Mrs. Gurnsey: Under 10 days. Bob: That's "pretty long."

At a dinner party later that week, Bob chats with Mrs. Farrell. She says her Aunt Laura's daughter Phyllis died in Cleveland of what they called peritonitis but what probably was infected teeth. She unsuccessfully recommended admirable New York X-ray specialist Dr. Julius to them. Bob confesses he needs X-rays "for pretty near everything," his symptoms being headaches, maybe gallstones, fever, toothaches, swollen ankles. Alarmed, he spends two weeks in March checked by 12 diagnosticians, 10 X-ray specialists, and eight dentists. Result? Medical bills, $2,800; confection bills, $1.90; teeth, "all right" but with 19 cavities. Medical orders? Be active, rest; exercise, get bed-rest; eat a lot including candy, eat only fish; don't smoke, try 12 cigars daily; take taxis to work, walk upstairs there. Bob tells Beth that Dr. Beistle recommends a solitary trip for Bob down south in April to avoid catching cold. Beth says Dr. Hastings said Bob requires constant companionship. Without preplanning, they go to tiny Stockridge, South Carolina, where its only taxi driver gets them to the Magnolia. Not the best hotel, he says, just the only and "worst." Take us there, urges Bob.

The moral of "How Are You?" would appear to be that you shouldn't ask someone "How are you?" unless you are prepared to engage in an organ recital complete with contagious melodies.

HOW TO WRITE SHORT STORIES [WITH SAMPLES] (1924). Ten short stories by Lardner.

F. Scott Fitzgerald* recommended Lardner to Maxwell Perkins,* editor of Charles Scribner's Sons, publishers. Perkins read "The Golden Honeymoon," admired it enormously, and wrote Lardner (July 2, 1923) to suggest their collecting several of his stories into a single volume. Lardner, Perkins, and Fitzgerald met later that summer on Long Island and enjoyed a drunken evening together, made memorable when, after Lardner left to go home, Fitzgerald drove Perkins for a little tour ending wheel-deep in a lily pond. Lardner suggested stories for the proposed collection but could not provide copies or even remember what magazines some of the stories appeared in. It took months for Perkins and Fitzgerald to locate all 10 in libraries and magazine offices. For example, Lardner sent Perkins his only copy of "Champion." Perkins was troubled by the foolish title of the book, which had been irresponsibly suggested by Fitzgerald. So Perkins asked Lardner to provide a satirical introduction for each story. Lardner gladly complied, because he wanted to parody Fitzgerald's unneeded tiny end-notes after stories in his own collection, *Tales of the Jazz Age* (1922). A silly example is the introduction to "A Frame-Up," in which Lardner calls the story "A stirring romance of the Hundred Years' War" and adds that it exemplifies "what can be done with a stub pen."

How to Write Short Stories was vital to Lardner's career for three reasons. The book sold well, enjoying six printings in 1924; reviews were laudatory, but also challenging; and its surprising success awakened in Lardner an awareness that he was not only a gifted sportswriter and newspaper humorist but also a respected literary figure. In a 1924 review, Edmund Wilson also objects to the title of the collection, saying that it should be *Champion and Other Stories*. Wilson continues by praising Lardner for demonstrating in the stories "an unexcelled, a perhaps unrivalled, mastery of ... the American language." (Sources: Berg, 50–53; Caruthers [1973], 2–3; Elder, 188; Lardner, Jr., 153–157; Wilson, 37, 39; Yardley, 266–268)

HOWARD ("The Busher Comes Back"). He manages the San Francisco team when Comiskey sells Keefe to it. Keefe likes Howard, who lets him pitch "regular," and who is "nice" and not "sarkastic like some of them big leaguers."

George Elmer Howard (1877–1956) played for the Pittsburgh Pirates (1905), the Boston Braves (1906), the Braves and the Chicago Cubs (1907), and the Cubs (1908–1909). George W. Hilton relevantly adds that Howard then managed the San Francisco Seals (1913–1914). (Sources: *Baseball Encyclopedia*, 1162; Hilton, 74)

HOWARD, FRED ("Absent-minded Beggar"). He is the chief clerk in the brokerage firm of J. L. Beasley and H. N. Comerford. When he breaks his leg and can't work, John Knowles, also clerking there, finds himself challenged but manages satisfactorily.

HOWARD, KID ("A Frame-Up"). He runs a Chicago gymnasium. Burke walks in and impresses Howard, who trains him quickly.

HOWARD, MRS. ("Absent-minded Beggar"). She is Fred Howard's wife and phones the brokerage firm he works for to report that he's broken his leg.

HOYT ("Lose with a Smile"). Hoyt pitched for Brooklyn against the Giants. According to Danny, a Brooklyn player, Ott hit Hoyt for a homer.

Waite Charles Hoyt (1899–1984) pitched for the New York Giants (1918), the Boston Red Sox (1919–1920), the New York Yankees (1921–1929), the Yankees and the Detroit Tigers (1930), the Tigers and the Philadelphia Athletics (1931), the Brooklyn Dodgers and the New York Giants (1932), the Pittsburgh Pirates (1933–1936), Pittsburgh and Brooklyn (1937), and Brooklyn (1938). Hoyt was elected to the Baseball Hall of Fame (1969). (Source: *Baseball Encyclopedia*, 2083)

HUB ("Back to Baltimore") *see* **PERDUE**

HUBBELL ("Lose with a Smile"). Danny Warner, playing for Brooklyn, was both "scarred" of this left-handed Giants pitcher and hopeful to "get a chance" to bat against him. Danny says Hubbell's screw ball "is just like a nuggle ball." "Carl" is mentioned in "'In Conference'" as a pitcher and a good card player.

Carl Hubbell (1903–1988) pitched for the New York Giants (1928–1943) and was elected to the Baseball Hall of Fame (1947). (Source: *Baseball Encyclopedia*, 2084)

HUGGINS In "Back to Baltimore," Dixon, narrator and manager of the Boston Braves, says that "Higgins [i.e., Huggins] trimmed us four straight," in their game against St. Louis. In "The Busher Pulls a Mays," Keefe says Gleason couldn't trade for Carl Mays, "and finely Huggins got him for the N.Y. club" in a big player exchange. In "Women," Mike Healy boasts that Huggins would have recruited him to replace Joe Dugin, third baseman for New York, except that a girlfriend lied to Huggins that Mike wasn't in his hotel room to meet him. Lardner capitalizes on Huggins's well-known diminutive stature by having Healy aware that Huggins was the potential recruiter through the girl's describing the unknown visitor to the hotel as "a little fella."

Cincinnati-born Miller James Huggins (1879–1929) earned a degree at the University of Cincinnati law school, became a member of the Ohio bar, then played for the Cincinnati Reds 1904–1909) and the St. Louis Cardinals (1910–1916), became their player-manager (1913–1916), then manager (1917), and finally manager of the New York Yankees (1918–1929). The Yankees in World Series play defeated the New York Giants (1923), the Pittsburgh Pirates (1927), and the St. Louis Cardinals (1928). Huggins was elected to the Hall of Fame (1964).

For the Bell Syndicate, Lardner reported on two of the three World Series in which Huggins figured — the 1923 World Series in seven columns (October 10–16) and the 1927 World Series in five (October 5–9). In addition, for the Bell Syndicate, Lardner covered the 1919, 1920, 1921, 1922, and 1925 World Series, in which Huggins was not involved. Jonathan Yardley quotes some of Lardner's humor concerning Huggins's size in his coverage of the 1927 World Series. He was 5' 6½" and 140 lbs. (Sources: *Baseball Encyclopedia*, 696, 1167–1168; Hilton, 304, 427–428; Yardley, 319)

HUGHES ("There Are Smiles"). He is from White Plains, drives carelessly near Manhattan traffic-cop Ben Collins, and doesn't quite recognize Ben, who has changed from genial to snarling because of Edith Dole's death.

HUGHES, PHIL ("Poodle"). He is a wealthy lunatic, just under 60, and a patient at Grave's Hospital. A physician calling himself Dr. Gregory allows Hughes dangerous freedom in return for sizable checks made out to cash.

HULL, GEORGE (*The Real Dope*). He is a South Bend friend of Finch's who gives Finch a bottle of bourbon.

HUMPHREYS, JOE ("A Frame-Up"). He is the ringmaster in a New York boxing program. When asked, he introduces Burke to the crowd.

HUNT, MRS. ("The Spinning Wheel"). She is Walter Hunt's wife, from Boston. After her birthday party in New York, the two, along with their guests, visit the hotel where the narrator is a roulette dealer. Enticed to put chips on the number indicating her age, which she declined to reveal at her party, she bets on No. 30 — and loses, because she is 34.

HUNT, WALTER ("The Spinning Wheel"). He throws a birthday party for his 34-year-old wife. When at the narrator's roulette wheel she "bets her age" by putting chips on No. 30, she loses. Walter later bets her real age, puts chips on No. 34, and wins.

HUNTER ("Freedom of the Press"). He is a *Ferret* reporter besieging Constance Warner for news. More successful than other newshounds, Hunter forces Constance Warner to speak with him, publishes sensational falsehoods about her life in France, follows her and her bridegroom Alexander Beardsley after their wedding, and even presents himself at their railroad compartment during their honeymoon trip.

HUNTER, ED ("The Maysville Minstrel"). He works as a trouble shooter and meter reader for the Maysville gas company. Stephen Gale is the only other employee. Both are bossed by Old Man Townsend, company owner.

HUNTER, PROF. ("Tour No. 2"). He is a teacher from Ohio. He and Prof. Baker are fellow tourists with Larry and Minnie Burns. Hunter is less tolerant of Larry than Baker is. When the tourists have a chance to escape from Brussels, Hunter decides to remain and write a book about the war.

"HURRY KANE" (*Cosmopolitan*, May 1927; RAB, RLR, RU). (Characters: Johnny Abbott, Ike Bloom, Joe Bonham, Bonner, Eddie Brainard, Bullard, Carney, Claymore, Lefty Condon, Evelyn Corey, Dave, Digman, Kid Farrell, Lefty Glaze, Hildebrand, Johnson, Hurry Kane, Helen Kerslake, King, Kramer, Fred Kruger, Jake Lewis, Frank Miller, Billy Moore, Sam Morris, Olds, Minnie Olson, Pierce, Robinson, Roy Smith, Smitty, Stout, Tierney, Topping, Bull Wade, Henry Wade, Welsh.)

The newspapers warn that the coming World Series can't be as thrilling as last year's was, between Chicago and New York. But the narrator, a catcher for his St. Louis team, knows better. His team needs a pitcher to bolster pitchers Carney, Olds, and Jake Lewis. Some recent trades by Dave, their boss, cost their team worthless Robinson, Bullard, and Roy Smith and brought only two — Frank Miller, who reports overweight to spring training at Fort Gregg, and Lefty Glaze, who seeks too much money and also "condition[s] himself on wood alcohol." Following a tip from his rich but seemingly ignorant friend Billy Moore, Dave drafts a "big sapper" named Kane, from Yuma and playing for Waco in the Texas League. He is 6 feet 3 inches in worn-out stockings, has few clothes in his bandaged luggage, and walks funny. But when Dave asks him to throw a practice pitch, its blazing speed almost knocks the narrator down. Cautioned to take it easy, Kane says he did.

Within a week Kane shows really phenomenal speed. Asked why he hid this ability, he says he was "stuck on a gal in Waco" and didn't want a scout to see him and have "to go 'up' [to the majors]," and leave her. He also had "a gal in Yuma for winters." He happened to see his Waco gal date Fred Kruger, Dallas's manager, got upset, and Moore happened to see him fan 15 Dallas batters next day. He "played sick" and went home to his Yuma gal. Dave and Kid Farrell train Kane to add curves and slow pitches to his repertoire and to field better. They also make him modify his gargantuan feeding habits. Dave warns everyone not to play practical jokes on Kane, because he was "simple enough" to believe anything. Nonetheless, Bull Wade kids him about his first name, Elmer, his suit, and his nickname, Hurry. It's a pun, Kane explains. Kidding continues, including "mash notes" inviting him to corners "to meet gals that never lived," and congratulatory telegrams from "Coolidge and Al Smith." The fellows encourage him to believe, first, that he resembles movie star Tommy Meighan, and, second, that Evelyn Corey wants to meet Kane. She is a retired Broadway star in their Florida hotel. He tries. No luck.

Kane mopes about his Yuma gal, loses his fast ball, and Dave grows worried. Kane overhears his roommate Johnny Abbott phone his fiancée so endearingly that he almost phones Minnie Olson, his Yuma gal, but decides long-distance calls are too expensive. Instead, he'll quit the team and go home to her — "where they ain't no smart Alecks kidding me all the while." Johnny informs Dave and Farrell, but no bribes of money and food dissuade Kane. Next morning there is a fire in their hotel. Evelyn, in a kimono, appears. Kane starts to rescue her when the alarm ends. She faints in her room. The two have a drink and agree to meet at the Ritz in New York, where she says she'll be staying. Kane returns to the team.

The team plays in New York, but Kane, trying hard and without help from teammates, never finds Evelyn again. In May he threatens to desert during their St. Louis games and head for Yuma. Bull Wade writes fake letters from Evelyn to Kane, sends them to his brother in Montreal to mail to Kane, to revive his interest in her. Johnny's "gal," Helen Kerslake, even introduces him some girls she knows; but he gets too amorous. Kane regularly wins games but in September decides to visit note-writing Evelyn in person in Montreal. Worried, the narrator gets Dave to wire Minnie money, confidentially, to come see Kane in New York. From El Paso she wires Kane, who forgets Evelyn, greets Minnie, "a plain, honest, good-hearted, small-town gal," and "I and Johnny and Helen" dine the happy couple. Next day Kane whitewashes the Detroit team.

For their final western swing, they take Minnie and Helen along. The White Sox need one victory of three games against the narrator's team. Kane, volunteering to pitch all three, does win the first two. A mysterious phone call causes Kane to rush out, return late, be sleepless, and fare badly during the first part of the third and final game. He keeps looking at the stands, forlornly — until Dave sends Topping, a young player, to check. Topping and Kane look at the stands, talk, and thereafter Kane pitches to a 6–4 victory.

St. Louis wins the World Series. Members get $5,300 each. Kane tells the narrator that Evelyn phoned him that ominous night to come see her. At her hotel, she promised him a spectacular European honeymoon if he could save $20,000 for it, and goodbye if he couldn't. A gambler persuaded him to throw the game, for $5,000 now and $15,000 when he did. It was Topping who told him that Evelyn, whom they saw in the stands, was crooked gambler Sam Morris's crooked gal. That's why Kane won. Should he return the $5,000? No, the narrator answers; split it with Topping. Kane later sends Topping $200. Johnny married Helen in November. Kane and his "Min" wed.

Lardner peppers "Hurry Kane" with names of well-known 1920s figures, including the dancing Bloomer Girls, Calvin Coolidge,* Tom Meighan,* Al Smith,* and comic Ed Wynn (1886–1966). Clifford M. Caruther comments that "'Hurry Kane' ... is indicative of his [Lardner's] deepening pessimism towards baseball." Douglas Robinson theorizes that "Hurry Kane" (and "My Roomy" and "Alibi Ike" as well) "might be read as recognizing both the vital importance and the terrible fragility and instability of 'lunacy,' of what the Other-as-majority defines as deviant behavior, but what the Other-as-minority knows is indispensable to human existence."

Lardner and George M. Cohan* collaborated on *Elmer the Great* (1928), a three-act play based on "Hurry Kane." The play failed, because, as Donald Elder, Jonathan Yardley, and Clifford M. Caruthers point out, Lardner saw the original as satire, whereas Cohan wanted to convert it into melodrama. After 40 performances on Broadway, it closed, despite admirable effort of its star, Walter Huston (1884–1950), who began his career on the New York stage in the 1920s before turning to movies. Two films were based on "Hurry Kane." The first was *Fast Company* (Paramount, 1929) — according to Jack Spear, the first talking movie about baseball. Playing Elmer Kane was Jack Oakie (1903–1978), a talented actor who debuted in the chorus of *Little Nellie Kelly* (1922), a musical comedy by George M. Cohan.* *Fast Company* involves Elmer Kane, cocky rube but natural hitter, who signs with the Chicago Cubs, does well when a beautiful actress favors him, badly when he learns she is toying with him, and fine again when she decides it's love after all. The other movie was *Elmer the Great* (Warner Brothers, 1934) starring Joe E. Brown,* whom Spears describes as portraying a "mulish braggart with a strong back and a weak mind." (Sources: Caruthers [1995], 212; Leiter, I, 239; Robinson, 129; Spears, 265; Yardley, 322–324)

HURST ("Meet Me in St. Louie"). Stengel, coaching for Brooklyn, tells Danny that the Phillies' short right-field fence confuses "young infielders," who might throw to Klein not Hurst.

Frank O'Donnell Hurst (1905–1952) played for the Philadelphia Phillies (1928–1933), then the Phillies and the Chicago Cubs (1934). (Source: *Baseball Encyclopedia*, 1172)

HUTCHINSON, JOCK ("Now and Then"). He is the golf "teacher" at Nassau, Bahamas. Bob borrows clubs from Jock so that Bob's wife Irma can try a round.

HUTTON, BILL ("Women"). He pitched for Springfield when Mike Healy was playing for Dayton. Hutton walked Mike, and therefore Mike couldn't show what he "could really do up there at the plate."

HYLAND, DR. ("DOC") He was John Winslow's physician and warned John about excessive use of coffee, cigarettes, and whiskey.

"I CAN'T BREATHE" (*Cosmopolitan*, September 1926; RLR, RU). (Characters: Frank Caswell, Gordon Flint, Barney Gallant, Helga, Aunt Jule, George Morse, Uncle Nat, Merle Oliver, Walter.)

An unnamed girl, 18, is vacationing from New York with Uncle Nat and Aunt Jule, each about 35, while her parents are abroad for a month. She decides to keep a diary.

July 12. She's been engaged to Walter, 22, for 16 days, plans to wed in December because he brought up marriage, can't wait. She saw two cute lads at dinner tonight.

July 13. She gets telegrams from Walter and also Gordon Flint, 21, just back from a trip around the world. She and Gordon were engaged last December. She didn't spoil his trip by writing him about Walter. Anyway, she forgot Gordon's "itinery," couldn't write. She pleads a headache to avoid playing golf with Nat and Jule, partly because Nat often feels her arms to guide her swing, and partly to ponder what to tell Gordon when he calls from Chicago. She is about to smoke when a fellow offers her a light. He is Frank Caswell, cute, from "Darthmouth" and 24, not "terribly old." She and Frank dance. Walter can't dance. Frank says in Hollywood last winter he met Norma Shearer, beautiful, like the diarist, he adds. She says the orchestra music reminds her of when she sat next to "Jack" Barrymore at Barney Gallant's.

July 14. Gordon phones. The connection is bad; so she whispers yes she loves him, hoping he won't hear. He does. She can't think, just now, about their meeting in New York when Walter is there. Walter wires again, sends flowers. So does Frank, who gets her to play golf. Jule laughs. No headache? Frank's golf drive is better than Walter's. Nat and Jule, too old to dance (or "really *do* anything"), watch Frank dance with her. Frank has her "in hysterics" with lines like "yes, sir, asthma baby" and "I underwear my baby is tonight."

July 15. Frank takes her for a drive, drinks from a flask. She tells him yes she loves him, figuring he's too "tight" to remember. If he does, she'll tell him about Walter and maybe Gordon. How "maddening."

July 16. Frank sends her flowers, phones. She gets a letter from Walter, forgets to read it. After lunch with Frank and during a drive, he says his father's rich and Frank plans for journalism and a novel-writing career. Asked, she reluctantly says California would be nice for their honeymoon. He says he'll introduce her to Hollywood people. That night they dance—briefly, because Jule is acting funny. She's gotta tell Frank the truth tomorrow, wishes she were dead.

July 18. Yesterday was bad. Gordon called from Chicago. The connection was too bad for her to tell all. During lunch with Frank, Walter called, complained slightly, said he had theater tickets for the 25th, when she would return home. Frank griped so much about her phone call that she couldn't break the truth to him then. Then golf and a drive with him. He wouldn't return her to the Inn until she promised December 10th for their wedding. She knows the 10th isn't Sunday because Saturday the 11th is her wedding date with Walter. Tomorrow she'll tell Frank everything, and write Gordon all, because right now she can't breathe, can't even live.

July 21. She wrote Gordon yesterday, but held off the entire truth until she sees him. She couldn't tell Frank because he's too sunburned to feel "his best." She wishes she could marry Frank, meet his Hollywood friends; after five years, let Frank go write novels; be only 23 herself, wed Gordon, tour the world with him; at 28 marry Walter, "the one I really love." At Nat's and Jule's ages, she wouldn't care to dance, but maybe have children with Walter. Why don't older people look at things properly? Suddenly the orchestra's playing "Limehouse Blues" reminds her that she and Merle Oliver first danced to it, two years ago. It's "funny," she's been thinking about Merle "all day." Will she see him again?

July 22. No "accident": Merle phones from Boston, is coming here today. "A whole year" he has loved her. He couldn't have believed it when she told him, earlier, she was engaged to George Morse. She couldn't love anyone but Merle. Home again Sunday, she'll have Walter and Gordon for dinner, and Merle can tell them both everything. They'll share the "hurt" more easily together.

"I Can't Breathe" is redolent of the Roaring Twenties, with names in it of "Jack" Barrymore (*see* Barrymore family), Buster Collier,* Marion Davies,* Barney Gallant,* Norman Kerry,* Lois Moran,* and Norma Shearer.* Jonathan Yardley reports that by the time "I Can't Breathe" was published Lardner was receiving $4,500 per story, adds that it "deserves to be ranked with Ring's best," and suggests that the prose of the diarist is based on "Floncy Rice's breathless conversation about her boyfriends." Florence Rice was the beautiful daughter of Grantland Rice* and his wife. Clifford M. Caruthers praises the story "for its masterful rendition of adolescent hyperbole." Douglas Robinson takes both story and diarist hyper-seriously, suggesting not only that the story is one of Lardner's several "bitter attacks on talkative women," but also that the girl "desperately attempts ... to land a husband ... and to pretend ... [she doesn't] really care." (Sources: Caruthers [1973], 128; Robinson, 101, 284; Yardley, 305, 312, 331)

"IDES OF JUNE" (*Saturday Evening Post*, September 5, 1932; LWS, RAB).

IGOE, BATTLING ("BAT") ("A Frame-Up"). He is a boxer in Boston. Nate matches Burke to fight him. Igoe takes a dive in the fourth.

In naming this Igoe, Lardner surely remembered Herbert A. "Hype" Igoe (1877–1945), reporter and cartoonist for the San Francisco *Examiner*, the New York *Evening Journal*, and the New York *Sun*. Igoe was on the sports staff of the New York *World* (1920s) and conducted "Pardon My Glove," a boxing column the title of which Irving Berlin* was said to have suggested to him. Hype Igoe rejoined the staff of the *Journal* (later the *Journal-American*) permanently (1927–1945). He was nicknamed Hype because he was so skinny that he resembled a hypodermic needle; the name stuck when used by friends, including cartoonist Thomas A. "Tad" Dorgan, Lardner's friend, whose brother Dick Dorgan illustrated Lardner's "You Know Me Al" comic strip (October 1923–September 1925). (Sources: Elder, 176–177; Obituary, *New York Times*, February 12, 1945; Yardley, 239)

ILLNESSES, LARDNER'S Lardner was born with a deformed left foot. When it was surgically repaired (1896), the result was that his left leg became thinner than his right leg but didn't prevent his swimming and playing baseball. He first suffered pulmonary pains (1917). He had his tonsils "pruned," as he put it (1918). After too many weeks-long binges, he tried a North Carolina retreat, perhaps to mend tobacco-damaged sinuses recently operated on but more likely in one of many vain efforts to combat acute alcoholism (1924). Though diagnosed as having tuberculosis (1926), he ignored advice to rest more, eat more sensibly, and avoid smoking and drinking. Ring Lardner Jr. writes about the family's fear that he and his brothers would contract tuberculosis from their father and also that Lardner's "two diseases, alcoholism and tuberculosis, progressed" together. His chronic pessimism began to descend into feelings of despondency and guilt, aggravated by restlessness (1927). Collaborating with George S. Kaufman* on the play *June Moon* (1929) was so enervating that Lardner was never even somewhat healthy again. He alternated hospital stays (1929–1931) with travel in search of good air, a search ruined for a time by dependence on alcohol to conquer insomnia. More travel only delayed inevitable hospital-hopping, until his fatal slide ended after a friendly family bridge game and a heart attack at home. (Sources: Lardner, Jr., 113, 118, 194; Yardley, 50, 206, 281–282, 309, 317, 319, 339–340, 345–346, 381)

"'IN CONFERENCE'" (*Liberty*, August 14, 1916; LN, RLR, WOI). (Characters: J. H. Carlisle, L. M. Croft, S. P. Daniels, K. M. Dewey, Mrs. Dewey, Galt, T. W. Havers, Harvey Hester, Z. H. Holt, R. L. Jamieson, Jennings, S. W. Kline, Kramer, A. M. Lansing, A. T. Lansing, Mrs. Lansing, Amy Leslie, Lundgren, C. T. Miller, H. J. Milton, Jimmie Montague, F. X. Murphy, B. B.

Nordyke, J. P., Paul Sickles, L. F. Wilcox, Minnie Wilcox.)

Harvey Hester enters the outer office of Kramer & Company, Efficiency Engineers, and asks to see A. T. Lansing. The secretary informs Hester that Lansing is in conference; Hester can wait or return later. Hester says he'll wait but "won't wait long!"

In conference are J. H. Carlisle, president, and vice presidents R. L. Jamieson, K. M. Dewey, W. P. Daniels, A. M. Lansing, T. W. Havers, and B. B. Nordyke, officers A. M. Lansing, A. T. Lansing, Z. H. Holt and F. X. Murphy, and secretary C. T. Miller, treasurer H. J. Milton, and non-officer Paul Sickles. With additional conferences yet ahead, all impatiently wait for L. M. Croft, another vice president, who has called this meeting, who enters late, and who has news. L. M. reports that J. P. on the phone just told him that the post office was holding an unstamped letter which is addressed to Kramer & Company and which it will forward upon receipt of a 2¢ stamp. Debate follows; everyone addressing one another using initials, except for Paul, addressed as Paul. Now, is the letter worth the time and expense involved in sending for it? Havers says his brother, G. K., answered such a post-office notice and what he sent for proved to be only a realtor's ad. Asked by A. T., Havers says he has two other brothers, N. D. and V. F. Nordyke says he has six brothers. Daniels says he's from Hingham, Massachusetts. They discuss other cities they once knew. Miller says he sold "Balzac complete for twenty-six dollars" in southern Ohio 15 years ago. F. X. Murphy asks Z. H. if he reads in the evenings. Z. H. says no and tells A. T. Lansing that at night, when tired, he plays the player piano or goes to movies. L. M. says his sister Minnie Wilcox reads free verse by Amy Leslie. To J. H. C.'s query regarding what to do about that unstamped letter, Z. H. mentions "an anonymous post-card" received by S. W. Kline in Marengo, Illinois, their home town. It might have been "a hoax" or some "blackmail" message. L. M. wonders if Z. H. knew any Lundgren in Marengo. Yes; further, when Z. H. was in Chicago, he saw Carl [Hubbell*] pitch. When J. H. C. asks about Kline, Z. H. says he never bothered with the letter. K. M. mentions a letter misaddressed to a company he worked for in St. Louis. Conversation by S. P. and Paul about Scotch triggers talk about Prohibition and "[e]ven nice women drinking." Again L. H. C. wonders what to do about "this letter." A. T. says that the post office should open it and see if it's important. He adds that he and his wife each open the other's "personal mail" when the other isn't home.

Harvey Hester asks the secretary to tell A. T. Lansing that the two were school friends and that he was just "tipped off" that Mrs. Lansing is eloping "for Chicago on the 12:05 train" and that since it's 11:53 now he can stop her if he hurries. The secretary: "But he's still in conference."

"'In Conference'" is partly clever for satirizing office priorities and partly tedious in also satirizing verbose, protracted, even prolix conversational rambling that many indulge in but fewer than many are amused by, or, perhaps, even tolerate, courteously, at least.

INCOME AND FINANCES, LARDNER'S

Lardner worked at sundry jobs in Chicago (1901) for $4 a week. As a reporter he started at $15 a week for the South Bend *Times* (by 1907); earned $18.50 weekly at the Chicago *Inter-Ocean* (by 1908); $25, Chicago *Examiner* (1908); $35–$50 and $100-to-$200, Chicago *Tribune* (1908–1910, 1913–1919); $50, St. Louis *Sporting News* (1911); $45, Boston *American* (1911). Meanwhile, he broke into the magazine market. *Collier's* paid him perhaps $100 for his first such item ("The Cost of Baseball," June 1912). His baseball stories started, including but not limited to what became *You Know Me Al* (1916). Jonathan Yardley reports that "[b]tween January [February], 1915, and February, 1917, he had twenty-nine magazine pieces published." Yardley figures that "one can assign an arbitrary average fee of $400 ... and come up with nearly $12,000 in ... two years." Ring Lardner Jr. recalled that his father's "income from [eight] books [1918–1921] came to about two thousand a year." Lardner signed a contract paying $2,700 (1918–1923) to write musical-comedy pieces for New York's Century Theater; he slaved over many, but none proved acceptable. The Bell Syndicate published "Ring Lardner's Weekly Letter" (1919–1927), which ultimately paid $30,000 a year. His "You Know Me Al" comic strips (1922–1925) became irksome to write but paid $17,000 annually. Yardley provides evidence that in 1927 Lardner's freelance income was $48,500. *Elmer the Great* (1928), the disastrous play based on his "Hurry Kane" short story, cost him $6,000. He earned $24,000 for 24 *Collier's* items (1928–1930). His play *June Moon* (1929), coauthored with George S. Kaufman,* was a money-maker. The New York *Morning Telegraph* offered Lardner $50,000 a year for two years for 4-a-week "Ring's Side" columns (1928–1929); lack of stamina caused a failure after 37 pieces. Clifford M. Caruthers reports that during its first year *Round Up* (1929) earned Lardner royalties from Scribner's of $11,873, plus $6,750 for being a Literary Guild selection. Lardner, a self-punishing wordsmith grievously ill, produced 69 daily columns, averaging 100 words each, under "A Night Letter from Ring Lardner," for $750 a week (Bell Syndicate, from February 2, 1931). After a flood (March 1931) endangered the Lardners' East Hampton house east of Great Neck, Long Island, they moved it to safety for $10,000. While hospitalized, Lardner wrote six baseball stories for the *Saturday Evening Post*, for $4,000 each (1932), republished as *Lose with a Smile* (1933). Caruthers totals Lardner's four years of royalties from Scribner's (1930–1933) at $2,130. The *Delineator* paid Lardner $750 for the posthumously published "Poodle" (1934).

Lardner and his wife were often in desperate financial straits, all owing to their extravagant Roaring Twenties lifestyle, frequent travel then and later, lavish and often renovated residences, servants and nurses, four sons' costly tuition, and foolish hotel and apartment hopping; also to Lardner's generosity to siblings for decades and often to friends, alcoholic binges at clubs and elsewhere, and insurance and medical bills. The stock market crash and the subsequent Great Depression spoiled many early investments, while bank deposits were uninsured, unlike supposedly secure banks in 21st-century America. But still.... At his death, Lardner's estate was worth $192,927, partly because of huge life-insurance policies. (Sources: Lardner, Jr., 149–150, 204, 217; Caruthers [1973], 129, 130–132, 145, 165; Caruthers [1995], 222, 232; Patrick, 31–32, 153; Yardley, 54, 59, 71, 83, 89, 113, 117, 132, 142, 183, 191, 207–208, 354, 305, 324, 327–239, 347–349)

INDIAN, THE ("My Roomy"). He is a "Cincy" pitcher. Buster Elliott, playing for Chicago, "hits one out o' the park off" him.

George Howard "Chief" Johnson (1886 or 1887–1922) pitched for the Cincinnati Reds (1913–1914). George W. Hilton says Johnson was a Native American of the Winnebago tribe. (Sources: *Baseball Encyclopedia*, 2100; Hilton, 342)

INGLES, DELLA ("Tour Y-10"). She and Paula Ingles, perhaps sisters, went unescorted on a vacation, according to Kate Hayes, who is trying to get her friend Violet Emerson to go with her to Yellowstone.

INGLES, PAULA ("Tour Y-10"). She and Della Ingles vacationed safely, according to Kate Hayes, who wants to do the same with her friend Violet Emerson.

INGRAM, EDITH ("EDIE") ("Poodle"). She is Jack Ingram's wife. They made friends with Mary, the narrator's wife. Mary tells boasting fibs to them to make them feel bad.

INGRAM, JACK ("Poodle"). He is Edith's husband. He works for the Boland Drug Company until released, after which they will move to Chicago, where he hopes to work for his brother.

"INSOMNIA" (*Cosmopolitan*, May 1931; SC). (Characters: Cora, Doc Early, Faulkner, Lucy Faulkner, Mrs. Faulkner, Holden, Mrs. Holden, Sam King, Harry Myers, Rogers, Spears, Spears, Allan Spears, Edith Spears, Gilbert White.)

The author tries to put himself to sleep by mental tricks. It's 10:00 P.M. He thinks of a song Bert Williams* sang; wishes he could write short stories as short as O. Henry's; remembers 10 baseball players whose records "I could recite" 20 years ago when "I was a baseball nut." And he remembers pretty Lucy Faulkner, whom he saw in church in Clayton, Michigan, when he was 16; he was embarrassed chasing Cora, the family cow, when she entered Lucy's yard; Lucy's parents objected when he and three other young beer-drinkers serenaded under her window one night.

It's 10:08 P.M. He could take that story Doc Early told him recently about Allan and Edith Spears of Rockford, Illinois, rename them Leslie and Amy Arnold to conceal their identities, and write it. Spears was an athlete at the University of Illinois. After graduating, he wasted an inheritance of $6,000 on drinking. Broke and sober, he fell in love with Edith Holden, and she with him. Despite her parents' objections and threats, Edith and Allan eloped to Chicago. In control of her private fortune of $200,000, Edith put $100,000 in bonds in a safety-deposit box available to both, $50,000 in her checking account, and $50,000 in one for him. Allan stayed sober four years, worked for $15,000 a year, had boy-and-girl twins with Edith, and took out a $70,000 life insurance policy naming the three as beneficiaries. Suddenly Edith's mother broke their parents' silence with a letter beginning "Dear Daughter." He resumed drinking, lost his job, wasted $35,000 at the races and partying. When Allan returned home after two months, disheveled, the doctor said another binge would kill him and Edith vowed if he drank again she would take the twins and leave him forever. After two weeks, Allan went downtown to seek work, found nothing, grew despondent, chanced to meet Gilbert White and Harry Myers, two Illinois alumni. At lunch, Gilbert made Allan drink in return for a stock tip from Harry. He awakened "in a Loop hotel" next morning, hung over, and with Harry's tip for "So-and-so" on a piece of paper. He consulted Sam King, an alumnus and a member of Rogers and King, a brokerage firm, asked about "So-and-so" stock, learned it was "the greatest buy there is," and ordered 7,000 shares on margin at 49 with orders to sell at 44 if it fell. He phoned Edit, confessed he was drinking and would continue until he could quit — a month? or maybe a year? — and she'd hear from him again only if "it's good news." Allan took $70,000 in bonds from the safety-deposit box, paid Rogers and King, and put the purchase receipt in the box. He figured if Harry was wrong, he'd get a job and pay everything back; if the doctor was right, Edith would get the insurance. Allan converted his checking account into travelers' checks, traveled to a "remote corner of the earth," and died. News reached Edith, whereupon she sold Allan's stock at 153, earning her "$728,000 minus commissions." This and her intact savings combined "to prove to her parents that she had loved wisely and just about well enough."

The author feels better with that story straightened out, thinks he might sleep better if he got some exercise, and checks the time. Only 11:18 P.M. Should he get up, write some notes about that story? Maybe have one cigarette? Then off with the lights, back to bed, and just "not think of anything"? That's how to fall asleep.

The author names 10 baseball players whose records he knew 20 years ago: Brown (William Verna Brown [1893–1965], or Delos Hight Brown [1892–1964], or James Donaldson Brown [1897–?], or Drummond Nicol Brown [1885–1927], or George Howard Brown [1876–1920]); [Frank Leroy] Chance (1877–1924); [John Joseph] Evers (1881–1947); [Arthur Frederick] Hofman*; [John] Kling (1875–1947); [Frank] Schulte*; [Samuel James Tilder] Sheckard*; [Harry M.] Steinfeldt (1877–1914); [Joseph Bert] Tinker*; and [Paul Glee and Lloyd James] Waner.*

Although some critics deny "Insomnia" short-story status, Donald Elder says, with acceptable certitude, that it is a "grim story [that] is not really written, merely sketched out among the musings of an insomniac." Jonathan Yardley defines it as "part stream of consciousness, part nostalgic reminiscence, part short story." (Sources: *Baseball Encyclopedia*, 688, 692, 698, 829, 830, 831, 834, 877–878, 1003, 1229, 1628–1629; Elder, 322; Yardley, 351)

IRENE ("Liberty Hall"). She is publisher Harms's secretary. Ben Drake arranges with her to send him fake emergency telegrams so that he can escape the clutches of hosts and hostesses, if he wants to. The scheme backfires when Ben and his wife are Hilda and Ralph Thayer's guests.

IRMA ("Now and Then"). She is Bob's naive wife. When they go to the Bahamas on a delayed honeymoon, his overly solicitous treatment pleases her. When they return three years later, she makes excuses for his hypocritically rationalized neglect of her.

IVES, MABEL ("The Venomous Viper of the Volga"). She is Sandy King's demanding girlfriend. She leaves him for the reluctant boxer Henry Goetz, known as "the Venomous Viper of the Volga," because she admires his tattoos.

JACK ("The Clubby Roadster"). He is Nan Cross's brother. He is rejected from officers' training during the war. This makes Nan cry, no doubt hypocritically.

JACK ("The Crook)." He was a White Sox coach in a baseball game in which Larry played against the Red Sox. Jack sent Larry home from third base, and he was called out by Bull, the umpire. Bull's silence when Larry bellowed a complaint caused him to notice Bull's unaccustomed sadness.

George W. Hilton believes that this Jack might have been Jack Lapp (1884–1920), who was a catcher for the Philadelphia Athletics (1908–1915) and the Chicago White Sox (1916). (Sources: *Baseball Encyclopedia*, 1252; Hilton, 550)

JACK ("Harmony"). He may be a baseball player. "Cap" Ryan tells the narrator that Bill Cole is such a liar that he would say Jack was the son of Walter Johnson.

JACK (*Own Your Own Home*). He is at police headquarters in Chicago. When Fred is arrested after his and Grace's big party gets too noisy, the authorities won't allow Fred to phone "Jack ... to come out and show them whose who."

"JACK THE KAISER KILLER" (*Saturday Evening Post*, March 23, 1918; LOW, TER).

JACKSON In "A Busher's Letters Home,"

Keefe, White Sox pitcher, boasts before the season opener in Cleveland that Jackson and Lajoie may be "great batters but the bigger they are the harder they fall." In "The Busher Comes Back," a grounder Jackson hit should have been thrown home but was fumbled, causing a run to score against Keefe. In "A New Busher Breaks In," Keefe doesn't want to take advantage of Jackson, therefore hopes the fellow is in good shape when he bats against him. In "Call for Mr. Keefe!," while Keefe was pitching for the White Sox, Jackson misplayed a fly ball hit by Cleveland's Roth. In *Treat 'Em Rough*, Keefe praises Jackson's hitting ability. In "The Battle of Texas," during practice Jackson hits the high foul that comes down on the rookie Cosgrove and knocks him unconscious. In "Along Came Ruth," Keefe continues to praise Jackson. In "The Busher's Welcome Home" and "The Yellow Kid," Joe Jackson is mentioned.

Joseph Jefferson ("Shoeless") Jackson (1887–1951) was born in Pickens County, South Carolina, into a poor mill family, was unschooled and illiterate into middle age, was a natural-born athlete, got the nickname "Shoeless" because a pair of new spiked shoes blistered his feet in a game (1908), and therefore played in his stockings (but only once). "Shoeless Joe" was a Cleveland Naps outfielder, then played for the Philadelphia Athletics (1908–1909), the Cleveland Indians (1910–1915), and the Chicago White Sox (1915–1919). He was the only rookie ever to bat over .400, and posted splendid statistics thereafter as a leftfielder with a fielding percentage in 1,332 games of .940 and a batting average of .356 (behind only Ty Cobb and Rogers Hornsby). Jackson was involved in the 1919 Black Sox Scandal. The White Sox lost to the Cincinnati Reds, and Jackson, and others, were banned from baseball. During the subsequent trial, Jackson said under oath that he accepted $5,000, that he tried unsuccessfully twice to return it, but that his share was incomplete. Charles Arthur Comiskey,* White Sox owner, pressured Jackson into these admissions. In the subsequent trial (1921), the jury acquitted Jackson of charges of criminality but found him guilty of failure to report the conspiracy. He sued Comiskey for back wages (1924), said under oath that he knew nothing of the conspiracy and did nothing to throw the games, denied knowledge of the conspiracy, but lost the case and was convicted of perjury. Jackson boasted in public that during the 1919 World Series games he played excellently, citing false figures in the process; in reality he played badly when doing so helped the Reds. Shoeless Joe has become a culture hero, tarnished, victimized, deserving of respect. *Eight Men Out: The Black Sox and the 1919 World Series* (1963) by Eliot Asinof (1919–2008) presents much information and was the basis for the movie *Eight Men Out* (1988). "Say It Ain't So, Joe" (1975) is a song by Murray Head. *Shoeless Joe* (1982), a novel by W. P. Kinsella (b. 1935) is excellent, but more memorable is *Field of Dreams* (1989), the movie it inspired. David L. Fleitz (b. 1955) presents the definitive account in *Shoeless: The Life and Times of Joe Jackson* (2001). Fleitz feels that Jackson told the truth in 1920, lied in 1924, deserved to be banned, but also deserved to be voted into the Baseball Hall of Fame. (Sources: *Baseball Encyclopedia*, 1178; Elder, 160–161; Fleitz; Hilton, 59–60)

JACKSON, MISS ("A Day with Conrad Green"). She is Conrad Green's efficient, intimidated secretary, about 45 or 50.

"THE JADE NECKLACE" (*Cosmopolitan*, November 1926). (Characters: L.N. Bauer, Earl Benham, Thelma Bowen, Dennis Byrne, Gifford Dean, Driscoll, Mrs. Garrett, Griffin, Maida Guthrie, Harrison, Kate Hollis, Maurice Kavanaugh, Quinn Martin, Harry Salsinger, David Wallace, Paul Wells, Wolf.)

The narrator no longer works for "the Griffin people" but is now "in the picture business," as L. N. Bauer's "half secretary and half valet." L.N. is "the big boss" of Colossal Films Incorporated. For $7,000 a week, the rival Supreme film company has just hired matinée-idol Dennis Byrne, whose movie *Danny Darling* thrills "the flappers." L.N. cables a Dublin friend to recommend another "beautiful Mick" as competition. The result? Gorgeous Maurice Kavanaugh agrees to cross the dangerous ocean and be hired at $8,000 a week. L.N. and Wolf, his vice president, are delighted, and their stenographers swoon when Kavanaugh walks through "the joint."

To outdo Supreme's "big guy" Harrison, Bauer of Colossal seeks Paul Wells and Quinn Martin, who recommend stories for films. They're out of town. He asks Harry Salsinger, a journalist, for an Irish story, but gets only a Pat-and-Mike joke. L.N. reads in "the picture news" that Supreme is offering David Wallace $25,000 for movie rights to *Harridan*, Wallace's novel. Figuring the film will star Byrne, L.N. and Wolf confer with Wallace without bothering to read *Harridan*. Wallace wonders what actress "would play in it," is told the cast is a secret, says money is less important than "pride in his work," and demands that his name appear on the credits. He is offered $50,000, faints, revives, and forgets "his scruples."

The narrator buys L.N. a copy of *Harridan*. Big words on the first of its 300 pages puzzle L.N. A slow reader anyway and partying tonight, he tells the narrator to read *Harridan* and provide him a synopsis. It is as follows: Widower, 55 or 60, goes abroad, cables two daughters and son he married Mrs. Garrett, whom children at first called "harridan." Children meet, find her "pretty and nice to them"; son, engaged to flapper, especially likes her. The narrator has to read some dictionary definitions to L.N. A harridan is formerly a loose woman, now a vixen; a vixen, formerly a female fox, is now an ill-tempered woman, a jade. The narrator suggests rewriting *Harridan* "for some woman star" and omitting Kavanaugh. But L.N. wants to insult Supreme by showcasing Kavanaugh, "handsomer" than Byrne, in a story L.N. gloats about outbidding Supreme for. So L.N. and Kavanaugh go to Hollywood, where Driscoll is "our star director," and Earl Benham is a scenarist.

Returning a month later, L.N. orders the narrator to fetch Wallace. L.N. explains everything. The picture is called *The Jade Necklace*. Gifford Dean plays a navy lieutenant. Thelma Bowen plays his wife. Dean sails to Japan. A Japanese girl, played by Maida Guthrie, falls in love with him. He marries her in a Japanese ceremony meaning nothing to him, goes home, returns to Japan with his wife. Both wives meet. The Japanese wife kills the lieutenant's baby and herself. Wallace asks if the lieutenant's name is Pinkerton. Bauer says no but adds that the movie does have a detective, a bit part for Kavanaugh, who recovers the jade necklace. Wallace wonders, "What jade necklace?" L.N. explains it belongs to the real wife, the lieutenant gave it to the mock wife, the real wife wants it back. Wallace hopes the photography is nice, doesn't mind having his name omitted, but thinks *Harridan* is a good title. L.N. totals the cost at over "half a million." The narrator won't return to Griffin. "It's fascinating" to be in movie work.

Lardner was variously motivated here. He satirizes American moviemakers' shameful extravagance and also their indifference to authors. He rebukes plagiarists. And he has fun while doing so by looting *Madame Butterfly* (1900), the play by David Belasco (1854–1931), based on "Madame Butterfly" (1898), a story by John Luther Long (1861–1927). Belasco (1854–1931) was an American playwright and theatrical manager. His *Madame Butterfly* became the grand opera *Madama Butterfly* (1904) by Giacomo Puccini (1858–1924). Lardner, who loved music in its various forms, was undoubtedly familiar with Puccini's opera. Does anyone need to have Pinkerton explicated?

JAKE ("Ball-A-Hole"). He is the narrator's friend, just under 16, and, a caddy like the narrator, 16. The two conspire to squeeze tips out of Mr. Conklin and Mr. Perkins, who are rich but stingy.

JAKE ("Sick 'Em"). He is the person to whom the unnamed narrator tells the story, and to whom he says, "I wouldn't lie to you, Jake."

George W. Hilton surmises that Jake is Jakey Atz (*which see*). (Source: Hilton, 267, 362)

JAKE, YOUNG ("Women"). He plays for Mike Healy's team. Healy warns him by way of tedious reminiscences to avoid women.

JAMES, SARGENT (*Treat 'Em Rough*). He is a non-com in Jack Keefe's army unit. James tells Jack and his buddies that "rifles was comeing." So Jack figures they won't be practicing with "broom sticks" much longer.

JAMES, WALLACE ("The Maysville Minstrel"). He is the fictitious editor of "James's Weekly," also fictitious. He is supposedly working in New York. In a cruel joke, Charley Roberts sends would-be poet Stephen Gale an invitation as from James to publish his verse. Gale mails an offering to Wallace, only to have it returned stamped "Not in Directory."

Lardner may have chosen the name Wallace James to combine parts of the names of two differently distinguished authors, Lew Wallace and Henry James.

JAMIESON, R. L. ("'In Conference'"). He and others work for Kramer & Company. While "in conference" they talk vacantly. He is a vice president.

JANNINY (*Treat 'Em Rough*). He is, according to Jack Keefe, "a wop or something" in Jack's army unit.

JANSON ("Women"). He played for Springfield against Mike Healy's Dayton team. Umpire Baldy Pierce dishonestly called Janson safe at home so that Pierce could have a picnic date next day.

JANSSEN, JOHN ("Stop Me — if you've heard This One"). He is the man who was frightened when he saw the beautiful blonde on the train bound from New York to Chicago. The blonde committed suicide by throwing herself onto the train tracks at Fort Wayne. Janssen shot himself to death on a Chicago street. All this according to Henry Wild Osborne's whopper spun out of Luke Garner's personal yarn.

JEFF, BIG ("My Roomy") *see* **TESREAU, JEFF**

JENKINS, JOE In "The Battle of Texas," he is a White Sox catcher who Keefe says is "still over there" in military service "acrost the pond." In "Along Came Ruth," Jenkins, back from France, bothers Keefe by talking about his wartime experience. Keefe says that "if they was any battles he wasn't in its because he can't pronounce them."

George W. Hilton reports that Joseph Daniel Jenkins (1890–1974) played for the St. Louis Browns (1914) and the Chicago White Sox (1917), was a lieutenant in the army (until 1919), and returned to the White Sox (1919). (Sources: *Baseball Encyclopedia*, 1185; Hilton, 237)

JENNIE ("Travelogue"). Hazel Dignan tells Dan Chapman that Jennie replaced her sister Lucy Kingston's Swedish maid, who got married; and that Jennie is 19 and "wild about movie actors."

JENNIE ("The Water Cure"). Jennie is Gullible's generic name for all mothers with babies aboard the Lake Michigan weekend boat.

JENNINGS In "A Busher's Letters Home," Keefe criticizes Jennings, a Detroit Tigers coach, for "yelling like a Indian" when Keefe was pitching in the White Sox game against the Tigers. In "A Busher Comes Back," Keefe is upset that Jennings bought Joe Hill from Providence and had Hill pitch and defeat the White Sox. Worse, Hill is marrying Violet, Keefe's girlfriend. In "A New Busher Breaks In," Keefe expresses willingness to pitch "every other day for Jennings" to assure him a pennant-winning season. In "The Crook," "Jennin's" was managing Detroit in games against the narrator Larry's White Sox. When Martin Gregory froze while batting, "Jennin's" taunted him from the bench. In *Treat 'Em Rough*, Keefe says that during army "lessons in trench takeing" he "kept hollering like Hughey Jennings or somebody." In "Call for Mr. Keefe!," Keefe complains that Florrie hired a girl whose "Swede talk" is as loud as Hughey Jennings. In "The Courtship of T. Dorgan," Keefe says Detroit is "Jennings club." In "The Busher Pulls a Mays," Keefe hints to Jennings, whom he praises, that he'd like to be traded to his team. When dumped on Philadelphia instead, Keefe vows to be winning when Jennings's club "will be in the old folks home." Gullible mentions "Hugh Jennin's" in "Three Without, Doubled." Keefe mentions "Hughey Jennings" once in "A One-Man Team" and several times in *The Real Dope*.

Hugh Ambrose Jennings (1869–1928) played for the Brooklyn Dodgers (1899–1900), the Philadelphia Phillies (1901–1902), the Dodgers (1903), and the Detroit Tigers (1907, 1909, 1912, 1918), and managed the Tigers (1907–1920) and the New York Giants (1924–1925). He was elected to the Baseball Hall of Fame (1945). George W. Hilton reports that Jennings was memorable for his antics and yells when he coached from the third-base box. (Sources: *Baseball Encyclopedia*, 697, 1185; Hilton, 69)

JENNINGS ("'In Conference'") *see* **GALT**

JESSIE ("One Hit, One Error, One Left," etc.) *see* **GRAHAM, JESSIE**

JIM ("My Roomy"). He is a friend of Buster Elliott. Jim writes the narrator about Elliott's final lunatic actions and subsequent confinement in a mental asylum.

JIM DANDY ("Widow"). He was a winning race horse at Saratoga, remembered by Frank Hastings, who would have bet on him until a drunk told him to.

JIMMIE (*The Young Immigrunts*). He is the narrator's brother, 5. He, their brothers John and David and their nurse go by train to "Grenitch Conn.," to meet the rest of the family.

JOE ("Alibi Ike"). He owns a spaghetti house in the home town of the narrator's baseball team. The narrator and his fellow players try to entice Alibi Ike, in love with absent Dolly, to go there on a date. They want to hear his excuses.

JOE (*The Real Dope*). He is a soldier with Keefe's unit in France. Jack Brady and others kid Simple Simon by telling him that Joe has so many souvenirs relating to the German army that he is nicknamed Souvenir Joe.

JOE ("The Spinning Wheel"). From Georgia, he is an honest roulette dealer in a New York hotel. When Macomber loses at his table and accuses him of cheating, Joe's boss rebukes Macomber.

JOE ("Women"). He is a pitcher on Mike Healy's team. Healy, on the bench, interrupts his own anti-woman story to shout praise of Joe.

JOEY ("How Are You?"). He is Mrs. Gurnsey's brother. She tells Bob Dayton that Dr. Benham saved Joey's life by extracting his infected teeth.

JOEY ("Meet Me in St. Louie") *see* **PHILLIPS, MR.**

JOHN ("My Roomy"). He manages the Chicago baseball team for which the narrator, Buster Elliott, and about 20 others play. John suffers Elliott's antics as long as he can but finally releases him — with near-fatal results.

George W. Hilton identifies John as "John Joseph Evers (1881–1947), manager of the third-place Chicago Cubs of 1913, the team on which the action is set." Evers played for the Cubs (1902–1913), the Giants (1913), the Boston Braves (1914–1916), the Braves and the Philadelphia Phillies (1917), the Chicago White Sox (1922), and the Braves (1929). (Sources: *Baseball Encyclopedia*, 1003; Hilton, 331)

JOHN ("One Hit, One Error, One Left"). Danny identifies "Mathews Mark and Luque and John" as "4 pitchers" of the House of David, "a religious sex."

JOHN (*The Young Immigrunts*). He is one of the narrator's older brothers and is 7. He, their brothers Jimmie and David, and their nurse go by train to meet the rest of the family in "Grenitch Conn."

JOHNNY ("Tour No. 2"). He is Larry's uncle. Larry would like to visit Ireland to see places Johnny told him about. He doesn't get to do so.

JOHNSON In "A Busher's Letters Home," he plays when the White Sox are divided into two teams for practice in Paso Robles. Keefe says he gave up one hit, a grounder "the recrut shortstop Johnson ought to of ate up." In "The Busher Comes Back," Keefe says Johnson played shortstop for Oakland team on "the training trip with the White Sox." (This Johnson is fictional.)

JOHNSON, BYRON BANCROFT (1865–1931). "Ban" Johnson was an important major-league baseball administrator. He was born in Norwalk, Ohio, and studied in Marietta College and at the University of Cincinnati Law School, without obtaining a degree in either school. He became a sports writer, then sports editor, for the Cincinnati *Commercial-Gazette* (1886–1887), met Charles A. Comiskey,* and the two helped form the Western League (1894) and its development into the American League (1900–1901), of which Johnson was president (until 1927). Johnson suspended Ty Cobb for attacking a heckler (May 15, 1912) but lifted the suspension five days later when Cobb's teammates went on strike to support him. (Source: Hilton, 39, 307)

In "A New Busher Breaks In," Keefe says that when he was in trouble with Comiskey, he "seen president Johnson the president of the league" and was given encouraging information. In "The Crook," Ban fires Bull for umpiring and fighting while supposedly drunk. After Larry tells Ban that Bull wasn't drunk but despondent over his love affair with Maggie Gregory, Ban lifts reinstates him. In "Call for Mr. Keefe!," Keefe explains he won't be quickly drafted into the army because authorities "promised Ban Johnson that they wouldn't take no baseball stars till the seasons over and maybe not then." In "The Busher Pulls a Mays," Keefe says that Ban Johnson "suspend it Mays" but wasn't able to suspend Ty Cobb. Ban Johnson is mentioned in "The Venomous Viper of the Volga."

JOHNSON, WALTER In "A Busher's Letters Home," Keefe, White Sox pitcher, boasts while training in Paso Robles that his ability will make his teammates think he is Walter Johnson. In "The Busher Comes Back," Keefe says Johnson, pitching for Washington, has "nothing but a fast ball" and later boasts he beat Johnson 1–0. In "Sick 'Em," the narrator says that Walter Johnson beat the Phillies when Smitty and Fogarty wouldn't pitch effectively, but that Smitty, finally goaded into pitching, "beat Johnson on the wettest grounds I ever seen!" In "A New Busher Breaks In," Keefe boasts that when pitching excellently against Washington's pitcher Joe Hill he could have done as well even if Johnson had been pitching against him. In "Horseshoes" Johnson is called as fast as a gun, too fast for Dick Grimes, of the Athletics, to hit. In "The Busher's Kid," Keefe says, "I will work against this here Johnson and show him up for giveing me that trimming in Washington, the lucky stiff." In "Where Do You Get That Noise?," Hawley complains that when he was playing with the Phillies in an exhibition game in Washington, Johnson was pitching, and no batters could hit because the sunlight blinded them. In "The Crook," Johnson pitched against the White Sox. When Weber, a rookie, came to bat, Johnson's speed terrified him and in frustration he shouted ineffectively at Bull, the umpire. In "The Yellow Kid," Lefty Crosby was praised as being "faster'n Johnson." In "Call for Mr. Keefe!," Keefe says that umpire Bill Evans favored Johnson, pitching for Washington, by calling a low ball a strike. Later, Keefe admits being defeated by Johnson but adds that Washington got only three runs against Keefe's pitching. In *The Real Dope*, Keefe remembers "pitching against the notorious Johnson." Jack plans to tell General Pershing about the event. In "The Battle of Texas," Kid Gleason says Keefe's fast ball resembles Johnson's. In "The Courtship of T. Dorgan," Keefe says that Gleason inserted him in the eighth inning in a game against Washington; and that although Johnson also came in "to try to hold the lead," the White Sox won. In "Hurry Kane," Johnson is said to be fast but Hurry Kane is faster. In "One Hit, One Error, One Left," Johnson is allegedly afraid of Carey's hitting ability. Johnson is mentioned In "The Busher Abroad," "The Busher's Welcome Home," "Good for the Soul," and "Harmony."

Walter Perry Johnson (1887–1946) was the Washington Senators legendary pitcher (1907–1917), managed the Senators (1929–1932) and the Cleveland Indians (1922–1925), and was a charter member of the Baseball Hall of Fame (1936). He threw so fast that he was nicknamed "The Big Train." George W. Hilton says that Johnson is "considered the greatest of all pitchers," and adds that "[t]he veneration with which Lardner's characters, both real and fictional, speak of Johnson is wholly consistent with the retrospective views of him of ... actual ballplayers." (Sources: *Baseball Encyclopedia*, 697, 2104; Hilton, 46)

JOHNSON, WILMA ABBY She was an early girlfriend of Lardner's. She lived in Goshen, Indiana, and then in Niles, Michigan. Her nicknames were "Johnny," "Ginnie," and "Ginseng." She liked Lardner very much. (Sources: Lardner, Jr., 33; Caruthers [1995], 193)

JOHNSTON ("The Busher Comes Back"). Keefe says that when he pitched for the White Sox against Cleveland, he walked Johnston.

Wheeler Roger Johnston (1887–1961) played for the Cincinnati Reds (1909), the Cleveland Indians (1912–1914), the Pittsburgh Pirates (1915–1916), the Indians (1918–1921), and the Philadelphia Athletics (1922). (Sources: *Baseball Encyclopedia*, 1193; Hilton, 82)

JOHNSTON ("A Busher's Letters Home"). Keefe boasts that when he was pitching for the White Sox against the St. Louis Browns, he "made Johnston look like a boob."

John Thomas Johnston (1890–1940) played for the St. Louis Browns (1913). (Sources: *Baseball Encyclopedia*, 1194; Hilton, 63)

JOHNSTON, RITA ("Reunion"). She is Bob Mason's brother and Stuart Johnston's wife. Rita and Bob were children together in Buchanan, Michigan. Her being named Rita after a well-to-do aunt led to her being separated from Bob and growing up in Philadelphia. The Johnstons' reunion with Bob and his wife Jennie, after Rita, 35, hasn't seen Bob, 34, for 20 years, is disastrous. They have nothing in common.

JOHNSTON, STUART ("Reunion"). He is Rita's well-to-do husband. From Philadelphia, he undoubtedly attended the University of Pennsylvania, since he met Rita after a Cornell-Pennsylvania football game. They live comfortably at Sands Point, Long Island. He plays golf in the high 80s and drinks enough to be called "Stu." His valiant efforts to entertain Rita's brother Bob Mason and his wife Jennie fizzle.

JONES (*The Real Dope*). He is mentioned as managing the St. Louis baseball team in notes that Jack Keefe, while in the army in France, prepares and intends to read to General Pershing.

Fielder Allison Jones (1871–1934) played for the Brooklyn Dodgers (1896–1900) and the Chicago White Sox (1901–1908), and managed the White Sox (1904–1908) and the St. Louis Browns (1916–1918). (Source: *Baseball Encyclopedia*, 697–698, 1197)

JONES, TED ("Who Dealt?"). While talking almost uninterruptibly, Mrs. Cannon reveals that her husband Thomas Cannon played football at Yale until he and the head coach, "Tex Jones, no, Ted Jones," had a dispute and Tom quit.

JORDAN ("There Are Smiles"). He is an old man who parked in front of Kaskel's. Traffic-cop Ben Collins tells Edith Dole that he got Jordan to move by gently saying, "Roll, Jordan, Roll!"

JOYCE ("Horseshoes"). He is the brilliant Athletics leftfielder. When he gets hurt in the sixth World Series game against the Giants, Dick Grimes must substitute for him.

George W. Hilton explains that Joyce, and also Grimes and Parker, are fictional characters. (Source: Hilton, 395)

JOYCE, MR. ("Ball-A-Hole"). He is mentioned as a golfer who always tips the narrator, his caddy. He and Mr. Davis play against Mr. Harper and Mr. McNally. After winning $30 last spring, Joyce tipped the narrator and Jake, another caddy, $2.50 each.

JOYCE, MR. ("A Caddy's Diary"). He and Mr. Clayton are golfers. Slow-playing Mr. Blake, Mr. Carter, Mr. Dunham, and Mr. Thomas let the two play through them.

J. P. ("'In Conference'"). J. P. works for Kramer & Company and just phoned L. M. Croft, a fellow worker, that a letter addressed to the firm is in the post office without a stamp. If the company sends a 2¢, the letter will be forwarded.

JUDGE In *The Real Dope*, Keefe, soldiering in France, describes in an essay Judge's wind-assisted hit for the Washington Senators when Jack was pitching for the Chicago White Sox. Keefe intends to tell General Pershing about the event. In "The Busher Pulls a Mays," Keefe boasts that when he pitched for the White Sox in relief against Washington, Judge hit a ball that Gandil could have fielded easily but for being ill.

Joseph Ignatius Judge (1894–1963) played for the Washington Senators (1915–1932), the Brooklyn Dodgers and the Boston Red Sox (1933), and the Red Sox (1934). (Sources: *Baseball Encyclopedia*, 1204; Hilton, 314)

JUDSON, MAY ("That Old Sweetheart of Mine"). She is supposedly a girlfriend that Will believes would return to him if he merely whistled.

JUDSON, MRS. ("Zone of Quiet"). She was the only patient whose death nurse Miss Eleanor Lyons says she didn't mind.

JULE, AUNT ("I Can't Breathe"). She is the young diarist's aunt. She and her husband Uncle Nat take her on a vacation while her parents are abroad for a month.

JULIA ("Sick 'Em"). She was Fogarty's girl at one point, supposedly prettier than Smitty's Marie.

JULIA ("Widow"). She is Alice Winslow's sister, in Minneapolis. Alice tells Margaret Winslow, her sister-in-law whose husband John has just died, that Julia was "alone when her husband [Bert] died."

JULIA, AUNT ("Freedom of the Press"). She is a Frenchman's wife and is Constance Warner's aunt. The three live quietly in a French village until Constance's dying father summons Constance home to New York.

JULIA, AUNT ("Good for the Soul"). She is Ethel Warner's aunt. When Ethel and Buck Warner were planning to marry as soon as he could manage financially, her aunt promised $2,500 as a wedding present. The two women argued when Julia fell in love with a much older Civil War veteran and said she would need the money. After Ethel married Buck and he turned grouchy, she threatened to go live with Julia in Dayton if he didn't confess his "crime."

JULIUS, DR. ("How Are You?"). He is recommended to Bob Dayton as an excellent X-ray specialist.

KAHN, GUS ("Rhythm"). He is a composer. Willis Merwin, a theatrical producer, is contracting with Kahn and Walter Donaldson for music to use in a new show.

Gus Kahn (1886–1941), German-born, was a popular musician and lyricist. He migrated to Chicago (1890), became a musician there and in New York (from 1913), and composed many songs with Walter Donaldson, including "Yes, Sir, That's My Baby" (1925).

KALMAR, BERT ("A Day with Conrad Green"). He and Harry Ruby wrote a successful musical comedy. Robert Blair stole the plot, and tried but failed to sell it to Conrad Green, who tries it as his on his librettist Joe Martin, who reveals the theft.

KANE ("Alibi Ike"). He was a player on the narrator's team. Alibi Ike is so good in spring training that he's hired to replace Kane.

KANE ("Ex Parte"). He owns the store where the narrator buys his antiquing tools — a blow torch and an axe.

KANE, BENNY ("Rhythm"). He is a lyric-thief who collaborates with tune-thief Harry Hart in musical comedies, until Hart is flattered into thinking he can be a creative composer. When Hart fails in this endeavor, the two resume their profitable relationship.

Is the name "Benny Kane" supposed to suggest an illegal mixture of benzadrine and cocaine?

KANE, ELMER ("Hurry Kane") *see* **KANE, HURRY**

KANE, HURRY ("Hurry Kane"). Hurry Kane, whose birth name is Elmer Kane, is a brilliant pitcher for the St. Louis baseball team. He is 20, 6' 3", and addicted to food. His love life is so tangled — what with his Waco gal, sweet Minnie Olson of Yuma, and scheming Evelyn Corey — that his fellow players must become ingeniously dishonest, to get him to stay. In one episode, Hurry Kane thinks he's as handsome as movie-star Thomas Meighan.* So his teammates advise him to quit playing baseball and become a movie star.

KANE, RAE ("Rhythm"). She is Benny Kane's new wife. Her objections to Harry Hart's tune thievery is a contributing factor to her husband's and Hart's temporary separation. Her objecting to the ensuing poverty helps the two men get back together again.

KASKEL ("There Are Smiles"). He may be the owner of a store named Kaskel, in front of which a man named Jordan parked until traffic-cop Ben Collins kidded him into moving.

KATE ("A Day with Conrad Green"). She is "the switchboard girl" who alerts Conrad Green that Mrs. Bryant Walker's secretary is calling him.

KATHLEEN MAVOURNEEN (*The Big Town*). This is the name Finch gives to the Irish colleen he and his wife Ella hire as a servant in New York. The name means "Kathleen My Darling."

KATHRYN ("The Facts"). She is Walter McDonald's current girlfriend. She giggles constantly.

KATIE (*The Big Town*). She is Ella Finch's sister, 20, attractive, stupid, and frivolous. Ella wants to find Katie a husband. They try in and near their home in South Bend, then in New York. On the train to New York, Katie is attracted to Francis Griffin, who, however, makes a play for Ella and Finch beats him up. When the Finches and Katie rent a Riverside Drive, their rich old neighbor Trumbull grows fond of Katie, who, however, prefers Trumbull's young chauffeur Ritchey — until it's revealed he is married with children. Katie accompanies the Finches to a Long Island hotel, where she meets Bob Codd, an aviator-inventor. She encourages him. She ruins Lady Perkins's chance to win big at bridge by shouting that the lady is holding four aces. Katie isn't grief-stricken when Bob crashes in his experimental "aeroplane" and dies, because, she concludes, his invention must have been worthless. She proves attractive to "horseman" Herbert Daley at the Decker, accepts his proposal of marriage to please Ella, but secretly dates Sid Mercer, Daley's dishonest jockey, and loses both men. She doesn't mind, because Finch bet successfully on Sap at the Belmont, after a tip from Sid. Returning to New York with Finch and Ella, Katie meets and falls in love with Jimmy Ralston, a Follies comedian, invests money in and plays Bridget in "Bridget Sees a Ghost," his failure of a play, but soon marries him. Katie often reveals her air-headiness. For example, when Daley explains bookmakers to her, she calls them "bookbinders." Finch says they are "bookworms."

Donald Phelps dismisses Katie as "lint-brained." (Source: Phelps, 97)

"KATIE WINS A HOME" (as "The Comic," (*Saturday Evening Post*, May 13, 1921; BT, PRL) *see* ***THE BIG TOWN***

KATZ ("Carmen"). It is at the Katzes' establishment that Mrs. Gullible gets Gullible's dress suit pressed before they attend the opera.

KAUFMAN, GEORGE S. (1889–1961). Playwright. Pittsburgh-born Kaufman was a New York journalist, witty friend of innumerable Manhattan literati, and author and coauthor of many plays. He is best remembered for collaborating with equally skillful fellow-dramatists. They include Marc Connelly (1890–1980), on *Merton of the Movies* (1922, spoofing Hollywood) and *Beggar on Horseback* (1924, with incidental music by Deems Taylor*; Edna Ferber (1887–1968), on *The Royal Family* (1927), described as "a veiled encomium" to the Barrymore family* of actors; and Moss Hart (1904–1961) on *Once in a Lifetime* (1930), *You Can't Take It with You* (1936), *The Man Who Came to Dinner* (1939), etc. Kaufman was also a sought-after friend able to touch up the work of lesser playwrights. Ring Lardner Jr. writes at great length about his father's often difficult but always amiable collaborative efforts with Kaufman to write and produce their play *June Moon* (1929), based on Lardner's "Some Like Them Cold." (Sources: Lardner Jr.; Leiter, I, 461)

KAVANAUGH, MAURICE ("The Jade Necklace"). He is a dazzlingly handsome Dublin actor. Movie-maker L. N. Bauer hires him at $8,000 a week to star in a movie and thus rival handsome Dennis Byrne, the Supreme company matinée idol. Ultimately Kavanaugh gets only a bit part in *The Jade Necklace*.

KEEFE, ALLEN In "A New Busher Breaks In," Florence Keefe gives birth to her husband Jack

Keefe's baby boy. They name him Allen after Florence's sister Marie Allen's husband. Keefe calls him "little Al." In "The Busher's Kid," the baby is the center of controversy when Florence hires a baby sitter and attends White Sox games Keefe pitches. In "The Busher Beats It Hence," Keefe decides not to go on the world tour because he wants to care for "little Al," decides to go, and asks Al Blanchard, if Keefe drowns, to prevent the boy from becoming left-handed. In "The Busher Abroad," Keefe during his tour sends little Al post cards from Cairo while aware the kid can't read. In "The Busher's Welcome Home," Keefe is disappointed when upon returning to Chicago he learns that Florrie has taken little Al to California. In "Call for Mr. Keefe!," Al, now three, can talk, wonders who Keefe is, and asks to go with "daddy" to war. In *The Real Dope*, when Keefe is in France with the army, he thinks of "little Al." He is happy to return home to him, and others in his family. In "The Busher Reënlists," Keefe is concerned about supporting the kid, now three, and also about missing him if he returns to playing baseball. In "The Battle of Texas," Keefe mentions having a family, including Al. In "Along Came Ruth," Keefe, when squabbling with his wife, wonders whether the authorities will "ward" him custody of Al and also Al's baby sister Florrie. In "The Courtship of T. Dorgan" and "The Busher Pulls a Mays," Keefe mentions his children. In *Treat 'Em Rough*, Jack, on week-end passes, sees little Al in Chicago and Houston, Texas. In *The Real Dope*, Keefe worries about little Al.

KEEFE, FLORRIE (FLORENCE) In "The Busher Comes Back," Keefe explains that Florence is the White Sox rookie pitcher Allen's wife's sister. Keefe says Florence "maybe ain't as pretty as Violet and Hazel." When dumped by those girls, however, he says he liked Florrie immediately and plans to marry her. In "The Busher's Honeymoon," Keefe reports their marriage, on October 15th in Chicago, where Florence gets him to remain during the winter so she can be near her sister Marie Allen and Marie's husband. Florrie dislikes Keefe's writing Al Blanchard, tries to disrupt his friendship with Al and his wife Bertha Blanchard, rationalizes Allen's sponging on Keefe, and when Keefe is in financial trouble deserts him and goes to Texas. In "A New Busher Breaks In," Florrie presents Keefe with their baby boy. The new parents dispute about how to care for "little Al." In "The Busher's Kid," Keefe is infuriated when he learns that Florrie hired a baby sitter so she could attend White Sox games when he's pitching, forgives her, and when she argues with Marie makes plans to move with Florrie and their baby from the Allens' flat in Chicago to Bedford. In "The Busher Beats It Hence," Keefe decides to go on the world tour, he asks Al Blanchard to see that she gets his life insurance and savings, if he drowns. In "The Busher Abroad," Keefe, on the world tour, worries when he doesn't hear from Florrie, and also when he does. In Kobe he buys "Kumonnes" for her, and from Cairo he sends her post cards. In "The Busher's Welcome Home," Keene gets no "male" from Florrie, and is sad when returning to Chicago he finds Florrie and little Al gone to California. In "Call for Mr. Keefe!," Florrie starts a beauty shop with Miss Nevins, makes money, is willing to lie on an affidavit to keep Keefe from being drafted, but calmly accepts his leaving to begin army service. In *Treat 'Em Rough*, Jack, in the army, visits Florrie in Chicago by "supprise," only to find her out. She returns. They argue, and her friends' arrival cuts short his free time with her. She visits Keefe in Houston, Texas, thus destroying his friendship with a letter-writer named Miss Lucy Chase. In *The Real Dope*, Keefe is sad when Florrie doesn't see his troop ship off, doesn't like it when she feels superior to Bertha Blanchard, and worries about Florrie's overspending and remarrying should he be killed. She seldom writes Keefe, and that mostly about her success and appearance. Her indifference prompts Keefe to seek fun with Miss Marie Antoinette. He is happy when Florrie gives birth to their daughter, returns home wounded, and wants to name the baby Florrie. In "The Busher Reënlists," Florrie shows her independence by what Keefe regards as excessive spending during the Christmas season. She says she'll miss him if he plays baseball again and has away games. In "The Battle of Texas," Keefe dates Miss Krug until Kid Gleason arranges for Florrie to come see Keefe pitch in St. Louis. In "Along Came Ruth," Florrie goes into partnership with a male beauty-parlor owner and his wife in downtown Chicago. This distresses Keefe, briefly. In "The Courtship of T. Dorgan," Keefe socializes with Florrie's beauty-parlor partners Dumont and his wife, this time including drives in the Dumonts' car and dinner events with Tom Dorgan and Miss Josie Mulvihill along. Florrie won't provide money to help Keefe buy a car. She is annoyed by Keefe's attentions to Miss Mulvihill. In "The Busher Pulls a Mays," Florrie dislikes the Dumonts, who buy her out. Florrie cries when she learns Keefe has been traded to Philadelphia but seems to agree that Philadelphia has some advantages.

KEEFE, FLORRIE She is Keefe's infant daughter. In *The Real Dope*, Keefe, in the army in France happily learns his wife Florrie has given birth to a daughter, named Florrie. In "The Busher Reënlists," "little Florrie" is the second child of Jack Keefe and Florence Keefe, and is about six months old. In "The Battle of Texas," Florrie has a new tooth and another on the way. In "Along Came Ruth," Keefe argues briefly with his wife and wonders, needlessly, who'll care for Florrie and her brother Al if the authorities "don't ward them to me." In "The Courtship of T. Dorgan," Keefe weasels out of a physical confrontation with Speaker, the tough Cleveland player, by staying home with "croopy" Florrie. In "The Busher Pulls a Mays," Keefe mentions his children.

KEEFE, JACK He is a baseball pitcher, then a soldier. In *You Know Me Al*, Keefe writes letters to his friend Al. In "A Busher's Letters Home," Keefe reports that he has been bought from Terre Haute to the White Sox, trains with them, does badly in several games, and is sold to "Frisco." In "The Busher Comes Back," Keefe gets experience pitching for San Francisco, is recalled to the White Sox, pitches with occasional success, and has trouble with three girlfriends. In "The Busher's Honeymoon," he continues pitching, boasting and rationalizing, marries Florence, tries to get a new baseball contract, and argues with Florrie, who leaves him. In "A New Busher Breaks In," he returns to the team chagrined without admitting it, travels and pitches with varying success, learns he's to be a father, and is reunited with Florrie. In "The Busher's Kid," he is home with his family, pitches in Chicago, travels with the team, does well and boasts, and does badly and explains. He argues with Florrie for hiring a baby sitter so she can see him pitch, forgives her, and they plan to move to Bedford. In "The Busher Beats It Hence," Keefe goes with the world-touring baseball players as far as the west coast, determines not to go "a round the world" with them because of obligations to Florrie and "little Al," but is persuaded by Callahan and McGraw to go.

In "The Busher Abroad," Keefe goes on the tour, writes Al Blanchard 32 letters, explaining about Japan, the Philippines, Ceylon, and Egypt, playing ball occasionally, and enjoying much. He misunderstands much of what he sees and is kidded effectively by fellow players.

In "The Busher's Welcome Home," Keefe, still on the tour, writes Blanchard eight letters from shipboard, Italy, France, and London, and then, home again, from New York and Chicago. He plays ball, continues to be fooled by his team mates and to misunderstand tourist sights, and is disappointed when he learns that Florrie has taken little Al to California.

In "Call for Mr. Keefe!," Keefe explains his part in games he pitched for the White Sox. He praises his successes, rationalizes his stupid mistakes. He tries to avoid the military draft by having Florrie cheat on an affidavit. Failing, he is drafted and boasts about his patriotism.

In "The Busher Reënlists," Keefe counts on his wartime service when he seeks employment in the business world, fails, figures on letting potential employers come to him, argues with Florrie about her Christmas purchases but lets her buy an expensive necklace for their new baby daughter "little Florrie," and signs with Comiskey to return to the White Sox for $2,400 instead of inflated figures he boasted he'd hold out for.

In "The Battle of Texas," Keefe boasts and rationalizes but evidently pitches better. He jeopardizes his marriage by flirting with Miss Krug until Kid Gleason brings Florrie down from Chicago to St. Louis to see him pitch — superbly, of course.

In "Along Came Ruth," Keefe creates trouble for himself off and on the playing field. Florrie neglects him to go partners with a beauty-parlor operator and his wife. Keefe pitches badly against Boston but, after reconciling with Florrie, defeats Philadelphia to earn a raise.

In "The Courtship of T. Dorgan," Keefe praises his good pitching, makes excuses for losing on the grounds of poor fielding by his teammates, retreats when Speaker objects to Keefe's macho remarks, bets on Willard against Dempsey, tries unsuccessfully to buy a car, and flirts with Miss Josie Mulville until she prefers Tom Dorgan and gets engaged to him.

In "The Busher Pulls a Mays," Keefe rationalizes his poor pitching while being mostly ineffective, blabs about wanting to be traded to Jennings's Washington team, drinks excessively, and goes along with $5,000 to Connie Mack's Philadelphia team in exchange for Page, their pitcher.

In *Treat 'Em Rough*, Keefe writes Al Blanchard 30 letters, including 29 from army camps. They concern his military training, buddies, willingness to serve in France, meetings with his wife

Florrie, and dishonest correspondence with a Texas "girlie" named Miss Lucy Chase.

In *The Real Dope*, Keefe's adventures include crossing the ocean on a troop ship to France, adapting to France ineffectively, being kidded by his "buddies," serenading "Miss Moselle" with a valentine poem, kissing a French flirt Ernestine and being scared by her father, kidding Johnny Alcock and being kidded in return, seeking friendship with a supposed Miss Marie Antoinette concocted by Alcock and others, and being wounded while trying to rescue Simon. Returning home, he sees his new baby daughter.

Nicholas Dawidoff reports that one model for Keefe was the White Sox pitcher Joe Benz (1886–1957). Walton R. Patrick usefully shows that "all the Keefe stories ... appeared in five related groups," and indicates when and where the 26 stories were first published. Carl Van Doren praises Lardner's characterization of Jack Keefe, "a pitcher expert enough to play with the White Sox and a fool complete enough to tickle even the stupid among the fans by his incomparable stupidity." Van Doren adds that Keefe "is more than a mirror of illiteracy; he is a treasure-trove." On the other hand, Donald Douglas dislikes Keefe, calling him "a braggart and a fool and a liar of the worst sort." Donald Phelps says that Keefe has an "earnest, ungrammatically glib voice." Robert J. Higgs analyzes Keefe as both comic and insidious, with redeeming traits, imagined versatility, vain, and disposed to rationalizing. Higgs adds that Keefe displays self-proclaimed qualities of royal heroism but sadly lacks a pal for comic contrast. James M. Cox, while comparing Lardner's use of vernacular and that of Mark Twain and J. D. Salinger, notes that Keefe "evolves a series of errors ... which intrude unassimilated correctness and abortive formality into ... primitive illiteracy." Tom Quirk remarks that "[w]hat in Huck Finn is innocence becomes in Jack Keefe debilitating ignorance. Huck's self-deprecation [Quirk adds] is transformed in Jack to exasperating self-deception." Elizabeth Evans analyzes Keefe's rhetorical devices, including sentence structures, misspellings, descriptions, double negatives, folksy imagery, formal phrasing, black humor, and diction. Ring Lardner Jr. is too kind in commenting on Keefe's facility with the pencil. After noting that "A Busher's Letters Home" has "misspellings and other writing errors," he opines that "[m]istakes are deliberately kept to a minimum and their main function is to remind the reader that these are letters, directed to one trusted intimate and dealing with the most private events as well as public ones." Even apart from the fact that neither Keefe (nor Lardner himself, for that matter) writes about "the most private [i.e., sexual] events," this statement isn't accurate, and less so when Keefe continues to flourish his pencil, beginning two short weeks later. Clifford M. Caruthers notes that "Lardner drew his protagonist with a tolerant pen that rendered Keefe vividly real and oddly sympathetic." (It ought to be added that the Keefe of *Treat 'Em Rough* and *The Real Dope* begins to fatigue the most enamored reader.) Edward A. Martin concludes, specifically, that Keefe's "genuine skill emerges briefly through the overlay of arrogance, paranoia, and desperate lack of self-growth," and, more generally, that "Lardner clearly respects and cherishes the skill of the athlete-artist and implicitly, sometimes bitterly, laments its loss."

Leverett T. Smith Jr. discusses Lardner's two favorite baseball players, Tyrus R. Cobb* and Christopher Mathewson,* and then remarks that "Jack Keefe is certainly the antithesis of Cobb and Mathewson, and is as certainly calculated to be so. Compared to the sensible, competent workmanship of their careers, he continually behaves like a lunatic." Matthew J. Bruccoli curtly defines Keefe as "not an innocent boob; he is dumb, dishonest, mean, and vain." George W. Hilton, however, goes into detail, describing Keefe as "immature, semiliterate, arrogant, unstable, miserly, and vain"; adds that "he manages to carry a self-image of shrewdness and great ability through all his experiences"; admits he's "likeable" and has "charm"; excuses his "shortcomings," which are owing to "limited education and some basic personality flaws, for neither of which he is responsible"; and concludes that "his principal trait is to be oblivious to himself" even as Lardner "is building character development" in him; and, in short, notes Keefe's "uneducated shrewdness." Patrick observes that "[t]he image of himself that Jack [Keefe] unconsciously presents to Al and the reader is ... the reverse of the one he has of himself." After listing Keefe's close to innumerable defects, Donald Elder manages to conclude thus: "He is not very much worse than anyone else; he is real. He is not quite like yourself, but he bears a fatal resemblance to your friends." Jonathan Yardley analyzes poor Keefe's imagined "wit and savvy" and liveliness "in any debate." (Sources: Bruccoli, xii; Cox, 320; Douglas, 584; Elder, 114; Evans, 31–35, 76; Higgs, 23, 24, 25, 25–26; Hilton, 7, 8, 9, 11; Lardner, Jr., 86–87; Martin, 160–161; Patrick, 43, 45;

Phelps, Quirk, 121; Smith, 144;Van Doren, 471, 472; Yardley, 166)

KELLOGG, DON ("Tour Y-10"). He is a friend of Violet Emerson. He and Bruce Patterson bid farewell to Violet Emerson, whom they like, on her vacation to Yellowstone. When Violet returns having flirted unsuccessfully, Don happily visits her again.

KELLY ("Back to Baltimore"). He is the Boston Braves secretary. When the team was in New York, Kelly showed Dixon, the Braves manager, the name of "William Baker Junior," in "the hotel book," as a team member.

George W. Hilton identifies Kelly as Peter F. Kelley (1870–1944), the Braves secretary in 1909–1912, not 1914, the date of the action of "Back to Baltimore." Hilton adds that Kelley worked for the Braves when Lardner was "covering the team for the Boston *American* in 1911." (Source: Hilton, 432)

KELLY ("The Busher Reënlists"). He is the manager of a department store. Keefe learns of a job opening there, but finds Kelly offensive and leaves. Kelly calls him "Mr. Smart" in a letter to Al Blanchard.

KELLY ("A Busher's Letters Home"). He is a White Sox player. Keefe tells Al that, when the team was practicing in Los Angeles, Kelly objected to Keefe's quitting while ahead in poker and the two almost fought.

KELLY ("Champion"). She is the daughter of Midge and Emma Kelly. Midge abandons Emma and their baby.

KELLY ("Holycaust"). Danny writes that Kelly, a Brooklyn player, walked in a game with Cincinnati, whereupon Danny was ordered to pinch hit.

George Lange Kelly (1895–1984) played for the New York Giants (1915–1916), the Giants and the Pittsburgh Pirates (1917), the Giants (1919–1926), the Cincinnati Reds (1927–1929), the Reds and the Chicago Cubs (1930), and the Brooklyn Dodgers (1932). He was elected to the Baseball Hall of Fame (1973). (Source: *Baseball Encyclopedia*, 1214)

KELLY, CONNIE ("Champion"). He is Midge Kelly's crippled, abused, but loyal younger brother. Connie lives with their mother in Chicago.

KELLY, ELLEN F. ("Champion"). She is the mother of Connie and Midge Kelly. She works at Faulkner's Steam Laundry in Chicago. She warns Midge after he abuses Connie, continues to love both, and appeals unsuccessfully to Midge for financial help.

KELLY, EMMA ("Champion"). She is Lou Hersh's sister, lives in Milwaukee, marries Midge Kelly, is abandoned by him when she's pregnant, and pleads unavailingly for financial support from him later.

KELLY, HUGO ("Tour No. 2"). He is an acquaintance of Larry's. Larry says that as "a wop" he would have fought only if armed with a knife, except that he had "a irish name."

Here, Lardner indicates racial prejudice of his characters and not of himself.

KELLY, MICHAEL ("MIDGE") ("Champion"). He is an unprincipled boxer. He abuses his crippled younger brother Connie Kelly, mistreats and abandons their mother Ellen F. Kelly and his wife Emma Kelly, and uses and viciously dumps one manager after another on his way to championship status.

Elizabeth Evans notes that Midge, among far worse defects, also "exemplifies the worst that wealth can produce ... [and] for new clothes ... selects with the taste of a hayseed barker given an unexpected bonus." Robert J. Higgs deplores Midge's uniqueness, saying that whereas Lardner's "baseball players are ... boobs, simps, and saps and ... generally more comic than mean," Midge "is not only mean but vicious as well." Earlier citing Midge's uniqueness, Donald Phelps continues by defining him as a "permanent outsider, an enemy alien to the human universe." (Sources: Evans 64; Higgs, 113; Phelps, 89)

KEMP ("Bob's Birthday"). Kemp and Warren were Bob Tyler's bosses until, for some reason, they discharged him two years ago.

KEMP, WILLIE ("A Frame-Up"). He is a New York boxer. Burke soundly defeats him in an effort to impress Esther Fester.

KENDALL ("Great Blessings"). He hired Tod Stewart two weeks before Thanksgiving Day, found him unsuitable, and fired him. Tod's mother is critical of "Old Kendall" and makes excuses for her useless son's behavior.

KENDALL ("Great Blessings"). He is the son of the man who hired and quickly fired Tod Stewart.

Tod's mother rationalizes that young Kendall was jealous of Tod.

KENDALL ("The Golden Honeymoon"). He is a grocer from Kingston, Rhode Island. Charley and Mother meet and like Kendall and his wife in Florida.

KENDALL, JIM ("Haircut"). This man, whose full name is James H. Kendall, was esteemed in Whitey's town for his clever jokes. But they were cruel. When he kidded Paul Dickson, called "cuckoo" because of a head injury, he went too far and got himself shot.

Lardner doesn't say so, or even hint at it; but one might say that when Paul killed Jim with his own shotgun, the wound was the village kidder's last haircut.

KENDALL, MRS. ("The Golden Honeymoon"). She and her husband meet Charley and Mother while the four are vacationing in Florida. Mrs. Kendall tells Mother that they have two sons, five grandchildren, and one great-grandchild.

KENDALL, MRS. ("Haircut"). She was Jim Kendall's wife and the mother of "their two kiddies." She would have divorced Jim, a faithless, alcoholic joker, but for lacking escape funds despite her efforts as a dressmaker.

KENNEDY ("The Crook"). He was a player on the narrator Larry's White Sox team. Larry explains that Kennedy, "in a battin' slump," was naturally enough "tryin' to take it out on the umps." He lost his shouting match with Bull, the witty umpire.

KENNEDY, FRANK ("Wedding Day"). He is a New York musical-comedy lyricist and a friend of comedian Jimmy Shane. On the evening of the day Jimmy marries Brownie Burt, Jimmy meets Kennedy at their club, not to discuss business, as Jimmy told Brownie, but to receive a phone call from another girlfriend.

KERR ("The Busher Pulls a Mays"), Keefe complains that when "Kerr and Faber and Lowdermilk" pitch for the White Sox, opposing batters get hits.

George W. Hilton summarizes the career of Richard Henry Kerr (1893–1963), who was a successful left-handed pitcher for the Chicago White Sox (1919–1921), associated with Edward Trowbridge Collins, Raymond William Schalk, and Urban Clarence Faber, was disliked by Arnold Gandil and his clique, was denied a raise by Charles Albert Comiskey, held out for the entire 1922 season, was suspended by the White Sox (1923–1924), pitched for them again briefly (1925), and then became a minor-league manager. (Sources: *Baseball Encyclopedia*, 2120; Hilton, 306)

KERRY, NORMAN (1889–1956). Born Arnold Kaiser, Norman Kerry player hero roles and villain roles, often with a waxed mustache, in many silent movies and then in several talkies (1916–1941). He is mentioned in "I Can't Breathe." (Source: Ephraim Katz, 745)

KERSLAKE, HELEN ("Hurry Kane"). She is Johnny Abbott's beautiful, well-educated fiancée. She befriends Hurry Kane and Minnie Olson. Helen marries Johnny in November.

KETTER ("Words and Music"). He is a music writer working for Roman Starr, the popular singer.

KILLIAN, JOAN ("Travelogue"). She is a girl from Elkhart. Hazel Dignan tells Dan Chapman about her. It seems that Bess Eldridge was engaged to Harley Bateman until she saw him with Joan Killian in Chicago.

KING ("Hurry Kane"). He plays for the White Sox. The narrator, the St. Louis catcher, drops King's foul ball in the crucial final game.

KING ("The Love Nest"). He is an elderly businessman from White Plains. Lou Gregg meets him and K. L. Latham in Tarrytown to discuss plans for a lavish new golf course.

KING, BERNARD ("Old Folks' Christmas"). He and Herb Castle are university classmates of Ted Carter. The three carouse when they are back home during Christmas vacation.

KING, JOSIE ("Wedding Day"). She is "the highest-salaried chorus girl" in New York musical comedies. She is a gossipy guest at the wedding of her cohorts Brownie Burt and Jimmy Shane.

KING, SAM ("Insomnia"). He was an alumnus of the University of Illinois, from which Allan Spears also graduated. Sam was the junior partner in Rogers and King, a brokerage firm. He advised Allan to invest in "So-and-so" stock.

KING, SANDY ("The Venomous Viper of the Volga"). He is an opportunistic press agent working for boxing promoter Luke Lewis. King converts Henry Goetz into the boxer known as Ivan

Ivanovitch, "the Venomous Viper of the Volga." King and Lewis are about to make a fortune matching the Viper against Frankie Fitzgerald, but the Viper and King's girlfriend Mabel Ives fall in love, and King beats him up.

KINGSTON, DICKIE ("Travelogue"). Hazel Dignan tells Dan Chapman that her sister Lucy Kingston's son Dickie, almost seven, "lost all his front teeth."

KINGSTON, JACK ("Travelogue"). Hazel Dignan tells Dan Chapman that this man married Hazel's sister Lucy and they live in Elkhart.

KINGSTON, LUCY ("Travelogue"). Hazel Dignan tells Dan Chapman about her "Sis." She is married to Jack Kingston, is Dickie's mother, and they live in Elkhart.

KINGSTON, MR. ("Freedom of the Press"). He is Robert J. Warner's attorney. When Warner dies, Kingston must go out of New York on business. He orders Warner's secretary Alexander Beardsley to manage Warner's daughter Constance Warner's affairs for a brief time.

KIRBY ("A One-Man Team"). He was an outstanding player on Marshall's football. Coach Belden recalls defeating Marshall one year because its "one-man team" was built on Kirby.

KIRK ("Mr. Frisbie"). He is a journalist who tries to interview rich Allen Frisbie. The narrator makes him leave.

KITCHELL (*The Big Town*). This is the name of Chicago friends of the Finches. Finch tells his wife Ella that the Kitchells owned their own furniture. Ella says she wants to rent an expensive furnished apartment on Riverside Drive in New York instead of renting anything unfurnished and having to buy furniture.

Lardner has harmless fun with the name Kitchell. His sister-in-law was his wife Ellis's sister Jane Abbott Kitchell,* the wife of Francis R. Kitchell, who was the brother of Howell W. Kitchell, who married Jane's sister Dorothy Abbott Kitchell,* another sister-in-law,

KITCHELL, DOROTHY ABBOTT. She was Lardner's sister-in-law. Like her sisters Ellis Abbott Lardner* and Jane Abbott Kitchell,* Dorothy attended Smith College. (Source: Lardner, Jr., 32)

KITCHELL, FRANCIS R. He was the husband of Lardner's sister-in-law Jane Abbott Kitchell.* He was the brother of Howell W. Kitchell, the husband of Lardner's sister-in-law Dorothy Abbott Kitchell.* Francis Kitchell evidently worked for a leather company. Lardner's called him "Kitch," and addresses him thus in humorous letters. In one letter (late 1919) Lardner jokingly says "F. R. Kitchell" wears glasses so people won't punch him. (Source: Caruthers [1995], 124, 147)

KITCHELL, HOWELL W. He was the husband of Lardner's sister-in-law Dorothy Abbott Kitchell.* His brother was Francis R. Kitchell, the husband of Lardner's sister-in-law Jane Abbott Kitchell.* In a letter (late 1919) to the Abbott family, Lardner mentions Howell Kitchell's being in the navy during World War I. In a family letter (May 11 [1921]) Lardner's humorously advises Howell that his "Indianapolis brother-in-law's first name" is spelled with "two l's." (See Torrence, Paull.) (Source: Caruthers [1995], 124, 133)

KITCHELL, JANE ABBOTT. She was Lardner's sister-in-law, often called Jeannette. Like her sisters Ellis Abbott Lardner* and Dorothy Abbott Howell,* Jane attended Smith College. She married Francis R. Kitchell.* Like Lardner and his wife, they had "four sons in a row," to quote Ring Lardner Jr. After the fourth son died in infancy, Jane bore yet another son. (Source: Lardner, Jr., 32, 207, 208)

KLABOR, MR. ("A Caddy's Diary"). He is a member of the golf club where the diarist caddies. Mr. Klabor's telling Mr. Thomas about Charley Crane's score means that Mr. Thomas must cheat to tie Crane and split first and second prizes.

KLEIN ("Freedom of the Press"). He is a *Ferret* photographer who was supposed to meet reporter Hunter at the Warner mansion to take a picture of Constance Warner. Hunter tells Constance that Klein, being a typical photographer, got confused and hasn't shown up.

Lardner evidently disliked photographers. Elsewhere in this story he mentions "a dozen photographers with unpronounceable names" outside the mansion.

KLEIN ("Meet Me in St. Louie"). Stengel tells Danny, both members of the Brooklyn baseball team, that the Phillies' short right-field fence confuses "young infielders," who might throw to Klein not Hurst.

Charles Herbert Klein (1904–1958) played for the Philadelphia Phillies (1928–1933), the

Chicago Cubs (1934–1935), the Cubs and the Phillies (1936), the Phillies (1937–1938), the Phillies and the Pittsburgh Pirates (1939), and the Phillies (1940–1944). Klein was elected to the Baseball Hall of Fame (1980). (Source: *Baseball Encyclopedia*, 1228)

KLEM, BILL In "My Roomy," he is the umpire in a game between the narrator's team and the Giants. In "The Busher Abroad," Keefe mentions Klem, along on the world tour. In "Horseshoes," Klem is an umpire when Dick Grimes and Speed Parker are playing for the Cubs in a game against Cincinnati. In "Where Do You Get That Noise?," Hawley jokes that everyone plays favorites, even "Woodruff Wilson" and Bill Klem. In "The Ides of June," Klem argued with Danny, told him to get his night shirt, and rest. Jessie was offended when Danny used the words "night shirt" in writing to her about the incident. Bill Klem is mentioned in *The Young Immigrunts*.

George W. Hilton identifies Klem as William J. Klem (1874–1951), the famous, long-serving National League umpire (1905–1940). James E. Elfers reports that Klem and Jack Sheridan were the two umpires on the world tour, that Klem and John J. McGraw were long-standing enemies earlier and during the tour, that Klem's game voice was memorably loud, and that he was "[t]erminally sullen." (Sources: Elfers, 8–9, Hilton, 357)

KLINE, S. W. ("'In Conference'"). He was a friend of Z. H. Holt, when both lived in Marengo, Illinois. While "in conference," Z. H. vapidly says Kline once received an unsigned postcard.

KLING ("Insomnia"). He is a baseball player the sleepless author remembers.

KLINKE ("Tour No. 2"). He is a German army officer whom Larry encounters in Brussels. Klinke is kind enough to the tourists, but when Larry seemingly insults the German emperor, Klinke and his fellow officers punish Larry by scaring him briefly.

KNABE ("Back to Baltimore"). He manages "the Baltimore Feds" team which Dixon, the narrator, begins his story by saying he is joining.

Franz Otto Knabe (1884–1961) played for the Pittsburgh Pirates (1905), the Philadelphia Phillies (1907–1913), and the Pirates and the Chicago Cubs (1916). He also played for and managed the Baltimore Terrapins (1914–1915). (Sources: *Baseball Encyclopedia*, 698, 1231; Hilton, 423)

KNOLL, PUNCH ("Sick 'Em"). He is a friend of Jack Barnett, who bet Punch $50 that Smitty would fail when traded to the Phillies. When Punch won, the narrator, a Phillies man, made up a $150 purse for Barnett, because Barnett had revealed to the narrator that Smitty could pitch well only when challenged by Fogarty, whom the Phillies therefore acquired.

George W. Hilton reports that Charles Elmer Knoll (1881–1960) played in the minor leagues, then for the Washington Senators (1905), then was a successful minor-league manager (1908–1930). When managing in Evansville, he observed Smitty and Fogarty (fictional pitchers). (Sources: *Baseball Encyclopedia*, 1232; Hilton, 375)

KNOWLES ("Absent-minded Beggar"). He is the deceased father of John Knowles and Charlotte Knowles. Charlotte, when nine, was puzzled when their widowed mother called both father and son "wool gatherers." After all, she thought, the father left them well provided for.

KNOWLES ("Take a Walk"). He is the Pittsburgh catcher in the game played against the team for which Agnew plays third base.

The real Pittsburgh Pirates never had a catcher named Knowles.

KNOWLES, CHARLOTTE ("CHARLEY") ("Absent-minded Beggar"). She is John Knowles's sister, Wallie Blair's girlfriend, and a partying customer of bootlegger Butch Harper.

KNOWLES, JOHN ("JOHNNY") ("Absent-minded Beggar"). He is the brother, three years older, of Charlotte Knowles. He is a bright but abysmally absent-minded poet, and persuades his mother to finance him for four years in Paris so he can write an opera libretto. When he returns home, he is not responsive to his long-time friend Beth Beasley, who loves him; but he lets her get him a job working for her broker father J. L. Beasley and falls in love with Irene Comerford, the daughter of Beasley's partner H N. Comerford.

KNOWLES, MRS. ("Absent-minded Beggar"). She is the widowed mother of John Knowles and Charlotte Knowles. She finances John's boondoggle abroad until the family money runs low and she becomes ill. When John returns home, he needs to get a job to defray her medical expenses.

KRAMER ("Along Came Ruth"). Keefe, frustrated by his wife Florrie's absence one evening, visits Kramer's for "a couple drinks."

George W. Hilton identifies George Kramer's Saloon in Chicago as "one of the principal haunts of White Sox fans" and adds that George Kramer (1868–1957) knew Charles A. Comiskey* well. (Source: Hilton, 269)

KRAMER ("Hurry Kane"). He plays for the White Sox and hits a homer in the crucial game against St. Louis.

KRAMER ("'In Conference'"). Officials and associates work in offices of "Kramer & Company, Efficiency Engineers," in New York. They talk vacantly.

KRAMER ("Three Without, Doubled"). She is a friend of Mrs. Gullible, who developed her ability at bridge by playing with Mrs. Kramer, Mrs. Pearson, and Bertha Hatch.

KRAMER, EDIE ("The Golden Honeymoon"). She is the daughter of Charley and Mother. Edie and her husband John H. Kramer live in Trenton, New Jersey. They suggest that her parents take a vacation in Florida.

KRAMER, JOHN H. ("The Golden Honeymoon"). He is the son-in-law of Charley and Mother. He is in real estate in Trenton, New Jersey. He suggests that the parents try St. Petersburg, Florida, if they didn't like Tampa four winters ago.

KRAMER, LEFTY (*Treat 'Em Rough*). He "pitchs in the Texas League," according to Jack Keefe, who was embarrassed when Lefty called him by name in a Houston hotel in front of Miss Lucy Chase, whom Jack was pusillanimously trying to avoid.

KRAUSE, H. L. (*The Real Dope*). He is or was the head of H. L. Krause and Co., a brokerage house on Wall Street, in New York. Francis Griffin works for the firm.

Lardner undoubtedly chose Krause's initials because of his friendship with H. L. Mencken,* Lardner's steady admirer.

KROM, CHARLEY ("Mr. and Mrs. Fix-It"). He is the manager of the Flamingo, a Miami hotel. Tom Stevens knows Krom and meddlesomely arranges for the narrator and his wife Ada to stay there instead of where they had reservations.

KRUG, MISS ("The Battle of Texas"). She is from St. Louis, drives with her mother down to Mineral Wells to have the old lady's rheumatism treated, and flirts with the baseball players, first with Belden, more seriously with Keefe. She follows the team and is in the stand when Keefe pitches in St. Louis. Keefe's wife Florence is also there; so all may be well in their marriage.

KRUGER, FRED ("Hurry Kane"). He is the manager of the Dallas minor-league baseball team. Hurry Kane was upset when he saw Fred on a date with Kane's Waco girlfriend.

KUHN ("A Busher's Letters Home"). Keefe says he warmed up with Kuhn before Keefe pitched for the White Sox against the St. Louis Browns.

Walter Charles Kuhn (1884–1935) was a Chicago White Sox reserve catcher (1912–1914). (Sources: *Baseball Encyclopedia*, 1242; Hilton, 63)

LACEY, BEN ("What of It?"). He is a talkative bore whom Dexter Cosset encounters on the train to New York. Said to be in his "late twenties or forties," Ben is a dry-goods salesman from Chicago. He rambles about his watch, his sister and her baby Ben, a friend named Fox, the Cragin murder case, the Trunkey elevator company, etc. Ben is squelched when Harrison Quolt replies to each of his speeches with "What of It?"

LACEY, MRS. ("What of It?"). She is Ben Lacey's wife, from Kenosha. Ben talks so much that it's lucky she "lost her hearing."

LA CHANCE (" The Battle of the Century"). He was the French promoter of Goulet, a French boxer. Larry Moon persuaded him by talk of big money to let Larry build enthusiasm for a match between Goulet and Larry's boxer, Jim Dugan. When Dugan won, the share of the million-dollar bout was $200,000 for La Chance and Goulet.

"LADY PERKINS" (as "The Battle of Long Island," November 27, 1920; BT, PRL) *see* ***THE BIG TOWN***

LAHEY ("The Hold-Out"). He was "the first sacker" purchased from Davenport by Mr. Edwards for his baseball team. He proved to be awkward, even though gritty. So Mr. Edwards and Frank Conley, his manager, ultimately signed first baseman Bill Hagedorn, who successfully held out for $6,000, rather than the $4,000 originally offered. Frank, who is the narrator, says he can't trust "the Three Eye Boys."

George W. Hilton explains that the Three-I League was a minor league, Class B, in Midwestern cities in Indiana, Illinois, and Iowa, all west of the Central League and including Davenport.

"The Three Eye" was long active (1901–1951), though with wartime and Great Depression interruptions. (Source: Hilton, 578)

LAHEY, SHORTY (*Treat 'Em Rough*). He is a member of Jack Keefe's army unit. He kids stupid Jack, is demeaned when Jack is promoted to corporal, but bothers Jack when he is promoted above Jack

LAIRD, ALEX ("A Caddy's Diary"). He is the alleged author of weekly golf articles, which Mr. Colby tells the diarist Laird actually pays someone to write for him.

When Lardner gave this man the first name he did, he may have been thinking of championship golfer Alex Smith (1872–1930), who is mentioned in "Mr. Frisbie," another golf story. Smith won the U.S. Open twice (1906, 1910). (Source: Sommers, 320)

LAJOIE In "A Busher's Letters Home," Keefe, White Sox pitcher, says just before the season opener in Cleveland that Lajoie and Jackson may be "great batters but the bigger they are the harder they fall." In "The Busher Comes Back," Callahan, Keefe's coach, ordered him to walk Lajoie. Instead, Keefe got him to line out. In "A New Busher Breaks In," Keefe hopes that both Cobb and Lajoie are in good shape when he pitches against them "because I don't want to pick on no cripples." In "The Busher's Welcome Home," Keefe and some teammates visited the graves of "Lajoies grate granfathers."

Napoleon Lajoie (1875–1959) played for the Philadelphia Phillies (1896–1900), the Philadelphia Athletics (1901), the Athletics and the Cleveland Indians (1902), the Indians (1903–1914), and the Athletics (1915–1916), and managed the Indians (1905–1909). Lajoie was elected to the Baseball Hall of Fame (1937). George W. Hilton reports that the Cleveland team, first called the Spiders, was renamed the Naps in Napoleon Lajoie's honor, because he was "a second baseman so distinguished," but that, "[u]pon his return to the Athletics in 1915, the Cleveland team was renamed 'Indians' following a popular contest." James E. Elfers reports that although Charles A. Comiskey* and John J. McGraw* tried hard to recruit Lajoie to go on their 1913–1914 around-the-world White Sox-Giants tour, "this fish wasn't biting." (Sources: *Baseball Encyclopedia*, 699, 1246; Elfers, 21; Hilton, 58)

LAMBERT, JOHNNIE ("Women"). He played third base for Mike Healy's team, was 35 and injured, and Healy would have replaced him except that Healy's fiancée from Ligonier, Indiana, caused Healy to miss a game and Smitty therefore to replace Lambert.

LAMONT, LEGS ("Greek Tragedy"). He is called a world champion wrestler whom Big Bill Buell may fight next after Greek Alexis lets Buell defeat him.

LAMONT, MISS ("Tour No. 2"). She, Miss Griffith, and Miss Lamont, all from What Cheer, Iowa, and each about 25, are touring with Larry and Minnie Burns. Larry judges them to be pretty but cocky. They see him as unaware of his ignorance.

LANDIS, KENESAW MOUNTAIN (1866–1944). Landis was organized baseball's first commissioner (1920–1944). Born in Millvale, Ohio, and raised in Indiana, he became an excellent baseball player, dropped out of high school, taught himself shorthand, was a county court reporter, attended Cincinnati Y.M.C.A. law classes, and graduated from the Union Law School of Chicago (1891). He advanced in law and politics in Chicago and Washington, D.C. until he was appointed a federal judge in northern Illinois (1905–1920). He was flamboyant in appearance, he made decisions often overturned on appeal. Before and certainly after the 1919 Black Sox Scandal, National and American league personnel recognized the need for a regulatory commissioner. Landis got the job. He banned for life the infamous eight Chicago White Sox players who threw the World Series to the Cincinnati Reds, even though they were acquitted by a Chicago jury (1920). He suspended Babe Ruth* for 40 games following a minor infraction of rules (1922), banned 11 other players for sundry offenses (1920s), tried unsuccessfully to block the St. Louis Cardinals' innovative farm system (1920s), sided with owners in their gaining lush radio contracts (1930s), prevented their hiring African-American players (1930s, 1940s), helped stop legendary Bill Veeck* (1914–1986) from buying the Philadelphia Phillies and improving that club with black players, but also helped prevent terminating and even disrupting major-league baseball during World War II. George W. Hilton calls Landis "despotic."

After Landis's death, owners of organized baseball teams saw to it that no subsequent commissioners had his sort of dictatorial power. (It may be worthwhile to mention that Landis's father named him as he did because the father was a surgeon in the Union Army during the Civil War and lost a leg at the Battle of Kenesaw Mountain, Tennessee [June 27, 1864]). David L. Fleitz writes much about Landis, often unfavorably, not least when he says that defenders of Shoeless Joe Jackson, one of the eight White Sox players banned by Landis in connection with the 1919 scandal, contended that "he was framed by ... Commissioner Landis" and others. Donald Gropman also writes sympathetically about Jackson.

Lardner mentions Landis in "Contract," "Mr. and Mrs. Fix-It," "The Venomous Viper of the Volga," and "Women." In covering the Yankees-Pirates 1927 World Series for the Bell Syndicate (October 5–9), Lardner humorously tells Landis how to tell spectators to treat the underdog Pirates. In "One Hit, One Error, One Left," Casey Stengel tells callow Danny Warner that during a Giants-Yankees world series game "the empires called the game on account of darkness at 3 pm with the sun shinning" and Landis "ast them to exclaim" and was told Stengel hit only doubles so it must have been dark. In a letter (November 5, 1932) to H. L. Mencken,* Lardner mentions "that ole devil H.R.M. Landis of Philly." John Sayles (b. 1950), wrote the screenplay and directed the movie *Eight Men Out* (1988), about the "Black Sox" scandal, and, for good measure, played the part of Lardner in it. Versatile Sayles's first novel was *Pride of the Bimbos* (1975), about baseball players in drag. Lardner would not have been amused. (Sources: Fleitz, 276–277; Gropman, 158–169; Hilton, 24, 304; Caruthers [1995], 265; Yardley, 319)

LANE, JUDGE ("The Golden Honeymoon"). He is from Paterson, New Jersey. Charley and Mother, at a church social in Florida, hear him lecture about business conditions.

Donald Elder quotes a minstrel song Lardner wrote for his singer-actor friend Bert Williams.* One line is "An' de things I seed a wavin' was de plumes on Jedge Lane's hat. Yes, sir." (Source: Elder, 246)

LANGDON, THE REV. MILES ("Widow"). He "read the service and toasted the deceased [John Winslow]" for so long that Gordon and Hastings, "dying for a smoke," would like him to "be muzzled."

LANGFORD, BILL (*The Young Immigrunts*). He is mentioned as an influential referee in Yonkers.

LANGLEY, MR. ("A Caddy's Diary"). He is a golfer for whom the diarist caddies one Sunday afternoon.

LANGUISH, LYDIA ("Words and Music"). She is the "lovely" heroine in *Amourette*, a movie starring Roman Starr as tenor. Hilda Harper finds their love scenes "unbearable" they are so poignant.

LANNIN, PAULINE ("Man Not Overboard"). She was novelist Benjamin Brainard's chorus-line girlfriend. Her heartlessness contributes to his decision to commit suicide. According to Brainard's friend Phil Runyon, she is an unattractive user of others.

Pauline Lannin's name is based on that of Lardner's friend Paul Lannin, vice president of the Red Sox, and then composer, musical director, and would-be collaborator with Lardner (1928) on an abortive musical comedy (to be called *All at Sea*). (Sources: Elder, 226, 227, 265–266, 273–276; Caruthers [1995], 228, 230)

LANSING, A. M. ("'In Conference'"). He, his son A. T. Lansing, and others work for Kramer & Company. While "in conference" they talk vacantly.

LANSING, A. T. ("'In Conference'"). He, his father A. M. Lansing, and others work for Kramer & Company. While "in conference" they talk vacuously. A. T. says to everyone that at night he tells his wife "everything that I've done down here during the day." The office secretary cannot let Harvey Hester, A. T.'s friend from schooldays, interrupt to report that A. T.'s wife is about to elope to Chicago.

LANSING, MRS. ("'In Conference'"). She is A. T. Lansing's wife. Harvey Hester is not permitted to interrupt a conference involving her husband at the Kramer & Company office to tell him that she is eloping.

LARDNER, ANNA *see* **TOBIN, ANNE LARDNER**

LARDNER, DAVID ELLIS (1919–1944). He was Lardner's fourth son. He attended Andover Academy, traveled in England, Ireland, France, and Germany, attended Yale briefly, married Frances Chaney, wrote for *The New Yorker*, served as a war correspondent for that magazine in during World War II (1944), and was killed when his jeep hit unearthed landmines near Aachen, Germany. Lardner delighted in all of his sons, wrote them when they were away, and wrote poems about them. Donald Elder quotes three clever ones concerning David. Ring Lardner Jr. writes affectionately about his younger brother. Two years after David's death, Ring Jr. married David's widow. (Sources: Elder, 221–222; Lardner Jr.)

LARDNER, ELLIS ABBOTT (1887–). She was Lardner's wife, the daughter of Frank Parker Abbott* and Jeannette Hascall Abbott.* Ellis grew up in Goshen, Indiana, had seven siblings, graduated from Smith College (1909), and taught in the elementary school of the Culver Military school in Indiana (1910–1911). She married Lardner (June 28, 1911) in the Abbotts' Goshen home. Ring Lardner Jr. quotes from the Niles *Daily Star* report that wedding gifts included a solid-silver vegetable dish from Guy Harris "Doc" White (1879–1969), who pitched for the Philadelphia Phillies (1901–1902) and for the Chicago White Sox (1903–1913); a 200-piece Haviland set of dishes from the Chicago Cubs; a cut-glass dish from American League president Byron Bancroft Johnson*; and a set of cut-glass tumblers and pitcher from James Joseph Callahan.* Lardner pampered Ellis, by present-day standards. At first, he (and she) insisted on servants to clean and cook. Additionally, their four sons—John Abbott Lardner,* James Phillips Lardner,* Ringgold Wilmer Lardner, Jr.,* and David Ellis Lardner*—had nurses and opportunities for excellent educations, and the family had a long-time chauffeur. Lardner and his wife were uncommonly happy, with adoring family, agreeable in-laws, friends often of varied talents, and travel opportunities. Lardner's death, an early tragedy for Ellis, was followed by two other personal tragedies: James was killed during the Spanish Civil War, then David, in World War II. (Sources: *Baseball Encyclopedia*, 2471; Lardner, Jr., 73, 281, 308)

LARDNER, HENRY (1839–1914). He was Lardner's father. He and his wife Lena Phillips Lardner* had nine children, three dying in childhood. The others were William Lardner,* Henry Lardner, Jr.,* Lena Lardner,* Reginald Lardner,* Anna Lardner,* and Ring Lardner. Henry Lardner Sr. inherited farm land from his father and invested well, mostly in mortgage loans. When a cousin died (1880), he inherited $180,000, became more active in mortgage loans, invested with his son William in a bank in Duluth, Minnesota (c. 1887), and Canadian mining (1895), and was wiped out. Soon after meeting Henry Lardner, Ellis Abbott (soon to marry Lardner) wrote a letter (October 17 [1909]) to her sister Florence (*see* Torrence, Florence Abbott), describing Henry as "an old *dear*." Alarming was Lardner's letter to Ellis (April 8, 1911) reporting that he sent his parents $10 weekly and would do so after their marriage. Henry Lardner was city treasurer of Niles before and after his financial reverses. (Sources: Elder, 12, 25; Lardner, Jr., 10–11, 19; Caruthers [1995], 36, 86; Yardley, 47, 58–59)

LARDNER, HENRY, JR. ("HARRY") He was Lardner's second oldest brother. In a letter (April 8, 1911) to Ellis Abbott, before the two married, Lardner says that "My brother Billy [William Lardner*] helps when he can. Harry has a crowd for a family of his own, so you see it's up to Rex [Reginald Lardner,* another brother] and me" to send money home to their parents. Ring Lardner Jr. notes that "Uncle Billy and Uncle Harry had drinking problems." (Sources: Lardner, Jr., 21; Caruthers [1995], 86)

LARDNER, JAMES PHILLIPS ("JIMMY") (1914–1938). He was Lardner's second son. He attended Phillips Academy and Harvard, was a song writer, was briefly in love with Florence Rice, the daughter of Grantland Rice,* worked for the New York *Herald Tribune* in New York and Paris, joined the Abraham Lincoln Brigade to fight on the Republican side against Francisco Franco's victorious Loyalist army, and was killed in action in the Sierra Pandols region (c. September 21, 1938). Ernest Hemingway tried to talk James out of enlisting, late and uselessly, in the Lincoln Brigade. Donald Elder writes that "Jimmy was always his [Lardner's] particular care and worry. There seemed to be a special understanding between them." Lardner wrote Jim careful and considerate letters, some concerning their mutual interest in football and music. (Sources Elder, 220; Lardner, Jr., 237–239, 267, 280–282; Caruthers [1995], *passim*).

LARDNER, JOHN ABBOTT (1912–1960). He was Lardner's first son. He attended Phillips Academy, worked for its semi-weekly paper, enrolled at Harvard, and studied French in France. When in declining health, Lardner sent John, then in Paris, bravely humorous letters, including one (March 15 [1931]) mentioning the flooded "Old Homme Seine." Returning to the United States, John became a New York *Herald Tribune* reporter and also published in other outlets. He and Thomas Sugrue (1907–1953) co-authored *The Crowning of Technocracy* (1933), a spoof that

Lardner spoofed in a letter to John (March 29, 1933) by wondering about "you and one Sorghum having written a tune or a book called 'The Grooning of Telegraphy?'" John was unhappily married to Hazel Hairston (d. 1962). Ring Lardner Jr. says that "drinking had been a bond between them" until she became addicted. John was a war correspondent during World War II (February 1942–June 1945, often overseas). John and Ring Lardner Jr. unsuccessfully collaborated (1945) on *Up Front*, a film scenario based on Armed Forces *Stars & Stripes* weekly newspaper cartoon strips featuring Willie and Joe by famous World War II illustrator-author William Henry "Bill" Maudlin (1921–2003). (A totally different scenario, also called *Up Front*, was filmed later [1951].) John continued to write for distinguished magazines, including *Newsweek* and *The New Yorker*. He also wrote *Southwest Passage: The Yanks in the Pacific* (1943), *It Beats Working* (1947), *Strong Cigars and Lovely Women* (1951), and *White Hope and Other Tigers* (1951). (See also *The World of John Lardner* [a collection of his essays], edited by Roger Kahn [1961].) (Sources: Garland, 201–202; Langman and Borg, 610; Caruthers [1995], 99, 215, 238, 278; Lardner, Jr., 199, 287, 335)

LARDNER, LENA She was Lardner's sister. Ring Lardner Jr. praises her as an accomplished musician and as a church organist who "later supported herself by giving piano and singing lessons" in her parents' home, which in time she inherited. (Source: Lardner, Jr., 12)

LARDNER, LENA PHILLIPS (1843–1918). She was Lardner's mother, born Lena Bogadus Phillips in Niles, Michigan, a preacher's daughter. She and her husband Henry Lardner* had nine children. Three died in childhood. Living were William Lardner,* Henry Lardner, Jr.,* Lena Lardner,* Reginald Lardner,* Anna Lardner,* and Ring Lardner. Ring Lardner Jr. describes his grandmother as a devout Episcopalian, fun-loving and home-schooling mother, skillful musician, and poet. Her two slim books of verse are *This Spray of Western Pine* (1903) and *Sparks from the Yule-Log* (1904). Donald Elder says that because of having "long-established wealth, gentility, and culture," she "wielded ... benign authority over her family, the church, and Niles society." Jonathan Yardley emphasizes the influence on Lardner of his mother's love of literature and music. Soon after meeting Lena Lardner, Ellis Abbott, later Lardner's wife, in a letter (October 17 [1909]) to her sister Florence (*see* Torrence, Florence Abbott), described Lena as "enormous and queer but very bright & a great talker." John Berryman oddly infers from Donald Elder's biography of Lardner that Lena Lardner's "rather wild, deeply religious personality appears to have been eight feet high." A more measured conclusion is that mother was a favorable influence on son with respect to religion, literature, and music. (Sources: Berryman, 417; Elder, 13; Lardner, Jr., 10–13; Caruthers [1995], 36; Yardley, 51)

LARDNER, REGINALD ("REX") (1881–?). He was Lardner's brother. Ring Lardner Jr. said that Rex and their sister Anna Lardner Tobin* were "the two members of his family that mattered most" to Lardner. Rex, a talented singer and musician, was in the chorus of *Zanzibar*, Lardner's musical comedy, when it was presented in Niles, Michigan (1903). Donald Elder describes Rex as "easygoing, affable, and scholarly; he was less given to worry and responsibility than Ring ... and for all but a few years of his life ... stayed close to him." Earlier than Lardner, Rex became a sports reporter, first for newspapers in Niles and Kalamazoo, Michigan, South Bend, Indiana, and later in Boston. He married Dora McCarley, of Nashville, Tennessee. For years, he and Lardner each sent $10 a week to help their parents after their father Henry Lardner* became almost insolvent (1907). Rex and his wife moved to Great Neck, Long Island, ahead of Lardner and his wife. Rex was an editor of *Liberty* and then of the *Cosmopolitan*. When Rex was released by the former (1925), Lardner promptly began sending his next short stories to the latter. (Sources: Elder, 31, 47, 218–219; Lardner, Jr., 21, 68, 77, 78; Caruthers [1995], 86, 127, 175; Yardley, 62, 118, 230, 287)

LARDNER, RINGGOLD WILMER, JR. (1915–2000). He was Lardner's third son. He attended Princeton University, became a reporter for the New York *Daily Mirror*, then worked on publicity for Hollywood movie-producer David Selznick (1902–1965). Young Lardner got into screenwriting, beginning as an uncredited script doctor. He collaborated on *Woman of the Year* (1942), which script won an Academy Award. He was married to Sylvia Schulman but soon divorced, then married Frances Chaney Lardner, the widow of his brother David Ellis Lardner.* Ring Lardner Jr. was sentenced (1947) to a year in prison for refusing to cooperate with the congressional House Un-American Activities Committee. Blacklisted, he was one of the so-called Hollywood Ten, wrote "underground" in Mexico,

New York, and London, using several pseudonyms, until he was regarded as rehabilitated (1962). He wrote the Oscar-winning script of *M*A*S*H** (1970); wrote two novels, *The Ecstasy of Owen Muir* (1954) and *All for Love* (1985); and, in all, wrote, co-wrote, or adapted at least two dozen movie scripts; one co-authored before his incarceration was the sensational *Forever Amber* (1947). His *The Lardners: My Family Remembered* (1976) is a treasure of information. (Sources: Gerald Horne; Ephraim Katz, 817–18; Lardner Jr.)

LARDNER, WILLIAM ("BILLY") He was Lardner's oldest brother. In a letter (April 8, 1911) to Ellis Abbott, before they married, Lardner explained that he and his brother Reginald Lardner* sent money to their parents and that "Billy helps when he can." Ring Lardner Jr. reports that William, backed by his father Henry Lardner,* invested in an insecure bank in Duluth, Minnesota, that Lardner and William were "never ... close," that Lardner sent William $100 a month until the Depression caused him to reduce the sum to $75, and that "Uncle Billy and Uncle Harry [Henry Lardner Jr.] had drinking problems. " (Sources: Lardner, Jr., 19–20, 21; Caruthers [1995], 86; Yardley, 58–59)

LARDNER ON WAR, edited by Jeff Silverman (Guilford, CT: Lyons Press, 2003). This collection contains *Treat 'Em Rough*, *The Real Dope*, and "Call for Mr. Keefe!"

LARRY ("The Crook"). He is the narrator. He plays first base for the unnamed White Sox. Larry reminisces with Tommy, an umpire, about Bull, another umpire; persuades Bull over some drinks to discuss his troubles; goes to Ban (Johnson) to get Bull reinstated; and through threatening Martin Gregory, a dishonest baseball player, enables Bull to reestablish his engagement to Maggie Gregory, Martin's twin sister.

LARRY ("My Roomy"). He is a Chicago baseball player. He hits fungos that Buster Elliott refuses to try to catch.

George W. Hilton identifies Larry as Laurence Russell Cheney (1886–1969), an ace pitcher who specialized in the spitball and the knuckleball. Cheney played for the Chicago Cubs (1911–1914), the Cubs and the Brooklyn Dodgers (1915), Brooklyn (1916–1918), and Brooklyn and the Boston Braves and the Philadelphia Phillies (1919). (See also Cheney.) (Sources: *Baseball Encyclopedia*, 1889; Hilton, 95, 336)

"THE LAST LAUGH" (*Red Book*, July 1915; OYH) *see* ***OWN YOUR OWN HOME***

"THE LAST NIGHT" (*Red Book*, November 1917). (Characters: Jay Arnold, Ben, Carney, Mrs. Crowell, Walter Crowell, Eddie, Fisher, George.)

Jay Arnold, an alcoholic Chicagoan, has heard, since he's "not stone deaf," that the United States is in a war "Over There"—or will be soon. This June 29 [1917], Arnold, whose "simple tastes" involve "rye and water" morning and night and reading newspaper articles about sports, is disturbed when on the streetcar heading toward a baseball game a fellow passenger tells him that President Wilson will be outlawing liquor to save grain for food for the troops. Arnold counters that drinking is a necessity, while eating is only a habit—else, why do saloons outnumber restaurants? Anxious for the truth, he leaves the game early to visit a "local stop." Eddie, the friendly bartender, provides a shot and agrees that by September all but beer and light wines may be prohibited. Heading downtown, Arnold decides to sample cocktails, since he's never tried any yet. At Carney's, Ben names "a raft of them." Arnold downs nine different ones, in succession, though Ben says chloroform would be quicker. After having some cordials, all new to him, and seeking "music and dancing," Arnold taxis, dozing, to the Red Duck. A waiter he names George suggests something new enough—an absinthe frappée. Arnold talks to a dancing couple, Walter and "Miss Gloom," as Walter calls her. Hearing that Arnold plans to sample "every drink that's made" before President Wilson outlaws liquor, Walter encourages him and says he likes the system of pretending every night is the last for drinking. He names julep and Swiss Ess as fancy drinks for Arnold, lists more drinks, gives him his card, then sends his date home by taxi.

Arnold, feeling awful, is jarred awake by an insistent telephone in a room in the Grand Hotel. It's Walter Crowell. He comes to Arnold's room, says that he put Arnold to bed, apologizes for last night, and adds that the morning paper doesn't mention prohibition. He explains that his "girl" is his wife and she's "forgiven me." Why? Because he has just now vowed to quit drinking, not to grouse about poor vision keeping him from enlisting to go "to France," and to save money for her for when the army will accept soldiers with less than fine eyesight—as it must. Enlightened, Arnold tells Walter to send him a drink—ice water—when he exits.

Arnold visits his doctor, who asks his age — 37 — tells him nothing is wrong with him except for his excessive drinking, and gives him some advice.

Arnold visits Eddie just as "the ticker" is recounting "the third inning." He surprises Eddie by saying "last night" was his last night of bingeing, that his doctor told him he'd be dead in two years unless he quit, that the army recruiters assured him that after boiling in "some springs ... awhile" and exercising they'd accept him in about nine weeks, that some Americans want to join but can't, that some Americans don't admire "a guy that can go and wont." He says the only shot that will get him doesn't need a chaser.

"The Last Night" has a clever title. It does not take place during "the last night" before prohibition, but it is "the last night" for Crowell's and Arnold's boozing. When Lardner has Jay Arnold explain to Eddie that the cost of going sober is simply having "nerve ... enough to carry me through the rye-fields without stopping to pick the fruit," Lardner is challenging himself to muster such nerve. It didn't work for him. "The Last Night," given its date of publication, is properly patriotic, but surprisingly so as well, when one considers Lardner's inherent pacifism.

LATHAM, K. L. ("The Love Nest"). He is a businessman. Lou Gregg meets him and King in Tarrytown to formulate plans for a lavish golf course.

LATTIMER, ROY ("Rhythm"). He is a guest of one of Peggy Leech's Sunday afternoon parties. When drunk, he plays the piano so badly that Harry Hart shoves him aside and takes over.

LAUDERMILK ("The Courtship of T. Dorgan," etc.) *see* **LOWDERMILK**

LAURA, AUNT ("How Are You?"). She is Mrs. Ferrell's aunt in Cleveland. Mrs. Ferrell tells Bob Dayton that Phyllis, whose funeral she just attended, needn't have died if Aunt Laura had taken her advice and sent Phyllis to New York's Dr. Julius. (Laura is probably Phyllis's mother.)

LAVELLE ("Bob's Birthday"). He and his wife belong to the club frequented by Bob Tyler's parents.

LAVELLE, MRS. ("Bob's Birthday"). She and her husband meet at their club with Bob Tyler's mother and father.

LAVENDER, JIM (JIMMY") ("My Roomy"). He is a member of the Chicago team the narrator plays for. Especially close, they play poker with a few others until Buster Elliott intervenes and soon ends the game.

James Sanford Lavender (born James Sanford Lemlein, 1884–1960) played for the Chicago Cubs (1912–1916) and the Philadelphia Phillies (1917). George W. Hilton notes that Vincent Starrett liked the name "James Lavender" so much that he asked for and received Lavender's permission to make "Jimmy Lavender" the name of his detective in several short stories. Starrett (1886–1974) was a Toronto-born Chicago author, bibliographer, and book collector. Ring Lardner Jr. mentions Starrett and himself as among several notable contributing writers for the first issue of *Esquire*, the new magazine coming out of Chicago (fall 1933). (Sources: *Baseball Encyclopedia*, 2150; Hilton, 336; Lardner, Jr., 223, 225)

LAWLOW, FLOSSIE ("Claude Diphthong, Student of Crime"). She was Flossie Campion, known as "Dental Flossie" because of her troubled teeth. She recently married Sir Arthur Lawlow. Flossie is wrongly suspected of murdering Gardner Lyle.

LAWLOW, SIR ARTHUR ("Claude Diphthong, Student of Crime"). He is the head of the towel department of the Pullman Company. He recently married Flossie Campion.

LAWTON ("The Crook"). He was an outfielder playing in a White Sox-Cleveland game. When he muffed a fly ball on a cloudy day and soon ran for sunglasses, Bull, the umpire, kidded him.

LEACH In "The Busher Comes Back," Keefe gripes that when pitching for the White Sox against the Cubs, he threw "Leach flatfooted off of second base ... but the umps wouldn't call it." In "My Roomy," Tommy Leach is one of several Chicago baseball players who refuse to accept Buster Elliott as a roommate. During a game with Cincinnati, Tommy didn't score Buster Elliott, who had hit a triple. In "The Busher's Kid," Keefe boasts that in a "city serious" game he retired "them good hitters Leach and Good and this here Saier." In "Horseshoes," Leach is a Cub outfielder when Dick Grimes joins the team in a utility capacity.

Thomas William Leach (1877–1969) played for the Pittsburgh Pirates (1900–1911), the Pirates and the Chicago Cubs (1912), the Cubs (1912–1914), the Cincinnati Reds (1915), and the Pirates (1918). George W. Hilton notes that Leach was mainly valuable for stealing bases. (Sources: *Baseball Encyclopedia*, 1259; Hilton, 96, 342)

LEACH, CHESTY ("Greek Tragedy"). He is mentioned as one of several supposedly world champion wrestlers.

LEE, BOB (*The Real Dope*). He is one of Jack Keefe's stateroom buddies on the troop ship. Jack finds him "funny," especially when Lee calls him "Jack Tar."

LEECH, PEGGY ("Rhythm"). She is a New York hostess whose Sunday afternoon parties are called "salons and ... a hot bed of culture." Spencer Deal brings Harry Hart to one, which helps to swell Hart's head.

There is no evidence that Lardner was enamored of spoonerisms; but assuming he was, he aptly named Peggy Leech.

LEER, HARRY ("A Caddy's Diary"). He is the caddy master at the golf club where the diarist caddies. Harry spreads the news of Charley Crane's crime and disappearance.

LEFTY ("Women"). He warms the bench with Mike Healy and others, and must listen to Healy's stories about women.

LEGRIED ("Holycaust"). Jessie writes Danny that "Mr. Legried," former resident in Centralia and now the state fire marshal, will determine what caused the Centralia fire and see if "it was larson."

LEIBOLD, HARRY LORAN ("The Battle of Texas," etc.) *see* **LIEBOLD**

LEMP ("Man Not Overboard"). He was Fred Lemp's older brother, according to Fred's fibs to Benjamin Brainard. Fred says he tried to help this brother when he committed murder, but the man was electrocuted anyway.

LEMP ("Man Not Overboard"). He was Fred Lemp's younger brother, according to Fred's fib to Brainard. Fred says he got the fellow out of trouble by paying off his gambling debts following his embezzling from the bank where he worked.

LEMP, EDITH ("Man Not Overboard"). Fred Lemp's fibs to Brainard include the yarn that Edith, his first wife, ran off with another man.

LEMP, FRED ("Man Not Overboard"). He is an upstate hosiery manufacturer, 61 but appearing to be about 55. He is a friend of Phil Runyon, who is novelist Benjamin Brainard's friend. To keep Brainard from contemplating suicide, Phil gets Fred to tell Brainard monstrous fibs about his own family troubles. Brainard then plans to write a novel about Fred's sad life.

LEMP, MARGARET ("Man Not Overboard"). Fred Lemp fibs to Benjamin Brainard that Margaret, his second wife, became insane and had to be committed.

LEMP, MIRIAM ("Man Not Overboard"). Fred Lemp fibs to Benjamin Brainard that Miriam is his daughter, was victimized by a bigamous policeman, has three children, and is a stenographer, and, further, that Fred supports the children.

LEMP, MRS. ("Man Not Overboard"). In Fred Lemp's fabrications to Benjamin Brainard, she is Fred's mother, whom he tried to be keep from sorrow by helping his two criminal brothers.

LENKE ("Harmony"). He is mentioned by Bill Cole as a member of the baseball team Cole plays for.

LESLIE ("Take a Walk"). He bats for New York in the game played against the team for which Agnew plays third base. The count is 3–2. Bleat, the umpire, calls the next pitch a ball, by simply saying, "Take a walk." Agnew rebukes Bleat once too often and gets slugged.

LESLIE, AMY ("'In Conference'"). She is a poet, who, according to L. M. Croft in talk with his associates, "got up this free verse." He says his sister Minnie Wilcox read one of Amy Leslie's poems.

Lardner is undoubtedly alluding to Amy Lowell (1874–1925), Massachusetts-born poet and critic, whose two finest free-verse poems are "Patterns" and "Lilacs" (both 1915). Clifford M. Caruther says that "Lardner deplored equally the works of Lowell and Guest," Edgar A. Guest (1881–1959) being the *Detroit Free Press* syndicated poet specializing in popular saccharine verse gathered in *Heap o' Livin'* (1916), *Just Folks* (1917), etc. (Source: Caruthers [1995], 219)

LESLIE, MR. ("A Chip of the Old Block"). He was a friend of Captain Evan Barnes and fought alongside Evan's father during the Spanish American War. Mr. Leslie sarcastically tells Evan, before he becomes a captain, not to worry about volunteering for wartime duty but "wait until the next draft."

LESTER ("Tour Y-10"). He and his friend Coles vacation to Yellowstone in the group including Violet Emerson and Kate Hayes. Violet becomes friendly with both men, tries to attract Coles, but fails. Lester tells Violet he thought she was more attractive than Kate and could fall for her himself if he weren't married, with children, in Kenosha.

LEVERENZ ("The Busher Abroad"). He is a pitcher aboard the ship taking baseball players on the 1913–1914 around-the-world tour. Keefe says Leverenz pitched in a game for the White Sox and defeated the Giants.

Walter Fred Leverenz (1887–1973) played for the St. Louis Browns (1913–1915). James E. Elfers reports that Chicago-born Leverenz's 1913 record with the Browns was 6–17 and that he therefore felt lucky to be given "the chance to represent his hometown in exotic locales in the States and around the world." (Sources: *Baseball Encyclopedia*, 2160; Elfers, 27)

LEVY ("Some Like Them Cold"). Levy's and Goebel's are New York publishers of songs, according to Chas. F. Lewis. They allegedly like his music.

LEVY, HAZEL In "The Busher Comes Back," Keefe says he met Hazel Carney, this "stropping" 160 pounder, in San Francisco. They became engaged, until she wrote him she was married to Kid Levy and to stay away. In "The Busher's Honeymoon," Keefe stupidly tells his wife Florence Keefe about both Hazel and Violet Hill.

LEVY, KID ("The Busher Comes Back"). Keefe tells Al that his girlfriend Hazel Carney is married to middleweight Kid Levy and warned Keefe that if he bothered them, Levy would "bust my jaw."

LEWIS ("A Day with Conrad Green"). He is Conrad Green's new confidential secretary, replacing deceased Herman Plant. Lewis, just under 30, gets more pay than Plant, is not obsequious, but does cover for Green.

LEWIS, CHAS. F. ("Some Like Them Cold"). He is an opinionated, selfish, would-be song writer who moves from Chicago to New York, can't sell his songs, and plays the piano at a hotel for less money than he feels he's worth. He and Mabelle Gillespie, of Chicago, correspond. She would like to marry him, until he writes of his engagement to Betsy Sears.

Donald Elder praises Lardner for avoiding any display of "scorn or hatred" of Chas and Mabelle, whose "shallowness and ineptitude" are evident; instead, Lardner treats both of them with "compassion." Less unforgiving, Jonathan Yardley says Chas is finally "conniving and contemptible." (Sources: Elder, 213; Yadley, 249)

LEWIS, DUFF In "The Crook," he was playing against Larry's White Sox, when Larry was waved past third by Keefe, only to be thrown out at home by Duff Lewis. In *The Real Dope*, Keefe recalls a lucky hit by Duffy Lewis that won the game Keefe was pitching for the White Sox.

George Edward "Duff" Lewis (1888–1979) played for the Boston Red Sox (1910–1917), the New York Yankees (1919–1920), and the Washington Senators (1921). (Sources: *Baseball Encyclopedia*, 1263; Hilton, 550)

LEWIS, JAKE ("Hurry Kane"). He pitched for the St. Louis team, injured his arm, and "was never no good" thereafter

LEWIS, LUKE ("The Venomous Viper of the Volga"). He is a shady boxing promoter. He and his press agent and associate Sandy King dishonestly groom Henry Goetz into an strong but inept boxer, call him Ivan Ivanovitch, "the Venomous Viper of the Volga," and parley him into a match against Frankie Fitzgerald — except that he and King's girlfriend fall in love and King beats him up.

LEWIS, MR. ("A Caddy's Diary"). He and Mr. Perdue are golfers at the club where the diarist caddies. They often play for money with Jack Andrews, the club pro. Andrews gives them a stroke a hole and still regularly defeats them, but only slightly, so they won't quit playing him.

"LIBERTY HALL" *Cosmopolitan*, March 1928; RLR, RU). (Characters: Buckley, Mrs. Buckley, Craig, Mrs. Craig, Ben Drake, Mrs. Drake, Joe Frazier, Harms, Irene, Marshall, Mrs. Marshall, Miss Miller, Shaw, Hilda Thayer, Ralph Thayer.)

The narrator is the wife of Ben Drake, successful score writer for New York musical comedies. She is alone now in New York, while Ben is in Atlantic City trying out a musical based on Charles Dickens' *David Copperfield*. Ben has grown tired of having his work interrupted by social engagements.

The Drakes used to go out with the Buckleys. When Buckley's business caused them to move to Albany, the Drakes visited them but found the guest room cold, bath water slow, no coffee in the morning, and reporters bothering Ben. Their visit to the Craigs in Stamford was even worse. Ben devised an "emergency exit" strategy. Irene, the secretary of Harms, his publisher, would send him a telegram, prepared by Ben, containing an urgent message for him to return to New York immediately, and signed "Ziegfeld or Gene Buck or Dillingham or George M. Cohan." Ben would act on such a wire, or not, as he chose. This scheme enabled the Drakes to get away from the Marshalls, at Spring Lake. Last September while Ben was conducting his "Step Lively" in Atlantic City, Hilda and Ralph Thayer of Lansdowne, outside Philadelphia, wanted to entertain the Drakes, were refused, persuaded Mrs. Drake to have lunch, and promised that Ben could utterly relax in their home. It would be his veritable "Liberty Hall." Ben succumbed. They arrived, by Thayer limo. Their guest room was perfect. But at breakfast next morning, Ralph queried Ben about his work habits almost like an inquisitive reporter, while Hilda elaborately forced Ben to take his requested black coffee with cream from the Thayers' cows, then recommended a modern book he didn't wish to read, made him discard his Jaquar cigarettes for her Tramps, made him drink rum instead of his preferred gin, wouldn't let him write at her piano a tune he had hummed to his wife and desperately wanted to record before it left him, and even rapped on their room door that night to offer blankets. Next morning, Hilda answered the only phone call and soon hung up. By noon, desperate Ben was inspired. He said that an hour ago he had a grave premonitory warning that he must return pronto to New York. Was it about "business or illness or what"? Hilda, averring she believes in hunches herself, expressed her regrets for not telling him that this very morning she took by phone a telegram that he must return to the theater at once to revise "Nile song, second bar of refrain," signed Gene Buck. His premonition was obviously involved. As Ben was happily rushing to catch the train, Hilda suddenly added that she had wired his office that Drake mustn't be disturbed for a week. Ben repaired to his Lambs' Club for an "interesting bender." The narrator tells Joe Frazier, an editor friend, that she would like to write a short story, and he agrees that her account of Ben's time at the Thayers' place would do fine, because plots are unnecessary; look at Ernest Hemingway's yarns; "it's his style that counts."

Cliford M. Caruthers notes that "the happy marriage [of the Drakes] is one of the few in Lardner's fictional world." Lardner makes "Liberty Hall" a Roaring Twenties document by peppering it with the names of Gene Buck,* librettist, song writer, theatrical producer; George M. Cohan,* actor, playwright, producer; Charles Bancroft Dillingham (1868–1934), theatrical manager, producer; George Gershwin,* composer; Florenz Ziegfeld,* theatrical producer; and his so-so friend Ernest Hemingway. According to Jonathan Yardley, Lardner admired Hemingway's work (apart from its use of obscenities and stress on sex), evidently met Hemingway only once (in 1928), but was meanly criticized by him in the early 1930s. (Sources: Caruthers [1973], 118; Yardley, 182–183)

LIEBOLD In "The Battle of Texas," he is a White Sox outfielder. When Keefe, pitching in a practice game, complains that Shano Collins hit a pitch that was over his head, Kid Gleason says it flew over Liebold's head also. In "The Courtship of T. Dorgan," while Keefe was pitching to Babe Ruth of the Boston Red Sox, "Liebold run back and catched the fly ball." In The Busher Pulls a Mays," Baker of the Yankees drove a pitch from Keefe past Liebold. In *The Real Dope*, Keefe mentions Nemo Liebold.

Harry Loran ("Nemo") Leibold (1892–1977) played for the Cleveland Indians (1913–1914), Cleveland and the Chicago White Sox (1915), the White Sox (1916–1920), the Boston Red Sox (1921–1922), the Red Sox and the Washington Senators (1923–1924), and the Senators (1924–1925). (Sources: *Baseball Encyclopedia*, 1263; Hilton, 246)

LINCKE, MR. ("Words and Music"). He is part of "Lincke Brothers," where Hilda Harper is a stenographer. He gives her permission to be absent from work one morning. She says she's going to the dentist but in reality goes to Roman Starr's apartment.

LINDSAY ("Anniversary"). This is the name of two sisters. Louis Taylor bores his wife Bess by recalling, yet again, how he and Harry Riker long ago visited the sisters one night but neglected to continue their friendship.

LINDSAY, MRS. ("Anniversary"). She was the two Lindsay girls' mother. When Louis Taylor and Harry Riker called on the girls, the mother politely suggested when it was time for the visitors to leave.

LINDSEY ("The Ides of June"). Danny mentions Lindsey as a pitcher in the "relief corpse" of Bill Street, the St. Louis manager.

James Kendrick Lindsey (1898–1963) played for the Cleveland Indians (1922, 1924), the St. Louis Cardinals (1929–1933), the Cincinnati Reds and the Cardinals (1934), and the Brooklyn Dodgers (1937). (Source: *Baseball Encyclopedia*, 2162–2163)

LINDSTROM ("Take a Walk"). He plays outfield well for Pittsburgh in the game in which Agnew plays third base for the opposing team.

Frederick Charles Lindstrom (1905–1981) played for the New York Giants (1924–1932), the Pittsburgh Pirates (1933–1934), the Chicago Cubs (1935), and the Brooklyn Dodgers (1936). He was a member of the Baseball Hall of Fame (1976). (Source: *Baseball Encyclopedia*, 1273)

LIPTON, SIR THOMAS JOHNSTONE (1850–1931). He was a Glasgow-born merchant, yachtsman, and plantation owner in Ceylon, now famous for tea sold under his company name. In "The Busher Abroad," Keefe meets "sir Thomas," doesn't especially care for tea, but thinks of sending some home to Bertha Blanchard.

James E. Elpers describes American-phile, baseball-fanatic Sir Thomas's hospitality to the baseball teams when they visited his main plantation at Colombo, Ceylon (January 22–23, 1914) for a lavish luncheon, tour, photo-op, darkness-shortened baseball game, and much else. A photo of the colorful fellow appears in *The Home Coming*. (Sources: Elpers, 177–181; *Home Coming*, 48)

LISTER, FRED ("The Venomous Viper of the Volga"). He is a waiter whom Willie Troy knows. Troy converts him into Dmitri Sashoff and has him act as Henry Goetz's manager and interpreter. Oddly, Lister drops from the story.

LLOYD ("Old Folks' Christmas"), Lloyd and Henry's is a fur store. Grace Carter bought a sealskin coat there as a Christmas present for her daughter Caroline Carter, who wants to exchange the coat for another one.

LLOYD, HAROLD (1894–1971). He was a popular movie actor. Born in Burchard, Nebraska, he starred in almost 500 comedic roles, first in silents, then talkies. His one-reel comedies (1912) stereotyped him as an inept daredevil, ever optimistic in wild chase scenes. His first feature was *A Sailor-Made Man* (1917). The first time he wore his horn-rimmed glasses was in *Over the Fence* (1917, a baseball movie). Next came *Safety Last* (1923), *Why Worry?* (1923), *The Freshman* (1925), *For Heaven's Sake* (1926), and *The Kid Brother* (1927). Later attempts to revive his career were mediocre. Lloyd received a special Academy Award (1952) as a master comedian.

In "Reunion," Jennie Mason boasts to her sister-in-law Rita Johnston that she and her husband Bob met Harold Lloyd in Los Angeles and gushes that he was handsome without his glasses. Donald Elder reports on Lardner's association with Lloyd. In 1931 Lardner "had an idea for a comedy for Harold Lloyd, but nothing came of it." When Lardner was ill and resting in La Quinta, California (1933), Lloyd visited him; they argued about the idea, causing Lardner to feel that he had wasted a couple of days writing uselessly for Lloyd, who didn't understand the limitations of synopses. (Sources: Elder, 290, 338, 339, 372–373; Spears, 258–59; Yardley, 373)

LLOYD, MARY ("The Yellow Kid"). She was the telegraph operator, beautiful, witty, and decent, in the Detroit hotel where the narrator Bill and his fellow baseball players stayed when playing the Tigers. She was smitten by the good looks of their shy pitcher Lefty Crosby. He was terrified of women but agreed to meet Mary to consider marrying her to avoid the military draft of young men. The two immediately fell in love.

Since Lardner loved the movies, and especially the performances of Mary Pickford* and Harold Lloyd,* it seems likely that he named Mary Lloyd with those two stars in mind. If Lardner were currently writing, he might name his young lady, say, Reese Affleck, Angelina Cruise, Britney Pitt; the short-lived possibilities are numerous.

LOBERT, HONEST ("The Busher Abroad"). Keefe mentions him as a baseball player on the world tour with other players. Keefe renders "Honus," Lobert's nickname, as "Honest."

John Bernard ("Honus") Lobert (1881–1968) played for the Pittsburgh Pirates (1903), the Chicago Cubs (1905), the Cincinnati Reds (1906–1910), the Philadelphia Phillies (1911–1914), and the New York Giants (1915–1917). Later he managed the Phillies (1938, 1942). James E. Elpers reports an unusual event involving Lobert, before the teams left the United States. During the seventh-inning stretch of the baseball game in Oxnard, California (November 11, 1913), Lobert raced a championship cattle horse around the diamond, losing "by half a length in 14 seconds." (Sources: *Baseball Encyclopedia*, 700, 1276; Elpers, 80–81)

LOGAN, MISS ("Widow"). She rents rooms. Alice Winslow will see if Miss Logan has a place for Margaret Winslow, her widowed sister-in-law. Margaret has other plans.

LOMBARDI ("Holycaust"). Danny, playing for Brooklyn, reports that Lombardi was traded from Brooklyn to Cincinnati, along with Babe Herman, whereupon they both hit home runs in a game against Brooklyn. Soon thereafter, Lombardi razzed Danny at bat.

Ernesto Natali Lombardi (1908–1977) played for the Brooklyn Dodgers(1931), the Cincinnati Reds (1932–1941), the Boston Braves (1942), and the New York Giants (1943–1947). Lombardi was elected to the Baseball Hall of Fame (1986). (Source: *Baseball Encyclopedia*, 1279–1280)

LOPEZ In "When the Moon Comes over the Mountain," he is a member of the Brooklyn baseball team, got a double against Boston, and Danny drove him in with a double, and Danny scored the winning run. In "Lose with a Smile," Danny bunts Lopez home in a game against the Giants.

Alfonso Raymond Lopez (1908–1959) played for the Brooklyn Dodgers (1928–1935), the Boston Braves (1936–1939), the Braves and the Pittsburgh Pirates (1940), Pittsburgh (1941–1946), and the Cleveland Indians (1947). He managed Cleveland (1951–1956) and the Chicago White Sox (1957–1969), and was elected to the Baseball Hall of Fame (1977). (Source: *Baseball Encyclopedia*, 700, 1282)

LOPEZ, SENIOR ("The Battle of the Century"). He and "Senior Pancho" were lower Broadway waiters. Larry Moon dressed them expensively and had them pretend to be Cuban fight promoters to inveigle Robert Crawley and Bill Guthrie into offering $500,000 for a boxing event featuring Larry's Jim Dugan and La Chance's Goulet — or lose out to the Cubans.

LORD In "A Busher's Letters Home," Keefe writes often about Lord, a White Sox teammate. Keefe, to show off his speed during batting practice in Paso Robles, nearly beaned Lord. The two discussed how to pitch against Baker, the Philadelphia "Athaletics" slugger. Keefe complains about Lord's inability to field. In "The Busher Comes Back," Keefe gripes that Lord muffed bunts by Boston hitters that he "ought to of eat up."

Harry Donald Lord (1882–1948) played for the Boston Red Sox (1907–1909), the Red Sox and the Chicago White Sox (1910), and the White Sox (1911–1914), and managed the Buffalo team in the Federal League (1915). (Sources: *Baseball Encyclopedia*, 700, 1283–1284; Hilton, 46)

LORIMER, GEORGE HORACE (1867–1937). He was a distinguished editor. Kentucky-born Lorimer studied at Yale (1888–1889), worked in the food industry in Chicago (1889–1896), failed and turned to journalism in Boston (1897–1898), was hired as literary editor of the weekly *Saturday Evening Post* (Philadelphia, 1898–1899), and became its editor (1899–1936). He revolutionized the magazine industry with down-to-earth, conservative articles, and attracted good writers by accepting or rejecting submissions in 72 hours and paying on acceptance, not on publication. Circulation skyrocketed from 2,000 (1898) to one million (1908). During World War I, Lorimer's editorial policy favored neutrality until America entered (1917), after which it reflected patriotic ideals. Until the Big Crash (1929), circulation was nearly three million, then fell during the Great Depression. Lorimer reflected his opposition to the New Deal measures of President Franklin D. Roosevelt, retired (1936), and died within months.

Lardner commenced a fruitful relationship with Lorimer and the *Post* when "The Busher's Letters Home" (*see You Know Me Al*) was rejected by the New York *Tribune* (1914) and he sent it to the *Post*. Lorimer bought it instantly for $250. More Jack Keefe stories netted Lardner $250 increases per segment (1910–1921), until Lorimer was paying $1,250 each, his top figure. When Lorimer unwisely rejected "The Golden Honeymoon" and advised Lardner (April 1922) to stick to sports stories, he stuck neither to such stories nor to the *Post* but turned to the *Cosmopolitan*, which published it (July 1922). Lardner's numerous letters to Lorimer remained courteous, but Lardner published nothing more with him for nine years. (Sources: Elder, 114; Lardner, Jr., 4, 87; Caruthers [1995], 104–105, 144, and *passim*; Yardley, 163)

"LOSE WITH A SMILE" (*Saturday Evening Post*, June 11, 1932; LWS, RAB).

LOSE WITH A SMILE (1933). This is a novel-like collection of six related stories. In each, Danny Warner, a Brooklyn Dodgers rookie, corresponds with his girlfriend Jessie Graham.

"One Hit, One Error, One Left" (*Saturday Evening Post*, April 23, 1932). (Characters: Boone, Max Carey, Clara, Clark, Dave, Clyde Day, Vivian

Duane, Grimes, Babe Herman, Jessie, John, Luque, Mark, Mathews, Lefty Odoul, Jack Quinn, Wm Robinson, Casey Stengel, Joe Stripp, Tommy Thompson, Danny Warner, Jack Warner, Hack Wilson.)

"*Clearwater fla mar 3.*" Danny Warner, on trial as an outfielder for Brooklyn, writes "Dear Jesse" of Centralia, Illinois that his "mgr Carey" has him rooming with coach Casey Stengel, whose nickname Casey "don't make sense" because he comes from Kansas City. Stengel explained two other nicknames: Tommy Thompson is "Al Fresco," since "he was born out doors like restrants"; and "Hack" Wilson was born in a hack and "takes a good cut at the ball." They nicknamed Danny "Rudy," right after they all "beggin to sing" and they asked "me wear did I lern to groon." Danny is "all tarred out" doing "calsthenics."

"Centralia, Ill. March 7." Jesse writes about her poor letter-writing, the cold weather, not holding him to his promise which "was just in fun," how his teammates must like his singing, her poor piano playing, how it's "quite in the store," how "cute" the first baby Clara and Dave just had is, how "Mr. Carey" may not want "men on his nine" to be married when young. "Yours, Jessie."

"*Clearwater fla march 12.*" Dave tells Jesse several players are married and have off-season jobs. He says her "piano plain ... will do till some body better comes a long." Carey sings pretty well and once "studded for the preist hood." Jesse should keep her "old bag packed" but "not breathe a word." Dave skipped going "to the picture" with "the boys" one night, found Carey and Stengel in his room discussing him, and learned they want him to bat "left hand it" as well as "right hand it." Stengel and "Max" Carey discussed switch-hitting. Next day they had Dave practice batting left-handed; so he think he'd get to play in place of "hole out" Babe Herman.

"*Centralia, March 16.*" Jessie read in St. Louis newspapers that "the Brooklyns ... played Cincinnati and Newark" but didn't name any players. She wonders why he would be asked to bat with his left hand, when she can't write left-handed. Dave told her he once saw "a world game in Pittsburgh," and Carey was so good that Walter Johnson would wish "Mr. Carey had stayed in church," whatever that meant. She's lonely, rereads his letters, but "I dont understand most of it."

"*Clearwater fla mar 23.*" Danny is now substituting for "Boone or Odoul"; Herman's being traded to Cincinnati may mean Danny will play center field, especially since Carey improved Danny's right-handed "stanch" and he hit well "again the As and ... the cards." He mentions taking Vivian Duane to the movies. She is the hotel phone operator and is nice despite her "funny drool." She wants him to find her a job "up north." He went with some others to a "caseno" in "Bellair." They "exclaimed" how its "rulette wheel" worked. He bet on red then black, forgot red again, was laughed at, but was "the only 1 that win." His team will play a "pm" baseball game with "a club called the House of David," a Michigan "religious sex" with beards. If Mathews, a "left hander" on Danny's team, pitches, he'll "give some of them outfielders a shave." Last week they visited "Tarpon springs," where "greeks ... fish for sponges." Danny bought two and will have Vivian "rap them up and male them" to Lessie and her mother. He'll "sine" this letter "Rudy."

"*Centralia, Ill., March 27.*" Jessie writes he'll always be Danny to her. He mustn't worry about that promise. Carey mightn't want Danny married so soon after making him Brooklyns' "pinch man." Jessie's mother feels better than she has for years. Jessie's father doesn't need her in the store, says they could "save money on coal" by closing until business improves. Jessie wonders how players' wives travel or maybe live "in some hotel" together. Or have summer Coney Island homes? The sponges haven't arrived. Did "Miss Duane" become jealous and not send them? Just kidding.

"*Clearwater fla march 24.*" Carey is probably assigning Danny to center field, if he learns to bat "left hand it ... again a left hander." He told Carey about his promise "to marry a little kid up home," but Carey told him that would "cause" him his job and "the right kind of a girl" would "release" him and "do" him "a flavor and wait till fall." Danny will let her decide. He doesn't want to go on "wafers" to "the Reds or Phila or St Louis." Stangel said it "would be plain a fine trick" making "your girl" leave her folks and live in "a human zoo like Brooklyn." Stengel said married players make more than Danny's $3,000 but Danny might better live "a lone" in Brooklyn "durn the 80 days" off-season. Danny "will go threw" with his promise if she insists. There is a "$1000.00" contest to rename the Brooklyn "Robins" now that "Wm Robinson" isn't "there mgr." Can Jessie think of a good name? Vivian suggested "Brooks" or "Bridges." Vivian plans to move to Brooklyn. Danny visited "her house for a few minutes last night"; she played the piano "like a street" while he "groon[ed] a few dittys." Maybe Jessie shouldn't leave her sick mother, should help at the store, would be "lone some a lone so much" in Brooklyn; Carey might blame Danny if he got married and then batted badly; Wilson is married but makes "$16500 witch is more then 5 times my salery." Danny will keep his promise, but he "only made it as a kind of a joke." Answer "by return male. Rudy"

"*Centralia, Ill. March 28.*" Jessie asks Danny to forget her yesterday's letter. She took his "crazy promise ... as a joke." She doesn't "consider it a promise for now or next fall or any other time." The sponges arrived. Miss Duane's handwriting is "pretty" and can play the piano in Brooklyn for him to sing. Learn from Mr. Stengel. Dave will tell her about "the Brooklyn nine ... [when] the season opens." Write if you "have a little spare time"; "please dont sign Rudy."

"When the Moon Comes Over the Mountain" (*Saturday Evening Post*, May 7, 1932). (Characters: Brant, Clara Burnett, Dave Burnett, Max Carey, Dave Driscoll, Vivian Duane, Fuchs, Graham, Jessie Graham, Mrs. Graham, Gross, Schofield Gross, Babe Herman, Lopez, Connie Mack, Odoul, Preston, Jack Quinn, Ruffing, Babe Ruth, Sherdel, Stengel, Welsh, Hack Wilson, Glenn Wright.)

"*Gulport Miss march 31.*" Danny writes Jessie about his prowess playing center field against Louisville "in mobile." Carey praised Jessie when "you insist it" on waiting to get married. Danny agreed, because he wanted to "pay all my tension" to baseball. When they were "plain the As in ft Myers," Danny charged into Glenn Wright, short stop and team captain, when both were fielding a fly ball. Wright's "solder" got hurt. "This pm" they'll play Baltimore, and Washington "at biloxi" and "Cleveland in new Orleans." Jessie should write Danny at "Norfolk va," since the club will be heading north. He'd marry her now "if you thot I ment it." Stengel told Danny instead of writing Jessie daily he should send her "jig sore puzzles."

"*Centralia, Ill. April 4.*" Jessie tells Danny not to write daily, not to send puzzles, not to write about marrying, since she'll stay single until her parents die. By then, "no one will want me." She hopes Miss Duane moves to Brooklyn so he can sing while she plays the piano.

"*Norfolk va apr 7.*" Danny will see Babe Ruth when they "open up the regular season with the Boston club." She can write Danny "care of the Brooklyn b b club Ebbets field Brooklyn n y." Stengel told Danny he could room "at the Aquarum in n y," but he'd get "tarred of fish" and might swallow bones. Danny hit well against "the Hartford club ... in macon." Vivian Duane wants a job in Brooklyn and sent him a photo of herself "in a batheing suit," which won't help her in applying for a phone job. Stengel wants Danny to ask Jack Quinn about when "Grant surrend it" here. Danny will "groon" instead.

"*Centralia, Ill. April 11.*" Danny needn't write often. Jessie hopes Danny's doesn't say "H — ... to girls." She's returning Miss Duane's photo to him, adding that she should perform in musicals where "women come out bare."

"*Brooklyn april 11.*" Danny sends Jessie his new Brooklyn "dress" for her to write him. He played the yankees in "2 games." In Brooklyn, the crowd "bood" when "the empire" called him out on strikes. When the air "presser" on the subway to "yankee stadum" hurt his ears, Stengel told him to hang his tongue out "like a dog" for relief. Danny didn't hit against their "left hander name Welsh." Hack Wilson pleased the crowd by swinging hard. Ruth homered twice "durn the series." Danny wishes Jessie were here "to cook my breakfast so I could lay a round the rm." He asks her to send "your picture kid." He's "tarred ... rideing the subway" with his tongue out "like I was a spaniel with the flu."

"*Centralia Ill. April 15.*" Jessie won't send an old picture of herself. Besides, Danny has one of "your friend Miss Duane," who's "prettier than I am or ever was." Jessie still has "a little pride though you may doubt it." Dave Burnett's report that Danny isn't mentioned in the St. Louis newspapers makes Jessie think he's sick. Papa said Danny should stuff cotton in his ears in the subway and not hang his tongue out. Every "umpire" should be "fair and partial." If Danny didn't play "against Boston's star man," it was because he isn't eating properly or resting in "noisy ... Brooklyn."

"*Brooklyn april 15.*" Danny says he "beggin to think" he was forgotten, until in a home game, against Boston, Brooklyn was behind 8–7 in the bottom of the 14th inning, with darkness falling. Carey ordered him to pinch hit for Quinn. Danny drove Lopez home with a double off "the fence in right center" and then scored on a wild throw by Boston's catcher. Everyone congratulated Danny. Stengel thought Danny was running fast because he'd missed a meal and told him to "go and eat some thing" and then write "that little girl in Centralia" about the victory. Danny replied that Jessie didn't understand baseball, and Stengel said then "you [two] ought to get along fine."

"*Centralia, Ill. April 19.*" Jessie is proud of Danny's game-winning "home run." He shouldn't write "H—" in letters to her, and the papers shouldn't call him "Rudy."

The title "When the Moon Comes over the Mountain" makes sense late in the story, when in his April 15th letter Danny explains that Carey as darkness was falling told him "the sun is set and you are back in Bloomington in the moon light league" and Stengel, coaching at third base "yelled come on Rudy your home in a night club" and Danny got that crucial double. The humor throughout "When the Moon Comes over the Mountain" is more forced than in the similarly formatted *You Know Me Al.*

"Lose With a Smile" (*Saturday Evening Post,* June 11, 1932) (Characters: Bancroft, Bergert, Carey, Cohen, Clark, Dazzy, Vivian Duane, Frank Earl, Mrs. Earl, Jim Elliot, Fitzsimmons, Frederick, Hogan, Hoyt, Hubbell, Jessie, Lopez, Maranville, Ott, Rigler, Seibold, Stengel, Terry, Vergez, Walker, Wilson, Glenn Wright.)

"*Brooklyn april 17.*" Danny writes Jessie he's not pinch-hitting in these home games. He had his "1st home cook meal since I left Centralia." It was at the Earls' Brooklyn apartment. Frank Earl, their rookie pitcher from Hartford, may not be kept on the team. His wife "plays the piano way down in the black keys." Danny boasted he could "groon like Rudy Valet," which she doubted. Frank understands Danny's "gag[s]," but she's "dum" and didn't understand Danny's pun about playing in minor keys and minor leagues. After playing "Phila," they'll go to Boston, then "open [with the Giants] ... here"—to a record crowd. Stengel told Danny even "the bench will be sold out."

"*Centralia, Ill. April 20.*" Jessie sympathizes with the Earls, says she couldn't understand his "pun" about "minors," and warns him not to sell his bench seat because he might be needed to play.

"*Boston april 23.*" Danny assures Jessie it's illegal to sell bench seats, says Carey will find Earl a minor-league position, and describes his own success against Boston. When Maranville kidded "Rudy" for running bases in near darkness, Danny commented on old Maranville's poor vision "day or night." Behind in "the 8th innings," Carey had Danny pinch hit. He got a scratch double over Maranville's head, stole third when "there 3d base man" dropped the ball, scored on Frederick's fly ball. Wilson and Wright got ninth-inning winning hits for Brooklyn. Next day Danny made rabbit "squeek[s]" from the bench at Maranville. (Maranville's nickname was "Rabbit.")

"*Centralia, Ill. April 20.*" Jessie says that since she wrote Danny earlier today and addressed the letter to Boston, she's sending this second letter to Brooklyn. She beseeches him not to sell his bench seat. Mr. Carey might want him to pinch and not find him.

"*Brooklyn april 23.*" Danny got both letters and says he'll get mad if she keeps "worring" he'll do something wrong. He's hoping to bat against some good Giant pitchers. The boys enjoyed hearing him "groon," but he got tired of the same songs. So Carey and Stengel suggested he write new words for an old tune, for example, for "life is just a bold of cherrys" make it "life is just a game of base ball." In his "rm" Danny wrote some words and "groon[ed]" to make them "fit." Stengel said he should add some verse to the chorus. Danny finished "the hole song," read the verse to the boys, and "grooned" the chorus. They all "went wild" and "want it a copy." Carey warned him to have a publisher get it copyrighted, to avoid theft by "some of the boys." Danny never "thot of writeing them [songs] only groon them." He'll copy "the hole song," verse and chorus," for Jessie. It advises people not to take life "so serious," because it's only "a game to play," "a game of base ball / so win or lose with a smile." Frank's wife rehearsed the song with him, said "a couple spots" weren't even, but Frank said publishers will fix them. Danny hopes for money "writeing songs," and Jessie knows "what that means."

"*Brooklyn april 27.*" Danny says he hasn't "the heart" to show his song to anyone in New York because of what happened in yesterday's home game against the Giants. Top of the 9th, 3–3; Ott homered off Hoyt; 4–3; bottom of the 9th, Lopez tripled; Carey ordered Danny to "bunt tords 3d base"; he did, Lopez scored. Danny was picked off first, argued with Rigler the "empire," called him a "big blind owl," got tossed. After Brooklyn lost 5–4 in the 11th, Danny was "groon a song" in the locker room when Carey came in, "says I dont know" whether Danny will remain with the team.

"*Centralia, Ill. April 28.*" Jessie writes Danny that Dave warns him not to steal "words or music" from anyone and thinks Bud Henderson and Brown wrote "Life Is Just a Bowl of Cherries." Jessie is glad Danny smiles at umpires "instead of getting mad."

In "Lose with a Smile," Danny Warner writes about taking a loss with a smile but doesn't; thus far, Jessie appears to be doing the losing with an occasional smile. Composer Ray Henderson (1986–1970) and lyricist Lew Brown (1893–1958) wrote "Life Is Just a Bowl of Cherries," which was a hit song in *George White's Scandals of 1931*, as was "This Is the Missus," which was sung by Rudy Vallée.*

"Meet Me in St. Louie" (*Saturday Evening Post*, July 2, 1932). (Characters: Mr. Abrams, Clara Burnett, Dave Burnett, Max Carey, Clark, Dizzy Dean, Edna, Mrs. Ferguson, Dr. Fred, Frederick, Gilbert, Graham, Ernie Graham, Mr. Graham, Haines, Hallahan, Hurst, Jessie, Joey, Kelin, Mr. Phillips, Rhem, Schwartz, Henry Splug, Stengel, Terry, Dazzy Vance, Walker, Warner, Danny Warner, Wilson.)

"*Phila april 28.*" Danny says he "ast mgr Carey" to trade him. Carey suggested sending him to Harry Splug, manager of the Alton team, a branch of the St. Louis team. Stengel advised Danny to stay with Carey, not "break his morals" by leaving. After playing in Chicago they'll go to St. Louis for games "the 9 10 and 11 of may." He invites Jessie, at his expense, to take the "5.26 am" train from Centralia for the 65 miles to St. Louis, arriving "7.30." She can watch batting practice, see the game, meet Stengel and Carey, have dinner with Danny, "maybe go to a picture," and leave St. Louis by "11 pm at night" for home. Best would be "Tuesday the 10 [May, 1932]." He'll send this letter "by air male"; she must reply the same way.

"*Centralia, Ill. April 30.*" Jessie, grateful for Danny's invitation, says "it is out of the question" [five times]. Her mother remembered at age 18 going to the St. Louis Fair with her parents and being accosted with a "Hello Jenny" by a stranger. Jessie's father suggested having her married friend Clara Burnett accompany her and offered to babysit the Burnett baby since Dave is "on the road all that week." To the objection that the baby isn't weaned, Papa offered to "cook him a wiener." Jessie says Danny was kind not to spike "Mr. Terry" and says players should wear tennis shoes. If Danny get spiked, Jessie recommends iodine for infections; she remembers that when Ernie cut his hand punching the screen door Dr. Fred used iodine. Jessie will give Mr. Phillips Danny's air mail stamp, for Joey.

"*Brooklyn may 3.*" Danny figured Jessie's "mother would put down her ft," expresses disappointment—"I was looking ford to seen you"—said no one would "make a mash on you," but he can't "get no wear argueing." After Brooklyn played the Giants in New York, Danny and Stengel went to Irving Berlin's office. Stengel asked for the manager. Mr. Abrams, "the mgr," agreed to hear Danny read his "Life is just a game of base ball," told Danny he can't use "the tune of Life is just a bold of Cherrys" because "[Ray] Henderson and [Lew] Brown" own it, and even objected that nobody "would be interest it in a base ball song." Stengel pleased Abrams by giving him a "sined" pass for his family to see Babe Ruth play next Sunday, plus a pass for Abrams' daughter, "a Giant fan," for a Friday game. Danny tells Jessie the first pass "aint ... good" and Fridays are free anyway for women at "the [Giants] polo grounds." Abrams suggested that Danny write "a ballot like My Mom." Leaving, Stengel said Danny should write "lyrics ... about your Pop" to the tune of "My Mom." Danny said his Dad died in Danville, but he'd try.

"*Centralia, Ill. May 6.*" Jessie writes that her father will close the store, Mrs. Ferguson will stay with Jessie's mother, and Jessie and her father will visit St. Louis at their expense. Jessie doesn't want to meet Mr. Carey or Mr. Stengel, because her clothes are shabby. She hopes she and her father can see Danny at least be "a pinch man" and hit one of his "home run steals." She likes the idea of "the 'Dad' song" but figures Mr. Abrams will be upset by Mr. Stengel's joke about those passes.

"*Chi may 8.*" Happy Danny will pay for everything because "I can ford it better then you," and explains that he promised Frank Earl's wife's "kid sister," who lives in St. Louis, to take her to lunch on the 10th, and that the two sisters, Jessie, and he can lunch together before the game. Danny hopes to play "the hole game" if they pitch "left hand it fire ball" Hallahan, and he says he'd like to hit against Dizzy Dean or Rhem. Stengel helped him with his "Dad song chorus," which he quotes completely and which ends "... my old pater. / He is my alma mater my pop." Stengel told him that "mater and pater are greek" with the same meaning. Stengel also told him about using numbers on players' backs in a scheme to win games.

"*Centralia, Ill. May 10.*" Jessie says she wired her refusal to come to St. Louis yesterday. They couldn't leave her sick mother; her father planned to go only for her sake; the trip would tire them both. Danny should agree that not coming is "wise."

"Holycaust" (*Saturday Evening Post*, July 30, 1932). (Characters: Chief Archbold, Bancroft, Jack Barry, Clara Burnett, Dave Burnett, Byrd, Al Capone, Carey, Clark, Cornell, George Cunningham, Douthit, Vivian Duane, Frank Earl, Edmiston, Miss Fleming, Glore, Graham, Jessie Graham, Mrs. Graham, Hausler, Dave Hecht, Babe Herman, Hogan, Kelly, Legried, Lombardi,

McGraw, E. B. Marshall, Nichols, Lefty Odoul, Pearson, Jack Quinn, Rixey, Silvers, Marion Sligar, Stengel, Stoneham, Fresco Thompson, Danny Warner, Watson, Hack Wilson, Glenn Wright.)

"*Cincinnati may 12.*" Danny is surprised Jessie "would throw me down," by not visiting him. Just planning for it cost him money. Also he got sick. He showed Jessie's telegram to Stengel, who said Danny was "a worst sap then you look even" for mistreating Jessie — Danny's "real girl." Danny wonders if Jessie was "jellus." Miss Fleming, Frank Earl's "sister and law," broke that lunch date to have a "scream test" with a "movie Co," was too excited to eat supper; so he took her to a joint called "the Nest." They "stang" him. He "eat some schrimps," bought a "qt" of gin, was called "Rudy" and was asked to "groon," rendered "2 encorps," had to tip the orchestra and too many others. When he wouldn't escort Miss Fleming away by taxi, she called him "cheep" — after "she cause me $42.00." He sneaked into the hotel "pretty near 3." Stengel promised not to tell Carey. Today, luckily, was a rain-out. The club returned Frank Earl to Hartford. Danny would have saved $42 if Earl hadn't joined the Brooklyn team and if Jessie had come to St. Louis as she promised.

"*Pittsburg may 16.*" Why hasn't Jessie replied? Is she "sore" about his "makeing that date" with "that crazy flabber"? Danny boasts about helping win a game in Cincinnati. Jessie "proudly dont remember" Brooklyn traded Babe Herman and Lombardi to Cincinnati. One day against Brooklyn both hit well and put Cincinnati ahead 3–2. In the 9th, their pitcher Rixey walked Brooklyn's Kelly; Danny pinch hit; he got a winning inside-the-park homer. Earl, writing from Hartford, said he was limiting opponents to "triples and doubles," and thus "trys to make a joke of it." Regards to "Dave and Clara and there baby" and Jessie's parents. And write.

"*Centralia, Ill. May 18.*" Jessie answers. She's not jealous; she's "not your 'real girl' or anybody else"; he can take any girl he wants "to entertain at speak easy music halls." He shouldn't disobey Mr. Carey or drink "boot legged gin." Her parents are "well as usual." Clara was sick, is better. There was an explosion in Silvers's Furniture that could be heard in Tamaroa; the resulting fire spread. It was a "holycaust," destroyed many stores, and will result in "a sweeping investigation." Jessie would like to remain Danny's friend, if that's what he wants; but he needn't believe she can feel the same toward him or quite believe him.

"*Brooklyn may 21.*" Danny tells Jessie to consider him the same as he always was and to write only if she wants to. He discussed that Centralia "holycaust" with the boys. Lefty Odoul said back home they had an annual fire and "roast it a hole ox." Glenn Wright thought such a fire was "a feast ... after easter." Stengel said a fire destroying all of Centralia "couldent be a thousand dollars damages." Danny says league rules denied players the right to talk with fans, because "1 of the boys" chatted with Al Capone. Recently "the govt rest it Sigar face" when he didn't pay "his hole income." He's "jail[ed] in Atlanta," which has a poor baseball team. Danny's league dropped the no-talk rule; the American league didn't. Danny discusses strategy for playing "an other series with the Giants." He praises Hack Wilson, booed "in Chi" partly because "the news paper boys is rideing him." Danny asks Jessie whether she wants him to "write like you was a stranger of mine," not write, or write the truth "like I always done." He hopes she "dont dissapoint me again."

"*Cantralia, Ills. May 24.*" Jessie replies apologetically. Not feeling well was "realy ... no excuse." He should write truthfully. He writes nicely and sees interesting things; her only excitement was the fire. The state fire marshal is conducting "a sweeping investigation." The cause was not "larson" but "a natural explosion or something." Jessie hopes Danny won't waste money and won't endanger his health "drinking ... poison like St. Louis."

"*Brooklyn may 27.*" Danny can't write a long letter, because that girl, Vivian Duane, has followed him, wired him, and is "stain at the St Geo hotel here," right "wear Stengel is stain." Danny visited her, and Stengel saw her in the lobby. She told them it's "to hot to stay in fla." Stengel told her he'd make it hot for her here and asked Danny to recall their discussion in St. Louis. Vivian cried. Danny "can't stand seen no woman crying specialy in a lobby"; so he's taking her to see some midnight spots "in n y." Danny mentions recent games against the Giants and is happy Jessie called him "dear" twice in that last letter.

"*Centralia, Ill. May 29.*" Jessie writes Danny to tear up her last letter; she didn't mean "dear" and tells him to write him only to say he's "tore up my letter." If he writes more letters, she'll destroy them "unopened before I read them. Jessie Graham."

The word "holocaust" is no longer to be toyed with. But Lardner's innocent title has simple humorous overtones and a touch of symbolism.

Danny's buddies joke about it, crudely; and the huge Centralia fire equates with the tiny emotional fires Danny's letters kindle in Jessie. The action of "Holycaust" has 1930s touches: Danny mentions Al Capone's arrest (1931), and Danny expresses happiness that the 4-piece speakeasy orchestra he had to tip wasn't "Susans band," i.e., that of John Philip Sousa, American composer-bandmaster (1854–1932), whose death (March 6) occurred four months before "Holycaust" was published.

"The Ides of June" (*Saturday Evening Post*, September 5, 1932). (Characters: Bancroft, Clara Burnett, Dave Burnett, Caldwell, Max Carey, Clark, Vivian Duane, Jumbo Elliot, Johnny Frederick, Graham, Jessie Graham, Bill Hallahan, Babe Herman, Klem, Lindsey, McGraw, Mungo, Fritz Nymeyer, Grace Nymeyer, Geo Olsen, Mrs. Olsen, Picinich, Richards, Stengel, Bill Street, Tommy Thompson, Danny Warner, Watkins, Whitney, Glenn Wright.)

"*Brooklyn june 2.*" Danny writes Jessie he wished she "hadent wrote" that last letter. He liked the earlier one where she called him "dear twict." He replied nicely, and she "jump all over" him and "sine your last name" as though they weren't friends for "21 yrs." That Centralia fire gave her fever, or she's "sore" about Vivian Duane. He took Vivian to a spot where "Geo Olsens band are the drawn cart." Vivian thought Olsen smiled at her, but a waiter said his perpetual smile was "pluging some toothe pest" and his wife sings with the band as "Ethel Schulte." Danny took Vivian to another place, brought along "a pt of real absent" he bought for $6 from a "ball pk" usher, drank some. She did too and "felt a sleep." Back at her "St Geo" hotel Stengel waited to criticize Danny. Danny would gladly pay Vivian's return to Florida to be rid of her but is almost broke. He asks Jessie to write "dear" again.

"*Brooklyn june 5.*" Danny says not hearing from Jessie makes him "scarred may be your sick." Vivian couldn't pay her hotel rent; so she had them hire her "as phone girl." Stengel made them "fix her hrs" days "10 to 2" and nights "6 to 10." Thus she rarely sees Danny. He describes part of Brooklyn's double header with Boston. He pinch hit for Clark; Jumbo Elliot walked him; Danny mistook Johnny Frederick's fly for a hit, spiked Picinich at "2d base," and was out. Carey and Stengel said they yelled instructions to Danny, who pleaded crowd noise. Danny would've played better "only I been so worred about you." He isn't bothered Brooklyn must reduce the roster to 23 men: The Giants would grab him, since McGraw isn't managing them and Bill Terry is and likes Danny. Sadly, Tommy Thompson, a good kidder, may be cut. Write. And "notus I call you dear."

"*Centralia, Ill. June 8.*" Jessie writes Danny isn't "quite fair." She'd "imajine" he misses her letters only because "Miss Duane" isn't around for him. He bothers his "old friends" by risking trouble. He should do his "duty to Mr. Carey and the Brooklyn nine." Jessie is feeling Danny is a stranger. He goes into debt buying "expensive poison" to drink with new friends. He shouldn't write "dear" in a mostly discourteous letter.

"*Brooklyn june 12.*" Danny apologizes, then boasts about his success in yesterday's St. Louis game. In the 8th they led by a run; their fire-baller Hallahan walked two; "Carey yelled Rudy"; Danny pinch hit for Mungo, homered on Hallahan's high-outside pitch; Brooklyn won 5–3 because they didn't score against Jack Quinn in their 9th. The boys wrote a poem, "For Rudy to Croon to His Favorite Tune," and left it in Danny's locker. It said it'll be "a pity" when he's "sent to Jersey City," because "Weel miss your croon." Danny notes they misspelled "groon." He's seen Vivian once, to say he can't see her again because Carey "put his ft down." Jessie, "dear," can write him nicely now.

"*Centralia, Ill. June 14.*" Jessie writes "Dear Danny" sounds like her old friend again. Mr. Carey should have the umpire Mr. Klem replaced if he uses improper language. Jessie heard bad talk by Dave and Fritz at Fritz and Grace Nymeyer's home, when she watched the three and Clara play whist. Jessie hopes that Miss Duane can receive money from home and return home, and that Danny will obey Mr. Carey, since Mr. Stengel "cant protect you forever."

"*Brooklyn june 15.*" Danny writes that yesterday Carey told him he was being sent to Jersey City, where a good manager will have him play daily and "lern things you cant lern only by plain every day regular." Danny objected. Carey said this: Danny couldn't play daily for Brooklyn in place of regulars; he made "to many mistakes"; his "mind was logey the last couple wks"; if better, he could be recalled next year; this is Danny's "chance." Danny didn't even "stay and watch the dam game" but got to his "rm and lade down ... and cride." Tonight Stengel arrived to report these developments: Carey sent Caldwell to Hartford; Carey can send Richards to Jersey City, sell Danny outright; maybe "the red sox" will like Danny; the Giants can't use him. When Danny said he's quitting baseball, Stengel told him to go with "that southren eye sore [Vivian] over to n y," spend his last cash "bat[ting] a round," and forget Jersey City, already full of "bums." Stengel tried to get Danny to wire "that little girl in Centralia" to come to Jersey City and marry her, because the Jersey City team likes young married players. Danny writes Jessie that she wouldn't want a failed ball player. He saw Vivian, who read about his release, agreed he'd be foolish to go to the minors, and wanted him to try for a grooning career. Danny tells "dear" Jessie his friends have failed him, he may or may not see her "in 10 days," he's sorry he can't offer her "nothing only my love."

"*Centralia, Ill. June 15.*" Jessie read in today's paper that Danny is going to Jersey City. He'll like playing every day. Jessie's father was paid an old debt, has money, and asked if she'd like a trip. Yes. He has a step-brother in Jersey City, visited him once, found the city interesting, and is letting her go there. She'll be at Penn Station, New York, 9:40, Saturday morning [June 18, 1932]. It's "leap year." She'll be "scared to death" if he doesn't meet her at the station. So "dont fail me dear. Yours, Jessie."

The ending of "The Ides of June" resembles that of "The Lady or the Tiger?" (1882) by Frank Stockton (1834–1902). However, the dice are loaded against Jessie, given Danny's nature and the fact that the Ides of March bode evil. To make "The Ides of June" timely, Lardner mentions Mrs. Hoover and Al Smith.* Mrs. Hoover's husband Herbert Hoover (1874–1964) campaigned successfully against Al Smith (1973–1944) to become president of the United States (1929–1933).

Jonathan Yardley reports that *Saturday Evening Post* editors wooed Lardner, when he was dangerously ill, to write more stories for $4,000 each. Though hospitalized, he wrote the above six, with what Yardley calls "unapologetic professionalism." When collected as *Lose with a Smile*, they disappointed most critics. H. L. Mencken* calls Danny Warner "a mephitic shape" and adds that "his girl is hardly better." Mencken continues: "They are far too elemental to come within the orbit of Freudism.... Lardner takes them as they are, and lets them tell their own story. It is vastly amusing, but there is a great deal more to it than a series of laughs." Ring Lardner Jr. seems prejudiced when he says that "[r]eaders ... reacted quite favorably to it." Gilbert Seldes objectively comments that "[i]n 1932, when Lardner reverted to his first theme [baseball stories], his heart was not engaged. He was no longer amused, and the book may be funny, but it is not amusing. It is melancholy." Walton R. Patrick says that it "is the work of a writer whose creative energies are fading, and the cheerful nostalgia of the autobiographical sketches is absent from its pages: rather its tone is that of hopelessness and despair." Elizabeth Evans dismisses it as "thin and disappointing," unable to "stand up under close analysis." Robert J. Higgs says that its faults are owing to Lardner's "allow[ing] sentiment to replace irony" in portraying Danny Warner, who is "the hero in search of the American dream [but who] is ... 'plumb pitiful.'" To George W. Hilton it as "a wan portrayal of an habitual loser, with none of Keefe's brash qualities." (Sources: Evans, 16, 38; Higgs, 28; Hilton, 23; Lardner, Jr., 218; Mencken [1933], 255; Patrick, 56; Seldes, 5; Yardley, 359, 362)

LOTTIE ("Rhythm"). She must be the title figure in a musical. Harry Hart tells Sam Rose that Benny Kane's lyrics for Hart's "two rhythm numbers" in "Lottie" were poor.

"THE LOVE NEST" (*Cosmopolitan*, August 1925; LN, PRL, RLR, RU). (Characters: Bartlett, Marie Blythe, Dennis, Ralph Doane, Forbes, Gregg, Celia Gregg, Grace Gregg, Lou Gregg, Norma Gregg, Harold Hodgson, Hortense, King, K. L. Latham, Morris.)

Bartlett writes for *Mankind*, a magazine edited by Ralph Doane, who knows Lou Gregg, president of Modern Pictures, Inc., in New York. Through Doane, Bartlett gets the chance to visit Gregg overnight, to interview and write about him. While Gregg and Bartlett "glided northward" in Gregg's Rolls to Gregg's mansion, located at Ardsley-on-Hudson, Gregg explains about his wife. He met Celia Sayles, starlet at 17, married her when she was 20, rescued her from movies; seven years later, she is ensconced in their "love nest" with three daughters. He wouldn't want sons.

The mansion resembles the Yale Bowl. Forbes, a servant, takes Bartlett's "things." The happy couple loft "sweetheart" at each other. Celia, "a striking brunette" with unneeded touches of makeup, floats in, meets Bartlett, and self-effacingly says not she but her "great" husband is Bartlett's interest. Remarking that he's from Chicago, Gregg has Forbes bring Bourbon, not scotch. Celia declines any. Gregg wonders why his fresh bottle is half empty. She blames the servants. When Gregg says Bartlett will be remaining overnight, Celia reminds "sweetheart" he's scheduled to meet K. L. Latham and King in Tarrytown tonight to formulate plans for their lavish new golf club. Gregg has Celia bring down Norma, 6, and Grace, 4, two of their three "kiddies." The third, 1½, is already abed. Bartlett asks each girl her age, responds "Well" each time, and up they go with Gregg, who must change his shirt and collar. Instead of showing Bartlett around, Celia chances a "sip" of Bourbon, a gulps two-thirds of a glass. Barlett freshens while Celia dresses in black lace for dinner, after which Gregg rushes off.

Celia can't let Bartlett drink alone, and doesn't. She turns the radio on briefly, dances alone with "unlabored grace," drinks more to "catch up," and wonders why she's high and he's sober. Because she isn't used to drink, he offers. Calling this comment "the cat's pajamas," she gushes gripes. She's drunk half the time. Wishes she'd never see Gregg again. Gregg loves only himself. She could've been a [Gloria] Swanson[*]. Instead, she's "a chronic mother." He wouldn't allow a divorce, and she's "got nothing on him." Potential lovers fear his moneyed power. Their "love nest" is "a baby ranch." Bartlett says she should get to bed and asleep quickly. She says she thought of it first and often pleads strategic headaches, then retires.

Gregg returns. Bartlett apologizes for sampling the Bourbon extensively, says Celia had a headache. Gregg says Celia reads so much she gets these headaches, and asks if Gregg has enough material for his article. Yes, "plenty." In the morning, Celia sleeps late but, unseen, shouts her apologies to Bartlett and a goodbye to "sweetheart."

Clifford M. Caruthers notes that "'The Love Nest'" was ... based on the Buck household," and that Gene Buck,* a song-writer for Florenz Ziegfeld,* was Lardner's neighbor at Great Neck, Long Island. In a letter (August 8, 1925) to F. Scott Fitzgerald,* Lardner reports that "Gene didn't make any comment on 'The Love Nest,' but evidently had no suspicion." Jonathan Yardley provides details: Lardner patterned the Greggs—"with matching His and Her tiny brains and elephantine egos"—after Buck and his wife Helen, and further that, when the Bucks read "The Love Nest," they evidently remained ignorant of the parallels. Is it true, as Donald Douglas contends, that when, "in 'The Love Nest,' you get used to the twisted grammar and the fun you stop laughing"? John Berryman dislikes "The Love Nest," and wonders "what can we say about this story except that it is undeveloped and manages to be both trite and implausible?" Douglas Robinson adds little when calling it an "overdone melodrama." The distinguished playwright Robert E. Sherwood (1986–1955) adapted "The Love Nest" into an unsuccessful three-act play (1927), which Samuel L. Leiter calls a "theatrical dud," in which Caruthers explains "the dipsomaniac Mrs. Gregg leaves her overly possessive husband by eloping with the butler." Incidentally, Lardner puts in a plug for "The Love Nest" when in his later story, "Poodle," he has the maritally frustrated narrator call his empty home "The Love Nest." (Sources: Berryman, 420; Caruthers [1973], 35, 47, 110; Caruthers [1995], 148, 181, 213; Douglas, 584; Leiter, I, 531; Robinson, 3; Yardley, 291, 322)

THE LOVE NEST AND OTHER STORIES (1926). Nine stories "by Ring Lardner with an Introduction by Sarah E. Spooldripper."

THE LOVE NEST AND OTHER STORIES (1928). Twenty-five stories "by Ring Lardner with an Introduction by Sarah E. Spooldripper" (British edition).

LOWDERMILK In "The Courtship of T. Dorgan," Keefe says "big Lowdermilk" pitched ineffectively on May 26th for the White Sox when Jim Shaw was pitching poorly for Washington. Gleason inserted Keefe as relief pitcher in the eighth inning, and he won against Walter Johnson, in relief for Washington. In *The Real Dope*, Keefe, soldiering in France, remembers a game "big Laudermilk" pitched and won against Keefe's White Sox. In "The Busher Pulls a Mays," Keefe gripes that White Sox pitchers "Kerr and Faber and Lowdermilk" are so ineffective that opposing batters easily get hits.

Grover Cleveland Lowdermilk (1885–1968) played for the St. Louis Cardinals (1909, 1911), the Chicago Cubs (1912), the St. Louis Browns and the Detroit Tigers (1915), the Tigers and the Cleveland Indians (1916), the Browns (1917–1918), the Browns and the Chicago White Sox (1919), and the White Sox (1920). George W. Hilton notes that Lowdermilk was "a journeyman righthander" the White Sox bought from the Browns (May 17, 1919) because the White Sox could not continue to rely exclusively on Cicotte and Williams. (Sources: *Baseball Encyclopedia*, 2170; Hilton, 282)

LUDERUS In "Sick 'Em," the narrator says that Luderus, Cravath, and Magee are good hitters for the Phillies. In "Back to Baltimore," Luderus was playing first base when William Baker, Jr., inexpertly playing for the Boston Braves, was hit by a pitch, went to first, and was out trying to steal second — because Luderus told him to run.

Frederick William Luderus (1885–1961) played for the Chicago Cubs (1909), the Cubs and the Philadelphia Phillies (1910), and the Phillies (1911–1920). (Sources; *Baseball Encyclopedia*, 1286–1287; Hilton, 369)

LUNDGREN ("'In Conference'"). L. M. Croft asks Z. H. Holt if he knew any Lungrens in Marengo, Illinois. "Yes, indeed, L. M.," Z. H. answers.

LUQUE ("One Hit, One Error, One Left"). Danny says that "Mathews Mark and Luque and John" are "4 pitchers" of the House of David.

LYLE, GARDNER ("Claude Diphthong, Student of Crime"). He is a handsome, talented New York banker, the ex-husband of Margalo Trawley, and the victim in a murder investigation in Hotel Baldwin.

LYNN ("Along Came Ruth"). Keefe explains that he was warming up with Lynn before pitching for the White Sox against Boston when he saw his wife Florrie sitting in the stand with a strange man. Thereafter Keefe blew the game.

Byrd Lynn (1889–1940) played for the White Sox (1916–1920). George W. Hilton comments that Lynn apparently was unaware of the 1919 Black Sox Scandal even though he roomed with Claude Williams, who was involved. (Sources: *Baseball Encyclopedia*, 1290; Hilton, 248, 276)

LYONS, MISS ELEANOR ("Zone of Quiet"). She is the day nurse, 25, assigned to a patient recovering from surgery and needing quiet rest. She chatters incessantly and inanely at him, largely about her B.F.s and G.F.s (boy friends, girl friends).

Elizabeth Evans dislikes Miss Lyons, saying that "[t]o dismiss the nurse as a mere featherbrain ... is to judge the story too lightly. Miss Lyons's youth and good looks do not compensate for her inept and somewhat sadistic behavior." Douglas Robinson applies the double-bind theory of critic Gregory Bateson (1904–1980) to Miss Lyons, when he says that her "breathless tales of nursing cry out with the double bind normatively imposed on mothers and other caretakers, of caring too much and too little, of needing so much that you pretend to need too little and minister instead to other people's needs (you 'need' to be needed)." Brian T. Cowlishaw says that the "implied reader" is expected to see Miss Lyons as vain ("by twisting insults into compliments"), stupid (by being unable to "decipher the simplest crossword puzzle" or to "recognize her beau's joke as a cliché"), and dangerous (by disobeying the doctor and risking on-the-job fatigue by too much night life). Jonathan Yardley dismisses Miss Lyons as ignorantly self-satisfied, "empty-headed," "also insensitive, selfish and opportunistic." (Sources: Cowlishaw, 210; Evans, 57; Robinson, 102; Yardley, 289, 290).

MAC ("Ball-A-Hole"). He is the pro at the golf club where the narrator and his friend Jake caddy. Mac, evidently from Edinburgh, is not friendly with the boys.

MAC ("Good for the Soul"). He was Buck Warner's manager when Buck slid around second base and crippled his knee. Mac promised not to reveal the injury.

MacGILLICUDDY, CORNELIUS ALEXANDER *see* **MACK, CONNIE**

MACK, CONNIE (1862–1956). He was a baseball administrator, born Cornelius McGillicuddy in East Brookfield, Massachusetts. Using the playing name Connie Mack, he was a catcher for the Washington Senators (1881–1889) and the catcher-manager of the Pittsburgh Pirates (1891–1896). He owned the Philadelphia Athletics, which he also managed (1901–1950). He was elected to the Hall of Fame (1937). He retained the presidency of the Athletics (to 1954). (Source: Hilton, 307)

In "Sick 'Em," the narrator says that Smitty pitched badly for the Phillies against "them Athaletics," because "them Mackmen" could hit. Jack Barnett tells the narrator that managers "down here in the sticks" work their players better than Mack and McGraw can. In "Horseshoes," Connie Mack is portrayed as managing the Athletics in the season before and then during the World Series in which his team is pitted against the Giants. In "The Crook," Connie Mack was persuaded by Bull, an umpire, to give Martin Gregory a try with the Athletics. Martin froze at bat in clinch situations, and Connie "canned" him. In "The Busher Pulls a Mays," Keefe, pitching for the White Sox, gripes to Gleason, his manager, and hints to Jennings, Washington manager, that he wants to be traded. Keefe's wife Florrie reads a newspaper report that Connie Mack, Philadelphia manager, sold his ace pitcher (fictional) Page to Gleason for Keefe plus $5,000. In "Back to

Baltimore," Dixon says that William Baker, Jr., idiotic Boston Braves player, resembles "the Baker Connie Mack's got" only because both Bakers have ears. In "When the Moon Comes over the Mountain," Casey Stengel told Danny Warner that Connie Mack "got his farm" in Baltimore. Danny wondered "what does he raze"? In *The Real Dope*, Keefe mentions how Connie Mack "waggle[s] his score card or something" (to signal a play).

MACK, JACK ("Alibi Ike"). He plays on the narrator's team. Alibi Ike defeats both of them, and Carey too, at billiards and then apologizes for his poor play.

MACOMBER ("The Spinning Wheel"). He is an ugly-looking but supposedly brainy banker. By doubling until he wins, he pockets $200 at the narrator's roulette table one night and $300 the next night at Harry's table, but loses $1,000 at Joe's table the third night. When he accuses Joe of cheating, Joe's boss gives Macomber "an earful."

MACOMBER, THE REV. WALLACE ("Freedom of the Press"). He is "a minister of the gospel" whom Alexander Beardsley, eager to avoid reporters, persuades to disguise himself as James Wyeth, plumber, come to the Warner mansion and quietly marry Beardsley and Constance Warner.

MAGEE In "Horseshoes," he and Oakes play outfield for St. Louis when Speed Parker of the Cubs hits a liner bouncing over infielder Hauser and between Magee and Oakes for a lucky three-run triple. In "The Busher Abroad," Keefe mentions "Maggie."

Lee Magee, whose real name was Leopold Christopher Hoernschemeyer (1889–1966), played for the St. Louis Cardinals (1911–1914), the Brooklyn Dodgers (1915), the New York Yankees and the St. Louis Browns (1917), the Cincinnati Reds (1918), and the Brooklyn Dodgers and the Chicago Cubs (1919). He managed the Dodgers earlier (1915). George W. Hilton reports that Magee was banned from baseball (1919) because while playing for the Dodgers he bet against them. (Sources: *Baseball Encyclopedia*, 1297; Hilton, 400)

MAGEE In "Sick 'Em," the narrator suggests that Magee, Cravath, and Luderus could be counted on to hit well for the Phillies. In "Back to Baltimore," Magee got a hit when playing against the narrator Dixon's Boston Braves and scored Cravath from third — in part because of William Baker Jr.'s mindless fielding.

Sherwood Robert Magee (1884–1929) played for the Philadelphia Phillies (1904–1914), the Boston Braves (1915–1916) the Braves and the Cincinnati Reds (1917), and the Chicago Cubs (1918–1919). George W. Hilton says that Magee was given a long suspension for punching Bill Finneran, an umpire (1911). (Sources: *Baseball Encyclopedia*, 1297–1298; Hilton, 369)

MAGGIE ("The Busher Abroad"). Keefe mentions Maggie as a baseball player on the world tour. He may be Lee Magee (*see* Magee).

MAJOR-LEAGUE BASEBALL TEAMS, IN LARDNER'S TIME During Lardner's creative years, the National League (1876–) was composed of the following teams: the Boston Braves,* the Brooklyn Dodgers,* the Chicago Cubs,* the Cincinnati Reds,* the New York Giants,* the Philadelphia Phillies,* the Pittsburgh Pirates,* and the St. Louis Cardinals.* The American League (1901–) was composed of the following teams: the Boston Red Sox,* the Chicago White Sox,* the Cleveland Indians,* the Detroit Tigers,* the New York Yankees,* the Philadelphia Athletics,* the St. Louis Browns,* and the Washington Senators.*

Early in his career, Lardner was a sportswriter covering major-league games (1907–1912), often traveling to do so. Later he reported six World Series for the Bell Syndicate — the Dodgers-Indians series (1920), three Giants-Yankees series (1921, 1922, and 1923), one Pirates-Senators series (1925), and one Pirates-Yankees series (1927). Lardner wrote 33 short stories (published 1914–1933) featuring real major-league teams, often with real-life players interfacing with fictional characters. (Source: Light, 22–25, 478–481, and *passim*)

MALDEN MURDERER, THE ("The Venomous Viper of the Volga") *see* **MORAN, MIKE**

"MAMMA" (*Good Housekeeping*, June 1930; SC). (Characters: Betty, Brother, Dad, Doctor, Miss Fraser, Mamma, Miss Parnell, Dr. Phillips, Steve.)

A woman about 30, too pale and tired to be still pretty, rides a street car in New York back and forth until the conductor tries to question her, unavailingly. She says that she wants to go home and bake a cake, and that a woman in a store stole her purse. She agrees to go to Grand Central Station, where she says her husband will come and take care of her. She sits on a bench there, smiles silently, and sleeps. A policeman questions her. She says only that her husband works in an office and will come for her, her name is Mamma, and her husband is Dad. Another policeman escorts her to the Travelers' Aid Guest House. She is bathed, allowed to sleep, and given breakfast in the morning.

Mamma, unable to answer questions, is taken to the psychopathic ward of the city hospital. She tells Miss Fraser and Miss Parnell that her husband will come and explain everything; he is going to surprise her for her birthday, that's what the cake's for; they have a son named Brother and a daughter named Betty; Dad, Brother, and Betty had the flu for two weeks; she cared for them a solid week, without sleep; Doctor, often there, praised her nursing ability; Doctor's bill is of no consequence, "as long as everybody got well." When Miss Parnell asks about money, Mamma says her husband "makes a good salary" but they spend disgracefully. Told she needs new clothes, Mamma says she just bought "what I'm wearing," only yesterday. She complains, "I'm tired of being nagged." Dr. Phillips nags her anyway. She tells him they live in an apartment, calls him "fresh," and says they prefer their own doctor. At night she rambles, unheard, about bright Brother, helpful Betty, and Doctor's bill. Next day she answers questions vaguely, loses her temper, and scolds those querying her. For two weeks she answers no one, cries and smiles, and tells fellow patients her husband is coming.

Authorities diligently try to locate Mamma's family, but lack of evidence prevents success. Suddenly Mamma blurts her last name: "Carns." Miss Fraser finds five persons in the telephone book named Carns. Four whom she phones say no family member is missing. Learning the fifth number is no longer in service, she goes to its Riverside Drive address. The janitor explains: Mrs. Carns's young husband, their "smart" daughter, and their "handsome" son all died of the flu two months ago; Mrs. Carns owed a month's rent and also money to the doctor, and also to a nurse the doctor brought, because Mrs. Carns "was the most useless, helpless woman you ever seen in a sick room"; she left, with maybe $10, looking for work.

Miss Fraser reports her findings to Dr. Phillips. He theorizes that if Mamma recalls her name she'll remember "the whole business" and be worse off. In the ward, Mamma asks Miss Fraser if she phoned Carns, her husband. Miss Fraser tells her there's no Carns in the book. Mamma says Miss Fraser probably got the wrong name and "Anyway he's coming for me this afternoon."

Donald Elder reports that this heart-wrenching story "was based on a case which Ellis [Lardner's wife] had observed while doing volunteer work in the hospital." Elder adds that the story "is 'true to life,' no doubt, but somehow not true to Ring. It could have been written by any competent imitator of O. Henry." Walton R. Patrick makes a better comparison: "The sheer horror and morbidity of 'Mamma,' as well as its surprise ending, suggest a typical Ambrose Bierce story." Although Jonathan Yardley thinks "Mamma" is close to "sentimental" and that Miss Fraser's detective work is "rather slick," he pronounces "the dialogue ... first rate." (Sources: Elder, 320; Patrick, 130; Yardley, 340)

MAMMA ("Mamma"). She suffers from amnesia induced when her husband, whom she now calls Dad, their son, called Brother, and their daughter, Betty, all died of the flu. Able to name herself only Mamma, she is found wandering in New York by police, taken to a psychopathic ward, and cared for. When she suddenly recalls her last name, Carns, Miss Frazer, a nurse, discovers details about her family losses and consequent indigence. She and Dr. Phillips are content when Mamma forgets her last name again and decide not to remind her of it — and of her misery.

"MAN NOT OVERBOARD" (*Cosmopolitan*, November 1927; RU). (Characters: Benjamin Brainard, Pauline Lannin, Lemp, Lemp, Edith Lemp, Fred Lemp, Margaret Lemp, Miriam Lemp, Mrs. Lemp, Phil Runyon.)

Benjamin Brainard, 30, wrote two popular novels but then a third novel that publishers don't want. His chorus-girl girlfriend, Pauline Lannin, has treated him heartlessly. He buys a gun and ships aboard the *Gargantua*. His friend Phil Runyon is pursar. Ben orders "three quick drinks" in the lounge, writes his mother and his sister explanatory farewells, and then 2,000 useless words to Pauline. He'll leave the letters with Phil and "embark ... to another World."

Brainard ignores the dinner bugle. A "robust" stranger, wanting to avoid drinking alone, introduces himself to Brainard as Fred Lemp, a businessman heading for Paris and Château-Thierry, and on learning Benjamin Brainard's name praises his novels for displaying a maturity surprising, he feels, in an author so young. On their sixth drinks, Brainard complains about his unappreciative "Girl." Lemp says forget her, write so well she'll be sorry. Brainard says he fought at Château-Thierry, and wishes he'd died there. Lemp says his son was killed there, and he annually visits his son's grave and also the Frenchwoman, unmarried but the mother of their child, now nine. Lemp says his first wife, Edith, left him for a well-to-do man, and his second wife, Margaret, is in a mental sanitarium. Over their eighth drinks, Lemp says one of his brothers embezzled, cost him a lot to prevent a scandal that would have destroyed their mother, paid lawyers to defend another brother who then was executed for murder anyway, and is supporting the children of his daughter who was betrayed by an adulterous husband. On their 12th drinks, Brainard offers his gun for Lemp to commit suicide and says he'll be doing the same at 11:00 P.M. No! is Lemp's rejoinder. Lemp is 61, enjoys life, tells Brainard to nap in his stateroom, and leave a call for 11:00 to kill himself then, and keeps the gun. A steward gets Brainard to bed in his cabin.

Phil appears and thanks his friend Fred for what he did. Their talk reveals that the gun was unloaded, that Brainard two nights ago saw his heartless Pauline with a dull old man, that Brainard was too drunk to make trouble then or even to remember telling someone later — actually Phil — about his suicide plans, and that Lemp must apologize to his wife for missing dinner this busy evening.

Next noon Brainard awakens, orders the steward to summon Phil, and says he met a Limp or a Lemp last night. Phil identifies Lemp is an upstate hosiery manufacturer. Brainard says Lemp gave him enough material for a great novel, and wants to talk details with him — but on deck and without liquor, which might "get" Lemp.

The World War battle at Château-Thierry occurred June 3–4, 1918. In a letter to Lardner (December 16, 1927), Maxwell Perkins* comments on recent stories by Lardner and says "I liked least ... 'Man Not Overboard' and yet I know several people who think that wonderful." Incidentally, the title "Man Not Overboard" is something of a giveaway, though probably a harmless one in a story so feeble anyway. (Source: Caruthers [1973], 114)

MANNING, MARJORIE ("A Day with Conrad Green") *see* **GREEN, MARJORIE**

MARANVILLE In "Sick 'Em," the narrator says that scrappy Davis is "not much bigger'n Maranville." In "Back to Baltimore," Maranville played second base well for the Boston Braves, despite William Baker Jr.'s inept throwing from first base. In "Lose with a Smile," Danny Warner, playing for Brooklyn against the Braves, got a double, bantered with Maranville there, and later made rabbit noises from the bench at him. Rabbit Maranville is mentioned in "The Hold-Out."

Walter James Vincent ("Rabbit") Maranville (1891–1954) 5'5", 155 lbs., played for the Boston Braves (1912–1920), the Pittsburgh Pirates (1921–1924), the Chicago Cubs (1925, managing them briefly), the Brooklyn Dodgers (1926), the St. Louis Cardinals (1927–1928), and the Braves (1929–1933, 1935), and managed the Cubs (1925). He was elected to the Baseball Hall of Fame (1954). George W. Hilton reports that Maranville was an alcoholic with a sense of humor — two reasons for Lardner's affection for him. Lardner knew and liked Rabbit Maranville, who, according to Donald Elder, visited him in East Hampton (1932), between his final hospital stays. (Source: *Baseball Encyclopedia*, 1307–1308); Elder, 363; Hilton, 387–388).

MARE OF VANILA ("The Busher Abroad"). Keefe, when in "the Philip Bean ilands," meets this official.

MARGARET ("Words and Music"). She is Hilda Harper's roommate, evidently in restricted quarters. She tells Hilda it would be easy to interview Roman Starr, the popular, conceited singer.

MARIAN ("Zone of Quiet"). She is Miss Eleanor Lyons's G.F. (girl friend), until they vie for Roy Stewart, Marian's B.F. (boy friend). Marian eventually gets engaged to him.

MARIE ("Sick 'Em"). She was Smitty's girl at one point and is supposedly prettier than Fogarty's Julia.

MARK ("How Are You?"). He was Hilda Pratt's brother. She tells Bob and Beth Dayton that Mark was diagnosed by Dr. Elston Gifford as having brain tumor, was operated on, and died.

MARK ("One Hit, One Error, One Left"). Danny names "Mathews Mark and Luque and John" as four House of David pitchers.

MARLOWE, RITA ("Rhythm"). She is an actress "of Goldwyn." Harry Hart is engaged to her but dumps her when he foolishly thinks he can discontinue successfully stealing tunes for musicals and starts composing grand music. When, down and out, he phones her, she generously readmits him to her friendship.

MARQUARD, BIG RUBE In "Alibi Ike," he

is the New York pitcher who strikes out Alibi Ike. Ike alibis strenuously, later misunderstands a bunt order, and hits a home run. In "The Poor Simp," Marquard was mentioned as one of McGraw's pitchers when the narrator's team played against the Giants.

Richard William ("Rube") Marquard (1889–1980) played for the New York Giants (1908–1915), the Giants and the Brooklyn Dodgers (1915), the Dodgers (1916–1920), the Cincinnati Reds (1921), and the Boston Braves (1922–1925). He was elected to the Baseball Hall of Fame (1971). (Sources: *Baseball Encyclopedia*, 2185–2186; Hilton, 355)

MARSANS ("Horseshoes"). He is a Cuban playing baseball for Cincinnati. In a game against the Cubs, Speed Parker, playing third and wrongly thinking there was one out instead of two, throws home in an elaborate misplay and luckily enables catcher Jim Archer to tag badly sliding Marsans.

Armando Marsans (1887–1960), born in Matanzas, Cuba, played for the Cincinnati Reds (1911–1914), the St. Louis Browns (1916), the Browns and the New York Yankees (1917, and the Yankees (1918). (Sources: *Baseball Encyclopedia*, 1309–1310; Hilton, 402)

MARSH ("The Facts"). This is the Chicago store where Billy Bowen and Tommy Richards shop for Christmas presents that Billy is to give members of the McDonald family. Billy, very drunk, naps while Tommy, rather drunk, does the shopping.

MARSH, HARRY ("Greek Tragedy"). He is a friend of wrestlers Big Bill Buell and Greek Alexis. Buell tells Alexis he saw Roy Clayton, another friend, and not Marsh.

MARSH, JOE ("The Hold-Out"). He was a member of Mr. Edwards's team. When Mr. Edwards had to cut costs, Joe agreed to play for $1,000 less than last year's salary. Joe, among others, had many opportunities to laugh at Lahey's poor fielding.

MARSHALL ("Liberty Hall"). He and his wife, who live in Spring Lake, are entertaining musical composer Ben Drake and his wife so unsatisfactorically that Ben decamps by executing his "emergency exit" — a fake alarming telegram from his publisher.

MARSHALL, DOC ("Reunion"). He and his wife Louise live in Buchanan, Michigan. Bob Mason gossips to his sister Rita Johnston, ad nauseum, about the Marshalls and about Tom Allen, Louise's father. Doc eloped with Louise and thought Tom would be upset, but he wasn't.

MARSHALL, E. B. ("Holycaust"). Jessie writes that the Centralia fire involved the E. B. Marshall Building.

MARSHALL, GEORGE ("Bob's Birthday"). He is Bob Tyler's worthless, sponging uncle. His wife is Lucille Marshall.

MARSHALL, LOUISE ("Reunion"). She and her husband Doc Marshall live in Buchanan, Michigan. Bob Mason gossips to his sister Rita Johnston repeatedly about the two and Louise's father Tom Allen.

MARSHALL, LUCILLE ("Bob's Birthday"). She is Bob Tyler's worthless, partying aunt. Her husband is George Marshall.

MARSHALL, MRS. ("Liberty Hall"). She and her husband live in Spring Lake and try unsuccessfully to play nice hostess and host to Ben Drake and his wife.

MARSTON, W. M. (*Own Your Own Home*). He is in charge of money being raised by a dance in Allison for the benefit of post-war Belgians.

MARTHA (*The Big Town*). She is Lady Perkins's servant, who cares for the lady's pet dogs during their stay at the Long Island hotel also frequented by Finch, Ella Finch, and Katie.

MARTIN (*Own Your Own Home*). He is a neighbor of Fred and Grace. When the Martins' party gets raucous one night, Fred tries to silence them by flashing his badge. Martin regularly commutes with Fred on the train to Chicago. Martin laughs when Fred laughs while reading the adverse newspaper publicity connected with Fred's own noisy party later, and may therefore laugh last. Martin often advises Fred about getting even with Hamilton, until Hamilton finally persuades Fred to believe that Martin is the neighborhood culprit. Hamilton and Martin are probably in cahoots.

MARTIN, GEN. (*Treat 'Em Rough*). He evidently is the commanding general at Camp Grant, where Jack Keefe begins his military training. Jack says "Gen. Martin ... will be sorry to see our bunch duck out" and be transferred to Camp Logan.

MARTIN, JAKE ("Harmony"). He is a member of "Cap" Ryan's baseball team. At one point he warms up pitcher Mike McCann, whose singing Jake likes.

MARTIN, JOE ("A Day with Conrad Green"). He is Conrad Green's "chief librettist." The two discuss Green's idea of a plot, until Martin tells him it was created by Bert Kalmar and Harry Ruby. Green then realizes that Robert Blair stole it from Kalmar and Ruby.

MARTIN, JOE ("The Yellow Kid"). He was a member of the baseball team on which Bill the narrator played. When others, especially vicious Harry Childs, kidded Lefty Crosby, who was scared of women and guns, Joe, "Crosby's best pal on the club," enabled Crosby to mature and get even with Childs.

MARTIN, MRS. (*Own Your Own Home*). She and her husband are neighbors living near Fred and Grace, whose "babys" are awakened by a loud party at the Martins' house. The Martins entertain Fred and Grace, whom Mrs. Martin demeans by sarcastic comments beyond Grace's comprehension. Fred regards Mrs. Martin as pretty, well-dressed, and a fragrant dancer. Hamilton makes Fred believe that Martin is jealous of Fred's attention to Mrs. Martin.

MARTIN, QUINN ("The Jade Necklace"). He is a friend of movie-mogul L. N. Bauer. Bauer reminds Wolf, his vice president, that he once asked Martin to suggest "a vehicle for Kate Hollis" and that Martin instantly suggested *Jane Eyre*.

Bauer adds, "and you know what a sensation it was." Lardner is fictionalizing when he suggests that Bauer produced a version of *Jane Eyre*. In reality, *Jane Eyre* was the subject of four movies, all post–Lardner (1934, 1943, 1970, 1996).

MARTIN, TIM ("There Are Smiles"). He is a Manhattan traffic policeman who follows Ben Collins when Ben comes off duty. He tries to entertain Ben with racial jokes.

MARTINEZ, MANUEL ("The Venomous Viper of the Volga"). He is an aging, impoverished boxer from Indiana, nicknamed "the Rugged Rock." Luke Lewis and Sandy King match him against their Henry Goetz in a rigged fight. Martinez stands with his arms down, is struck, and soon dies.

Lardner's having his narrator casually report this death makes it all the more shocking.

MARTINGALE, LINCOLN H. ("Claude Diphthong, Student of Crime") *see* **FAILING, LEONARD K.**

MARY ("Poodle"). She is the narrator's self-deceiving, shrewish wife. She enjoys demeaning everyone by boastful lies. When she learns that her husband has been released from work but is lying about it (only to delay hurting her), she accuses him of having an affair and goes home to her mother.

MASON, BOB ("Reunion"). He is Rita Johnston's sister. They were children together in Buchanan, Michigan, a small town, but were separated when he was 14 and she was 15. He became a Los Angeles real-estate agent, married Jennie, and moved back to Buchanan. Now 34, he has a reunion with Rita that is miserable, and brief.

MASON, JENNIE ("Reunion"). She was from San Bernardino. Bob Mason married her when he was working in Los Angeles. The two moved to Buchanan, Michigan, and try for a reunion with Bob's sister Rita Johnston, of Long Island — with dismal results. Jennie, 35, is characterized as having prominent gold teeth.

MASON, JIMMY ("A Frame-Up"). He is a boxer Burke defeats in Milwaukee.

MATHER, LIEUT. (*The Real Dope*). He is an army officer in the unit in which Keefe serves in France. Keefe obtains Mather's permission to go see Capt. Seeley.

MATHEWS ("One Hit, One Error, One Left"). Danny names "Mathews Mark and Luque and John" as four bearded pitchers for the House of David. Danny adds that Mathews is a left-hander, hopes he gets a hit off Mathews, and if so will give "them outfielders a shave."

MATHEWSON In "Back to Baltimore," Matty is mentioned by McGraw, managing the Giants, as too valuable to be traded. In "My Roomy," Matty pitches for the New York baseball team. Mac inserts him in relief during a game against the Chicago team for which Buster Elliott pinch hits. In "Horseshoes," Matty is a left-handed pitcher for the Giants in the World Series against the Athletics. He loses the second game, wins the fourth. In "The Busher's Kid," Keefe says that if he had pitched only against the Cubs this season, his "record ... would make Johnson and Mathewson and some of them other swell heads look like a dirty doose." In "The Busher Beats It Hence," Keefe says Mathewson is going with McGraw as far as the west coast but not on the world tour thereafter. In "The Poor Simp," Mathewson is mentioned as one of McGraw's pitchers when the narrator's team played Giants. Matty is also mentioned in "The Busher Abroad," "The Busher's Welcome Home," "The Crook," "Good for the Soul," and "The Water Cure."

Leverett T. Smith, Jr., offers proof of Lardner's admiration for Mathewson, partly by citing Lardner's early essay "Matty" (*American Magazine* [August 1915]). Christopher ("Christy," "Matty") Mathewson (1880–1925) pitched for the Giants (1900–1915) and the Giants and the Cincinnati Reds (1916), then managed the Reds (1916–1918). Mathewson attended Bucknell College, was a U. S. Army captain (1918–1919), was gassed during World War I while serving in France (1918), became a coach for the Giants (1919–1920), was named president of the Boston Braves merely as a publicity stunt (1923), and died early of tuberculosis. He was a charter member of the Baseball Hall of Fame (1936). (Sources: *Baseball Encyclopedia*, 701, 2191–2192; Hilton, 155; Smith, 142, 144)

MATTY ("Back to Baltimore," etc.) *see* **MATHEWSON**

MAVOURNEEN, KATHLEEN (*The Big Town*) *see* **KATHLEEN MAVOURNEEN**

MAYER In "Sick 'Em," He is a competent Phillies pitcher, but less able than fellow-pitchers Alexander and Rixey. In "The Busher Pulls a Mays," Keefe gripes to Al Blanchard on August 6 [1919] that Gleason is managing the White Sox so badly that "he has signed up Mayer that has been in the National League 20 or 30 years."

James Erskine Mayer, also identified as Erskine James Mayer (born James Erskine, 1891–1957), pitched for the Philadelphia Phillies (1912–1917), the Phillies and the Pittsburgh Pirates (1918), and the Pirates (1919). George W. Hilton adds that Mayer joined the Chicago White Sox August 6, 1919, appearing in only six games, with a 1–3 record. (Sources: *Baseball Encyclopedia*, 2195; Hilton, 311)

MAYNARD ("Absent-minded Beggar"). This is the owner of a lake cottage where Wallie Blair is staying when Wallie asks John Knowles to come for the week-end.

MAYOR, THE ("Nora"). In Hazlett's play "Nora," he is the city official in whose honor a party is given. Guests include Nora Crowley, John Collins, and Dick Percival. Dick falls in love with Nora, who loves John, who loves Nora.

MAYS In *The Real Dope*, Keefe when soldiering in France remembers a game he pitched for the Chicago White Sox against Carl Mays, pitching for Boston. He says Mays "didn't have nothing on the ball only the cover." In "Along Came Ruth," Keefe says Mays and Babe Ruth will pitch for Boston in successive games against the White Sox. Gleason told Keefe he could choose which opponent to pitch against. He chose Ruth. In "The Busher Pulls a Mays," Keefe says that Carl Mays "walked out on the Boston club" and wasn't suspended, "other clubs in the league begun biding for him," and "Huggins got him for the N. Y. club." This makes Keefe complain to his manager Gleason and hint unsuccessfully to Washington manager Jennings of his willingness to "pull a Mays" by jumping to his team.

Carl William Mays (1891–1971) was a submarine pitcher for the Boston Red Sox (1915–1918), the Red Sox and the New York Yankees (1919), the Yankees (1920–1923), the Cincinnati Reds (1924–1928), and the New York Giants (1929). George W. Hilton reports that Mays deserted the White Sox during a game between the White Sox and the Boston Red Sox in Comiskey Park, alleging poor teammate support (July 13, 1919), was suspended by his general manager, and switched to the Yankees (July 29). (Sources: *Baseball Encyclopedia*, 2195; Hilton, 271, 303–304)

"THE MAYSVILLE MINSTREL" (*Cosmopolitan*, September 1928; RLR, RU). (Characters: George Balch, Mrs. Gale, Stella Nichols Gale, Stephen Gale, Mrs. Harper, Ed Hunter, Wallace James, Mrs. Arnold Peters, Charley Roberts, Old Man Townsend.)

Stephen Gale, 31, has been bookkeeper and overdue-bill collector for the gas company in Maysville, population 5,000, for 12 years. He works with troubleshooter and meter-reader Ed Hunter, the company's only other employee. Both are bossed by Old Man Townsend, who owns several gas companies in the region.

Stephen and his wife Stella have two children. His long-unraised weekly pay of $22.50 keeps them poverty-stricken. Stephen reads poetry by Amy Lowell, Edgar Guest, and others, and secretly writes verses. Charley Roberts, New York–based drummer for instant water heaters, learns of Stephen's poetry. Stephen reluctantly shows Roberts his wretched, heart-felt 17-line birthday poem to Stella. Roberts says that he knows a New York *Standard* columnist who would publish the poem, and that Stephen might make $1 a line, write prolifically, and get rich.

In due time, Stephen receives a copy of the *Standard* including "To Stella—A Maysville Minstrel Gives His Mrs. a Birthday Treat." Stephen writes more doggerel, entitled "The Lackawanna Railroad" and "The Gas Business." When shown them, Stella is delighted and suggests that Stephen split long lines in two to make more money. He receives a letter signed Wallace James, New York editor of "James's Weekly," praising "To Stella" and requesting more poems. He resigns from his gas job, despite Townsend's offering him a slight raise. Stephen mails his two new poems to Wallace James. The envelope is returned marked "Not Found." Townsend agrees to rehire Stephen at $23.50, and "don't let's have no more foolishness." Stephen advises Townsend not to trust Roberts, but Roberts has recently sent Townsend six instant heaters and is coming to Maysville to demonstrate them. Stephen yearns "grimly" for revenge but immediately feels powerless.

Jonathan Yardley notes that this late story "uses the device of the cruel practical joke, ... dating back to his [Lardner's] earliest fiction." Clifford M. Caruthers defines "The Maysville Minstrel" as "at once the most poignant and the bleakest of Lardner's stories." Douglas Robinson takes the admittedly acerbic story too seriously, first by rebuking Stella for praising Stephen's poem to her—generalizing that "[a]ll praise is suspect"—and second by concluding that "[t]he moral for Lardner is clear: be wary of all praise and all ambition." (Sources: Caruthers [1995], 219; Robinson, 75; Yardley, 331)

McBRIDE In "The Busher Comes Back," Keefe boasts that when pitching for the White Sox against Washington, he "made McBride and their catcher look like suckers with my speed." In "Horseshoes," McBride is a Washington infielder that Dick Grimes, playing for the Athletics, grounded out to. In *The Real Dope*, Keefe recalls that when in a game he was pitching "Geo. McBride booted one."

George Florian McBride (1880–1973) played for the Pittsburgh Pirates and the St. Louis Cardinals (1905), the Cardinals (1906), and the Washington Senators (1908–1920), and managed the Senators (1921). (Sources: *Baseball Encyclopedia*, 702, 1328; Hilton, 90)

McCANN ("Champion"). He was an associate with Tommy Haley in Philadelphia and was counting their money in a "s'loon" when Midge Kelly entered.

McCANN, MIKE ("Harmony"). He pitched for the baseball team Bill Cole plays for. Cole tells the narrator that McCann sang so beautifully in the quartet including Art Graham, Lefty Parks, and Cole that, according to Cole, "C'ruso, McCormack, or Gadski ... had nothin' on him for a pure tenor." When Mike's "old souper" went bad, he was cut, and the abandoned singers scrambled to replace him—with Waldron.

Lardner makes his story especially appealing to those of his contemporary readers who not only endured baseball quartets but also appreciated fine singing. He mentions "C'ruso" and "Car*us*'" (Enrico Caruso [1873–1921]), one of the world's greatest Italian operatic tenors, and John McCormack (1874–1945), nonpareil Irish operatic and concert tenor. Lardner satirizes ballplayers' incomplete knowledge of celebrated singers by having Cole include Joanna Gadski (1871–1932), German soprano, in his list of tenors.

McCHESNEY, BONES ("The Hold-Out"). He played baseball on the team Mr. Edwards bought. To save money, Mr. Edwards sought to reduce McChesney's salary from $3,500 to $3,000. He refused and was sold to Toronto.

McDONALD ("Alibi Ike"). He plays on the narrator's team. When Big Rube Marquard, the New York pitcher, walks McDonald, Alibi Ike is told by Cap to bunt, instead hits a home run, then equivocates about the wording of Cap's order.

McDONALD ("Women"). He was a scout for McGraw. According to Mike Healy, bad calls by Baldy Pierce, umpiring a crucial game between Dayton, Healy's team, and Springfield, prevented McDonald from appreciating Healy's fielding and batting.

McDONALD, BOB ("The Facts"). He is Ellen McDonald's hirsute brother and Florence McDonald's husband. Billy Bowen observes Bob's frothing jealous when Billy innocently converses with "temporarily dumb" Flo. So Tommy Richards sends the couple a book entitled *The Green-Eyed Monster* as Billy Bowen's Christmas present.

McDONALD, EDITH ("The Facts"). She is Ellen McDonald's athletic sister. Edith and their sister Wilma are students in the Northampton region. Tommy Richards sends heavy Edith and skinny Wilma a book entitled *Eat and Grow Thin* as Billy Bowen's Christmas present.

McDONALD, ELLEN ("The Facts"). She is an attractive young lady, 21. She and Billy Bowen, both living in Chicago, fall in love. Billy temporarily swears off drinking, tries hard to be acceptable to her big family but fails when Tommy Richards, an old college chum, appears on the scene, gets him drunk, and shops for him for inappropriate Christmas presents for the McDonald clan. Tommy causes Ellen special consternation by sending her a cheap wrist watch, with Violet Moore's card, containing a request for Billy to phone her about a job with him.

Lardner insufficiently develops Ellen as a credible character with a real personality.

McDONALD, FLORENCE ("FLO") ("The Facts"). Florence is Bob McDonald's obedient wife. They live in Evanston, visit his parents' home in Chicago, and meet Billy Bowen, Bob's sister Ellen's fiancé. Billy bothers Bob by trying to chat innocently with Flo.

McDONALD, LOUISE ("The Facts"). She is Sam McDonald's sister and Ellen McDonald's aunt. Louise, Aunt Harriet, and Mary Carey do "settlement work" in Chicago. Louise has thin hair; so Tommy Richards sends her a yellow-colored "switch" as Billy Bowen's Christmas present.

McDONALD, MRS. ("The Facts"). She is Sam McDonald's wife, and the mother of Bob, Edith, Ellen, Walter, and Wilma McDonald. Mrs. McDonald has written two books on how to play bridge. She tells Billy Bowen, who is in love with Ellen, that her book on auction bridge is useless now that bridge rules have changed. So Tommy Richards sends her *The First Principles of Auction Bridge* as Billy Bowen's Christmas present.

McDONALD, SAM ("The Facts"). Samuel McDonald is the pompous, hypocritical father of Bob, Edith, Ellen, Walter, and Wilma McDonald. He lectures Billy Bowen, in love with Ellen, on the dangers of cigarettes, gambling, and drinking. So Tommy Richards sends Sam a cigarette case as Billy's Christmas present.

McDONALD, WALTER ("The Facts"). He is the skirt-chasing schoolboy brother of Bob, Edith, Ellen, and Wilma McDonald. Walter's father, Sam McDonald, ineffectively rebukes Walter for misbehavior. Having dumped Beth, Walter dates giggling Kathryn. So Tommy Richards sends Walter a poker set as Billy Bowen's Christmas present.

McDONALD, WILMA ("The Facts"). She is the intellectual sister of Bob, Edith, Ellen, and Walter McDonald. Wilma and Edith are students in the Northampton region. So Tommy Richards sends thin Wilma and heavy Edith a book entitled *Eat and Grow Thin* as Billy Bowen's Christmas present.

McGILL ("Oh, You Bonehead!"). He was a quarterback on the Coach's Leighton football team. He cooperated with Joe Draper in their game against Pelham.

McGOWAN ("The Yellow Kid"). He played for Dallas in the Texas League with Buck Means. Buck heartlessly told the narrator Bill that McGowan kidded girl-shy Lefty Crosby, a Dallas pitcher drafted by Bill's boss.

McGRAW, JOHN JOSEPH (1875–1934). Mac McGraw, born in Truxton, New York, played baseball for the St. Louis Cardinals (1900) and the New York Giants (1902–1906), then became the durable manager of the Giants (1902–1932) who won ten pennants. His Giants beat the New York Yankees in the World Series twice (1921, 1922) and the Washington Senators once (1933). By the late 1920s his annual income was upwards of $70,000. However, he was overly generous with indigent former baseball players and also lost $100,000 in the Florida land bust (1926). McGraw became a member of the Baseball Hall of Fame (1937).

Lardner knew and greatly respected McGraw. Lardner covered both Giant-Yankee World Series in rollicking columns for the Bell Syndicate (October 3–14, 1921; October 3–7, 1922). In several stories published both before and after 1921–1922, Lardner includes McGraw, whose name is often given as "Mcgraw." In "My Roomy," McGraw won't accept Buster Elliott from the Chicago team, managed by John, because Charlie Faust doesn't need to be replaced. In "Sick 'Em," Jack Barnett boasts that managers "down here in the sticks" can "get the work out of a man" better than McGraw or Mack can. In "Horseshoes," McGraw manages the Giants in the fictional World Series against the Philadelphia Athletics. In "The Poor Simp," Carey kidded Skull Scoville, a naive pitcher, by telling him to pump McGraw for information on how to pitch against his Giant batters. In "Back to Baltimore," Dixon, managing the Boston Braves, says McGraw's pitchers were in poor shape and "we skun 'em three out o' the first four." In "The Busher Beats It Hence," Keefe reports that while McGraw was assembling his Giants for the world tour he kidded Keefe, tried to persuade him to join his pitching staff, and finally succeeded. Keefe spells his name "Mcgraw." In

Treat 'Em Rough, Keefe mentions that McGraw on "Sun. P.M." [October 7, 1917] started another lefty against the White Sox in "the world serious." In "The Busher Abroad" and "The Busher's Welcome Home," McGraw treats Keefe gently during the world tour while other men kid him relentlessly. James E. Elpers, in his history of the 1913–1914 Giants-White Sox tour around the world, devotes more space to McGraw than to any other man, including this for openers: "John McGraw, ... the greatest manager in the history of the National League, stood just five feet six inches tall. He was balding, pudgy, and acerbic. Behind his close-set beady eyes operated a keen, almost criminal, managerial mind." On the trip, McGraw combined professional skill, fun, praise, and ridicule. According to Mike Healy in "Women," McGraw sent McDonald to scout him; dishonest calls by umpire Baldy Pierce in the game between Dayton, Healy's team, and Springfield prevented McDonald from hiring Healy. In "The Ides of June," Danny reports to Jessie that McGraw quit managing the Giants "on a count of bad helth" but remained as its "V P." McGraw is mentioned in "The Hold-Out," "Holycaust," and "Lose with a Smile."

Lardner wrote a letter (June 4, 1932) while in the hospital to McGraw, who was also in poor health and was retiring because of that fact. In his letter, Lardner praises McGraw for representing what he liked best about baseball. Decades earlier, if Lardner ever saw the baseball movie, *One Touch of Nature* (1917), he would have delighted in the part McGraw plays in it as well as bit parts in which several of his Giants are featured. (Sources: *Baseball Encyclopedia*, 702, 1340–1341; Elder, 361–362; Elpers, 2 and *passim*; Hilton, 172; Caruthers [1995], 257–158; Spears, 256, 260)

McINERNY, J. M. ("Absent-minded Beggar"). He is a customer whose order for Murray Corporation stock John Knowles and Miss Davenport handle in the brokerage firm owned by J. L. Beasley and H. N. Comerford.

McINNES, JACK In "Horseshoes," he plays for the Athletics, gets a hit against Washington, and makes an error but hits well in the second game of the World Series against the Giants. In "A New Busher Breaks In," Keefe writes Al that at the moment he "was makeing McInnis look like a sucker" as a pinch hitter, his wife Florrie Keefe was giving birth to their baby Allen Keefe.

John Phalen McInnis (1890–1960) played for the Philadelphia Athletics (1909–1917), the Boston Red Sox (1918–1921), the Cleveland Indians (1922), the Boston Braves (1923–1924), the Pittsburgh Pirates (1925–1926), and the Philadelphia Phillies (1927), and managed the Phillies (1927). George W. Hilton reports that McInnis also coached for Norwich University and Harvard University. (Sources: *Baseball Encyclopedia*, 702, 1343; Hilton, 142)

McMAHON (MAC) ("Claude Diphthong, Student of Crime"). He and Burke are New York detectives who investigate Gardner Lyle's murder.

McMULLIN ("Call for Mr. Keefe!"). Keefe, pitching for the White Sox, criticizes White Sox infielder McMullin's performance, by saying that when Keefe was pitching against Washington and "the scorer give them 3 hits," the scorer "must be McMullins brother in law or something."

Frederick William McMullin (1891–1952) played for the Detroit Tigers (1914) and the Chicago White Sox (1916–1920). George W. Hilton notes that McMullin played "the most minor role" in the 1919 Black Sox Scandal but nevertheless was banned from baseball (1920). (Sources: *Baseball Encyclopedia*, 1348; Hilton, 213)

McNALLY, MR. ("Ball-A-Hole"). He is mentioned as a golfer who plays with Mr. Harper against Mr. Davis and Mr. Joyce for $1 to $5 a hole.

MEANS, BUCK ("The Yellow Kid"). He was a fellow Dallas baseball player with Lefty Crosby and McGowan in the Texas League. When Crosby went to the narrator Bill's team in the majors, Means became envious and told the narrator Bill that Crosby was scared of women.

MEEKS ("Oh, You Bonehead!"). He was a member of the Coach's Leighton football team.

"MEET ME IN ST. LOUIE" (*Saturday Evening Post*, July 2, 1932; LWS, RAB).

MEIGHAN, THOMAS ("TOM") (1879–1936). Pittsburgh-born Meighan was a teenage stage performer, gained prominence on Broadway, became a leading man in movies (from 1913), and in the 1920s portrayed engaging heroes in at least 19 films. When Lardner and his family moved to Great Neck, they were neighbors of Meighan and his wife Frances, whose nephew A. Edward Sunderland was a movie director. Ring and Tom became drinking-party partners. Ring

Lardner Jr. says, with no shred of even implicit criticism, that Meighan was "one of the few drinkers whom Ring classified with himself as a genuine 'two-bottle man.'" Jonathan Yardley reports that when Lardner and his wife went to California (1926) with Grantland Rice,* his wife Kate, and their daughter Florence, they were allowed to watch the filming of some movies. A year earlier Lardner had written the scenario and titles of *The New Klondike* (1926), a silent movie starring Meighan, and in addition Lardner was popular with filmmakers. In the movie, Meighan is a baseball player who quits the big leagues to make money in Florida during the real-estate boom. In a letter (November 8 [1925]) to F. Scott Fitzgerald* and his wife, Lardner says he balked at writing "a picture scenario for Tom Meighan" until he was offered $7,500 for what took him only "four days to [do] the job." Lardner mentions Meighan in two stories. In "Travelogue," Hazel Dignan says Meighan was "Wonderful!" in *Old Home Week* [1925]. In "Hurry Kane," Hurry Kane is jocosely told he resembles Meighan and should try for the movies. (Sources: Lardner, Jr., 150; Caruthers [1995], 183, 188; Spears, 235, 245, 261; Yardley, 298–301).

MELLON, ANDY ("Stop Me — if you've heard This One"). This man met Henry Wild Osborne on the train from New York to Chicago, according to Osborne's false boast.

Andrew Mellon (1855–1937), born in Pittsburgh, was financier, industrialist, and philanthropist, and Secretary of the Treasury (1921–1932) during the administrations of presidents Warren Harding, Calvin Coolidge,* and Herbert Hoover. (Source: Streissguth, 378).

MENCKEN, H. L. (1880–1956). He was the famous Baltimore-born journalist, editor, critic, and essayist. He worked for the Baltimore *Morning Herald* (1899–1906), the Baltimore *Evening Sun* (1906–1956), and *The Smart Set* (1908–1923), which he coedited (1914–1923) with critic George Jean Nathan (1882–1958). Mencken and Nathan cofounded the *American Mercury* (1924), which Mencken edited (1924–1933). He was a war correspondent in Germany (1916–1917). He thoroughly relished blasting aspects of American culture in a series of *Prejudices* (1919–1927) and in more than a dozen other books. He significantly surveyed ever-involving patterns of American writing and speech in *The American Language* (1919, often revised and supplemented).

Edward A. Martin says that "cultural indictment formed the background of much of Lardner's writing ... and Mencken was its expository source," but then adds that "[l]ike Mencken, Lardner both needed and attacked the culture that had nourished him." In *The American Language* (1919), Mencken praises Lardner's "grotesque tales of base-ball players" for capturing their "common speech not only with humor, but also with the utmost accuracy," for presenting "in a single story ... almost every logical and grammatical peculiarity of the emerging language," and in the process "very stoutly [resisting] the temptation to overdo the thing." Donald Elder reports that Lardner and Mencken "attended the Republican convention of 1920 and ... [saw] much of each other. Ring respected Mencken above almost all other contemporary critics." Clifford M. Caruthers adds that at the convention "Lardner and Mencken became good friends. They shared a number of views, notably distrust of the American politician and skepticism of an electoral process dependent on the good judgment of the American 'boob.'" Lardner chortled when Mencken sent him a copy of his revised *American Language* (1921) inscribed to Lardner " the eminent philologist." Mencken reviewed Lardner's subsequent writings as they came out in book form, and often with half-embarrassing overpraise. Over the years, Lardner and Mencken met too seldom to please either. Their letters, however, particularly when Lardner was hospitalized (1932, 1933), indicate deep friendship and dying Lardner's undying humor. (Sources: Elder, 122, 332; Caruthers [1995], 109, 139, and *passim*; Martin, 126, 169; Mencken [1919], 190–191; Yardley, 236–237, 286–287, 295–296)

MERCER, SID (*The Big Town*). He is wealthy "horseman" Herbert Daley's well-paid, dishonest, alcoholic jockey. Sid secretly dates Katie, Daley's fiancée, rides Daley's horse Only One at the Belmont, and deliberately loses. Daley knows about Sid and Katie, but still bets heavily on Only One, and loses. Both dump flighty Katie.

MERKLE In "Horseshoes," he plays for the Giants in the third game during their World Series against the Athletics. In "The Busher Beats It Hence," Keefe complains that when he was pitching for the White Sox in "a exibishun" game in Chicago, he tried to "waist" a ball that Merkle luckily "hit in to the seats."

Frederick Charles Merkle (1888–1956) played for the New York Giants (1907–1915), the Giants and the Brooklyn Dodgers (1916), the Dodgers and the Chicago Cubs (1917), the Cubs (1918–1920), and the New York Yankees (195–1926). (Sources: *Baseball Encyclopedia*, 1358; Hilton, 171–172)

MESSENGER, MRS. ("Three Without, Doubled"). She is married to Robert Messenger, who owns apartment buildings in Chicago. She invites the Gullibles to join the San Susie bridge club. Mrs. Gullible gets Gullible to agree. At a bridge party hosted by Mrs. Garrett and her husband, Gullible and Mrs. Messenger are "pardners" at one table and lose playing against Garrett and Mrs. Gullible.

MESSENGER, ROBERT ("Three Without, Doubled"). He owns several Chicago apartment buildings, including one where the Gullibles live, and another where the Garretts live. When the Gullibles attend a San Susie bridge club dinner party at the Garretts' home, Gullible is so gauche that he asks Garrett what rent they pay. Gullible describes Messenger as exceedingly thin.

MEUSEL ("Women"). He is a batter on the team playing against Mike Healy's team. He gets a hit off pitcher Lefty, who explains his hook "didn't break."

Robert William Meusel (1896–1977) played for the New York Yankees (1920–1929) and the Cincinnati Reds (1930). "Long Bob," 6' 3", 190 lbs., appeared in the movie *The Pride of the Yankees* (1942). (Sources: *Baseball Encyclopedia*, 1361; Spears, 271)

MEYER, GUY (*The Real Dope*). This is the name of a French ace, according to Jack Brady, an American soldier in France who enjoys spinning stories to gullible Simon, a fellow soldier.

MEYER, JOE (*The Big Town*). He is a bookie whom Finch casually meets at the Jamaica racetrack. Finch prefers to place a big bet with Haynes, another bookie.

MEYERS ("Alibi Ike"). He is the New York catcher who throws out Alibi Ike trying to steal second. Ike alibis that the batter missed a nonexistent hit-and-run sign.

MEYERS ("Horseshoes"). He is mentioned as the Giants catcher playing in the fourth game of the World Series against the Athletics.

MEYERS, HOD ("Haircut"). He was Jim Kendall's fellow village joker.

MEYERS, TOM ("Greek Tragedy") *see* **ALEXIS, GREEK**

MIKE ("Three Without, Doubled"). He is the custodian of the apartment building where Gullible and his wife live. After the disastrous San Susie bridge club meeting at the home of Mrs. Garrett and her husband, Mrs. Gullible is so angry at Gullible that, to escape, he "went down to help Mike close up."

MILAN In "The Busher Comes Back," Keefe boasts that when pitching for the White Sox and a Boston player was on first, he offered nothing Milan could bunt, and he flied out. In "Sick 'Em" the narrator gloats that "Milan and Gandil ... might just as well of used jackstraws as bats," when Smitty, pitching for the Phillies, defeated Washington. In "Horseshoes," Milan plays outfield for Washington and makes a lucky catch of a fly hit by Dick Grimes, playing for the Athletics after they have clinched the pennant. In "The Crook," Milan hit a fly ball that Larry, the narrator playing first base for the White Sox, missed. Later errors caused Larry to be upset and shout at Bull, the umpire. In "Call for Mr. Keefe!," Milan bunted, could have been "throwed" out by McMullin, but was given a hit. In *The Real Dope*, Keefe remembers a wind-blown hit Milan got one day against his pitching.

George W. Hilton reports that Jesse Clyde Milan (1887–1953) played outfield for Washington (1907–1922) and was the Milan referred to in "The Busher Comes Back" and in "Horseshoes," but that Clyde, as he was called, was sick, did not play in the game described in "Call for Mr. Keefe!," and was substituted for by his brother Horace Milan. Horace Milan (1894–1955) played outfield for Washington (1915–1917). (Sources: *Baseball Encyclopedia*, 1364; Hilton, 88, 213)

MILBURN, FRED ("Widow"). He is the second husband of Mrs. Milburn, who met him in Miami while she was vacationing after Archie, her first husband, died.

MILBURN, MRS. ("Widow"). She lost her first husband, Archie, when they were living in Louisville, Kentucky. She tells Margart Winslow, whose husband John has just died, that "time is a great healer," that her religion helped her, that Dr. Sampson advised her to take a trip, that she met Fred Milburn in Miami, and that in a year "this may all seem like a bad dream that never happened." The Milburns and Margaret live in the same city.

When "the Fred Milburns" send a "floral tribute" labeled "Gates Ajar" to John Winslow's funeral, could this be Mrs. Milburn's way of telling John's widow Margaret that her terrestrial future is wide open?

MILLER ("My Roomy"). He is one of several Chicago baseball players who refuse to accept Buster Elliott as a roommate. Miller first tells John that Elliott won't try to catch fly balls.

Ward Taylor Miller (1884–1958), played for the Pittsburgh Pirates and the Cincinnati Reds (1909), the Reds (1910), the Chicago Cubs (1912–1913), and the St. Louis Browns (1916–1917). (Sources: *Baseball Encyclopedia*, 1370; Hilton, 335)

MILLER, C. T. ("'In Conference'"). He and others work for Kramer & Company. He is the treasurer. He tells T. W. Havers that he sold "Balzac complete" when he was "a bibliopolistic actuary in southern Ohio."

MILLER, FRANK ("Hurry Kane"). He and Lefty Glaze are traded to the St. Louis baseball team from the Boston baseball team for Bullard, Robinson, and Roy Smith. All five are ineffective players.

MILLER, MISS ("Liberty Hall"). In one of the "emergency exit" wires pre-prepared by Ben Drake, Miss Miller and Shaw are supposedly suffering from laryngitis and Ben must return to New York to rewrite "the score ... half tone lower."

MILLER, RUDY ("Cured!"). He and his buddies Joe Gale and Paul Stroud drink with their friend Dick Streeter at Mike Clayton's bar. Their challenge to Dick to have too much renders him unable to meet his wife Mary for their dinner engagement with friends.

If Lardner's wife ever read this story, she must have been embarrassed, for it would have reminded her of when Lardner's own excessive drinking with his buddies meant that she had to make excuses, as Dick's wife Mary must.

MILTON, YOUNG ("Champion"). He is a boxer scheduled to fight Midge Kelly in New York soon after Joe Morgan interviews Wallie Adams, Midge's dishonest manager.

MIN ("A Frame-Up"). She is a girl the narrator says one can see in Chicago dancing at "St. Joe" but then to be found mid-week at "the Draperies." (The references are unclear.)

MISSUS, THE ("The Clubby Roadster"). She is the narrator's wife. His fellow office-worker Harry Cross takes his wife Nan Cross, the narrator, and his wife on a drive out of Chicago.

MISSUS, THE ("A Friendly Game"). She is the narrator's quietly demanding wife. They give a poker party in their home. Their guests are Jim Hatch and Mrs. Hatch, Harry Quinn and Marion Quinn, and Joe Tuttle. The Missus tries to defuse arguments during the inept, cheating play, and serves sandwiches and coffee.

"MR. AND MRS. FIX-IT" (*Liberty*, May 9, 1925; LN, RU). (Characters: Ada, Crandall, Mrs. Crandall, Peggy Flood, Charley Krom, Belle Stevens, Tom Stevens, Thayer, Mrs. Thayer.)

The narrator and his wife Ada have been in this town only three days, and already people have come to ask if they are comfortable and to offer help. Why he and Ada came here is the narrator's long story:

In Chicago, my old drinking friends came with their wives to my house, but my wife Ada disliked their not liking bridge or mah jong or crossword puzzles. Ada's friends were no better. Crandall boasted of his war valor; his wife was on the Boardwalk in Atlantic City when a movie crew was shooting, and she was in it and her friends said if she became an actress she could outdo Gloria Swanson.* Thayer mimicked birds, played the ocarina, recited Kipling and "Robert H. [make that W.] Service"[*]; Mr. Crandall taught elocution, would read when asked — or when not — and talked baby talk. Peggy Flood was happy only when going into or recovering from surgery. Ada's newest friend, Belle Stevens, however, was "the cat's nightgown."

Ada and Belle met by chance on the Elevated. Belle insisted on showing her around and even told her that her husband Tom knew law well enough to help us break our one-year lease and move from the South Side to the better North Side. Belle and Tom came calling. Tom wanted to examine our lease, which I lied was elsewhere. Tom saw my safety razor, recommended his regular one, wanted to take me to his razor salesman. At this point, I labeled Tom and Belle "Mr. and Mrs. Fix-It." Belle disliked Ada's dress and suggested taking her to a dress shop where Ada could buy better garments, at a discount. Ada reluctantly bought three expensive dresses there that she didn't want. The mail brought me three razors, a bill, and a note that "Thomas J. Stevens" had selected them. Ada and I accepted an invitation to visit the Stevenses, where the owner of the apartment building was waiting to meet the "prospective tenant" Tom wanted to introduce. I declined, to everyone's distress.

After two months, the Stevenses practically lived with us. One day Ada was critical of our cook; next day "a Jap come to the apartment," sent by Belle as replacement. Ada sent him away. After complaining her feet hurt, Ada fibbed to Belle to keep her from making an appointment with her chiropodist. The Stevenses heard that Ada and I wanted to see "Red" Grange play in a scheduled Illinois-Chicago game but lacked tickets. Tom promised to get good tickets for all four of us, since "Stagg and I is just like that." The seats were awful. But Tom did have influential friends. I "got pinched for speedin' one night" and happened to tell Tom. He phoned a judge and had my ticket "wiped off the book."

Nonetheless, the Stevenses interfered with everything. "I and Ada" planned a winter trip to Miami, vowed to keep mum, but when the Stevenses invited us to join them for a post–New Year's California vacation, we felt safe in mentioning our plans. Tom made us cancel our "Big Four" railroad reservations for better ones he obtained on "the C. & E. I.," through his knowing its general passenger agent. He also changed our reservations from the Royal Palm to the Flamingo, whose manager was Charley Krom, a childhood pal. Belle persuaded Ada to exchange her beach togs for better ones at her better shop. I told Ada we'd soon be in Miami away from the Stevenses, who, however, phoned to say they'd canceled California and would join us aboard their C. & E. I. bound for Miami.

That's why "we happened to come to Biloxi."

When "Red" Grange and Stagg are mentioned, Lardner is providing some 1920s local color. Harold Edward "Red" Grange (1903–1991) was an All-American football player at the University of Illinois (1923–1925), played professionally for the Chicago Bears (1928–1935), and was elected to the Football Hall of Fame (1963). Amos Alonzo Stagg (1862–1965) played football and baseball at Yale, and became an innovative football coach at various colleges and universities, notably at the University of Illinois (1892–1932). Donald Elder says that "'Mr. and Mrs. Fix-It' is not a very remarkable story; ... but it is amusing in connection with a paragraph in the introduction." Elder didn't explicate the amusing paragraph, which may escape the unwary. It is simply that once "I and Ada" escape to Biloxi, they are barraged by do-good meddlers no more welcome than Tom and Belle of "Chi." Biloxi is then mentioned at the ending. Elizabeth Evans notes that "Biloxi ... [is] hardly a traveler's paradise." Walton R. Patrick notes that the meddlers in "Mr. and Mrs. Fix-It" are "less cruel" than villainous ones in other Lardner stories but are "more significant because ... more common." (Sources: Elder, 239; Evans, 54; Patrick, 107; Streissguth, 230–231, 372)

"MR. FRISBIE" (*Cosmopolitan*, June 1928; RLR, RU). (Characters: Florence Craig, Henry Craig, Allen Frisbie, Mrs. Frisbie, Robert Frisbie, Holt, Junior Holt, Kirk, Vischer.)

The narrator is one of the three chauffeurs and is the golf caddy of ultra-wealthy Mr. Allen Frisbie. He is about 60, and that is not his real name. The narrator ejects Kirk, a journalist who wanted to interview Frisbie about his golf game, which is wretched. The narrator decides to write an essay himself about Allen Frisbie, his golf, and his family:

Frisbie bought the Vischer estate. It included a 9-hole golf course, which Frisbie would have plowed to use the land otherwise except that his golf-playing brother-in-law happened by and asked Frisbie to try a golf drive. He drove uniquely well, once, and became such "a slave of the game" that he added nine more holes to his links. When he played badly, he was a grouch. So I secretly helped him improve his score. Once, I surreptitiously tossed Frisbie's golf ball out of a sand trap, thus helping him shoot 112 for 18 holes — his new record.

Mrs. Frisbie liked music, couldn't play the piano, and asked Frisbie to buy her a player piano. No was his reply; "pianos were made to be played by hand." I intervened. When Frisbie happened to make a good shot, I whistled for Mrs. Frisbie, placed strategically, to ask for her piano. "Why certainly dear." The Frisbies' son Robert, 16, wanted to drive a car. No; "There is plenty of chauffeurs." So I secretly improved Frisbie's bad golf-ball position at one point, therefore was cheerfully permitted to give Robert car-driving lessons. The Frisbies' daughter Florence wanted to marry attractive but impoverished Henry Craig. Frisbie, learning that Craig was an unemployed "tramp" who cadged drinks, ordered her instead to wed Junior Holt, the pudgy, sneering son of Frisbie's former partner or be "cut ... off without a dime." Siding with Florence, Mrs. Frisbie appealed to me. I suggested that Florence should seemingly relent, and tell Junior, a splendid golfer, to ask to play with Frisbie, who, she was to say, would appreciate tips to improve his game but was too shy to ask. In reality, Frisbie loathed advice. After Frisbie "swang" badly at the first tee, Junior advised him as to stance, balance, grip, back swing, and follow-through. Holt's own drive off the second tee was so excellent that the game ended there, with his profane dismissal. Frisbie allowed Florence to marry Craig, probably to "rile Junior Holt." In truth, when Frisbie said Craig "would never amount to anything," he proved to be correct.

Lardner gives this story temporal local color by mentioning golf champions Walter Hagen (1892–1969), Bobby Jones (1902–1971), Gene Sarazen (1902–1999), and Alex Smith (1872–1930), and one president — Calvin Coolidge.* Lardner played golf once with his sportswriter friend Grantland Rice.* Not also with Coolidge, it needn't be said, but actually with President Warren G. Harding (in April 1921). Don Van Natta Jr. narrates the event. Jonathan Yardley notes that "'Mr. Frisbie' is [only] a variation on ... 'A Caddy's Diary' [1922]." Nevertheless, the sincere but semi-illiterate narrator's mangled English and unconscious humor make it uproarious. For one example among many, at one "junction" the Frisbies "disgust" something. Better, the narrator attended "the polo at Meadowbrook" because he loved "horse's flesh." (Sources: Sommers; Van Natta, 272–273; Yardley, 229, 331)

MR. SMART ("The Busher Reënlists") *see* **KELLY**

MOLLA ("Old Folks' Christmas"). She is Grace and Tom Carter's Scandinavian maid.

MOLLNITZ, FRITZ ("Where Do You Get That Noise?"). Fritz Mollnitz, Heine Groh, Count Von Kolnitz, Wagner, Schneider, and Herzog are Reds players. Carey, a Cub, says their names should help the Reds break attendance records in Cincinnati, which is full of citizens of German background. Hawley wonders what about away games.

Frederick August Mollwitz (1890–1967), born in Hoburg, Germany, played for the Chicago Cubs (1913), the Cubs and the Cincinnati Reds (1914, 1916), the Pittsburgh Pirates (1917–1918), and the Pirates and the St. Louis Cardinals (1919). (Sources: *Baseball Encyclopedia*, 1377; Hilton, 513)

MONTAGUE, JIMMIE ("'In Conference'"). While "in conference," F. X. Murphy asks Z. H. Holt if he read Jimmie Montague's poem in this morning's *Record*. Z. H. replies, "No, F. X."

MONTANA, BULL ("Greek Tragedy"). He is a wrestler presumed to be ugly. He is known to Big Bill Buell and Greek Alexis, both definitely ugly.

MOON, FRANK ("Nora"). He is a successful lyricist, and works with Jerry Morris, successful tunesmith, to create musical shows which Louie Brock produces. Brock introduces the two to Hazlett, the plot of whose play "Nora" they completely revise to their liking.

MOON, LARRY ("The Battle of the Century"). He is the narrator Pinkie's friend. Larry managed Jim Dugan, a professional boxer. Larry matched Dugan against three fighters, enabling Larry to match Dugan against Goulet, an admired French boxer. Larry conned wealthy Robert Crawley and Bill Guthrie out of $100,000 and got Charley Riggs to create a million-dollar purse, most of which went to Larry, Riggs, and Dugan, and $200,000 to La Chance, French manager of Goulet, whom Dugan defeated.

Larry Moon is based on Jack Kearns, who was manager (1917–1925) of the championship boxer Jack Dempsey,* as Lardner explains in a letter (August 4, 1921) to a *Saturday Evening Post* editor, and as Clifford M. Caruther annotates. Kearns, born in Michigan as John Leon McKernan (1882–1963), also later was manager (1931–1932) of lightweight champion Benny Leonard (1896–1947). (Source: Caruthers [1995], 134)

MOORE, BILLY ("Hurry Kane"). He is an oil-rich Texan, is a friend of Dave, the St. Louis baseball team manager, and recommends Hurry Kane to Dave.

MOORE, MARIAN ("Pity is Akin —"). She is a sultry singer at New York's Cozy Club. Henry Spalding tries to get her to violate liquor laws, testifies against her in court, but seems relieved when she is acquitted. He locates her again, now singing at The Snug for better pay. For revenge, she has her associate Joe Schwartz slug him.

Lardner snidely reports in this 1929 story that although poor Marian's crooked smile "gave her face a childish appearance," she was old enough to "have voted for Hughes." Charles Evans Hughes (1862–1948) ran for president and lost when Woodrow Wilson was reelected (1916).

MOORE, VIOLET ("The Facts"). She applies for the position of secretary for Billy Bowen. Her leaving him a note on her business card to phone him "any night after seven" causes Billy woe because Tommy Richards put the card with Billy's

Christmas present, a cheap wrist watch, and dispatched the gift to Ellen McDonald, Billy's fiancée.

MORAN, JACK ("The Hold-Out"). He and Hype Corliss were both inadequate pitchers; so Frank Conley traded them for Johnny Gould.

MORAN, LOIS (1908–1990). Actress. Pittsburgh-born but reared in France by her widowed mother, Lois Moran danced professionally with the Paris National Opera (1922–1924) and was featured in three French movies. Returning to America, she debuted in *Stella Dallas* (1925). She appeared in 24 more American films in the 1920s, left Hollywood (1931) to appear in Broadway musical comedies (to 1935), including *Of Thee I Sing* (1931) by George S. Kaufman* and George Gershwin.* She taught drama, was featured in television productions, and was the model for several characters in fiction by Lardner's close friend F. Scott Fitzgerald,* including Rosemary Hoyt in *Tender Is the Night* (1934), in which Abe North, another character, is partly patterned after Lardner. The name Lois Moran appears in "I Can't Breathe."

MORAN, MIKE ("The Venomous Viper of the Volga"). He is a boxer. Though dubbed "the Malden Murderer" and winning over Eddie Brock, Moran is defeated by Frankie Fitzgerald.

MORAN, PAT In "The Busher Pulls a Mays," Keefe says his White Sox teammates boast that their pitchers Cicotte and Williams will defeat Moran's Cincinnati team. In "Back to Baltimore," Pat (Moran) coached for the Phillies at first base in a game against the Boston Braves. He told inept William Baker, Jr., playing first base for Boston, to throw to second, which he did — with no one covering second. In "Where Do You Get That Noise?," it is said that Pat Moran traded Hawley away from the Phillies because he could no longer stand listening to him talk constantly. See also Pat ("Sick *'Em*").

Patrick Joseph Moran (1876–1924) played for the Boston Braves (1901–1905), the Chicago Cubs (1906–1909), and the Philadelphia Phillies (1910–1914), then managed the Phillies (1915–1918) and the Cincinnati Reds (1919–1923). George W. Hilton observes that Moran had been "an undistinguished catcher ... but ... led the Phillies to their first pennant in his first season as manager, in 1915." (Sources: *Baseball Encyclopedia*, 703–704, 1384; Hilton, 315)

MOREHEAD (*Own Your Own Home*). He and his wife are neighbors in Allison on whom Grace calls briefly (and evidently without social success).

MOREHEAD, MRS. (*Own Your Own Home*). She and her husband live near Fred and Grace Gross. Grace visits them once.

MORGAN, JOE ("Champion"). He is a New York *News* reporter who interviews Wallie Adams, Midge Kelly's manager, about Midge. Joe writes and prints Adams' lies about Midge's clean, unselfish life.

MORGAN, MISS ("A Frame-Up"). She gives a benefit show at "the Garden," with the receipts going "to devastated France." The Leonard-Mitchell boxing match is a main feature (January 14, 1921).

MORIARTY In "A Busher's Letters Home," Keefe says that when he was pitching for the White Sox against the Tigers, he "got mad" at Schalk, his catcher; so he walked Moriarty. In "A New Busher Breaks In," Keefe says that he saw Violet Hill applaud when he made Moriarty "pop up in the pinch." This seems doubtful, because Violet's husband, John Hill, was pitching well for Detroit at the time.

George Moriarty (1884–1864) played for the Chicago Cubs (1903–1904), the New York Yankees (1906–1908), the Detroit Tigers (1909–1915), and the Chicago White Sox (1916). George W. Hilton reports that Moriarty then became an American League umpire (1917–1926, 1929–1940). (Sources: *Baseball Encyclopedia*, 1388; Hilton, 68)

MORRIS ("The Love Nest"). He is a "fat old ... hotel man" that Celia Gregg boasts to Bartlett she "could have" if she wanted. She says the only reason Morris is regarded as "a model husband" is that he is "too stingy" "to step out more."

MORRIS, IKE ("Greek Tragedy"). He is wrestler Big Bill Buell's manager.

MORRIS, JERRY ("Nora"). He is a successful tunesmith and works with Frank Moon, a successful lyricist. When Louie Brock, their successful producer, introduces them to playwright Hazlett, the three revise his play "Nora" to their liking.

MORRIS, JOE ("What of It?"). He is a New York producer who has accepted Dexter Cosset's play *Ghosts*. He wants it to be renamed *Carlotta's Corns*, because, as he wires Cosset, "man named Ibsen has a farce that title [i.e., *Ghosts*]" The new title is inane, because Carlotta, the heroine of the play, doesn't have corns.

MORRIS, SAM ("Hurry Kane"). He is a crooked gambler and Evelyn Corey's associate. Morris pays Hurry Kane to throw the final game his St. Louis baseball team is playing against the White Sox. Topping informs Kane that Evelyn is faithful to Morris and won't marry Kane. Morris also bribes Digman and Stout, who try to throw the game by making errors but don't succeed.

MORSE, GEORGE ("I Can't Breathe"). The diarist says she can't believe Merle Oliver meant it when she said she was engaged to George Morse.

MORSE, GEORGE ("Zone of Quiet"). He is Miss Eleanor's latest B.F. (boy friend). She tells her patient that she danced with him and that Marian, her rival for Roy Stewart's attentions, is welcome to him.

MORSE, HELEN ("Anniversary"). She was a friend of Grace, Florence Hammond's sister. To explain how irresponsible Grace's husband Ed has always been, Florence tells Bess that he was to elope with Grace, who was staying with the Morse family, but forgot to pick her up as planned. The two got married later.

MORSE, HELEN ("Rhythm"). She is a guest at a party given by Buck and his wife. She is "enraptured" to meet Harry Hart and asks him to play "Something of your own!" He confesses he steals all of his memorable tunes, then plays something he stole and used in Conrad Green's "Upsy Daisy" musical.

MORSE, MRS. ("The Golden Honeymoon"). She is from Rutland, Vermont, and plays roque with Mother, Mrs. Hartsell, and Mrs. Ryan in Florida.

MORTON ("High-rollers"). He played high-stakes poker with Kenneth Hart, Dick Parker, and Alex Spears. Jack Bowen tells his friend Walter Finch that he sat in one night and watched Hart win $200,000 from Spears. Walter asks Jack if Spears paid. Jack replies that "he will."

MOSELLE, MISS (*The Real Dope*) *see* **PALMER, RUTH**

MOTHER ("The Golden Honeymoon"). She has been Charley's affectionately named wife for 50 years. Her maiden name was Lucy Frost. She was engaged to Frank M. Hartsell until Charley came along. Mother, now 70 or 71, and Charley have a daughter, Edie Kramer. Edie suggests that her parents celebrate their golden wedding anniversary by going to Florida. They do, with a predictable combination of pleasure and boredom.

MOTHER (*The Young Immigrunts*). She is the devoted mother of the narrator Bill, and his brothers John, Jimmie, and David. She is also the long-suffering wife of their father. She endures his grumpy sarcasm when he drives her and the narrator to "Grenitch Conn.," but launches a few effective barbs in response.

MOVIES BASED ON LARDNER'S WORKS *The New Klondike* (1925), a silent, was filmed from an original scenario by Lardner. *Fast Company* (1929), *Elmer the Great* (1933), and *The Cowboy Quarterback* (1939) were based on "Hurry Kane" and the play *Elmer the Great. June Moon* (1931) and *Blonde Trouble* (1937) were based on *June Moon*, which was adapted from "Some Like Them Cold." *So This Is New York* (1948) was based on *The Big Town. Alibi Ike* (1935) was based on "Alibi Ike." *Champion* (1949) was based on "Champion." Efforts were also made, unsuccessfully, to convert both *You Know Me Al* and "I Can't Breathe" into movies. (Sources: Elder, 288–289; Lardner, Jr., 150–153; Caruthers [1995], 194; Spears, 265, 266; Yardley, 301)

MOWREY ("Horseshoes"). He and fellow Pittsburgh infielder Gibson collide going for a grounder by Cub player Speed Parker, who gets an undeserved two-run double.

Harry Harlan Mowrey (1884 or 1887–1947) played for the Cincinnati Reds (1905–1908), the Reds and the St. Louis Cardinals (1909), the Cardinals (1910–1913), the Pittsburgh Pirates (1914), and the Brooklyn Dodgers (1916–1917). (Sources: *Baseball Encyclopedia*, 1394; Hilton, 400)

MOXEY ("A One-Man Team"). He plays halfback, as does Byron, for Doane, the team Coach Belden plans to defeat by stressing defense against Davis, Doane's "one-man team." Moxey proves to be a formidable offensive player.

MULVIHILL, MISS JOSIE ("The Courtship of T. Dorgan"). Keefe says that Dumont and his wife, who are Florrie Keefe's beauty-shop partners, escorted Miss Josie Mulvihill, "a mighty sweet looking doll," to a baseball game. The five begin partying with Tom Dorgan, whom Keefe brought into the picture. Although Keefe distressed Florrie by flirting with Josie, the girl preferred Dorgan and became engaged to him.

George W. Hilton says that, given Lardner's "puritannical" nature, Keefe's holding hands with Miss Mulvihill "was the worst offense he could be expected to put in print." Hilton adds that "the total absence of sexual urges in his characters" is a weakness in Lardner's writings and that "an actual busher would have attempted more than the ... handholding he allowed Jack Keefe." (Source: Hilton, 16, 29)

MUNGO ("The Ides of June"). He is a Brooklyn player. Danny mentions to Jessie that he was sent to pinch hit for Mungo in a game against St. Louis.

Van Lingo Mungo (1911–1985) played for the Brooklyn Dodgers (1931–1941) and the New York Giants (1942–1945). (Source: *Baseball Encyclopedia*, 2244)

MURDOCK, BEATRICE ("Old Folks' Christmas"). She and her brother Paul are Caroline Carter's friends. Caroline parties with the two over Christmas vacation so extensively that she totally ignores her parents, Tom and Grace Carter.

MURDOCK, PAUL ("Old Folks' Christmas"). He is Beatrice Murdock's brother, 19. The two socialize over Christmas vacation with siblings Ted and Caroline Carter. Caroline likes Paul. Ted likes Paul's sports car.

MURPHY ("Horseshoes"). He plays for the Athletics. When they have clinched the pennant, Dick Grimes, another Athlete, substitutes for him in a game against Washington, strikes out and grounds out. During the second game of the World Series, Murphy grounds to the Giants' third base man, Speed Parker, whose foot deflects the ball to another infielder for an out.

George W. Hilton identifies Murphy as probably John Edward Murphy (1891–1969), who played for the Philadelphia Athletics (1912–1915), the Athletics and the Chicago White Sox (1915), the White Sox (1916–1921), and the Pittsburgh Pirates (1926). (Sources: *Baseball Encyclopedia*, 1401; Hilton, 407)

MURPHY ("MURPH") ("Oh You Bonehead!"). He is the coach of Leighton's track team. He released Joe Draper, his crack track runner, to the Coach of Leighton's football team. When Joe made a "bonehead" play that enabled Pelham to defeat Leighton, the Coach rebuked him, with tragic consequences. Only after Murphy told off the Coach did he realize that experienced coaches should consider their youthful players' inevitable inadequacies.

Murphy, obviously Irish, boasted to the Coach that if his track team didn't win with Joe's brilliance, "my name's Goldstein." This could rank as anti-Semitic — but on Murph's part, not Lardner's. Ring Lardner Jr. repeatedly asserts that his father was not anti-Semitic. (Source: Larder, Jr., 26–27, 145)

MURPHY, EDDIE (*The Real Dope*). He played right field well in a White Sox game in which Keefe boasts to fellow soldiers that he brilliantly pitched.

John Edward Murphy (1891–1969) played for the Philadelphia Athletics (1912–1914), the Athletics and the White Sox (1915), the White Sox (1916–1921), and the Pittsburgh Pirates (1926). (Source: *Baseball Encyclopedia*, 1401)

MURPHY, F. X. ("'In Conference'"). He and others work for Kramer & Company. While "in conference" they talk ramblingly. He asks Z. H. Holt if he read a recent poem by Jimmie Montague.

MURRAY ("Absent-minded Beggar"). This is the name of the corporation J. M. McInerny tells John Knowles he wants to invest in.

MURRAY ("Horseshoes"). He plays for the Giants. In the first game of the World Series against the Athletics, he lines out to Barry. In the second game, Murray hits a line drive to Speed Parker, who boots the ball to Doyle at second base for a lucky out.

John Joseph Murray (1884–1958) played for the St. Louis Cardinals (1906–1908), the New York Giants (1909–1914), the Giants and the Chicago Cubs (1915), and the Giants (1917). (Sources: *Baseball Encyclopedia*, 1403; Hilton, 411)

"MY ROOMY" (*Saturday Evening Post*, May 9, 1914; ABS, HTW, LOB, RAB, RLR, RU). (Characters: Amos, Archer, Benton, Bert, Brid, Carter, the Chief, Buster Elliott, Charlie Faust, Griner, Heinie, Hobby, Hofman, the Indian, Big Jeff, Jim, John, Bill Klem, Larry, Jim Lavender, Tommy Leach, McGraw, Matty, Miller, Tom Needham, Oakes, Perdue, Pierce, Richie, Rigler, Rube, Saier, Sallee, Schulte, Sheckard, Dummy Taylor, Big Ed Walsh, Martin Walsh, Whitted, Charlie Williams.)

I. The narrator plays professional baseball for Chicago. John, their manager, hears that Buster Elliott is a fine semi-pro hitter and a fast runner, and hires him. Elliott arrives without baggage at spring training in Tampa, hasn't eaten in three days, makes up for it by "inhal[ing] ... four meals at once." At practice, he refuses to chase fungoes but batting left-handed he fiercely wallops every type of pitch they try him with. He plays infield so badly that John will use him as pinch hitter.

II. John assigns Elliott to room with one fellow player after another. Heine calls him a "bug" (i.e., insane). Nor can Archer, Schulte, Larry Miller, or Leach stand him. Saier even fears his potential for violence. Elliott runs bath water all night, since it reminds him of a dam back home. Carter starts a fight with Elliott and is almost killed. Elliott shaves nightly before a mirror and waves his razor over ostensible sleepers. The month of May gives way to June. In Indianapolis, John says Elliott likes the narrator and gets the narrator to accept Elliott as his "roomy" when they open in Cincinnati.

III. In their room, the narrator turns on the bath water and starts shaving at night. Elliott turns the water off and accepts the narrator's suggestion that shaving in the morning might improve his fielding ability, thus emulating Cobb more.

IV. Against Cincinnati, the narrator's team loses two games despite Elliott's excellent pinch-hitting. They win the third game without Elliott. When Elliott violates night curfew, the narrator warns him; but Elliott says John couldn't fine him because he's broke, and anyway he's hitting well. The narrator tells Elliott his hitting might get worse. During the first game against St. Louis, Elliott could have snatched victory from defeat in the eighth, but after slamming two vicious fouls strikes out, deliberately, to save the St. Louis pitcher from embarrassment, he explains. He adds that he's saving for $500 with which to marry an infatuated girl from Muskegon. She isn't pretty but sings loud. The narrator foolishly asks whether Elliott can sing. He bellows "Silver Threads Among the Gold" after midnight. The hotel night clerk and the hotel detective make him stop. He sings in the street. Next day, instead of firing Elliott, tempted though the bosses were, John has him pinch hit in the ninth, down 3–1, with the bases full. He hits a triple and next play steals home. The team has a two-week series at home in "Chi." Elliott tells the narrator during that time he went to violent "nickel shows," so as to learn how to kill people, which he may do "some day." Elliott wins two home games, against Pittsburgh, and against "Cincy."

V. In Pittsburgh the fellows are playing poker in the narrator's room. Elliott enters, hints at ignorance but plays, wins, then loses, wants to sleep, and orders everyone out. The narrator praises his "busting" homers but not his poker playing. Elliott says his "business" is "bustin' things," hurls a water pitcher through the window, and when calmer says he and his wife-to-be will do vaudeville singing. Elliott predicts their team won't win the pennant and play in the World Series, but, told of fall city-series games maybe gaining him $500–$800, depending, says he'll try to "behave."

VI. Against Boston, the team loses, partly because Elliott hit a triple and, in defiance of John's order, was thrown out trying to steal home. That night Elliott seizes the elevator, with two timid ladies and the narrator aboard, and rides it up and down ten times. The team gets to New York without further incident.

VII. Elliott receives a letter from his girl, destroys it unopened, and says, "Girls always writes the same junk." He plans to void his contract, play for New York instead, and thus earn money to get married. Tied in the tenth with two on: John sends Elliott to pinch hit. Elliott asks New York's manager McGraw if he'll hire him if he whiffs. Yes; so he strikes out and helps lose. Furious, John waivers Elliott and sells him to Atlanta. The narrator beseeches Elliott to try Atlanta and hit the majors again. Instead, he weeps about losing both money and girl, lacerates his hand by smashing the mirror, smears blood on the narrator's face, and bolts wildly from the hotel.

VIII. Without Elliott, the narrator's team plays only in the city series, loses, and each player's share is $607. The narrator eloquently persuades his 20 teammates to send Elliott a share, so he and the "other songbird" could wed. This reduces each player's share to $580, with a like sum sent to Elliott.

The narrator began his account by mentioning a letter concerning Elliott. It is from "Jim —." In it he explains he used the money to get his friend Elliott into a comfortable asylum in Kalamazoo. Elliott's girl wrote him she was marrying Joe Bishop, a soda-fountain man. He didn't read the letter. When he learned the bad news later, he found the pair and nearly killed both with a baseball bat, then sang "Silver Threads Among the Gold" He was adjudged crazy. In an enclosed note to "Old Roomy," Elliott explains "he was at bat twice and made two hits," both though are still alive, and he hopes there are good pitchers where he's "goin.'" The narrator concludes that he won't room with a "bug" ever again.

Donald Elder says that Lardner's "My Roomy" "is one of his earliest [stories] and ... has some technical crudities; yet Elliott's wild idiosyncrasies are so skillfully underplayed that his violence at the end comes as a breathtaking climax...." Leverett T. Smith Jr. regards "My Roomy" as "one of his most admired and one of his most enigmatic [stories]." It may be added that when the story is re-read, Lardner's unobtrusive use of foreshadowing emerges as breathtakingly skillful. Douglas Robinson offers the insight that "My Roomy," when the reader subtextually explores "Lardner's masculine self-management," becomes "an athletic allegory of Lardner's psychic economy," to be studied "as recognizing both the vital importance and the terrible fragility and instability of 'lunacy.'" (Sources: Elder, 208; Robinson, 129; Smith, 147)

MYERS, HARRY ("Insomnia"). He is an alumnus of the University of Illinois, from which Allan Spears also graduated later. Myers is reputed to have cleaned up on the stock market. He and fellow-alumnus Gilbert White persuade Allan Spears to have a drink, on the promise that afterwards Myers will give Allan a sure-fire tip. Allan agrees.

MYRTLE, AUNT ("The Clubby Roadster"). She was Nan Cross's aunt who at age 39 died and left Nan $2,500.

NAP, MRS. ("Three Without, Doubled") *see* **OLD SLUMBER**

NASH, CAPT. (*Treat 'Em Rough*). He is one of Jack Keefe's commanding officers. At one point, he gives "some of the boys a nice baling out" for disorderly appearance, but not Jack.

NAT, UNCLE ("I Can't Breathe"). He and his wife Jule take their young niece, the diarist, on a brief vacation.

NATE ("A Frame-Up"). He is Burke's manager and schedules him for many fights. Nate and the narrator are close friends.

NEEDHAM, TOM ("My Roomy"). He pitches for the Chicago baseball team. John, the manager, sends him to scout Buster Elliott in Michigan. Tom recommends him as "a whaler of a hitter."

Thomas J. Needham (1879–1926) was born in Ireland, played for the Boston Braves (1904–1907), the New York Giants (1908), and the Chicago Cubs (1909–1914). George W. Hilton adds that Needham later was a Chicago White Sox coach and scout. (Sources: *Baseball Encyclopedia*, 1409; Hilton, 334).

NELSON ("Who Dealt?"). Helen Gratz tells Mrs. Cannon she bought the dress she is wearing at Crandall and Nelson's.

NEVIN (*Treat 'Em Rough*). He was a singing instructor whose efforts failed with Jack Keefe and many of his fellow soldiers.

Is Lardner capitalizing on the name Nevin? Ethelbert Woodbridge Nevin (1862–1901) and his brother Arthur Finley Nevin (1871–1943) were American composers.

NEVINS, MISS ("Call for Mr. Keefe!"). She is Florrie Keefe's partner in a successful beauty parlor venture. They divide a June profit of $400.

"A NEW BUSHER BREAKS IN" (*Saturday Evening Post*, September 12, 1914; YKM).

NEW YORK GIANTS A National League baseball team. It was established in 1883, was active through 1957, after which it moved to San Francisco. (Sources: Light, 492–295; Streissguth, 65, 112, 234)

NEW YORK YANKEES An American League baseball team (1903–). (Sources: Light, 499–505; Streissguth, 41, 65, 112, 233–235, 243–245, 259)

NEWELL, MRS. ("The Golden Honeymoon"). She is a bird mimic from Westfield, New Jersey. Charley and Mother hear her perform at a church social in Florida.

NEWMAN ("Words and Music"). He is a lyricist who writes for Roman Starr, the popular singer.

NICHOLS ("Holycaust") *see* **EDMISTON-NICHOLS**

NIEMANN ("Champion"). This is a Milwaukee saloon where Midge Kelly runs up a tab, which he ignores.

NOONAN ("There Are Smiles"). He is a traffic policeman at Forty-seventh Street and whistles at Edith Dole's car for speeding down Fifth Avenue.

NORA ("Absent-minded Beggar"). She was the Knowleses' family maid when John Knowles was an absent-minded high-school student. She tried to help him.

NORA ("Rhythm"). She is the title figure in "Nora's Nightie," with lyrics by Sam Rose.

"NORA" (*Cosmopolitan*, February 1928; RLR, RU). (Characters: Louis Brock, Mrs. Brock, Collins, John Collins, Crowley, Nora Crowley, Enriqueta, Hazlett, the Mayor, Frank Moon, Jerry Morris, Dick Percival, Count Pizzola, Joe Stein, Charlie Williams.)

Louis Brock is a successful producer of musicals written by Jerry Morris, tunesmith, and Frank Moon, lyricist. Brock introduces the pair to Hazlett, who has written a play entitled "Nora." They are to convert it into a musical. Morris creates innovative "melodies and rhythms"; Moon specializes in "fast triplets" and incomprehensible "three-syllable rhymes." They tell Hazlett to summarize "Nora." He does, timidly, thus: Crowley, an avaricious Irish immigrant and wealthy from "the building business" in New York, knows a Collins, a crooked politician influential in "letting ... city building contracts." To gain favor with Collins, Crowley throws him a party, at which John Collins, his son, 23 or 24, sees the picture of Nora, Crowley's gorgeous niece, in Ireland. John vows to marry only her. Crowley cables Nora, over she comes, and she and John fall in love. Dick Percival, "transplanted Englishman" and sugar millionaire, also loves Nora. Crowley orders Nora to dump John for Dick. No. Old Collins, caught in a "bribery scandal," is imprisoned. He also gambled his fortune away. Crowley feels that Nora will dump penniless John, hosts a party announcing her engagement to Dick, lets her invite John, and is surprised when she says Crowley printed her fiancé's name wrong on the invitations and it should be John. She and John leave together.

Moon, Morris, and Brock quickly order revisions for "Nora," with appropriate song contents. For examples, John sings to Nora's picture, a duet "between she and the boy," "a Wop or a Heeb" comic, not an Irish one "these days." Brock wants a Spanish heroine, not Irish, because Enriqueta is under expensive contract and needs work. Moon figures her lover can be "a wop." Moon and Morris sing and play "La Paloma" and "Cara Roma," which Hazlett says are stolen tunes. He is squelched. The duo add their already-composed song ending "Montgomery, Alabam'" and featuring a girl "black as coal" who'll "be tickled pink." Joe Stein, also under contract, can be a "dinge" doing blackface. To Hazlett's queries about these grotesqueries, Morris trumpets his past successes, praises Hazlett's "good novelty idear," but says it requires changes that Hazlett can script in 30 minutes, thus. Act One: Make Nora Spanish and played by Enriqueta, make her uncle her father, make his establishment a restaurant where she is cashier, make her boyfriend rich Count Pizzola. Pizzola lends Enriqueta his sister's clothes and takes her aboard his yacht. A villainous Frenchman, also aboard, hates Pizzola, fancies Enriqueta, steals a diamond brooch from her borrowed clothes to make Pizzola despise her. To avoid being searched, innocent Enriqueta escapes via a sailor's launch. Act Two: At the Saratoga racetrack, Enriqueta's bankrupt father seeks work; after all, he trained Spanish bullfight horses. Enriqueta, with him, encounters the Frenchman and Pizzola. Pizzola asks the Frenchman for a light, getting which exposes that stolen brooch. Enriqueta won't accept lovestruck Pizzola's apology. Joe Stein sings the Alabam' song in a nearby clubhouse. All proceed to a Southern plantation. Pizzola sings his unforgotten love song to Enriqueta. His sister persuades Enriqueta to accept Pizzola, who mentions his wealth.

Morris orders Hazlett to write a finale for the lovers, over in Japan, because he and Moon have "a cherry-blososm number." He praises Hazlett's "idear" of John's falling in love with Nora's picture. Hazlett goes home, phones his bootlegger, who says he has some fine Scotch but some uncertain rye. Hazlett asks for rye.

In "Nora," Donald Elder comments, "Ring wrote of the treatment accorded the hapless writer by producers and composers. It is very close to his own experience." (Source: Elder, 270)

NORDYKE, B. B. ("'In Conference'"). He and others work for Kramer & Company. He is a vice president. They converse vacantly "in conference." He tells T. W. Havers, among others, that he is "one of a family of seven boys."

NORTON (Poodle"). Norton's Store for Men is a New York establishment. Mr. Waldron gives the narrator, one of his employees, a $50 haberdasher order to buy something there, in place of a promised Christmas bonus.

"NOW AND THEN" (as "Then and Now," *Cosmopolitan*, June 1917; RLR, RU). (Characters: Bob, Miss Cutts, Esther, Granville, Griffin, Mrs. Griffin, Jock Hutchinson, Irma.)

Irma, married to Bob for seven months but only now having "our honeymoon," writes "dearest friend" Esther four letters from Nassau, Bahamas. Three years later, Irma writes Esther four more letters, three from Nassau again, and a final one from Miami.

Feb. 3 — I enjoyed being seasick voyaging "down" (from New York) because good-sailor Bob was angelically attentive. We passed liquor-seeking British customs officials, went by two-seat carriage drawn by a "Negro" with a half-comprehensible British accent. Bob unpacked, to spare me. Once-sociable Bob demanded a corner table at lunch, to have me to himself. We enjoyed a tea dance. Bob avoided liquor, to keep his vision unblurred on me.

Feb. 6 — Since I haven't learned bridge, Bob declined a game by fibbing that we were going sailing, which we therefore did so Bob wouldn't have lied. Good-swimmer Bob disliked others' seeing me in a bathing suit, also wouldn't swim far and leave me alone, said sharks bite lonely women near shore. During a sail in a glass-bottom boat, Bob grimaced when someone spoke to me. We dined alone in our room.

Feb. 10 — I shot 92 for nine holes with golf-expert Bob. He praised my swing. He snubbed a Chicagoan (Granville) he knew, to be alone with me. I bought one copy of each photograph taken of me. Bob wouldn't let me buy extras to send to friends. The hotel's assistant manager wanted to dance with me, but Bob said I hurt my ankle swimming and told me to ignore the fellow. I read at night to Bob, so he could gaze at me.

Feb. 13 — I can't write more, Esther. "Bob don't" want me to, "for two reasons." He won't tolerate my old friends competing with his unique devotion, and details of our honeymoon are sacredly secret.

Feb. 5 — Three years later, here I am in Nassau with Bob again. He asked for a conspicuous table in the dining room, and let me unpack while he golfed with men he met dining on the boat when I bothered him by being seasick in our stateroom. He promised to finish in time for a dance but was probably delayed.

Feb. 7 — Bob is playing bridge tonight with three people he met on the boat — a man (Griffin), his wife, and her sister (Miss Cutts). This morning, Bob said swallowing salt water made him afraid to swim and told me to let recently widowered Granville, seen three years ago, teach me to swim. I wouldn't let nice Granville teach me. I'm reluctant to have fun while Bob is ill. He played afternoon golf but not with me. He called me awkward. He wouldn't try the glass-bottom boat again. Why see dirty seaweed? He was too tired from golf to dance with me, said I should dance with Granville. Bob's four highballs meant he lied that golf tired him. I offered to read in bed to him. He said I mumbled incomprehensively and should go to our room while he drank and talked business with new friends. He phoned he had to play bridge and I shouldn't wait up. I wanted to, to hear his amusingly told business anecdotes.

Feb. 8 — I ate in my room. That trio Bob met made him, though tired, play more bridge. While I was returning from the beach with Granville, a photographer took my picture. Seeing us, Bob said I must think I'm a movie star. I said the pictures were for him. He said he has plenty of photos of me, I should send them to friends. I went driving with Granville. We saw Bob swimming with Miss Cutts. Bob promised me a moonlight sail, but I saw him later with Miss Cutts and I hinted I was lonesome. Angry, he said I read too much and should write my troubles to you, Esther. This place would be "heavenly" if poor Bob could get away from talking business with the Griffins.

Feb. 11 from Miami — I'm here alone. Bob, staying in Nassau two more weeks, says I'm not "strong enough to stand the pace" there. When I return home, Esther, let's get tickets and attend some "things ... you will want to see." Please don't disappoint me.

In "Now and Then," poor Irma calls the Bahamas "heavenly" 13 times. The Bahamas, and, indeed, the world in general, would be closer to "heavenly" without monsters like Bob, of whom too many populate Lardner's fiction. This story was originally published as "Then and Now" (*Cosmopolitan*, June 1917).

NYMEYER, FRITZ ("The Ides of June"). He and his wife Grace played whist with Clara and Dave Burnett. Jessie wrote Danny that she was a guest, watched them, and was displeased by the men's bad language.

NYMEYER, GRACE ("The Ides of June"). She and her husband Fritz hosted a game of whist with Clara and Dave Burnett, and Jessie was their non-playing guest.

OAKES In "My Roomy," he and Whitted are St. Louis outfielders. Buster Elliott hits "a shot" between them for a triple. In "Horseshoes," Oakes and Magee let a ball hit by Speed Parker of the Cubs get between them for a lucky three-run triple. In "Where Do You Get That Noise?," Carey of the Cubs jokes to Hawley that his ideas are as senseless as a "trade [of Walter] Johnson to the Pittsburgh Federals for Oakes."

Ennis Talmadge Oakes (1886–1948) played for

the Cincinnati Reds (1909) and the St. Louis Cardinals (1910–1913). His middle name is also recorded as Telfair. (Sources: *Baseball Encyclopedia*, 704, 1424; Hilton, 347)

O'DAY, HENRY FRANCIS ("HANK") In "Sick 'Em," the narrator explains that without the good pitching by Smitty and Fogarty, the Phillies played the Cubs and lost three straight games to Hank (the Cubs manager). In "Horseshoes," as Hank, he manages the Cubs when Dick Grimes and Speed Parker are Cubs. In "The Busher's Kid," Keefe mentions that O'Day, Cubs manager, was reluctant to waste his pitcher Cheney against Keefe, a sure winner. In "Back to Baltimore," Mrs. Hayes, president of the Boston Braves, wanted Dixon, her manager, to tell O'Day not to let Cheney pitch, because spitballs are unsanitary.

Henry Francis O'Day (1862 or 1863–1935) played for the Washington Senators (1886–1888) and the Senators and the New York Giants (1889), then managed the Cincinnati Reds (1912) and the Chicago Cubs (1914). George W. Hilton adds that O'Day was a National League umpire "at various times from 1888 to1926." Hilton also reveals an anachronism in "Horseshoes": O'Day was not managing the Cubs in 1912, the time of the action. (Sources: *Baseball Encyclopedia*, 704, 1429; Hilton, 158, 377, 399)

ODOUL, LEFTY In "One Hit, One Error, One Out," Danny mentions Odoul and Boone as Brooklyn outfielders that he sometimes replaces. Danny also says that in the winter Lefty Odoul sells shoes. In "When the Moon Comes over the Mountain," Danny says that owing to darkness Odoul missed a fly ball in a game against Boston. In "Holycaust," Danny relays some of Lefty Odoul's jokes to Jessie.

Francis Joseph Odoul (1897–1969) played for the New York Yankees (1919–1922), the Boston Red Sox (1923), the New York Giants (1928), the Philadelphia Phillies (1929–1930), the Brooklyn Dodgers (1931–1932), and Brooklyn and the Giants (1933). (Source: *Baseball Encyclopedia*, 1429–1430)

"OH, YOU BONEHEAD!" (*Saturday Evening Post*, October 30, 1915). (Characters: Ashton, Benson, John Bentley, Bixby, Carey, Chandler, the Coach, Conrad, Dana, Dickie, Joe Draper, Eaton, Bert Harris, McGill, Meeks, Murphy, Smith, Warner, Winslow.)

The Coach's football team has just lost a game 3–0 on Saturday. Dana expects the Coach to criticize Dickie violently for pulling a costly boner. They would have won, 7–3, as crestfallen Dickie admits. Instead, the Coach praises Dickie and even says he kept the team from losing 20–0.

A few days later, Bert Harris, the Coach's "trusty scout," reports that a rival school called Doane has a very capable team, hears Dana describe how gently the Coach let Dickie off, and wonders why. The Coach replies that he was tempted to reprimand him for ignoring "common sense" and going "out of his way to pull a boner." But the Coach soon cooled off, "gave him the glad hand," and proceeds to tell Harris and Dana "a little story" so they'll understand:

When I was Leighton's coach my final year, my senior quarterback was Joe Draper. Remember about him? Much like Dickie. Joe, from little Cedarville, Iowa, was an intercollegiate track star, an excellent student, a member of the important Alpha Delt fraternity, and a clean lad. His "only dissipation" was his beautiful girlfriend. She was a junior from a fine St. Louis family, whose family all liked him. The two planned to marry when he graduated. Joe had made the freshman team at quarterback. I planned for him to be halfback, behind McGill, his quarterback. But Joe broke his arm in scrimmage and became a star runner under Murphy, Leighton's track coach. I was irate when Murphy said Joe promised to quit football and be a winning track man. The next two seasons were victorious for us, with McGill as quarterback, young Bixby playing halfback, and Conrad and Meeks "shoot[ing] through the holes." We beat Pelham 27–0 in 1911. But McGill, Conrad, and Meeks were graduating seniors. So in January I persuaded Murphy to release Joe, wrote him "a nice little spiel about comin' to the old school's rescue," and said with his speed we'd beat Pelham and Marshall too. Joe wrote me courteously: If Murphy released him, he would be my quarterback but would have to miss September's first two weeks because of previous "engagements." I learned later that he had to visit his girlfriend's family in St. Louis. I worried about Bixby, now our team captain, and also about Ashton, subbing for Conrad earlier and available as a fullback. I needed another halfback and a kicker. I wasn't aware then about Joe's kicking ability.

In early September practice, no one could kick. When Joe reported, he surprised us by drop-kicking and punting marvelously. Bixby and Joe secretly practiced formations so Joe could drop-kick from forty yards. Without showing Joe's kicking and while holding Bixby back, we beat Brandon,

Barnes, Riverside, and the Indians, even though we didn't "plunge" or "smash" very well. I was intent on winning our "two big games," against Pelham and Marshall. New York papers criticized me but remained ignorant of my strategy. Just before facing Pelham, I told my players our plans — opening lanes, faking, lateraling, but mainly relying on Joe's long punts and surprise drop-kicks. I also stressed our one surprise: "Number 91," which was a sudden shout meanng "Wait a minute! Signals!" to get Pelham's defense to relax a fatal second; then we'd run. My only strong players were Joe and Bixby, and also big Carey, my valuable guard.

Saturday, Pelham Field. Spectators from Leighton crowded in, including Joe's beautiful girlfriend. I met her, praised Joe, and said he'd win for us. She proudly called him clever. First quarter: Pelham had the offense and the wind. Carey tackled well. Second quarter: Joe punted long, soon caught one of their short punts, and on first down kicked for 3 points. Third quarter: Pelham tacklers roughed Joe, but he stood "the gaff all right" and didn't call time. Bixby and "my whole bunch" were tiring. Fourth quarter: Eaton, Pelham's quarterback, faked a kick; their Winslow ran past Bixby; Joe stopped him on our 12-yard line. But they scored, making it 7–3. After tiring back-and-forth plays and with three minutes left, I sent a sub in to tell Joe to bluff to Bixby, get close, try an onside kick. It worked, but when Bixby retrieved it Pelham's Smith nailed him unconscious on their 8-yard line. I signaled "Number 91," but Joe lined up, kicked for 3 useless points, and we lost 7–6.

I called Joe an ignorant "bonehead." When Bixby came to, he also reviled Joe, who said he confused 91 and 19 and lost his head. Later, Marshall beat us 40–0 for my final game at Leighton. Joe was so humiliated and scorned by all our students that he never graduated and also lost his girlfriend. I wrote her too assume all the blame, but she replied that she and Joe "weren't suited to each other."

Last spring I visited Leighton to brief my successor and ran into Murphy, who snubbed me until I demanded an explanation. He vigorously replied that Joe's not being on Murph's track team was insignificant. What mattered was that I knew football after 15 years of it, sought my glory by a big victory, was mad at the loss, and mercilessly rebuked a 20-year-old kid incapable of fast thinking and inevitably making a mistake. I told my wife the truth, and she sympathized with poor ruined Joe. Fellows, that's why I went easy on Dickie, who simply made a hasty mistake, just the way Joe did. Anyway, you'll see Dickie's "smoke" this Saturday against Doane!

The critics have totally ignored "Oh, You Bonehead!," which has both a complex structure — rapid introduction, flashback, and two climaxes — and an obvious but simultaneously an everlasting, solid moral. Which is that more than sticks and stones can hurt some boneheads. In "A One-Man Team" (1916), Dana, Dickie, and Harris are again involved in football, under the watchful eye of Coach Belden and eagerly hoping to defeat Doane.

OHMAN, PHIL (1896–1969). Philmore Wellington Ohman was a talented pianist and pipe-organ player whose family lacked funds to finance advanced training for him. He sold pianos in New York (1915), worked for the QRS Piano Roll Company (1919), and while there met Victor Arden,* his future partner. First, however, Ohman was an arranger-composer for singers and was a pianist for the popular band-leader Paul Whiteman* (1922). Ohman and Arden teamed up (1923) in vaudeville and club shows, and conducted pit orchestras for several musicals by George Gershwin,* beginning with his *Lady Be Good* (1924). The two also provided musical backgrounds in silent-movie theaters. "Ohman and Arden" were best known for making countless records of songs and dazzling piano rolls. After separating from Arden (1934), Ohman worked in Hollywood for a night club, as a movie scorer, as a composer, and the piano player for actors simulating their on-screen performances (to the 1950s).

"Ohman and Arden" are mentioned in "Lose with a Smile" and "There Are Smiles," and also in "A Crooner" (part of a radio review, "An Infant Industry," *The New Yorker* [February 25, 1933]).

"OLD FOLKS' CHRISTMAS" (as "Old Folks' Xmas," *Cosmopolitan*, January 1929; RLR, RU). (Characters: Caroline Carter, Grace Carter, Ted Carter, Tom Carter, Herb Castle, Henry, Barnard King, Lloyd, Molla, Beatrice Murdock, Paul Murdock, Signe.)

Christmas Eve. Tom and Grace Carter are at home, tingling with anticipation. Their son Ted, 19, a university freshman, and their daughter Caroline, 17, a boarding-school student, arrived just this morning, napped, and are now off with friends. Tom became wealthy by inventing a weather-proof paint that General Motors bought.

He and Grace will surprise Ted with a new Gorham car, hidden in the garage, and will surprise Caroline with a sealskin coat and jewelry featuring opals, Grace's favorite gem. Plus other lavish gifts. The parents are eagerly awaiting their children's return. Caroline is having a dinner-theater date with Paul Murdock, 19, and his sister, Beatrice Murdock. Ted is at a hockey game with his classmates Herb Castle and Bernard King. Paul, Beatrice, and Caroline drive up at 3:20 A.M. and sit in the car outside until 4:00. Caroline, "rumpled," comes in. She and her parents retire. Ted stumbles in, drunk, at 5:50.

Ted and Caroline appear at noon, say they're breakfasting at the Murdock home, and have time to see just a couple gifts now. Caroline adores her sealskin coat but gets permission to exchange it for something she prefers, and isn't "so crazy" about opals. Ted likes the car idea but hopes that, if undriven, it can be exchanged for a sporty Barnes model like Paul's, though with "a different color scheme." The Carters' servants, Molla and Signe, express "Scandinavian thanks" for their presents and leave. Ted drives himself and "Sis" in Tom's old Gorham to the Murdocks' place, promising "pretty sure" to be back for dinner. Caroline gifts her parents with tickets for tonight for "Jolly Jane," the show that she, Paul, and Beatrice relished last night. While the parents will be at the show, Caroline plans to entertain here at the Carter house the Murdock siblings and some more friends. The parents dine early and alone, on part of a 16-pound turkey Signe prepared. By 7:00 P.M., no children. The old folks take the train to town, see "Jolly Jane," but dislike it as a "rehash" of two earlier shows. Returning, they find their house in a shambles. Empty glasses, cigarette butts, burned carpet, etc. In the untouched music room, Tom and Grace locate their forgotten presents to each other — diamond studs and cuff buttons for him, opal ring for her. They plan to dine out tomorrow, decked out in studs and ring. They rush to bed tonight.

"Old Folks' Christmas" was aptly published in January. It is subtle enough to deserve re-reading. Ominous foreshadowing lurks in the children's changing of their names from Tom to Ted and Grace to Caroline. Tom is less worried, more sardonic, and sooner perceptive than Grace, who, however, is the one coyly suggesting a rush upstairs for what she calls "a good night's *rest* [emphasis added]" when it becomes obvious that the oldies have only each other and will be dining out, as Tom requests, "somewhere tomorrow night." Their plight, doubtless, found and finds echoes in parental dismay in the 1920s, the 1960s, the 2000s, and in other decades. The most poignant touch comes when Tom tells Grace not to worry when the kids are out very late and adds, "You were young once yourself," and Grace replies, "That's just it! When I was young, I was young." Douglas Robinson calls "Old Folks' Christmas" a story of "martyred resignation." (Source: Robinson, 138)

"OLD FOLKS' XMAS" (*Cosmopolitan*, January 1929) *see* **"OLD FOLKS' CHRISTMAS"**

OLD FOX, THE (Good for the Soul") *see* **WHISKERS**

OLD 1 LEGGED MIKE (*The Real Dope*), this is the name the imaginary flare thrower in the German army is given by Jack Brady, an American soldier, to kid Simple Simon.

OLD SLUMBER ("Three Without, Doubled"). When Gullible and his wife attend a San Susie bridge club party at the Garrett home, his "pardner" at one table is "a woman about forty-eight, and she acted like it was way past her bedtime." So he dubs her Old Slumber, and later Mrs. Nap and Mrs. Sleeper.

OLDRING In "The Busher Comes Back," Keefe complains that when he was pitching for the White Sox, the reporters wrongly scored a double for Oldring of the "Athaletics" that "Weaver had to duck to get out of the way from." In "Horseshoes," Rube Oldring plays for the Athletics. When he breaks a leg, Joyce replaces him, which causes Dick Grimes of Baltimore to be transferred by manager Dunnie to the Athletics as a utility outfielder. In *The Real Dope*, Keefe remembers a game he was pitching when Rube Oldring lined to Gandil, who misplayed it.

Reuben Henry Oldring (1884–1961) played for the New York Yankees (1905), the Philadelphia Athletics (1906–1915), the Athletics and the Yankees (1916), and the Athletics (1918). George W. Hilton notes that Oldring did break his leg, though earlier (1910). (Sources: *Baseball Encyclopedia*, 1432; Hilton, 78, 405)

OLDS ("Hurry Kane"). He is a pitcher on the St. Louis team the narrator catches for.

O'LEARY, CHARLIE In "A New Busher Breaks In," Keefe complains that when he was pitching to Charlie O'Leary, who was batting for San Francisco, O'Leary tried to avoid a fast ball, which by luck hit his bat for a single. In "The

Busher Reënlists," Charley [*sic*] O'Leary, Joe Benz, and Artie Hofman are baseball players. Keefe is upset when he meets "the boys" in a Chicago hotel and they don't ask about his war experiences.

Charles Timothy O'Leary (1881 or 1882–1941) played for the Detroit Tigers (1904–1912), the St. Louis Cardinals (1913), the San Francisco Seals (1914), and for one pinch-hit performance with the St. Louis Browns in a successful effort to improve his batting average (1934). George W. Hilton suggests that O'Leary would indeed be in Chicago looking for work because he had discontinued managing the Texas League's San Antonio team (1917) and only later was to manage the semi-professional Gunthers (Chicago West Side, 1919). Hilton mentions that O'Leary and Herman A. "Germany" Schaefer, who were teammates with the Tigers, tried a vaudeville act together. (Sources: *Baseball Encyclopedia*, 1432–1433; Hilton, 88, 130, 222)

OLGA ("Bob's Birthday"). She is the Tyler family servant. She bakes a cake for Bob Tyler's birthday.

OLGA ("Cured!"). She is Mary and Dick Streeter's maid. When Mary telegraphs Dick she's returning after visiting her aunt in Maine, she tells Dick to have Olga make their house ready.

OLIVER, MERLE ("I Can't Breathe"). He is from Boston. When he phones the diarist, she remembers she loves and will marry him, not Gordon Flint or Walter, to both of whom she is engaged.

O'LOUGHLIN, SILK In "Call for Mr. Keefe!," Keefe complains that umpire Silk O'Loughlin called a low ball from Johnson, pitching for Washington, a strike, which outraged White Sox coach Kid Gleason, who remarked about Silk's eyesight and was ejected. Silk O'Laughlin is mentioned in *The Real Dope* and "The Yellow Kid."

George W. Hilton reports that Francis H. O'Loughlin (1870–1918) was a respected American League umpire (1902–1918) and that he died in the 1918 influenza epidemic. (Source: Hilton, 199)

OLSEN, GEO ("The Ides of June"). He is a Brooklyn band director. Danny took Vivian Duane to his performance twice. She was foolishly encouraged by his set smile. Olsen's wife sings with the band.

OLSEN, MRS. ("The Ides of June"). She sings with her husband Geo Olsen's Brooklyn band. Her professional name is Ethel Schulte.

OLSON, MINNIE ("Hurry Kane"). She is Hurry Kane's Yuma girlfriend. After tribulations, all's well with Hurry and "Min."

OMAR (*The Big Town*). He and Allah are Trumbull's twin-like servants. Finch describes Omar as "a rug peddler."

"ONE HIT, ONE ERROR, ONE LEFT" (*Saturday Evening Post*, April 23, 1932; LWS, RAB) *see* ***LOSE WITH A SMILE***

"A ONE-MAN TEAM" (*Red Book*, May 1916). (Characters: Ainslee, Barrows, Benjamin, Byron, Coach Belden, Dana, Davis, Dickie, Flynn, Harris, Hayes, Hosteller, Kirby, Moxey, Robbins, Smith, Wallace, Wickham.)

After lunch on Monday at the training table, Coach Belden tells his football players to cut classes if necessary, but get to the 2:30 practice. The players leave, including Dickie and Wickham, who say they may be delayed. Belden and his three assistants, Harris, Wallace, and Dana, discuss the upcoming game with a school called Doane. Harris scouted Doane's game against Monroe last Saturday and reports that Doane is "a one-man team" and would be weak but for Davis, their backfield star. Wallace gloats with Belden about their success against Monroe, whose Benjamin was supposedly "their whole team." Dana worries, though, because Monroe's coaches stressed offense and didn't defend Benjamin, whereas Smith, Doane's coach, will protect Davis. Harris responds by praising Belden's defensive strategy. Belden boasts of previous proofs thereof and adds that "a one-man team" is his "favorite dish." Dana and Harris are concerned that Bryon, Doane's big halfback, will protect Davis whether he passes or runs. Belden says his men will tackle or intercept Davis, who can't "plunge"; so Belden will loosen his linemen.

Thursday night Belden dreams that Davis caught the kickoff, was tackled, lined up defensively, but then passed for a touchdown. Morning finally comes. Belden describes his dream to his players and says they won't get varsity letters if Doane passes successfully. Wickham promises to tackle Davis. Robbins promises to block an end if Davis passes. Barrows promises to "get" Davis twice or more. Belden orders his 15 players out for afternoon practice, sings "Hang Doane's Davis on a sour-apple tree," and all depart. Barrows furtively mimicks Belden's "raucous voice."

They get to the town called Doane. While the players are asleep in the hotel the night before the game, Harris reads Belden and the other coaches these comments from the *Doane Daily*: Davis's record is perfect; this is his final game; Belden's traditional defense is against one man; Belden's scouts know Doane's strengths; Davis has outwitted "all opponents"; when his running is stopped, he passes; Davis skipped tonight's meeting, at which Smith, Doane's coach, spoke confidently. Belden's assistants turn in. He too sleeps, and dreams Davis got tackled into hopeless disgust.

Both bands introduce the game to 10,000 shouters. Belden's "sour-apple tree" song evokes Doane smiles, and "Yea, Davis" follows. Belden's men lose the coin toss, must kick; a Doan tackle receives, "was thrown" at once. Belden expects his open defense to succeed. But Doane's "quarter," not Davis, is centered to, gains merely four yards. Belden won't be drawn in. Next, their "quarter" trips. On purpose? Barrows yells to warn of a Davis pass. Davis is behind his halfbacks Byron and Moxey; Byron, not Davis, receives, scores when Moxey blocks Barrows, the defender least surprised. Davis kicks the point after. Although Dana suggests defending differently, Belden won't be "scare[d] into tightening up," knowing Davis wants to shine during "his last appearance." Later, Doane's repeated "quarter-through-center play" is foiled: Belden's center, Wickham, "dive[d] in" to blunt two slight gains. Davis next? No, the "quarter," receiving, lateraled to Byron for a first down. Belden sends Ainslee to substitute for Hayes and to tell the team to close until they see Davis handle the ball. Ainslee arrives late. Harris fears a Davis pass; Belden says he must chance it. Doane's ends flank, are followed. Again Byron and Moxey line close, but one of their tackles laterals to Byron, who outruns an opposing end along the sidelines, dodges Barrows, scores. Davis's point after means 14–0. Belden expects Davis to drive his team back with his vaunted first-down punts, but Moxey does the punting with surprising hang-time. When Barrows tries to catch one such punt but "made a square muff," Doane scored its third touchdown. Score: 21–0.

At halftime Belden tells his players that he was "mostly" at fault, they must forget Davis, they must win, and if they do "the credit's all yours." They fight spiritedly, to 21–7. Moxey keeps outpunting and thus driving Belden's boys back. Toward the end, Davis is subbed for. After his defeated players "had shed their armor and departed," Belden and his aides talk. Belden thinks something was "funny." Harris says his scouts concentrated on Davis, not on Byron, Moxey, or their ends. Belden remembers Davis never handled the ball but only kicked points-after. Harris praises smart Smith, who, Dana adds, "crossed us" by having them "laying for Davis." But Belden says not even Napoleon would keep "his best army in the stable during a big battle, just to fool the other side."

Belden finds Smith amid "wild Doane rooters" in the hotel café, lures him away, and asks how he kept Moxey and Byron "under cover" from his scouts. Smith says that "Lady Necessity" helped him, that last Wednesday he learned how capable Moxey and Byron could be, right after right-handed Davis broke his right wrist in practice.

"Oh, You Bonehead!" obviously is followed by "A One-Man Team," in which Dana, Dickie, and Harris figure, all masterminded by Coach Belden.

ON WATCH (*The Big Town*). He is a horse mentioned as running at the Jamaica track.

O'NEILL, JOE ("The Busher Pulls a Mays"). Keefe says that Gleason asked Joe O'Neill to buy Cicotte and Keefe railroad tickets for the two to go from Boston to Philadelphia ahead of the other White Sox players.

George W. Hilton reports that Joseph O'Neill (c. 1885–1920) was the White Sox traveling secretary (ending 1919), shortly before his death of tuberculosis. (Source: Hilton, 309)

ONLY ONE (*The Big Town*). He is Herbert Daley's prize racehorse, ridden successfully in race after race by Sid Mercer, until Sid falls in love with Finch's sister-in-law Katie, Daley's fickle fiancée. Sid then deliberately causes Only One to lose at the Belmont.

"ONLY ONE" (*Saturday Evening Post*, February 12, 1921; BT; PRL) *see* ***THE BIG TOWN***

ORR, MILDRED ("Travelogue"). She is Hazel Dignan's friend and traveling companion on the train from Chicago to San Francisco. Mildred is mentally slow, knows it, and is self-effacingly quiet while Hazel talks endlessly to Dan Chapman. He finds Mildred pretty and asks for a date when they get to San Francisco.

OSBORNE, HENRY WILD ("HARRY") ("Stop Me — if you've heard This One"). He is a "famous globe-trotter, raconteur, and banquet-hall fixture." And liar. Osbourne listens to Luke

Garner's story about a beautiful brunette and a mysterious Spanish-looking man he saw on the train from New York to Chicago. Then two years later Osborne converts the anecdote into his own supposedly true account of a beautiful blonde and a handsome Scandinavian.

OSBOURNE, ED ("EDDIE") ("Ex Parte"). He used to be the narrator's best friend. The narrator leaves a written account of his troubles with women in his will, for Osbourne to reveal in due time.

OSBOURNE, MRS. ("Ex Parte"). She is Ed Osbourne's wife and has prevented Ed from remaining the narrator's best friend.

OTT ("Lose with a Smile"). He played for the Giants and hit a homer off Brooklyn pitcher Hoyt, according to Danny's letter to Jessie.

Melvin Thomas Ott (1909–1958) played for the New York Giants (1926–1947) and was elected to the Baseball Hall of Fame (1951). (Source: *Baseball Encyclopedia*, 1444)

"OWN YOUR OWN HOME" (*Red Book*, January 1915; OYH) *see* ***OWN YOUR OWN HOME***

OWN YOUR OWN HOME (1919). Novel-like set of four stories, entitled "Own Your Own Home" (*Red Book*, January 1915), "Welcome to Our City" (*Red Book*, May 1915), "The Last Laugh" (*Red Book*, July 1915), and "Uncivil War" (*Red Book*, September 1915). Fred A. Gross writes his brother Charley Gross a series of 44 letters.

"OWN YOUR OWN HOME," subtitled "It's the Only Life." (Characters: Annie, Gross, Charley Gross, Ed Gross, Fred A. Gross, Grace Gross, Mary Gross, May Gross, Guy Walters, Mrs. Walters.)

Fred Gross writes his brother Charley 17 letters. The first 15 are from Chicago, the last two, from "Allison, Ill."

May 3. Fred and his wife Grace, who is tired of being "cooped up in the flat all day" with "little Ed & and the baby," will let their "lease run ... out in Oct.," go to "them subburbs," and either rent a house or buy a lot and "build a house not a grate big house of corse." Charley and Mary should do so also. Grace has $800; Fred, $300. They can "build a bungello" for $1,200 and have it "payed for in 1 yr." at "$25 per wk." by not spending on "cloths & nickle shows."

May 5. An agent showed them a $1,500 "bargun" lot in Allison, "16 mi. west of the Loop," with "100 ft. frontidge" and "3 big trees." Grace liked it immediately. Fred can commute to town in "40 min." by train, instead of "35 ... on the L." Fred gave the agent $100, promised to get $700 from the bank, will "borry" the rest, and pay all "in 2 yrs." Charley should also "get in to the game." Fred sends "Kindest to Mary."

May 7. At the bank Fred learned he'd have to pay $25 for the lot title "garantee polisy" and $700 more toward the lot before getting a $1,200 bank loan "for 2yrs. with 6 percent int. per annum" for funds to build. When Fred "told Grace I thot shed cry," but they soon decided to pay the $700, save "30 per wk. ... if we live pretty clost," renew the flat lease, and start building "in Nov."

Nov. 2. Grace's father gave her $100 "on her berth day ... to buy cloths." They put it toward the lot. Its owner charged them "$20 int." Grace's brother-in-law calls "bungellos" old-fashioned. So Fred got "a young archateck" who'll build them a "2 story house for $2000." After Fred paid 5 percent ($100 toward it), this "univ." graduate "will over look the hole busness" and says he'll easily find "a contrackter" during this "dull season." Everything will cost "a bout $3700." Better than "being cooped up in a 4 room flat" for "$25 per mo. rent."

Nov. 15. Fred describes their "7 rms. 3 down stares & 4 up stares," including a spare bedroom when "you & Mary ... vissit." They'll have "gas & electrick lts. & all moderate conveenyenses," and "the contracker" gets only $2,000, and "the archateck ... does all the worring for $100."

Nov. 16. Why is it "the papers keeps after us for not halling in all the stick up men" robbing banks? [Fred is a policeman.] Banks "is the worst stick ups they is." Fred is saddled with extras at his banks, demanding $330 more for lights, hardware, wall paper, insurance. Charley shouldn't be "mixed up in nothing like this."

Nov. 20. Fred gave the bank $330 Grace got from her father but also must pay "6 percent int. twict a yr. ... on the prinsipal" plus paying on it "for 5 yrs." And "yet the papers ... pans ... us" about an occasional "stick up."

Nov. 29. The men "dug the foundashun the rong way of the lot." Winter freezes may delay redoing it because "concreet" might "crack some time and brake & ... the house might ... fall." Still, Fred tells Charley "liveing in a house is the only way" and asks about "little May."

Dec. 23. To save every "nickle," Grace will send "little May" only homemade candy for "mary xmas." Extra "gradeing" cost $60. Replanning for bedroom closets cost an "extra $50." The house "out side is most all up."

Jan. 21. With "the price of ivorys" up, Fred must pay about $30 more for something better than "a tin ... bath tub." Allison officials sent "a notise to day that I owe $40 taxes." Also, "the archateck ... made a misstake a bout ... radiators"; so the house needs more. But soon "they wont be no more trouble."

Feb 2. Fred has been "busy down to the station ... for 2 wks." He finds no work done on the house, though "the weathers been grand." It seems "the lumber Co." wouldn't trust "the contrackter" until Fred "garantee[d] the money." The bank told him to call "the contracker," who complained "he wasent going to do no job where he was loosing money." He had agreed to finish "by the 1 of march," but a banker said Fred couldn't sue him because "hes probly broke." The "archateck" got Fred to hire "a boss carpenter to finnish the job" using "sub contrackters." Fred has "sub letted [their flat] to a family from the 1 of march to the 1 of May"; so they'll move into a hotel and store their "furnitur for a couple wks." There's no use finding that "contrackter" to "brake his jaw."

Feb. 24. Now "the archateck is sick ... & left the work to his cousin," who "is worse ... a bout asking questions that I dont know nothing a bout." Also "the mill work people" are delaying. Charley's lucky he "aint in no jam like this."

Feb. 27. Some "swedes" brought the lumber after they made Fred "sine a paper garanteeing ... that the bank all ready" held money for them. Fred and his family are boarding out at "$12 a wk." plus "$6 to store the furnitur." All this after he paid $30 to move it and $10 to move it "to the house if the house is ever ready."

March 29. The "lts. fixtures" Grace liked cost $50 more than the $50 "we stuck in the bank for them." The painter is charging an extra $30 for a third "cote." The cousin of the sick "archateck" is missing.

April 13. Their house is "near finnished" and "looks fine." But Allison authorities require a $100 "cement sidewalk" plus "a side walk ... to the house." A man charged $150 for a "cement & gravvle" driveway and grading and seeding the yard. That "finnished hard ware" cost $70. Fred is also "paying the carpenter all the time" for "fixing up the flors with pollish."

"Allison, Ill., May 6." Now "we been here 2 hole days." The movers "busted" their "furniturs"; "the gas stove aint come yet"; "the gas aint conected." When the architect's cousin came and called the house great for only $2,000, Fred summed up everything and said "what was suposed to cost me a bout $3600 or $3700 is going to cost me $5300." Also, "theys int. do the 1 of July," and he must "buy cole" for "a cole heater" because the cousin didn't install the promised gas water heater. The doors and windows stick open or shut. Screens "cost $50 more," and "the roof of the house leeks." Still, "the kids seems to be haveing a h-ell of a time ... running a round." Fred won't worry if he owes money, and his "hares turned gray," and "the papers is paning ... the dept. because [of] ... stick up men a round town." Anyway,"coles only $8 a ton out here." He must find "a plumer" to pump "the celler" and "coax the sewer to stay out doors." The kitchen is small for a stove and a table.

June 25. They've been in the house "6 wks. now," and the stove "4 days," and "the screens isent here yet." The "archateck" claimed his cousin wanted 5 percent of the "$1600 extras" of overruns. Fred shut the door on him, "as clost as it will shut." The bank wants more "int." Grace will "write & ask her old man." He'll "come acrost," especially knowing "he wont never half to give Grace no more berth day pressents" no matter how long he lives. The Walters visited and liked the house. Charley should "get busy & get in the game," since "its the only life."

"WELCOME TO OUR CITY." (Characters: Arnold, Mrs. Arnold, Carpenter, Mrs. Carpenter, Carry, Mrs. Carry, Curtis, Mrs. Curtis, Gross, Charley Gross, Fred Gross, Grace Gross, Mary Gross, Hamilton, Mrs. Hamilton, Wm. Marston, Morehead, Mrs. Morehead, Walters, Mrs. Walters.)

Fred sends Charley 12 more letters from Allison.

July 8. Everything is "smoth." Fred "payed the 1st. int. on my lone down to the bank." They depended on Grace's father less when they were back in Chicago. The house is damp and the paint smells. But the "babys" are safer than when "cooped up ... in Chi" or in danger on streets there. He wishes the Walters and the Arnolds, their old Chicago friends, would visit them.

July 24. Rains have filled the basement so "you could dive off the top step of the stares ... & not bump your head." A "plummer" charged "$.50 cents" to lie to Fred that "the dranepipes could carry" the water away. Grace enjoys burning their spare lumber in the fire place because it's pretty and she's "lonesom" and can't "dress the babys up & go out" since she lacks good clothes. Fred had to give her "$20.00 dollars" to have new dresses made.

Aug. 13. Sunday. Fred is staying home to watch the kid while Grace, with "her close made & all finnished," will call on some neighbors. He had his business cards printed so while visiting neighbors she can "stick them on the piano" to show Fred "wanted to come but couldent." Grace will "go from house to house." Fred figures the Hamiltons next-door may have a "swell big house" but Hamilton will be friendly because "all men was crated free."

Aug. 16. Grace "was toged up in her new close & looked like a million $," and called on "4 famlys a long the street." The Hamiltons were first. A "hire girl" asked for her card. Grace gave her one of Fred's. The cards "set me back $.50 for 200 of them," and Grace has lots of them. They "says on them F. A. Gross asst. Chief of Detectives Chicago Police dept" and indicate his "20 years in the service in red tipe." Mr. Hamilton spoke to Grace. He thought he was being charged with something until Grace told him her husband Fred was the detective. Hamilton laughed, but his wife wasn't amused. Hamilton named other neighbors the Carpenters and suggested Grace show them a card. She did, and Grace and the Carpenters chatted with her "pretty near a hr." Hamilton went to Carpenter's front door and "ast was he arested." The two men went outside, laughing and "come pareing nots a bout the joke." When Mrs. Carpenter asked if Grace had more neighbors yet to visit, Grace went next door and met Mrs. Carry, who said her husband "keeps the grosery store or 1 of them." When Grace explained the joke with their neighbors, Mrs. Carry said neither the Hamiltons nor the Carpenters had ever called on the Carrys. After Grace called on the Moreheads, she returned home and told Fred that Mrs. Carry said Grace could leave her babies with Mrs. Carry's "hire girl" to watch over them.

Aug. 31. Water has been shut off for "2 or 3 days" in Allison. Grace took the children to the Carrys, who have a sister. So have the Hamiltons, but Mrs. Hamilton has snubbed poor Grace. Leaving the kids with Mrs. Carry, Grace has called on "15 or 20 famlys," and the Carrys have been visiting the Grosses for card games. Without water, Fred and Grace can drink beer and the kids have milk. Still, they "cant take no bath in beer or milk."

Sep. 14. Fred is planning a surprise "to cheer Grace up." He told her the Walters were coming for "dinner Sun. noon" but is inviting the Hamiltons and the Carpenters instead. She'll be "supprised & tickeled to deth." He had trouble writing the invitation; so he "ast the tipewriter in the chiefs office" to do it. She typed once, using "a peace of this here copy paper" and changing "the names on the top."

Sep. 18. Fred "got the supprise and not Grace." The guests never showed up. Fred had to confess the truth to Grace, who "scolded me like Id stole some money or something." Fred offered to go check with the guests. No! She'd take the kids and leave him if he did. She went into "histeriks & all the rest of it." He remembered he "dident male the letters" but put them "under there doors." Grace, feeling better soon, said she'd "do the inviteing to the house." When the Carrys come "tonight to play cinch," they can share the Sunday dinner the Grosses didn't "have the heart to eat."

Oct. 3. A boy delivered a letter to Fred. It was addressed to the Hamiltons, who "if we got theres they got ourn." It's "a invatation to a dance here in Allison the 17 of this month," to "benifit ... the Bellgiums that was killed in the war." Now "where the Bellgiums needs help any more than I need it" is puzzling. Anyway, Fred threw away the envelope, showed Grace the "invatation," and she cried until he agreed to take some "danceing" lessons with her to learn the new "1 step walk & the foxs trot." The "ticket ... costs $2.00 dollars," and the lesson "probly ... a 5 spot."

Oct. 8. Fred wishes he'd "left Grace bellow." Dance lessons are $2 already and more needed. He wanted "to ware the uneform" saved from before he "was put in plane close," but Grace ordered him to rent "a evning dress sute" for $3. If Mrs. Carry isn't going, she can babysit "the childern"; if she is, they'll "higher a girl."

Oct. 11. When the Carrys were playing cards at the Grosses' house, Grace mentioned the dance. Mrs. Carry said they hadn't been invited. Grace asked them to babysit, because she and Fred were going. Mrs. Carry said if the Grosses went "that will show you think your better than us." Fred said their not being invited "was probly a miss take." Mrs. Carry said the Grosses' being invited "was the miss take." Then "Carry & his wife & Grace & I all lost our temper." Mrs. Carry "couldent keep her mouth shut." It was good the Carrys left, because if she babysat she might "cloraform" the kids.

Oct. 18. Fred says "its pretty lucky" he didn't take his "gat" to the dance. It would have looked "funny ... in my evning dress sute." He would've been charged with "murdring some body" instead of just "takeing money from stick up guys & dips." Grace let out the pants of Fred's rented "sute." fixed her hair, and they got to the dance "close to 9 a clock." A man told him their "invatation" was a mistake. When Grace saw "the Hamiltons come & the Carpenters" enter, she named them to Fred. After "the music beggin" and partners danced, a "comitty"—"2 ladies & 3 gents ... & 1 ... was Carpenter"—explained everything. The Grosses got the Hamiltons' "invitation" when "the boy made a miss take," and the Grosses weren't invited. Fred "would of soiled some of there collars," but Grace bellowed and they went home. He had to "douse camfer all over her face" to get her to sleep. Fred "this A.M." phoned "the chief" that Grace was sick and he "couldent come down" and he's had no breakfast.

Oct. 22. Grace is so unhappy that Fred plans to sell their house for about "$1000.00 more then it costed all to gether." Somebody must pay for expenses for their "danceing," etc. He wants cash or someone to "asume the morgidge." Grace felt even worse when her "old man" for her "berth day" didn't send another "1 of them $100.00 checks" but instead "a reciet for $100.00 ... we all ready borryed off of him."

Nov. 1. The Grosses will remain in Allison. The agent told Fred he'd sell for a loss and "You wont find no better town no wheres." And the Walters visited and "wisht they had a home like ourn in the subburbs" and not "a dirty flat" in Chicago. And Grace made up with Mrs. Carry, and the Carrys will be playing "cinch" here "to-night." And being out here is best for "the childern." In a "P. S." Fred says he "tore this letter open again" to add that a neighbor named Curtis, who sells wood and coal, and his wife moved here just ahead of the Carrys. The Curtises are "as nice peopl is youd want to meet." The Grosses, Curtises, and Carrys played "rummy 6 hand." Grace made "a welch rabbit." Fred provided beer. The Curtises asked Fred and Grace to visit them and dance to their "phonagraf." So "money wasent waisted" on dance lessons, "eh Charley."

"THE LAST LAUGH." (Characters: Bob Barnes, Bishop, Mrs. Bishop, Carpenter, Mrs. Carpenter, Carry, Mrs. Carry, Curtis, Mrs. Curtis, Farrell, Mrs. Farrell, Grimes, Mrs. Grimes, Gus Goetz, Gross, Charley Gross, Ed Gross, Fred Gross, Grace Gross, Mary Gross, Hamilton, Mrs. Hamilton, Jack, Martin, Mrs. Martin, Parker.)

Fred writes Charley seven more letters from Allison.

Jan. 2. Fred won't complain about this "rotten weather," because "a mans waisting time when you wish for some thing they cant have." He'd could wish to be "chief of police all ready" and have "big money." He and Grace play cards with guests who "lap up our beer," but "you couldent drownded you self in the beer they give us when wear at there house." Still, "Grace is haveing the time of her life." For "$.50" they can hire a 17-year-old "irish girl" nearby "to come & set in the house wile wear out nights." The girl has "a bow" who's so "stuck on her" he babysits with her, but they're "probably to busy smacking each other to hear" if the "babys" should cry. The "bow" should pay the Grosses, because "it would cost him more then $.50" to take his girl "to Hofmanns garden ... a way from her perants." Fred won't let Grace show the two "where we kept our beer." Fred gripes to Charley that "postige stamps in N.Y. city" must cost more than Fred pays, because "you dont write onct in a wile."

Jan. 11. Allison is livelier than Chicago "when your a good dresser and peopl likes you." Last night Fred and Grace went "to Curtis house" for a party. The Carrys were also there. Curtis gets "$20.00 per mo. out of us for 2 & ½ ton of coal" but served us "not hardley enough [beer] ... to wet your tungue." Grace expected "a regular meal," but they got only "ice cream & cake & coffee." Next time Fred will take along "crackers in my pocket & a little cheese." Mrs. Curtis started a game called "auction bridge." She said since Fred knew whist he'd have no trouble. But soon his woman partner took his bid of spades away by bidding hearts, which he lacked. He put his hand down and got "balled ... out" until he called her a monkey and everyone laughed. Fred didn't mind not winning the prize, which was a box to hold collars, since he has only "3 or 4 of them." "The womans prize" was black stockings, which Grace didn't mind not winning because "she aint in morning." Fred told Carry he preferred "rummy or cinch" to bridge and would have liked more beer. The party is at the Carrys "next wk."

Jan. 16. The Carry party "last night" was bad—weak punch not beer, and not enough food for "a canery" when "splitted up for 16 peopl ... & the Carrys runs a grosery store" and could get food cheap. Later, on the street, Grace was upset because she tried to speak to Mrs. Carpenter and Mrs. Hamilton and they snubbed her. Fred plans to get revenge, and "you know Im the 1 that can do it."

Jan. 25. Grace decided to give a party. Their guests will be the Bishops, Carrys, Curtises, Farrells, and Grimeses. Grace will gladly let Fred "tend to the refreshmunts a speshaly the drinks." They won't invite the Carpenters and Hamiltons, who "will want to go hide in a hole some wheres" when they see Fred not "giveing no cheap party." He printed "invatations" specifying "3 tables proggresive cinch," "refreshmunts," "Gents prize 1 qt. whisky," and "hansome pare of corsets" for "Ladys prize." A requirement is "Dress sutes." Gus Goetz sent Fred a case of whisky "for xmas," and the corsets were what Mary sent Grace "2 yrs. a go last xmas" that didn't fit. Fred plans "frank forters," "potato sellid," "of corse beer," etc. If the winner opens his whisky up, Fred will provide "the excelsior water to make high balls." Fred has told the "weakly paper" editor to report the party. The Martins, recent neighbors, made too much noise at their "new yrs. eve party." So Fred went over at "2 ... A.M.," flashed his badge, and made them quiet down. Fred and Martin commuted to Chicago "on the same train to gather" the next morning, and Martin said Fred "dident spoil our fun you just add it to it." He's surely "a good fellow." Still, Martin and his wife would make 14 at the party; so they won't invite them.

Feb. 1. The papers reported Fred and Grace's party, and he's embarrassed. During the card playing, Fred got dry and began mixing high balls. Curtis got drunk, threw the cards around, "pertend it like he was the orchuster," sang, got the others to dance outside, "sliped & fell down on the ice," was carried back inside, tried to quiet the crying "babys," then rested. The night watchman came and said they were reported for "disturbing the piece." Fred tried but failed to see a "warant." Curtis tried to "take a crack at the guy." The watchman returned with "2 others ... [and] pulled his gat," and took Fred down to jail overnight. Fred "figger[ed] ... Hamilton & Carpenter" did the complaining. Fred appeared before the justice. The "good fellow" released him, and "the oficer ... says he was sorry." Back home, Grace was reading the newspaper about their "party ... doing the foxey trot" in the street.

Feb. 4. Fred has a plan to get even with Hamilton and Carpenter, because "the 1 that laughs the last gets the best of it." His friend Bob Barnes, "the sherrif of Cook Co.," agreed to send Parker, a deputy he wants to get rid of, to the Hamiltons' house next Thursday afternoon, where Fred's "little irish girl" heard from Mrs. Hamilton's maid about her "auction bridge whist club" party and that they play for $12 prize money. Parker will make a pinch, and if "theys any trubble," he will "face the music." The newspaper account will make "these birds" at the party start "cralling on there hands & niece."

Feb. 7. Parker "pored ... currage down his throte," went to the Hamiltons' house, waved his gun at Mrs. Hamilton, told her "the place was pinched ... for being a gambleing house," and sat down. Mrs. Hamilton, "a pretty game bird," phoned her husband, who phoned the sheriff, who phoned Parker to return to the office. This morning on the train, Martin—you know, that noisy neighbor—watched Fred laughing and "reading the peace in the papers" about "a deputy sherrif radeing a swell gambleing joint in Allison." The Hamiltons and Carpenters must be ashamed. When questioned, Fred told him the "secrit" and Martin also laughed. Fred reminded him about "the 1 that laughs the last," and Martin laughed even harder. So, Charley, "them swell heads" won't "put on heirs" before their betters any more.

"UNCIVIL WAR." (Characters: Ed Gross, Charley Gross, Fred Gross, Grace Gross, Mary Gross, Hamilton, Mrs. Hamilton, Martin, Mrs. Martin.)

Fred sends eight more letters from Allison.

Feb. 3. It's funny that Fred's neighbors on the left are friendly Martins but on the right are mean Hamiltons. While "comeing home" on the train recently, Fred sat next to Martin and invited him "and his Mrs. ... some night and play cards." Martin replied "he dident need nothing to put him to sleep." He "ment ... probily" Fred's beer would "fill him up." Last night over they came. Mrs. Martin is "prety as a pitcher and dresses as good is a coarse girl." And has flashing "dimonds." She asked Grace if she sewed "her own close." Grace said not "sence 3 yrs. a go when little Ed was born." Grace was pleased when Mrs. Martin added that she'd seen nothing like Grace's dress "in the stores wile she was shopping." The four played rummy, because the Martins don't know cinch. At "$.01 a pt." Fred "loose $1.50 and Grace loose $.80"; still, "it was ... fun." There was a noise on the back porch. The Hamiltons' cat knocked down the Grosses' "garbidge pale." Grace said this often happened. Martin figured the Hamiltons "starved their cat" so she would "undisterb us evry night." Fred told Martin about the rude Hamiltons and how he got a deputy to embarrass Mrs. Hamilton, but "onily ... to get even." Martin told Fred he should play a trick on Hamilton so "he would quitt monking with me." Fred won't shoot the cat, because "it aint the cats falt ... and a cats got to eat the same as a human bean." Charley should see Mrs. Martin—"pretter then Edna Tangay [Eva Tanguay*]," with a dress that almost "would fall off" because it was hardly "attacked," showed "her arms and neck and soldiers," and resembled "a batheing sute." She wore "tacklum powder" and smelled like "a Green house or ... a funeral." Grace gripes about the cold even though Fred burns "near a ton of cole a wk."

Feb. 12. Fred plans to get even with the Hamiltons. Grace's "little irish girl" learned that the Hamiltons plan a party for "Valentine day." Martin suggested hanging a sign at the Hamiltons' door warning that "the residence has got some decease and got to be quarnteed." The guests will see it, leave, and the Hamiltons will "set all evning wondring why dident there friends come." For a valentine message Fred will "male" Hamilton "a pitcher of a big hog" and a poem saying that "you" should be "in a pen" unlike "other men" because "Your ... just a big ... greasy pig." That's "dirty" but better than "starveing your cat" so she'd "knock over a mans gabidge pale over" plus "yowel[s] a round the house."

Feb. 15. Grace is mad at Fred, but he has "a right to feel sore." He didn't tell her what happened. Before Fred sent his valentine, Hamilton must have been the person who sent him one. It pictured "a stick up guy" giving a bandaged detective "a role of bills." Beneath "was a pome sane all detectives was cheap grafters." Fred told Martin about it on the train. Martine figured Hamilton sent it but advised Fred not to "bust his jaw" but plant "the small pox sine." Fred did. But Hamilton didn't turn on the porch light, and the guests went right in, and "I could hear them singing and enjoin them self." Fred takes nothing from "stick up men ... [but] abuse." That "swell head pup" shouldn't send "these here valentines" that are "a bout as comical is a hanging over to the county jail."

March 1. Fred and Grace went to the Martins' house last night. Charley's wife Mary might not have wanted to go because Mrs. Martin dresses so well. She said she wished she could "borry" Grace's "close" to "ware ... to a mask raid." Martin mixed "cock tales," and Mrs. Martin taught "Grace the ballad dance." When Fred danced with Mrs. Martin to "phonegraf" music, it was like "a arm full of flowers." Martin said Fred and Grace "was suckers" if they didn't get even with the Hamiltons. Martin said he'd think of something.

March 9. "Martins idear" was for Fred to slash the tires on Hamilton's automobile, "out side there house on the st." Fred said "destroying a mans property" could get him "in bad down town." Martin said "unscrew[ing] the valves" would let "the wind ... come out," and since air belongs to everyone "they wouldent be no property destroyed." Fred did it while the Hamiltons "was in the house." When Hamilton saw "what had came off" he swore in front of Mrs. Hamilton, blamed "the neighbors hood" children, and said no "groan up man [would] pull some thing like that." Fred says if he "aint groan up yet" he'll "be a gient" later. Hamilton "can cuss as good is the chief." Martin persuaded Grace "to enter tane a good eel"; so "next Fri. night" they'll have a party based on Martin's "tips a bout how." It should "cost us some money" and include "drug store" ice cream and 16 guests—"the cream of Allison socitey"—and not the Hamiltons.

March 14. Fred would like to shoot "some body with out naming no names." No guests showed up. Mrs. Martin phoned "near 10 a clock" and explained that "krape on the front door" of Fred's house made all the guests fear "some body [was] dead," and they left. Fred "explained it was 1 of the Hamiltons dirty tricks" and still wanted the party, but Grace said "her party close was all off" and it was too late to "get drest again." Grace called other guests, but their "party close [was] off" also and, besides, that "krape" upset them. Fred says they saw it because, unlike that "cheap stiff" Hamilton, he left his porch light on. Grace said Fred shouldn't go shoot Hamilton. It "probly wasn't Mrs. Hamiltons falt," and she might be a widow without "enough to live on." Fred told Grace they should keep the "krape" because "I and her cant live for ever."

March 18. Martin told Fred to bother Hamilton until he comes over "on my side" and got Fred to phone Hamilton day and night and hang up. Fred told "the girl down to the tellephone office" that he and Hamilton were friends and it was all a joke. The telephone girl soon got "scarred she will get fired"; so Fred figured Hamilton was "reddy to ... call evry thing quits."

March 20. Fred says that for a long time he suspected Martin, who "dident never act right some way." So "I and Hamilton is good friends now." Hamilton said "the cat was geting enough to eat" and he'd "never think of mixxing up in no brall with his neighbors." It was "Martin trying to make trubble." Fred "never relay liked him." Martin was mad that Mrs. Hamilton was unfriendly toward his wife. Both Hamiltons "seen ... that Martin wasent no good." He "couldent horn in" with "high socitey" and "used me for a Tool." Fred tells Charley not to tell his wife Mary the following: Martin saw his wife flirting with Fred and "thot may be I was trying to steal his wife." Though Fred doesn't do "that busness," he'd be blind not to "notice" her. When Fred's house suffered "dammige," Hamilton said not to go after Martin, that Hamilton would get the town to pay, that "we will run him out of town" if he misbehaves again. What happened was that Fred and Grace "wasent hardily no more then in bed" when "the fire enjine and hose cart" came to their house. He rushed out in his "night gown" and got soaked. Hamilton suddenly appeared, ordered "the 2 guys ... holding the nozzle" to "shut off the water insolently," told them he suspected Martin, and they said "Martin had told them to do it ... [as] a joke between friends." Fred figures Martin bribed the firemen and got them drunk. Hamilton told them he's "1 of the [town] bord" and "to beet it" at once. Hamilton said he and his wife knew what harm Martin caused Fred but wouldn't "but in unlest they was some real dammige." Seeing "the fire dept." by Fred's house, he knew he should "enter fear." Fred thanked him, shook his hand, and agreed to await a chance to "get Martin good." Fred can't blame Mrs. Martin "for looking at an other man onct in a wile." When Martin returns, he'll see "I and Grace hobbling a round with the Hamiltons and the other high monky monks hey Charley."

The stories in *Own Your Own Home* are slightly autobiographical, reflecting some of Lardner's own problems following his purchase of property west of Chicago, building a house, and moving into it, where he and his family lived for several years (1914–1917). Grace's frequent money gifts from her father is Lardner's unpleasant reworking of the fact that when his father-in-law Frank Parker Abbott* died (1912), his will provided, as Clifford M. Caruthers reports, "some money with which she [Lardner's wife] and Lardner bought property in west suburban Riverside [near Chicago] and began to build a house." Jonathan Yardley remarks that in *Own Your Own Home* Lardner satirizes "middle-class suburban life," that he did it better in *Gullible's Travels* later, and that Gross's narration is "now rather difficult to read because of the proliferation of misspelling, abbreviations and colloquialism." (Sources: Caruthers [1995], 102, 107, 108; Yardley, 184)

OXFORD, MRS. ("The Golden Honeymoon"). She sings at a church social attended by Charley and Mother in Florida. Although Mrs. Hartsell calls the performance "grand opera," Charley says his daughter Edie could do better without making "such a hullaballoo."

PAGE ("The Busher Pulls a Mays"). He is an effective pitcher for Philadelphia. Keefe criticizes him, especially after Gleason sends Keefe and $5,000 to Connie Mack's team in exchange for Page.

George W. Hilton explains that Page, a fictional character, is "vital to the denouement of the story": "The White Sox [in 1919] were endeavoring unsuccessfully to secure a pitcher, Scott Perry from the Athletics, and Perry was presumably the model for Page." Herbert Scott Perry (1891–1959) played for the St. Louis Browns (1915), the New York Giants (1916), the Cincinnati Reds (1917), and the Philadelphia Athletics (1918–1921). (Sources: *Baseball Encyclopedia* 2291; Hilton, 306, 311)

PAINTER, LESLIE ("The Facts"). He clerks at the Chicago railroad station and sells Tommy Richards a ticket to Minneapolis, where Tommy lives.

PALMER, RUTH (*The Real Dope*). She is a Red Cross canteen worker in France. In Keefe's presence, Frank Carter, an army buddy, addresses her as "Madam Moselle," according to Keefe, who then call her "Miss Moselle." Encouraged by her amiability, Keefe writes and gives her a valentine poem. Sargent Avery informs Keefe that she is Ruth Palmer, daughter of a wealthy "N.Y. city" man.

PANCHO, SENIOR ("The Battle of the Century"). He and "Senior Lopez" were lower Broadway waiters. Larry Moon had the two, both Spanish, pretend to be Cuban fight promoters so that Robert Crawley and Bill Guthrie would be suckered into outbidding them for a Dugan-Goulet boxing event.

PARDEE, E. M. ("Contract"). He and his wife are friends of Gale Bartlett and his wife. Bartlett persuades his friend Shelton to quit playing bridge with Cameron and his wife, Carl Dittmar and his wife, and Robert French and his wife, and instead to play with the Pardees.

PARDEE, MRS. ("Contract"). She and her husband E. M. Pardee are asked by their friend Gale Bartlett to invite Bartlett's friend Shelton and his wife to their supposedly hospitable home to play bridge. The Sheltons go. Mrs. Pardee quickly calls Shelton "Mr. Shevlin" and criticizes his bridge-playing.

PARELLI, SIGNOR ("Rhythm"). He is introduced by Peggy Leech to Harry Hart as "one of the Metropolitan's conductors." When Parelli says he'd like to conduct an opera by Hart, he retorts that he won't have an opera by him "ruined by a foreigner."

PARKER ("The Crook"). He was a rookie catcher on Larry's White Sox. Larry says Parker was so "spike-shy" that when Tyrus Cobb headed to home plate, Parker "backed off."

PARKER (*Own Your Own Home*). In "The Last Laugh," he is a deputy serving under Bob Barnes, the Cook County sheriff. Fred gets his friend Barnes to send Parker to Mrs. Hamilton's home when she is entertaining her bridge club, and arrest her for running a gambling house. Paker arrives drunk and waving his gun. Mrs. Hamilton has her husband phone Barnes to call off Fred's vengeful prank.

PARKER, DICK ("High-rollers"). He graduated from Harvard, is rich, and plays golf and cards for money at a Hampton Dunes club on Long Island with Dick Parker, Alex Spears, Jack Bowen, and Jack's friend Walter Finch. Walter learns how these fellows win and lose but don't pay up.

PARKER, DOROTHY (1893–1967). New Jersey–born Dorothy ("Dottie") Rothschild was a witty author before, during, and after the Roaring Twenties She began as a drama and book reviewer. She married Wall Street broker Edwin Pond Parker (1917; they divorced, 1928). She was fired from *Vanity Fair* (1920) for writing adversely about Billie Burke, the second wife of *Follies* impresario Florenz Ziegfeld.* She continued published several volumes of flippant, wry verse, collected in *Not So Deep as a Well* (1936), and several volumes of gloomy short stories and sketches, reprinted in *Collected Stories* (1942). She wrote for the movies (1929–1941). She was an alcoholic (by 1922), attempted suicide (1923, 1926, 1932), and married Alan Campbell (1932 or 1933). They were Hollywood screenwriters in Hollywood, soon made $5,000 a week, then were war correspondents to Spain to report Loyalist actions for the Communist *New Masses* (1937) during the Spanish Civil War. They divorced (1947), remarried each other (1950), and Campbell died (1963, perhaps by suicide). Dorothy Parker was blacklisted in Hollywood (1949), was called a Communist by the FBI (1950), was ruinously defiant before the House Un-American Activities Committee (1952), and much later died alone in a New York hotel room.

Parker cofounded the Algonquin Round Table (1920), the famous Manhattan lunch club. Lardner, always welcome, occasionally dropped in and soon associated with the following eminent men and women of letters, among others: Franklin P. Adams (1881–1960), newspaper columnist, humorist; Robert Benchley (1889–1945), humorist, critic, actor; Heywood Broun*; Marc Connelly (1890–1980), journalist, screenwriter, playwright; Edna Ferber (1885–1968), fiction writer, playwright; George S. Kaufman*; Margaret Leech (1893–1974), historian, novelist; Harold Ross (1892–1951), editor of *The New Yorker* (1925–1951); Robert Sherwood (1896–1955), playwright, editor, critic; and Alexander Woollcott (1987–1943), writer. In a letter (January 9, 1925) to F. Scott Fitzgerald,* Lardner mentions a recent Algonquin party hosted by "Dorothy, Beatrice [Mrs. Marc] Kaufman, and Peggy Leech." He wrote Fitzgerald again (July 27, 1825), to describe Dorothy Parker's week-long visit to the Lardners and his taking her, with other drunks but without his wife, to a restaurant at Manhasset, Long Island. Ring Lardner Jr. writes about his father's friendship with Dorothy, praises her for saying Lardner's stories reveal his "strange, bitter pity," but denies the rumor perhaps started by Dorothy herself that she and Lardner had an affair.

(Sources: Elder, 200; Lardner, Jr., 159, 189, 189–191; Caruthers [1995], 171, 181–182; Streissguth, 380)

PARKER, LEFTY ("Harmony"). He is a baseball player on "Cap" Ryan's team and appears to be mainly notable for singing an acceptable baritone in the quartet including Bill Cole, Art Graham, and sometimes Mike McCann and Waldron.

PARKER, MRS. ("High-rollers"). She is wealthy Dick Parker's wife. Mrs. Parker, Mrs. Hart, Mrs. Spears, and Peggy Bowen play bridge. When Mrs. Spears goes abroad for the summer, Peggy gets her friend Marion Finch to replace her at their parties.

PARKER, SPEED ("Horseshoes"). He and Dick Grimes have been rival baseball players for years. Speed has good luck and winds up with the Giants; Grimes has bad luck but winds up with the Athletics. During the Athletics-Giants World Series, with Grimes playing left field and Speed playing third, luck is finally reversed. Grimes makes a phenomenal catch of Speed's sure homer, slugs him when he calls Grimes "Horseshoes" (meaning dumb-lucky), and wins the girl both are after.

PARNELL, MISS ("Mamma"). She is a nurse in the psychopathic ward of New York's city hospital. When Miss Fraser, another nurse, can't successfully question Mamma, an amnesiac, she refers her to Miss Parnell, who is also unsuccessful.

PARRISH, ELLEN (MRS. CHARLES) ("Absent-minded Beggar"). She is the gracious hostess at her lake cottage when John Knowles mistakenly goes there. His good looks so impress her that she asks her week-end guest Irene Comerford if she invited this "beautiful sheik." Mrs. Parrish's having to go to a party held by the Tuttles results in John's being alone with Irene.

PARVIS ("Take a Walk"). He is a young man, 19 or 20, who plays the ukulele for a radio station in the town where Edith and her mother live. Parvis rents a room in their home. Edith is in love with Bleat, the umpire, until Bleat makes calls regarded by the townspeople as wrong. Edith then favors Parvis over Bleat.

PARVIS, THOMAS ("Anniversary"). He is a rich man with a controlling interest in Milton's interurban railway system. Louis Taylor is his well-paid secretary and traveling companion.

PASKERT In "Sick 'Em," he plays outfield for the Phillies. The narrator says that when Smitty was pitching badly for the Phillies, "Paskert ast Red [his manager] to send him a taxi" so he could go after distant fly balls. In "Where Do You Get That Noise?," Dode tells the narrator that the Phillies traded Hawley to the narrator's club because Pat Moran, Phillies manager, became sick of Hawley's incessant talk.

George Henry ("Dode") Paskert (1881–1959) played for the Cincinnati Reds (1907–1910), the Philadelphia Phillies (1911–1917), the Chicago Cubs (1918–1920), and the Cincinnati Reds (1921). George W. Hilton notes that Paskert played centerfield with "exceptional range" and that he was a "favorite of Lardner's because of their days in the Central League." (Sources: *Baseball Encyclopedia*, 1455; Hilton, 370–371)

PASS, SAMMY (*The Big Town*). He was a friend of Finch's sister-in-law Katie. She remembers betting him once that Cincinnati would beat the White Sox. She won "a five-pound box of candy."

PAT ("The Golden Honeymoon"). He is the subject of a story about "Pat and the motorcycle" that Charley recites in a brogue when he is persuaded to speak at a church social in Florida.

PAT ("Sick 'Em"). He is a member of the Phillies' baseball club. While scouting, he observed Smitty and Fogarty, both superb Fort Wayne pitchers. He recommended both men to Phillies manager Red, who got Smitty; Fogarty, however, went to the Cubs. When both pitchers worked for the Phillies, Pat, Red, and the narrator goad Smitty into doing better by praising Fogarty, and vice versa. See also Moran, Pat.

George W. Hilton glosses Pat as "Pat Moran, coach of the Phillies," adding that he replaced Dooin as Phillies manager (1915). (Source: Hilton, 365)

PAT ("Tour No. 2"). He is a friend of Larry's. Larry recalls that last winter at French Lick [Indiana] "evry body accept I & Pat was on the wagon."

PATRICK ("The Yellow Kid"). He was an outfielder drafted from the Coast by the narrator Bill's team. When Patrick was injured, Harry Childs replaced him and did so well that he felt he could afford to marry Mary Lloyd.

PATTERSON, BRUCE ("Tour Y-10"). He and Don Kellogg both like Violet Emerson and see her off on her vacation to Yellowstone. Violet prefers the men she tries to attract on the tour, but fails, returns home, and encourages Don.

PAUL ("Good for the Soul"). He is Ethel Warner's brother. He put up $2,500; Buck Warner, engaged to and then marrying Ethel, put up another $2,500. The two men bought an automobile garage in Hopsboro and now run it together.

PAXTON, JOE ("Ex Parte"). He is the narrator's friend in New York. When Joe and his wife, Marjorie Paxton, invite the narrator to dine, he meets Florence, whom he later marries.

PAXTON, MARJORIE ("Ex Parte"). She is the wife of Joe Paxtron, the narrator's friend in New York. They invite the narrator to dinner, and he meets fellow-guest Florence, Marjorie's friend from school days. The narrator marries Florence — to his regret.

PEARSON ("Holycaust"). Danny names Pearson as a pitcher for the Giants. According to Fresco Thompson, Pearson will be traded to Bridgeport.

Montgomery Marcellus Pearson (1909–1978) played for the Cleveland Indians (1932–1935), the New York Yankees (1936–1940), and the Cincinnati Reds (1941). (Source: *Baseball Encyclopedia*, 2284)

PEARSON ("Three Without, Doubled"). He is the husband of a woman Mrs. Gullible played bridge with.

PEARSON, MRS. ("Three Without, Doubled"). She is a friend of Mrs. Gullible, who developed her ability at bridge by playing with Mrs. Pearson, Mrs. Kramer, and Bertha Hatch. Mrs. Gullible boasts to Gullible that when the two of them were invited to join the San Susie bridge club, the Pearsons weren't.

PECK ("The Busher Pulls a Mays"). Keefe of the White Sox explains that a hangover made him dizzy and he mistakenly walked Peck, at bat for New York.

Roger Thorpe Peckinpaugh (1891–1977) played for the Cleveland Indians (1910, 1912), the Indians and the New York Yankees (1913), the Yankees (1914–1921), the Washington Senators (1922–1926), and the Chicago White Sox (1927), and managed the Yankees (1914) and the Indians (1928–1933, 1941). George W. Hilton adds that Peckinpaugh was also the general manager of the Indians (1941–1946). (Sources: *Baseball Encyclopedia*, 705, 1458–1459; Hilton, 321)

PECK, BILL ("Sick 'Em"). Jack Barnett tells his friend the narrator that Central League players Bill Peck, Joe Hammond, and Bull Harper were involved in recent trades.

George W. Hilton annotates the three players as "presumed fictional." (Source: Hilton, 375)

PEEBLES, EZRA ("A Day with Conrad Green"). He is a friend of Conrad Green and "a fellow entrepreneur." Peebles recommended Lewis to replace Green's deceased confidential secretary. Green tells his new secretary Lewis that Peebles is a crook.

PENCE ("The Golden Honeymoon"). He is over 80. He drove, with his wife as passenger, 1,641 miles from Brady, Texas, to attend the Tin Can Tourists in St. Petersburg, Florida. Charley and Mother see them there.

PENCE, MRS. ("The Golden Honeymoon"). She accompanied her husband to the Tin Canners' meeting in Florida.

PERCIVAL, DICK ("Nora"). In Hazlett's play "Nora," he is a Englishman and a sugar millionaire. He falls in love with Nora Crowley, who prefers John Collins, who also loves Nora.

PERDUE In "My Roomy," he is a Boston Braves pitcher against whom Buster Elliott, of the Chicago team, tries to steal home from third and is "out as far from here to Seattle." In "Back to Baltimore," the narrator Dixon and Hub Perdue, both with the Braves, discuss two Southern League teams, Nashville and New Orleans. Hub says he played for Nashville last year.

Hubbard E. ("Hub") Perdue (1882–1968), played for Nashville (1910), the Boston Braves (1911–1913), the Braves and the St. Louis Cardinals (1914), and the Cardinals (1915). Hilton adds that Lardner was "fond of Perdue" and accurately rendered "his speech habits" here. Jonathan Yardley offers proof of Lardner's affection for Hub, by quoting references to him in Lardner's "Pullman Pastimes" (*Chicago Tribune*, December 15, 1910–February 16, 1911). (Sources: *Baseball Encyclopedia*, 2288; Hilton, 351, 435–436; Yardley, 114–117)

PERDUE, MR. ("A Caddy's Diary"). He and Mr. Lewis are golfers at the club where the diarist caddies. Jack Andrews, the club pro, plays the men for money, giving them a stroke a hole and defeating them but not so badly that they quit playing him.

PERKINS (*The Big Town*). He is married to Lady Perkins and is on business in Texas when Finch, Ella Finch, and Katie meet her while vacationing on Long Island.

PERKINS, LADY (*The Big Town*). She is a guest at the Long Island hotel where Finch, Ella, and Katie are summering. She is said to be English with a husband in Texas on business. At the hotel she is with two dogs and Martha, her dogs' nurse. Finch tells Lady Perkins, whom he calls Perk and Perkie in his account of events, that he can cure her dogs (which aren't sick) with an anti-rash medicine. She is grateful and lets Finch, his wife Ella, and her sister Katie all watch her play bridge — until Katie spoils everything. Perk then snubs Finch but soon, fortunately, leaves to join her husband in Texas.

PERKINS, MAX (1884–1947). Born in New York City, Maxwell Evarts Perkins graduated from Harvard (1907), was a *New York Times* reporter (1907–1910), joined the publishing firm of Charles

Scribner's Sons (1910), became a member of their editorial staff (1914), saw military service on the Mexican border (1916), then by brilliant work helping several excellent authors rose to be Scribner's vice president (1932). Three such authors were novelists F. Scott Fitzgerald,* Ernest Hemingway (1899–1961), and Thomas Wolfe (1900–1938), also critic Edmund Wilson (1895–1972). And also Lardner, whom Fitzgerald recommended to Perkins (1923). The result was Lardner's *How to Write Short Stories* (1924), followed by his *What of It?* (1925), *The Love Nest and Other Stories* (1926), *Round Up* (1929), *June Moon* (1930), and *Lose with a Smile* (1933).

Lardner and Perkins became personal friends. Clifford M. Caruthers summarizes their activities: Perkins and his wife Louise Saunders Perkins were guests at the Lardners' Long Island home (May 9, 1924). Perkins had trouble locating Lardner's periodical publications for reissue, exercised patience when Lardner procrastinated, retained his composure in answering Lardner's whimsical letters, and tried but failed to blandish Lardner into writing a full-length novel. Several letters Lardner wrote to Perkins are especially revealing. Lardner expressed contrition at being slow in sending Perkins his sole copy of "Champions" for republication (December 5 [1923]); praised Fitzgerald's short story "Absolution" (1924), though partly "over my partly bald head" (May 27, 1924); asked whether Max liked the Lardner title *What of It?*, which Grantland Rice* suggested (January 31, 1925); griped about George M. Cohan* (October 13, 1927); complained about his health—"I guess I am paying for my past" (February 13, 1931); expressed sadness that some of the stories that became *Lose with a Smile* displeased *Saturday Evening Post* editors (August 16, 1932); and offered gallows humor about illness and money (February 3, 1933). (Sources: Caruthers [1973], xix–xxiii; Caruthers [1995], 151, 156, 173, 213, 232, 263, 270–271)

PERKINS, MR. ("Ball-A-Hole"). He is a church warden, pious, rich, and stingy. He is inveigled by the narrator and Jake into playing golf with Mr. Conklin. The two men dispute but ultimately become amiable.

PERRY, BUCK ("The Busher's Honeymoon"). He is a pitcher obtained from Boston by Tinker. Tinker delays in seeing Keefe. So Keefe goes out drinking with Perry, who reveals his $5,000 contract plus $500 bonus.

PERSHING, GENERAL In *Treat 'Em Rough*, he is the subject of rumors heard and repeated by Jack Keefe. In *The Real Dope*, Keefe is encouraged when he receives a letter purportedly from Black Jack Pershing praising his essay comparing baseball and war. Keefe replies, addressing his response to "Folies Bergere, Paris." When Pershing inspects Keefe's regiment, the two don't meet. Keefe hopes to be an "intelligents" agent for Pershing. Rumor has it that Pershing fears a German attack on Africa. Pershing in mentioned in *The Big Town*.

John Joseph Pershing (1860–1948), an experienced military officer, was the commander of the American Expeditionary Force in World War I (1917–1919).

PETERS, MRS. ARNOLD ("The Maysville Minstrel"). She is the biggest gas consumer in Maysville, according to Stephen Gale's poem entitled "The Gas Business."

PETERSON ("Contract"). He was Mrs. Dittmar's "impudent" butler. When she says she "didn't object to him going," Shelton corrects her mismodification of a "participle used as a substantive."

PHELON, DR. GEORGE ("How Are You?"). He is a New York diagnostician recommended to Bob Dayton.

PHILADELPHIA ATHLETICS An American League baseball team. It was established in 1901 and was active through 1954, after which it moved to Kansas City. (Source: Light, 551–553)

PHILADELPHIA PHILLIES A National League baseball team (1883–). (Source: Light, 554–557)

PHILLIPS ("What of It?"). This is the name of people "in the furniture game." The narrator has a friend who "travels out of Grand Rapids" to work for them. The friend finds useful the narrator's story about how to silence talkative fellow salesmen.

PHILLIPS, DR. ("Mamma"). He works in the psychopathic ward of New York's city hospital. He tries to cure Mamma of amnesia. But when he learns that her condition was owing to the death by flu of her husband, their son, and their daughter, he hopes that her amnesia is permanent.

PHILLIPS, MR. ("Meet Me in St. Louie"). He is a friend of Jessie, who will give him and Joey some air-mail stamps, including the one used on Danny's letter to her. Joey, in the hospital, is probably Phillips's son.

PHILLIPS, MRS. ("Three Without, Doubled"). During the San Susie bridge club party at the Garrett apartment, Gullible's first "pardner was a strappin' big woman with a name somethin' like Rowley or Phillips."

PHILLIPS, TED (*The Real Dope*). He is a soldier in Keefe's unit in France. "Sargent" Crane orders Keefe to go with Phillips to the listening post, where Phillips kids and scares Keefe. Jack Brady, another soldier, distresses Simple Simon by telling him that Phillips has a collection of German souvenirs superior to Simon's.

PHYLLIS ("How Are You?"). She was a Cleveland relative of New Yorker Mrs. Ferrell. Mrs. Ferrell tells Bob Dayton that Phyllis was diagnosed with peritonitis and died. Mrs. Ferrell thinks that what killed her was infected teeth and she should have been diagnosed by Dr. Julius in New York. Mrs. Ferrell says she so advised Aunt Laura. Phyllis was probably Laura's daughter.

PICCOLINI ("Claude Diphthong, Student of Crime"). He taught Claude Diphthong in Florence how to play the bugle.

PICINICH ("The Ides of June"). He plays baseball on the Brooklyn team. Danny reports that he started a winning rally "in the 7th innings" by doubling off Jumbo Elliot, pitching for Boston.

Valentine John Picinich (1896–1942) played for the Philadelphia Athletics (1916–1917), the Washington Senators (1918–1922), the Boston Red Sox (1912–1925), the Cincinnati Reds (1926–1928), the Brooklyn Dodgers (1929–1932), and Brooklyn and the Pittsburgh Pirates (1933). (Source: *Baseball Encyclopedia*, 1472)

PICKFORD, MARY (1893–1979). Toronto-born as Gladys Smith starred on Broadway (1907) as Mary Pickford and in silent films (from 1909), had shrewd business sense, established her film company (1916), and often made $350,000 per movie. She and movie figures Charlie Chaplin,* D. W. Griffin (1875–1948), and Douglas Fairbanks Sr. (1883–1939) established the United Artists (1919). She married Fairbanks (1920) — it was the second marriage for each — and created their dream palace Pickfair. Finding him incurably alcoholic, she divorced him (1936). She starred in 14 or so 1920s movies, bought many of her silents, including upwards of 150 Biograph classics, intended to have them destroyed at her death, but willed 50 to the American Film Institute. Lardner enjoyed her acting and mentioned her in "Good for the Soul" and "Harmony." (Sources: Spears, *passim*; Streissguth, 380–381; Yardley, 204)

PIERCE In "My Roomy," he is a left-handed pitcher for the Chicago team. During batting practice, he throws "a flock o' curves" to Buster Elliott, who is trying out for the team and who "slammed 'em right along." In "The Busher's Kid," Keefe boasts that O'Day substituted "this here left-hander Pierce" for Cheney, O'Day's ace pitcher, knowing Keefe was pitching for the White Sox and would win so why waste Cheney? In "Hurry Kane," Pierce is the White Sox relief pitcher, against whom "Bull [Wade] and Johnny Abbot and myself [St. Louis catcher-narrator] had some luck" late in the crucial game.

George Pearce (1888–1935) played for the Chicago Cubs (1912–1916) and the St. Louis Cardinals (1917). (Sources: *Baseball Encyclopedia*, 2284; Hilton, 158, 337)

PIERCE, BALDY ("Women"). He umpired the game between Dayton, Mike Healy's team, and Springfield. Pierce and Healy were rival boasters about their success with women. Pierce made bad calls against Healy, both to assure his having a pleasant date with Helen Buck next day and also to increase Healy's discomfiture.

PIERCE, CHARLEY ("Zone of Quiet"). He was Miss Eleanor Lyons's B.F. (boy friend) in Baltimore, until her G.F. (girl friend) lied to him about her and married him.

PIERCE, TED ("The Crook"). He managed the Montgomery baseball team. Bull, a major-league umpire, conferred with Pierce in an effort to help Martin Gregory get a chance to join Connie Mack's Athletics. Wanting to be rid of Martin, who was offensive, Pierce recommended him.

PIERSON, CAPT. (*The Real Dope*). He is a soldier in Keefe's company in France. Pierson starts a regimental newspaper, encourages Keefe to write about baseball for it, and publishes a short version of Keefe's essay comparing war to baseball.

PINKIE ("The Battle of the Century"). Pinkie, the narrator, is Larry Moon's rather idle friend. Larry, who managed boxer Jim Dugan, asked Pinkie to talk to and play rummy with Dugan while he was training to fight Goulet, the popular French boxer.

Lardner makes awkward use of Pinkie as narrator here, instead of adopting an omniscient point of view. He does this to present an ungrammatical, slangy narrative. For three examples, Pinkie says "Further and more" (twice), "Moon ordered for him and I," and "knocked" instead of "knocked out." Lardner, never Pinkie, is responsible for the controlled ambivalences in Chapter VIII of the story — until resolution comes in the last four short paragraphs.

PIPP In *Treat 'Em Rough*, Jack Keefe, a White Sox pitcher now in the army, mentions Pipp as an opposing batter he formerly faced. In "The Courtship of T. Dorgan," when Keefe's White Sox play "the N.Y. club," Keefe will "make Pipp and some of the rest of them think they have got the pip, eh Al?"

Walter Clement Pipp (1893–1965) played for the Detroit Tigers (1913), the New York Yankees (1915–1925), and the Cincinnati Reds (1926–1928). (Sources: *Baseball Encyclopedia*, 1476; Hilton, 289)

PITTSBURGH PIRATES A National League baseball team (1887–). (Sources: Light, 572–577; Streissguth, 234–235)

"PITY IS AKIN —" (*Cosmopolitan*, September 1929). (Characters: English, Marian Moore, Joe Schwartz, Betty Spalding, Edith Spalding, Henry Spalding.)

Just after midnight Henry Spalding and his wife Edith try a New York night spot called the Cozy Club, get a table after the head waiter removes the "Reserved" sign, and consult menu cards. Edith orders expensive "viands" she lacks taste for. Henry flourishes two $1 bills, requests dry martinis, but must settle for ginger ale and a pint of rye. Edith breaks her habitual silence only when children are mentioned. After a high ball, she wonders if Betty, their three-year-old daughter back home in Toledo, is lonely. This enables the two to jibe at each other.

Regular patrons stream in. A dozen "negro musicians," who are "hot" recorders and Palace performers, play for customers crowding the dance floor. The Spaldings aren't dancing tonight. Marian Moore, the club's husky-voiced, ultra-slow singer, offers "Where Is My Man Gone?" twice. It would have sounded better had she avoided liquor and cigarettes. She sits drinking with friendly customers, then with the tough-looking Club manager. He introduces himself as Joe Schwartz to the Spaldings, who name themselves Travers and wife. When "Mrs. Travers" says Marian's singing "had me almost in tears," Joe praises Marian and says he'll bring her to their table, and does — after 3:00 A.M.

Henry compliments Marian. She demands a drink. He offers to buy another bottle of rye. Instead, she tells "sweet" Joe to fetch the special liquor from her locker. Henry tells Marian they're from Toledo. She says everyone "has to come from somewhere." The waiter brings Henry his fourth pint of rye while Joe produces what Marian calls her 100-year-old rum. He pours her a drink. She won't share because, she gripes, Henry's dozing wife must think "my club" is a hotel to sleep in. She says that she played vaudeville with Bill Abbott in Toledo and adds that this revelation has "foxed" Joe, who wrongly thinks he knows everything about her. Joe tells her to drink up and take a taxi home. Not alone, Marian replies; "Travers" will escort her home and Joe can give Travers's wife a bottle when she comes to. This inspires Henry to yell "Edith." She awakens, says she was asleep a second, and dreamed about "my children." "'Children!' said Marian," and begins sobbing on Edith's breast. Joe says he'll handle Marian and the Traverses should return to their hotel. Henry pays his $73 check and gets a taxi. On the way to their hotel, Henry says he disliked Marian but felt sorry for her when she cried about children. Edith blurts that "she'd have acted just the same" if ring-worm not children had been mentioned.

A court trial ensues. Porter is government prosecutor. English is defense attorney. Spalding and Miss Moore, sobbing, are questioned. Porter: Mr. Spalding, describe events that occurred. Henry: My wife and I, "in evening clothes," got table near dance floor; I bought four pints of rye; Miss Moore sang, drank, came to our table; manager Schwartz introduced her and himself; Henry called himself Travers, offered her rye; she wanted her rum, which Schwartz brought. Porter: Did Miss Moore know you were buying rye? Henry: I think so. English: Was Miss Moore drunk? Henry: Yes; she talked silly. English: You tasted her rum? Henry: No. English: Discuss your rye. Henry: In three hours, my wife had two drinks; I drank the rest, was sober leaving. English: Was Miss Moore part owner of club? Henry: She called it "her club." English to Miss Moore: Are you part owner of club? Miss Moore: No. English: Were you drunk that night? Miss Moore: I never drink; that so-called rum was my cough medicine. Summations follow. Porter stresses enforcement of laws and finds "the defense's only witness" incredible. English stresses "sanctity of womanhood and wolves in evening clothes." The jury finds the defendant not guilty. Marion stops crying, kisses English and all 12 male jurors, and takes "some cough sirup" from her maid in the ladies' room. One juror says, "Golly" and "Her breath had me reeling."

After four nights, Henry buys two quarts of Scotch from his hotel bell boy, drinks copiously, and makes notes for his report implicating the hotel. He "musters enough courage" at 2:00 A.M. to locate Marian at The Snug, where she sings now that the Cozy is padlocked. She tells him to buy her a drink, since her rum supplier is tardy. He begs her forgiveness for his testimony, says her weeping broke his heart, and if she'll forgive him he'll tell her something. She says she's happy; front-page publicity got her this Snug job "at twicet the Cozy" pay; so "I really ought to love you." Now he can tell her he fell in love with her when she cried on his wife's bosom. Marian says he seems to "love people when they're miserable"; so maybe she could love him too if he too cried. He says he'd like that but doesn't "cry easy." She says only Joe is sore because losing part-ownership of the Cozy cost him $2,000. Joe approaches, bearing her rum. Marian tells Joe that "Travers-Spalding" loves her because she cried and she might "love him back" if he cried and maybe Joe could make him cry. Willing to try, Joe slugs Henry, after which Marian says Henry will cry all right but only "out of one eye" hereafter.

"Pity is Akin —" is ignored by most critics. Walton R. Patrick, however, astutely defines it as "a fictionalized presentation of two pet grievances which Lardner touched on more frequently in his nonfiction than in his fiction: the tendency of a jury to acquit a woman regardless of the evidence indicting her; and the sheer folly of attempting to enforce a law to which the general public objects, as was the case with the Volsted Act." Wrongly, however, Patrick downgrades "Pity is Akin —" as "mere hackwork." It requires re-reading to appreciate Lardner's brilliant use of foreshadowing. Not only is it a subtle satire on Prohibition-era enforcement and hypocrisy; it is also a seemingly light-hearted revelation of one woman's descent into alcoholic hell. (Source: Patrick, 127)

PIZZOLA, COUNT ("Nora"). In the play which Louie Brock, Frank Moon, and Jerry Morris mangle Hazlett's play "Nora" into becoming, Count Pizzola, an Italian, falls in love with the Spanish heroine played by Enriqueta, in a role originally written by Hazlett for his Irish heroine Nora Crowley.

PLANK ("Horseshoes"). He is an Athletics pitcher. In the second Athletics-Giants World Series, he is put out by Doyle of the Giants at second base. But Plank defeats Matty, who is pitching for the Giants.

Edward Stewart Plank (1875–1926) played for the Philadelphia Athletics (1901–1914) and the St. Louis Browns (1916–1917). He was a member of the Baseball Hall of Fame (1946). (Sources: *Baseball Encyclopedia*, 2300; Hilton, 411)

PLANT, HERMAN ("A Day with Conrad Green"). He was Conrad Green's long-serving, faithful confidential secretary, recently deceased. Green begrudges the $45 bouquet his secretary Miss Jackson sent for him to Plant's funeral, then lies to avoid going.

PLATT, DOCTOR In *The Big Town*, he plays bridge with Lady Perkins, Mrs. Snell, and another man. When Finch fibs that he has a dog with a disease called blanny, Doctor Platt becomes suspicious. In "Travelogue," Hazel tells Dan Chapman that Platt, a dentist, cured her rheumatism by extracting one of her teeth. (Are these two doctors one and the same?)

PLEAT, ORVILLE ("What of It?"). He is Dexter Cosset's possible rival for Carlotta's affections. Pleat is "in the automobile game on Vistula Avenue," in South Bend.

POND, HY ("The Busher Reënlists"). Keefe bumps into Hy Pond after chatting with other baseball players in the Chicago hotel where American League officials are having a meeting. The two "histed a couple beers" and talk about when both were in the Central League.

George W. Hilton presents evidence suggesting that Hy Pond is a fictional character but says that Pond "appears in a context in which Lardner would be expected to use an actual figure." (Source: Hilton, 222–223)

POODLE ("Poodle"). This is the nickname given to a man by a rich lunatic who calls himself Phil Hughes and who also pretends that Poodle's real name is Ben Collins. Poodle, having worked well until discharged by his boss Mr. Waldron, lies to his wife Mary that he's still working, and meets and is hired as a paid companion by

Hughes. When Mary learns that her husband is no longer working for Waldron, she leaves him.

Donald Elder is optimistic when he says that "Poodle philosophically awaits her [Mary's] ultimate return, meanwhile passing his leisure hours drinking." Howard W. Webb Jr. says that although this "nameless victim of the depression" is a "man of decency and common sense," Lardner gives him "little solace." (Sources: Elder, 369; Webb, 444).

"POODLE" (*Delineator*, January 1934; SC). (Characters: Boland, Felton, Graves, Dr. Gregory, Phil Hughes, Edith Ingram, Jack Ingram, Mary, Norton, Poodle, Mr. Waldron.)

The narrator, 34, has been married to Mary for eight years. He tells his story to a patient fellow drinker at a New York bar:

When I drink, I talk too much. Well, Mary talks constantly and also spends extravagantly. I worked faithfully and well at Waldron's. Last Christmas Mr. Waldron would have given me a $600 bonus except for what he called "a temporay slump in business." All I got was a haberdasher order for $50. When informed, Mary loudly suggested my suing Waldron, or spreading false rumors about his shoddy manufacturing practices, or getting fellow employees to strike. I knew that once I agreed with any idea, she'd change tactics or forget about "plotting about how to fleece Mr. Waldron."

When we first came to New York, we stayed in a hotel before finding an apartment to rent. Mary met Edith Ingram, who was with her husband Jack in the same hotel waiting for a house they fully purchased in Bayside to be completed. Jack made $7,500 a year "before the crash" as a chemist for the Boland Drug Company. We week-ended with the Ingrams when their house was ready. Then we rented a place in Bayside. Mary bought a Parker car at a Bayside dealership, drove it around with Edith sleeping in front and Jack and me bored in back. Mary would drop me at the station so I could get to work by train, then pick up Jack for a later train.

Edie and Jack visited us on Christmas Eve. Mary fibbed about my big bonus, since Jack got none. In fact, as of New Year's Eve, Jack was to lose his job. The Ingrams left their house with a real-estate agent "to hold" for an offer and made plans to move January 8th to Chicago, where Jack could work for his brother, who owned two hotels.

On January 7th, my birthday, Mr. Waldron apologized for not giving me that $600 bonus and promised "to more than make [it] up to me." He didn't say "how much." Puzzled, I visited a saloon that afternoon, took the 6:15 train rather than my usual 5:12, got home late, and bothered Mary, because when I drink I talk too much. I blurted about being promised big money from Mr. Waldron. When the Ingrams appeared, Mary, having exaggerated the likely sum, gloated, embarrassed them, and sent them away miserable, especially "her best friend" Edith.

My weekly pay checks reflected no raise. On Monday, January 30 [1933], Mr. Waldron went to Florida without saying goodbye. Next morning I found a note from him dismissing me after February 4th. Since Mary regularly took my pay and gave me a weekly $10 allowance and bought my monthly commuter tickets by check to the Long Island Railroad Company, I had "to practise deception." Starting Monday, February 6th, I began loafing at "the talkies and the speakies" and lying to Mary that I was now to be paid monthly not weekly. She enjoyed multiplying that monthly pay by 12 for ever-increasing annual sums. Instead of feeling "mean," I was happy: Mary was briefly hopeful. I was peaceful. I read dozens of job ads, applied to many, stood in lines, but found nothing suitable. Just today I tried for three jobs, failed, wasted time answering ads requiring mailed replies, knew I wouldn't succeeded there either, and avoided another 50¢ blue-plate lunch by attending a show at the Paramount.

While I was there, a fellow began talking loudly at me. He explained he was an outpatient from Graves' Hospital, called himself Phil Hughes, said he recognized me as Ben Collins from Oconomowoc, Wisconsin, and said my nickname was always Poodle because I resembled a poodle. I couldn't silence him and humored him by saying I was unemployed. He said if I could prove I was really out of work he would give me a job. We left before the usher could kick us out for talking. Hughes, almost 60, didn't look like a bum, insisted he really knew me, took me by taxi to his hospital, and introduced me to a nurse as hometown-friend Mr. Collins, and asked for Dr. Gregory, who, Hughes explained, let him out from 9:00 A.M. until time to return for lunch but urged him to hire a companion to see that he didn't overspend. Hughes offered me the job. I told him I wasn't from his town. He said I could keep my secret, we should "let it go at that," he'd pay me $7,200 a year, but first he needed "the doctor's approval of me as a man." Alone with the doctor, I lacked time to explain myself because he said his real name was Tyson and yet Hughes insisted he knew Dr. Gregory in Cleveland and paid him in "checks to cash" so Tyson needn't endorse checks made out to Gregory. Approving of me, the doctor said he didn't want Hughes to fritter away his huge trust-fund checks by foolish purchases, and the doctor didn't want to lose his own $3,600-a-month checks. If I could simply be Poodle, I could escort this harmless "fella" to matinées and movies, and also to baseball games when summer came. The doctor called Mr. Waldron's office, and his treasurer and vice president evidently gave me satisfactory recommendations.

I figured I'd make $7,200 a year as Poodle, an 8-hour-a-day day-nurse for a crazy man, and make nothing by living with a crazy woman the rest of the time. But not so. Mary phoned Waldron's just before lunchtime today, and a new switchboard girl said she'd never heard of me, inquired, and reported my leaving after February 4th. Home again, I found a note from Mary accusing me of lying about my work but in reality consorting with a "huzzy." Mary added that maybe she'd return to me and resume her "humiliating position" as my slave if I give up my "deceptions and frauds and infidelity." I plan to let her enjoy a long vacation. Meanwhile, I'm having some more drinks here with you, because "Every dog must have his night."

"Poodle" has its problems. The narrator at one point tells his drinking pal, "You've been drowsing and not listening." In reality, attentive readers who have not nodded, but have "listened," have surely been puzzled. "Poodle" gives evidence of hasty writing by Lardner, who was mortally ill when he wrote it. Mary is at the wheel of a car without details of its purchase provided. After Jack's move to and employment in Chicago are detailed, he and Edie are still in New York. The narrator mentions pocketing Poodle's first-month's pay—$500 plus $100 in cash—before explaining his interview with the physician. Finally, the narrator says that the doctor phoned Waldron's office in the afternoon and got good news about him but then says that Mary phoned the office earlier and got bad news. In a letter (February 3, 1933) to Max Perkins,* Lardner says that he started "Poodle" in July 1932 and finished it in January 1933 and, further, that it was rejected by *Collier's* and *Cosmopolitan* before the *Delineator* accepted it.

Jonathan Yardley reports that Lardner was surprised that the *Delineator*, a woman's magazine, accepted it and even paid him $750 for it; then Yardley dismissively defines it as "a story about the young man facing Depression job difficulties." Yes, indeed. But many readers in 1934, probably aware that Lardner had recently died and knowing firsthand about the corrosive effects the Depression had on families, might see "Poodle" as a humor-muffled nightmare parable, actors in which are hypocritical boss, unemployed good worker, self-absorbed wife, man unemployed and with wife and unsold house, lunatic rich man, dishonest physician.

To make "Poodle" timely, Lardner has the narrator say Mary gave Jack a record of "Tea for Two," a popular song by Vincent Youmans* and Irving Caesar (1895–1986); make goofy references to Richard Byrd (1888–1957), who led first flights over both the South Pole (1926) and the North Pole (1928), and to Benito Mussolini (1883–1945), Fascist dictator of Italy (1922–1945); and see and hear Paul Whiteman* and *Rhapsody in Blue* by George Gershwin* at the Paramount. Ring Lardner Jr. notes that "Poodle" is the only story his father "ever wrote concerned with the Depression and its effects on people's lives ... and it was, for him, a quite serious treatment of the subject." (Sources: Lardner, Jr., 220; Caruthers [1995], 270; Yardley, 371)

POOLE, CLINT ("Travelogue"). Hazel Dignan tells Dan Chaman that this man, from South Bend, is Harley Bateman's brother-in-law.

"THE POOR SIMP" (*Saturday Evening Post*, September 11, 1915; ABS, RAB). (Characters: Jack Andrews, Red Burns, Cap, Carey, Conahan, Mary Conahan, Bill Garwood, McGraw, Marquard, Mathewson, Robbie, Rucker, Skull Scoville, Smitty, Tesreau, Uncle Zeke.)

I. The narrator plays baseball [for the Cubs] honorably, unlike some. Jack Andrews, for example, bat after Bill Garwood and regularly spiked him trying to run ahead; and Jack does well now, "runnin' a halfway house outside o' Chicago." Also, Red Burns had to be paged "when it was his turn to hit," and he's in a profitable "contractin' business in Cleveland." But when the narrator, in his seventh year, earning $4,500, retires, he'll starve or get a foundry job. Although he's not "heavy with brains," brains in general are "the worst handicap a man can have in this business." Ask Carey to talk about Skull Scoville. Or listen to the narrator's story:

II. When Carey returned from scouting college players, he asked me about that new player, preening like Francis X. Bushman.* I told Carey he was

Skull Scoville, a pitcher recruited from the Carolina League. I told Carey he didn't want a good-looking player but "somebody to pick on." Carey agreed, saying he'd kidded college players with "the old junk" and needed a new victim. He approached Skull and mentioned a Utah baseball team managed by women. Asked where Utah was, Carey told Skull he could get there by taking a St. Louis streetcar going past Michigan City to Shreveport. Cap pleased Carey by liking Skull well enough to keep him. Though wild, Skull's phenomenal speed scared batters.

III. Scheduled to play Brooklyn in May, our team went by train. Carey, undressing, warned Skull not to follow the players to the dining car but to undress and grab one of the 12 lower berths, since 12 speedy players would get the lowers and the others would get the uppers, which are dangerous when the train went "through them Indiana mountains." Smitty, Carey, and I told Skull that the train avoided a storm in Fall River via Evanston, where the fireman's mother-in-law was selling chicken and potatoes at the station. To save his berth, Skull paid Carey to go buy their dinner at the Evanston stop (really Toledo); Carey tried but said he dropped "your supper" in rushing back. Skull was as hungry as Jess Willard* "in the diner next mornin.'"

IV. After two days of rainouts in Brooklyn, the sun shone next morning. Carey told Skull in their hotel at Eighty-first and Columbus to rush breakfast because they were playing three games. The "gang" hid, pretending to be already gone. Carey told Skull to take a taxi, which the club would pay for. Skull arrived alone so early that Robbie suspected he'd been sent to steal signs of his Dodgers, at early practice. I told Robbie the fellow was Scoville, our ace. Robbie said he was too handsome to pitch well. That afternoon Skull won, though Rucker "outpitched him." While Carey, Skull, and I returned to the hotel, Carey said he tried to phone Skull to explain there'd be only one game after all, but Skull had already left. Skull said no problem, he'd be reimbursed $8.75 for the cab. Carey replied that "the sec." of their "cheap club" said that Skull took the wrong taxi, that a second taxi had already been paid to take him.

V. About to play the Giants at the Polo Grounds, Carey suggested Skull go early to watch the polo game. Carey couldn't go see again, because repeat visitors weren't allowed, for fear they'd "learn secrets o' the game." I started to tell Skull how to get to the Polo Grounds; but Carey interfered, told him to go south to the Battery, take an Elevated to Harlem, and guard against girl pickpockets. He learned the way eventually, though too late for polo. He was scheduled to pitch the third game. Carey said Cap told him to tell Skull to quiz McGraw about which pitches his players can hit and can't hit, who's going to pitch, etc. After talking with Mac, who's too used to nuts to be "excite[d] no more," Skull returned to announce that Mathewson, Marquard, or Tesreau would pitch against us, and that Mac said his men couldn't hit anything. When Cap wanted Skull to warm up, he said it wasn't necessary because Giants "can't hit nothin.'" Who said so? Their manager. Who is he? Mac. Cap said he thought George Cohan managed the Giants. Skull pitched but soon "went to the shower."

VI. Skull pitched badly "over in Philly," giving up five walks and one hit in his first and only inning, and was hardly better in Boston before "Cap yanked him." Carey razzed Skull. Did pickpockets steal his control? Should we enlarge home plate when we returned home? Carey acted surprised when Skull said he couldn't pitch where he was "aimin.'" On "the cute little jump" train trip from Boston to St. Louis, Carey terrified Skull. Carey made him stay up all night, armed with the engineer's empty gun, accompanied by the obviously uneasy porter, patrolling in and out of the washroom. They must prevent "the James Boys," namely train robbers as well as two uninvolved pitchers, one for Boston and the other for St. Louis, from robbing Skull of his money, watch, "clo'es," control, and nice complexion. Next morning, Skull reported "Not a sign" of the James Boys but also said he was sleepy.

VII. He didn't pitch that afternoon, but next day he was so wild after 14 straight balls that Cap took him out and immediately "ast" waivers on him. No team wanted him. After nearly two weeks, Cap was about to "leave him go outright." So Carey tried a final joke on "the poor simp." When Skull returned from shagging flies in the outfield, Carey told him that two beautiful "dames" in the stand wanted to meet him. The blonde was "a bear cat"; the other, even classier. Carey identified the blonde as Lizzie Carnegie, "the richest girl in the country," and the other as her sister-in-law. Strutting over, Skull "got two nice smiles." After the game I saw "Skull and the pair o' them hikin' for the exit." Released by Cap, Skull said he might try Utah, where women are baseball managers. Instead, however, when we returned from Cincinnati on July 3rd, Skull told us he was getting married to that blonde. He explained she is Mary Conahan, not Lizzie Carnegie, and her companion was "just a friend o' her'n," not an in-law. Mary's father was rich, brewed Silver Tip beer, and was ailing, and Skull was "goin' to kind-a look after the business." Carey and I proceeded to seek some Silver Tip, not "to help out old Skull" but to relieve ourselves.

For a little verisimilitude, Lardner has Carey compare Skull Scoville's good looks to those of matinée idol Francis X. Bushman* and has Carey mention George M. Cohan,* popular musical-comedy actor, writer, and producer.

THE PORTABLE RING LARDNER edited by Gilbert Seldes (New York: Viking Press, 1946). This collection contains 22 short stories.

PORTER, CHARLEY ("A Frame-Up"). He is a boxer from Benton Harbor. Burke trains, at first, only to defeat Porter and thus impress Porter's girlfriend. Burke succeeds but then dumps the girl for prettier, rich prey.

POTTER, MRS. ("Gullible's Travels"). She is a famous Chicago socialite. While vacationing at Palm Beach, she mistakes Mrs. Gullible, accidentally or purposely, for a hotel maid and asks for towels.

Lardner in naming this thoughtless woman has in mind the art-collecting, much-traveled wife of Potter Palmer (1826–1902), the Chicago merchant-capitalist. Their $700,000 mansion was on the Lake Shore Drive.

POTTER, PAUL ("The Facts"). He is a boyfriend of Ellen McDonald, who breaks a date with him to await Billy Bowen's return to Chicago.

PRATT ("A Busher's Letters Home"). Keefe boasts that his pitching combination of spitters and fast balls made "Mister Pratt ... a dead baby.' Keefe was pitching against Pratt of the St. Louis Browns.

Derrill Burnham Pratt (1888–1977) played for the St. Louis Browns (1912–1917), the New York Yankees (1918–1920), the Boston Red Sox (1921–1922), and the Detroit Tigers (1923–1924). (Sources: *Baseball Encyclopedia*, 1484; Hilton, 63)

PRATT, HILDA ("How Are You?"). She and her husband Wallie are Bob and Beth Dayton's friends. After a bridge party at the Daytons,' the Pratts stay overnight. In the morning, Hilda and Bob discuss symptoms of ailments. She recommends Dr. Elston Gifford as New York's best diagnostician, says her brother Mark went to him, was diagnosed with a brain tumor, was operated on, and died.

PRATT, MR. ("The Facts"). He sings "Fear Ye Not, O Israel!" at the church service attended by Sam McDonald and his sister-in-law Mary Carey.

PRATT, WALLIE ("How Are You?"). He and his wife Hilda are guests at a bridge party at Bob and Beth Dayton's home. It is late and is raining; so Wallie agrees, reluctantly, to remain overnight. He makes witty comments. He has a wolfhound named Dmitri.

PRENDERGAST, JACK ("Rhythm"). He has written a book that producer Conrad Green wants for a musical. Green asks Harry Hart, tune-thief, to collaborate with lyric-thief Benny Kane on it. Hart, turning cocky, prefers to have Sam Rose as their lyricist.

PRENDERGAST, MRS. ("Absent-minded Beggar"). She was a friend to whom Mrs. Knowles complained that both her late husband and their young son John Knowles were "wool gatherers."

PRENTISS ("The Venomous Viper of the Volga"). He is a ventriloquist performing at the Palace when Sandy King and Mabel Ives go there. King spots Henry Goetz, Prentiss's huge actor in the show, and hires him to become the boxer known as Ivan Ivanovitch, "the Venomous Viper of the Volga."

PRESTON ("When the Moon Comes over the Mountain"). This is the name of a family that Jessie tells Danny she visited two years ago. A picture taken of her then doesn't resemble her now, she adds.

PRESTON, JIM ("Women"). He was a relief pitcher for Springfield, in their game against Dayton, Mike Healy's team. He relieved Bill Hutton in the ninth inning, during which the umpire Baldy Pierce made bad calls against Healy to end the game.

PRESTON, JIMMY ("Reunion"). He is an old neighbor of Bob and Jennie Mason. They ask him to tend their garden in Buchanan, Michigan, when they have a reunion with Bob's sister Rita Johnston on Long Island, New York.

According to Donald Elder and Clifford M. Caruthers, Lardner's many neighbors in East Hampton, Long Island, included his friends James and May Preston. (Sources: Caruthers [1973], 122; Elder, 294, 306)

PRINCE, CHARLIE ("That Old Sweetheart of Mine"). He is a business associate of Will's, or he may be fictitious. In order to meet the suddenly available Stella Crane, Will breaks his date with Betty, a New York girlfriend, by phoning Betty and lying that Charlie Prince is coming from Buffalo to see him. When romance proves impossible for Will with Stella, he phones Betty again, to say that Charlie has been delayed and Will is available. Betty is willing.

"PRIVATE VALENTINE" (*Saturday Evening Post,* August 3, 1918; RD) *see* ***THE REAL DOPE***

PURDY ("Haircut"). Whitey, the narrator, says Purdy owes him for unpaid haircuts.

"PURLS BEFORE SWINE" (*Saturday Evening Post,* June 8, 1918; TER) *see* ***TREAT 'EM ROUGH***

"QUICK RETURNS" (*Saturday Evening Post,* March 27, 1920; BT, PRL, RLR) *see* ***THE BIG TOWN***

QUINN, HARRY ("A Friendly Game"). He is Marion Quinn's husband, 23 or 24, a seemingly talentless and callow "fourth assistant head shippin' clerk" in the office where the narrator works. But when Quinn and his wife play poker as guests of the narrator and "The Missus," the Quinns defeat their five rivals.

QUINN, JACK In "One Hit, One Error, One Left." he is a Brooklyn pitcher, who Danny writes Jessie "aint got nothing on the ball." Later Danny adds that Quinn "was married when Carey was lerning to talk." Danny fibs to Jessie that young baseball players aren't encouraged to get married. In "When the Moon Comes over the Mountain," Quinn pitched in a long game against Boston. In "Holycaust," Danny says Jack Quinn thought "holycaust" was a college where Jack Barry coached. (Yes, Quinn's pun is about Holy Cross College.)

John Picus Quinn (1883–1946) played for the New York Yankees (1909–1912), the Boston Braves (1913), the Chicago White Sox (1918), the Yankees (1919–1921), the Boston Red Sox (1922–1924), the Red Sox and the Philadelphia Athletics (1925), the Athletics (1926–1930), the Brooklyn Dodgers (1931–1932), and the Cincinnati Reds (1933). George W. Hilton reports that Byron Bancroft Johnson,* president of the American League, awarded Quinn's contract in 1918 to the Yankees and not to the White Sox. This angered Charles Albert Comiskey,* owner of the White Sox. Charles F. Faber and Richard B. Faber demonstrate that Quinn was a magnificent spitball pitcher, third in prowess only to Red Faber and Burleigh Grimes, but add that after Quinn's wife died he "lived in comparative obscurity" and that his death was "perhaps brought on by alcohol abuse." (Sources: *Baseball Encyclopedia,* 2311; Faber and Faber, 64, 187; Hilton, 39)

QUINN, MARION ("A Friendly Game"). She is Harry Quinn's pretty but seemingly air-headed wife. After marrying, the two room and board with her parents. Professing to know little or nothing about poker, she wins $28 when the narrator and his wife host a poker party including the Quinns, Jim Hatch, Mrs. Hatch, and Joe Tuttle. The narrator calls Marion "Cutie" and "Sweetness."

The narrator says the following of hysterically giggling Marion: "If she was a theater audience, you could put Frances Starr in this here play, Justice, and call it a minstrel show." Frances Grant Starr (1881–1973) played the doe-eyed ingénue in many productions (1904–1922) mounted by impresario David Belasco (1853–1931); but neither Starr nor Belasco ever had anything professional to do with *Justice* (1910), the sombre play by John Galsworthy (1867–1933) criticizing solitary confinement as a punishment for prisoners.

QUOLT, HARRISON ("What of It?"). He happens to be traveling on the train to New York with Dexter Cosset and Ben Lacey. When Ben complains to Quolt that Ben's constant talk prevents his thinking about his play *Ghosts,* Quolt silences Ben by answering each of his string of words with "What of It?" When Dexter expresses grateful relief, Quolt replies, "What did you say?"

R., MRS. ("Contract"). She is a bridge-playing friend of Lardner, who hopes in a postscript she won't take his story personally.

RAGAN, PAT ("The Busher Pulls a Mays"). Keefe writes Al Blanchard on August 2 [1919] that "Gleason has went plain cuckoo" because he "signed up Pat Ragan," a pitcher for so many clubs that his only recommendation is "acquaintences in all the big citys."

Don Carlos Patrick Ragan (1888–1956) pitched for the Cincinnati Reds and the Chicago Cubs (1909), the Brooklyn Dodgers (1911–1914), the Dodgers and the Boston Braves (1915), the Braves (1916–1918), the Braves and the New York Giants and the Chicago White Sox (1919), and the Philadelphia Phillies (1923).

George W. Hilton, agreeing with Keefe that Pat Ragan was "shopworn," says that Ragan pitched for five clubs before the White Sox obtained him "at the waiver price" (August 2, 1919) and that he pitched without a decision in only one game thereafter for them. Lardner is right, if heartless, to have fictional Keefe expose a living athlete this way, regardless of his professional statistics. Hilton notes that in 11 seasons with the National League, Ragan's "record was 75–104." (Sources: *Baseball Encyclopedia*, 2313; Hilton, 306)

RAISA, ROSA ("Dinner"). Miss Coakley tells Harry Barton that the soprano Rosa Raisa, of the "simply gorgeous opera company in Chicago," is married to Ruffo or perhaps Rimini, both being "barytones" anyhow.

RALSTON, JARVIS ("The Spinning Wheel"). This "automobile man" is a gambler. The narrator, a roulette dealer, recalls how one evening Ralston lost $15,000, almost walked away, but then won it back plus $500 more. The narrator says that Ralston was the sort of man to lose without squawking, unlike many losers.

RALSTON, JIMMY ("JIM") (*The Big Town*). He is the handsome, sponging, lying comedian in the Ziegfeld Follies in New York. He attracts well-to-do but stupid Katie, Ella's unmarried sister. Katie invests money in Ralston's hopeless play, "Bridget Sees a Ghost," which fails, after which Ralston returns to the Follies and marries Katie. Finch, though aware of Ralston's shady character, is happy to be rid of his sister-in-law.

RANDALL, DICK ("Widow"). He has evidently been Margaret Winslow's secret lover. But when her husband John Winslow dies and she seeks to reunite with Dick, he tells her he cried when John, a fellow Rotary member, died, makes excuses, and says "it's all different now." Margaret laments the loss of Dick only briefly.

Lardner was not the sort of writer to describe this pair's assignations in any sort of detail. Walton R. Patrick makes Randall out to be more honorable than is probable when he says that Randall "comes to tell her [Margaret] that he can have nothing further to do with her because of his respect for her dead husband." (Source: Patrick, 130)

RASCOE, BURTON (1892–1957). He was a Kentucky-born journalist and critic. While attending classes at the University of Chicago (1911–1913), he was employed by the *Chicago Tribune* as campus reporter and married Hazel Luke (1913; they were to have a son and then a daughter). Rascoe continued to report for the *Tribune* (1913–1920), but was discharged for criticizing Mary Baker Eddy, founder of Christian Science. The Rascoes moved to New York, where he worked for the *New York Tribune* (1922–1924). He was editor of the board of editors for the Literary Guild of America (1927–1937). He worked for the *Bookman* (1927–1928), the *New York Sun* (1930–1932), *Esquire* (1933–1938), the *American Mercury* (1940–1941), the *Chicago Sun* (1941–1942), and the *New York World-Telegram* (1942–1946). He was also a free-lance writer; among his several books were a brief study (1925) of the novelist Theodore Dreiser, a subjective literary history (*Titans of Literature*, 1932), two autobiographical volumes (*Before I Forget*, 1937; *We Were Interrupted*, 1947), and a biography (1941) of Western gun moll Belle Starr (1848–1889).

Lardner knew Rascoe when they worked for the *Chicago Tribune* together and later when both worked in New York. In a letter (June 5, [1924]) Lardner sent to F. Scott Fitzgerald,* Lardner says that Rascoe's wife Hazel "was on the wagon, but her husband was *not*." Rascoe was a member of the Literary Guild selection committee and, with others, voted *Round Up* as one of the Guild's monthly selections. This resulted in a printing of 70,000 special Guild copies. Lardner was asked by a *World-Telegram* reporter for his opinion of Dreiser and was misquoted as saying something derogatory (December 18, 1931). When Rascoe repeated the misstatement, Lardner wrote him (December 16, 1931) in vigorous protest and also wrote Dreiser three times to explain and praise him (January 2, 6, 11, 1932). (Sources: Hensley; Caruthers [1995], 159, 222, 250–255)

THE REAL DOPE (1919; RD, LOB, RD). Novel-like series of 54 letters from Jack Keefe to his friend Al Blanchard, originally published in six parts, entitled "And Many a Stormy Wind Shall Blow" (*Saturday Evening Post*, July 6, 1918), "Private Valentine" (*Saturday Evening Post*, August 3, 1918), "Stragety and Tragedy" (*Saturday Evening Post*, August 31, 1918), "Decorated" (*Saturday Evening Post*, October 26, 1918), "Sammy Boy" (*Saturday Evening Post*, December 21, 1918), and "Simple Simon" (*Saturday Evening Post*, January 25, 1919).

"AND MANY A STORMY WIND SHALL BLOW." (Characters: Sargent Bishop, Al Blanchard, Bertha Blanchard, the Colonel, Doran, Sam Hall, Al Keefe, Florrie Keefe, Jack Keefe, Bob Lee, Freddie Smith, Capt. Seeley, Capt. Somebody, the Swede.)

Jack Keefe addresses 11 letters to Al Blanchard, the first 10 from "On the Ship Board," and the eleventh from France.

Jan. 15 [1918]. Jack Keefe tells Al he'll mail several letters from the other side of "the old pond." They will be "the real dope," not like reporters' writings. The convoy includes "four boat loads of soldiers" and six war ships to look for submarines. Jack isn't sea sick but is "a little home sick." Florrie and little Al didn't come to see them off. The men were supposed to sail secretly, but families were there kissing and saying goodbye. It's time for "chow." That means food.

Jan. 17. The men are "jammed like a sardine or something," with four strange "roomys" to each "state room." He is with Smith, criminal looking; Sam Hall, a "grouch" who smokes; and Lee, who's funny. They have daily lifeboat drills and roll calls. Seeing Jack "writeing," Lee said everything would be censored. They put the slowest ship — which Lee calls "the censor ship" — in the convoy first. Why not the fastest, to set the pace?

Jan. 19. Bob Lee says Jack didn't get seasick, like the others, and should be called Jack Tar, meaning experienced sailor. Freddie Smith, a Milwaukee "resturent" waiter, knows French, will teach "Lee and I," so they can order food when on leave in France.

Jan. 20. Jack was sick "from something I eat." He got mad at Hall's kidding. Uncle Sam shouldn't feed "his boys" bad "canned beans."

Jan. 21. Doran, a sailor, warned Jack that "subs might fire a periscope," sinking their ship. Those Camp Grant "smart alex" taught Jack less French than Smith. Now "I and Lee" can order "beef steak und brot mit butter schmieren." Al, it's "lebe wohl" for now.

Jan. 22. In "the danger zone," Jack stays on deck to see anything exciting. Also he "maybe ... could help out in some way." They proceed so slowly that Jack calls the lead ship "a he---ll of a censor ship." Lee tried some French on some French officers aboard, and they "smiled and bowed."

Jan. 23. Sargent Bishop said Capt. Seeley said in emergencies let the privates get into lifeboats first, because "the N. C. O. officers" are coolest. Doran said Gen. Pershing standardized this procedure. Reporters don't hear this kind of "dope." Doran says the subs seek this heavy ship because it'll sink fast. Jack's hunch may be right; he won't see France, because he must save the privates first. He feels faint, like after pitching against St. Louis.

Jan. 23 again. Jack is afraid "a bang against the side of the boat" will sink them. He must write Al carefully. He's sorry he and Florrie never visited the Blanchards in Bedford. Florrie always felt superior. She once said something kind about them, that the Blanchards' wedding photo was of "honest homely ... people" you "could always depend on." Al, visit Florrie if Jack is "laying at the bottom of the ocean tonight," and see she doesn't waste Jack's "$10000 dollars soldiers insurence" buying expensive "widows weeds" that people "will think ... are flowers." Money isn't everything; kindness counts. Jack asks Al to check on Florrie. If Jack dies, her "mind will be effected," she might marry some "horse Dr.," and little Al would have a bad "father in law." Blanchard shouldn't take Bertha to see Florrie. Jack won't "last long in France," will send presents from there, but probably won't "never get there" and also lacks money. Well, "be proud of me."

Jan. 24. Trouble. Jack saluted and said "Schones tag" — some French that Smith taught him — to a French officer. Jack got hauled before "my Capt. Seeley" and others, and was criticized for saying "we had a he---ll of a censor ship." When Jack explained what Lee said about the lead ship and Capt. Seeley smiled, "I knew I was O.K." The French officer was mad until Jack explained he didn't know German and had been deceived. Capt. Seeley put Smith, Lee, and Doran "up on the carpet" for the Colonel to "give ... a fierce balling out" to, because the war "wasn't no practicle joke." Capt. Seeley told Jack he was too "dam innocent" to be a corporal. He's glad, because now he can "pal around with the boys," and, as a private, can jump quick into a lifeboat. Still, he'd help others first.

Jan. 25. In port now. Away from the subs, which "between you and I" he never thought of "all the way over," except when others mentioned them. Why worry?

"Somewheres in France, Jan. 26." Any "Shylock" knows where they are by the post mark to be on this letter. Rumor says a German "periscope" missed hitting "our ship" because American destroyers dropped "death bombs" and "nine subs sank." Jack "had a hunch" earlier about danger, but there was "no alarm" because why "get everybody up at night for nothing"? The girls in this

French town are "some girls." Jack won't flirt much. Everybody's busy anyway.

"PRIVATE VALENTINE." (Characters: Sargent Avery, Al Blanchard, Bertha Blanchard, Frank Carson, Al Keefe, Florrie Keefe, Jack Keefe, Ruth Palmer, Capt. Seeley, Stoops.)

Jack sends "Friend Al" nine letters from "Somewheres in France."

Feb. 2. Jack comments on French pronunciations, the soldiers' uncertainty about getting to the front, French trains, their cold billets in a barn, the traffic of "motor Lauras."

Feb. 4. Jack is "writeing this in the Y.M.C.A." to get warm. There's so much noise he can't spell right. French officers are training them about "trenchs" in "mud and slush." They don't say "miles" but "kilometts." The Germans boast of a spring "drive" but are like "birds come up to hit in baseball" whose only drive was "a hump back liner to the pitcher." Drink here is weak beer and "red and white" wine, cheap because "a frank isn't only worth about $.19 cents." The French don't put stamps on envelopes. Jack knows why Al isn't writing much — because "in Bedford you haven't got nothing to write." Jack is where "big" things happen — baseball and this "bigger game." He'd like "a Chi paper." He asked Florrie, but no luck.

Feb. 7. Jack says Al probably reads articles about the war "wrote over here by reporters." One asked Jack if he was "the White Sox pitcher," said he couldn't name Jack in writing, but could discuss a certain star American League pitcher and readers would identify him. The reporter wants Jack to write patriotic "poultry" he'd try to get published for him, and maybe a song could be made out of it. Jack is "to busy to monkey with it." There are many songs about "the boshs." Germans, being "full of bunk," are called that. Jack relates the history of Jonah Vark, "a young gal" around "a 100 yrs. ago" in a war. Jonah "carried a white flag." The Dutchmens regarded it as "a flag of truants." She captured New Orleans. If a German shouts "Conrad" to Jack to surrender, he'll "perculate them with a bayonet."

Feb. 9. Last night Jack composed "poultry" for that reporter to use, because "censors smeers out" what he writes and he lacks material. The poem warns Germany, sympathizes with each soldier's "girl so dear," and says "the stars and stripes / Will always fight for their rights." Jack and Frank Carson, his "buddy" — which means an army "pal" — went to "the Red X canteen" for decent food at "$.19 cents." They met one of "3 janes" from America. Carson said, "Bon soir Madam Moselle" to her. Jack understood but said Carson meant his bones were sore. Miss Moselle understood and laughed. Carson had to go ask about Jack's "Mrs." and went on that Jack was a baseball pitcher, which "popped her eyes out." Jack mustn't see her again, though; somebody might get hurt.

Feb. 11. For a soldier's birthday, his buddies bought "enough champagne to bathe in" for about "60 franks." The "revelry" cost them fines, confinement, and a warning from Capt. Seeley about "a fireing squad" next time. The reporter didn't ask for his "verses." French women here wouldn't impress "a scout for the Follys." Unlike some, Jack longs to get to the front.

Feb. 13. Returning to the canteen, Jack bumped into Miss Moselle. She asked how he liked this town. He said he preferred her. She blushed. He happened to drop his "verses." When she wanted to copy them, he offered to write her "a comical valentine." He won't come back, though, but maybe he'll write something not "mushy." She's "a darb" he wouldn't want to hurt. The boys "begged" him to give a baseball talk at the Y.M.C.A. on Saturday. He "don't hardly feeling like refuseing."

Feb. 15. Jack reluctantly wrote that valentine he promised. It says it would be fine if he could call her his valentine and show her a good time. He gave it, one day late and sealed, to Miss Moselle. She knows he's married. It should "let her down easy" and not cause "more tensions from me." Jack saw some "fine looking" German prisoners. They were surely "wondring if all the U. S. soldiers was big stroppers like I." They proved the "storys ... about no soap in Germany." And "finely" a letter from Florrie — about little Al needing shoes, her beauty parlor success, her heel "callous," and "a snapshot" of her in a "war bride" dress.

Feb. 17. Jack is irate at "a certain bird in this camp." Jack was asked to speak at a show. He introduced himself, mentioned his baseball background, and summarized a game he pitched for the Chicago White Sox against Detroit. Ninth inning, two Tigers on base: Tyrus Cobb was at bat; Jack waived off his catcher Ray Schalk's curve signal in favor of "my floater"; Cobb lined to Eddie Murphy; the Sox won. Jack then says war is like baseball, "because it is stratejy that wins" in both, and regardless of his troop strength "a gen. ... won't get nowheres without he uses his brains." Jack was applauded. Then Sargent Avery rose, praised Jack as "stratejest," pitcher, and poet, and then read Jack's "beautiful valentine ... to a certain lady" that everyone knew and that returned "to

Paris to resume other dutys." The troops "hollered ... and razed he---ll." Miss Moselle probably left for Paris through embarrassment. When Jack finds who gave stole her valentine, "they will be one less snake in this regt."

Feb. 18. Jack confronted Avery, who identified "Miss Moselle" as Ruth Palmer of "N.Y. city" and said she gave him the poem with a laugh. Jack bought some champagne with "a 20 frank note" and got so drunk and sick that Capt. Seeley didn't let him ship out with the others. Before any possible "court marshall," though, he'll get some of "these birds" that started calling him "Private Valentine."

"STRAGETY AND TRAGEDY" (Characters: Johnny Alcock, Ernestine, Al Keefe, Florrie Keefe, Jack Keefe, Gen. Black Jack Pershing, Corp. Pierson, Robbins, Capt. Seeley.)

Jack sends eight more letters to Blanchard, from "Somewheres in France."

March 2. It has rained. The army should "page" the navy to bring one of its "supper dread 0" ships for us to use as "Lauras." The German won't attack those ships, which are as safe as "a private yatch." If the French had baseball games, "the no game sign" would be up until little Al had kids. Good training at Camp Grant would be for soldiers to take showers "with their close on." One soldier called Jack's billet "Noahs Ark." Remember that "gag" concerning Noah, "his folks, and a married couple of every kind of animals"? Jack wishes helmets were wide like "a bumber shoot."

March 4. The French give lots of "meddles." Since "the U. S. and the English uses the same language," the French should adopt English because nobody but the French understand French. French uniforms are different colors for different service branches. Corp. Pierson of Jack's company is starting a weekly newspaper, wants Jack to write about baseball. He said no. He recalls a White Sox game "in Phil.," poor play by Weaver, Collins, and Gandil for the Sox, Rube Oldring's liner for Phil., Bill Dinneen's poor umpiring. Florrie got upset when she read the column about it by Robbins, a "Chi" reporter, who criticized Jack.

March 9. Pierson didn't hear right; so Jack wrote an essay called "War and Baseball: Two Games Where Brains Wins." It compares "the stragety of baseball" and "the stregety of war" and showing how in both games "brains wins." To illustrate, he describes his pitching one time against Boston's Carl Mays. Ninth inning: 2–2, two out; Larry Gardner of Boston doubled because Weaver and Jackson "layed down and died"; Jack walked Hoblitzel because weak-hitting Scott was up next; Scott struck out. Eleventh inning: Duffy Lewis got a triple against Jack when Jackson "layed down and died" near the ball; Lewis "scored on a past ball"; Boston won 3–2. Jack's correct "stragety" made him walk Hobby. Too bad "our gens. is so old" they don't know "much about baseball since it become a test of brains like it is now." Johnny Alcock saw Jack writing, read his essay, and told Jack that their officers should apply "my idears ... to war fair" and promote Jack "to the gen. staff." Jack wouldn't want to go stick pins on maps with them. He'd prefer carrying "a riffle" and sticking his bayonet into Germans' maps. Still, he'd wear his "fingers to the bone writeing" if it would "give them a few hints."

March 13. Jack says "somebody must of sent a coppy" of his essay, which was partly published, to Gen. Pershing, who answered. Jack provides a "coppy" for Al. It praised Jack's essay, expressed unhappiness that the general's staff lacked the ability to play professional baseball like Jack, and asks Jack to send him suggestions for "a campaign against our enemy." Noting the bond between them through having the same first name, he signed the letter "Black Jack Pershing, Folies Bergere, Paris, France." The letter is confidential; so Jack showed it to "only 3 or 4 of my buddys," including Alcock, whose eyes popped and who said it was "realy" from Pershing, because it was signed Black Jack, which was "a private nickname." Alcock advised Jack to reply carefully, so as to get "summons ... to Paris," work there, and not "wrist my life and probably get splattered all over France." Jack will "sacrifice my own feelings," as he did in baseball, and go. Alcock advised him to brush up on his French. If Black Jack hires him, they'll make "some pair of Jacks eh Al"?" If the two open the pot, the Germans would be "sucker[s] ... to stay in."

March 14. Jack sends Al a "coppy" of his answer to "Gen. Pershing." In it, he says that being a baseball pitcher, he obviously has courage to die in the "trenchs." But if "you figure that I can serve old glory" with you, "I am willing." War is like baseball, but not like "football or bridge whist"; to win, "use ... brains." War and baseball "stragety" is similar. He can help but should know Pershing's aims first. They can't write each other because of "censors." But they can talk. Can Pershing write Capt. Seeley for Jack to get "leave to go to Paris"? Until "I hear from you," Jack wrote, he'll be working on "idears." Being "a pair of jacks," the two "could put up a good bluff."

While awaiting Gen. Pershing's answer, Jack visited "a estaminet"—it's "kind of a store"—met a French girl with a brogue, and they agreed to "learn" each other French and English. She smiled so much that Jack "won't stand for no foolishness." He'll chill the next woman looking "X eyed" at him

March 16. Capt. Seeley informed the regiment that Gen. Pershing is coming soon, supposedly "to overlook us"; in reality, Jack knows and Alcock agrees, it's to confer with Jack. Jack might be too nervous to speak to Gen. Pershing; so he'll write out his "idears" to read to him. That estaminet girl, Ernestine, is bothering Jack by some winning looks. He'd tell her he was married but can't explain in French. She'll cry after he leaves. He might wear his gas mask as a disguise "to have a little peace."

March 18. Here are "bear outlines" of "idears" Jack will "spring" on the gen.

1. Rowland, White Sox manager, would tell his players the opposing team's weakness. Before a battle, "the gens." should decide to "work on the other side's weakness" too.

2. In baseball as in war, "getting the jump on your oppts." is necessary. Jack recalls a game when they tried to get the jump, but "the wind raised havioc with the ball," and the Washington team won.

3. In baseball, each team has nine men. This means a gen. has an advantage over a baseball manager. The gen. can muster "2 to 1" against an enemy, and then if he can't win he should join "the G.A.R." St. Louis lacked good pitchers in a game once; thus Rowland had an advantage in numbers, could have called the game because of cold weather, didn't, but still lost.

4. A gen. has an advantage over baseball managers. Both sides of a game start at the same time. But a gen. could plan at night to attack early, bring up men and "supplys" against the enemy, and "take them by supprise."

Jack is a $30-a-month "doughboy"—"a fine nickname"—but soon may be on a staff with higher-paid lieuts. Since Florrie isn't "writeing" him, he's suspicious; so "Jack the Kisser" might just "give ... Ernestine a smack" if she "bulges her lips" again.

March 20. Bad luck. After too much marching Jack's feet hurt, and he was excused from "riffle practice." He visited Ernestine, who called him "cherry" (meaning "dearie") and was about to cry when he hinted at leaving soon. He kissed her, as you would a hurt "kid." Her father burst in and jabbered fast French. Since was too old to hit, Jack slipped him 20 franks. Back at the Ark, Alcock told Jack that Gen. Pershing "overlooked" the men's "riffle practice," glanced around "like he mist somebody," and left. A kind letter came from Florrie. So Jack is miserable: Pershing didn't find him; he wouldn't have kissed Ernestine but for Florrie's not sending letters earlier; and "gone ... is my 20 franks."

"DECORATED." (Characters: Johnny Alcock, D., Florrie Keefe, Jack Keefe, Lieut. Mather, Capt. Seeley, George Shaffer.)

Jack sends Al eight more letters from "Somewheres in France."

April 2. Jack pulled one on Johnny Alcock. He wrote "April Fool" on some paper, put it in an envelope that had contained Alcock's girlfriend's letter in it, sealed it, and gave it to him like new mail. Alcock "tore it open," read it, and vowed revenge on Jack. Reports "about the Dutchmens starting a drive" are meaningless. Paris newspapers are useless, "all printed in la la la." If Van Hindenburg attacks, it's because he's homesick and wants to leave France.

April 6. Jack read that Foch is named "gen. of all the Allys." It would be better if Foch spoke English; if he ordered "feu," meaning "fire," soldiers speaking English wouldn't understand. Still, "in war like in baseball ... you got to have 1 man running it." Imagine baseball with "3 or 4 mgrs" or one general saying "charge," and another saying "pay cash." It's safe "writeing" about the Americans "along the Moose river," because Germans lack money to buy "U. S. papers" to read about it. Anyway, they'd confuse it with the Elks. "Jokeing a side," it's no "supprise" that Jack is "a A No. 1 marksman," because he had "control in pitching." He may become "a snipper," stationed in a tree not "trenchs." Since Alcock got "a reel letter" from his girl, he's no longer mad at Jack. Men should take jokes and be "a monkey" and not "acid" and be "a corps." People don't mind Jack's jokes because he smiles often.

April 11. Jack is becoming "a dick" and will "get the goods on a certain bird" named "Geo. Shaffer" in his outfit. He has "a German name," wrote a letter, and dropped one page when he went looking for an envelope. Jack saw that the page had "x" written 11 times at the bottom. He hid it when Shaffer returned looking for it. Jack showed the page to Alcock, who agreed it looked "off color," and suggested that Jack should get more "evidents" against Shaffer and report him to Capt. Seeley, temporarily away. The letter had more "fishy" parts to it, for example "I. L. U." and "I am W. C. T. U." mostly. Alcock wishes he'd found the letter, which he thinks may help Jack "get a commission in the intelligents dept." and get "the dope" on "pro German spys." Alcock told Jack to converse with Shaffer, "lead him on," and "trap" him. Shaffer is so huge that "the fireing squad" can simply "face their riffles ... and let go."

April 14. Shaffer can't "wrinkle out of" a "net of evidents" Jack is "closeing." Jack conversed with Shaffer. Jack: Where do you live? Shaffer: "Milwaukee Ave. in Chi." Jack, who knows about German traffic there: Are you married? Shaffer: No. Jack: Where were you born? Shaffer: Hell, are you "the personal officer?" When Shaffer mentioned Van Hindenburg and Jack "traped" him by asking who revealed Van Hindenburg's plans, the answer — "Oh he---ll my mother in law." Later, Alcock agreed that a single man couldn't have "a mother in law without marrying into one."

April 16. Thanks to Lieut. Mather, Jack will see Capt. Seeley tomorrow. Alcock found a letter yesterday printed in German to "Field Marshall Van Hindenburg" and signed "G.S." Alcock, knowing German, translates the German for Jack, saying it's about advising when 500,000 Americans will attack (but it's really about losing stockings and therefore being unable to walk home). Alcock said he talked to someone "in the int. dept." who said "their dutys was to keep" from avoid being seen; advised Jack therefore to do the same; and said in Paris he might make love to women "that's been the tools of some Dutchmens," get information from the "girlies," and then dump them, though sadly. Jack hit a slump in "riffle practice" and won't be a snipper. When they saw "Lauras ... takeing wounded back to a base hospital," Alcock said everyone wounded was a snipper. Jack and the boys want to "get ... to the front and get even."

April 18. Jack reported to Capt. Seeley and showed him both letters. He read them, laughed, told Jack to destroy them, said someone was tricking him, and interpreted those "x" marks as "kisses" — which Jack says he already knew. Alcock and some others "framed up" that letter supposedly from Shaffer, and Jack would like to "bust them in the jaw." He confronted Alcock, threatened to punch him, and was told to take a joke the way he told Alcock to earlier. Jack is pleased he won't be "double crossing women" in Paris but will "fight fair like man to man."

April 23. Sad news. When Jack was reading a letter from Florrie, about a cute "new suit" she bought, in came Shaffer. He accused Jack of reading his "male" and asked him to stand up. Jack thought he was being friendly but instead received "a black eye and a bad nose," also a "swole" jaw. Jack "triped," or he "would of made a punching bag" out of Shaffer. Alcock was scared of tackling Jack himself; so "he told big Shaffer a peck of lies." Jack will be "Handsome Jack" again soon.

April 25. Big news. Jack's unit is ordered to the front. He hopes the Germans start something; if so, "we will run them ragged." Alcock and some others "pertend" to be glad but wouldn't cry if ordered to stay "here till the duration of the war" in "this class D burg." Suddenly the men started laughing at a regimental newspaper report that Private Jack Keefe was wounded in action by "Gen. George Shaffer" firing "four ... shells," decorating him with "Schwartz Auge," "Ros Nase," "Blumenkohl Ohren," and even "Right Cross" placed "on his jaw." Let them laugh while they can.

References here are to Paul Von Hindenburg (1847–1934), German general and president, who after several victories was promoted to field marshal and commander of the German army (1917–1918); and to Ferdinand Foch (1851–1929), French marshal, who in World War I was commander in the Battle of the Marne (1914), the first Battle of Ypres (1915), and the Battle of the Somme (1916), and was named supreme Allied commander (March 26, 1918) and marshal of France (August, 1918)

"SAMMY BOY." (Characters: Johnny Alcock, Marie Antoinette, Al Blanchard, Bertha Blanchard, Jack Brady, the Colonel, Sargent Crane, Harry Friend, Florrie Keefe, Jack Keefe, Ted Phillips, Capt. Seeley.)

Keefe treats Blanchard to nine letters from "In the Trenchs."

May 6. Keefe's regiment didn't take "motor Lauras" to "the reserve trenchs" but marched. It's so "motonus" waiting that he wants the regiment fighting ahead to "get messed up tonight" so that his bunch "will jump right in." Maybe France is suffering "casualities" but none "amist the cuties." A soldier named Harry Friend "loves the ladys," gets many letters, and replies in a fancy way; "between every word he sores up and swoops down again" and is slow "get[ting] within writeing distants of the paper." Friend showed the men a picture of "some dame in Chalons" so pretty that Jack would like to meet a similar "baby doll" there. He's married, though, and won't flirt "with the parley vous."

May 9. Keefe told Jack Brady, who's "1 of the boys," about Friend and his girls, and said he'd like to meet one. Brady asked a "lieut ... he stands pretty good with," and got the name of the last girl on the officers' female list. Jack Keefe wrote this one, "Miss Marie Antoinette, 14 rue de Nez Rouge, O. D. Cologne," saying he was an Uncle Sam soldier fighting for France, was a tall baseball athlete, hoped to obtain leave, and would like to visit her and be shown around Cologne. Jack figures nothing will happen, but still "a man has got to amuse yourself ... in a dump like this or they would go crazy." Meanwhile, he wants to participate in military action "in the front row."

May 11. Since the army likes "haveing things come by supprise," Keefe's outfit moved to the front "2 days ahead of time." Someone heard Capt. Seeley talking about "the next drive" by the Dutchmans, a retreat by front-line Americans, Gen. Pershing's figuring an attack by "Jerry" on Africa. Capt. Seeley wants the men to rest. But Keefe fears their "sentrys" may miss warning signs, and he wants to be awake when he's killed, to have an "idear who done it." This may be Keefe's last letter to Al.

May 14. Big "supprise"! Marie Antoinette replied, mostly in English, which she's "just learning to write." She wants to show Keefe around Cologne. She'll dress "comme un cheval" for him, and signs with "l'amour und kussen." Keefe must tell her he's married and can't flirt. Meanwhile, the chow is poor, the Germans shell the American "back arrears," shoot flares over "Nobody's Land," aren't sending patrols, and an attack would be welcome to "break the motley."

May 16. The "Col." asked for volunteers to learn about the "new Dutch regt." ahead. Keefe almost volunteered, felt he shouldn't crowd the others, and was "to late and ... lost out." That patrol never returned. Those soldiers' "wifes," assuming "they got any," may learn "they are missing in actions." Florrie writes so little that she might not recognize Keefe's name on a "casuality list." But "they's other gals." Keefe wrote "Mon cher Marie," telling her that each can learn the other's language and unless for "bad luck" he might be sent to Cologne. He signs "Your Sammy Boy, Jack Keefe." He feels he deserves "something" distracting when he "come so near" being on that patrol.

May 18. Sargent Crane asked Keefe how he liked trench life. When Keefe said there was no excitement, Crane ordered him to accompany Ted Phillips to "the listening post" that night, stay "quite," and report enemy talk. Keefe complained that the shelling made him "a little deef," but Crane said Phillips would hear fine for both. They went. All was "quite." Phillips turned "crazy." He said the two should yell to get fired at, and laugh at the Germans' "waisting their ammunitions." He also suggested mewing like a cow to attract hungry Germans. They "crall[ed] back" safely. Jack complained about Phillip to Crane, who said "the quite" crazed most soldiers but, strangely, not Keefe.

May 19. Keefe writes Al not to disclose this to Bertha. After all, Florrie "has wrote ... [only] 3 letters" in about "4 months." After ten days at the front the men will enjoy "rest billets somewheres." Brady said he got a "lieut." to agree they could go to Cologne. Someone gave Keefe a letter from Marie to "Dear Sammy Boy": Cologne is "the prettiest town in France"; we'll see "shows etc."; "bring along beaucoup francs"; arrive "toot sweet." Although they seem fated to meet, Jack hopes Marie won't be "likeing me to well." Most "women back in the U. S." don't understand.

May 20. Brady says they might have to march the "18 miles" to Cologne. They have seen no action, not even "aeroplanes" lately. He signed "Sammy Boy" to a letter to Marie about arriving soon. Why did "a censor" have "to spill" his name to his buddies? Now they're calling him "Sammy Boy."

May 22. "Well Al its all off." Jack asked Crane when they'd be "releived," because he wanted to go to Cologne. Crane indicated Cologne was "back of the German lines" and the next patrol would head that way. So Alcock, Brady, and others were "playing another 1 of their gags." Keefe is ordered to go on that patrol. After all, he "come across the old puddle to fight."

"SIMPLE SIMON." (Characters: Johnny Alcock, Marie Allen, Al Blanchard, Bertha Blanchard, Jack Brady, Corp. Evans, Guy Meyer, Joe, Al Keefe, Florrie Keefe, Florrie Keefe, Old 1 Legged Mike, Ted Phillips, Capt. Seeley, Jack Simon, the Swede, Charlotte Warren.)

Keefe sends Blanchard nine more letters, the first seven from "In the Trenchs."

May 29. Keefe writes about fellow-soldier Jack Simon, who is such an open-mouthed butt of jokes that he is dubbed "Simple Simon." Keefe learned that Simon likes souvenirs, told Johnny Alcock, and Alcock and Jack Brady sell him items supposedly from Germans. Keefe hopes Al will write, since Florrie rarely does.

June 4. It would be "quite" here except "our batterys" fire and "the Dutchmans" reply. In "some of the other sections," there's action and "the Dutchmans" are winning. The "Allys" appear to be waiting "till the other side has wore themself out," then plan "to strike back." The "stragety" in baseball is "the same like in war," but no manager would want his team "to not try and score till the other side had all the runs they was going to get." When "the Germans" are exhausted, they'll rest again in fine Parisian hotels. Alcock said the military police wouldn't let such Germans into Paris. When the boys joked to Simon that the German "trenchs" opposite them were empty, he suggested occupying them but the boys said the American "trenchs" were farther south, hence warmer.

June 7. The boys kidded Simon about the empty "trenchs" so much that "it finely downed on him" to ask who was "throwing up them flares." Brady said the Germans left one flare thrower for that work. Simon thought one man couldn't move around fast enough. Alcock said the Germans put one one-legged soldier on a motorcycle to manage the job. Brady recommended Ted Phillips if Simon wanted more souvenirs. So Simon bought a cracked "speegle" from Phillips for "4 franks down" and six more "when he got hold of some jack."

June 11. Capt. Seeley "is raveing" because even though "Gen. Pershing told Gen. Foch" to "throw" American soldiers in anywhere, "our regt." has never been "over the top," has seen no "actions," has taken no prisoners, and only "makes repairs in the ['bob'] wire and etc." Rumors swirl that the Germans "opp. us" are Saxons who hate Van Hindenburg and therefore are "friendly towards us." Brady told Simon that a soldier "in the regt." has so many souvenirs they call him "Souvenir Joe" and Simon should either buy more items or throw his little collection away. Questioned about Joe's sources, Brady said he "crall[ed] out in Nobody's Land" when "Old 1 Legged Mike" was some distance away and retrieved shell fragments from shell holes. Keefe was tempted to tell "poor crum" Simon "to not pay no tension to these smart alex," but decided Simon was so dumb that "he is better off dead so let him go."

June 13. Keefe reports "wonderfull news Al": Florrie's sister Marie Allen wrote that Florrie has given birth to a daughter. Marie must stay to help. However, "rm. in the apt." is limited; so the "ski jumper" Swede will have to go. Keefe says Al and Bertha should "adopt 1 of these here Belgium orphans that's lost their parents." Little Al must be tickled with his sister. Now the soldiers "call me Papa."

June 14. Simon is missing. Corp. Evans asked Keefe what he knew, and he told Evans about how Alcock and Brady mentioned German souvenirs in shell holes. Evans said to tell Capt. Seeley nothing. Alcock told Simon if he collected a Saxon he'd be nicknamed Souvenir Simon and outclass Souvenir Joe. Keefe is "the only 1 of them that has got a heart," hence might have warned Simon, but was busy talking about his new "little gal." Keefe will be "on post duty tonight." It is "no Elks carnivle" listening "for a cry from out there," from "that poor ½ wit." Brady calls Simon "nothing but a Mormon." Keefe feels "its our duty" to help him. He says this letter may be his last.

"In the Hospital, July 20." Keefe writes Al after a five-weeks' silence. He went to that post that night with Evans, heard a cry, and they thought it was Simon. Keefe inched ahead, without his "riffle," since he wouldn't "pick Simon up with a bayonet." The man Keefe found wasn't Simon. The two fought. The man bit Keefe. Keefe kept slugging him. He suddenly saw lights and heard bullets, was wounded in the leg and left arm, and was hospitalized. Meanwhile, Simon brought in a dead German. Two weeks ago Keefe learned that his beat-up enemy was Alcock, just out of the hospital. Keefe can walk in "a couple wks.," but his left arm is bad. There's a pretty nurse here.

"Somewheres in France, Aug 16." Keefe is "homewards bound." His left arm will be "pretty good" later, and his right arm — his "old souper" — is unhurt. This "old sea port town" will hate to see big-spending Americans depart. Authorities want Keefe, among many other "poplar idles," to get home and help with the "next Liberty Loan." The nurse, Charlotte Warren, gave Keefe a sad look when he left the hospital two days ago. Keefe gotta now and drink some "Vin Rouge" with the boys.

"Chicago, Aug. 29." The trip "across the old pond took ... to long." New York looked fine. He got "outside a big steak." Everybody at the restaurant cheered "like ... when I use to walk out there to warm up." Then home to "supprise" Florrie. She "give a running hop" to hug him. Little Al hugged him. They showed him the "little gal," who is pretty, whereas most babies "3 mos. old" resemble "a French breakfast." Keefe didn't want Florrie to call the baby Marie. When she asked what name he wanted, he paused and then suggested Charlotte. Florrie said that he couldn't return home and name her "after none of your French nurses," that only the name Florrie "she wouldn't be suspicious of." Keefe wishes he could return to France and help his "regt." but can't leave home now.

In "Simple Simon," Keefe mentions Foch, Pershing, and "Van" Hindenburg again, but this time adds another historical name. He says the boys could tell Simon during a lull in the action that "Capt. Seeley and Ludendorf married sisters" and therefore "agreed to lay off each other." Erich Friedrich Wilhelm Ludendorff (1865–1937) was a German general effective in World War I, and later a confused politician supporting and then deserting Adolf Hitler.

Lardner wrote a letter (December 23 [1918]) to his long-time friend Hewitt H. Howland, editor of Bobbs-Merrill Publishing Company, which had published several of his early books and was to issue *The Real Dope* in book form, to express trouble in giving the book a title but to reject *Let's Go* as a title. (Source: Caruthers [1995], 120)

RED ("Sick 'Em"). He is the Philadelphia Phillies manager. On Pat's recommendation, Red trades to get Smitty but can't also get Fogarty. Smitty and Fogarty are superb pitchers but only when on the same team and competing for glory. Red tries fruitlessly to shame Smitty into pitching well. The narrator enables Red to acquire Fogarty from the Cubs, after which the two pitchers help the Phillies defeat the Washington Senators in the World Series. (See Dooin, Red.)

RELL ("Dinner"). He is Miss Rell's father. She tells Harry Barton that her father is 54, knows Congressman Burleigh of South Chicago, plays golf, and shoots 60, 160, or perhaps 120.

RELL, LOU ("Dinner"). He is Miss Rell's brother, as she explains to Harry Barton. She adds that he and their father "read the sporting page religiously every day."

It is undoubtedly only a coincidence that the name Lou Rell is similar to that of Louis Riel (1844–1885), Canadian politician whose leadership of the Métis French-Indians led to his execution for treason.

RELL, MISS ("Dinner"). She is a "strikingly pretty[,] ... rather tall, slender blonde." Harry Barton finds her attractive at Grace Halpern's dinner party in New York, until she rattles unstoppably, jumps from subject to subject, and disregards his courteous attempts to chime in.

RENNIE, MISS ("A Caddy's Diary"). She is a pretty golfer at the club where the diarist caddies. She is engaged to Charley Crane. The diarist cheats to help Mrs. Doane buy Miss Rennie's unwanted $100 dress for $50.

REULBACH In "The Busher Abroad," Keefe mentioned "Ruleback" as a fast pitcher. In *Treat 'Em Rough*, Reulbach was a pitcher known to Keefe, who in the army says that the instructor in grenade throwing is as awkward as Reulbach.

Edward Marvin Reulbach (1882–1961) played for the Chicago Cubs (1905–1912), the Cubs and the Brooklyn Dodgers (1913), the Dodgers (1914), and the Boston Braves (1916–1917). George W. Hilton notes out that Lardner's "Pullman Pastimes" (St. Louis *Sporting News*, December 15, 1910—February 16, 1921) contains "funny and penetrating character sketches" of eight Chicago baseball players, including Ed Reulbach. (Sources: *Baseball Encyclopedia*, 2322; Hilton, 5)

REUM, FRANZ ("The Venomous Viper of the Volga"). He is a boxer (perhaps fictitious) who Sandy King reports in a fake letter was recently defeated by Ivan Ivanovitch.

"REUNION" (*Liberty*, October 31, 1925; LN, RU). (Characters: Tom Allen, Dean, Gates, Stuart Johnston, Rita Johnston, Doc Marshall, Louise Marshall, Bob Mason, Jennie Mason, Jimmy Preston, Rita.)

Rita Mason and Bob Mason are siblings, originally from Buchanan, Michigan. When Rita was three or four, the aunt in Philadelphia for whom she was named persuaded Rita's mother to bring her east. Reared thereafter by her aunt, Rita rarely saw Bob, who at 14 lived with cousins in California for health reasons. Rita married well-off Stuart Johnston, and they live at Sands Point, Long Island. Bob did well in Los Angeles real estate, married a San Bernardino girl named Jennie "for some reason," inherited his father's Michigan homestead, and now resides in Buchanan with Jennie. They like small-town life. For a change, they go to Chicago to see *Abie's Irish Rose*, repeatedly.

Jennie invites Rita and Stuart to come visit. But Stu, aptly nicknamed, won't waste his time. Rita invites Bob and Jennie. Accepting, they take a train from Niles, Michigan, to New York's Grand Central Station. Bob, shabby at 34, and Rita, beautiful at 35 and dressed like movie stars, reunite there after 20 years. Rita notices the gold teeth of Jennie, also 35. Gates, Rita's chauffeur, whisks the three through dense traffic, upsetting Bob, and past ugly Long Island scenes that Jennie calls beautiful, to the Johnston residence. Jennie marvels at the guest room. Bob dozes. Stu meets his in-laws. Stu and Rita deplore Bob's and Rita's clothes and Rita's dental work. Dinner, cum conversation, stumbles: Bob and Rita won't break the law by drinking; Bob never played golf, can't go with Stu to Piping Rock, as Stu offers; Bob and Rita won't smoke; Rita and Stu do; neither guest ever learned to play bridge; Stu has no radio for his guests to listen to; they praise *Abie's Irish Rose*, which Rita calls "terrible"; Bob won't play tennis or take a launch ride with Stu, because he can't play tennis and he fears the water. Bob gossips about three residents from Buchanan, Michigan — how Tom Allen's daughter Louise eloped with Doc Marshall — to Rita, who barely remembers them. Rita mentions author Michael Arlen,* whom Jennie never heard of. Upstairs, while Stu wonders what he and Rita can do with Bob and Jennie for two anticipated weeks, Bob and Jennie are wishing they had a radio in their room.

In the morning, Rita ignores Jennie's desire to compare the New York version of *Abie's Irish Rose* to Chicago's. The two discuss movies; Rita says in California they met movie-actor Harold Lloyd.* After a seven-highball lunch, Stu naps. Jennie tries to read something. Bob discusses Tom's Louise's Doc again. Bedtime finally supervenes. Next morning Bob tells Stu he might sample his proffered scotch. To get rid of their guests, Stu and Rita are about to pretend that sick relatives or friends are demanding their immediate presence, but Jennie says Bob just read in one of Stu's New York newspapers about a drought in Michigan requiring Bob's attention to their garden. "Well," says Rita. "Well," says Stu.

Bob gets Rita to get Gates to get him and Jennie to New York efficiently; Bob insists they can see a bit of New York by themselves before train time. Instead, once there they engage a room in the Biltmore, at $56 for a week, they plan to see *Abie's Irish Rose* twice, plus the Woolworth Building and "Coney."

The Home Coming, the book by Lardner and Edward G. Heeman about the return of the White Sox and Giants after their 1913–1914 world tour, includes illustrations of the New Biltmore Hotel, opposite New York City's Grand Central Station, together with a description of its sybaritic features. Elizabeth Evans writes that in "Reunion" "Ring Lardner, himself at home in Niles, Michigan, and in Long Island, presents the small-town couple as limited, but sensible," and adds that "[t]he suburbanites are less gently treated." In *Abie's Irish Rose* (1922), a comedy by Anne Nichols (1891–1966), Abraham Levy, Jewish youth, and Rosemary Murphy, Irish girl, are in love on New York's East Side. Their fathers object to their interreligious relationship. They get married by a Methodist minister, a rabbi, and a Catholic priest. All is well once their twins, Patrick and Rebecca, are born. The play had a poor start. Once Nichols obtained financial support from Arnold Rothstein (1883–1928), New York gambler, racketeer, and bootlegger, it became incredibly popular, running for 2,327 performances at the Fulton Theatre, New York, and uncounted ones with road-show companies. Meyer Wolfsheim in *The Great Gatsby* (1925) by Lardner's friend F. Scott Fitzgerald* is patterned after Rothstein, who helped fix the 1919 Black Sox Scandal and later became an unsolved-murder victim. The theme of *Abie's Irish Rose* is familial accommodation, which fails in "Reunion." One wonders why Jonathan Yardley, in criticizing Lardner's story "Champion," says that its tone "is ... so out of character for Ring that it is as if he had written 'Abie's Irish Rose.'" (Sources: Evans 83; *The Home Coming*, 10–11; Yardley, 191)

RHEM ("Meet Me in St. Louie"). He is a St. Louis Cardinal pitcher that Danny, Brooklyn hitter, says he'd "like to get a sock at."

"RHYTHM" (*Cosmopolitan*, May 1926; PRL, RLR, RU). (Characters: Guy Bolton, Buck, Mrs. Buck, Elinor Deal, Spencer Deal, Walter Donaldson, Eulalie, Mrs. Wallace Gerard, Conrad Green, Mira Hampton, Harry Hart, Gus Kahn, Benny Kane, Rae Kane, Roy Lattimer, Peggy Leech, Lottie, Rita Marlowe, Helen Morse, Nora, Signor Parelli, Jack Prendergast, Sam Rose, Sheila, Miss Silloh, Dave Stamper, Frank Tours, Thelma Warren, Max Wise.)

Harry Hart, successful composer of "rhythm numbers" for musicals, tells Sam Rose, a lyricist, he'd like to work with him. Hart argued with Benny Kane, his former lyric-thief collaborator, who recently married and whose wife has made him too honest. She recognized that Hart's "Catch Me," a song in Hart and Kane's "Yes, Yes, Eulalie," was stolen from some opera. Not "Gioconda," boasts Hart; he took it from "Donizetti's 'Linda di Chamounix,'" and says the "millions" of "dumb-bells that goes to our shows" will enjoy "hearing a beautiful piece of music that they wouldn't never hear otherwise." Hart stops Benny by accusing him of liking an old song going "I love you" and thereafter using "I love you" in his own lyrics. Hart tells Sam that musical-producer Conrad Green wants Hart to turn Jack Prendergast's show book on "Cinderella" into a musical, and Hart persuades Sam to replace lyricist Benny. Hart assures Sam that he's got new tunes, for example, one he plays out of *Aïda* that only opera experts would recognize. It would've become popular except "Verdi didn't know rhythm."

Hart is invited to the Bucks' home on Long Island, is begged to play some of his compositions on the piano, does so but explains they're filched, and stops midway in one taken from Friml when that real-life composer appears as a fellow-guest.

Hart is at a football game with his fiancée, actress Rita Marlowe, when the band plays "Yes, Sir! That's my Baby!" He praises it. She says his tunes are as good. Denying it, he adds that people are staring not at him, as she believes, but at her. He boasts of his high income.

The popularity of Green's "Upsy Daisy" has everyone whistling Hart's stolen melodies, Musicologist Spencer Deal not only writes an article about Hart but takes him to a Peggy Leech Sunday salon. Hart refuses when Mira Hampton, a pretty actress, asks him to play. Peggy introduces him to Signor Parelli, opera conductor who wants to conduct an opera by Hart if he ever composes one. Hart insults him by saying no foreigner will ever do so. When a drunk tries to play the piano, Hart rudely replaces him and plays until all guests leave, except sycophantic Deal.

Flattered, Hart writes a symphony, which gets so-so reviews. He becomes conceited anyway, rebuffs several insistent girls, and chills Rita at the Plaza. Deal arranges for Hart to meet Mrs. Wallace Gerard, "known to give ... substantial aid" to young composers. She invites him to play the piano at her apartment on Park Avenue. Cockily acting on the assumption that she wanted petting, he found himself never welcome again. Green hires Hart to compose music for a new show, based on Guy Bolton's book. Hart finds Sam Rose's lyrics "proletarian" and instead wants Deal, whose lyrics are soon pronounced unworkable by Frank Tours, Green's musical consultant. Hart brashly threatens to sue Green for breach of contract. Green counter-threatens to see Hart in court for 40 years. Harry, soon impoverished, chances to read that Otto Harbach is writing a book for Willis Merwin, who wants a composer. Seeking Merwin at their old Friars' Club, Hart requests work but is rebuked as a writer now of "ponderous junk." Hart and Kane see each other at the club. Kane looks seedy. Hart visits his old publisher, Max Wise, who suggests that he collaborate with Kane again, since they co-produced smashes. But for pride, Hart would call Kane, who phones about "an idear" for a song. They joyfully meet, decide to rework "I love you" etc. into a Dave Stamper melody, and are happy. Hart calls Rita, who rebukes him but says her piano is retuned, so come play it.

Lardner displays his knowledge of music by describing Hart's playing one of his tunes "first in F sharp — a catchy refrain that seemed to be in waltz time in the right hand and two-four in the left" — then "again, just as surely, in B natural, a key whose mere mention is henbane to the average pianist." Lardner outdoes himself in "Rhythm" by having his name-dropping characters mention a score of real-life figures prominent in the 1920s: Michael Arlen;* Irving Berlin;* Heywood Broun;* Charlie Chaplin*; Giulio Gatti-Casazza (1869–1940), Italian-born New York Metropolitan Opera impresario (1908–2935); Alma Gluck (1884–1938), Rumanian-born lyric soprano; Noël Coward (1899–1973), British playwright, actor, producer, composer; George Gershwin;* Jascha Heifetz (1901–1987), Lithuanian-born concert violinist; Jerome Kern (1885–1945), New York–born composer, musical-comedy producer; Max Reinhardt (1873–1943), Austrian-born theatrical director; Leopold Stokowski (1882–1977), London-born maverick conductor; Deems Taylor*; Gene Tunney (1897–1978), boxer; Paul Whiteman;* Vincent Youmans;* and other notables less well-known, especially to 21st-century readers.

Donald Elder links Lardner to Hart, noting that Lardner "had ... a naïve distrust of highbrows" and that Hart "was nearly ruined by being taken seriously by intellectuals." (Source: Elder, 200, 200–201)

RICE, GRANTLAND (1880–1954). Tennessee-born Rice was educated at Vanderbilt University (1897–1901) with a degree in Greek and Latin, and became a reporter in Atlanta and then Cleveland (1901–1911). He married Katherine ("Kate") Hollis (1906). Their daughter was Florence ("Floncy") Rice. Rice covered sports events for the New York *Evening Mail*, *Tribune*, and *Sun*. "The Sportlight," his column (beginning 1911), was nationally syndicated (from 1930). *The Home Coming* includes his "At Journey's End," a 32-line poem inspired by the 1913–1914 White Sox-Giants world tour; in it, two players say watching good baseball players is preferable to anything they saw abroad. Rice was a U.S. army second lieutenant (1918–1919, partly in France). Rice was president of a film company producing sports documentaries. He was a radio broadcaster (1920s, 1930s). His books include *The Duffer's Handbook of Golf* (1926) and *The Tumult and the Shouting: My Life in Sport* (1954, his autobiography). Interesting is Rice's "The President's Golf Game: Wherein Your Correspondent and Ring Lardner Mingle in Fast Company over the Chevy Chase Links" (*American Golfer*, April 23, 1921). Rice's prose is often florid, poetic, and metaphorical; he likens athletes to classical and mythical heroes. He estimated that he published 22,000 columns, 7,000 verses, and 1,000 magazine pieces, totaling 67,000,000 words. (Doubtful? Doing so would mean writing an average of more than 3,600 words *every* day for his half century.) Lardner would agree that Rice's famous statement (first used in 1908) that winning and losing are less important than "how you play the game" is nice but hardly honored; nor, Lardner might add, is enough else in professional sports today. Columbia University established The Grantland Rice Fellowship in journalism (1951).

Lardner and his wife relished their long, close friendship with "Grant" Rice and Kate and often vacationed together. Lardner revered Floncy, whose problems with boyfriends Lardner is said to have modified for use in "I Can't Breathe." (Sources: *Home Coming*, 50; Yardley, 311)

RICHARDS ("The Ides of June"). He is a member of the Brooklyn baseball team, whom Danny says Stengel said "Max [Carey, manager] had to sell ... right out."

Paul Rapier Richards (1908–1986) played for the Brooklyn Dodgers (1932), the New York Giants (1933–1934), the Giants and the Philadelphia Athletics (1935), and the Detroit Tigers (1943–1946), and managed the White Sox (1951–1954, 1976). (Source: *Baseball Encyclopedia*, 706, 1512).

RICHARDS, MISS RUTH ("Wedding Day"). She is the single sister of Alice, who is married to Ed in New York. Ruth visits them from Detroit and, as ill Alice's substitute, goes with Ed to the wedding of Brownie Burt and Jimmy Shane, who are in show business, as are their gossipy guests. At the party afterwards at Ben Seaton's apartment, Ruth loosens up, dances with Jimmy, resists his slick advances, and learns from some of the guests of the crassly materialistic basis of the marriage.

RICHARDS, OLD MAN ("Greek Tragedy"). He is a friend of Roy Clayton. Big Bill Buell scares Greek Alexis, fellow wrestler, by saying that Richards read about Buell in some Phoenix newspapers. Clayton knows Alexis is really Tom Meyers.

RICHARDS, TOMMY ("The Facts"). He is Billy Bowen's college friend. Returning from a western business trip, Tommy rendezvouses with Billy in Chicago before returning home to Minneapolis. Tommy gets Billy to drink excessively after a period of abstinence, generously volunteers to shop for Christmas gifts for Billy's fiancée Ellen McDonald and members of her family, and sends presents for him in his name. The presents are inappropriate, offensively but hilariously.

RICHARDSON, MISS CLAIRE ("Words and Music"). She is the *Bulletin* columnist who interviews the self-centered singer-actor Roman Starr. Hilda Harper finds Miss Richardson's write-up so full of "levity" that she would like to slap her.

RICHIE ("My Roomy"). The narrator recalls Richie, Hofman, and Sheckard as former Chicago baseball players who sang together loudly. Buster Elliott's solitary singing is louder than their combined "harmonizin.'"

Lewis A. Richie (1883–1936) played for the Philadelphia Phillies (1906–1908), the Phillie and the Boston Braves (1909), the Braves and the Chicago Cubs (1910), and the Cubs (1911–1913). Jonathan Yardley quotes Lardner's *Chicago Tribune* dispatch (June 16, 1910) in which he gives "Turkey" as his friend Richie's nickname. George W. Hilton comments that "Lurid Lew" Richie, sang second tenor, "teamed with Lardner in pantomimes and pranks on long train trips, and is thought to have been one of the major inspirations for Lardner's first efforts at fiction." (Sources: *Baseball Encyclopedia*, 2327–2328; Hilton, 345; Yardley, 102)

RICKARD ("A Frame-Up"). He manages boxer Willie Kemp, whom Burke defeats to impress a girl he thinks is named Esther Fester. She is really Mary Holt.

George Lewis ("Tex") Rickard (1871–1929), premier sports promoter of the 1920s, was a Texas-born cowboy, unsuccessful Alaskan gold-field miner, successful Alaskan saloon owner, and unsuccessful diamond miner in South Africa, before promoting boxing events in Goldfield and Rawhide, Nevada, and elsewhere (1906–1910). After cattle-ranching in Paraguay (1910–1915), Rickard became a boxing promoter in New York (1916–1927). He promoted Jess Willard* and

Frank Moran (1916; no decision), Willard and Jack Dempsey* (Toledo, July 4, 1919; Dempsey won), Dempsey and Georges Carpentier (Jersey City, 1921; Dempsey won), Dempsey and Luis Angel Firpo (New York's Polo Grounds, 1923; Dempsey won), Dempsey and Gene Tunney (Philadelphia, 1926; Tunney won), and Tunney-Dempsey ("Battle of the Long Count," Chicago, 1927; Tunney won after Dempsey delayed moving to a neutral corner; Tunney is frivolously mentioned in "Great Blessings"). Rickard helped make professional boxing more respectable. He built a new and bigger Madison Square Garden (1925). Although Rickard amassed millions, he was careless with money and left an estate under $170,000. He was elected to the International Boxing Hall of Fame (1990).

For the Bell Syndicate, Lardner wrote 13 columns concerning the Dempsey-Willard fight (June 22–July 5, 1919), 15 for the Dempsey-Carpentier fight (June 19–July 3, 1921), 14 for the Dempsey-Firpo fight (September 3–15, 1923), and one for the 1926 Dempsey-Tunney fight (September 24, 1926). (Larry Moon, in "The Battle of the Century," mentions some false publicity for a boxing match that never materialized in a place called "Nugget, Nevada." Lardner probably had in mind Tex Rickard's puffed-up promotions in Goldfield and Rawhide, Nevada.) (Sources: Hilton, 84, 298; Streissguth, 232, 243)

RICKETTS, TEX ("The Courtship of T. Dorgan"). Keefe reports that "Tex Ricketts" is in charge of the Jess Willard*-Jack Dempsey* fight. Keefe bets on Willard and loses $600. See Rickard.

RIGGS, CHARLEY ("The Battle of the Century"). He was a New York boxing-match promoter. Larry Moon hyped the coming match between his boxer, Jim Dugan, and Goulet, handsome French boxer, so cleverly that Riggs established a million-dollar purse, much of which Riggs, Larry, and Dugan shared when Dugan won.

Charley Riggs is based on George Lewis ("Tex") Rickard (*see* Rickard), as Lardner explains in a letter (August 4, 1921) to a *Saturday Evening Post* editor. (Source: Caruthers [1995], 134)

RIGLER In "My Roomy," he umpires a Chicago-St. Louis game. Griner pitches a curve to Buster Elliott, who is pinch-hitting for Chicago and whom Rigler calls out on a third strike looking. In "Back to Baltimore," Rigler, sometimes called "Rig," umpired a game between the Phillies and the narrator Dixon's Boston Braves. When William Baker, Jr., the stupid Braves batter, was hit by a pitch and Rig told him to take first, he didn't understand. In "Lose with a Smile," Rigler called Danny, playing for Brooklyn against the Giants, out at first. When Danny argued too long, Rigler ejected him. In "Take a Walk," Agnew, loud-mouthed third baseman, criticizes Rigler's calls and later boasts that he was tempted to "sock ... Rigler" for having it in for him. The narrator says Agnew's body is about the size of Rigler's chest. Rigler is mentioned in "The Poor Simp."

George W. Hilton identifies Rigler as Charles Rigler (1882–1935), National League umpire (1905–1922, 1924–1935). Hilton adds that since Rigler umpired in the Central League while Lardner was a reporter for the South Bend, Indiana, *Times* (1905–1907), he knew Rigler and Rigler often appears in Lardner's baseball stories. (Source: Hilton, 26, 343)

RIKER ("Anniversary"). He was the father of Louis Taylor's friend Harry Riker.

RIKER, HARRY ("Anniversary"). He and Louis Taylor were childhood friends. Louis repeatedly tells his bored wife Bess how he and Harry borrowed Riker's horse to go call on the Lindsay sisters, who lived out of town. The horse wandered home, and the boys had to walk home in the rain. Nothing developed from the friendships.

RIMINI ("Dinner"). Miss Coakley tells Harry Barton that soprano Rosa Raisa, of the "simply gorgeous opera company in Chicago," is married to Ruffo or perhaps Rimini, both "barytones" anyway.

RING AROUND THE BASES: THE COMPLETE BASEBALL STORIES OF RING LARDNER, edited by Matthew J. Bruccoli (Columbia: University of South Carolina Press, 1992). This collection contains 34 short stories.

RIPLEY ("High-rollers"). He was Walter Finch's employer in New York until Walter accepted a better-paying job with Bernard and Craig.

RITA ("Reunion"). She is or was the aunt in Philadelphia for whom Rita Mason was named. Wealthy, the aunt persuaded the mother, perhaps her sister, of little Rita, then three or four, to bring the girl east. This resulted in her separation from her brother Bob Mason. Aunt Rita encouraged her niece to marry Stuart Johnston.

RITCHEY (*The Big Town*). He is the liveried chauffeur who drives Trumbull's "Rools-Royce." Katie prefers this young employee to his old employer until she learns that Ritchey is married and has two children.

"RITCHEY" (as "Beautiful Katie," *Saturday Evening Post*, July 10, 1920; BT, PRL) *see* ***THE BIG TOWN***

RIVERS, JOE ("A Frame-Up"). He is a Chicago boxer. Kid Howard assigns him to spar with Burke to see how capable Burke is. Burke won't hurt Rivers because he doesn't dislike him.

RIXEY, EPPA In "Sick 'Em," he is a steady Phillies pitcher, along with Alexander, but was briefly sidelined by "a pair o' busted fingers," according to the narrator. Smitty and Fogarty, more than Rixey and Alexander, formed the pitching combination that won the World Series against Washington. The narrator humorously says that the real name of Smitty, an Italian-American, is "longer'n Eppa Rixey," an allusion to Rixey's height. In "Back to Baltimore," when Rixey was pitching to William Baker, Jr., batting for the Boston Braves, he rolled balls to him, because Baker was so inept at bat, and elsewhere. In "Meet Me in St. Louie," Casey Stengel kids callow Danny, when both are with Brooklyn, that Rixey's name is Effie Jessica Rixey, that he "is 7 ft tall," and that when he pitched "cross fire" once, he caught "his little finger in the right field scream." In "Holycaust," Danny describes how he got a home run when Rixey "throwed [him] a fast ball." Rixey is mentioned in "The Ides of June."

Eppa Rixey, Jr. (1891–1963), 6'5" and 210 lbs., played for the Phillies (1912–1920) and the Cincinnati Reds (1921–1933), and was elected to the Baseball Hall of Fame (1963). Hilton, who writes a great deal about Rixey, says that he earned a bachelor's degree in chemistry and a master's degree in Latin (University of Virginia, 1912, 1914). (Sources: *Baseball Encyclopedia*, 2331–2332; Hilton, 363–364)

ROACH, WALLIE ("Wedding Day"). He is an "eccentric" New York dancer in musical comedies. He attends the wedding of fellow-entertainers Brownie Burt and Jimmy Shane.

ROBBIE ("The Poor Simp"). He managed the Brooklyn Dodgers when Carey, playing for the narrator's opposing team, sent Skull Scoville to the baseball park long before a game, as a practical joke. Robbie told Carey he suspected Skull was spying during the Dodgers' practice to learn their signs. Wilbert Robinson is mentioned in "The Hold-Out." In "One Hit, One Error, One Left," Danny writes Jessie that the Brooklyn team was called "the robins because there mgr was Wm Robinson but Carey is the mgr now so robins dont make no sense." Danny says that there is a contest to rename the team.

George W. Hilton identifies Wilbert ("Robbie," "Uncle Robbie") Robinson (1863–1934) as the Dodgers manager. He played for minor-league teams (1886–1899, 1901–1902) and the Cardinals (1900), replaced McGraw as manager of the Baltimore Orioles (1902), managed the Dodgers (1914–1931), and was elected to the Baseball Hall of Fame (1945). (Sources: *Baseball Encyclopedia*, 706–707, 1526; Hilton, 492–493)

ROBBINS (*The Real Dope*). He was a sports reporter whose critical comments on Keefe's pitching against "Phila." Keefe and his wife Florrie resented.

ROBBINS ("A One-Man Team"). He plays football for Coach Belden, who encourages him to block an end playing for their opponent, the Doane team. Robbins doesn't do so.

ROBERT, GENERAL ("A Chip of the Old Block"). He is an officer in Washington, D.C. Captain Bellows introduces Captain Evan Barnes to him. At lunch Barnes so disgusts the general that he says he is "nauseated" and asks the two to leave. Barnes thinks the old fellow "is in a decline."

ROBERTS, CHARLEY ("The Maysville Minstrel"). He is a wise-cracking drummer who sells instant water heaters out of New York. He calls on Old Man Townsend's gas company in Maysville. Stephen Gale, an company employee, reluctantly shows Roberts his wretched poems. Concocting a cruel joke, Roberts has his friend, a New York *Standard* columnist, publish Stephen's birthday poem to his wife Stella Gale, for laughs. Roberts also has Stephen send two more poems to a fictitious editor, only to have them returned to him.

ROBERTS, LEE ("Dinner"). He and his wife are friends in Chicago of Miss Rell, or so she tells Harry Barton. To praise Miss Rell's swimming, Lee called her, she says, Gertrude Ederle

Gertrude Ederle (1906–2003) was the first woman to swim the English Channel (on August 6, 1926, in 14 hours and 31 minutes).

ROBERTS, MRS. ("Dinner"). Miss Rells says that she and her brother Lou Rell know Mrs. Roberts and her husband Lee Roberts, in Chicago.

ROBINSON ("Hurry Kane"). He, Bullard, and Roy Smith are traded from the St. Louis baseball team to Boston for Frank Miller and Lefty Glaze. All five are ineffective players.

ROCKEFELLER, MAGGIE ("Gullible's Travels"). She is someone at the Poinciana in Palm Beach whom Mrs. Gullible points out to Gullible. In the swirl of supposedly important guests, Gullible probably gets names wrong and says he "didn't know Pat Vanderbilt from Maggie Rockefeller."

ROSE, MR. ("Second-Act Curtain"). He is an officious theatrical manager for whom Booth and Chambers have written a play. Everyone, including Mr. Rose, says it needs a "second-act curtain." He interferes with Booth's efforts to write one by phoning him often.

Lardner may have been inspired to name Mr. Rose after Billy Rose (1899–1966), whose talents as a theater manager were beginning to be evident on Broadway with successes by 1927. Admittedly, he hit his stride only after Lardner's death, sustaining it until 1960.

ROSE, SAM ("Rhythm"). He is a competent lyricist in the musical-comedy world populated by Harry Hart, Benny Kane, and Conrad Green. Hart, tune-thief, tells Sam about his discontent with Benny, lyric-thief. When Hart gets cocky, he calls Sam's lyrics "hopelessly proletarian."

ROTH In "Call for Mr. Keefe!," Keefe, pitching for the White Sox, wound up when Roth was at bat for Cleveland, enabling both Chapman, on second, and Speaker, at first, to steal. In "The Busher Reënlists," Keefe sees Bobby Roth in the Chicago hotel where American League officials are having a meeting. The two exchange sarcastic remarks about their supposed ability on the field.

Robert Frank Roth (1892–1936) played for the ChicagoWhite Sox (1914), the White Sox and the Cleveland Indians (1915), the Philadelphia Athletics and the Boston Red Sox (1919), the Washington Senators (1920), and the New York Yankees (1921). (Sources: *Baseball Encyclopedia*, 1538; Hilton, 204)

ROUND UP: THE STORIES OF RING LARDNER (1929). A collection of 35 stories.

Lardner didn't like the title *Round Up*, which was suggested by his editor Max Perkins.* The two considered several other titles, including "Our Kind," "Some of Ours," "Sorts and Conditions," and "Such as We." Sales, already substantial. were augmented by 70,000 copies when *Round Up* was chosen as a monthly selection by Lardner's friend Burton Rascoe* and other members of the board of the Literary Guild of America. (Source: Caruthers [1995], 217, 221)

ROUSH ("The Busher Pulls a Mays"). White Sox pitcher Keefe boasts that "we will see if Roush and Groh is such wales when they get up vs. real pitching," if their Cincinnati Reds meet the White Sox in "the world serious."

Edd J. Roush (1893–1988) played for the Chicago White Sox (1913), the New York Giants and the Cincinnati Reds (1916), the Reds (1917–1926), the Giants (1927–1929), and the Reds (1931). He was elected to the Baseball Hall of Fame (1962). Roush died during a spring-training game with the Reds. George W. Hilton notes that, of all the real-life baseball players in the stories in Hilton's edition, Roush "was the last to die." See also Vick. (Sources: *Baseball Encyclopedia*, 1539; Hilton, 315–316)

ROWAN (*Treat 'Em Rough*). Jack Keene, when in the army, recalls playing baseball in Terre Haute and getting a hit "off big Jack Rowan."

John Albert Rowan (1887–1966) pitched for the Detroit Tigers (1906), the Cincinnati Reds (1908–1910), the Philadelphia Phillies and the Chicago Cubs (1911), and the Reds (1913–1914). (Source: *Baseball Encyclopedia*, 2342)

ROWLAND In "Call for Mr. Keefe!," Keefe hopes that Rowland, after succeeding Callahan as White Sox manager, "handles the club right and don't play no favorites." In *Treat 'Em Rough* and *The Real Dope*, Keefe, now in the army, reminisces about Rowland. In "The Busher Reënlists," Keefe bumps into Rowland at the Chicago hotel where American League officials are having a meeting. The two don't discuss Keefe's desire for a contract nor the wartime wound in his left arm.

Clarence Henry Rowland (1879–1969) managed the Chicago White Sox (1915–1918) and later was Pacific Coast League president and an administrator for the Chicago Cubs. (Sources: *Baseball Encyclopedia*, 707; Hilton, 192–193).

ROWLEY, MRS. ("Three Without, Doubled") *see* **PHILLIPS, MRS.**

THE ROYAL TIN CAN OPENER OF THE WORLD ("The Golden Honeymoon"). He was elected the president of the Tin Canners at their national convention in Gainesville, Florida. Charley and Mother, while in St. Petersburg, hear about this important man, from Fredonia, New York. The Tin Canners are so named because they camp in their cars and eat mostly from tin cans.

RUBE ("BIG RUBE") In "My Roomy," he pitches a winning game for New York against the Chicago team. In "Horseshoes," he pitches for the Giants in the first game of the World Series against the Athletics, whose pitcher, the Chief, wins.

George W. Hilton identifies this pitcher as Richard William "Rube" Marquand (1889–1980), an ace right-hander for the Giants (1908–1915) and then for other major-league teams (until 1925). He was elected to the Baseball Hall of Fame (1970). (Source: Hilton, 355)

RUBY, HARRY ("A Day with Conrad Green"). He and Bert Kalmar wrote a musical comedy. Robert Blair stole its plot and wants to sell it to theatrical-producer Conrad Green. Green refuses it, then presents it as his to his librettist Joe Martin, who reveals the theft.

Imaginative readers may wish to put an image to the name "Harry Ruby."

RUCKER In "Back to Baltimore," he was pitching for the Brooklyn Dodgers when Dixon, playing first base for the Boston Braves, came to the plate. Mrs. Hayes, Braves president, asked Dixon to hit a home run. He struck out. In "The Poor Simp," Carey asked Robbie, managing the Dodgers, not to pitch Rucker against his team.

George Napoleon Rucker (1884–1970) pitched for the Brooklyn Dodgers (1907–1916). (Sources: *Baseball Encyclopedia*, 2244; Hilton, 429)

RUFFING ("When the Moon Comes over the Mountain"). Danny mentions that an "empire" called him out when this right-handed Yankee was pitching against Danny's Brooklyn team.

Charles Herbert Ruffing (1904–1986) played for the Boston Red Sox (1924–1929), the Red Sox and the Yankees (1930), the Yankees (1931–1946), and the Chicago White Sox (1947). Ruffing entered the Baseball Hall of Fame (1967). (Source: *Baseball Encyclopedia*, 2345)

RUFFO ("Dinner"). Miss Coakley tells Harry Barton that soprano Rosa Raisa, of the "simply gorgeous opera company in Chicago," is married to Ruffo or perhaps Rimini, both "barytones" regardless.

RULEBACK ("The Busher Abroad") *see* **REULBACH**

RUNKLE ("Who Dealt?"). Mrs. Cannon says that an editor, "Runkle or Byers, or some such name," didn't read her husband Tom Cannon's short story.

RUNYON, DEMON ("The Busher's Welcome Home"). Keefe says that Demon Runyon joins the baseball players in Paris during their 1913–1914 around-the-world tour, and accompanies them to London and New York.

Damon Runyon (1884–1946), Kansas-born author and journalist, was most famous for his *Guys and Dolls* (1932), which became a hit musical comedy (1950). Jonathan Yardley reports that Lardner met and drank with Runyon and Grantland Rice,* among others, when he was in New York on his way to France as a reporter (1917). Yardley adds that "Runyon ... was well on his way to becoming the most prominent and financially successful Lardner imitator in journalism, transposing Ring's use of Middle Western vernacular to the Broadway world of show-biz people and small-town punks he himself knew well." (Source: Yardley, 200)

RUNYON, PHIL ("Man Not Overboard"). He is the *Gargantua* purser. To circumvent his friend novelist Benjamin Brainard's half-baked scheme to commit suicide aboard, Phil has Fred Lemp get Brainard drunk and tell him horrifying stories involving his own family, which Brainard, when sober, feels inspired to write about.

When he gave silly Phil his last name, Lardner was thinking about his friend Damon Runyon (1880–1946), journalist, sports columnist, and popular short-story writer. Jonathan Yardley remarks that Runyon was Lardner's drinking buddy starting in New York (about 1918) and that Runyon was "the most prominent and financially successful Lardner imitator in journalism," because of his success in "transposing Ring's use of Middle Western vernacular to the Broadway world of show-biz people and small-time punks he knew so well." Douglas Robinson also notes Lardner's influence on Runyon. (Sources: Robinson, 101; Yardley, 200).

RUSSELL In "A Busher's Letters Home," Keefe mentions warming up with fellow-pitcher Russell in Paso Robles. In "The Busher Comes Back,"

Keefe says Callahan is saving Russell and other pitchers for the city series. In "The Busher's Kid," Keefe says Kid Gleason dislikes left-handers "even if he does jolly Allen and Russell along and make them think they can pitch." In "The Busher Abroad" and in *Treat 'Em Rough*, Keefe remembers Russell.

Ewell Robert Russell (1889–1973) pitched for the White Sox (1913–1919), especially well when Keefe was on the team (1913). Ewell's middle name is also listed as Albert. (Source: *Baseball Encyclopedia*, 2347–2348; Hilton, 44–45)

RUSSELL, FRANK ("How Are You?"). He was Bob Dayton's secretary Annie's sister's husband. Bob releases Annie from work to attend Russell's funeral.

RUTH, BABE In "Along Came Ruth," Keefe explains that when Gleason told him he could choose to pitch against Mays one day or Ruth the next, Keefe chose Ruth. Trouble: Keefe and Ruth were warming up before the game, and Keefe saw his wife Florrie in the stand with a strange man. Keefe's bad pitching ended that day when Ruth hit a home run "into the right field bleachers where the black birds sets." In "The Courtship of T. Dorgan," Keefe says Ruth is appropriately nicknamed "Babe" because "I had him swinging like a baby in a cradle" and fouling twice. In "When the Moon Comes over the Mountain," Danny says that when Ruth was playing for Boston against Brooklyn "he hit a couple out of the park durn the series." In *The Real Dope* and "Meet Me in St. Louie," Keefe mentions Ruth.

George Herman ("Babe") Ruth (1895–1948), played for the Boston Red Sox (1914–1919), the New York Yankees (1920–1934), and the Boston Braves (1935). George W. Hilton explains that in 1919 Comiskey Park had left- and right-field bleachers, and that the latter "was never literally a Jim Crow section, but many of the team's black fans sat there." Ruth became a charter member of the Baseball Hall of Fame (1936). (Sources: *Baseball Encyclopedia*, 1546, 2348; Hilton, 272–274, 277; Streissguth, 382)

RYAN, "CAP" ("Harmony"). He is the long-suffering captain of the baseball team mainly featuring harmonious singers Bill Cole, Art Graham, and Lefty Parks.

RYAN, DR. ("Champion"). This Chicago physician treats Connie Kelly after Midge Kelly, his older brother, beats him up.

RYAN, JACK ("The Venomous Viper of the Volga"). He is a championship boxer, defeated by Beau Burton. When promoter Luke Lewis's Venomous Viper of the Volga falls out of contention, Lewis seeks to arrange a match between his Frankie Fitzgerald and Ryan.

RYAN, MRS. ("The Golden Honeymoon"). She is a roque player from Eagle, Nebraska. Mother, Mrs. Hartsell, and Mrs. Morse play together in Florida.

SAIER In "My Roomy," he is one of several baseball players rejecting Buster Elliott as a roommate. In "Horseshoes," Saier plays for the Cubs in a game against St. Louis. With one out, Saier hits a sure-out fly. Speed Parker, on first and thinking there are two outs, runs home. The ball is muffed. Speed says he had a hunch the ball would drop. In "The Busher's Kid," Keefe boasts that in a "city serious" game he sent "them good hitters Leach and Good and this here Saier" back to the bench.

Victor Sylvester Saier (1891–1967) played for the Chicago Cubs (1911–1917), saw military service, and then played for the Pittsburgh Pirates (1919). (Sources: *Baseball Encyclopedia*, 1549; Hilton, 159)

ST. LOUIS BROWNS An American League baseball team (1902–1953). (Source: Light, 633–634)

ST. LOUIS CARDINALS A National League baseball team (1892–). (Sources: Light, 634–637; Streissguth, 234, 259)

SALLEE "My Roomy," he pitches for St. Louis against Chicago. Buster Elliott hits him for a triple. When Sallee forgets him and winds up, Elliott steals home. In "Sick 'Em," the narrator says the new Philly pitcher Smitty has "a cross fire like Sallee's!" In "Alibi Ike," Sallee is the St. Louis pitcher off whom Alibi Ike, happy after meeting Dolly, gets three hits. In *Treat 'Em Rough*, Jack Keefe says Sallee pitched a ball to Felsch that he "hit ... out of the park." (This is a reference to the October 6, 1917 World Series game between Sallee's New York Giants and Felsch's Chicago White Sox.)

Harry Franklin Sallee (1885–1950) played for the Cardinals (1908–1915), the Cardinals and the New York Giants (1916), the Giants (1917–1918), the Cincinnati Reds (1919), the Reds and the Giants (1920), and the Giants (1921). (Sources: *Baseball Encyclopedia*, 2352; Hilton, 347)

SALSINGER, HARRY ("The Jade Necklace"). He is a friend of movie-mogul L. N. Bauer. When Bauer asks Salsinger if he knows any Irish stories, Bauer means any "Irish romance" he can use to star his Irish actor Maurice Kavanaugh in. Salsinger barely starts a Pat-and-Mike story before being interrupted.

SAM ("Alibi Ike"). He is on the team the narrator Carey and others also play for. Carey, to hear his response, tells Alibi Ike he has bet Sam about Ike's possible engagement to Dolly.

SAM ("Women"). He plays on the team Mike Healy, Young Jake, Lefty, and Gephart are warming the bench for. They criticize Sam for making a bad play.

"SAMMY BOY" (*Saturday Evening Post*, December 21, 1918; RD) *see* ***THE REAL DOPE***

SAMPSON, DR. ("Widow"). He was the physician in Louisville, Kentucky, who advised Archie's widow to find relief by vacationing. She went to Miami, met Fred Milburn, and married him.

SAMPSON, RED (*Treat 'Em Rough*). He is one of Jack Keefe's army buddies, notable for kidding Jack. Red shoots well during rifle practice.

SAP (*The Big Town*). He is a racehorse that defeats Only One at the Belmont when Sid Mercer, Only One's jockey, double-crosses Herbert Daley, owner of Only One, by briefly reversing Only One's direction.

SASHOFF, DMITRI ("The Venomous Viper of the Colga") *see* **LISTER, FRED**

SATTERLY, JIM ("Anniversary"). He was a young man in Milton. Bess could have married him but chose Louis Taylor. After high school, Satterly worked for the Milton Gas Company, ultimately earning $22 a week. He married a girl who bore three children and gives piano lessons for 50¢ per half-hour. Jim, now 35, and his wife go to the movies occasionally.

SAWYER ("The Crook"). He was a "kid" pitcher that "Jennin's," the Tigers manager, ordered to face the White Sox. Sawyer's wildness inspires Bull, the fun-loving umpire, to say that his "right arm needs a good rest" in a humorous exchange with Stanage, who was trying to be Sawyer's catcher.

SAYER, SMILEY ("Champion"). He is a boxer whom Midge Kelly "stopped [in Philadelphia] ... so quick that Smiley thought sure he was poisoned," according to Tommy Haley.

SAYLES, CELIA ("The Love Nest") *see* **GREGG, CELIA**

SCHAEFER, DUTCH HERMAN In "The Busher Comes Back," Keefe praises this Washington coach for his ability to "cut up" with fellow-coach Altrock "on the infield" before their game with the White Sox. In "The Busher Beats It Hence," Keefe says McGraw is happy that Steve Evans and Dutch Schaefer are going on the world tour, because "both ... [are] funny." Keefe summarizes Schaefer's kidding of him, which he both excuses and doesn't fully understand. In "The Busher Abroad," Schaefer and Keefe go on the world tour, during which Schaefer makes Keefe a laughing stock, partly by encouraging him to write poems. In "The Busher's Welcome Home," all this continues, when Schaefer, Schalk, and Steve Evans get Keefe to try, briefly, to quit playing for the White Sox and jump to the Federal League. In *The Real Dope*, Keefe thinks fellow-soldier George Shaffer is a German spy because his name resembles that of Schaefer, who was called "Germany" and "use to play ball in our league." Schaefer is mentioned in "Good for the Soul."

Herman A. ("Germany") Schaefer (1877 or 1878–1919) played for the Chicago Cubs (1901–1902), the Detroit Tigers (1905–1908), the Tigers and the Washington Senators (1909), the Senators (1910–1914), the New York Yankees (1916), and the Cleveland Indians (1918). George W. Hilton says Schaefer showed little ability but had a great sense of humor with the Senators (1913) and briefly tried vaudeville with Charley O'Leary. James E. Elfers details Schaefer's delight in participating in the 1913–1914 around-the-world tour. (Sources: *Baseball Encyclopedia*, 1559; Elfers, *passim*; Hilton, 87–88, 535)

SCHALK In "A Busher's Letters Home," Keefe, pitching for the White Sox, praises Schalk, his catcher, for understanding St. Louis Browns batters well; then gripes that when he was pitching against the Tigers and Schalk told him to shut up and pitch, he lost his temper and walked some Tigers who then stole on him. In "The Busher Comes Back," Keefe gripes after a later game that if "Schalk had of let me throw ... spitters instead of fast ones" he could have kept Cobb from getting Detroit's one hit off him. In "A New Busher Breaks In," Keefe says Schalk got a single off

Detroit's pitcher, Joe Hill. In "The Busher's Kid," Keefe complains that he would have done better against New York "eccept for Schalk dropping the ball at the plate." In "The Busher's Welcome Home," Schalk continues to kid Keefe. In "Call for Mr. Keefe!," Keefe, when pitching against Cleveland, gripes that "Schalk made me waist 2" on Speaker, who then got a hit — when Keefe failed to cover first base. In *The Real Dope*, Keefe remembers ignoring a curve sign from Ray Schalk, pitching a "floater" instead to Tyrus Cobb, and winning the game. He also plans to tell General Pershing how Schalk in another game "dropped a third strike on me." In "The Battle of Texas," Keefe praises "Schalkie." In "Along Came Ruth," Keefe explains that after seeing his wife Florrie in the stand with a strange man he wasn't able to warm up with Schalk and pitched so badly against the Red Sox that Schalk wondered what was wrong. In "The Courtship of T. Dorgan," Keefe says he had "Cracker Schalk" look over the car the Detroit salesman was offering him. He also says that young Tom Dorgan doesn't have much chance to be a regular White Sox catcher "with a man like Ray Schalk" on the team. In "The Busher Pulls a Mays," Keefe complains that when the White Sox were doing badly at one point, even "Cracker Schalk has to be wheeled up to the plate and back." In "The Hold-Out," Stremmle was praised as possibly "a second Schalk."

Raymond William Schalk (1892–1970) played for the Chicago White Sox (1912–1928), was their manager (1927–1928), and played for the New York Giants (1929). He was elected to the Baseball Hall of Fame (1955). (Sources: *Baseball Encyclopedia*, 707, 1560; Hilton, 63).

SCHANG In "Horseshoes," he catches for the Athletics and figures in their World Series with the Giants. In "The Busher Abroad," Keefe explains that "Lie Hung Schang," a Chinese phrase that "steve Evans" taught him, is not a reference to the "Athaletics" Schang. In "Along Came Ruth," while Eddie Cicotte was pitching for the White Sox, Schange bunted for the Red Sox to advance Scott from first, and got on when Cicotte threw errantly past second.

Walter Henry Schang (1889–1965) played for the Philadelphia Athletics (1913–1917), the Boston Red Sox (1918–1920), the New York Yankees (1921–1925), the St. Louis Browns (1926–1929), the Athletics (1930), and the Detroit Tigers (1931). (Sources: *Baseball Encyclopedia*, 1560; Hilton, 271)

SCHNEIDER ("Where Do You Get That Noise?"). Schneider, Heine Groh, Fritz Mollwitz, Count Von Kolnitz, Wagner, and Herzog play for the Reds. Carey, a Cub, says their names should help the Reds break Cincinnati attendance records, because Cincinnati has many citizens of German background. Hawley wonders what about away games.

Peter Joseph Schneider (1895–1957) played for the Cincinnati Reds (1914–1918) and the New York Yankees (1919). (Sources: *Baseball Encyclopedia*, 2362; Hilton, 513)

SCHOBINGER (*Treat 'Em Rough*). He is a soldier in Jack Keefe's unit. Capt. Whiting recruits Schobinger, "from Champlain college here in Ill.," to play football.

SCHULTE In "My Roomy," Schulte is one of several baseball players who won't tolerate Buster Elliott as a roommate. In "The Busher Comes Back," Keefe complains that when he was pitching for the White Sox, Schulte of the Cubs got a lucky hit "past first base" that "Chase must of been asleep" to miss. In "Sick 'Em," the narrator, a Philly man, talks with Frank Schulte during batting practice before a Cubs game. When asked, Schulte speaks sarcastically about Fogarty's ineffective pitching. In "Horseshoes," Schulte is a Cub outfielder when Dick Grimes joins the team in a utility capacity. In "The Busher's Kid," Keefe gripes about Schulte's being accorded a hit on a ball "Weaver throwed away." Larry Burns mentions Frank Schulte in "Tour No. 2." In "Insomnia" the sleepless author remembers Schulte.

Frank Schulte (1882–1949) played for the Chicago Cubs (1904–1915), the Cubs and the Pittsburgh Pirates (1916), the Pirates and the Philadelphia Phillies (1917), and the Washington Senators (1918). Donald Elder explains that when Lardner traveled with and reported on the Cubs during their 1909 spring tour, he got to know Schulte and that the two became close friends. (Sources: *Baseball Encyclopedia*, 1568; Elder, 61–63, *passim*; Hilton, 96)

SCHULTE, ETHEL ("The Ides of June") *see* **OLSEN, MRS.**

SCHULTZ, DAVY ("DAVE") ("Ball-A-Hole"). He is a callow young caddy at the golf club where the narrator and his friend Jake are more experienced caddies. The two bet Davy that they can inveigle Mr. Conklin and Mr. Perkins, both stingy though wealthy, into giving them tips. The boys win but don't accept Davy's payment.

SCHRADER ("Haircut"). He owns the hardware store in Whitey's town. Jim Kendall sent Paul Dickson there to fetch a key for the baseball pitcher's box. A joke, you understand.

SCHUPP ("The Hold-Out"). He, Smith, and Tyler were praised by Frank Conley, the narrator, as such good pitchers that Mr. Edwards's spotty team would have trouble against them.

Ferdinand Maurice Schupp (1891–1971) played for the Giants (1913–1918), the Giants and the St. Louis Cardinals (1919), the Cardinals (1920), the Cardinals and Brooklyn (1921), and the Chicago White Sox (1922). George W. Hilton reports that Schupp, like many other baseball players, was less effective after his World War I military service. (Sources: *Baseball Encyclopedia*, 2364; Hilton, 584)

SCHUYLER ("A Day with Conrad Green"). He and his wife attended Mrs. Bryant-Walker's party. When Conrad Green reads about the event in the newspapers, it bothers him that the Schuylers were mentioned and he wasn't, although he and his wife Marjorie Green were also guests.

SCHUYLER, MRS. ("A Day with Conrad Green"). She also attended Mrs. Bryant-Walker's party.

SCHWARTZ ("Meet Me in St. Louie"). Stengel and Danny play for the Brooklyn baseball team. Stengel took callow Danny to see the manager of Irving Berlin* and asked to see Mr. Schwartz, knowing he was non-existent. The secretary showed the two to Mr. Abrams.

Lardner may present this episode as he does in order harmlessly to indicate the dominance of Jewish persons in the show business. Jonathan Lardner notes that Lardner "moved in the markedly Jewish world of the theater with no discomfort, and he caused none." (Source: Yardley, 54)

SCHWARTZ, JOE ("Pity is Akin—"). He is manager and part-owner of New York's Cozy Club. He sells Henry Spalding illegal rye and is with cahoots with singer Marian Moore there. Spalding reports them to authorities, and Marian is tried but acquitted. Spalding finds Marian at The Snug. Also working there is Schwartz, who lost $2,000 when the Cozy was padlocked, and who is happy to obey Marian's hint to slug Spalding.

SCHWARTZ, LOU ("Greek Tragedy"). He is wrestler Greek Alexis's manager.

SCOTT In "The Busher's Welcome Home," Keefe and Scott are on the around-the-world tour. Keefe says he won't sell Scott his lucky scarab. In *The Real Dope*, Keefe, a Chicago White Sox pitcher, recalls while soldiering in France that Scott of the Boston club "couldn't take the ball in his hand and make a hit off a man like I." "Along Came Ruth," Keefe explains that when Eddie Cicotte was pitching for the White Sox, Schang of the Red Sox bunted to advance Scott, who was at first, and got on first himself when Cicotte threw to second wildly. Keefe mentions Scott in *The Real Dope*.

Lewis Everett Scott (1892–1960) played for the Boston Red Sox (1914–1921), the New York Yankees (1922–1924), the Yankees and the Washington Senators (1925), and the Chicago White Sox and the Cincinnati Reds (1926). George W. Hilton reports that Scott, "[a] notable iron man, ... held the major league record for consecutive games played, 1,307, before being displaced by Lou Gehrig." (Sources: *Baseball Encyclopedia*, 1571; Hilton, 271)

SCOTT, JIM In "A Busher's Letters Home," Keefe says Callahan, White Sox coach, worked him in Los Angeles as a pitcher more often than he did Scott. In "The Busher Comes Back," Callahan didn't let Scott pitch against Detroit but saved him for the city series. In "A New Busher Breaks In," Keefe explains that when he was having trouble pitching against Detroit because Joe Hill was their pitcher, Callahan ordered Scott to warm up to replace Keefe. However, Keefe continued pitching, beaned Hill, and got into real trouble. In "The Busher's Kid," Keefe gripes that Weaver and Scott spitefully dislike him. In "The Busher Abroad," Keefe and Jim Scott are on the world tour. Keefe mentions pitching against him in an exhibition game. In "The Busher Reënlists," Keefe recalls a double-header the White Sox played against St. Louis, and how "Jim Scott lose the 1st. game," how Keefe "had eat something that didn't set very good," and told Kid Gleason "I'm not myself." Gleason said that in that case Keefe might win a game.

James Scott (1888–1957) played for the Chicago White Sox (1909–1917). James E. Elfers reports that when the world-touring baseball players visited Tokyo, Scott, "[a]fter shaking off the cobwebs of idleness and seasickness," pitched successfully for the Americans against a well-mannered Japanese university team (December 7, 1913); but that, far more important, "[w]hat had started as a sporting event became a delightful encounter between cultures." (Sources: *Baseball Encyclopedia*, 2366; Elfers, 116; Hilton, 44)

SCOTT, JOHN ("Haircut"). He and his wife live seven miles beyond Whitey's town. Jim Kendall got Whitey the barber to go shave Scott, supposedly dead. But he wasn't. Doc Ralph Stair later found Jim Kendall's body at the Scotts' lake shore.

SCOTT, MRS. ("Haircut"). She and her husband own lakeside property outside Whitey's town.

SCOVILLE, SKULL ("The Poor Simp"). He was a wild but fast pitcher recruited from the Carolina League to play for the narrator's team. Skull, a handsome strutter, was so naive that Carey, the narrator's buddy, played unkind practical jokes on him. When, at last, Carey told him that rich "Lizzie Carnegie" was enamored of him, Skull made himself acquainted with her; but she was really Mary Conahan, a rich man's daughter, and will marry "the poor simp." Skull is compared to the handsome movie star Francis X. Bushman.*

SEA MIST (*The Big Town*). He is a horse mentioned as appearing at a Belmont race.

SEARS, BETSY ("Some Like Them Cold"). She is the sister of Paul Sears, a New York song lyricist. Chas. F. Lewis, would-be song writer, writes Mabelle Gillesie, living in Chicago, that Miss Sears is cold. Later he writes Mabelle that he's marrying Betsy.

Grant Overton (1887–1930) says that Lewis was "vamped by an icicle [Betsy]." Jonathan Yardley labels her "a venal shrew." (Sources: Overton, 49; Yardley, 349)

SEARS, PAUL ("Some Like Them Cold"). He is a New York song lyricist. He meets and befriends Chas. F. Lewis, would-be song writer from Chicago. Lewis writes Mabelle Gillespie, living in Chicago, of his plan to marry Paul's sister Betsy Sears.

Song-writer Sears's first name was surely suggested to Lardner because of his friendship with Paul Lannin,* composer and musical director, and a friend of Vincent Youmans* and Florenz Ziegfeld,* among others involved in music. Lardner and Lannin collaborated (1928–1930) on a musical to be called *All at Sea*, but nothing came of it. (Sources: 274–276; Yardley, 303)

SEATON, BEN ("Wedding Day"). He is described as "a juvenile" (in New York show business). He attends the wedding of Brownie Burt and Jimmy Shane. After the ceremony, Ben hosts a dinner, drinking, and dance party in his apartment for Brownie, Jimmy, fellow show-people Dorothy Drew, Josie King, and Wallie Roach, and publicist Ed and his sister-in-law Ruth.

It seems like a plot miscue that when the party breaks up, Ben leaves his own residence in a taxi with Dorothy, Josie, and Wallie.

SEBASTIAN, MRS. (*Treat 'Em Rough*). She is Nick Sebastian's wife. She brings a box of attractive food when she visits Camp Grant. Jack Keefe finds her more considerate than his own wife, Florrie Keefe, but describes her as ugly.

SEBASTIAN, NICK (*Treat 'Em Rough*). He is one of Jack Keefe's army buddies. He is not "Nick the Blade," the dangerous fighter that Shorty Lahey identifies him as being, to scare Jack. Nick's friendly wife visits Nick and other soldiers at Camp Grant. Another visitor is Jack's wife Florrie, whom Nick calls "beautiful." Jack's response is that if Nick's wife "is a good mother and willing to work," it doesn't matter that "she is no Eva Tanguay[*]."

"SECOND-ACT CURTAIN" (*Collier's*, April 19, 1930; SC). (Characters: Booth, Chambers, Mr. Rose, Mr. Youmans.)

Mr. Rose manages a play by Booth and Chambers. It was "liked ... pretty well" in Washington and did better in Newark; but everyone, especially Mr. Rose, thinks it "lacked a second-act curtain." Chambers, who has "a mansion in the lower sixties," tells Booth, rooming in a hotel all summer, they should separately think about the needed rewriting. Booth goes to "a speakeasy to buy himself some thinking powders" before entering his $4 room. He tries to peep again into the room across the court, "occupied by a comely and frank lady of about twenty-six"; but it's dark. He samples his bottle. His typewriter "*I* key" is broken. He orders food, delivered by an aging, talkative chambermaid he dismisses. He rummages his room for something to read. The Holy Bible he rejects as an "anonymous ... steal of Gideon's novel of the same name." *The Insidious Dr. Fu-Manchu* by Sax Rohmer he delays sampling, because he glances first into *Heart Throbs*, "a collection, by Joe Mitchell Chapple, of favorite bits of verse or prose of well-known Americans." One poem almost brings tears; another cheerily gives him an idea. After another swig, he lies down, thinks, then phones Chambers to suggest ending the second act with a song rather than unfunny lines. Chambers says the song better be "damn' funny." The light in that girl's room goes on, then off. Perhaps she's a buyer from out of town, finished with work for now, changing her clothes, planning to see a movie, maybe having to eat alone, hoping someone come to dance with her, returning to her $4 room to fall sleep "read[ing] the confessions of John Gilbert and Rudy Vallée." Booth sleeps.

Mr. Rose phones him at 2:30 A.M. demanding that second-act curtain. Booth says he's got an idea, sees a man in the girl's room. Good. She's married. Maybe unhappy. Anyway, not alone. Feeling "resentful," Booth gulps a huge drink. A pretty tune flashes into his head. He writes "half the refrain," hoping to match "silly, incongruous words" to it, but is interrupted again by Rose's phoning again. He orders a second-act close in words, not music, and hangs up. Booth writes more words for his nice tune, then fears he's heard it before, phones Mr. Youmans at 3:10 A.M., and whistles the tune. Youmans says it's from his own *Great Day* musical. Booth destroys his composition, sees a man leaving the girl's room across the court, phones to ask the switchboard operator to tell that girl he tried but couldn't compose anything for a second-act curtain. A 7:00 A.M. phone gurgle awakens him. The cord is around his neck. He summons the house dick, and tells him someone emptied his bottle of "good stuff" and tried to strangle him. The detective says he'll "run down the clues" and probably concludes that drinker and would-be strangler are "one man."

Lardner furnishes Booth's hotel room with only three books. The Gideon Bible occasions a joke. *The Insidious Dr. Fu-Manchu* (1913) is one of 15 popular novels by British-writer Sax Rohmer (pseudonym of Arthur Henry [Sarsfield] Ward [1883–1959]) featuring the villainous, canny Chinese criminal. Joe ("Joseph") Mitchell Chapple (1867–1950), Iowa-born editor and author, assembled *Heart Throbs* (1906) and *Heart Throbs of Famous People* (1929), and produced a movie series called *Heart Throbs*. The reference to Rudy Vallée* is obvious. John Gilbert (1899–1936), Utah-born John Cecil Pringle, was a romantic leading man in silent movies (from 1916), so handsome that he was dubbed "the great lover." He was best in *The Big Parade* (1925), a realistic, popular war movie. (Source: Spears, 54, 55–56)

SEELEY, CAPT. (*The Real Dope*). He is one of Keefe's officers. Aboard their troop ship, he forgives Keefe for spouting German words to a French officer, since Keefe thinks he's speaking French. Seeley rebukes some soldiers for celebrating a buddy's birthday with too much champagne. He holds Keefe back from a unit's being shipped out, for getting drunk. When Keefe is kidded into believing that General Pershing needs his advice, he figures Pershing will order Seeley to give him leave to rush to Paris. Keefe goes to Seeley to report George Shaffer as a German spy in their midst. Keefe shows the phony evidence to Seeley, who smilingly tells him he's been tricked by his pals. Soldiers tell Keefe that Seeley is the source of rumors they concoct. At one point, Seeley tells his men to rest, "on acct. of what's comeing." Keefe chafes at inaction. When "the boys" kid Simple Simon, they realize they mustn't tell Seeley.

SEIBOLD ("Lose with a Smile"). Seibold was pitching for the Boston Braves when Danny, playing for Brooklyn, got a hit. Danny writes Jessie that Seibold is so slow "you can count the seems on ... [his] fast ball."

Harry Seibold (1896–1965) played for the Philadelphia Athletics (1916–1917, 1919) and the Boston Braves (1929–1933). (Source: *Baseball Encyclopedia*, 2369)

SELEE, FRANK ("Back to Baltimore"). Dixon, managing the Boston Braves, says that if Mrs. Hayes hadn't become their interfering president he would have "finished higher with that gang than they finished since Frank Selee had 'em."

George W. Hilton reports that Frank Selee (1859–1909), manager of the Boston Braves (1890–1901), won five pennants, managed the Chicago Cubs (1902–1905), then, suffering from tuberculosis, helped recruit players for the highly successful Cubs (1906–1910). (Source: Hilton, 425)

SENA DAY (*The Big Town*). He is a horse that Herbert Daley, supposedly on "a hunch," bets on and wins for himself and also for Ella Finch and her sister Katie, at the Jamaica race track.

SERVICE, ROBERT W. (1874–1958). British-born poet. He emigrated to Canada (1897), visited the Pacific coast, worked in the Yukon, learned much concerning the Klondike gold rush, and led a literary life in Paris before and after the First World War, during which he was a correspondent and a Canadian Army ambulance driver. Service wrote novels but was popular only for wretched poetry, typically "The Shooting of Dan McGrew" (1908). Lardner has Mabelle in "Some Like Them Cold" and Thayer in "Mr. and Mrs. Fix-It" reveal their lack of critical discernment by liking Service's works.

SHAFER ("Horseshoes"). He is a Giant third baseman. When he abruptly quits baseball, McGraw trades to replace him with Speed Parker of the Cubs.

George W. Hilton says that Arthur Joseph Shafer (1889–1962), who played for the New York Giants (1909–1913), did indeed quit at the end of the season, and adds that he graduated from the University of Santa Clara, became a Los Angeles real-estate businessman, and was a fine amateur golfer. (Sources: *Baseball Encyclopedia*, 1577–1578; Hilton, 405)

SHAFFER, GEORGE (*The Real Dope*). He is a big soldier in Keefe's army unit in France. Keefe peeks at part of a harmless letter Shaffer wrote home, is encouraged by Johnny Alcock, another soldier, to believe Shaffer is a German spy, goes to Capt. Seeley with the "evidence," and is told he's been tricked. Alcock tells Shaffer, who beats up Keefe.

SHAFFER, LOUIS ("Tour No. 2"). He is Minnie Burns's cousin. Larry, Minnie's husband, has Shaffer handle his gardening business while he and Minnie go to Europe. When Larry returns, Shaffer isn't around.

SHANE, JIMMY ("JIM") ("Wedding Day"). He is a highly paid spendthrift "funnyman" in New York musical comedies. He marries Brownie Burt, his long-time girlfriend, also in musicals. They don't wed for love. After a cold ceremony and a drink-filled party hosted for their few guests by Ben Seaton, Shane fibs his way that very evening to go to a club to await a phone call from his Philadelphia girlfriend.

SHANKS ("The Busher Comes Back"). Keefe says that when Shanks, a Washington outfielder, misplayed White Sox Bodie's fly ball, Callahan reluctantly let Keefe bat. He boasts he "slapped" a single over first base.

Howard Samuel Shanks (1890–1941) played for the Washington Senators (1912–1922), the Boston Red Sox (1923–1924), and the New York Yankees (1925). (Sources: *Baseball Encyclopedia*, 1578; Hilton, 89)

SHANO ("The Crook"). He was a White Sox outfielder. A sacrifice fly scored Hooper, who was a Red Sox player. Cahill, a hotheaded White Sox player, made trouble with the umpires on the play and called Bull, an umpire, a "crook." Bull got into trouble by pummeling Cahill.

SHAW ("The Courtship of T. Dorgan"). According to Keefe, Shaw pitched ineffectively for the Senators in a game against the White Sox.

George W. Hilton reports that James Aloysius Shaw (1893–1962) compiled a losing record pitching for the Washington Senators (1913–1921), after which he discontinued playing because of a hip injury. (Sources: *Baseball Encyclopedia*, 2373; Hilton, 282)

SHAW ("Liberty Hall"). In one of composer Ben Drake's "emergency exit" telegrams, Shaw and Miss Miller are reported to be suffering from laryngitis; so Ben has to return to New York and rewrite the score a little "lower."

SHAW ("Women"). He played shortstop on the Dayton team for which Mike Healy was playing on that bad day when umpire Baldy Pierce made dishonest calls.

SHAW, BOBBIE (*The Big Town*). He is the infant son of Captain Francis Shaw and his wife Maizie Shaw in "Bridget Sees a Ghost," Jimmy Ralston's play.

SHAW, CAPTAIN FRANCIS (*The Big Town*). He is the soldier in "Bridget Sees a Ghost," Jimmy Ralston's play. The captain returns home after the war, learns his wife Maizie Shaw has remarried, and leaves.

SHAW, MAIZIE (*The Big Town*). She is Captain Francis Shaw's wife, Bobbie Shaw's mother, and, by the time Francis returns from war, Thornton's wife. Francis promptly disappears without seeing her or Thornton.

SHAYNE ("Take a Walk"). He is a pitcher, a knuckle-ball specialist, for the team on which Agnew plays third base.

SHEARER, NORMA (1900–1983). Actress. Montreal-born Edith Norma Shearer, stunningly attractive, won a beauty contest (1914), was taken by her mother in an unsuccessful effort to get an audition with Florenz Ziegfeld,* modeled, took movie bit parts (1920), and was discovered and signed (1923) by Irving Thalberg (1899–1936), whom Jack Spears labeled "the boy mogul of Metro-Goldwyn-Mayer." Even before she married Thalberg (1927), Shearer's career skyrocketed, because of his tutelage and her clever insistence on varied roles. In the 1920s she appeared in upwards of 40 films, notably *The Bootleggers* (1922), *The Student Prince* (1927), *The Trial of Mary Dugan* (1929), and *The Last of Mrs. Cheyney* (1929). She declined the starring roles in *Gone with the Wind* (1939) and *Mrs. Miniver* (1942).

Norma Shearer's first name may be consciously echoed in that of pretty Norma Gregg in "The Love Nest." Norma Shearer is also mentioned twice in "I Can't Breathe." (Sources: Ephraim Katz, 1281; Spears, 56)

SHECKARD ("My Roomy"). The narrator recalls Sheckard, Hofman, and Richie as former Chicago baseball players. They sang loudly, but soloist Buster Elliott is louder. In "Insomnia" the sleepless author remembers Sheckard.

Samuel James Tilden Sheckard (1878–1947) played for the Brooklyn Dodgers (1897–1898, 1900–1905), the Chicago Cubs (1906–1912), and the St. Louis Cardinals and the Cincinnati Reds (1913). Jonathan Yardley quotes a *Chicago Tribune* article by Lardner (June 16, 1910) indicating that he knew Sheckard, Hofman, and Richie well. (Sources: *Baseball Encyclopedia*, 1582; Hilton, 345; Yardley, 102)

SHEILA ("Rhythm"). She is the title figure in "Sheila's Shirt," with lyrics by Sam Rose.

SHELTON ("Contract"). He is the associate editor of a magazine. He and his wife are invited to play bridge with Cameron and his wife, Carl Dittmar and his wife, and Robert French and his wife, only to have their misplays jumped on. Shelton gets revenge by criticizing his critics for their grammar, repetitious diction, mispronunciations, and stale jokes. Shelton's friend Gale Bartlett recommends E. M. Pardee and his wife as refined bridge-playing host and hostess, only to be rebuked by Mrs. Pardee for mistakes.

SHELTON, MRS. ("Contract"). She is her magazine-editor husband's socially lonely wife. When they move to Linden, a suburb, he tolerates her desire to mingle with bridge-playing neighbors, only to experience criticism of their faulty play by harsh bridge fiends.

SHEPPARD ("The Hold-Out"). Frank Conley, the narrator, says that "young Sheppard showin' up so good [on Mr. Edwards's basebell team] helped a lot." Nothing more is said about Sheppard.

SHEPPARD, MILT ("Haircut"). He had a big Adam's apple, about which Hod Meyers and Jim Kendall kidded him when Whitey, the town barber, was shaving him.

SHERDEL ("When the Moon Comes over the Mountain"). Danny boasts that when Sherdel was pitching for Boston against him, he hit a game-saving double and then scored the winning run.

William Henry Sherdel (1896–1968) played for the St. Louis Cardinals (1918–1929), the Cardinals and the Boston Braves (1930), the Braves (1931), and the Braves and the Cardinals (1932). (Source: *Baseball Encyclopedia*, 2375)

SHERIDAN, JACK ("The Busher Beats It Hence"). He is a baseball umpire. When Keefe tells him about Dutch Schaefer's remarks to him concerning the dangers of going on the world tour, Sheridan says he was only "kiding me."

George W. Hilton reports that John F. Sheridan (c. 1852–1914) was a minor-league player before becoming an umpire, was an American League umpire (1901–1914), and participated in the world tour (1913–1914). (Source: Hilton, 188)

SHIVERICK (*Treat 'Em Rough*). He is a soldier in Jack Keefe's unit. Capt. Whiting recruits Shiverick, who "played with the Ithaca club down east," to play football.

SHOTTEN ("A Busher's Letters Home"). Keefe complains that when he was sent in as relief pitcher against the St. Louis Browns, he was insufficiently warmed up and walked Shotten.

Burton Edward Shotten (1884–1962) played for the St. Louis Browns (1909–1917), the Washington Senators (1918), and the St. Louis Cardinals (1919–1923), and managed the Philadelphia Phillies (1928–1933), the Cincinnati Reds (1934), and the Brooklyn Dodgers (1947). (Sources: *Baseball Encyclopedia*, 708, 1587; Hilton, 63)

SHUBERT ("Anniversary"). The Shuberts are mentioned as theater persons for whom Ed is "a publicity man."

SHULTZ, CONGRESSMAN ("A Chip of the Old Block"). He gets Captain Evan Barnes his commission, when Barnes's mother requests his help.

"SICK 'EM" (*Saturday Evening Post*, June 25, 1914; ABS, LOB, RAB). (Characters: Alexander, Jack Barnett, Bill, Boehling, Jack Burke, Cravath, Davis, Mrs. Davis, Fogarty, Gandil, Hank, Honus, Jake, Joe Hammond, Bull Harper, Walter Johnson, Julia, Punch Knoll, Luderus, Magee, Marie, Mayer, Milan, Paskert, Pat, Bill Peck, Red, Eppa Rixey, Sallee, Frank Schulte, Smitty.)

The narrator assures Jake that he is telling him the truth. The two are fellow baseball players. This is what happened:

Red managed our Phillies last fall, and we won the "World Serious." Red had Pat (one of his coaches) scout some Central League teams. He saw teammates Lefty Smith and Fogarty, recommended both as superb pitchers, and "the big boss ... bought Smitty." But the Cubs got Fogarty. Smitty had a fine "record, full o' no-hit games and shut-outs," was "a wop, but ... handsome," and we watched him during training in the South. He was fast, could "cross fire" well, but relaxed and was hit "acrost the state line." Against Richmond, the same; Red kept him in the game, and they scored 11 runs on him. In exhibition against "them [Connie] Mackmen" in Philadelphia, Smitty lobbed his pitches as usual and Red rebuked him. I read in "the Chi papers" that Fogarty was also dogging it and told Smitty about his "sidekick." Smitty called Fogarty "a false alarm" and said Fogarty won games earlier because other teams pitied him.

The season began. Our pitchers Alexander and Rixey won regularly. Our best hitters — Cravath, Magee, and Luderus — "pole[d]" homers. Red started Smitty only "onst," and seven straight Boston batters got hits. Red benched Smitty, criticized him sarcastically, and he sat meekly. Trouble in June: Alexander's arm weakened; Rixey broke two fingers; and only Mayer was an experienced pitcher. Losses weren't better when Red had Smitty pitch in relief.

Red sent me to Dayton to scout "a big spitter" pitching there against Evansville. No good. But I saw Jack Barnett, my friend from our Utica days together, on Evansville's bench. I asked him about Smitty. Barnett knew him from their Evansville time together. Barnett explained that Smitty, the handsome "wop," pitched badly for Evansville — but not after they traded for Fogarty, who was cocky about his good looks but also formerly pitching badly for Grand Rapids. Both Smitty and Fogarty pitched excellently after the Evansville coaches got them mad at each other by telling each one that the other was handsomer. The two, "strong for the skirts," pitched shutouts and other victories on alternate days practically. Barnett told Smitty that "Fogarty's Marie was prettier than his Julia." Barnett had predicted that when Smitty went to Philadelphia and Fogarty to Chicago, the two would flop as pitchers.

I rejoined the club when we played the Cubs in Chicago. I asked Frank Schulte, a Cub, about Fogarty and learned that the handsome fellow was useless except to pitch in batting practice and to primp before his pocket mirror. I told Red about the Smitty-Fogarty rivalry and persuaded him to get Fogarty from Cubs manager Hank on waivers. Fogarty traveled by train to St. Louis with us for our games there. When Smitty first glimpsed Fogarty, whose red hair Red praised, he called Fogarty "a swell-headed pup" and asked to pitch today. When Fogarty, my new roommate, asked whether that "burg ... Philly" had a satisfactory "female population," I told him that I was married but Smitty could explain adequately, because "the real dolls in the burg is bugs over him"; I added that Smitty, sore of arm until recently, was pitching today against St. Louis. Smitty did, and though "hog wild" and walking eight, pitched a two-hitter and won 5–2. I goaded Fogarty, who said Smitty was "so dam' homely" that he scares hitters whereas Fogarty was so attractive in Fort Wayne that he "could of married any dame" there. I said Red lacked a good pitcher for tomorrow; Fogarty bit and volunteered. Next day he won, pitching mostly fast balls and few "hooks or spitters," walking none, and allowing three hits. Pat praised Fogarty to Smitty, who after two rainy days won, followed by another win by Fogarty, to whom I praised Smitty. And so it went. By August we were second only to the Giants. Red ordered "I and Pat" to "ride ... in private" those "two handsome birds" and not tell our teammates about the scheme. Alexander and Rixey were well again and pitching, which bothered the pair. When Smitty beat Brooklyn both games of a double-header, Fogarty "ast" about the next double-header; Red let him pitch the two "agin the Cubs," and he won both. The two were razzed into clothes-buying and singing competitions. Pat and I wrote love letters to the two, from the same fictitious girl praising the recipient, mentioning his handsome rival, and saying she'd be sitting in the stand "right back o' your bench." The "birds" fell for the trick and "rubbered for that dame" the two final months of home games. We had telephone girls in our away hotels call Smitty, ask for Fogarty, hang up, and vice versa. In Pittsburgh, Pat told Smitty that Fogarty generously tipped "the hops and waiters." That started an expensive rivalry.

After we cinched the pennant in "Cincy" on September 15, Red permitted wild celebrations. Someone — never knew who — told Fogarty that

Smitty was a huge wine drinker and told Smitty the same about Fogarty. At a café the two tried outdoing each other, got so drunk we took them away, put them in bed together in Pat's room, found them in the morning "both poundin' their ear," and awakened them. Neither dared admit being too drunk to know how they happened to become roommates. Nor would either admit being hungover. Both tried to down some breakfast. Neither asked to pitch that day. Both quickly recovered, however, "wanted to pitch in Chi," but were told they'd be rested carefully for "the World Serious."

Trouble came in Boston, toward the season's close. A beautiful girl was in the stands. Smitty, Fogarty, Davis, who was our scrappy infielder just acquired from the Boston team, and I were sitting on the bench. Smitty and Fogarty smiled at the girl. She smiled back at all of us. As the game ended, Smitty and Fogarty, having rushed to get dressed, flirted at the rail with her — until Davis rushed up with a bat, hit Smitty's left hand and Fogarty's right arm. Red would have shot Davis, but he identified the girl as his bride, who had been smiling at him, not at strangers. A doctor examined Smitty's swollen hand and Fogarty's limp arm. On to Philly. More doctors there. More dire fears. Rixey, Alexander, and Mayer were pitching badly. In the World Series against Washington, Johnson beat us. In Philly, Boehling beat us. After four days of rain in Washington, I had a hunch, obtained Red's permission to try something, told Smitty that Fogarty's doctor, who treated the president and congressmen, said he was ready to pitch tomorrow, then told Fogarty that Smitty was likewise cured. Both pitchers reported to Red ready to pitch. Red let Smitty pitch the third game, a shutout against Johnson. Next day Fogarty was "even better." Finally, Smitty outpitched Johnson, who got Washington's only hit. Fogarty was mad that the newspapers praised Smitty's two victories compared to his one.

I spoke at the clubhouse about Jack Barnett's helpful information, collected a $150 purse, and sent it to him. I didn't care when the doctors said both Smitty and Fogarty might be ruined for next year by pitching when out of shape, because I'm going to manage and maybe play for Mobile next year myself. Now just tell me I can't manage.

George W. Hilton praises "Sick 'Em" for its "cleverness of plot and freshness of baseball environment," but then calls its "chronology ... an impossible mishmash of the 1913 and 1914 seasons," all of which he corrects by extensive footnotes. (Source: Hilton, 20, 25, *passim*)

SICKLES, PAUL ("'In Conference'"). He and others work for Kramer & Company. They converse vacantly "in conference." Since he is the only worker not a company officer, "they called Paul instead of by his initials."

SIGNE ("Old Folks' Christmas"). She is the Scandinavian cook of Grace and Tom Carter. Signe prepares a big Christmas turkey for the Carters. Ignored by their children, Ted and Caroline Carter, old Grace and old Tom nibble on it alone.

SILLOH, MISS ("Rhythm"). She and Harry Hart are guests at the Bucks' Long Island home. At the piano, Hart quits playing a melody he tells Miss Shilloh he stole from Friml, because, he explains, he has just heard that Friml is also a guest.

(Charles) Rudolf Friml (1879–1972), Prague-born American composer, helped with music for the *Follies* (1921, 1923, 1924, 1925) of Florenz Ziegfeld,* and composed for musical comedies and for movies. Two of his loveliest songs are "Rose Marie" and "Indian Love Call."

SILVERS ("Bob's Birthday"). Grandfather Tyler was a bookkeeper for Silvers & Co. but was released.

SILVERS ("Holycaust"). Jessie writes that the Centralia fire involved "Silvers's store."

SIMON, JACK (*The Real Dope*). He is a soldier in France with Keefe's unit. He is so naive that his fellow soldiers call him Simple Simon. They kid him about collecting German souvenirs in shell holes. They persuade him to seek "a Saxon" in "Nobody's Land." He goes missing awhile but later returns with a German corpse.

In real military, such heartless "jokes" in combat situations quickly lead to casualties.

SIMPLE SIMON (*The Real Dope*) *see* **SIMON, JACK**

"SIMPLE SIMON" (*Saturday Evening Post*, January 25, 1919; RD) *see* ***THE REAL DOPE***

SISLER In "The Battle of Texas," Keefe boasts that in a game against St. Louis he "sent him [Sisler] back twice for a drink of water." In "Along Came Ruth," Keefe again pitched to Sisler, who this time swung "at a ball he couldn't hardly reach" but got a hit that scored Tobin. In *The Real Dope*,

Keefe praises George Sisler. Finch mentions Sisler in a complimentary way in *The Big Town.*

George Harold Sisler (1893–1973) played for the St. Louis Browns (1915–1927), the Washington Senators and the Boston Braves (1928), and the Braves (1929–1930), and also managed the Browns (1924–1926). He became a member of the Baseball Hall of Fame (1939). George W. Hilton says that Sisler had a University of Michigan engineering degree, was a premier first baseman comparable in greatness to Lou Gehrig, and scouted for the Browns and was their batting instructor. (Sources: *Baseball Encyclopedia,* 708, 1594–1595; Hilton, 253)

SLEEPER, MR. ("Three Without, Doubled"). At the bridge party hosted by Mrs. Garrett and her husband, one of Gullible's "pardners" is so sleepy-looking that he dubs her Old Slumber, Mrs. Nap, and Mrs. Sleeper. He calls her husband Mr. Sleeper.

SLEEPER, MRS. ("Three Without, Doubled") *see* **OLD SLUMBER**

SLIGAR, MARION ("Holycaust"). Jessie writes that during the Centralia fire Marion Sligar rescued George Cunningham from the Byrd-Watson building.

SLIGHT In "The Busher Abroad," he is a catcher aboard the ship taking the baseball players around the world. Keefe is told that Slight wears his mask to avoid being pecked by birds known as Thomas Hawks. In "The Busher's Welcome Home," Keefe mentions Slight.

James E. Elfers identifies "Andy Slight" as a "[m]inor leaguer assigned to the [White] Sox for some seasoning" on the world tour. Elfer adds that Slight had "the best singing voice" among the touring baseball players, and that "[a]lthough destined never to make a Major League roster, as a tourist Slight was a star." (Source: Elfers, xix, 102)

SLOAN ("Great Blessings"). He owns a market where Clara Stewart can no longer shop, because she can't get more credit there.

SMALL, HERB ("That Old Sweetheart of Mine"). Stella Crane remembers attending the theater with Herb Small and his wife. Stella boasts to Will that Herb got better tickets to *Journey's End,* when she saw it earlier with the Smalls, than tickets Will has bought for her to see it with him.

Journey's End (1928) by R. C. Sherriff (1896–1975) was a gripping drama about World War I trench warfare.

SMALL, MRS. ("That Old Sweetheart of Mine"). Stella Crane remembers that she has attended the theater with Mrs. Small and her husband Herb.

SMITH ("Back to Baltimore"). In a tall tale that Hub, Boston Braves pitcher, told gullible William Baker, Jr., who ineptly played for the Braves, it seems that Smith and Hub were playing for Nashville against New Orleans. The game, 6–6, was in the 21st inning. Since Smith was hitting .600, the New Orleans pitcher walked him, the first baseman stepped viciously on Smith's foot, but Smith eventually hopped home for a win, after which two toes fell off and one leg was amputated. Baker lauded Smith for his nerve.

SMITH ("A Busher's Letters Home"). Keefe says Smith told him that Kid Gleason said if Keefe didn't learn to field better he'd be released.

George W. Hilton unearthed that fact that businessman Louis D. Smith (1861–1925) owned the Terre Haute Hottentots (1901–1911), shortly before Keefe left Terre Haute (1912) to join the White Sox. (Source: Hilton, 49)

SMITH ("The Hold-Out"). Frank Conley, the narrator, regarded Smith, Schupp, and Tyler as such good pitchers that the team Conley managed would have trouble against them.

Sherrod Malone Smith (1891–1949) played for the Pittsburgh Pirates (1911–1912), the Brooklyn Dodgers (1915–1921), Brooklyn and the Cleveland Indians (1922), and Cleveland (1923–1927). (Source: *Baseball Encyclopedia,* 2390)

SMITH ("Oh, You Bonehead!"). He ran well for Pelham in their football game against the Coach's Leighton team.

SMITH ("A One-Man Team"). He coaches the Doane football team. When he discovers that Davis, supposedly his "one-man team," requires help against Coach Belden's opposing team, he uses his halfbacks Byron and Moxey effectively.

SMITH, AL (1873–1944). New York–born politician, Alfred Emanuel Smith left school at 13 to support his Irish immigrant family. He clerked for the Tammany political machine (beginning 1895), was elected a state assemblyman (1904), and became governor of New York (1919–1920, 1923–1928), during which times he sponsored labor, park, housing, and welfare reforms. Smith, who was Catholic, urban, and anti-Prohibition, was the unsuccessful Democratic candidate for the presidency (1928), losing to Republican Herbert Hoover (1874–1964). Smith lost the Democratic nomination for president (1932) to Franklin D. Roosevelt (1882–1945), after which Smith became a lobbyist in opposition to Roosevelt's New Deal policies.

Al Smith is mentioned in "Hurry Kane," "The Jade Necklace," and *The Young Immigrunts*.

SMITH, FREDDIE (*The Real Dope*). He is a soldier aboard Keefe's troop ship. Smith, a German-speaking waiter from Milwaukee, teaches Keefe some German phrases but calls them French, which causes Keefe to be ridiculed. The Colonel rebukes Smith for doing so.

SMITH, HENRY ("Haircut"). He owned a drygoods store in Benton, a town near Carterville, where Jim Kendall used to work. Jim liked to send Smith anonymous postcards suggesting that when Smith was away other men kept Mrs. Smith "from gettin' lonesome." As a joke, you know.

SMITH, LEFTY ("Sick 'Em") *see* **SMITTY** ("Sick 'Em")

SMITH, MRS. ("Haircut"). She is or was Henry Smith's wife in Benton.

SMITH, RED ("Back to Baltimore"). He played for Brooklyn in a game against the Boston Braves, for whom Dixon the narrator managed and played. Rucker, Brooklyn's pitcher, walked a Brave, and Red Smith made an error, putting a second man on. Dixon then came up and struck out.

George W. Hilton reports that James Carlisle Smith (1890–1966) played for the Brooklyn Dodgers (1911–1914), then was sold to the Boston Braves (August 13, 1914), for whom he played (through 1919). (Sources: *Baseball Encyclopedia*, 1607; Hilton, 429)

SMITH, ROY ("Hurry Kane"). He, Bullard, and Robinson are traded from the St. Louis baseball team to the Boston baseball team for Frank Miller and Lefty Glaze. All five are ineffective players.

SMITTY In "Alibi Ike," he plays on the team (the Cubs) the narrator is with and figures in action on and off the diamond. In "The Poor Simp," Smitty witnessed a practical joke Carey played on gullible Skull Scoville on the train taking the team to a series with Brooklyn. In "Where Do You Get That Noise?," Smitty finds Hawley's talk idiotic, not least when Smitty praises his kid brother's shooting 71 in golf and Hawley replies that his own 73 score is better.

SMITTY ("Hurry Kane"). He played on the Waco team, in the Texas League, for which Hurry Kane pitched. Kane recalls that Smitty spoiled his no-hitter by misjudging a fly ball he "could have caught in a hollow tooth if he hadn't drunk his lunch."

SMITTY ("Sick 'Em"). He is a dark, handsome, vain pitcher, also called Lefty Smith. Smitty and Fogarty are Central League pitchers, effective only when on the same team, because they compete for success then. When Fogarty is sold to the Cubs and Smitty to the Phillies, each fails. The narrator, a Philly, learns of their rivalry from his friend Jack Barnett. So he persuades Red, the Phillies manager, to obtain Fogarty, after which both men pitch successfully. In an effort to outdo Fogarty, Smitty even pitches with a badly bruised throwing hand. The narrator says Smitty is not his real name, which is a long one.

Smitty is frequently called "the wop." The word was less offensive in Lardner's time than it is now.

SMITTY ("Women"). He plays third base instead of Mike Healy. Healy explains that he would have replaced injured Johnnie Lambert, but Healy's girlfriend demanded his attention out of town and Smitty got the call.

SMYTHE-CARTER ("What of It?"). This is the dry-goods company for which Ben Lacey's sister Bertha's husband works as a traveling salesman, about whom Ben tells Dexter Cosset.

SNELL (*The Big Town*). He is, according to Ella Finch, "the sugar man" husband of Mrs. Snell, the excellent bridge player.

SNELL ("Take a Walk"). He is the manager for the baseball team for which Agnew plays third base.

SNELL, MRS. (*The Big Town*). She plays bridge with Lady Perkins, Doctor Platt, and another man at the Long Island hotel where Finch, Ella Finch, and Katie are summering. Ella says Mrs. Snell's husband is "the sugar man." Ella longs to meet her and does. But Katie ruins any friendship Ella and Mrs. Snell might enjoy by revealing the contents of Lady Perkins's hand at a crucial moment.

SO-AND-SO ("Gullible's Travels"). This is Gullible's generic term for socially prominent Chicagoans whose going to or returning from Palm Beach he and his wife read about in "the society news at breakfast." Doing so triggers her determination to vacation there.

SOME CHAMPIONS: SKETCHES & FICTION BY RING LARDNER edited by Matthew J. Bruccoli & Richard Layman (New York: Charles Scribner's Sons, 1976). This collection contains nine short stories and also "Insomnia," sometimes considered a short story.

"SOME LIKE THEM COLD" (*Saturday Evening Post,* October 1, 1921; HTW, PRL, RU). (Characters: Edith, Mabelle Gillespie, Mrs. Gillespie, Sis Gillespie, Goebel, Levy, Chas. F. Lewis, Betsy Sears, Paul Sears, Charlie White.)

Chas. F. Lewis met a young woman in Chicago's Lasalle Street railway station, obtained her address, and went to New York "to make my liveing in the song writeing game," as he explains in a promised letter from "*N.Y., Aug. 3.*" He bet her he'd write. So he's writing. He sweat trying to sleep on the train. He gave the brush-off to "a dame" trying "to make me," which displeased him. His hotel room "at 47th st. right off old Broadway," cost "$21 per wk.," with bath. He likes bathing "in the A.M." and often nightly.

Mabelle Gillespie replies from "*Chicago, Ill., Aug. 6.*" She calls him "wonder man" and "Mr. Man," is willing to pay since she lost that bet, but she's just a poor "working girl," unlike that woman on the train. She doesn't normally speak to men without being introduced. She usually regrets being impulsive, hopes he won't make her regret having been "dazzled" upon seeing him. "Sis" arrived by train that day, saw her blushing, but she blamed the heat. Sis would die of shock on learning the truth. She knows that "Mibs" (Mabelle's nickname) squelches "fresh" men. She showed Sis the city sights, though she'd be happy just hearing Mabelle "rattle on," with her well-known sense of humor. Edith, Mabelle's roommate, praises her for making their tiny place "cozy," "homey." Little money isn't a handicap. She reluctantly admits she likes "good jazz music" more than "classical." He must visit Chi and play his songs on the piano. She couldn't fulfill her "threat" to see him in New York unless a rich, loving man took her there. She must bake Sis a pie, for which she's famous. For "pastry" too. But why mention "common things" to a "genius"?

Chas writes "Dear Girlie" August 10. Calling her "Miss Gillespie" would be cold. In New York two women "flopped" in this hellish heat, though wearing few "cloths." He won't see anyone but important theatrical people, now on vacation. Invited to the "Friars club" for dinner, he was inveigled into playing the piano. Everyone, including song-writer Paul Sears, "went crazy over his stuff." Someone took him to some woman on Riverside Drive. He declined to be "made." He'll follow "the right gal"—she'll have to "know a dish rag from a waffle iron" to marry him—"till she says yes."

Mabelle writes "Dear Mr. Man" August 13. She can't write "Dear Charles," though that was her father's name too. Dying, he left mother, Sis, and herself "enough insurance." She flew the "home nest" to avoid being a "drone." Chi is also hot. She can will herself not to feel heat or other "disagreeable things." Edith says she's a pleasant "breeze" to be near. Mabelle uniquely appreciates Mr. Man's witticisms. She has a priceless "sense of humour" herself, recognized by Sis, gone now, and "Edie," who likes "the pictures," whereas she prefers to read. Does he also like "high-brow" poems by Robert W. Service*? She likes hearing someone properly play popular music on the piano. She's glad he resisted those "ladies." She resists men but judged Mr. Man's exceptional "right kind" of "character." Do tell about that Riverside Drive girl. She won't say whether she's jealous.

Chas replies August 20, explaining his delay. He and Paul Sears collaborated on a song. Paul's song starts "Some like them hot, some like them cold, / Some like them when they're not too darn old," and ends "Some like them fickle, some like them true, / But the time I like them is when they're you." Chas provided the music. The song should make them "$25,000 apiece." Chi is a dirty burg compared to this "Mecca." "Girlie" needn't worry about that Riverside girl. She wore too much makeup, would likely want a husband with a "5th ave." house and servants. He wants "a real help mate" wife, to entertain his friends, see shows with, never nag. The only girl he's met here is Paul's sister, who treats men "like dirt" and is "the coldest," Paul says. Off for dinner at "Paul's place."

Mabelle replies August 23. She'd love to hear him play his new song, so money-making he'll likely not "remember ... 'old' friends." How clever he wrote about being "busier than a one armed paper hanger." She'll be thought clever repeating that and pretending she invented it. Luckily, her natural complexion is so attractive that a girl in a restaurant expressed envy. Oh, how Mabelle envies Mr. Man's life in New York. Chicago is so dirty she enjoys bathing often. Edie wondered if Mabelle's in love, writing him instead of going to movies with her. Though mainly "a home body," she does like "catchy" musicals, also having friends drop in, for whom she, not Edie, prepares "nice things to eat." Homemaking is special for women. She just bought a chair, a substantial one economical "in the long run." Her mother, in failing health, will give her some nice things, including a piano, when she has her own home. Will Mr. Man write a song for her? Write soon.

Chas replies September 8, briefly. He can't answer topics in her letter, which isn't right before him now; anyway, he must attend a party, show, and dinner "with the Sears." He's the one who wrote that song and whose sister is that "cold fish." Chas will start living with them, to save money, being short until royalties gush. Meanwhile, he's been hired to play a hotel piano for $60 per week. He hopes her father "is better." When idle, write.

Puzzled, she answers "Mr. Lewis" September 11. Is he mad at her? She'll apologize if she wrote anything hurtful. She'd never do that. Maybe he's glum because of his publishers' delay. Better to smile than worry about "temporary troubles." A salary of $60 is enough, if well managed, to marry and start a family on.

Chas writes "Miss Gillespie" September 24. He's marrying Paul's sister Betsy and they're all going to Atlantic City, where he'll be playing the piano. Though Betsy is "so cold," she says she dislikes him less than some men Paul "brought round." She also says she'll "run wild" unless he takes her to nightly shows, and says she won't be a house "slave." He wouldn't expect a wife to "live ... in druggery." She uses rainproof makeup and will allow him to write former girlfriends if she doesn't have to read their replies. He hopes Miss Gillespie finds a man who likes her furniture but cautions her against accosting any man on the make, unlike himself.

In her September 27th answer Mabelle tells him to thank his "fiance" and adds that her "man friend" would object to her "continuing [such] a correspondence," and he has asked her to end it with "this note." She closes by saying she'd like to meet "Miss Sears" and ask how to run wild on $60.

Thomas Boyd observes that "Some Like Them Cold" concerns "a man and a girl on a treadmill, seeking to rise above it, but being drawn more firmly to it in their attempt to escape." Boyd adds that the story "evokes a greater feeling of the uncertainty of existence and of active sympathy than all of Charlie Chaplin's pathetic shoes." Elizabeth Bibesco says that "Who Dealt?" and "Some Like Them Cold" "belong to the universal masterpieces that know no frontiers."

Ernest Hemingway found fault with most of Lardner's fiction but did offer grubby praise for "Some Like Them Cold," because, he allowed, it was "about someone that he [Lardner] was sorry for, and in his sorrow, forgot to be superior." Donald Elder writes about "Some Like Them Cold" thus: "These characters reveal themselves ... with the utmost clarity; ... their whole history from the first spark of mutual attraction to the time when it is stifled by their pitifully small ambitions is contained in these few letters." Elder calls the story "a masterpiece" and regards it as Lardner's "most artful story." Jonathan Yardley notes that in it "a young man who had seemed amiable and naïve turns out to be gullible and ignorant, and a young woman who had seemed hopeful and sympathetic is shown to be conniving and contemptible." Was Chas, however, ever unsubjectively "amiable"? His admiring Paul's dumb song indicates otherwise. Further, was Mabelle ever disinterestedly "sympathetic"?

In a letter (February 28, 1929), Maxwell Perkins* tells Lardner that he "always thought it ["Some Like Them Cold"] was an almost perfect story." It was the basis of *June Moon* (1929), a plot-altered three-act comedy by Lardner and George S. Kaufman.* *June Moon* is a tune-filled, biting satire of commercial song-writing. Samuel L. Leiter calls *June Moon* "[t]he laugh riot hit of 1929–1930" and reminds readers that it was "selected by Burns Mantle as a Best Play." In it, lyricwriter Fred meets Edna on a train to New York. Eileen is the mistress of Hart, Fred's publisher. Hart tires of Eileen, to whom Fred is attracted. Eileen's brother-in-law is Paul Sears, a composer with whom Fred writes "June Moon." It makes money. Eileen gets Fred to promise marriage. Maxie, who plays the piano, persuades Fred and Edna to reconcile, easily done when Paul explains Eileen's previous misbehaviors to Fred. Ring Lardner Jr. reminisces about *June Moon*, difficulties connected with its being written, the cast in it, and his father's later responses to it. (Sources: Bibesco, 367; Boyd, 602; Caruthers [1973], 135; Elder, 213, 278; Hemingway, 158B;

Lardner, Jr., 181–187; Leiter, I, 461; Yardley, 249, 333–339)

SOMEBODY, CAPT. (*The Real Dope*). Keefe refers to a French officer aboard the troop ship as Capt. Somebody.

SOMEBODY, MRS. (*Treat 'Em Rough*). She is one of Florrie Keefe's bothersome friends in Chicago, so designated by Jack Keefe.

SOMERS, MRS. ("Widow"). She consoles Margaret Winslow, whose husband John has died, by saying that she'd want to go hide if anything happened to Paul, her own husband.

SOMERS, PAUL ("Widow"). He accompanies his wife to offer comfort to Margaret Winslow, whose husband died. Paul asks Margaret's brother-in-law Ed Winslow about John's financial situation.

SOTHORON ("Along Came Ruth"). Keefe explains that he watched Sothoron pitch for St. Louis in the Cleveland-St. Louis game.

Allen Sutton Sothoron (1893–1939) pitched for the St. Louis Browns (1914–1920), the Browns and the Boston Red Sox and the Cleveland Indians (1921), the Indians (1922), and the St. Louis Cardinals (1924–1926), and managed to Browns (1933). Charles F. Faber and Richard B. Faber laud Sothoron as an excellent spitball pitcher, but add that his early death was owing not only to heart trouble and hepatitis but also to alcoholism. (Sources: *Baseball Encyclopedia*, 709, 2393; Faber and Faber, 150; 187; Hilton, 266)

SOULE, HARRY ("The Venomous Viper of the Volga"). He is the Palace theater stage manager. He helps Sandy King locate Henry Goetz.

SPALDING, BETTY ("Pity Is Akin —"). She is mentioned by Henry Spalding and his wife, while they are drinking at the Cozy Club, as their daughter back in Toledo.

SPALDING, EDITH ("Pity Is Akin —"). She is Henry Spalding's wife. They go with him for illegal drinks at the Cozy Club. She speaks only about children, otherwise is silent. When that subject comes up, Cozy singer Marian Moore, dining with them, falls weeping on Mrs. Spalding's breast. Henry calls Mrs. Spalding Edith once. At the Cozy, Spalding says their last name is Travers.

SPALDING, HENRY ("Pity Is Akin —"). He is a prohibition agent. He and his wife go to New York's Cozy Club, posing as Mr. and Mrs. Travers. He buys illegal rye, begins to like the singer Marian Moore there, and observes her drinking only from her stock of supposed rum, brought to her by manager Joe Schwartz. Later Spalding reluctantly testifies against Marian, but she is acquitted. When he locates Marian singing at The Snug, he reveals his love for her. In revenge, she gets Joe, also working at The Snug since the Cozy has been padlocked, to slug Spalding.

SPARKS, MR. ("Three Without, Doubled"). He and his wife are guests at the San Susie bridge club dinner party at the Garrett home. Gullible catches the names of "Mr. and Mrs. Sparks" but doesn't mention them again.

SPARKS, MRS. ("Three Without, Doubled") *see* **SPARKS, MR.**

SPEAKER In "The Busher Beats It Hence," Keefe reports that when the teams proceeded to the west coast before the world tour was to begin, they "got Speaker from the Boston club." Keefe contends that Speaker was afraid to bat against him until Callahan said it would be good practice for him. In "The Busher Abroad,"Keefe says Speaker, on their world tour, swings the bat so well that he could safely ward off the dangerous Thomas Hawks birds without having to wear a catcher's "mast." Speaker buys Keefe a fez in Cairo. In "The Busher's Welcome Home," Keefe mentions Speaker's being sold to the "Boston club." In "Call for Mr. Keefe!," Keefe, pitching for the White Sox, complains that Speaker, batting for Cleveland, got a hit when Gandil, playing first base, gloved the ball but then "messed it all up." In reality, Keefe failed to cover first. In *The Real Dope*, Keefe remembers Speaker as "gabby" but hitting a high pop fly ball when Keefe pitched against him. In "Along Came Ruth," Keefe is looking forward to playing against Cleveland, partly because "Mr. Speaker ... hasn't been going any to good against ... Detroit and St. Louis." In "The Courtship of T. Dorgan," Keefe gets into trouble when "Spoke," as he calls Speaker, slid into Chick Gandil, and the two began fighting and got ejected. To be macho, Keefe told Jack Graney that Speaker better not mess with him. Speaker confronted Keefe about the remark. Keefe backed down.

Tristram E. Speaker (1888–1858) played for the Boston Red Sox (1907–1915) and the Cleveland Indians (1916–1919), managed the Indians (1919–

1926), and played for the Washington Senators (1927) and the Philadelphia Athletics (1928). He was elected to the Baseball Hall of Fame (1937). James E. Elfers notes that "Comiskey ... talked ... Speaker of the Boston Red Sox into coming along [on the world tour]. Speaker produced box office magic. Comiskey, no doubt, hoped Speaker's drawing power would repeat itself around the globe." Elfer's later comments indicate that it did. (Sources: *Baseball Encyclopedia*, 709, 1615; Elfers, 22–23 and *passim*; Hilton, 203)

SPEARS, ALEX HART ("High-rollers"). He has played golf and cards for big stakes at a Hampton Dunes club on Long Island with Dick Parker, Alex Spears, and Jack Bowen. Spears and his wife are abroad this summer. Jack gets his friend Walter Finch to replace Spears.

SPEARS, MRS. ("High-rollers"). She and her wealthy husband are vacationing abroad. Marion Finch replaces her at Hampton Dunes bridge parties including Peggy Bowen, Mrs. Hart, and Mrs. Parker.

SPEED, CHARLEY ("Stop Me—if you've heard This One"). He is an actor, a member of the Lambs' Club, and a friend of young playwrights Jerry Blades and Luke Garner. Speed introduces them to Henry Wild Osborne, well-known "raconteur," probably to give the well-known fibber an opportunity to deceive or amuse Blades and Garner.

"THE SPINNING WHEEL" (*Cosmopolitan*, July 1927). (Characters: Amy Bennett, Jess Dorsey, Harry, Mrs. Hunt, Walter Hunt, Joe, Macomber, Jarvis Ralston.)

The narrator, 56, operates a roulette wheel at a New York City hotel for an honest owner. Three nights ago in came a bald, pimply-faced, chinless bank director named Macomber, known as a brainy "giant of finance." Holding $100 in $5 "checks" [i.e., chips], he bet $20 on red, lost, doubled, lost, doubled, finally won $200, and quit. Ditto at Harry's wheel here two nights ago, winning $300. Last night, accompanied by some cheering ladies, he tried the same method at Joe's table, but black kept coming up and he lost $1,000. He told Joe he was "fleeced." When Joe said he'd report him to the boss, Macomber said he'd deny the statement. The boss heard and rebuked Macomber. Macomber should know about car dealer Jarvis Ralston. He bet at Joe's wheel last month, lost $15,000, told Joe to put one overlooked check on No. 11, hit, eventually won back his $15,000 plus $500, and left. Ralston, unlike Macomber, wouldn't have "squawk[ed]" if he'd lost. Too many otherwise "nice," "smart" people, though, accuse dealers of being crooked, even though they'll lose money on rigged boxing events without questioning them.

The narrator has been dealing in gambling establishments for 30 years, in Florida, New York, Cuba, and elsewhere, and has "never yet seen a crooked wheel." Owners never cheat, for three reasons: They wouldn't know how; their employees would tell on them if they tried; and they'd be shut down if suspected, even where they pay almost "a quarter of their receipts in graft."

Here's a story. The narrator worked for "a crook at heart" who ran "straight" wheels in Cuba. The two men disliked each other. One night a drunk quit playing hazard, griped about being cheated, turned to the narrator's wheel, and put $300 on No. 32. Although the limit was $25, the boss nodded his permission. No. 32 hit, and the drunk staggered out with $10,500. The boss denied nodding and fired the narrator.

Here's a story about "a woman that cheated herself and her friends." Walter Hunt gave his wife a birthday party "wringing wet" with drinks, then brought the revelers here "the night after we opened up." Hunt played so-so at Joe's table and sent drinks to his wife and four of her "crowd," who were playing $1 checks at the narrator's table. A friend suggested pooling their five separate checks, remembered she wouldn't reveal her age at her party, and told her to bet her age with stacks of $5 checks. She put pile after pile on No. 30. No. 34 repeatedly came up. She lost and went with her friends for drinks and bridge in another room. Hunt approached the narrator's wheel with his remaining $25, asked what to bid on, was told by his pal to try his wife's age, bet on No. 34, and won $875.

Now about Jess Dorsey. He was handsome, used to deal but hated to see anyone lose too much, and got especially "blue" three years ago after his wife's death. One night two seasons ago "a beautiful young gal," about 23, approached Jess's table, lost $10 worth of 50¢ checks, and stayed chatting with him, with "pleading" eyes. Next night she lost another $10. Jess told the narrator that Amy Bennett was her name, she was lonely, she couldn't fall for "a fella" like Jess, they talked about the beach, and her appearance reminded him of his wife. The two met at the beach one morning; that evening he told the narrator he was in love again. Amy kept returning and losing money. One night she asked Jess what number to play. He suggested No. 35. She won. Next night Jess told her "to split the O's." She won again, this time about $80. Jess told her to quit because he surely couldn't pick more than "a winner two nights in succession." Amy said if he liked her he'd keep recommending winners because "You see you can't fool me." She said she couldn't swim tomorrow with him because her brother would be visiting, but if "you're awfully good to me tomorrow night" they can "have a party" the following day without her brother. Before leaving, she had Jess explain betting limits. He said $25 on a number, with exceptions for plunging. She said her brother would be betting tomorrow night. When asked, he showed about betting $25 on No. 26 for example, "walling" it at Nos. 25, 26, and 27, then betting $1,000s and $500s so as to risk $4,600 and maybe win $10,700. Smiling and leaving, Amy said her brother would "split with me" if he won.

Obviously that "fella" wasn't her brother. But he believed "poor, simple Jess" when she told him that dealers can spin any numbers they wish and that Jess liked her so much they couldn't lose. When "the moron" bet, he bet $600 on No. 26, would've won $5,700, except the ball hit No. 4. Amy tossed an ashtray at Jess and called him "names that she'd never learned from a brother." Workers "wrestled them out of the place." That's why Jess quit dealing and now runs elevators in some Broadway office building — maybe No. 26.

Lardner reveals more knowledge about roulette betting than most of his readers knew, or know. When Amy says her brother will split with her, does Lardner have her mean "divide with me," or is Lardner anticipating later slang — thus, "disappear with me"?

SPLUG, HARRY ("Meet Me in St. Louie"). Max Carey, Brooklyn's manager, kidded Danny, playing unhappily on their Brooklyn team, that he might trade him to the St. Louis Cardinals, which has a "retail branch in Alton." It was run, Carey went on, by Harry Splug, who is happiest when cry-baby players irritate him and cause him to lose his temper.

STACEY, LOUIE ("How Are You?"). He is the husband of Mrs. L. S. Stacey, who tells Bob Dayton about Louie's gallstones.

STACEY, MRS. L. S. ("How Are You?"). She is one of Bob Dayton's few clients. She tells him that her husband Louie had gallstones and was successfully treated by Dr. Troutman.

STAIR, DOC RALPH ("Haircut"). He came to Whitey's town, already cared for by Doc Foote and Doc Gamble, though not very well. Younger and handsome, Stair was popular. When coroner Ken Beatty died, Stair replaced him. Jim Kendall's kidding Julie Gregg when she fell passively in love with Stair, who was uncomprehending, led to Stair's telling mentally challenged Paul Dickson that the perpetrator of such a joke didn't deserve to live. Paul took action.

STALLINGS ("The Hold-Out"). Frank Conley says that Mr. Edwards' baseball team, "with a little pep at first base," might cause trouble for "George Stallin's, Wilbert Robinson and John J. McGraw."

George Tweedy Stallings (1867–1929) was a catcher for the Brooklyn Dodgers (1900) and the Philadelphia Phillies (1897–1898), and managed the Phillies (1897–1898), the Detroit Tigers (1901), the New York Yankees (1909–1910), and the Boston Braves (1913–1920). Leverett T. Smith Jr. makes use of Lardner's "'Braves' Is Right" (*American Magazine* [March 1915]) to show that "Lardner credits him [Stallings] with inspiring the team [Braves] to the heights it achieved," namely, winning the pennant (1914). (Sources: *Baseball Encyclopedia*, 709, 1622; Hilton, 573; Smith, 139)

STAMPER, DAVE ("Rhythm"). He is a composer whose melodies Harry Hart does not play during a Sunday afternoon party at Peggy Leech's apartment. Hart is willing, however, to steal from Stamper when he and Benny Kane agree to collaborate again.

STANAGE In "A Busher's Letters Home," Keefe, pitching for the White Sox, says he walked Stanage, a Detroit Tiger. In "A New Busher Breaks In," Keefe says that Joe Hill, Detroit pitcher in a later game, got him so mad that he walked Stanage, "who if I had of been myself could not foul me." In "The Crook," Stanage was the catcher when Sawyer, rookie Tiger pitcher, was so wild that Bull, the witty umpire, told Stanage that his right arm needed a rest anyway. Keefe mentions Oscar Stanage in *The Real Dope*.

Oscar Harland Stanage (1883–1964) played for the Cincinnati Reds (1906) and the Detroit Tigers (1909–1925). (Sources: *Baseball Encyclopedia*, 1622; Hilton, 68)

STANDING ("Widow"). He is a tenor and part of a quartet including Miss Wells at John Winslow's funeral service. She pitches "In the Hour of Trial" too high for him, or for her.

STARK, KATHRYN ("A Chip of the Old Block"). She is "a peach" whom Captain Evan Barnes meets in Washington. When her fiancé is badly wounded in France, she dumps him and agrees to marry Barnes.

STARR, MRS. ("Words and Music"). This may be the name of Roman Starr's ill-tempered wife. Starr may be only his professional name.

Mrs. Starr indicates limited knowledge of music when she seems to be telling Starr that his snoring is so low-pitched that "Gatti-Cazoozis would have you doubling for Chaliapin's grandfather." Giulio Gatti-Casazza (1869–1940) managed the Metropolitan Opera House in New York (1908–1935). Feodor Chaliapin (1873–1938) was an operatic basso there (1907–1923).

STARR, ROMAN ("Words and Music"). He is the popular, conceited tenor appearing on stage and in movies. In an article he composed, he says his "Art" will improve if he has an unhappy love affair. Hilda Harper is so smitten by seeing his performances and reading about him that she enters his apartment posing as a reporter seeking an interview. She is disillusioned when by eavesdropping she learns he's married to a harridan and behaves grossly himself. His wife calls him "Gus."

STEELE ("Good for the Soul"). He was a superb pitcher recruited by A.T. Grant for his minor-league team. Buck Warner both praised him for his speed and accuracy, and felt sorry for him for having to play among losers. Buck predicts ultimate success for Steele.

STEIN ("Champion"). This is the name of a Milwaukee saloon frequented by Midge Kelly, in preference to Niemann's and Duane's, where he owes for numerous drinks.

STEIN ("A Day with Conrad Green"). He is mentioned in a newspaper item as possibly becoming Conrad Green's partner. Denying the report, Green calls Stein "a crook."

STEIN, HAP ("A Frame-Up"). He is a good boxer from Grand Rapids. Burke defeats him in Benton Harbor but since he doesn't dislike Stein, he doesn't hurt him.

STEIN, JOE ("Nora"). He is an actor under contract with musical-producer Louie Brock. Brock tells his lyricist Frank Moon and his tunesmith Jerry Morris to write a comic part for Stein into their revision of Hazlett's play "Nora."

The racial insensitivity of Lardner's characters, not Lardner, is manifest when Morris, Brock, and Moon agree that Stein can play "a Wop" or "a Heeb" or "a dinge."

STEINFELDT ("Insomnia"). He is a baseball player the sleepless author remembers.

Harry F. Steinfeldt (1877–1914) played for the Cincinnati Reds (1898–1910) and the Boston Braves (1911). (Source: *Baseball Encyclopedia*, 1628–1629)

STENGEL, CASEY In "One Hit, One Error, One Left," Danny, playing baseball for Brooklyn, writes Jessie that Stengel is "asst mrg and coach of the club" and that "mgr Carey" has assigned Stengel to room with him. Both men encouraged and kidded callow Danny. In "When the Moon Comes over the Mountain," Stengel now kids Danny about sponges, a baseball team's "farm," and Danny's appetite. In "Lose with a Smile" Sengel chatted with and coached Danny. In "Meet Me in St. Louie," Stengel continued to help and kid Danny, who describes him to Jessie as "a hit skech" she'd enjoy meeting. Stengel helped Danny with his "Dad song chorus." In "Holycaust," Stengel offered help to Danny, not least when he tried, unsuccessfully, to persuade him to treat Jessie better. In "The Ides of June," Stengel kidded Danny but offered him sensible advice when he was finally cut from the Brooklyn team.

Charles Dillon Stengel (1889–1975) played for the Brooklyn Dodgers (1912–1917), the Pittsburgh Pirates (1918–1919), the Philadelphia Phillies and the New York Giants (1921), the Giants (1922–1923), and the Boston Braves (1924–1925). He managed the Dodgers (1934–1936), the Braves (1938–1943), the New York Yankees (1949–1960), and the Giants (1962–1065). Stengel was elected to the Baseball Hall of Fame (1966). Jonathan Yardley notes that Lardner "followed Stengel's career since ... 1912," and that Stengel "met Ring's prime requirement of playing to his full potential, and he had a quirky sense of humor in which Ring obviously delighted." Robert J. Higgs says that "[i]f there is a genuine hero in Lardner's work, it is Casey, a man who appears to have taken baseball for what it is, not as a Big Deal, but as a 'game to play.'" (Sources: *Baseball Encyclopedia*, 709, 1629; Higgs, 29; Yardley, 360)

STERRETT ("Bob's Birthday"). He belongs to the club frequented by Bob Tyler's parents.

STETSON, DOCTOR ("Absent-minded Beggar"). He gave the baccalaureate address at the high-school commencement John Knowles absent-mindedly missed.

STEVE ("Mamma"). This is the name of the New York policeman who takes Mamma, an amnesiac, to the Traveler's Aid Guest House, from which she is transferred to a hospital.

STEVENS ("Freedom of the Press"). He is a *Blaze* reporter hounding Constance Warner for news. He sneaks into her mansion, pounds on her bathroom door, and when she screams filches a photograph of her Aunt Julia, which he doctors and publishes as a picture of Constance.

STEVENS ("Sun Cured"). She is the girlfriend of Ben Drew, Ernie Fretts's friend. Ben and Stevens join Fretts and Bonnie Werner, Fretts's girlfriend, in a Florida vacation. They all dance and drink, and the girls also shop.

STEVENS, BELLE ("Mr. and Mrs. Fix-It"). She and Ada, the narrator's wife, chance to meet on the Elevated in Chicago. Thereafter, Belle and her husband Tom Stevens meddle unacceptably in the lives of Ada and her husband.

STEVENS, TOM ("Mr. and Mrs. Fix-It"). Thomas J. Stevens is a well-connected Chicagoan who constantly meddles in the lives of the narrator and his wife Ada. So does Tom's wife Belle. Tom means well but grows intolerable.

Donald Phelps says that Tom and Belle Stevens "tramp like affable Attillas through the rubble of their neighbors' privacy." (Source: Phelps, 94)

STEWART ("The Busher Abroad"). Keefe thus names one officer aboard the ship taking the baseball players around the world.

STEWART ("The Busher Abroad"). He is the manager of a prison in "Vanila," in the Philippines. Keefe meets him.

James E. Elfers identifies M. L. Stewart as "the director of prisons," in the Philippines, and adds that when the baseball players on their 1913–1914 world tour stopped in Manila, Stewart "sent word that at 11:00 A.M. [December 18, 1913] the Bilibid Prison would be available for tours." Elfers adds that the players, some of whom were "former jailbirds," visited it and were impressed by how humanely it was managed. (Source: Elfers, 142–143)

STEWART In "Horseshoes," he is a Cub outfielder when Dick Grimes joins the team in a utility capacity. In *Treat 'Em Rough*, Jack Keefe remembers replacing an outfielder named Stewart in Terre Haute.

Charles Eugene Stewart (1883–1934) appeared in only a few games for the Chicago Cubs (1913–1914). George W. Hilton notes that Lardner presents him anachronistically in "Horseshoes," since the events in it occur in 1912. (Sources: *Baseball Encyclopedia*, 1633; Hilton, 399)

STEWART, BEN ("Great Blessings") *see* **STEWART, FATHER**

STEWART, CLARA ("Great Blessings"). She is Tod Stewart's wife and Myrtle's mother. Now 35, Clara married when 23 instead of accepting more stable Dave Bonham. For years Tod's parents have derided her. After serving them a Thanksgiving Day dinner both nice and unappreciated, Clara watches Tod scoot to visit his bootlegger Frank Butler's flirtatious sister Mamie, later puts drunken Tod to bed, and thinks about Dave.

Is Lardner hinting that Clara may escape her wretched marriage by going to Dave, and taking Myrtle along, whom Dave likes? Regardless, canny readers should conclude that Clara is too spineless in the face of her demonic in-laws ever to escape. Walton R. Patrick cites "Great Blessings" as typical of Lardner's ability to treat characters in a "sympathetic manner" while placing them in "grim situations." Patrick concentrates on Clara, who "suffers great misery [not 'great blessings'], which she hardly deserves despite her wrong choice of a husband." (Source: Patrick, 128)

STEWART, FATHER ("Great Blessings"). Stewart is Tod Stewart's useless father, long-suffering Clara Stewart's father-in-law, and the grandfather of Myrtle Stewart, whom he spoils with candy. His wife calls him Ben.

STEWART, GRACE ("Great Blessings"). She is Harry Stewart's wife. They live in Detroit, distant from her critical mother-in-law. Grace, who is childless, drinks, smokes, and plays bridge.

STEWART, HARRY ("Great Blessings"). He is Tod's brother, Grace's husband, and a Detroit hotel manager. Harry and Tod were brought up by an overly indulgent mother and drink too much.

STEWART, MOTHER ("Great Blessings"). She and her husband are the parents of alcoholic Harry Stewart, married to Grace, and of alcoholic Tod Stewart, married to Clara. The two oldsters used to have Thanksgiving Day dinner with Grace and Harry, until Grace and Harry moved to Detroit. Now they dine at Clara and Tod's home. Mother Stewart rationalizes her behavior when her sons were pampered children, criticizes and praises Grace and Clara, and finally orders Clara around at Thanksgiving Day and excuses unemployed Tod's behavior. Clara suffers too long; so, when the in-laws are about to move in, she possibly ponders escape plans.

Mother Stewart is the mother-in-law from Hell, so grotesquely presented as to resemble a cartoon.

STEWART, MYRTLE ("Great Blessings"). She is Clara and Tod Stewart's daughter, 10. Clara's domineering mother-in-law encourages the child's addiction to sweets and says her nervousness and chronic bouts of sickness are Clara's fault.

STEWART, ROY ("Zone of Quiet"). He is someone Miss Eleanor Lyons and her friend Marian vie for. Marian wins him, by which time Miss Lyons is turning to George Morse.

STEWART, TOD ("Great Blessings"). He is the son of indulgent, rationalizing parents, and is Harry Stewart's brother, long-suffering Clara Stewart's husband, and sweets-addicted Myrtle's father. Tod is an unemployed alcoholic. He flirts with his bootlegger Frank Butler's sister Mamie Butler. After Clara has thanklessly served this fifth Thanksgiving Day dinner for Tod, Myrtle, Mother Stewart, and Father Stewart, Tod decamps, consorts with Mamie, returns home drunk, and flops asleep — unaware that at last Clara maybe thinks of escaping.

STONE, CAPTAIN F. CONKLIN ("A Chip of the Old Block"). He is identified by Tracy in conversation with Captain Evan Barnes as a member of the Monument Department.

STONEHAM ("Holycaust"). McGraw and Stoneham, both in the Giants' baseball administration, are the butt of a joke by Stengel, who said that since the Giants are so good on paper they should put paper on "the polo grounds" for home games.

STOOPS (*The Real Dope*). He is a soldier in Keefe's army company in France. Keefe gets Stoops, an artist in civilian life, to decorate the valentine poem he has written for Miss Moselle.

"STOP ME — IF YOU'VE HEARD THIS ONE" (*Cosmopolitan*, July 1929). (Characters: Jerry Blades, Captain Byrne, George Cohan, General Charles Dawes, Luke Garner, Wallace Gore, John Janssen, Andy Mellon, Henry Wild Osborne, Charley Speed.)

The year is 1927; the scene, the Lambs' Club. Actor Charley Speed introduces Jerry Blades and Luke Garner, young playwrights, to famous "raconteur" Henry Wild Osborne, and then attends a committee meeting elsewhere. Osborne tells some Irish, Jewish, and Scottish jokes, seemingly funny. He laughed heartily anyway. Then he expatiates on his friendships with numerous celebrities. He and Charles Lindbergh, with a borrowed hat as usual, walked through admiring throngs and flew over Long Island. He was with comedian Fred Stone when Stone pummeled two bothersome Princeton athletes. He also mentions a dozen other famous people, from Irving Berlin to Flo Ziegfeld. Garner is thrilled. So is Blades, who says Osborne should write his memoirs. Osborne laments that his "chronic *Wanderlust*" prevents his doing so. Garner confesses to a wanderlust that does him no good. Blades says poor Garner would be happy living on trains, has been out of New York state only once, but had "a queer little experience" that time, and should tell Mr. Osborne. Garner says it was only a little mystery that involved him on his way to Chicago. Osborne assumes "a polite interest." Garner says, "I'll try to make it brief":

I was writing a play last year and read an act to George Cohan. He liked it and wanted to see the finished play. I completed it, learned Cohan was in Chicago, borrowed money, and took the Century heading west. In my section was a beautiful woman, about 25, holding a book, but staring, also bound for Chicago. At my dining-car table, a handsome, Spanish-looking man was also eating, as were "an elderly couple," who soon vacated their seats. The beautiful girl entered, sat at one seat, then saw the Spaniard. Both panicked. The Spaniard put $5 on the table and rushed from the diner. The girl clutched the table, blanched, and wrote her order with shaking hands. I finished my dinner quietly, and was paying when the waiter asked whether the other man would return. The girl blurted "No," then "bit her lip" in embarrassment, and left. Back in our section, she stared, gave me a note, asked me — not the porter — to deliver it to the Spaniard, undoubtedly in the club car, and please report back. I found him, handed him the note, and described everything to the girl. She was immensely grateful. I returned to the club car to clear the way for him to go see her. He was writing at a desk but left soon. When I returned to my section, her berth was curtained and dark. I arose at Elkhart, couldn't see the girl anywhere, or at Englewood. I questioned the porter. He said she got off the train at Toledo and, no, he saw no handsome dark man with her. She wasn't among passengers disembarking at Chicago's La Salle Street station. But the Spaniard was there, grabbed by "two men obviously detectives." I found nothing about my "mystery" in the papers. Incidentally, Cohan rejected my play.

Osborne praises Garner's anecdote but says he would have followed the escorted Spaniard. Speed returns and takes Osborne away. Blades tells Garner someone told him about Lindbergh's pushing through crowds to take off in his plane. Garner tells Blades that author Rex Beach told him he was with Stone when he confronted those athletes.

Two years later Blades and Garner, now successful Broadway playwrights, attend "a 'small' dinner" hosted by publisher Wallace Gore. Fellow-guest Osborne doesn't recognize the two writers when introduced. Osborne, betwixt "adoring women," tells some racist jokes, pauses, and agrees when Gore beseeches him to relate that story of his about "your Chicago trip[,] ... the girl and the foreigner." Osborne says his listeners mustn't tell reporters about his story, which follows:

Last month General Charles Dawes wired me to come to Chicago to discuss a certain subject. I boarded the Broadway Limited, started reading my Maupassant, but a beautiful blonde settled opposite me, looking ineffably sad. Andy Mellon's strolling by to chat interrupted my thoughts about romancing her. Declining Andy's invitation to dine privately, I went to the dining car, sat with a florid man, his fat wife, and a "healthy specimen of ... Scandinavian young manhood." The oldsters finished and left. The "young giant" began eating. The blonde entered, sat, then saw him. He saw her. Their glance "struck ... terror in each." Laying $10 by his plate, he left. She seemed about a swoon, then displayed "pseudo-calmness." I bolted my food. The waiter saw the giant's money and asked if he were returning. "No," the girl shouted, then "bit her lip" for speaking. Past Harrisburg, in our sleeper, the blonde gave me an envelope, had me — not the porter — give it to that young man, return, and tell her. I did. At Pittsburgh, when after trying to read in the club car I took to my berth, hers opposite me was dark and curtained. We neared Englewood. No sign of her. The porter, George, said she left the train at Fort Wayne not continuing to Chicago. At Chicago's Union Station, she didn't appear, but that man did. He taxied to "Stevens House"; I, to the Sherman, to refresh myself and prepare for "the General." The afternoon papers reported that an "unidentified young woman" had thrown herself before the Broadway Limited out of Fort Wayne and died. I reported details to the police, was assigned Captain Byrne to accompany me to Stevens House, where on the sidewalk we saw that "viking," a suicide by his nearby pistol. He was identified as John Janssen, son of a Chicago millionaire, and with "a wife and children in Lake Forest." The police revealed the blonde's name to me but not to the family of the other suicide, whose death they ascribed to "temporary insanity induced by illness." I know better.

Osborne ceases. The dinner ends. Blades quietly asks Garner what Osborne has "against brunets." Garner quietly wonders why Osborne doesn't travel via the New York Central.

Lardner gives this slight tale a flavor of contemporaneity, by having Osborne include in his acquaintance Irving Berlin;* Gerald Chapman; General Charley [Charles Gates] Dawes;* Marshal [Ferdinand] Foch (1851–1929, French soldier); Kid [William J.] Gleason;* boxers Jim Jeffries and Jack Johnson, [Charles] Lindbergh, Andy [Andrew] Mellon*; General [John Joseph] Pershing*; Herman Rosenthal; Fred Stone (1873–1959, actor); Lloyd Waner;* and Flo [Florenz] Ziegfeld.* To boot, Lardner even has Garner recall knowing novelist Rex Beach (1877–1949).

THE STORY OF A WONDER MAN: BEING THE AUTOBIOGRAPHY OF RING LARDNER (1927). Clifton Fadiman regards this "burlesque autobiography ... [as] really a savage, if not particularly interesting, piece of self-exposure." Fadiman thus reveals misguided and ingrained prejudice against Lardner. In truth, it is zany, self-satirizing, and partly fictional. For example, Lardner explains his being captain of the Yale football team. Jonathan Yardley rightly laments the fact that some readers up to 1976 regarded as truth this *Story*, which includes "inspired nonsense" if sometimes "silly." (Sources: Fadiman, 315; Patrick, 139–140; Yardley, 306)

STOUT ("Hurry Kane"). He plays first base on the St. Louis team the narrator is catcher on. Sam Morris bribed Stout and Digman to throw the game. They try, but St. Louis wins anyway.

"STRAGETY AND TRAGEDY" (*Saturday Evening Post*, August 31, 1918; RD) *see* ***THE REAL DOPE***

STREAK OF LIGHTNING (*The Big Town*). He is a racehorse defeated at Belmont by Herbert Daley's horse, Only One, ridden by Sid Mercer and making money for Daley, Finch, Ella Finch, and Katie.

STREET ("The Ides of June"). He managed the St. Louis Cardinals when they played the Brooklyn team. Danny was happy when Street left Bill Hallahan in to pitch to him. Danny calls Street "Big Bill."

Charles Evard ("Gabby") Street (1882–1951) played for the Cincinnati Reds (1904), the Reds and the Boston Braves (1905), the Washington Senators (1908–1911), the New York Yankees (1912), and the St. Louis Cardinals (1931). Street also managed the Cardinals (1929–1933) and the St. Louis Browns (1938). (It is unclear why Danny Warner refers to Street as "Big Bill.") (Source: *Baseball Encyclopedia*, 710, 1638)

STREETER, DICK ("Cured!"). He is a successful syndicated cartoonist in New York. His chronic alcoholism causes him to bribe Sammy Burns, his assistant, to do the work for him. Dick goes on and off the wagon so often that when he binges with three buddies for 40 hours, his wife Mary makes him consult Dr. Wendell. The result? He pretends to be cured so as to return to their marriage.

The Story of a Wonder Man: Being the Autobiography of Ring Lardner (1927) contains a reference to Ed Streeter, a probably fictional neighbor.

STREETER, MARY ("Cured!"). She is Dick Streeter's loving wife. They have no children. She makes excuses for his alcoholism, until, rebelling, she persuades him to consult Dr. Wendell. Dick pretends to be cured, because he prefers his wife to his drinking and his boozing cronies. Mary thinks her "hunch" that Dick could be cured was "right."

STREMMLE ("The Hold-Out"). Frank Conley, manager of Mr. Edwards's baseball team, was encouraged to believe that Stremmle, obtained from Indianapolis, was a seasoned player. Stremmle proved to be reliable.

Lardner probably derived the unusual name Stremmle from that of Philip Stremmel (1880–1947), who played for the St. Louis Browns (1909–1910). (Source: *Baseball Encyclopedia*, 2409)

STRIPP, JOE ("One Hit, One Error, One Left"). He was a Cincinnati baseball player and, according to Brooklyn player Danny, was the subject of trade rumors when Brooklyn was about to play "the reds" during spring practice in "Tampa the capitol."

Joseph Valentine Stripp (1903–1989) played for the Cincinnati Reds (1928), the Reds (1929–1931), for the Brooklyn Dodgers (1932–1937), and Brooklyn and the Boston Braves (1938). (Source: *Baseball Encyclopedia*, 1639)

STRONG, HELEN BIRD ("Who Dealt?") *see* **GRATZ, HELEN**

STROUD, PAUL ("Cured!"). He and his buddies Joe Gale and Rudy Miller are alcoholics. They drink with their friend Dick Streeter at Mike Clayton's establishment, challenge him to have too much, get him to join in song, and cause him to break an engagement to attend a dinner party with his wife Mary.

STRUNK In "Horseshoes," he plays utility outfield for the Athletics during their World Series against the Giants. In "Along Came Ruth," Keefe mentions Strunk's playing with the Boston Red Sox when Eddie Cicotte pitched well for the White Sox. In a later game, Keefe, upset when he saw his wife Florrie in the stand with a strange man, pitched badly when Strunk was at bat and later.

Amos Aaron Strunk (1889–1979) played for the Philadelphia Athletics (1908–1917), the Boston Red Sox (1918), the Red Sox and the Athletics (1919), the Athletics and the Chicago White Sox (1920), the White Sox (1921–1923), and the White Sox and the Athletics (1924). (Sources: *Baseball Encyclopedia*, 1639–1640; Hilton, 274)

SULLIVAN In "The Busher Comes Back," Keefe says that "Bill Sullivan the old White Sox catcher" talked him into accepting Comiskey's selling him to San Francisco to gain experience there, in the hope of being recalled to the White Sox. In "The Busher's Kid," Sullivan advised Keefe to "go over to the park the next 3 days and warm up a little," to prepare for "the city serious." Keefe says he "don't need to be in no shape to beat them Cubs."

William Joseph Sullivan Sr. (1875–1965) played for the Boston Braves (1899–1900), the Chicago White Sox (1901–1914), and the Detroit Tigers (1916), and managed the White Sox (1909). (Sources: *Baseball Encyclopedia*, 710, 1643; Hilton, 72)

SULLIVAN ("Tour No. 2"). He was the subject or the host of "the sullivan banquit" that Larry recalls buying a dress suit to attend.

SULLIVAN, TED In "Back to Baltimore," Mrs. Hayes, Boston Braves president, informed Dixon, her disgruntled manager, that she told "Mr. Sullivan" to scout for more gentlemanly players, "round the colleges." In "The Busher Beats It Hence," Keefe says that Ted Sullivan was among the speakers entertaining the crowd during a rain-out in Abilene, Texas.

George W. Hilton explains that Timothy Paul Sullivan (1852–1929) helped found the Northwestern League, the Western League, the Texas League, and the Southern Association. He gave Charles A. Comiskey his start in baseball (1879) and associated with him later. Sullivan managed several minor-league teams (1880s). He was managing director of the world tour (1913–1914) and wrote a pamphlet describing it (1914). Hilton adds that Mrs. Hayes's order to "Mr. Sullivan" to go scouting "is probably a reference to Ted Sullivan," although there is no evidence that Ted Sullivan, who did scout, ever did so for Boston. (Source: Hilton, 178)

"SUN CURED" (*Cosmopolitan*, January 1927; RLR, RU). (Characters: Jim Allison, Jess Andrews, Miss Clancy, Drew, Ben Drew, Ernie Fretts, Garvey, Leo Hargrave, Stevens, C. L. Walters, Bonnie Werner.)

Ernie Fretts, a successful insurance agent in Brooklyn, meets C. L. Walters, fellow New Yorker, on a train bound for Florida. Loud-mouth Fretts talks about himself and stops Walter from interruptions concerning himself. Fretts excessively partied with drink, poker (won $700 drunk), and on a double date with his friend Ben Drew, his girl named Stevens, and his own hopeful girl named Bonnie Werner ("Fine chance" he'd marry her). So his secretary, Miss Clancy (built like "a Channel swimmer"), tells him to vacation a month or so in Florida, and just "lay around in the sun and ... relax yourself." He agreed. When he couldn't find his old vacation items, he replaced everything. He bought golf clubs ($70+), tennis racket $14), terrific bathing suit ($32), and fishing tackle ($30+). He won $100 shooting 87 at golf some years ago "out on Long Island," plans in Florida to rise early daily, polish his tennis, swim, shoot 18 holes, "lay around on the beach," then "go to bed around nine, ten o'clock." Within three weeks he'll "be in the pink!" But after New Year's eve, Fretts and his Bonnie and Drew and his date all partied. He abandoned Bonnie, played poker again, and drank Drew's scotch. Bonnie came to his office, squeezed promises from him that he broke. That's when Miss Clancy — that's his secretary — ordered him to Florida. He's never been there, will look it over, might find "some great bargains" for vacation property. He hates to freeze during winters in New York.

A month later, Fretts and Walters chanced to return from Jacksonville by train together. Walters briefly queries Fretts, who at first doesn't recognize him. Walters soon learns that Fretts stayed at Miami's Flamingo, found two bottles of gin in his room left by the previous occupant who had to pack fast, phoned Leo Hargrave, of Cleveland, the "fella" who taxied with him from the station to the hotel, and in Hargrave's room they enjoyed "ten, eleven Tom Collinses" fast. They filled the empty bottles with water, carefully resealed them, greeted the owner when he soon returned, accepted his grateful thanks, and left. Fretts gloats he'd "like to heard" the man "when he took his first swig." He and his Hargrave went to Hialeah, drank, played roulette, and Hargave phoned a girlfriend he knew. Instead of double-dating with her girl friend, Fretts wrote Bonnie "to jump in an upper" and join him. Awaiting her, Fretts met "a couple dandy fellas" and enjoyed barbershop harmonizing with them. Six people — Hargrave, his girl, Ben Drew and his girl — they also came down — and Fretts and Bonnie — all had fun. The three men also played "the w'eel" and some "stud," and slept afternoons while the girls shopped. Fretts would try California's climate sometime, except for travel time wasted in getting there. Walters asks about golf. No. Tennis? No. Fishing? Takes all day; further, there was no swimming until noon. What about Ben, Bonnie, Stevens? They're asleep in their berths right now, wasted from the trip. Walters tells Fretts he looks great, to which Fretts replies that this trip was what he needed and that Miss Clancy — she's his secretary — has handled business just right.

The title "Sun Cured" is clever. Perhaps night-crawler Fretts's curative vacation combined maximum alcohol and minimal sun; or his Florida jaunt "cured" him of any desire to "just lay in the sun." Fretts says his New Year's hangover lasted until Monday, January 3; this date fell on 1927, apt since "Sun Cured" hit the news stands in January 1927. Walton R. Patrick properly calls the meeting of Fretts and Walters on the train returning them home a "farfetched coincidence." (Source: Patrick, 114)

SUTTON ("A Day with Conrad Green"). Like

the Schuylers, he and his wife attended Mrs. Bryant-Walker's party.

SUTTON, MRS. ("A Day with Conrad Green"). She too went to the Bryant-Walker party.

SWANSON ("The Water Cure"). Gullible scares Elmer Bishop in a fib that the only passenger that survived when a "boat turned a turtle" on Lake Michigan and sank was "a tailor named Swanson."

SWANSON, GLORIA (1897–1983). Actress. Chicago-born, she had bit parts in movies (from 1913), married (1916) popular actor Wallace Beery, accompanied him to Hollywood, and divorced him (1916). (She tried five more marriages.) She started her meteoric career once she met (1919) famed director Cecil B. De Mille (1881–1959). Financed by Joseph P. Kennedy, father of President John F. Kennedy, she produced her own films (from 1927). One of her 29 1920s movies was the classic *Sadie Thompson* (1928). She retired (1934) but returned, notably with *Sunset Boulevard* (1950). Gloria Swanson is mentioned in "The Love Nest" and "Mr. and Mrs. Fix-It." (Source: Ephraim Katz, 1362–63)

SWEDE, THE In *Treat 'Em Rough*, she is a servant helping Florrie Keefe with cooking, cleaning, and handling "little Al," the Keefes' son. Because she is Scandinavian, Keefe calls her "the ski jumper." She screams when she sees Keefe at the apartment unexpectedly. She tells him Florrie is briefly absent with friends. In *The Real Dope*, Keefe hopes Florrie isn't leaving their small son in the Swede's care too much. In "The Busher Reënlists," Keefe takes offense when Florrie threatens to fire the Swede and have him replace her. In "Along Came Ruth," the Swede works harder for Florrie, who is away from home establishing a beauty parlor. The Swede relays Gleason's message to Keefe, who again calls her "the ski jumper." In "The Busher Pulls a Mays," Keefe rationalizes that Al Blanchard can't visit the Keefes in Chicago because they lack a room for him "what with the Swede."

SWEET AND PRETTY (*The Big Town*). He is a racehorse at the Belmont. Herbert Daley gets a tip on him, bets, and wins, thus impressing Finch, Ella Finch, and Katie.

"THE SWIFT SIX" (*Red Book*, July 1916). (Characters: Jerry Donahue, Mrs. Dutton, Gross, Charley Gross, Ed Gross, Fred A. Gross, Grace Gross, Mary Gross, Alec Welsh,)

Fred A. Gross writes 11 letters, from Allison, Illinois, to his brother Charley.

Jan. 1. It's "going to be a lucky yr. for me." Fred has nothing "dew" on house payments until July. He won't throw "money a round like it was a drunkard sailor." He'll quit smoking and not "hawk and cough like you was going to loose a lunge." He used to "never take more then say 5 or 6 drinks a day and mostly beer," but he'll "cut out the booze all together" and also "make my cloths last as long is theyll hold together." Women "cant hold on to a chunk of money." Although Grace used to "be blowing it for cloths," she gave Fred $600 out of the "berthday present" from her father "to keep for her" in the bank because she couldn't "trust herself with that amt. in her own name." Fred wishes "prosterity to you and Mary."

Jan. 22. Grace was "scarred" to tell Fred something. He said even if she confessed murder he "wouldent squeal" on "the mother of my childern." She said she and Mrs. Dutton saw a $250 piano for sale at $110. She said even if they couldn't play it, it would look nice in their home. He said if she wants "a music instermunt" buy a flute, which she could "use ... for a roling pin." She sulked, thinking he'd let her "buy her old piano and higher a forner to come out evry night and play it." But no. So where "funs conserned" at home, "things is dull."

Jan. 24. Fred and his friend Alec Welsh saw "a grand" automobile show "up to the Coliseum" yesterday. You can get a "big size 5 passenger car ... for $550." With one, Fred wouldn't "half to patternize them suburban trains" where there's no "rm. enough to set down" without starving "your self for a few months 1st." Grace dislikes "leting loose of a little money on pleasure." With a car he could upstage his Allison neighbors, the "cheap stiffs." Still, he dislikes "liveing behind your means."

Jan. 27. Fred told Grace he had a "suprise." Was it that piano? No. He showed a "pitcher" of a "Swift Six," a fast $550 6-passenger car he put $490 on, "fob Detroit." He can "rake up $60.00 some wheres ... [from] freinds." Grace "got sarcastical." He offered to get his deposit back. She said "youd borry $550 some wheres and ... [not] take me rideing" because she wasn't willing to "spend a nichol" toward the car. They "argude a wile about what use was a piano." He "agrede to her proposition." Today they bought the piano "and payed $110.00 cash." When he showed her the Swift Six in the Coliseum, "she couldent help from likeing it." It starts with "your ft. on a peddle," has handy tools for repairs, "but they claim it dont hardley ever need nothing done to it." There's a top; "1 man can put it up or put it down." Everything looks "spick and spand." Fred took one "lesson driveing." After another tomorrow he'll drive his Swift Six "to hellangone" once "they got 1 to spare for me." He signs "F. A. Gross. motorist."

Feb. 15. "2 wks. late and not no sine of a car." The man offered to return the money Fred was "entittled to," but he didn't want the man "looseing his sale" and said he'd wait until today. Today, no car. The piano "come out the day after we bought it." Fred's kids climb on the stool, fall, and holler. Grace "tackles over the waves with 1 finger." The salesman gives Fred more "driveing lessons." He'd willingly be "runing up ... gasoline bills" rather than simply using gasoline "takeing gravey spots" off his overcoat.

March 3. The car came today. Fred "borried [$60] off of the chief to pay the bal.," learned "the freight from Detroit to Chi" was $20 more, promised to "pay it next month," and drove toward home. His hands got "pretty near froze." So he stopped "in a salloon and ..."thawed out." At 7:30 "in front of the house ... I tuted the horn." Grace appeared, saying she thought Fred was on the wagon. He showed her this wagon. They had no babysitter; so Grace sat in the car all "exited," but got cold, and cried. Fred promised "I and the babys and all of us would have a ride 1st. thing in the A.M." He'll worry later about a "garrage," since "2 above zero is to cold for rain or snow ... to nite."

March 5. The family hasn't had a ride yet. Grace is almost crying. The kids are "balling ... in the window." The car was frozen. Fred pressed "the self starting peddle" too hard. He got so cold he had to go sit on the stove. He called a "garrage man" who charged "the battrys up" and took "2 hrs. to get her runing again." A garage does nothing "as good as it can charge." Grace called Fred at work and ordered him "to buy a couple robes to help keep the kids warm in the car." They cost "$11.00 for the 2 cheapest." It will cost $10.00 per mo." to "keep your car in the town garrage." Fred is glad he "dident get a [more costly] dodge or a saxon 6."

March 9. Fred would sell Charley the car "fob Chicago." They "finely" fixed it yesterday and "give me a bill for $7.50." It made Fred sick, and Grace phoned the chief he was sick. Fred drove the car today, "a little shakey going in the loop." His pal Jerry Donahue stopped him at "5th ave. and Washington st.," and told him he needed a "Lisence." Stalled, Fred started but not "in neutruls and ... shot ahead." Jerry "yelled to the people to duck." Fred drove to headquarters. The boys working for him wouldn't take a ride. He called them "a cheap skate." One of them "for a fine trick" let the air out of "1 of the back end tires." Fred "dident never know it" at first. A nearby mechanic said he must "get a hole new wheel and a new tire." While the two conversed, "flames begin shooting out the front part." Fred said his "fine bunch of freinds" must have also been trying to "burn me up." Saying no, the mechanic asked if he put water in the radiator, laughed when Fred said "never put none in," and said he should have known better at first. Retaliating, Fred told him he probably first thought soap "was cheese and ett it." Back home, "Grace had a grouch." The house seemed like "the home for deef and dum muts," and "Grace snuck off to bed."

March 18. Fred has been "borring money." A new garage will cost "near $200.00 dollars," the tire and wheel $30. Fred "would brake ... in 2" whoever deflated his tire, but no one will "squeal." The boys say the tire might have been punctured. Fred said not a "tire that hadent had no ware." Someone said Fred's brains "aint had no ware" but "could get puntured." Fred's "lisence" cost $3.00. Grace griped about not having a ride yet in "your present to your famly." He replied that her piano "rented the hole liveing room" uselessly. A car "insurence" salesman came by, warned him his car might burn up, might kill someone, someone might steal it "when its laying in the st." Fred said not "a car that bellonged to 1 of the detective bureau." The man replied "probily not," since that "would be like stealing pennys from a blind man," and told him fire and "libilty insurence" would cost $40 a year. Fred said $40 around him resembles "whiskers on a flute."

March 22. "I got no car and who evers got it can keep it." Anyway, "Grace and the kids had 1 ride ... 4 or 5 miles," and can say "they road in their own car." Fred got the car yesterday. The day was beautiful, "and the sky dident have no sine of a cloud in them." They "was just turning in to Ogden ave. tords town" when it started raining. Grace insisted on continuing. It poured. Fred couldn't get the top up. They dashed "in to a salloon with a family entrence." They removed the kids' wet things, and "the props wife ... rapped the kids up" with blankets. "Grace begin howling ... and I thought Id be better off in the storm."

Outside, "the car wasent nowheres ... no body a round ... or nothing." Fred returned by the saloon front "to phone headquarters," saw "a big turk policeman," identified himself, and rebuked him for ignoring his beat. While Fred called the chief to report the theft, the "turk" disappeared. They all got home by "st. car and ... transfer[ring] twice." So many Swift Sixes are around that "it aint nothing but luck when you identify witch is yourn." Grace is bathing the kids as though the rain wasn't enough "till the last Saturday this yr." Fred is "in the pianos room" reckoning that the car cost him $849 including everything. Grace shouldn't be "splurgeing on pianos and cars ... they cant nobody aford unlest there millionares." Charley should keep Mary from having money, "or 1st. thing you know youll be like I," in trouble.

May 22. All's well. Fred "set down on Grace spending her money." They can't meet the July 1 mortgage, but the house is so "valuble" they mustn't "loose" it. Fred is learning to play the piano. It's better than a car. You "put your ft. down ... on the peddle with out unchargeing no baterys," it needs no "lisence," "new tires," "nor gasoline," etc. With practice on "hard cords" Fred "will be a reglar Crusoe." He has a "nice garrage" even though the piano doesn't need one.

Of interest regarding that $250 piano is Jonathan Yardley's report that soon after their marriage Lardner and his wife "blew $250 of $300 that Mr. Abbott [her father] had given them as a wedding present on the piano." (Source: Yardley, 129)

T., MR. ("Contract"). He is a bridge-playing friend of Lardner, who hopes in a postscript he won't take his story personally

"TAKE A WALK" (*American Magazine*, October 1933; RAB). (Characters: Agnew, Bleat, Edith, French, Horner, Hornsby, Knowles, Leslie, Lindstrom, Parvis, Rigler, Shayne, Snell, Terry, Traynor, Vaughan, Waner, Warren.)

The narrator, a baseball umpire, finds it strange being in this town when Bleat, a former umpire, is gone. Many people think umpires are crazy, inhuman, busy studying the rule book, and lacking fun outside work. Many umpires have lots of fun.

When games end, umpires rush out, well dressed. Some like foul tips so they can turn and ogle girls in the stands. Married umpires are different. Umpires avoid hotels putting up players, see movies and boxing matches, play pool, read and write letters in our hotel rooms, and dine with old friends but avoid talking baseball with them. The narrator's story follows:

I used to go to movies and take walks with Bleat, read newspapers, and write my wife briefly each week. Bleat wasn't that way, except in this town. He'd get long letters from Edith, his fiancée. Each time one would come, he'd treasure it until after breakfast, then read and re-read it for hours, write a lengthy reply, and sometimes get to the ball park too late for a comforting hot dog even.

Bleat avoided shop talk, raved about Edith instead, and solicited reinforcing comments from me on his age and goodness. I miss him most here, his home town for 14 happy years. Entering the big leagues to play, he arrived from Texas and answered Edith's mother's room-for-rent sign, and began always staying there when in town. He was 22; Edith, nine and cute. He was nicknamed Bleat because, despite his huge bulk, his voice was high-pitched.

Bleat paid $12 a week for room, breakfast, and supper, and occasionally insisted on paying more. A spinster school teacher and summer guests rented other rooms. When his arm failed, Bleat at 28 he became an umpire. Edith was 15, still a kid. Two years later he found himself eager to return from road games, and no longer for the customary sisterly kiss. Being stuck on Edith scared him.

Bleat figured Edith would begin regarding him as grandfatherly or an uncle with three feet in the grave. Finally, disliking suspense, he told her he loved her and, surprisingly, she responded and asked only why the long wait. Her mother was happy he'd waited until he was an umpire. The two lived with her mother, and Bleat became a well-paid fall-and-winter garage mechanic. By now, they would have been married five years except but for some luck. Was it fortunate or not? Well, Bleat had a sister in Texas. Her husband directed a small-town bank that failed, wrecking his moderate savings and requiring Bleat to support his sister, his brother-in-law, and their four children. Bleat's wedding was suspended.

Bleat stayed in this town, happy here with Edith. I liked seeing him happy. The town is really wretched; but we stayed, even though I got badly abused once while umpiring.

A year ago last May, Bleat and I were assigned to umpire here. The local team was doing far better than expected. Edith had seen Bleat umpire a few times, and now she and her mother began to attend regularly. Bleat got tickets for them and for Parvis. He rented the schoolteacher's room after she died. He was 19 or 20 and a ukulele player on the radio.

Pittsburgh came to town to play against the local club, which had won nine straight. Bleat umped behind the plate. Agnew, local third baseman, was hitting better than usual. He fumed when Pittsburgh's Traynor in the fourth inning spoiled his sure extra-base hit with one of his spectacular catches. In the seventh, French, Pittsburgh's fine pitcher, struck Agnew out, and to show contempt for Bleat he threw his bat at the bat boy.

Bottom of the ninth. Pittsburgh ahead 1 to 0. Two out. Agnes hit one off the fence, rounded third, slid past home plate, and tried to crawl back; but Pittsburgh's catcher Knowles tagged him, and Bleat called him out. Agnew, jumping up and griping, stood on Bleat's feet spiking them, grabbed him, and Bleat pushed him away. He fell, pretending to be hit. I tried to interfere but was knocked unconscious when the crowd swarmed the plate, angry at the loss. Bleat, though battered and bruised, visited me in the hospital, and I guessed something was amiss regarding Edith.

During the league's investigation, Bleat said only that he pushed Agnew, who claimed he was slugged. Bleat let me partly support his story without letting me say Agnew deliberately fell. Sadly, Edith saw by Bleat's bruises that he wasn't superhuman, felt Agnew was safe or should have been generously called safe anyway, and believed Bleat knocked Agnew down. She couldn't marry a bad-tempered man. Parvis sided with Edith, met Agnew, and offered him ukulele lessons; but Edith told him to wait until Bleat could meet Agnew socially and recognize his goodness. Bleat's eyes stopped merrily twinkling.

We stoically umped the rest of the series, despite our injuries and despite being booed. A newspaper manufactured a picture of Bleat standing over Agnew with fist doubled. Agnew's lies were believed. Our boss even rebuked Bleat. When we returned here again, the local team played New York, and Agnew's batting average was about the number in attendance—122.

Bleat went to Edith's mother's house. Edith was rushing to meet Parvis at the radio station but required Bleat to be home that evening to meet Agnew there. Coming to bat, Agnew jibed that Bleat was too old for Edith, that Agnew himself might like her, or he might let Parvis have her. Bleat remained silent. Agnew bat badly. But in the ninth, his team was a run ahead. With the bases full and no outs, Agnew, thinking there was one out, played a grounder by stepping on third and throwing to first instead of home. With the score tied, local knuckler Shayne filled the bases. Horner relieved him. Leslie, the New York pinch hitter, worked a full call. Then came the final pitch, a trifle out and law. "Take a walk," bleated Bleat.

The rest of the story? Agnew rushed Bleat, cursing and spiking his feet again. Bleat told Agnew any photo of the ensuing action would prove that the earlier photo of Agnew was phony, then slugged him six times. In attendance were Parvis and Edith. She got sick. Parvis told me afterwards that they were engaged and hoped Bleat wouldn't harbor hard feelings. Bleat now lives with his sister's family in Texas, works in a garage, and spoils her children with toys—but never a ukulele.

In "Take a Walk," the narrator presents Bleat's sad story in a folksy way but moseys too easily along a confusing time line. Lardner's handling of baseball details, however, is as sure as ever. The National League teams opposing vicious Agnew's team—Brooklyn, Chicago, Cincinnati, New York, and Pittsburgh—permit the conclusion that Agnew's unnamed home town could be Philadelphia, Washington, or St. Louis. It is most likely St. Louis, because the narrator says that fans will frequently ask an umpire they are friendly with "what happened to Hornsby the last place he was at." Rogers Hornsby (1896–1963) was the record-setting darling of St. Louis. He played second base for the St. Louis Cardinals (1915–1926, 1933) and the St. Louis Browns (1922–1937), managed the Cardinals (1925–1926) and the Browns (1933–1937, 1952), and played and managed elsewhere only briefly. He was elected to the Baseball Hall of Fame (1942). Four other real baseball players—Lindstrom, Terry, Traynor, Vaughan, and Wan—are mentioned in "Take a Walk" (and in other Lardner stories). Other baseball players in the story are fictional but with last names identical to those of real players, all of whom Lardner might well have known about. Agnew here is not Samuel Lester Agnew (1887–1951, active 1913–1919). French isn't Charles Calvin French (1883–1962, active 1919–1910), Richard James French (1893–1969, active 1917), Raymond Edward French (1895–1978, active 1920–1923), or Walter Edward French (1899–1984, active 1923–1929). The Pittsburgh Pirates had no catcher named Knowles. Leslie isn't Roy Reid Leslie (1894–1972, active 1917–1922) or Samuel Alexander Leslie (1905–

1979, active 1923–1929). And Snell isn't Charles Anthony Snell (1893–1988, active 1912), or Walter Henry Snell (1889–1980, active 1913). Robert J. Higgs applauds Lardner's satirical treatment of fans both in "Take a Walk" and in *Lose with a Smile*, which appeared at about the same time. Higgs says that "Lardner's most trenchant satire ... is directed not at the heroes but at the worshipers, the faithful fans, " who are part of "the masses," and whose "taste and judgment" Lardner "distrusted" because they foolishly "long for the miraculous and sensational in sports as well as in religion, drama, fiction, and the movies." Higgs then quotes, as many other critics do, the statement by Britain's brilliant Virginia Woolf (1882–1941) that Lardner's best fiction is "about games," which give him "a meeting place for the diverse activities of people whom a vast continent isolates," and where "there is baseball instead of society." (Sources: *Baseball Encyclopedia*, 726, 1034, 1158–1159, 1268, 1609; Higgs, 30; Woolf, 123).

TALMADGE, NORMA (1893–1957). Actress. Brooklyn-born, she appeared in about 250 Vitagraph silent movies (1910–1915), in other films (1916–1930), and occasionally with her brother-in-law Buster Keaton (1895–1966), the comedian. She failed after starring in two poor talkies, married three times, and died of arthritis aggravated by drug abuse. Lardner may have been thinking of beautiful Norma Talmadge when he named pretty Norma Gregg in "The Love Nest." Norma Talmadge is also mentioned in "Zone of Quiet." In a letter to family members (March 29, 1933), Lardner hints at Keaton's drinking problem. (Source: Spears, 397–400; Caruthers [1995], 277–278)

TAMARISK (*The Big Town*). She is a filly racehorse Herbert Daley bets on and wins at the Belmont. He also bets for and thus impresses Ella Finch and Katie.

TANGUAY, EVA (1878–1947). Quebec-born vigorous acrobat, vaudeville gyrating dancer, and brassy singer. She appeared the *Follies of 1907*, the first of the famous Florenz Ziegfeld* *Follies*; financed her own 5-reel film, *Energetic Eva* (1916); lost heavily in the Big Crash (1929); and returned to the stage (1930–1933). Eva Tanguay is mentioned in *Own Your Own Home* and *Treat 'Em Rough*.

TAYLOR ("Ex Parte"). He sold his family barn and four adjacent acres, near the Turnpike, to Jim and Mildred Dwan, after the Taylor family house burned. The Taylors may have torched the place for the insurance.

TAYLOR, BESS ("Anniversary"). She is Louis Taylor's wife. They live in Milton. Childless after 12 years of dull married life, Bess is so bored that she thinks passively of rejected suitors Walter Frayne and Jim Satterly. Walter and Jim also still live in Milton. When her friend Florence Hammond tells her that Florence's sister Grace was recently hit by her alcoholic husband Ed, Bess asks Louis, who has forgotten their anniversary this day, to give her not flowers but a punch in the eye. He calls her funny and continues reading his newspaper.

Elizabeth Evans concludes that "to Bess, violent abuse surpasses boredom and neglect," adding that "Lardner indicates that Bess's dilemma is not to be taken lightly." (Source: Evans, 68)

TAYLOR, DEEMS ("Absent-minded Beggar"). He is a librettist who goes to Europe to write his own libretto. John Knowles is inspired to seek Taylor in Naples and Paris.

Lardner oddly writes here about "a famous American composer, whom we will call Deems Taylor." Deems Taylor (1885–1966) was popular and influential as a New York composer, music critic, music consultant (for CBS, from 1936), journalist, and editor. He wrote for the New York *World* (1921–1925) and the New York *American* (1931–1932). His most ambitious compositions are *The King's Henchman* (opera, libretto by Edna St. Vincent Millay, 1927) and *Peter Ibbetson* (opera, 1931). Ring Lardner Jr. says that his father had "more than a casual acquaintance" with Taylor in New York. (Source: Lardner, Jr., 136)

TAYLOR, DUMMY In "My Roomy," The narrator says that Buster Elliott's loud singing makes "a boiler factory sound like Dummy Taylor." In "The Busher Beats It Hence," Keefe says that when he spoke to help entertain the crowd in Abilene, Texas, after a rain-out, "the boys" praised him by saying he "done just as well as Dummy Taylor could of." This alleged joke is cruel. In *The Real Dope*, Keefe cruelly says the only pitcher he knew who "couldn't talk ... was Dummy Taylor." In "The Courtship of T. Dorgan," Keefe says that Tom Dorgan was as tongue-tied in Miss Josie Mulvihill's presence as "Dummy Taylor."

Luther Hayden Taylor (1875–1958) played for the New York Giants (1900–1901), the Cleveland Indians and the Giants (1902), and the Giants

(1903–1908). George W. Hilton explains that Taylor was a deaf-mute and that after his baseball career ended he worked for the Illinois School for the Deaf. (Sources: *Baseball Encyclopedia*, 2422; Hilton, 179)

TAYLOR, LOUIS ("Anniversary"). He is Bess Taylor's husband. Their childless marriage of 12 years is safe but boring. He is rich Thomas Parvis's secretary and traveling companion, at $4,000 a year. He bowls on Wednesday nights. He reads newspaper reports aloud to Bess and repeats stale stories of his past and present. He doesn't hear all of her sarcastic rejoinders, and those he hears he misinterprets.

Louis Taylor may be likened to but is more hurtful than the earlier George F. Babbitt, in Sinclair Lewis's *Babbitt* (1922); each reads news items to his bored wife. Elizabeth Evans notes that Taylor "keeps her [Bess] in a comfortable condition, utterly oblivious to her as a woman or as a person. She is Celia Gregg [of 'The Love Nest'] ... enduring life with solitaire instead of bourbon. ... Her death wish and plea for attention go unnoticed." (Source: Evans, 68)

TELWELL ("Claude Diphthong, Student of Crime"). The mysterious Telwell bombing was solved by New York detectives Burke and McMahon.

TERRY In "Take a Walk," he is the playing manager of the New York baseball team in the game against Agnew's team. In "Lose with a Smile," Terry was playing first base when Danny, playing for Brooklyn, bunted successfully but was then picked off. In "Meet Me in St. Louie," Danny tells Jessie he was picked off first base because he wouldn't spike Terry. Jessie is proud of him and says players should wear spikeless tennis shoes. In "The Ides of June," Danny thinks Bill Terry will remember him fondly because Danny didn't spike him.

William Harold Terry (1896–1989) played for the New York Giants (1923–1936), managed the New York Yankees (1932–1941), and was elected to the Baseball Hall of Fame (1954). (Source: *Baseball Encyclopedia*, 711, 1661)

TESREAU, JEFF In "My Roomy," Big Jeff pitches for the New York baseball team and is "wabblin'" against Chicago. Buster Elliott pinch hits and deliberately strikes out, hoping stupidly that McGraw, New York's manager, will keep his word, said in jest, and hire him for doing so. In "Horseshoes," Big Jeff Tesreau is mentioned as the winning pitcher for the Giants during the third game of the World Series with the Athletics. In "The Poor Simp," Tesreau is mentioned as one of McGraw's pitchers when the narrator's team faced the Giants.

Charles Monroe ("Jeff") Tesreau (1889–1946) played for the Giants (1912–1918), after which he coached baseball at Dartmouth College (1919–1946). (Sources: *Baseball Encyclopedia*, 2426; Hilton, 355–356)

"THAT OLD SWEETHEART OF MINE" (*Cosmopolitan*, November 1929). (Characters: Betty, Boyer, Bess Cooper, Ralph Crane, Stella Crane, Fields, Lillian Fields, Gillespie, Hammond, May Judson, Charlie Prince, Herb Small, Mrs. Small, Fannie Towns, Will.)

Stella Crane, 39, has been married 15 years to Ralph Crane, a patent lawyer in New York. She is lonely and bored. Ralph keeps promising they'll have more gregarious activities when they can afford it. One morning she answers the phone, because her maid tends "to confuse names as similar as Gillespie and Hammond." A somewhat familiar male voice bets she can't guess who's calling. She hesitates before saying "Will," a former boyfriend she rejected when Ralph proposed and got her away from their "deadly" town. Queried, Will says he's not married "yet." Stella replies that Ralph is in Washington on business for two days. Although he disapproves of "wives who went around with other men," she sees no harm in accepting Will's invitation for lunch and a matinée. Asked for place and time, she decides on the Biltmore at 1:00, and tells him to pick the show. She dresses carefully, notes those extra pounds, and practices her cultivated smile.

Will remembers 50 women, including Fannie Towns and May Judson. Each, he knows, would return to him if he whistled. But right now he's to rendezvous with the only woman he ever loved and desired. Stella seemed "easily persuaded." The matinée won't end this day for him, he feels. He phones Betty, and lies that his colleague Charlie Prince just wired he's coming from Buffalo to meet Will all evening. Sorry; he'll call Betty tomorrow.

Will and Stella meet and have lunch. She seems a bit plumper, and her smile is different. His hair is thinner, and he seems slightly touched by dissipation. He boasts he's working again for Boyer, rehired at $15,000, $5,000 more than originally. She says Ralph makes $30,000, but city expenses for married couples prevent their saving very much. He suggests *Journey's End* for their show. She says she'll happily see it again. He suggests seeing *Follow Thru* tonight. She equivocates. He says he's had no love affair "since you." That appealing line he doesn't follow up, because their food arrives. Will attacks the scallops, which she says she loves how they're prepared at the Ritz. She says she still likes him. That appealing line he doesn't follow up. He's concentrating on the spumoni. To prove he's not stingy, he taxis her to the nearby theater and suggests dinner at the Ritz. She equivocates.

At the theater, Will admits he got these poor seats through his hotel clerk. Stella names a friend who got better seats when she saw the show earlier. Throughout the performance Stella whispers what's to happen next. She thinks a "Ssh!" is aimed at someone else. She says the drama will be made into a movie and asks if he likes "talking pictures. "'No,' says Will. 'Or people.'" Rattling on, she explains that what the captain in the drama drinks must be "colored water," asks whether Will "drink[s] much," and says he was silly when he did. He replies that he may fall off the wagon soon, would be silly again if he did, and when drunk hit women.

After the show, Stella declines dining with Will, saying she's tired and Will looks tired. He says "rye will fix me up." She says Ralph might return. Will tells her to use her judgment, puts her in a taxi, rushes to his hotel, and calls Betty. He explains: Charlie Prince just wired about car trouble in Binghamton and won't arrive till tomorrow. Will is glad to hear that Betty is still available.

Walton R. Patrick downgrades "That Old Sweetheart of Mine" when he says it merely "shows a wife and her former boyfriend fatuously attempting to warm up their old romance, though neither is really any longer interested in the other." Although Stella descends into a cardboard figure later in the story, Lardner's opening presentation of her as an isolated, lonely, and perilously bored urban wife is poignant. *Journey's End* (London, 1928; New York, 1919) was a grippingly realistic play about World War I trench warfare by British-playwright R[obert]. C[edric]. Sherriff (1896–1975). Sherrif served with the East Surrey Regiment, rose to the rank of captain, was wounded at Ypres (1917), and later became a popular playwright and novelist. The operative word in "That Old Sweetheart of Mine" is "old." Moreover, the titles *Journey's End* and *Follow Thru* ironically micro-symbolize Will's libido. (Source: Patrick, 127)

THAYER ("Mr. and Mrs. Fix-It"). He and his wife are Chicago friends of Ada, the wife of the narrator, who describes Thayer as mimic, yodeler, ocarina player, reciter of poetry, magician, and knot expert.

THAYER, HILDA ("Liberty Hall"). Hilda's husband Ralph, and mainly Hilda herself, prevent Ben Drake and his wife from enjoying "Liberty Hall," as she defines a restful time in the Thayer mansion, to which she invites them.

Jonathan Yardley defines the Thayers as "two pushy, nosy do-gooders who will not leave him [Ben] alone." (Source: Yardley, 333)

THAYER, MRS. ("Mr. and Mrs. Fix-It"). She is a friend of Ada, the wife of the narrator, who says Mrs. Thayer taught elecution, "gives readin's," and "gets a headache playin' bridge, so it's mah jong or rhum when she's around."

THAYER, RALPH ("Liberty Hall"). He and his wife Hilda invite Ben Drake and his wife to rest in their lavishly appointed home in Lansdowne, outside Philadelphia, only to bother him relentlessly after he reluctantly accepts.

"THEN AND NOW" (*Cosmopolitan*, June 1927; RU) *see* **"NOW AND THEN"**

"THERE ARE SMILES" (*Cosmopolitan*, April 1928; RLR, RU). (Characters: Arnold, Mary Arnold, Barney, Carmody, Ben Collins, Grace Collins, Edith Dole, Hughes, Jordan, Kaskel, Tim Martin, Noonan, Wurtz.)

Ben Collins, about 30 and married to Grace, is a huge, good-natured traffic policeman at Fifth Avenue and Forty-sixth Street in Manhattan. Instead of berating law violators, he criticizes with good-natured sarcasm. For example, he would say you must like London since you're on the wrong side of the street. Those ribbed are sometimes even "rather glad ... [they] had done wrong." One September morning, a girl in a blue-and-yellow Cadillac roadster is speeding south, despite the whistles of cops at Forty-eighth and Forty-seventh. Ben stops her by standing in the street. She has "the prettiest face he had ever seen," with an "ill-timed" and yet uniquely "irresistible smile." He pulls his London gag. She calls him "cute," says she's already late for a date on Eighth, asks when he gets off—"Four o'clock"—and says she might see him again when heading north. His relief appears; so Ben walks south to Thirty-sixth, watching northbound cars—no luck—then, too late to hitchhike as usual, takes the subway to his Bronx home.

Remembering that smile, Ben kisses Grace with surprising fervor. Knowing Grace's dislike of anecdotes about pretty women, he typically tries her patience with half-fictional yarns about fender-benders and his defusing quips. During an "unaccustomed silence," she asks what he's thinking. He foolishly mentions "a gal in a blue Cadillac." He "give her hell." "Was she pretty?" He "didn't notice." "[Y]ou probably just smiled at her." Instead of describing her smile, Ben suggests taking in a show, featuring Joe Frisco and Charlie Chaplin.

After 4:00 next week, that girl stops and asks if she can drive Ben home. He explains his four-to-midnight shift this week, but eight-to-four next week. She promises to drive by when he's off Monday afternoon. "If you live," he joshes. She says he's her "incentive." That night he can't find "insentive" in Grace's dictionary.

After Ben's week, the girl arrives on Monday and Ben jams himself into her roadster at four to be driven home. Although he complains that she drives recklessly, he makes no effort to get out. They talk flippantly. He says that drivers giving him a lift question him, and that he avoids tedium by fibbing. Saying "grand! ... lie to me!," she interviews him as others do. Does he get cold in the winter? He says an old lady asked that, and he replied he'd halt traffic and lean against a hot radiator. Does he get hit? He's seldom run over. Tired standing on your feet all day? Better than standing on his hands. Angry I called you "cute"? Never. They drive past his home. He insists on hitching back. She says she often visits her sister in Greenwich Village on Mondays. They make a date two weeks hence.

That Monday he spots her heading south in the rain. She picks him up on returning. Seeming somber, she asks his name. He tells her and says he could get hers by demanding her driver's license. Confessing she lacks a license, she says she's Edith Dole. She asks if he's married. No. She says she'll marry, hesitantly, a man from Buffalo who'll be her eager father's partner. Extricating himself from the top-up roadster near home, he beseeches her to drive carefully, for her fiancé's sake — and his! Her radiant smile is memorable. Grace, soaked by rain after a card game, tells Ben to have a hot bath, and plays her favorite "Ohman and Arden record" again.

Before breakfast Ben reads a newspaper account that motorist Miss Edith Dole, 22, of Rye, was killed skidding into a street-car on Fordham Road, the Bronx, at 4:30 P.M. yesterday. Ben, stunned, lies to Grace that he must attend a parade at 7:00 A.M. A few weeks later Ben snarls at a Mr. Hughes of White Plains, when in his Studebaker he violates traffic regulations. The man apologizes, offers to give him a lift to the Bronx as he's done before, but then says Ben looks so different that he must not be the "fella" he thought he recognized.

The title of "There Are Smiles" comes from the popular 1917 song "There Are Smiles," by Lee S. Roberts and J. Will Callahan. The time of action in "There Are Smiles" is mid–1920s, evidenced by references to "a 1922 Buick," Phil Ohman* and Victor Arden,* Joe Frisco, and Charlie Chaplin,* and, sadly, by Tim Martin's talking twice about "Heebs" unrebuked. Joe Frisco, really Louis Wilson Joseph (1889–1958), born in Milan, Illinois, was an illiterate, stuttering jazz dancer. He debuted in the 1918 *Follies* of Florenz Ziegfeld* and became famous for his vaudeville "Jewish Charleston" (1920s, 1930s). Compulsive gambling caused him to die penniless. Clifford M. Caruthers presents evidence that Lardner's friends highly praised "There Are Smiles," which Douglas Robinson dismisses as merely sentimental. Anyway, memorably so. Matthew J. Bruccoli in admiration says that "[a]ny one who has not read 'There Are Smiles' ... has an imperfect understanding of Lardner's genius." (Sources: Bruccoli, xi; Caruthers [1973], 122; Robinson, 166)

THOMAS, CHARLIE ("Anniversary"). He is a car mechanic in Milton. Walter Trumbull has him repair his car. Charlie finds it was out of gas.

THOMAS, MR. ("A Caddy's Diary"). He is the vice president of a local bank and is a member of the golf club where the diarist caddies. Mr. Thomas won't play golf on the Sabbath but regularly cheats. He even cheats to share first prize, 9 golf balls, instead of taking second prize, 6 balls, and letting Charley Crane, his employee at the bank, gain first prize, 12 balls.

THOMAS, MR. ("Fore!"). He is the richest man in Allison, Illinois, and is a member of its golf club. Mr. Carlton is a better player, but Mr. Thomas's handicap enables him to advance above him in the tournament. Fred defeats Mr. Thomas by cheating. He and Mr. Carpenter, another golfer Fred mistreated, get even by stiffing Fred for a wine bill.

THOMAS, MRS. ("A Caddy's Diary"). She is Mr. Thomas's fat wife. She plays golf badly and cheats Miss Rennie to win 25¢.

THOMAS, MRS. ("Fore!"). She is rich Mr. Thomas's wife. He deliberately keeps her from witnessing his golf game against Fred, telling him she had better things to do. Fred erroneously concludes that Mr. Thomas fears playing before a crowd.

THOMPSON, TOMMY In "One Hit, One Error, One Left," Danny writes Jessie that "there is a infielder Tommy Thompson" whose nickname, according to Casey Stengel, is "Al Fresco," not because he is from Frisco but because he was born outdoors. In "Holycaust," Danny says that Fresco Thompson believed that Pearson, a Giants pitcher, is due to be sent down to Bridgeport. In "The Ides of June," Danny feels "scarred" because Tommy Thompson might be "sent some wear" and they'll miss his jokes. To cut the Brooklyn squad to 23, Max Carey sent Thompson to Hartford.

Rupert Lockhart ("Tommy") Thompson (1910–1971) played for the Boston Braves (1933–1936), the Chicago White Sox (1938), and the Chicago Cubs and the St. Louis Browns (1939). (Source: *Baseball Encyclopedia*, 1669)

THORNTON (*The Big Town*). He marries the supposedly widowed Maizie Shaw in "Bridget Sees a Ghost," Jimmy Ralston's play. Not to worry. The bigamy prevails.

THORPE, JIM In "The Busher Beats It Hence," Keefe reports that the world-tour baseball teams have "some ... real stars," including Thorpe. In "The Busher Abroad," Keefe mentions "jim Thorpe" and says that "indian Thorpe" knows how to fight the dangerous birds called Thomas Hawks allegedly encountered in "the indian Ocean."

James Francis Thorpe (1886, 1887, or 1888–1953) played for the New York Giants (1913–1915), the Cincinnati Reds and the Giants (1917), the Giants (1918), and the Giants and the Boston Braves (1919). George W. Hilton, noting that James Francis Thorpe was "America's finest all-around athlete of the period," reports that he was an Olympics star (1912), a great football running back, and a fine baseball outfielder but a weak hitter. This may be added: Thorpe was a Native American of Sac and Fox ancestry. He won his Olympic gold medals in the pentathlon and the decathlon. His victories were disallowed (1913) when it was discovered he had played semi-professional baseball. In later life he played more football, appeared in a few movies, lectured on Native-American culture, and was a seaman in the merchant marines in World War II. He was elected to the Professional Football Hall of Fame (1963). His Olympic medals were restored to his record posthumously (1982). James E. Elfers, when narrating the events of the 1913–1914 world tour, enthusiastically praises Jim Thorpe, as well as Thorpe's wife. The two were honeymooners on the trip, and she kept a journal. (Sources: *Baseball Encyclopedia*, 1670; Elfers, xix and *passim*; Hilton, 179, 180; Light, 487; Spears, 388)

"THREE KINGS AND A PAIR" (*Saturday Evening Post*, March 11, 1916; GT) *see* ***GULLIBLE'S TRAVELS***

"THREE WITHOUT, DOUBLED" (*Saturday Evening Post*, January 13, 1917; GT, RLR) *see* ***GULLIBLE'S TRAVELS***

TIERNEY ("Hurry Kane"). He is standing near the plate when Hurry Kane shows his newly met St. Louis baseball players his stuff. The pitch is so fast it that blows Tierney's cap off.

TIM ("The Water Cure"). He owns an establishment which Gullible visits to check on White Sox statistics.

TINKER In "The Busher's Honeymoon," Tinker was a Federal League official that Keefe approached for a pitching assignment after Comiskey refused Keefe's demand for more money. Tinker couldn't negotiate, because Keefe was under contract with Comiskey. In "The Busher's Welcome Home," Joe Tinker is named as the president of the federal league Keefe is fooled into unavailingly trying to negotiate joining. In "Insomnia" the sleepless author remembers Tinker.

Joseph Bert Tinker (1880–1948) played for the Chicago Cubs (1902–1912) and the Cincinnati Reds (1913, 1916), and managed the Reds (1913) and the Cubs (1916). In between, he managed the Chicago Whales of the Federal League (1914–1915). Tinker was elected to the Baseball Hall of Fame (1946). (Sources: *Baseball Encyclopedia*, 710–711, 1672–1673; Hilton, 114)

TOBIN ("Along Came Ruth"). Keefe complains that when he was pitching for the White Sox against the St. Louis Browns, Tobin scored the Browns' only run because Felsch, White Sox centerfielder, misplayed his position. Keefe notes that in the Cleveland-St. Louis game later, Francis, Cleveland's rookie pitcher, hit a triple over Tobin's head.

John Thomas Tobin (1892–1969) played for the St. Louis Browns (1916–1925), the Washington Senators and the Boston Red Sox (1926), and the Red Sox (1927). (Sources: *Baseball Encyclopedia*, 1673–1674; Hilton, 263)

TOBIN, ANNE LARDNER (born 1883). Lardner's sister, christened Anna. She graduated from high school at Niles, Michigan (1901). When *Zanzibar*, the musical comedy for which Lardner wrote most of the music and lyrics, was performed in Niles (1903), Anne played the piano. Donald Elder describes her as "a musician of professional calibre." She married Richard G. Tobin* (1908), who roomed with Lardner when the two worked on the Chicago *Inter-Ocean* (1907–1908). Lardner brought Tobin home to Niles, and introduced him to Anne. Lardner and his brother Rex Lardner* shared a Chicago apartment with Anne and Richard Tobin (1908–1910). Ring Lardner Jr. says that "Rex [Reginald Lardner*] and Anne ... [were] the two members of his family that mattered most" to Lardner. After Lardner's marriage (1911), he and his wife and the two Tobins remained close friends and often socialized. The Tobins' son Richard Lardner Tobin graduated from the University of Michigan and was briefly a reporter, as was Lardner's son John Abbott Lardner* at the same time, for the New York *Herald Tribune.* Clifford M. Caruthers notes that Richard Tobin was later senior vice president of *Saturday Review*. (Sources: Elder, 10, 31, 58, 243; Lardner, Jr., 43, 68; Caruthers [1995], 20, 242, 259)

TOBIN, RICHARD G. Lardner's brother-in-law, called Dick and Tobe.

TOMMY ("Anniversary"). He replaces Berger, too drunk to bowl one night, according to Louis Taylor's dull story to his bored wife Bess.

TOMMY ("The Crook") *see* **CONNOLLY**

TOMMY ("My Roomy") *see* **LEACH**

TONIO ("The Facts"). At Tonio's New York restaurant Billy Bowen meets Ellen McDonald. Both fall in love, with dire consequences.

TONY ("Back to Baltimore"). Doc, the Boston Braves sprint trainer, took William Baker, Jr., to Tony's restaurant in St. Louis in an unsuccessful effort to get him drunk and therefore fired.

George W. Hilton names and provides addresses of two St. Louis eateries, Tony Faust's and John Tony's, as possible sites of Baker's sandwich and lemonade lunch. (Source: Hilton, 443)

TOPPING ("Hurry Kane"). He is a young player on the St. Louis baseball team. He informs Hurry Kane that Kane's supposed girlfriend Evelyn Corey is really gambler Sam Morris's intimate associate.

TORRENCE, FLORENCE ABBOTT Lardner's sister-in-law. She married Paull Torrence. An Abbott family story has it that Florence fainted when Paull proposed to her in a rowboat on Lake Wawasee, where the Abbott family owned a vacation cottage. (Source: Lardner, Jr., 49)

TORRENCE, PAULL He was the husband of Lardner's sister-in-law Florence Abbott Torrence, and was from Indianapolis, Indiana. (Source: Caruthers [1995], 133)

"TOUR NO. 2" (*Saturday Evening Post*, February 13 and 20, 1915). (Characters: Prof. Baker, Ed Burns, Kate Burns, Lawrence Martin Burns, Minnie Burns, Callighan, Chambers, Mrs. Chambers, Flynn, Mrs. Flynn, Fogarty, Mrs. Fogarty, Miss Griffith, Joe Harding, Miss Hendricks, Prof. Hunter, Johnny, Hugo Kelly, Klinke, Miss Lamont, Mike, Pat, Pat, Louis Shaffer, Sullivan.)

Larry Burns, who calls himself L. M. Burns, Larry M. Burns, and Lawrence Martin Burns, writes 21 letters to his brother Ed ("Eddy") Burns. Both men are "irish."

From "Chgo." are the first three letters. "July 1.19.14." Larry reluctantly promises Minnie, his "dutch" wife from Milwaukee, to take her to "europe." He'll leave his "over $1000.00 a mo." garden business in her cousin Louis Shaffer's hands but wants to return for "the primeries." He wishes Ed and Kate, Ed's Irish wife, could go too, but he says it would cost Ed too much.

"Chgo. Ill. July 3. 19.14." Larry has planned with "a steam boat co." for a $500, three-week trip to "plymouth & England" and back, maybe including Ireland. When Minnie returns from visiting her mother in "milwaukee," she'll agree.

July 10. Minnie demands a trip to real "europe." Since "a man dont feel like being nasty to a woman even his wife," they'll take the "prince S. N. katrina" on "tour no. 2" from "N.Y. city to bremen & from there to Germany," where Minnie says "the dutch word for beer is the same as american," fortunately for Larry. Other places include "brussels & Bellijum" and Paris. All for 64 days and almost $1,300. Such a trip "would bankrup you wouldent it Ed. so your lucky you dident marry no dutch girl or no pretty 1 thats got these nosions ... a bout travveling."

"N.Y. city. July 22." Larry's friends gave him "some send off," and he arrived at the train "lit up." Minnie, with "new close," was "dressed up like a horse." In their hotel Minnie is mad because he wouldn't let her buy "more close" along "5th. av." Their fellow travelers are a married couple, two male teachers, and three girls, about 25, pretty but "proud & stuck on there self." Larry said the girls could have "1st. cabin," thus "brakeing the wind for us" in "2d. cabin." That shut the girls up. Before readying their voluminous "bagage," Larry will slip in some "towls thats got the king charles [hotel] printed on them," to show when "Minnies folks ... comes to visit." Larry advises Ed not to take "wooden nickles" or "no bad money."

Six letters follow from "on the prinzessin Katrina." July 25. Professor Baker, one of the teachers, explained how letters to Ed could be placed in "a male box right on the boat," to be "put ... in a brrl." for "speed boats" to take to New York. He also showed Larry the steerage where "steerage is done at." Minnie "chin[s] with the other skirts" on deck. Three "saloons" are enough for Larry, though there are four. The boat is huge, with "4 hunerd pgrs." in first cabin and only 330 in Larry's less crowded "2d." The meals are enough "to choke a horse," especially when Minnie made Larry "ware the soup and fish at supper." The teachers dress that way. Their table includes their seven fellow tourists: Professor Baker; Professor Hunter, from an Ohio college; the Misses Griffith, Hendricks, and Lamont, all from "What Cheer iowa"; and Mr. and Mrs. Chambers, from "down south some wheres." Minnie told Chambers that Larry was a doctor. She won $3 playing rummy.

July 26. Larry writes Ed with "pensil," because he can't find "there pen & ink." He boasts of winning $120.00 in a $1.00 limit [poker] game" lasting "till 6 this A.M." Baker, calling him "doc," suggested he could win more by playing richer first-class passengers.

July 28. Larry "took them" for $55 more at cards, then had to play that "rummy game" with Minnie and the three girls. They called him "dr. Burns," asked how to treat hay fever, and laughed when he "kided a long" by calling "hit the hay" a cure. Miss Hendricks got Miss Griffith to tell Larry his "fortun" with cards. She said he'd have only "good luck from now on." Annoyed, Minnie said he gave Miss Griffith 50 cents simply because she was pretty. He was bored walking with Minnie "70 miles" on deck, with "no new senery but nothing but the same ocean." Voyages are "all ok" if you don't want "no excitment for a wile."

July 30. Larry told a joke with "nothing wrong ... only just them 2 words." But the girls, the Chamberses, and Minnie were offended. He asked "the profs" to have wine with him. They let him "lap up the most of it," then played poker with him. He lost $185. He couldn't get more money from Minnie "with out a shot gun." The three men went on deck, but a storm broke so bad that soon "no prgs. was to be a loud" there. For two days and nights Larry was so sick he wished some one would shoot him "threw the tempul." He was sicker than when "we was kids & laped up them manhattan cock tails." Minnie is "still in her birth." Instead of hanging a murderer they should make him take "a bout 2 trips like this here ... [to] finnish him." All "them swell meals ... [is] waisted."

July 31. The weather turns "grand." The captain says even the ship lost some cargo. Baker kidded "dr. Burns" about seasick remedies. The girls become friendly, but not the Chamberses or Minnie, who thinks Larry "was ruff & not the ocean." Still, he's glad he "fixed it up to come & let Minnie come a long." Life for you, Ed, must seem "pretty slow ... shut up in Det."

Aug. 1. Ed, some "news ... on the boat" from "a wire lest tel." reports "theys a war bet. germany & England & france & russia and pretty near all the countrys in europe accept norway & ejypt." If he'd known earlier, Larry would have ordered the captain to drop him off in England or Ireland. Baker says that in Bremen if a man don't speak "dutch" they "murder him a live." Baker says at least Larry's "wifes a dutch man" and if he's killed "a pretty girl like she" will be safe, because "may be the zar him self will fall for her." Larry is too "nervus" for Baker to "lern" him "dutch." He doesn't want, if not killed "right a way," to be "lockd up" with those "no good" Chamberses. Larry writes that if the "dutch" get Minnie, Ed and not her "people" must inherit Larry's "place." Her "dutch friends" must have "tiped her off" how to have Larry disposed of. He'd marry "some old stiff without no looks" if he could "do it over again." Ed should tell "pres. Wilson" what "these dutch" have done to him. Baker promised to "male this letter" and look up Ed later. Larry won't "be burred in the semmitery" he bought the lot in. Minnie has locked her "st. room door" and is crying, because he told her she "insisst[ed] on us comeing." Larry wishes he'd married "a plain irish girl like you," Ed.

Two letters follow from "Bremen, Germ." Aug 2. Nothing happened; so Larry, not Baker, "maled the [last] letter." Nobody looks angry. If "there soldiers ... start after us," the tourists can say ""wear america citizens" and "pres. Wilson" would handle matters. But everyone speaks "dutch," even Minnie. Some "dutch man" might call her "deary" or ask "would she pass the pickles," and Larry "wouldent know." Baker is asking about the next boat home. While Minnie is "laying down" in the hotel, Larry wishes they'd vacationed "at cedar lake or st. Joe." But "you cant tell a woman nothing." The "What Cheer ia." girls want to tour "Germ. & up to Venice," etc., and say the war will end soon. Baker and Hunter disagree. Baker explained: Somebody "from Hungry" with his wife was shot, and "both ... croked." The police blamed "Servia," whose "people ... got sore." Everyone took sides, the way Ed would "if 1 of your freinds got mixed up," hurt, and Ed could help. Why fight people from "diffrunt countrys" talking "diffrunt languidges," when they can't even understand what you're calling them? Larry will wire Ed from New York about visiting in "Det."

Aug. 2. Larry writes to say "wear all o k." Baker couldn't find "a boat leaveing tomorrow" and learned from "the america counsil" that they should take "a train ... to some new trull country," where, Baker explained, war is "against the law." The "2 new trull countrys" are "holland & Belljum." Since the Chamberses, the girls, and Minnie wanted "holland," to keep speaking "dutch," Larry talked Minnie into "Brussels," which is "the capitle" of "Belljum," by promising to get her a "Brussels carpet," which is cheaper than "a Orentul rug" she wanted. Hunter will "stay here in germ. & write a book a bout the war." Baker will accompany Larry and Minnie in order, Baker insists, to "hear some more of my storys."

Seven letters from "Brussels, Bell." follow. Aug. 4. "Baker says england had declaired war on the dutch men for walking on Belljum & I don't see what is it to england." If someone wanted to "walk from 35 to 34 st.," Larry wouldn't allow him onto his sidewalk but would make him "walk out in the middle of the st." Also, why fight Germany "2 or 3 days" and only then declare war? It's like Larry's hitting "you in the jaw & then ... say Im sore at you." Baker says they're safe because the "dutch men" aim for Paris and won't detour through "Belljum," any more than someone would go "to new Orleans from Chgo ... threw Omaha." Also, "the irish has called off there quarl with england" and plan to help "clean up germ." Minnie enjoys Brussels "1st. strate." It's "a live town." They can go "a short distence" to "Austin," then "england to N.Y. city." Larry can't play cards here, because he lacks money and can't understand their talk.

Aug. 6. It seems "the little Belljums ... licked ... the dutch men down to Liege." And Minnie thought "the dutch men" was tough. The town has "went plum nuts ... holering like ... collidge boys thats had a bronix cock tale." It's "like the old 1st. ward ball a bout 5 a m." Rumor says "4 hunderd thousend dutch men" were killed by "little Belljums"; so "the war is pretty near over." Larry can "pick a winner eh Ed?" When home again, he'll kid any "dutch man" coming "to the place ... & make them sore."

Aug. 10. Now the truth now is "the Belljums ... may of killed 2 or 3 dutch men," not thousands. "The dutch men beat them Belljums down to Liege," which they don't pronounce "like the national or american Liege." They're coming indirectly toward Brussels, the way "a dutch man" might go "from Det. to Chgo." by way of "st. Louis." They want Paris. The Brussels "mare" says he won't "try & stop" them. If Larry were "mare," he'd give them "the fight of there life," except "for geting Minnie and prof. Baker in trouble." He must mind his "own busness."

Aug. 16. There are "so many diffrunt storys" about "the dutch men" that Larry has quit "worring" about what to "beleive." H's "near broke" and must save for "our fair from Austin to england," then get more money there for "our ticket acrost the ocean." Baker has friends Larry can "borry ... off." They could walk to Austin but for "Minnies feet hurting her."

Aug. 22. "The mare surenderd the town to the dutch men yest." It was like when Larry's "elks had the convenshon in denver" and were told "the town is yrs." Larry has seen so many "dutch" soldiers he thinks they may be marching "threw" town twice. Baker says not so. They all look so "a like" that maybe "none of them know weather he was himself or some body else." Ed resembles Larry, but "would you like to look like a bout a million other dutch mens ... walking a long"? When in Paris, "there wont be enough hotels & bording houses" for them. Paris will also lack "liver worst & pretsils ... to feed the hole Germ. army." Larry wishes he owned a "paris brewry." Baker warned him that the "dutch" might read one of his critical letters; if so, he'd "get the P O dept. after them & its a peneteniary ofense."

Baker talked with "dutch officers in dutch" and said some Germans will occupy Brussels while the rest enter Paris. Larry says where "Im consernd" let them "all go down to paris or Pittsburgh." When "things is quited down," he and Minnie can leave.

Aug. 24. Baker has talked to "some dutch officers in there own languige." One, named "Klinke or how ever you spell it," also talks "america," is planning a party with welcome food for Baker, Larry, and Minnie, and will "send us down to Austin in a auto mobile" free. Larry would like to get home in time "for the primerys" and before Shaffer has "played to many tunes on the cash rejister."

Aug. 26. Klinke invited the three Americans to lunch. Larry ordered plenty, including wine, because "my stumick felt like the colliseem." Baker "coxed" him into telling "irish" stories. Then the officers wanted stories "a bout dutch men." The last one he told was about an Irishman drinking with a German and shouting "hock the kiser," meaning "hurah for the kiser in dutch"; the two argued, and the German asked the Irishman for a dime to go drink elsewhere; the Irishman said "why dont you hock the kiser?" The German officers weren't amused. One hauled Larry to a prison in the hotel and ordered him to shout "hock the kiser" once every hour. Larry did so "4 or 5 times" but only because an officer pointed a gun at him; "no dutch man could make me do nothing with there bear fists." Klinke appeared, told him Baker and Minnie were being driven to Austin, and said Larry could leave but would have to walk there.

"Austin, Bell. Sept. 1." Baker and Minnie went by car to "Ostend," as "they spell it ... over here." The Germans promised to scare without hurting Larry, for "insulting the emper of Germ." He walked until his feet got so sore that he wished "dutch feet was as sore." Part of the time he was "rideing in farmers waggons" and had to beg "like a bum" for "a couple peaces of bread." Baker got "money off of the america counsil," for passage to Dover and then "N. Y. city." Minnie wanted to "in joy our self" in London first but figured Larry would "tell them some storys," insult "king Geo. & ... may be get us all shot." She said "you look like you should ought to sleep in the bath tub." Austin is "full of refuges." Baker caused all this trouble by "interduceing us to them dutch officers."

"Chgo., Ill. Sept. 11." Larry, Minnie, and Baker went by crowded boat to "dover," then "lay a round London 2 days," then went by "train to south Hampton." For their return to New York they had "rotten rooms" for "the longest 7 days I ever seen." There weren't card games; anyway, Larry lacked spare money. The Chamberses and "them 3 girls" were also aboard. They wanted Baker to tell what happened, but he got Larry to do so instead. Larry explained how he was jailed "by the dutch men," broke out to avoid being shot spying, slugged a "dutch officer" for flirting with Minnie, and saved a "Belljum woman" from having her house burned. Baker said the "storys" got better on retelling. Larry must "remmember" everything, for when Eddy and Kate come visit. The trip cost "a bout 8 hunderd dollars all to gather ... includeing what I lost in the poker game." Larry's friend "Joe harding" says Shaffer hasn't been around lately. Minnie lost some "close" and demands "a hole new out fit." She also wants a real trip, this time "to black Lake Mich. where her sisters been all summer ... up in Mich. near holland." "Near Holland, I says." He won't leave "the 3rd. ward again." Minnie can go visit the "lincoln pk." zoo. Baker "promussed" to visit and hear "them storys of mine" again.

"TOUR Y-10" (*Metropolitan*, February 1917). (Characters: Boler, Mr. Coles, Mrs. Emerson, Violet Emerson, Mr. Garrett, Hetty Gould, Kate Hayes, Della Ingles, Paula Ingles, Don Kellogg, Mr. Lester, Bruce Patterson.)

Violet Emerson keeps a diary of her vacation from Chicago to Yellowstone and back:

"Saturday August 26 [1916]." Kate Hayes bravely sprang the idea on me in June. I figured we lacked money. She said I could save by not "plunging in silk stockings," further, if I needed some money she'd help. We'll leave "grimy old Chi" for two weeks. Dear Kate isn't pretty, being big, tall, dark, with glasses. I'm a slender blonde. I tell her "beauty is only "skin deep, or something." When I wondered if it's "proper for two girls" to travel alone, Katie reminded me that Della and Paula Ingles vacationed happily two years ago. I called some girls to tell about our trip. Bruce Patterson and Don Kellogg will see me off; hope they're friendly to Katie.

Sunday, August 27. Mr. Garrett, in charge of our trip, says trains are safe. He's "grand" and helpful. Bruce and Don saw me off last night. Don brought a "dear bouquet"; Bruce, some chocolates. Only Kate's sister and brother-in-law saw her off. Bruce and Don "looked daggers at each other." Don asked me to kiss him good-bye. I said only a fiancé could do that. The train started. I pitied Kate, told her I wished I was ugly "as a mud fence or something." I probably won't marry, since I love my independence. Katie said she'd sleep in the upper berth. I didn't like undressing behind that curtain. The train's "noise and jar" bothered me. Next morning washing in "one dinky little room" gave me "a fright." Mr. Garrett said about 35 people are on our trip. Some couples are "elderly," about 40. Two old women hogged the mirror combing their hair. I like the looks of some college lads, but encouraging them would make Katie jealous. She doesn't have much pleasure and "to hide her inner feelings" jokes a lot.

August 28. I forgot my promise to sleep in the upper, took the lower, and in the morning while Kate was dressing in the lower I started breakfast in the dining-car ahead of her. To avoid being rude, I sat blushing with the two college boys. Mr. Garrett approached and introduced me—Miss Emerson—to Mr. Coles and Mr. Lester. Kate appeared, called me "girlie," and said she was half starved, half hungry. Mr. Garrett introduced her—Miss Hayes—and left. Mr. Lester joked about Mr. Coles's "truck horse" appetite and made me laugh, then blush, when he said he liked the scenery inside better than the Wyoming scenery outside. Mr. Lester said we should be glad that Nebraska corn wasn't on "your feet." Kate, speechless, was happy to start eating. Mr. Lester is witty; Mr. Coles, serious. He would conquer "poor little ... me" if he wanted. I must avoid but not "wound a man like he." He's tall, dark, and we'd be a "striking" contrasting pair.

August 29. Today was perfect. We didn't tour Salt Lake City. Last night Kate, fatigued after riding the Yellowstone train, refused my invitation to stay up and play cards with "the boys." She called Mr.Coles and Mr. Lester "chorus boys." I said they're college graduates. She said yes, of a barber school. I said attractiveness isn't everything and when they knew her they'd like her. I went to tell the men that "our card game was off." Mr. Lester called Kate "a prune," me "a pippin." I defended Kate, felt guilty hearing his wittiness, and left. This morning four stage coaches drove our group through Yellowstone Park. I found myself sitting between Mr. Coles and Mr. Lester; Kate and Mr. Garrett, with the driver. I simply can't describe the "Xmas tree park," the river, the mountains. We lunched at the Fountain Hotel, saw wonderful geysers. Mr. Coles agreed they were more beautiful than anything "not human." I called him "a jollier." He turned to Kate. She stayed silent, unused to chatting "with men of the other sex." At the Paint Pots, Mr. Garrett said a guide fell in and died "though he was a good swimmner on account of the water being so hot." Some bears began eating discarded food. Frightened, I clutched Mr. Coles's arm. Kate and I roomed together in Old Faithful Inn, near the beautiful Old Faithful Geyser. Mr. Lester escorted me to see it. Mr. Coles pleaded sleepiness. So did Kate. She's bored. I'll quite writing now—"a certain little girl ... [must] get her 'beauty sleep.'"

August 30. Today's coach seating was awkward. Kate told "Girlie" to sit up front with Mr. Garrett. I was embarrassed for her, stuck between Mr. Lester and Mr. Coles. Mr. Garrett entertained some "chatterboxes" by explaining park slang terms like "dudes," "rotten-logging," etc., and by saying soldiers near Yellowstone Lake prevented dangers from nearby Mexico. After lunch I got Kate to trade places with me and sat by Mr. Coles. I said his sitting beside Kate embarrassed him. He admirably defended her, then grew pleasantly silent. I smiled at his boyishness. Seeing the beautiful "Sleeping Giant" by "Lake Hotel" caused me to grasp Mr. Coles's arm, causing me to blush and apologize, causing him to smile. After dinner, the men disappeared. When I started writing my diary Kate humorously said she was going for a walk and might wake up that "Sleeping Giant."

August 31. This morning Mr. Coles sat behind in the coach, obviously hoping I'd join him. To show I wasn't chasing him, I sat with Mr. Garrett, causing him to blush. He'd been casting eyes at me earlier. Though he controlled himself, I scarcely enjoyed the riverside drive. I wish "I had of" relished the "Upper Falls" view too. During lunchtime at the Canyon Hotel, I apologized to Katie for making her sit by Mr. Coles and confessed that Mr. Garrett was "growing too fond of me," though unencouraged, because Mr. Coles and I are practically engaged. I even said I'd dress Kate up as my maid of honor. Kate flopped on her bed. Mr. Lester, saying Mr. Coles had a headache in his room, accompanied our group to the Great Falls, near which Mr. Lester made cheering jokes. Dinner was awkward. Mr. Lester asked me why Kate, Mr. Coles, and Mr. Garrett seemed "sore at each other," even said Kate broke two dates to walk and rotten-log with Mr. Coles. I doubted all this. Lester suggested that we rotten-log. Regarding him as comical but forward, I declined.

September 1. A railroad strike set for next Monday forced our early departure. Riding toward Yellowstone Station, I sat in the coach with silent

Mr. Lester and Mr. Coles, who ignored Kate. While I was washing for lunch, Mr. Garrett drove off with the others, and I had to board a coach with strangers. At the station, I confronted them. Mr. Garrett apologized and said he was hurried. Kate said being "upset" kept her from revealing that Mr. Coles proposed to her. I bravely avoided fainting before strangers. Then Kate said I could have Mr. Coles because she's marrying Mr. Garrett. Silence followed between Kate and me. We boarded the train to Ogden. Approaching, Mr. Coles said he lost Kate's love and Mr. Garrett's lucky. Ignoring Mr. Coles, I told Mr. Garrett to schedule me straight home from Ogden. He said Kate, Mr. Lester, and Mr. Coles want to return via Salt Lake. The old ladies kidded me about a budding "romance." I said they'd have none; they retorted I wouldn't either. Mr. Lester chanced by, expressed surprise that Mr. Garrett and Mr. Coles both liked Kate, said he could love me except he's married in Kenosha. I'm so betrayed I hope to die.

September 3. The conductor said President Wilson stopped the strike. My "friends" are welcome to enjoy Colorado Springs, etc. I'll be home, will read there for my second vacation week, won't associate with "a man of the opposite sex" again. Mr. Coles is probably flirting with some lonely girl now. Kate and Mr. Garrett are alike, and unlike me. Kate bid me an early farewell at Ogden, tried to make amends, said that Mr. Garrett foolishly fell for her despite her ugliness and that "You pretty girls cannot expect to get all the men." I told her to hide because if Mr. Garrett saw her "the way she looked" now, "still in her kimona," he'd faint. My conclusion: A girl shouldn't surrender freedom to "any man." Why drudge for him? I'll consider some noble Red Cross work.

September 4. Instead of destroying this diary, I'll keep it for containing my Yellowstone Park "impressions." I would be with mother at a movie tonight but for remembering Don Kellogg borrowed a book I plan to read. I phoned him. He's coming over. He'll be surprised about Kate's engagement. If I take another vacation trip, it might be on my honeymoon.

Lardner offers no discernible reason for calling this story "Tour Y-10." Jonathan Yardley regards it as "a pale version of the far more successful 'Travelogue,'" published six years later. Neither story is among Lardner's best, and — in truth — Miss Emerson is too prolixly depicted as gushingly revealing her tactless, self-deluded, self-absorbed nature. If Lardner were writing today, he wouldn't condone Miss Emerson's writing about a railroad employee as a "darkey." (Source: Yardley, 183)

TOURS, FRANK ("Rhythm"). He is Conrad Green's musical adviser. Tours calls Harry Hart's collaboration with Spencer Deal "Terrible!"

TOWNS, FANNIE ("That Old Sweetheart of Mine"). She is a girlfriend that Will feels would return to him if he whistled.

TOWNSEND, OLD MAN ("The Maysville Minstrel"). He owns the Maysville gas company and similar companies in the region. He bosses Stephen Gale and Ed Hunter, his only Maysville employees. He warns Stephen not to quit his job and try to become a successful poet. When Stephen does so but fails, Townsend hires him back with a rebuke.

TRACY (*The Big Town*). The Decker Hotel is located at the Tracy Estates on Long Island. Finch, Ella, and Katie have a summer vacation there.

TRACY ("A Chip of the Old Block"). He is a Cincinnati reporter. Captain Evan Barnes meets him on the train to Washington, D.C., where Tracy, concluding that Barnes is useless to the military effort, treats the foolish fellow to sarcasm he misunderstands.

TRACY, YOUNG ("Champion"). He is a boxer who fights Midge Kelly in Milwaukee. Kelly throws the fight for $80 but later defeats Tracy three times.

"TRAVELOGUE" (*Cosmopolitan*, May 1926; RLR, RU). (Characters: Babcock, Harley Bateman, Dan Chapman, Hazel Dignan, Bess Eldridge, Mrs. Ina Gilbert, Dave Homan, Jennie, Joan Killian, Dickie Kingston, Jack Kingston, Lucy Kingston, Mildred Orr, Doctor Platt, Clint Poole, Margaret Trumbull, the Rev. N. L. Veach, Wannop.)

Hazel Dignan, a self-absorbed motormouth, and her friend Mildred Orr are on the Chicago-to-California train. At lunch they meet well-traveled Dan Chapman, who encourages the girls to talk. Hazel mentions "Frisco." He cautions against saying that "in front of them native sons." Hazel boasts of wide travel. Mention of one place after another reminds her of one friend after another, mainly Bess Eldridge and Harley Bateman, who drinks too much. Neither Hazel nor Chapman listens well. Mildred is silently puzzled.

They visit the observation car. "For no possible reason," Chapman admits, Nebraska reminds him of Michigan. Hazel recalls her sister's six-year-old Dickie's teeth. Chapman says he had a tooth pulled, bravely without his taking gas — after all, he faced 16 months of German artillery fire. Hazel slept better after her rheumatism-causing tooth was extracted. Chapman and Hazel contrast their ability to sleep on trains. Mildred silently envies these "interesting, traveled people." Chapman's naming "San Antone" requires Hazel to mention "dirty Mexicans," swimming in Salt Lake's buoyant lake, and elsewhere. Hazel notices that Mildred is asleep and disputes Chapman's calling Mildred pretty. Chapman jump-starts Hazel by naming Atlantic City. Hazel says she'll wire her sister, in Elkhart, doing so from Grand Island before they "change time."

Past North Platte, Chapman finds Hazel and Mildred again. He says they're in Mountain time now. Mildred wonders if that's why people say "it's high time," feels embarrassed for speaking, and turns to a book. Talk involves Washington, D.C., locales there, and teeth. Mildred, grateful that these two travelers restrict their reminiscing to "geography and dentistry before her," courteously goes for a nap. Chapman mentions Lake Louise, which reminds Hazel — been there, seen that — of people mentioned before, prompting Chapman, who again calls Mildred pretty, to go for a nap.

At dinner Mildred regards Chapman's staring at her as astonishment at her dumbness, wishes she could chat him up like clever Hazel, and absents herself from next day's lunch, where Chapman's mentioning time changing in Ogden spurs Hazel's memories of her watch, bought in New York, where she knows friends and saw a show with Bess and bumped into Dave Homan, who took them to the aquarium and had Mr. Fish paged. She admits she laughed but poor Mildred lacks a sense of humor. Hazel confides that she wouldn't marry Dave — never serious — nor Harley — often drunk. Chapman interrupts Hazel's comments about Harley's brother-in-law to announce Ogden. Hazel departs to wire her sister. Chapman asks Mildred to breakfast with him — without Hazel.

At breakfast, Chapman gets dazzled Mildred to say that neither Harley nor Bess is her friend and that Hazel broke off two marital engagements; to commiserate with him about his tooth extraction; and to let him, yes, phone her in San Francisco — when Hazel is off seeing her aunt in Berkeley.

The moral of "Travelogue," which crawls like a train, is surely that simple Mildred instinctively knows how, given one opening — namely the hole where Chapman's tooth was — to attract a man, dumb though he too is. Critic Ludwig Lewisohn (1882–1955) feels that the characters in the story are "pretentious fools of a ghastly emptiness." Nonetheless, Jonathan Yardley judges "Travelogue" to be "more successful" than the earlier "Tour Y-10" and to be actually "a refinement" of it. (Sources: Lewison, 515; Yardley, 183, 331)

TRAVERS ("Pity Is Akin —") *see* **SPALDING, HENRY**

TRAVERS, MRS ("Pity Is Akin —") *see* **SPALDING, EDITH**

TRAWLEY, MARGALO ("Claude Diphthong, Student of Crime"). She is the beautiful "Follies' ... show girl" that Gardner Lyle married. They were recently divorced.

TRAYNOR ("Take a Walk"). He is the Pittsburgh outfielder whose spectacular play robs Agnew, doing well before his home-town crowd, of a sure extra-base hit.

Harold Joseph Traynor (1899–1972) played for the Pittsburgh Pirates (1920–1937) and was also their manager (1934–1939). (Source: *Baseball Encyclopedia*, 711, 1680)

TREAT 'EM ROUGH; LETTERS FROM JACK THE KAISER KILLER (1918; TER). Novel-like series of 30 letters from Jack Keefe to his friend Al Blanchard, originally published in three parts, entitled "Jack the Kaiser Killer" (*Saturday Evening Post*, March 23, 1918), "Corporal Punishment" (*Saturday Evening Post*, April 13, 1918), and "Purls before Swine" (June 8, 1918). (Characters: Gen. Barry, Al Blanchard, Bertha Blanchard, Bishop, Bowen, Tom Castle, Chambers, Miss Lucy Chase, Crane, Mrs. Crane, Corporal Daly, Eddy, Gardner, Col. Gould, Corp. Haney, Hess, Sargent James, Janniny, Al Keefe, Florrie Keefe, Jack Keefe, Lefty Kramer, Shorty Lahey, Sargent Leslie, McGraw, Gen. Masters, Capt. Nash, Nevin, Red Sampson, Schobinger, Shiverick, Mrs. Sebastian, Nick Sebastian, Mrs. Somebody, the Swede, Capt. Whiting.)

The first 15 letters are from Camp Grant, Illinois.

Sept. 23 [1917]. Jack writes "Friend Al [Blanchard]" about his "bunk," his sore left arm "where I got vacinated," "drawing $30.00 per mo. from the Govmt.," pride because in "50 yrs." he'll be mentioning Berlin, whereas all "Cicotte and Faber and Russell" can discuss is "what they done to the Giants." Jack is "out of baseball now and in the big game." Goodbyes in "Chi Wed. noon" were full of kisses. Florrie, his wife, said she shouldn't "blubber" and spoil her looks. Little Al, their "game" three-year-old, didn't cry. On the train, two recruits played a cornet and a trombone. Many got drunk. Jack was sick after eating a sandwich "a wop give me on the train." They got blankets in camp. He skipped supper. In the morning "the buggle" called them for what's called "mess."

Sept. 24. Jack writes about working to "buggles," cleaning the barracks, having shots for "small pox or tyford fever," being examined by a doctor and called "a fine specimen," being issued shoes too big and other items including "2 cocky suits." Questioned by an officer about his vocational background, Jack indicated he was only a pitcher and figured he could "throw one of them bombs" exactly at "a German's right eye." Training included "upseting exercises." Breakfast was oatmeal, bread, steak, coffee. He saluted well. But why salute officers with "a stick of wood in their right hand"? Jack figures Capt. Nash will pick him to train others "on acct. of knowing all about the drills etc." There were lectures about what to do "if we got stewed or something," about conduct before officers. Though Jack was in great shape, the corporal wouldn't let him skip exercising. Dinner included chicken, potatoes, corn. Supper featured beans, steak, cake, coffee. But they had to eat too fast. It's risky to sleep in total silence, because a snooper might cut your throat.

Sept. 26. Lahey, a soldier they call Shorty "on acct. of him being so short," warned Jack about a grouchy soldier named Nick Sebastian. He's been arrested for stabbing people and carries a knife. If soldiers laugh at "Nick the Blade" in the shower, he might stab them. Teddy Roosevelt gave a speech to "about 20 thousand" soldiers here.

Sept. 29. Nick, who eyes Jack, bunks on one side of him; on the other is a new guy Shorty calls Tom the Trigger who kept asking God "Do you want me to kill?" But "the connection couldn't of been very good," because he got no answer. At "inspections day," Capt. Nash was "baling out" some untidy men, but not Jack. Why bother being neat, anyway? Nick might stab him, or Tom might shoot him if "the lord says Fire."

Oct. 3. Jack hopes for leave to see Florrie, little Al, and "the world serious" with the White Sox in Chicago. He is tired. After having to run 20 minutes "to improve our wind," he had no wind to improve; also his feet hurt. He was relieved to learn that Nick was too afraid of officers to stab anyone, and that Tom Castle, called the Trigger, lacked a gun and also objected to killing. But then Shorty told Jack that Nick planned to "cut you up in slices" outside camp and then desert the army.

Oct. 7. Jack is upset today, Sunday. Shorty warned him that Nick would go with him to Chicago and kill him, Florrie, and little Al. Jack stayed in camp yesterday, hoping to be promoted. He asked a soldier named Bishop, going to Chicago, to phone Florrie and tell her to visit camp today. On returning, Bishop said that when he got to Chicago his wife had a baby and he forgot about Florrie. Jack resisted hitting "the little srimph." Jack looked in vain for Florrie here today.

Oct. 10. Florrie wrote Jack that she and Al "cried themself to sleep Saturday night" when he didn't arrive, and that they attended the ball game Sunday. Shorty was only kidding him about Nick Sebastian. Far from looking at Jack to kill him, Nick told Jack he was a groundskeeper "at Washington Pk.," saw Jack pitch, admired his "prettiest wind up," didn't have "leave last Sat.," and proved it by producing a letter from Mrs. Sebastian. Jack noted she "don't spell very good." Jack plans to pull a better joke on Shorty than "no fizzle like some of his." Tom Castle is gone, reassigned to "quarter masters."

Oct. 12. Jack is "writeing" at the Y.M.C.A., to avoid soldiers in the barracks "jabbering ... in foreign languages." He will attend free French languages classes. When in France he can be "an interpeter" between "a French genl." and "our genl." When Jack told Shorty, he said Jack "better learn to talk English to." Florrie and little Al are visiting camp Sunday. She'll bring "some daintys" she or "the swede girl" cooked.

Oct. 14. Florrie and little Al visited. Al thought Jack was the captain, which he might be soon. The men "staired at Florrie." Mrs. Sebastian visited Nick with their "2 kids." Jack suggested for them to return to Chicago on the same train with Florrie, but Florrie "ball[ed] me out" because, she said, Mrs. Sebastian "looked like she had left home before she got up." Florrie can be mean. What if Jack got wounded and had "no nose"? Would she make him "a grass widower" because he couldn't "smell the cooking"? Later, Nick said Florrie was "beautiful." Jack replied that he shouldn't worry, because "your Mrs. is a good mother." The wives brought boxes the men opened later. Mrs. Sebastian's contained doughnuts, pie, cake; Florries, candy "for 60 cts" that all "ran together like chop sooy" with a cover picturing a girl which you can't eat. Florrie didn't cook but "spent [her time] toneing up her ear lobs."

Oct. 16. Jack addresses this letter to "My Cher Ami" and explains he's learning "a dozen words" to jabber in French. The men are learning to dig "trenchs" so "we can go through them Dutchman like they was fly paper." Red Sampson, a soldier, says his brother, "Gen. Pershing's right hand bower," wrote that Pershing asked for good-looking men; therefore, they'll probably be sent when "each Co. had a rifle." Red said we'd avoid "submarine U boats" by traveling via Japan and then help the Russians. Shorty saw Red was kidding. They had a lecture about German gas. The Russians don't worry about "gastritis." Jack comments on the White Sox $3600.00 pay for winning the "world serious." If a private sends $15 of his monthly $30 pay to his "wife or who ever," then "the govt." sends a matching $15. So Jack plans to send his entire $60 to Florrie and have "the govt." match that. Jack won't write letters in French to "old pal bon sore," which means "good night," which "they couldn't nobody in Bedford" understand.

Oct. 18. Capt. Nash promoted Jack to corporal. He commands "7 men": Nick, Red, Shorty, "a wop named Janinny or something," "a stropper" named Hess, Gardner, and Bowen. They're "pretty rough," but he can handle them. His monthly pay is $36. He wrote Florrie, who can say she's "Mrs. Corp. Keefe please." To be ready to throw bombs, they practiced with stones and tomato cans. The training office "kept his arm stiff like he didn't have no elbow joint" and ignored Jack's suggestion to cock it. But "I kept my temper."

Oct. 22. They trained in trench warfare but without "real rifles and bombs." Shorty got mad at Jack's yelling and asked if Jack thought he was "Jonah Vark." Capt. Nash challenged them to imitate drilling like West Pt. cadets he showed "some pictures" of. A soldier named Chambers was promoted to corporal but went on leave to Chi, returned late, and was drunk. The captain "busted him," not on the jaw but "reduced to a private." Red said maybe Chambers couldn't stand responsibility and wasn't "a born leader" like Jack.

Oct. 23. Jack knows enough French now, has enough responsibility, and also quit because the "crazy" instructor said you pronounce "tres," meaning "very," as "tray," because the "e" is "a" and the silent "s" is "just the French of it." Red said his brother wrote of 2500 Frenchmen killed. Shorty: All privates? Red: No, the French put "corporals and sargents" up front, not privates.

Oct. 24. A baseball game was organized. Though urged to pitch, Jack thought it wouldn't "be fair." Corp. Haney told him the "govt." wouldn't match his "whole salary" if sent to Florrie. What with buying "soldiers insurance" and liberty bonds, Jack makes "$.60" a month. Florrie would get a lot if Jack became disabled. Some "birds in the big leagues" pitch as bad as though disabled. Red said French corporals charge unarmed to attract German fire. Not being in the French army, "I should worry."

Oct. 26. General Pershing won't say, but according to Red, their "regt." may go to France in about a week, though whether by the Atlantic or the Pacific is unclear. Jack wishes if he's killed he could leave money for Blanchard and his wife Bertha, as well as for his own family. Still, he'd be dying for "Al and your familys." Red inspired Jack by saying that Jack's men are more concerned about their corporal than "danger to themselfs." The men of Napoleon, also a corporal, "looked up to him" that way.

Chicago, Oct. 28. Jack is home on brief leave. He wishes he were a private again, because he's "got attached to my boys" and doesn't want to "quit them" by going to France. Shorty and Red told him that Pershing is sending for "non commission officers" to increase his regiment, but not privates. Jack figures he'll be killed in France. Shorty said the Germans will capture some corporals to "get information off them." Jack said he won't "spill anything." Shorty said the Germans will cut some toes off Jack, then, since he'd remain silent, "finish you off" or make him work "without no food." Shorty said this information came from "his wife's 2 brothers ... in the German army." Jack felt sick all night. Florrie will soon "get up for breakfast." If he were a private, he might remain at Camp Grant "and see Florrie and he [little Al] every month."

The next 10 letters are from Camp Grant.

Oct. 30. Jack was caught returning to camp late. Capt. Nash denied him leave for one month, told him he was still needed as a corporal, and said that corporals wouldn't go to France ahead of privates. Jack's men were "tickled," but Jack felt "dissappointment."

Nov. 4. The "riff and raff" in Jack's camp are

being sent south to increase the national guards there. They'll go to France first. Jack and his men, being more competent, will remain here. Jack, wanting action in France, plans to enter "officers training camp" they're starting "here in Jan.," and with "my lieut. or capt. bars" should "take command" in France fast. "Sarah Bernhart the French comedian" visited, gave "the boys a treat," but didn't impress Jack, who prefers his Florrie to "a dozen like she."

Nov. 7. Jack's unit got "a bunch" of knitted sox "from the Red X." One contained a note addressed to "Dear Soldier Boy" from a Lucy Chase, with her Texas address included. She is "oh so lonesome" and please write. Jack "shouldn't ought to be monking around," wouldn't write, but if he did he'd say he's married. He wonders if she saw him playing baseball in Texas during "the spring trip." He cautions Al not to tell Bertha. Jack says a singing instructor named Nevin tried to lead "3000 of us" with "Keep the home fires burning" but failed. Being mostly "from Chi," Jack's "gang ... leave takeing care of the furnace to the janitor." Nevin quit. Then while returning "to quarters," the men "cut loose and sung." Some college men in camp under Capt. Whiting are planning to play football against a Great Lakes navy team and a Camp Custer team from "up in Mich." Though never having played football, Jack, being "a born athelete," could be better than "college Willy boys," too busy "doing the foxy trot and ... stewed on chocolate and whip cream."

Nov. 10. The story is false about "a gang of [German] spys" on the troop train sent from Camp Grant to Camp Logan. They were burglars and included Shorty. Jack decided to write Lucy Chase, to ask where she saw him and to send him her picture, which he'd tear up. If Florrie should find out and object, he'd tell her to "jump in the lake." Florrie never knit or even mended sox for him. Jack started practicing football. Capt. Whiting asked him what position he played, and where he played. He said "center rush or tackle back," and at Harvard. He got kicked in the head and quit, because "what is the use of takeing chances"? He must "think about ... winning this war."

Nov. 14. They had target practice with rifles, during "a rotten day," which was windy and dark. A "smart aleck" officer hit the bulls eye at 100 yards 8 out of10 times. He was lucky, because the wind helped him. Before firing, the men were ordered to "lay on their stomach," thus presenting an enemy "less mark" to shoot at. Foolish, because standing up you might get a "flesh wound or something" and survive. Jack hit the target 8 times. Red kidded him that he deserved "a expert rifle shooter's meddle." Jack says he hasn't heard from the "girl down in Texas." Maybe she's "over her infatuation."

Nov. 17. That "girlie" wrote Jack, praising his being an officer and leaving "the big league" to join up, offering to make her "needles fly" to make him "a helmet or a sweater or something," refusing to say where she saw him or to send him a photo that his buddies would ridicule, hoping he'll be transferred to Texas. Jack feels this correspondence "got to end." It's going to "be pretty hard for her" when he writes he's married. He can't remember where they must have met. Jack regrets that Al can't "advice me" because girls were never "looseing their heads ... for you." In the football game, the Great Lakes sailors "cleaned up 9 to 6" over Capt. Whiting's college Willys.

Nov. 22. Jack's camp is depleted by men being sent south to the national guards. Jack and the other best soldiers are held back. He won't go to officers' school after all. The only applicants are those that "talk all the languages of the ally countrys." Red overheard "2 of the lieuts." say even college boys would have trouble "between now and Jan." learning. Jack might learn "French and maybe 1 or 2 others" but not "Roman and Australian." Florrie doesn't write. Is she dead? Jack wrote the Texas girl he already had a helmet, didn't say he was married, said he was too busy to write much, and maybe they should "forget it." But girls "don't forget so easy."

Dec. 2. With his in-camp month of punishment over, Jack went to Chicago for a weekend. Wanting to surprise Florrie, he didn't write. No one was home, not even "the Swede." A girl at the beauty parlor said Florrie was away until Monday morning. A neighbor woman said she was out. Keefe sent for "a doz. bottles of beer," had two, had supper out, returned, and drank the rest. Next morning the Swede entered, "screemed" on seeing Jack, then explained how Florrie was away with friends. Florrie returned with little Al, explained her absence, and they argued. Her women friends barged in, met Jack, and they discussed the army endlessly. In an hour Jack had to catch the train to camp.

Dec. 4. That "little girlie" wrote Jack again. He probably shouldn't answer, but he'd feel guilty "if she done anything to herself on my acct." The soldiers went on a cold "19 mile hike." Jack kidded Red for "the whole regt. ... [being] out of step but you."

Dec. 7. Great news. The best men are being sent "to fill up the national guards"; so "they's a big bunch of us leaveing soon for Camp Logan." They're warned "we musent spill nothing about it" for fear "spys" would torpedo the train. They won't head for France soon because "they have closed up navigations for the winter." Camp Logan is in Texas; so "you can bet" he won't tell that "girlie." He wrote her to ask for her picture, to "make her feel a little happier." He may get promoted in Texas.

Camp Logan, Dec. 14. They're "in sunny Texas," somewhat warmer "being further south." On the way "we seen some bad eggs ... that looked like Germans." Shorty is promoted to "sargent." Therefore, Jack should make "gen. in a month." He wrote "the little girl" again to send a picture, because if she sent one to Camp Grant "some rummys might get a hold of it" and write her. He "didn't give her no encouragement" but did joke they might meet in Houston, which is "100 miles from home" for her. If they met, he'd ignore her.

Camp Logan, Dec. 16. "Well old pal," here's danger. That girl wrote she's visiting her aunt in Houston and Jack must meet her 1:00 P.M. next Sunday [December 23, 1917] at the Rice Hotel for dinner. Otherwise, "I will do something to make you sorry." She'll present "your sweater" she knit. Jack has decided he'll meet her, accept her kind gift, tell her everything, and "hope she is a game bird and will take it O.K." Jack adds that, unfortunately, he's handsome and not "a littls scrimp or ugly."

Houston, Tex., Dec. 24. On Saturday Jack hoped he'd be denied leave, but he got it. He went to the Houston hotel promptly, saw one woman who was alone, "about 35," and when she approached he said he was looking for a man. She got sarcastic. Then Jack Kramer, a Texas League lefty, saw Jack and shouted "old Jack Keefe." She introduced herself to Kramer as "Miss Chase." Who should appear but Florrie and little Al, "down to give me a Xmas supprise." She'll stay "3 wks.," partly with her sister in Beaumont. As the Keefes departed, Miss Chase "looked right at me." He felt that "a woman her age" shouldn't write to strangers and probably Kramer has that sweater now. Florrie will give him a sweater for Christmas; thus, he "won't loose out after all."

Camp Logan, Jan. 4 [1918]. Jack writes Al about being picked to sail overseas. Florrie almost broke her heart at the news. He won't betray the army's confidence in him. Bertha is lucky her "husband ... didn't enlist." Jack will write when he can.

The Chicago White Sox played the New York Giants in the 1917 World Series, defeating the Giants 4–2. Jack's sour comments on the October 6 White Sox victory imply that he was annoyed they could win without him. Lardner may have remembered that he had Jack say that Florrie can jump in the lake when, a dozen years later, Lardner wrote "If I Were You Love (I'd Jump in the Lake)," among other songs, for the musical comedy *Smiles* (1930), with music by Vincent Youmans* and produced by Florenz Ziegfeld.* Sarah Bernhardt (1844–1923) was the French actress, famous as a tragedienne of legendary skill, but not as a comedienne. Although an accident resulted in the amputaion of one leg (1915), "the divine Sarah" played at the Front in France and toured in America (1917).

TROY, WILLIE ("The Venomous Viper of the Volga"). He is a retired boxer and now a well-to-do, fun-loving trainer. He colludes with Sandy King to train Henry Goetz, whom they dub Ivan Ivanovitch, "the Venomous Viper of the Volga," as a fighter by housing and training him in the Bronx until he's allegedly ready for the ring.

TRUDY, DICK ("Women"). He is "a veteran usher" in the stand during a game watched by Mike Healy from the bench. He brings Healy "a mash note" from a pretty girl that Healy and fellow bench warmers have been eyeing.

TRUMBULL (*The Big Town*). He is the rich old neighbor of Finch, his wife Ella, and her sister Katie. They all live on the sixth floor of the Lucius, a Riverside Drive apartment building in New York. Trumbull entertains his neighbors generously and grows fond of Katie. She likes the old man's chauffeur Ritchey better, until Trumbull mentions that Ritchey has a wife and two children.

Finch says that Ella sat in a chair in Trumbull's over-furnished apartment so large that Finch says it "was made for Eddie Foyt's family." Eddie Foy (1856–1928), born in Greenwich Village, was a popular Broadway vaudeville and musical-comedy performer. His "family," some of whom acted with him, included, in all, four wives and seven children.

TRUMBULL, MARJORIE ("Anniversary"). She is Walter Trumbull's wife. Louis Taylor knows both and tells his bored wife Bess about the two.

TRUMBULL, MARJORIE ("Travelogue"). Hazel Dignan tells Dan Chapman that she and Marjorie Trumbull visited the House of David in Benton Harbor.

TRUMBULL, WALTER ("Anniversary"). He and his wife Marjorie are friends of Louis Taylor. They all live in Milton. Louis bores his wife Bess by repeatedly telling her how the Trumbulls were once driving toward nearby Harper City to see a movie but ran out of gas.

TRUNKEY ("What of It?"). This is the name of people in "the elevator game," as is Ben Lacey, according to Ben's unstoppable comments to Dexter Cosset.

TURNER ("The Busher Comes Back"). He is one of several Cleveland players that Keefe of the White Sox says he pitched to in relief. Keefe gripes about getting "rotten support" in the ninth inning.

Terrence Lamont Turner (1881–1960) played for the Pittsburgh Pirates (1901), the Cleveland Indians (1904–1918), and the Philadelphia Athletics (1919). (Sources: *Baseball Encyclopedia*, 1684–1685; Hilton, 82)

TUTTLE ("Absent-minded Beggar"). This is the name of a family whose party Ellen Parrish tells Irene Comerford and John Knowles she must leave them to attend. The two are delighted.

TUTTLE, JOE ("A Friendly Game"). He and his wife are friends of the narrator. He attends the disastrous poker game held at the home of the narrator and his wife.

TUTTLE, JOE ("A Friendly Game"). He is the little son of Joe Tuttle and Mrs. Tuttle.

TUTTLE, MILLICENT ("A Friendly Game"). She is the Tuttles' little daughter.

TUTTLE, MRS. ("A Friendly Game"). She is Joe Tuttle's wife and the mother of their young children, Joe and Millicent. Her husband is a guest at the poker game held by the narrator. Mrs. Tuttle stayed home babysitting and missed the event.

TYLER ("Bob's Birthday"). He is Bob Tyler's father. Unemployed, he lets Bob support the whole family while he is pompous, frequents his club with his wife, and makes excuses.

TYLER In "Horseshoes," he is a left-handed pitcher for Boston when Dick Grimes and Speed Parker are playing for the Cubs against Boston. Grimes plays badly and is released to Indianapolis. In "Back to Baltimore," Dixon, managing Boston, told Tyler to play practice catch with William Baker, Jr., who complained that the pitches stung both of his hands. In "The Hold-Out," Frank Conley, the narrator, said Tyler, Smith, and Schupp were such good pitchers that the team he managed would "be a set-up" for them.

George Albert Tyler (1889–1953) played for the Boston Braves (1910–1917) and the Cubs (1918–1921). Hilton mentions that Tyler helped Boston win the pennant in 1914, the date of the action of "Back to Baltimore." (Sources: *Baseball Encyclopedia*, 1686, 2442; Hilton, 402)

TYLER ("Zone of Quiet"). He is a hospital interne. Miss Eleanor Lyons tells her patient that Tyler praised her small ankles, which, he added, resemble Miss Helen Halsey's.

TYLER, BOB ("Bob's Birthday"). He is a talented musician, 17, denied a career and even a life of his own because he plays in local orchestras to support his sponging parents, uncle, aunt, and even grandfather, and loves but will lose Kathleen Dennis. Only Bob's sister, 14, remembers his birthday properly.

TYLER, GRANDFATHER ("Bob's Birthday"). He is Bob Tyler's grandfather, 62. When he is released from employment as the Silvers & Co. bookkeeper, he moves in with the Tyler family, and Bob must support him.

TYLER, MISS ("Bob's Birthday"). She is the narrator of the story. She is Bob Tyler's loving sister, 14, respectful of her elders but disapproving of them. She gives Bob a biography of Richard Wagner for his birthday. She is friendly with Bob's girlfriend Kathleen Dennis.

In addition to praising Bob at the expense of the musician Rudy Vallée,* his sister laments that Bob couldn't study in Europe and become "a second [Fritz] Kreisler [1875–1962]," who was a renowned American violist and composer. Lardner skillfully presents this young girl's timidly frank account of her family's shoddiness. Not revealing her name, she is ambitious to write, composes steadily but inevitably not well, and at best can only partly understand her imposed-on brother's fate. Nor does she realize that she is also likely to be a loser in life and, like Bib, a giver to takers.

TYLER, MRS. ("Bob's Birthday"). She is Bob Tyler's mother, utterly ignorant of the misery that she, her husband, her brother, her sister-in-law, and finally her father-in-law are causing Bob.

TYRUS ("Horseshoes"). He is evidently a great baseball player. The narrator says he can talk to Tyrus without getting nervous.

TYSON, DR. ("Poodle") *see* **GREGORY, DR.**

"UNCIVIL WAR" (*Red Book*, September 1915; OYH) *see* ***OWN YOUR OWN HOME***

UNCLE ZEKE ("The Poor Simp"). When Carey was planning a joke on Skull Scoville, he told the narrator that he would tell Skull that a pretty girl in the stand admired Skull, and that the girl's Uncle Zeke had died and left her and her companion "three hundred iron men." What Carey said started Skull's friendship with Mary Conahan (the girl's real name), whom Skull will marry and for whose rich father he will work.

UNDERHILL, HARRIETTE ("Wedding Day"). She is a friend of Jimmy Shane. At the party after the wedding ceremony of theatrical personalities Shane and Brownie Burt, Dorothy Drew, an actress who knows the couple, sarcastically reminds Shane that he boasted to Harriette Underhill that he wrote his own comedy lines.

Is it possible that Harriette is one of Shane's other girlfriends and that he goes to his club the very evening of his marriage expecting and receiving a telephone call from her?

VAIL, CHARLES M. ("Haircut"). Whitey, the barber-narrator, recalls that Charley Vail's shaving mug is on the shelf next to that of the late James H. Kendall.

VALLÉE, RUDY (1901–1986). Born at Island Pond, Vermont, Hubert Prior Vallee was a popular musician and actor. He played drums in high school, played the saxophone and the clarinet on New England tours, entered the navy (1917) but was released as too young, and took his small band to London (1924–1925). He transferred from the University of Maine to Yale, where he earned a degree in philosophy. His softly voiced "crooning," accompanied by the seven-piece "Rudy Vallee and the Connecticut Yankees," led to decades of recording contracts (from 1928) and radio broadcasting (from 1929). His handsome, juvenile looks led to appearances in at least 33 movies (1929–1976), including *The Vagabond Lover* (1929), *Glorifying the American Girl* (1929), and *International House* (1933). Remarkably durable, Vallée starred opposite Claudette Colbert in *The Palm Beach Story* (1942), performed with the Coast Guard Band during World War II, was sensational in the Broadway production of *How to Succeed in Business Without Even Trying* (1961), and was married four times.

In "Lose With a Smile," Danny Warner boasts of his ability to "groon" like Rudy Vallée. Danny's teammates nickname him Rudy and kid him by saying they could tell the difference between a Rudy Vallée recording and one by [Phil] Ohman* and [Victor] Arden.* Part of "An Infant Industry," a radio review by Lardner (*The New Yorker* [February 25, 1933]), is "A Crooner." In it, Lardner cutely discusses "Rudy Vallée and ... suggestive songs," one of which, named by Rudy, is "Let's Put Out the Lights and Go to Sleep." Lardner says Rudy offered to sing and thus "purge it with the hyssop of his immaculate larynx." Lardner needn't but does say for "Sleep" read "Bed." Donald Elder gets hot and bothered about Lardner's objection to Vallée's verbal sanitizing. In "Bob's Birthday," Bob's sister favorably compares Bob to performers like Vallée with greasy hair. In "Second-Act Curtain," Booth imagines that the girl in his hotel may put herself to sleep reading "the confessions of ... Rudy Vallée." (Source: Elder, 357)

VANCE In "When the Moon Comes over the Mountain," Danny, playing for Brooklyn, mentions Vance as a fast right-handed pitcher on their team. Off a Hartford pitcher, reputedly "faster then Vance," Danny hit his "fire ball' so far that "the fire ball burnt up a cotton field in the next league." In "Lose with a Smile," Danny says that Dazzy pitched for Brooklyn in a game Hubbell pitched for the Giants. In "Meet Me in St. Louie," Danny says that Max Carey, Brooklyn manager, was "saveing Vance" until he could pitch against the St. Louis Cardinals' Dizzy Dean, thus featuring "Dazzy again Dizzy." In "The Ides of June," Dazzy is mentioned as a fast pitcher.

Clarence Arthur ("Dazzy") Vance (1891–1961) played for the Pittsburgh Pirates and the New York Yankees (1915), the Yankees (1918), the Brooklyn Dodgers (1922–1932), and the St. Louis Cardinals (1933). Vance was elected to the Baseball Hall of Fame (1955). Lardner, when mortally ill, was still following Vance's career to such an extent that he wrote a letter to family members (February 28, 1933) wishing "some one would tell me whom Brooklyn got in exchange for Vance."

(Source: Caruthers [1995], 275; *Baseball Encyclopedia,* 2446)

VANDERBECK ("A Day with Conrad Green"). He was at the Bryant-Walker party, as were the Schuylers and the Suttons.

VANDERBECK, MRS. ("A Day with Conrad Green"). She was also at Mrs. Bryant-Walker's party.

VANDERBILT, PAT ("Gullible's Travels") *see* **ROCKEFELLER, MAGGIE**

VANDEVENTER ("Gullible's Travels"). He is "the biggest street-car conductor in Philadelphia," according to Mrs. Gullible, who elbows her husband and points out Mrs. Vandeventer to him in Palm Beach.

VANDEVENTER, MRS. ("Gullible's Travels"). Mrs. Gullible happily tells her husband that this important woman is vacationing in Palm Beach, as are the Gullibles.

VAN HALTREN, GEO. ("The Busher Pulls a Mays"). Keefe complains that Gleason, White Sox manager, is handling his pitching staff so badly that he may soon "be sending for Geo. Van Haltren or somebody" to help out.

George Edward Martin Van Haltren (1866–1945) played for the Chicago Cubs (1887–1889), the Pittsburgh Pirates (1892–1893), and the New York Giants (1894–1903). George W. Hilton remarks that Van Haltren was "a pitcher ... of no great merit ... in nine seasons" for five teams (1887–1901) but was a "thoroughly respectable" outfielder, mostly for the Giants (1894–1903). Hilton suggests that the record of Van Haltren, who would have been 53 in 1919, makes him "an excellent choice for this passage" containing Keefe's sarcasm. (Sources: *Baseball Encyclopedia,* 711, 1692–1693, 2448; Hilton, 311–312)

VAUGHAN ("Take a Walk"). He plays third base for Pittsburgh excellently in the game in which Agnew is playing for the home team.

Joseph Floyd Vaughan (1912–1952) played for the Pittsburgh Pirates (1933–1941) and the Brooklyn Dodgers (1942–1948). He was elected to the Baseball Hall of Fame (1985). (Source: *Baseball Encyclopedia,* 1694)

VEACH In "A Busher's Letters Home," Keefe rationalizes that when he was pitching for the White Sox against the Tigers, he "got mad" at his sassy catcher, Schalk, and therefore walked Veach, then complains that Veach stole a base on him. In "The Busher Comes Back," Keefe felt so insulted by Schalk that he walked Veach, continued to do badly, and was subjected to Callahan's sarcasm. In "A New Busher Breaks In," Keefe reports a game against Detroit, when Joe Hill was pitching. Hill tried to bean Keefe, who hit "a bullet ... [that] got between Cobb and Veach and goes clear to the fence," scoring Bodie and Schalk. In "Along Came Ruth," Keefe felt that he had enough stuff when he was about to pitch against St. Louis even "to make a monkey out of Cobb and Veach." In "The Busher Pulls a Mays," Keefe feels that he merits being traded to Detroit "for Bob Veach and no money on the side." Bob Veach is mentioned in "The Yellow Kid."

Robert Hayes Veach (1888–1945) played for the Detroit Tigers (1912–1923), the Boston Red Sox (1924), and the Red Sox, the New York Yankees, and the Washington Senators (1925). (Sources: *Baseball Encyclopedia,* 1695; Hilton, 67)

VEACH, THE REV. N. L. ("Travelogue"). He gave Mildred Orr a book identified as "Carlyle on Cromwell and Others." Bored on the train, Mildred at least opens the book (above the sweet girl's comprehension though it likely is).

VELEY, DR. ("Freedom of the Press"). He is a friend of Alexander Beardsley. Beardsley gets him to spike drinks for the troublesome reporters, so they will slumber a couple of hours and thus enable Veley to conduct the marriage of Constance Warner and Beardsley secretly.

"THE VENOMOUS VIPER OF THE VOLGA" (*Cosmopolitan,* September 1927). (Characters: Eddie Brock, Red Burke, Beau Burton, Jem Cook, Jimmy Donohue, Frankie Fitzgerald, Henry Goetz, Mabel Ives, Sandy King, Luke Lewis, Fred Lister, Manuel Martinez, Moran, Prentiss, Franz Reum, Jack Ran, Dmitri Sashoff, Harry Soule, Willie Troy, Duke Wallace, Teddy Walsh, Barney Williams, Larry Woltz.)

In October Luke Lewis, boxing promoter, and Sandy King, his press agent and associate, puzzle over winter and spring matches featuring Beau Burton, the heavyweight who took the championship from Jack Ryan. Burton was booed in public yesterday. Too bad they can't put Burton against Jem Cook, "a colored gentleman" from Biloxi who despite being aging is seen by moronic fans as a contender. Next week Cook fights Teddy Walsh in Buffalo. The referee, Larry Woltz, is a southerner; therefore, it's "good night Cook."

King says Jimmy Donohue has a good punch. Luke replies that matching underweight Donohue against Burton would be a joke. King recalls the "Carpenteer"-Dempsey mismatch. Luke says only Carpenteer's being "a frog" drew fans. Lewis wants "any guy from some place abroad" — maybe "Spain or Greece or somewheres." Deciding to match some nondescript fighters for now, Lewis promises King a "five grand" bonus to locate a likely foreign boxer.

King has an afternoon date with Mabel Ives, his girlfriend, whose "beauty was shown to its best advantage in the dark." With $5,000, he can marry her. They attend a variety show at the Palace. King spots a big "silent sentry" in a silly scene in "Master Ventriloquist" Prentiss's show. Figuring he may do as Lewis's "foreign" boxer, King locates him through the stage manager. He is Henry Goetz, born in Pennsylvania to a German father and a Russian mother. Illiterate and often unemployed, Goetz is 24, "six feet two, weighed 208 pounds, and had not been in a fight since he was old enough to apologize." At a speakeasy featuring "thirty-proof Scotch," King persuades Goetz he can make money boxing, at first against "push-overs" for maybe $30,000, then upwards of $75,000 against Jack Ryan, whose deadliness Goetz fears until King minimizes it. Goetz goes with King for $50 a week. Paid only $100 a week by Lewis, King introduces Goetz to Willie Troy, a rich, fun-loving boxing promoter who orders Goetz to abandon his friends — probably few, anyway — grooms him as Russian-born Ivan Ivanovitch, known as "The Venomous Viper of the Volga," and tells him "don't talk at all."

Troy houses the Viper in his Bronx home and trains him, somewhat, at his gymnasium. King writes himself a fake letter as from Berlin touting Russian-champ Ivan Ivanovitch for KO-ing Franz Reum, a leading German heavyweight, and including semi-nude "snap-shots of the new Slav fistic marvel" showing wonderful muscles. King shows everything to Lewis and says Troy has been writing the Slav's European manager for American rights. Staring knowingly at King, Lewis assures him that regardless of the Slav's identity — Milwaukee Dane or Montreal Mexican — he can have his $5,000 provided Lewis can "do business with Troy." Told the Slav's nickname in Russia is "the Venomous Viper of the Volga," Lewis says that's fine even if King and Troy invented it. The promoters stage a crowd-appeasing, phony fight between Eddie Brock, at 140 pounds, and 206-pound Moran, which Brock, betting $5,000 on Moran, loses by fouling Moran thrice "just above the knees."

In January the Viper "arrived" by boat, sick, gutteral, and accompanied by a Troy employee named Fred Lister. He becomes Dmitri Sashoff, is the Viper's manager-interpreter, and knows the word "ruble." Troy hustles the pair to his Bronx home, away from reporters. Lewis tells Troy they'll introduce the Viper to the public as Welsh's contender. At the ring just before a bout between Red Burke and Barney Williams, Troy has the announcer introduce "The Ven-ominous Viper of the Vodka," then whisks him away, because he's never seen a boxing match.

By February Troy has failed to train the Viper in defense and can rely only on his muscular offense, thus far limited to an obvious roundhouse. Luckily, Duke Wallace, Manuel Martinez's manager, offers to match the popular Martinez, aging, consumptive, but needing money, to Troy's "new foreigner" Duke heard about. Agreed, if Martinez can "take his dive in Round One," and if Troy pays Wallace $5,000 from big profits that Lewis, this fight's impresario, will give Troy. Brief exhibitions by each show Martinez slow against his opponent and the Viper clumsy against "four big hams" diving for $50 each.

Fight time. The huge Arena crowd applauds Martinez but is wild about the Viper, tattooed, on Lewis's orders, with a lady on each arm and Nevsky Prospect across his chest. The Viper quickly delivers a fierce right that floors Martinez and sends him to the hospital. Everyone lauds "the new Killer, a foreigner with a punch." Lewis is ecstatic and unconcerned whether Ryan comes out of retirement, because he plans for Fitzgerald to fight Moran, his Viper to knock out the winner in July, and the Viper to meet Burton for a "fifty-million-dollar" gate in September. First, though, he bribes Donohue to avoid fighting Fitzgerald, then reports that the Viper won't fight again — since Martinez has died — until he faces the sturdy Fitzgerald-Moran victor.

Trouble in May. Fitzgerald impressively defeats Moran; and the papers announce that Fitzgerald has signed to fight the Viper, the winner to meet Burton July 8 for the world championship. On July 7 King can't locate Mabel, even after phoning her mother, guesses she's with the Viper, and goes to Troy's home. The Viper boasts that Mabel has been enamored of him ever since seeing his tattoos, unfurled when he clobbered Martinez. King tattoos the Viper with numerous punches. Troy, back from conferring with Lewis and

Fitzgerald's manager, finds the Viper moaning with black eyes and bleeding from "a remodeled and unbecoming mouth and nose." Lewis starts negotiating for an early Ryan-Fitzgerald bout, on any terms.

Lardner was not inventive in naming characters in this story. He has a Harry and a Henry, and a Frank, a Franz, and a Fred, and perhaps named Burke, Lewis, Moran, Walsh, and Williams while thinking of the following baseball players he had written about: Jack Burke, George Lewis, Patrick Moran, Edward Walsh, August Williams, and Fred Williams. Lardner quotes Bill McGeehan as calling professional boxing "the cauliflower industry." William O'Connell McGeehan (1879–1933) was a sports writer. After army service during the Spanish-American War, he worked in San Francisco (1900–1914), wrote for New York newspapers (1914–1917), served in the American army again (1917–1918), and returned to sports writing (1919–1925). In his "Down the Line" column, McGeehan praised and encouraged amateur athletes, lauded clean professional sports, but castigated the commercialism of some professional sports, especially boxing.

VERGEZ ("Lose with a Smile"). Danny bunted when Vergez was playing third base in a Giants game against Brooklyn. Danny writes Jessie Graham that Vergez and Walker, pitching for the Giants, "was still trying to kick the ball foul" when "I was a crost 1st base."

John Lewis Vergez (1906–1991) played for the New York Giants (1931–1934), the Philadelphia Phillies (1935), and the Phillies and the St. Louis Cardinals (1936). (Source: *Baseball Encyclopedia*, 1697)

"VIA THE CANAL" (New York *Sunday News*, January 7, 1934). Searched for, unsuccessfully.

VICK ("The Busher Pulls a Mays"). Keefe says that while pitching for the White Sox to Vick, playing for New York, he had such a hangover that Vick "looked like he was hitting from both sides of the plate and I tried to throw a ball between him." Result? Keefe beaned Vick.

Samuel Bruce Vick (1895–1986) played for the New York Yankees (1917–1920) and Boston Red Sox (1921). George W. Hilton comments that Vick's "chief claim to historical notice is being the man whom Babe Ruth replaced upon joining the Yankees." Hilton adds that despite "the fictional beaning" Vick lived to age 91. Of players Lardner named, only Edd J. Roush lived longer. (Sources: *Baseball Encyclopedia*, 1698; Hilton, 315–316, 321)

VINCENT ("Gullible's Travels"). Among the supposedly prominent people Mrs. Gullible sees vacationing at Palm Beach, she mentions "The Vincents, ... the canned prune people."

VIOLET ("A Busher's Letters Home") *see* **HILL, VIOLET**

VISCHER ("Mr. Frisbie"). He was the owner of the estate Allen Frisbie bought. The fact that it included a golf course was the indirect cause of Frisbie's taking up golf— to his family's consternation.

VITT, "OSKAR" ("The Busher Comes Back"). Keefe boasts that when he pitched for the White Sox against Detroit he got "that bird" Vitt to pop out while he was trying to bunt.

Oscar Joseph Vitt (1890–1963) played for the Detroit Tigers (1912–1918) and the Boston Red Sox (1919–1921), and managed the Cleveland Indians (1938–1940). (Sources: *Baseball Encyclopedia*, 711, 1700; Hilton, 80)

VON KOLNITZ, COUNT ("Where Do You Get That Noise?"). Count Von Kolnitz, Heine Groh, Fritz Mollwitz, Wagner, Schneider, and Herzog play for the Reds. Carey, of the Cubs, says their names should help the Reds to break attendance records in Cincinnati, which is full of citizens of German background. Hawley wonders what about away games?

Alfred Holmes Von Kolnitz (1893–1948) played for the Cincinnati Reds (1914–1915) and the Chicago White Sox (1916). (Sources: *Baseball Encyclopedia*, 1701; Hilton, 513)

VOYANT, CLARA (The Water Cure") *see* **GULLIBLE, MRS.**

W., MRS. ("Contract"). She is a bridge-playing friend of Lardner, who hopes in a postscript she won't take his story personally.

WADDELL In "Sick 'Em," when the narrator, a Phillies man, first observes Smitty, he says that his fast pitch is comparable to Rube Waddell's. In "The Yellow Kid," the narrator says that he has faced all the fast pitchers, "from Rube Waddell down," and that Lefty Crosby was as speedy as any of them.

George Edward ("Rube") Waddell (1876–1914) played for the Pittsburgh Pirates (1900), the Pirates and the Chicago Cubs (1901), the Philadelphia Athletics (1902–1907) and the St. Louis Browns

(1908–1910). George W. Hilton describes Waddell as "brilliant, erratic, and unstable." Even so, he was elected to the Baseball Hall of Fame (1946). (Sources: *Baseball Encyclopedia*, 2452–2453; Hilton, 365)

WADE, BULL ("Hurry Kane"). He plays for St. Louis and kids Hurry Kane, their star pitcher. When Kane threatens to quit the team, Bull steadies him by composing fake letters to Kane, supposedly from Evelyn Corey, one of Kane's girlfriends. Bull sends the letters to Bull's brother Harry Wade, who addresses them to Kane from Montreal, where Harry lives and where Evelyn is supposedly on tour.

WADE, CHARLEY ("Good for the Soul"). He was a former Boston catcher recruited, along with other experienced baseball players, by A.T. Grant for his minor-league team. In a failed effort to improve the generally inept team, Billy Carmody, the manager, switched players around, including Wade.

WADE, HARRY ("Hurry Kane"). He is the brother of Bull Wade, who is a member of the narrator-catcher's St. Louis baseball team. A Montreal resident, Harry forwards pleasant phony letters from Evelyn Corey, to keep Hurry Kane, St. Louis pitcher and enamored of Evelyn, from visiting Minnie Olson, Kane's "Yuma gal."

WAGNER ("Where Do You Get That Noise?"). Wagner, Heine Groh, Fritz Mollwitz, Count Von Kolnitz, Schneider, and Herzog are Reds ballplayers. Carey, who plays for the Cubs, says that their names are enough for the Reds to break attendance records in Cincinnati, full as it is of citizens of German background. Hawley wonders about away-game attendance.

Joseph Bernard Wagner (1889–1948) played for the Cincinnati Reds (1915). (Sources: *Baseball Encyclopedia*, 1703; Hilton, 513)

WAGNER, JOHN PETER ("HONUS") See Honus. Larry Burns mentions "Wagner" in "Tour No. 2." Undoubtedly, the reference is to Honus Wagner.

WALDRON ("Harmony"). He is a natural-born baseball player. Some of his cohorts, however, value him more for his outstanding tenor voice and therefore want him to make a fourth with Bill Cole, Art Graham, and Lefty Parks when Mike McCann has to be cut from the team.

WALDRON, MR. ("Poodle"). He is the narrator's boss. He promises the narrator a $600 Christmas bonus, gives him a $50 haberdasher order instead, discharges him effective after February 4th, and goes on vacation to Florida without speaking to him.

WALKER In "Lose with a Smile." he pitched for the Giants when Danny bunted successfully for Brooklyn, only to be picked off at first base by Walker, who, as Danny wrote Jessie, "is left handed it." In "Meet Me in St. Louie," Max Carey, managing Brooklyn, kidded Danny for being picked off.

William Henry Walker (1903–1966) played for the Giants (1927–1932) and the St. Louis Cardinals (1933–1936). (Source: *Baseball Encyclopedia*, 2455)

WALL ("Champion"). He has a dance hall in Milwaukee where Midge Kelly, Emma Hersch, Emma's brother Lou Hersch, and Lou's date all "danced half the night away." Midge later marries Emma. (See Kelly, Emma.)

WALLACE ("A One-Man Team"). He is an overly optimistic assistant coach under Coach Belden. Their cockiness gets its comeuppance when they play the Doane team.

WALLACE, DAVE ("Dinner"). He is the other bachelor who, with Harry Barton, is invited for gender balance to attend Grace Halpern's dinner party. Both men endure inane talk by Miss Coakley and Miss Rell. Miss Coakley addresses Wallace as Walsh, Walters, Welling, and Wolheim.

WALLACE, DAVID ("The Jade Necklace"). He is a novelist. L. N. Bauer buys movie rights to Wallace's novel *Harridan* by outbidding the Supreme film company. Bauer's scenarist Earl Benham and Bauer's director Driscoll convert *Harridan* into *The Jade Necklace*— something totally different. Wallace willingly pockets his $50,000.

WALLACE, DUKE ("The Venomous Viper of the Volga"). He is the manager of the aging boxer Manuel Martinez. He agrees to have Martinez take a dive in a fight with "the Venomous Viper of the Volga," a fight resulting in Martinez's death.

WALSH In "A Busher's Letters Home," Keefe says that Callahan, White Sox coach, pitched him in Los Angeles more often than he did Walsh, praised as a fine hurler. In "The Busher Comes Back," Keefe praises Ed Walsh for having "a loud high tenor" voice and mentions that Callahan was saving Walsh for the city "serious." In "The Crook," Walsh was pitching when, as Larry the narrator-player puts it, he caught Carney, an opposing runner, "flat-footed off o' third base." Bull, the umpire, answered Carney's complaint with gentle sarcasm. In "The Busher Reënlists," Keefe complains that if he pitched regularly he would outdo "Walsh and all the rest of them big [regularly pitching] 4 flushers."

Edward Augustine Walsh (1881–1959) played for the Chicago White Sox (1904–1916) and the Boston Braves (1917), and managed the White Sox (1924). He was elected to the Baseball Fame of Fame (1946). (Sources: *Baseball Encyclopedia*, 1710, 2458; Hilton, 35)

WALSH ("Freedom of the Press"). He is a *Star* reporter hounding Constance Warner for news. He publishes unsigned falsehoods about Alexander Beardsley, Constance's new friend.

WALSH, BIG ED ("My Roomy"). He is mentioned as Martin Walsh's brother.

WALSH, MARTIN ("My Roomy"). He formerly pitched for Chicago. The narrator says that he sang so loudly "he could drownd out the Subway." Big Ed Martin is his brother.

George W. Hilton identifies Martin Walsh (1889–1954) as only a minor-league pitcher (1906–1921), who attended the Cubs' spring training but was not signed (1908), and who indeed had a fine tenor voice. (Source: Hilton, 346)

WALSH, TEDDY ("The Venomous Viper of the Volga"). He is scheduled to fight Jem Cook in Buffalo. Since Cook is African American and the referee, Larry Woltz, is a racist, Walsh is going to win.

WALTER ("I Can't Breathe"). This young man, 22, is engaged, temporarily, to the diarist, 18.

WALTERS, C. L. ("Sun Cured"). He is a passenger on the train from New York to Florida and, a month later, on the train back to New York. He does nothing but listen as Ernie Fretts talks about himself without allowing interruptions of more than a few words. Fretts is so self-absorbed that after wondering twice whether Walters is married he pays no attention to the answers. Walters is single.

WALTERS, GUS (*Own Your Own Home*). In "Own Your Own Home," he is evidently Fred's wife Grace's brother. The Walters live in Chicago. (The relationship is confusing, because Fred, in one of his semi-illiterate letters to his brother Charley Gross, says that Grace "lerned [something] from her brothers wife Gus Walters.") The Walterses like the house that Fred and Grace built and move into, in Allison, Illinois. In "Welcome to Our City," they visit the Grosses and praise their home.

WALTERS, MRS. (*Own Your Own Home*). In "Own Your Own Home," she is Grace's sister. In "Welcome to Our City," she is Fred's wife Grace's sister. In "Welcome to Our City," she and her husband visit Fred and Grace with pleasure.

WANER ("Take a Walk"). The narrator, in describing home-team Agnew's fence-hitting drive off French, Pittsburgh's pitcher, says it went beyond "half a dozen Waners." Bleat, however, correctly called Agnew out at home plate.

The reference is to the Waner brothers. Paul Glee Waner (1903–1965) played for Pittsburgh (1926–1941). He was elected to the Baseball Hall of Fame (1952). Lloyd James Waner (1906–1982) also played for the Pittsburgh Pirates (1927–1940), the Pirates and the Boston Braves and the Cincinnati Reds (1941), the Philadelphia Phillies (1942), the Brooklyn Dodgers and the Pirates (1944), and the Pirates (1945). He was elected to the Baseball Hall of Fame (1967). In "Insomnia" the sleepless author feels that "Nowadays I hardly know which Waner bats second and which third." (Source: *Baseball Encyclopedia*, 1712, 1716)

WANNOP ("Travelogue"). Hazel Dignan tells Dan Chapman that Bess Eldridge married Wannop, who owns flour mills in Minneapolis.

WANNOP, BESS ("Travelogue") *see* **ELDRIDGE, BESS**

"WAR BRIBES" (*Red Book*, April 1916). (Characters: Dr., Charley Gross, Fred Gross, Fred A. Gross, Grace Gross, Mary Gross, Dick Harger.)

Fred A. Gross sends 11 letters from Allison, Illinois, to his brother Charley Gross.

Aug. 12. "Bro. Charley," there "was a epidermis of whopping cough all a round town." Fred told his wife Grace to keep the kids inside. Therefore she took them outside. The two, including "little Fred," got sick and big Fred then "catched it." Fred wanted the kids to "cough there heads off" and then get well. Grace feared it was worse. Fred joked about "there simpsons" indicating "gout or some thing." Grace "beggin whinning" and called "the Dr." He said the kids had "whopping cough," visited almost daily for "2 mos." and billed each time for $1.50 just "lissening to them cough 10 minutes." Fred "lissened ... [longer] and got not nothing not even sleep." He attended one of "them banquits" — with beer — and next morning turned dizzy. "Grace drug me in to the parler and lade me on the lunge." Only when "the Dr." visited the kids did Grace let him examine Fred. He said Fred "was billius" and prescribed some pills and water. In July Fred had to "borry" from the chief, paid "intrust on my [house] lone" and let the doctor's bill lapse. In August the doctor added $6 to the bill. When Grace was invited to play cards, she cried because her dresses were all winter ones. So "there gos $14.50 for a party dress." She played "action bridge" badly and "loose $2.45."

Aug. 29. Fred writes "Chas." asking to borrow "$100 till the 1st. of Oct.," to pay "the bucher and groser." He won't ask "Graces old man," whose "down to his last $50000," or ask the chief for more. It's untrue "a bout a detective haveing a soft graft." He "wouldent do nothing crookit." He "wisht we hadent ... built no house." Fred sends "kindest to Mary." He's "fond" of her.

Sep. 15. Charley's not coming through with money "wont make no diffrunts in my feelings tords you and Mary." Grace's father sent $100 for her "berth day" but could have "trippled the amt." Fred wishes he had some "real money." He gets "tips on the stock markit strate from head quarters." He would have "trippled" a stock investment, or made even more if he had bought "on the margins" and could live "on the intrust"; but he "wouldent run no wrist" like that but would buy "the stocks right out" and sell when he "got the tip." The best tips are on "what they call the war bribes." The companies profiting most are not only "steal Cos.," making "bullits," "riffles," "shells," but also automobile companies and "boat factorys." — all "for the armys over in europe," who "give them big bribes to get the work done." And "theys danger" because if a factory supplied "the servias," some "french spy" might know and get the factory blown up "with dinahmite." Most plants work "night and day and there stocks is sky high." Some stocks are "still low," and you can "get in on the ground flr." If he knew about "bethleham steal," once "$.50 a share" and now $500.00, he "could of boughten 2 hundred shares" and now have "$100 thousand dollars." If he hadn't been broke, he'd "probly" be rich and would give, not "lone," Charley "money for a xmas present." About "Gen. Moders," Fred says "hes making some thing for the war." Sadly, Fred lacks money. It wouldn't be "gambolling ... when you get the info strate." The chief wants Fred to "go in with him." Fred won't try margins. If he could sell his house and buy "right out," he could make "my little pile" and then build a big place.

Oct. 23. Fred will be rich soon. He borrowed $100 from the chief, got a tip from Dick Harger about "crucial steal," "maxwell commons," and "Rumley." When the papers said Rumley was "8," he thought it was "8 cts." It was $8, and he could buy only 12 and ½ shares. Dick and his broker got him to buy 10 shares on margins for $100, figuring to make $10 on each point up. The broker asked Fred about life in Allison and laughed pleasantly. After drinking with Dick, Fred went home, didn't tell Grace and planned to drop a nice check in her lap soon instead. Rumley is a "war bribe" factory "down in Ind." making "riffles." Dick says Rumley may go to "$25 a peace," but Fred wants to hold until it's $500 like"bethleham Steal." Explaining margins to Charley, Fred says he will outwit the broker since "they aint room enough" for Rumley to "fall ... 10 pts."

Oct. 28. These "stock markit games got working beat to deth." Fred has a paper profit of "$60.00 in 5 days," plans to make $12 a day for a year, or "pretty clost to $4500.00." If Charley can send Fred $100, he'll "get some body [else] to place it," because his broker is "probly ... sore" about Fred's profits.

Oct. 31. The papers printed "junk a bout a U.S. boat geting sank by a German boat." "Steal" and other stocks went down, "rumley went a long," and "it was a falts report." Fred would "sew the papers" except he "hold[s] a public office" and doesn't want "no jam." He's now "$20.00 to the bad but of coarse it aint only temperary."

Nov. 4. Fred spoke with the broker, who "wasent gambolling with me" but was "a go between between I and the man" in New York that sold him that "rumley stock," which was "a fliver." Fred sold his stock, down to "$3.00 a peace," had to pay a commission, lost $56 altogether, but he "wont make no misstake the next time," and "will make ... [it] back" in "the game."

Nov. 6. Fred has bought 10 shares of "maxwell commons" at $85 on margins. It was $70, is already $90, but he can't sell yet. The more U.S. boats that sink the better, because "maxwell" make cars, and they'll replace boats. The man who gave him this tip says "maxwell" should go to $150. So Fred will have "prophet of $650.00."

Fred writes "Bro. Charley" an undated letter about that "bunch of crooks." A rumor about "a U.S. fish [that] was dying" caused the whole market to drop, including "maxwell" to $74. The broker demanded another $100 for the lost 10 points. When Fred threatened to refuse, the broker said he'd "loose the $100 you all ready put up," plus $10, plus "commision and intrust." Fred got $100 more from his chief, plans to hold to $85, then sell, and won't be "dubbling in stocks" again. Grace wants Fred to buy some coal, but he can't right now.

Nov. 15. Fred is "threw with this stock markit game." They're welcome "to build a bond fire" with "there stock," but they'd need bonds instead of stocks "for a bond fire." See, he can "still joke yet." Maxwell "dropped to $67.00," and the broker demanded another $100. Fred refused, and they sold him out and sent him a refund he "couldent buy supper for a flee on." He'll slug the next man with any tip for him. He must repay the chief $200. The whole family needs "new close." Maybe the chief will assign him "back to travvleing beat," with a uniform. So "nothing from us this xmas Charley." Grace's father from Milwaukee will "spend a wk. with us," and "Thats ... all as he will spend."

Nov. 20. Grace's father visited and gave her $3,000. She and Fred "huged and kissed the old man." He explained he just "cleaned up $30000" by "corting the war bribes." He bought "crucial Steal," sold, and profited $5,000. Then he "pertended" to his Milwaukee broker he had 500 shares of "bethleham Steal" at $550, gave him $10,000 to wire a Chicago broker who sold the 500 shares, and when they fell to $500 he and the Milwaukee broker bought 500 shares and delivered them to Chicago for $550. Fred "allways knowed" the old man was smart. Fred has paid his "dedts now, "boughten" some coal, and plans to play this "best game of all" with "some broker" secretly. If he sells "some rumley at $14" and instead of going down it goes to $20, he'll "jest say" he can't "fine it no wheres and it must of been stole." Charley and Mary can expect "xmas" gifts after all. "O you war bribes."

The critics have ignored "War Bribes," which admittedly does nothing to improve the reader's respect for gross Gross.

WARNER ("Meet Me in St. Louie"). He was Danny Warner's father. Danny writes Jessie that his father died in a Danville hospital years ago.

Danny's father probably died in Danville, Indiana, since Danny is from Bloomington, Indiana, south of Danville. There are 21 Danvilles in the U.S.A.

WARNER ("Oh, You Bonehead!"). He was a halfback on the Coach's Leighton football team.

WARNER, BUCK ("Good for the Soul"). Robert Frederick "Buck" Warner is a retired baseball player. He voluntarily dictates a confession to the Baseball Writers' Association of America telling how he obtained $2,500 in extra pay when he played right field for A.T. Grant's minor-league team. He had crippled his knee in the majors but hid the fact from Grant, couldn't marry Ethel of Dayton at the end of the season without obtaining an extra $2,500, and did so by extorting that sum in extra pay by agreeing to play shortstop for Grant as an emergency measure. Buck's confession is the story. At one point Ethel called him "Sidney Gloom."

WARNER, CONSTANCE ("Freedom of the Press"). She is Robert J. Warner's daughter, 22. When she was 11, Warner's wife died. He sent Constance from New York to live in France with her Aunt Julia and her French husband. Warner summons Constance home but dies before she arrives. She moves into the family mansion in Hempstead, is besieged by reporters, is befriended by Alexander Beardsley, Warner's former secretary, and they fall in love and marry.

WARNER, DANNY In "One Hit, One Error, One Left," Danny writes letters to and receives replies from his girlfriend Jessie (Graham) about his experiences when he is trying out in Clearwater, Florida, for a position in the outfield for the Brooklyn team. He boasts about his ability, makes excuses when things go poorly, and vacillates on the subject of his promise to marry Jessie, especially when he meets Vivian Duane in Clearwater. His manager Max Carey and Casey Stengel, who is Carey's assistant manager and coach, kid Danny in ways he can't comprehend. Danny likes to sing and boasts that he can "groon"—"kind of soft," he explains. In "Meet Me in St. Louie," Danny continued to play unsteadily, tried to write lyrics for a song about his father, was encouraged by Casey to do so, invited Jessie to visit him in St. Louis, but caused her to decline by saying they'd be lunching with two other young women. In "Holycaust," Danny got key hits for Brooklyn, dated Frank Earl's "sister and law" Miss Fleming, encouraged Vivian Duane once she arrived in Brooklyn, and further affronted Jessie, who wrote him to write her no more. In "The Ides of June," Danny was an effective pinch hitter, was shepherded by Stengel, continued to upset Jessie by seeing Vivian, and was cut from the team by Max Carey. Jessie felt encouraged by one of Danny's letters, and wrote him asking him to meet her in New York.

Danny Warner and Jack Keefe, of *You Know Me Al* and other stories, are both semi-literate letter-writing baseball players. Otherwise they are quite unlike. Danny may be a better athlete; but, unlike Jack, is unattractively and unpleasantly self-absorbed, selfish, humorlessly tactless, and stupid. Readers should like Jack but ought gradually to despise Danny. His teammates nickname him "Rudy," after Hubert Prior ("Rudy") Vallée,* the popular musician, band leader, and crooner. Howard W. Webb, Jr., after describing Danny negatively, concludes that "[e]ven his chances for a happy marriage seem dim." (Source: Webb, 443)

WARNER, ETHEL ("Good for the Soul"). She is Buck Warner's wife. They live in Hopsboro. Before they were married, Ethel, living in Dayton, learned that Buck was in debt, promised to wed only after he was in the clear financially, was briefly encouraged by her Aunt Julia's abortive promise of $2,500 for a wedding present, but happily learned that Buck obtained sufficient money to enable him and her brother Paul to buy a garage in Hopsboro and go into business together. Buck became a conscience-gnawed grouch until she persuaded him to confess how he obtained the tainted money.

WARNER, JACK ("One Hit, One Error, One Left"). He is a member of the Brooklyn baseball team. Casey Stengel says that since Jack Warner is already on the team they might nickname Danny Warner "bench."

John Ralph Warner (1903–1986) played for the Detroit Tigers (1925–1928), the Brooklyn Dodgers (1929–1931), and the Philadelphia Phillies (1933). (Source: *Baseball Encyclopedia*, 1715–1716)

WARNER, ROBERT J. ("Freedom of the Press"). He is a rich, reclusive New Yorker. When his wife died 11 years ago, he sent their daughter, then 11, to live with an aunt in France. Dying, he sends for Constance but dies before seeing her again.

WARREN ("Bob's Birthday"). Kemp and Warren employed Bob Tyler's father, but for some reason he was fired two years ago.

WARREN ("Take a Walk"). In the game against Pittsburgh, Warren, playing for the home team, hit a triple, but Agnew followed by striking out and griping about the calls made by Bleat, home-plate umpire.

WARREN, CHARLOTTE (*The Real Dope*). She is an American army nurse from Minneapolis, serving in France. When Keefe is in the hospital after being wounded, he has designs on her, unavailingly. In Chicago again with his wife Florrie, Keefe stupidly suggests the name Charlotte for their new baby daughter. Florrie retorts that "you can't come home and name my baby after none of your French nurses."

Since Keefe wrote only to Al Blanchard about Charlotte, the reader may assume Al tattled on Keefe.

WARREN, THELMA ("Rhythm"). She is evidently an important society figure. Harry Hart grows cocky and boasts of "hobnobbing" with her.

WASHINGTON SENATORS An American League baseball team. It was established in 1901, was active through 1960, after which it moved to Minneapolis and became the Minnesota Twins. (Source: Light, 779–781)

"THE WATER CURE" (*Saturday Evening Post*, October 14, 1916; GT) *see* ***GULLIBLE'S TRAVELS, ETC***

WATKINS ("The Ides of June"). He played baseball for St. Louis. Danny, batting for Brooklyn, boasts he hit a Bill Hallahan pitch so far that Watkins "never even tipped his cap to it."

George Archibald Watkins (1900–1970) played for the St. Louis Cardinals (1930–1933), the New York Giants (1934), the Philadelphia Phillies (1935), and the Phillies and the Brooklyn Dodgers (1936). (Source: *Baseball Encyclopedia*, 1719).

WATSON ("Cured!"). He owns the Duane Syndicate for which Dick Streeter is a cartoonist. When Dick, an alcoholic, reports to sign his new contract, Watson commends him for looking fine but asks how long he'll stay on the wagon.

WATSON ("Holycaust") *see* **BYRD-WATSON**

WEASEL, GWENDOLYN ("A Frame-Up"). She is the daughter of the man who owns the Lower Level of Grand Central Station, according to Jack Grace's silly talk, which Burke believes.

WEAVER ("The Golden Honeymoon"). He is from Danville, Illinois. Charley defeats him in checkers while both are vacationing in Florida.

WEAVER, BUCK In "A Busher's Letters Home," Keefe complains that Weaver, his White Sox teammate, made a bad throw during an Oakland game that cost a run, then another poor fielding play in their game against the Detroit Tigers. In "The Busher Comes Back," Keefe says that when he was pitching for the White Sox, Weaver's poor fielding in a game against Washington was costly again. In "A New Busher Breaks In," Keefe complains that during a disastrous game against Detroit's pitcher Joe Hill he struck out, after which Weaver and Blackburne also failed to score. In a game against Detroit in which Keefe pitched, Weaver "catched a lucky line drive off" Cobb. In "The Busher's Kid," Keefe complains twice about Weaver. Against Washington, he deliberately "throwed" badly so Keefe would lose the game; in a game against the Cubs, Weaver misplayed a ball hit by Schulte, who was wrongly given a hit for it by the reporters. In "The Busher Abroad" and "The Busher's Welcome Home," Keene mentions Buck Weaver as one of the baseball players on the world tour. In "The Battle of Texas," Keefe complains twice about Buck Weaver's playing badly while Keefe was pitching. In *The Real Dope*, Keefe recalls a game which he was pitching against "Phil." and in which Weaver fielded as though paralyzed. In "Along Came Ruth," Weaver earns Keefe's praise. When Keefe was pitching against Detroit, Weaver "stabbed" Ty Cobb's line drive and stepped on third to complete a double play. In "The Courtship of T. Dorgan," Keefe complains about Weaver's and Collins's play during a Washington game. In "The Courtship of T. Dorgan," Weaver and Keefe bet on the fight between Jack Dempsey* and Jess Willard,* and Weaver won. Buck Weaver is mentioned in "The Hold-Out."

George Daniel ("Buck") Weaver (1890–1956) played for the Chicago White Sox (1912–1920). George W. Hilton reports that Lardner met Weaver, then a rookie, at the White Sox training camp in Texas (1912) and liked him immensely. James E. Elfers begins the first of many comments on Weaver by saying that he "was easily the most talented of the White Sox to go around the world." Elfers describes how Weaver dazzled "the crowd ... of British and Egyptian soldiers" when, moving "like a sleek desert cat," he initiated a triple play during a game the world-touring teams played in Cairo (February 2, 1914). Weaver helped to plan what became the 1919 Black Sox Scandal. Although he backed out and didn't participate in the crime, his failure to report the plot to authorities caused him to be banned for life from professional baseball. Donald Elder says that "Ring, who had known Weaver back in the Central League, particularly regretted the injustice, and [Charles Albert] Comiskey[*] himself would have liked to save Weaver." David L. Fleitz says that "[i]f any member of the Black Sox deserves sympathy, it is Buck Weaver, who didn't receive any of the gamblers' cash and played all out in the Series." Fleitz, however, is critical of Comiskey. (Sources: *Baseball Encyclopedia*, 1720; Elder, 42, 71, 160, 161; Elfers, 25, 192, 193; Fleitz, 285; Hilton, 51; Yardley, 213)

WEBER ("The Crook"). Larry describes "Poor little Weber," his White Sox teammate, as terrified when he first faced Walter Johnson, the Senators' fast-ball hurler. Weber struck out and tried to cover his embarrassment by complaining to Bull, the umpire. Bull gently answered that he could hardly see some of the pitches himself.

"WEDDING DAY" (*Cosmopolitan*, July 1928). (Characters: Alice, Brownie Burt, Dorothy Drew, Ed, Fred, Frank Kennedy, Josie King, Wallie Roach, Miss Ruth Richards, Ben Seaton, Jimmy Shane, Shubert, Harriet Underhill.)

Miss Ruth Richards, of Detroit, has been visiting her sister Alice and her husband Ed, a New York show-business publicity man. Alice catches the flu. Ruth substitutes to attend the wedding of Jimmy Shane, stage and screen funnyman, and Brownie Burt, beautiful actress. While taxiing to the church, Ed tells Ruth that Shane is unfunny in private life. The other guests are theatrical people: Ben Seaton, "juvenile"; Wallie Roach, "eccentric dancer"; "soubrette" Dorothy Drew; and Josie King, high-paid chorus girl. Beautiful Brownie is becomingly nervous. Jimmy arrives, foppish and serious, in a chauffeured car. The ceremony is quick. Jimmy kisses everyone. Documents get signed. Jimmy in his car escorts Brownie, Dorothy, Wallie, and Ed to Ben's home. While Ben gets Josie and Ruth there, he and Josie talk shop but not about the newlyweds. This surprises Ruth, who says "Miss Burt" looked lovely. Ben and Josie tell Ruth that the bride and groom were engaged about six years, that money couldn't have delayed them, that Jimmy wastes money on three cars and slow racehorses, and that Brownie invested badly in Florida land. His $4,000 a week and her $3,500 aren't enough.

Ben's modest "suite" in a Fifty-fifth Street apartment hotel is alive with photographers, reporters, and cocktails. Brownie flashes her new diamond and sapphire bracelet, which Jimmy, refusing to say where they will honeymoon, admits cost about $10,000. When the outsiders leave, Jimmy orders Ben to play some records, and dancing begins. Jimmy, partnering with Ruth, says she and Alice are pretty enough to be in show business. When Ruth praises Brownie's bracelet, he offers to buy Ruth one just like it. Ruth replies that he's "as funny off the stage as on." No; he's serious and promises to dance again with her later. More dancing and drinking. Ben orders room service. Two waiters bring elaborate food and wine, the latter being especially appreciated. The guests toast Brownie and then Jimmy, at whom Ruth, "feeling more at home," shouts "Speech!" When Dorothy tells her not to encourage Jimmy, he accuses Dorothy is being jealous of Brownie. Dorothy replies that she'd like to have Brownie's "looks," "voice," and "figure," but not "her taste in men." Gulping wine, Jimmy intones seemingly sincere praise of Brownie and their deep-down loyal friends. After 10 or 12 minutes of it, Josie rudely interrupts by demonstrating her lithe tap-dance routine. When the dinner tables are removed, Ruth, Dorothy, and Josie "renew their make-up" in Ben's bedroom. Dorothy tells Ruth, who is inquisitive, that the newlyweds have no honeymoon plans. Josie, after saying the couple avoided being alone by attending this party, says she has rehearsal tomorrow and must leave. Despite Jimmy gripes that it's only 9:00 P.M., Ben calls for an "adjournment." Kisses all around, until Ruth "eluded" Jimmy's try. Brownie thanks Ruth for coming and hopes to see Alice soon. Everyone exits. Ed and Ruth decline Jimmy's offer to drive them home, hail a taxi, and watch "bride and groom start off in Jimmy's car."

Ruth wouldn't like hearing what follows in that car. Jimmy and Brownie agree that Ruth is dumb, without personality. Brownie urges Jimmy to return the bracelet. He admits it's not paid for and agrees he could return it after she flashes it a while. He says he's meeting Kennedy at his club tonight to consider his idea for a show set in a barber shop, kisses "Mrs. Shane," has his driver drop her off, will phone her tomorrow, and heads for Kennedy.

Back home, Ed won't answer Ruth's queries beyond saying Shane and Brownie are "a queer couple." However, while Ed has a cocktail in their kitchen, Alice explains: Brownie may still love Jimmy after years with him, "is used to him" anyway, and is too proud to "give him up without a struggle." She hired a lawyer to threaten a $200,000 breach-of-promise suit that might attach his salary for years; so he stymied her by agreeing to this marriage. She will be too proud, at least for a few years, to divorce him for alimony "if he doesn't behave." By then Jimmy figures he could escape "cheaper."

At the club Jimmy tells a desk clerk he's expecting a phone call from Philadelphia and plays billiards with lyricist Frank Kennedy. They don't discuss any "barber-shop scene." Jimmy gets his call, tells his "dear" yes it happened, he feels no different, he'll return that bracelet when the clasp is repaired by those busy jewelers, he'll try hard to "be over tomorrow." Kennedy tells Jimmy it's his shot. Jimmy tells Kennedy it was tough placing them [his two women?] as he did.

Though ignored by the critics, "Wedding Day" is a stunning indictment of Roaring Twenties "show biz" personalities. Since Ed calls Jimmy Shane, among others, "queer," is it possible that Jimmy's Philadelphia friend was a homosexual?

WEEGMAN ("The Busher's Welcome Home"). Keefe names Weegman as the owner of the federal league Keefe is deceived into trying unsuccessfully to join.

James E. Elfers explains that Charles Weeghman and James A. Gilmore in 1914 were trying to develop the Chicago Whales in the Federal League but were frustrated by Charles A. Comiskey* and Ban Johnson* (Source: Elfers, 170, 237–238)

"WELCOME TO OUR CITY" (*Red Book*, May 1915; OYH) *see* ***OWN YOUR OWN HOME***

WELLS, JACK ("Greek Tragedy"). He is the *Record* sports reporter. He goes to wrestler Alexis Greek's manager Lous Schwartz and offers to publicize him for a fee, is declined, but succeeds when he offers aid to Alexis's opponent Big Bill Buell's manager Ike Morris.

WELLS, MISS ("Widow"). She is a soprano, who leads a quartet including a tenor named Standing at John Winslow's funeral service. She pitches "In the Hour of Trial" so high that neither does a good job.

WELLS, PAUL ("The Jade Necklace"). He is a friend of movie-mogul L. N. Bauer, who reminds Wolf, his vice president, that Wells often identifies "a type of story to fit a certain star" for them.

WELSH ("Hurry Kane"). He plays for the White Sox in their crucial final game with the narrator-catcher's St. Louis team. He is safe when Digman makes an error.

WELSH ("When the Moon Comes over the Mountain"). Danny mentions "a left hander name Welsh" pitching for the Yankees. He "throwed" when Danny was "rubing dirt" on his hands. Welsh seems to be fictional.

WELSH, ALEC ("The Swift Six"). He is one of Fred A. Gross's friends. The two go to an automobile show in Chicago's Coliseum. Fred likes a car called a Swift Six so thoroughly that he buys one.

WELSH, FREDDIE ("Champion"). He is mentioned as a boxer Midge Kelly says he isn't afraid of. Midge grows too heavy to box him.

WENDELL, DR. ("Cured!"). He is the foreign-looking, mustachioed "kind of psychologist and psychiatrist" who drives "an expensive car" to the home of Dick Streeter, an alcoholic, and his wife Mary. Her friend Murna Evick recommended Dr. Wendell to treat Dick. The doctor, who says alcoholism is a disease not a bad habit, puts Dick on a seemingly successful regimen of hotel life and visitations. Dick cheats to appear cured, with the doctor's connivance.

A note, both ominous as to the patient's future and critical of the doctor's professionalism, is sounded when it is said that "Dr. Wendell was released and paid off a month ago."

WERNER, BONNIE ("Sun Cured"). She is Ernie Fretts's girlfriend. Fretts explains to C. L. Walters that she mistakenly thinks he'll marry her. Instead, he gets long-suffering Bonnie to board a New York train alone and join him for a vacation in Florida, during which he and she and two other couples dance and drink. While the men play poker and sleep in the afternoon, the girls shop and watch polo games.

WHALIN ("Back to Baltimore"). Dixon, Boston Braves manager, and narrator, explains that in a game against Philadelphia, Whalin, playing for Boston, "makes a perfect peg" to William Baker, Jr., who caught the ball but didn't put out the runner.

Albert James Whaling (1888–1965) played for the Boston Braves (1913–1915). (Sources: *Baseball Encyclopedia*, 1728; Hilton, 439)

"WHAT OF IT?" (*Liberty*, June 7, 1924; LN, WOI). (Characters: Bertha, Ben, Carlotta, Carlotta, Carter, Dexter Cosset, Cragin, Ellsworth, Fox, George, Ben Lacey, Mrs. Lacey, Joe Morris, Phillips, Orville Pleat, Harrison Quolt, Smythe, Trunkey.)

The narrator told a friend of his who is a traveling salesman "in the furniture game" about Ben Lacey, a bothersome talker on trains, and how he was effectively silenced:

"Well, ... a fella named Dexter Cosset," who was a South Bend clerk, wrote a play called *Ghosts*, sent a copy to a friend in New York who knew Joe Morris, a producer, whose reader liked it. Cosset was called to New York to discuss it. Cosset was distressed because the heroine was named Carlotta, after his girlfriend, and the New York people wired him that his title *Ghosts* won't do because a "man named Ibsen has a farce that title." So they plan to call it *Carlotta's Corns*. This would make Carlotta, who doesn't have corns, so mad she "would of give him the air and submitted to the caresses of Orville Pleat," a car dealer.

On the train to New York, Cosset had to smoke to think. He went to the Pullman washroom but encountered Lacey, whom he knew as a salesman out of Chicago. Lacey transitions non-stop from topic to topic — his accurate watch, Fox who knows watches, Cragin the Los Angeles murder victim, Lacey's sister, her son named Ben, Trunkey the elevator people, [Calvin] Coolidge.* Saying he had to check his luggage, Cosset escaped. A fellow passenger named Harrison Quolt entered his car, saw Cosset's agitation, and asked why. After Cosset summarized "all the circumstances," Quolt said he too was bothered by "these Pullman elucutionists" until he "mastered the art of putting the quietus" on them. Quolt took Cosset back to the washroom, sat down facing Lacey, and stared constantly at Lacey's knee. After Lacey jabbered about being hired by the Trunkey people and then stopped, Quolt, continuing to stare at Lacey's knee, said, "What?" Lacey repeated his commentary. Quolt, still staring, said, "What of it?" Lacey replied that he was lucky. Quolt: "What of it?" Lacey said their train was approaching "Kendallville or Ligonier." Quolt: "What of it?" The three men sat immobile 30 minutes. Finally Cosset said that "the treatment's worked" and he will rename his play "What of It?" Quolt: "What did you say?"

Lardner's use of *Ghosts* (1881) by Henrik Ibsen (1828–1906), though tangential, is apt. In it, misleading talk disconnects from reality with consequences — far more tragic, to be sure, than Cosset or Lacey will ever suffer. Lardner liked the put-down line "What of it?" so much that he used it as a title for *What of It?* (1925), a grab-bag book of 31 previously published essays, nonsense plays, satires, newspaper pieces, and also has Father use the put-down query twice, and Mother once, in

The Young Immigrunts. In a letter to Max Perkins* (January 31, 1925), Lardner credited his friend Grantland Rice* with the idea for the title. (Source: Caruthers [1995], 173)

WHEAT ("Where Do You Get That Noise?"). He is a Brooklyn player who hits a triple in a game against the narrator's team. Then Carey, playing center field, catches Cutshaw's fly ball but throws home so wildly that Wheat scores the winning run.

Zachariah (Zachary) Davis Wheat (1888–1972) played for the Brooklyn Dodgers (1909–1926) and the Philadelphia Athletics (1927). He was elected to the Baseball Hall of Fame (1959). (Sources: *Baseball Encyclopedia*, 1728; Hilton, 519)

WHEELER, BIG ("The Battle of the Century"). He was a boxer whom Jim Dugan defeated in Ohio to win the title, before the main action begins.

"WHEN THE MOON COMES OVER THE MOUNTAIN" (*Saturday Evening Post*, May 7, 1932; LWS, RAB) *see* ***LOSE WITH A SMILE***

"WHERE DO YOU GET THAT NOISE?" (*Saturday Evening Post*, October 23, 1915; ABS, RAB). (Characters: Bishop, Bobby, Cap, Carey, Clarke, Cutshaw, Dale, Dode, Griffith, Groh, Hawley, Hawley, Mrs. Hawley, Zeke Hawley, Hermann, Herzog, Johnson, Klem, Pat Moran, Mollwitz, Oakes, Schneider, Smitty, Von Kolnitz, Wagner, Wheat.)

I. The narrator is with a baseball team (the Cubs, 1915) that traded two worthless players for a Philly named Hawley. He "had went better this spring" than ever. The narrator asks his Philly friend Dode why Hawley, only 27, was released. Dode says, "I and Bobby ... figured that Pat just plain got sick o' hearin' him talk." When the narrator doubts this, Dode says that there "wasn't no subject that he didn't know all about it better'n anybody else," whether it was chess, towns, relatives, surgeries, etc., and adds that Carey (the Cubs jokester) will "get sick of him" like everyone else.

II. The narrator briefs Carey, who quickly challenges Hawley, by saying European artillery firing has caused this summer's wet weather. Hawley explains that he's seen far worse weather. It rained every day 19 years ago May till September, then it cleared "for the world serious." Carey counters that there wasn't a world series in 1896. Hawley agrees that European artillery caused this summer's rain, which Carey ventures to doubt. Hawley adds that dynamite causes rain.

III. During batting practice (in Chicago), Carey's line drive hits the fence. To admirers, Hawley explains it's hard to hit well in this smoky town's dirt- and cinder-filled air, whereas Cobb and Crawford are great hitters in clean Detroit. Carey mentions Wagner of Pittsburgh, to which Hawley replies that Wagner would've hit over .500 if "in New York or Detroit all the wile." The narrator's mentioning Washington primes Hawley to say his Uncle Zeke is Senator Hawley, personal friend of "Woodruff Wilson." The narrator wishes he could live in clean Washington but wonders why "fellas in the Washington Club" are poor hitters. Carey theorizes that "the silver dust from the mint gets in their eyes." Responding "Where do you get that noise?," Hawley explains that the Washington baseball players sit too much under Washington's shady trees and therefore sudden ball-park sunlight blinds them. The narrator's and Carey's jokes about cutting Washington trees outside the park and others planted near home plate and elsewhere don't unsettle Hawley.

IV. They wonder why attendance is so poor when they play "down in Cincy." The narrator blames the ineffective Reds and adds that the war hurts business, golf provides better exercise than sitting in ball parks, and cars are so cheap that people drive around with friends. No, says Hawley, then explains "about the war hurtin' baseball." Spectators favor either "the Dutchmen or the Alleys." It's fine if the Reds, full of players with German names, win at home, because Cincinnati is full of Germans; but if they win in Boston, there could be trouble. The lucrative solution? Field a team "o' fellas from countries that ain't got nothin' to do with the war — Norwegians, Denmarks, Chinks, Mongrels and them fellas." Carey opines that such a club couldn't find a team it could defeat.

V. Smitty, from Lansing, Michigan, reads in his hometown paper that his kid brother is competing in Michigan's Wolverine Club golf championship, says he's likely to win, because he can shoot 71. Hawley steps in, claims he learned golf at Wolverine, has shot 73, better than 71. Encouraged, he says he could shoot even higher but is out of practice and played with only one heavy club costing $50. Did he slice with it? Yes, so fiercely that it cut balls in two. Smitty volunteers that his brother lost last year's city tournament when "stymied by a bumblebee." Hawley says applying raw meat to such stings is better than cauterizing, which was Carey's suggestion. Hawley confesses he quit golf because hitting golf balls spoiled his aim at baseballs. Also when playing golf you wait for golfers ahead of you so tediously that when you're batting you automatically wait and the pitcher sneaks strikes on you. Also you don't hit a golf ball hard, for fear of losing it. Just the same in baseball, because you forget "balls is furnished by the club."

VI. The narrator's team's bunting ability worsens; therefore, after July 4th Cap orders hit-and-run plays. Carey fails, however, three days in a row, hitting instead into double plays. When he sarcastically gripes "that's about a record," Hawley boasts that he hit into four double plays in one Philly game. Irate, Carey strikes out all next week. Hawley advises him to choke up his bat. Instead of encouraging Hawley's nonsense, Carey derides him. In mid–July against Brooklyn, with the game tied in the ninth, their man Wheat is on third, Carey in center field catches their Cutshaw's fly ball, Wheat scores because Carey's peg home — normally he's deadly — misses by 20 feet, and Brooklyn wins. Hawley, rushing to sympathize, tells Carey he could have thrown precisely if only a white stripe guided centerfielders to home plate the way foul-line stripes guide left-fielders and right-fielders. Monumentally upset by Hawley, Carey tells the narrator that he "won't cripple him up or nothin' like that" but that "he's goin' to get himself in wrong" — and tonight.

VII. Carey "framed it up so's" he, Cap, and the narrator meet Hawley "to supper." The narrator recalls that Cap is immensely proud of his wife, a blonde "and — believe me — she dresses!" Since she's caring for her sick mother "out there in St. Joe," Hawley has never seen her. Hawley wonders why Carey, hitting badly, can be all smiles now. Because, he says, he has just seen a gloriously beautiful woman. Cap asks about her. Like the prettiest girls, she's a blonde, Carey answers. This remark obliges Hawley to insist that a beautiful brunette outclasses all blondes. Carey responds that the prettiest woman in the U.S. is a certain Missouri blonde he remembers. Hawley says he went to school in Missouri with that state's prettiest girl. A blonde? Carey asks. No, Hawley retorts, adding that all blondes dye their hair, whereas girls' black hair is always natural. Hawley admits "I forget" that stunning Missouri brunette's name. Cap explodes, reviles Hawley in detail, says he'll rid the team of him on waivers, and storms out. Alone with the ostensibly shocked narrator, Carey predicts that without Hawley around he'll hit well again. Pittsburgh takes Hawley from Cap. One day later, Carey is hitless at five at-bats. And Hawley? He is "doin' good" and likely advising Wagner how to bat.

The arresting title "Where Do You Get That Noise?" is Hawley's intemperate, off-putting refrain, blurted six times to stop rational opposition or uncomprehended jibes. For variety, he also uses "stuff" instead of "noise" a few times.

WHICHONE ("Widow"). He was a race horse at Saratoga, remembered by Frank Hastings.

WHIFFLETREE, MILDRED ("A Frame-Up"). She is the niece of ukulele-king Bud Fisher, according to Jack Grace's silly talk, which Burke believes.

WHISKERS ("Good for the Soul"). He guarded the field where A.T. Grant's mostly inept baseball players practiced in Dixie Springs. Buck Warner usually designated the cranky fellow "Whiskers" but also called him "the Old Fox."

WHITE, CHARLIE ("Some Like Them Cold"). He is some sort of performer to whose "show" Chas writes Mabelle that he and the Searses will see.

WHITE, GILBERT ("Insomnia"). He is an alumnus of the University of Illinois, from which Allan Spears also graduated. White and fellow-alumnus Harry Myers tell Allan that if he has a drink, Myers will give Allan a stock-market tip. Allan agrees.

WHITEMAN, PAUL (1890–1967). Musician. Denver-born Whiteman led a jazz-like band in San Francisco (1918) and in New York (1920), and became a fabulous showman. He toured England (1923, 1926), commissioned *Rhapsody in Blue* (1923) for piano and orchestra by George Gershwin,* and featured it with Gershwin at the piano in New York's first completely symphonic jazz concert (February 24, 1924). Whiteman's first movie was *The King of Jazz* (1930), which included Bing Crosby's film debut. Whiteman became a recording, radio, and television artist. He is mentioned in "Poodle," "Rhythm," and "Zone of Quiet." Jonathan Yardley quotes from a radio review Lardner wrote late in his life ("The Perfect Radio Program," *The New Yorker* [August 26, 1933]), in which he highly praises Whiteman. (Sources: Evans, 112–113; Yardley, 368)

WHITEY ("Haircut"). He is the barber-narrator. His real name is Dick. At and near Whitey's shop, Jim Kendall concocted his string of jokes, which were usually cruel and the last of which proved fatal — to Jim.

The black humor in "Haircut," typical of much in Lardner, is enhanced here by Whitey's abysmal ignorance. Brian T. Cowlishaw notes that "Whitey ... is too stupid to see that Kendall's 'jokes' aren't funny" or "to understand what narratee (haircut recipient) and implied reader understand clearly"; meanwhile, Whitey's mangling of standard English "also reveals a careless, unreasoning mind." (Source: Cowlishaw, 213)

WHITING, CAPT. (*Treat 'Em Rough*). He is one of Jack Keefe's commanding officers. When he organizes a football team, partly made up of former college players, Jack joins them, but soon quits and demeans them for playing "a college Willy Boy game."

WHITNEY ("The Ides of June"). He played third base for Boston in a game against Brooklyn. Danny, a Brooklyn player, explains that after he was walked, Johnny Frederick hit a fly to Whitney and Danny was caught off first base.

Arthur Carter Whitney (1905–1987) played for the Philadelphia Phillies (1928–1932), the Phillies and the Boston Braves (1933), the Braves (1934–1935), the Braves and the Phillies (1936), and the Phillies (1937–1939). (Source: *Baseball Encyclopedia*, 1736)

WHITTED ("My Roomy"). He and Whitted are St. Louis outfielders. They can't field a vicious smash by Buster Elliott that goes between them for a triple.

George Bostic Whitted (1890–1962) played for the St. Louis Cardinals (1912–1913), the Cardinals and the Boston Braves (1914), the Philadelphia Phillies (1915–1918), the Phillies and the Pittsburgh Pirates (1919), the Pirates (1920–1921), and the Brooklyn Dodgers (1922). (Sources: *Baseball Encyclopedia*, 1736–1737; Hilton, 347)

"WHO DEALT?" (*Cosmopolitan*, January 1926; LN, RLR, RU). (Characters: Gertie Baker, Ken Baker, Byers, Jack Brooks, Mrs. Cannon, Thomas Cannon, Crandall, Ned Frawley, Arthur Gratz, Helen Gratz, A. L. Guthrie, Mrs. Guthrie, Hammond, Hastings, Ted Jones, Nelson, Runkle.)

Mrs. Cannon is the monologist-narrator of this account. She has been married to Thomas Cannon for three months. They are playing bridge with Arthur and Helen Gratz at the Gratz home somewhere far east of Portland (Oregon), which Mrs. Cannon feels is "out there," as she repeatedly says. In the course of simultaneously babbling and playing bridge carelessly, like the thoughtless person she is, the narrator uninterruptably and despite Tom's growing uneasiness reveals the following:

Tom said that he and Helen were childhood "pals"; Tom solemnly vowed to quit drinking; she heard that Helen and Arthur eloped four years ago; Tom got a raise and is a vice president; he has secrets she tries to worm out of him; Tom quit playing football at Yale after a dispute with Ted Jones, "the main coach"; Tom's friends Ken and Gertie Baker happened to see Tom and the narrator during their honeymoon in Chicago, tried to get Tom to drink but couldn't; Tom might run for mayor; they played bridge "out there" with lumberman A. I. Guthrie and his nice but ill-dressing wife; the Guthries were really too different ever to get married (but there's "a proverb ... about like not liking like. Or is it just the other way?"); the narrator and Tom agree on what's good for breakfast and about pajamas; "feel just the same about everything" (except music); Tom wrote a short story he intended to destroy until she made him save it. That story concerns an impoverished Yale man and a handsome, "well-off" Princeton athlete (handsome like Arthur here), both in love with the same girl, who promised to wait for the Yale man to do well but instead eloped with the Princeton man, who didn't know about the girl's broken promise. Tom's story was rejected by magazines; their editors probably never read it; it included a poem. Despite Tom's anguish, the narrator recites the poem — about the persona's divine beloved who broke her promise, left him crushed, and "has flown!" The narrator expresses shock that Helen has just revoked and Tom is suddenly guzzling scotch.

Lardner played bridge and was intrigued when contract bridge began to supplant auction bridge (mid–1920s). Charles Goren reports that Lardner as a journalist covered the famous 150-rubber contract bridge tournament (December 11, 1931–January 8, 1932) between Eli Culbertson and his wife Josephine Murphy Dillon Culbertson vs. Sidney Lenz and Oswald Jacoby. It was held at the Chatham Hotel in New York. Other reporters were Lucius Beebe, Robert Benchley, Heywood Broun,* Henry McLemore, Grantland Rice,* Westbrook Pegler, Damon Runyon,* and H. Allen Smith, many of whom were Lardner's personal friends. By 8,980 points, the Culbertsons won the $1,000 prize and invaluable publicity. Elizabeth Bibesco, praising "Who Dealt?" as well as "Some Like Them Cold," says that they "belong to the universal masterpieces that know no frontiers." Martin Seymour-Smith may have had "Who Dealt?" in mind when he generalizes that Lardner often locates his fiction in "the realm of the horrible-as-funny." (Sources: Bibesco, 367; Goren, 20–22; Seymour-Smith, 203)

WICKHAM ('A One-Man Team"). He is the big football center playing for Coach Belden, who tells him to cut a class, if he must, in order to practice. In the game against Doane, Wickham is ineffective.

"WIDOW" (*The Red Book Magazine*, October 1935; SC). (Characters: Archie, Belden, Flora Belden, Bert, Mrs. Bishop, Miss Brent, Fleming, Mrs. Fleming, Gallant Fox, Joe Gordon, Mrs. Gordon, Hamlin, Frank Hastings, Hastings, Dr. Hyland, Jim Dandy, Julia, the Rev. Miles Langdon, Miss Logan, Fred Milburn, Mrs. Milburn, Dick Randall, Dr. Simpson, Mrs. Somers, Paul Somers, Standing, Miss Wells, Whichone, Alice Winslow, Ed Winslow, John Winslow, Margaret Winslow.)

John Winslow, who indulged in coffee and cigarettes excessively and had trouble breathing, was reticent about answering disinterested questioners concerning his health, felt bad Sunday, and died Tuesday.

Margaret, John's wife six years and now his widow, phones his brother, Ed Winslow, and his wife Alice Winslow, to come stay with her. Alice tells Margaret so often to get hold of herself that she finally cries on Alice's shoulder. Ed takes time off and makes funeral arrangements. Visitors, mostly women, come to sympathize with Margaret on Wednesday and Thursday. Mrs. Hastings tells her she'd want to die or go into seclusion if her Frank died. Mr. Somers advises Margaret to rest for Friday's funeral and says if her Paul died she'd just hide. Mrs. Gordon says that she and her Joe will help Margaret if needed, remembers that Mrs. Gordon's sister Julia lost her husband, who was wealthy and left her "comfortably off," but concludes that one "doesn't think of money at a time like this." Mrs. Bishop visits, but cries, and is comforted outside by Alice. Mrs. Milburn suggests that time heals, that after her Archie died she found solace in religion, her doctor told her to take a trip, and that luckily she "had enough money to do what he said." She went to Miami, and bumped into her old friends the Beldens, who coaxed her into attending a party at the Casino. Despite having brought only two evening gowns, she went and "met Fred — it was the beginning of a new life." She believes her heart has room for both Archie and Fred. She theorizes that in time Margaret's John's death will resemble "a bad dream." Margaret won't answer questions about money but silently reckons her checking account, savings bank, and John's insurance would make $26,900. While Mrs. Fleming says John seemed too healthy to die so suddenly, Mr. Fleming listens in another room as Ed tells Paul Somers that John's doctor knew about his weak heart and tried unsuccessfully to make him quit coffee, cigarettes, and whiskey, and to quit acting like a high-strung colt. This reminds Frank Hastings to tell — again — about when he would have bet at Saratoga last summer on Jim Dandy, a horse that won, except a drunk insisted he should. Meanwhile, no male mourner — all are light-hearted — tries to make John's brother Ed cry.

Friday. The home funeral. Many "floral tributes," notably expensive ones from "the Fred Milburnes" and the Gordons. A mixed quartet from John and Margaret's church. A 25-minute eulogy by the Rev. Miles Langdon. It makes Gordon and Hastings long "for a smoke." Margaret's thoughts? Awareness that she should weep. The cost of all those carnations. Is Mrs. Hastings crying because this funeral isn't her husband's? Why hasn't Dick Randall been in touch, and what could Alice know? Twelve cars proceed to the cemetery, where Ed does cry, as do other men. This distresses Margaret, who believes therefore that "John must have been nice."

Home again, Margaret wishes Alice and Ed would leave. On Saturday Alice says Margaret should answer the piled-up condolence notes; well, a little later. Margaret discards them all. On Sunday Alice says Margaret needs advice from Ed. He says she can void her lease next month, must rent some place reasonable, will have roughly $26,000 after paying John's few debts, and should invest in good bonds or mortgages at, say, 6%, meaning, "let's see," about $130 a month to be "careful" with, oh, minus a little state inheritance tax. Alice expresses gladness Margaret has no children. Earlier, she thought they'd be "such a comfort." Asking Ed to check investments and Alice to check rooms, Margaret announces tentative thoughts about a brief getaway.

Alone at last Wednesday evening, Margaret wishes John had died after the Hamlins' costume party next Saturday, to which she and Dick Randall would have been guests. She also wishes John had died of an accident, which would have added $15,000 to his insurance. Also, remembering their dancing and warmly kissing, and his saying, "If you were only free!" She wishes Dick had called by now. Next day she phones him. Reminding her of flowers he sent for John's funeral, Dick agrees to visit briefly before his lodge meeting. Arriving when "it was quite dark," Dick gradually says they had fun but if they continued he'd be thinking of John, a fellow lodge member. She urges Dick to get to his meeting. Alone again, Margaret figures Los Angeles would be a better vacation spot than Miami, where she might encounter "another Fred Milburn."

WILCOX, L. F. ("'In Conference'"). He is "the tire people," according to L. N. Croft, a Kramer & Company vice president. L. N. adds that his sister Minnie is Wilcox's wife.

WILCOX, MINNIE ("'In Conference'"). She is L. M. Croft's sister and L. F. Wilcox's wife. L. M. tells his Kramer Company associates that Minnie "was over to the house last night" and "was reading us" a free-verse poem by Amy Leslie.

WILL ("That Old Sweetheart of Mine"). He was a boyfriend whom Stella Barnes abandoned to marry Ralph Barnes quickly, in order to escape what she recalls as "that deadly place." Fifteen years later, Will phones Stella in New York. Hoping to rekindle their affections, they have lunch and go to the theater together. But each observes too much wrong in the other, and they separate in relief. Will, who has broken a date with his standby Betty, phones her again and will see her pronto.

WILLARD, JESS (1881–1968). Professional boxer. Born on Potawatomi land, Kansas, Willard was a farmer, wagon handler, and then a professional heavyweight boxer (from 1909). Willard, white, defeated world-champion John Arthur "Jack" Johnson (1878–1946), black, by a 26th-round knockout in Havana (1915). Johnson had made a deal to throw the fight to avoid a prison sentence but was jailed anyway. Jack Dempsey* defeated Willard (1919) by a third-round technical knockout. Willard fought in 36 matches, winning 20 by knockouts and losing two by knockouts. He later worked in circuses and appeared in some silent movies. Lardner mentions Willard in *The Big Town*, "The Busher Pulls a Mays," "Champion," "The Clubby Roadster," "The Courtship of T. Dorgan," "The Poor Simp," *Treat 'Em Rough*, and *The Young Immigrunts*. Lardner covered the Willard-Firpo fight for the Bell Syndicate (July 13, 1923). Firpo won. (See also Rickard.)

WILLIAMS ("Back to Baltimore"). He is the Boston Braves vice president. He retains little authority once Mrs. Hayes becomes president, principal owner, and stupidly domineering boss.

WILLIAMS In "The Battle of Texas," "Lefty" Williams is on the White Sox pitching staff with Keefe, who says that "Williams ... was pretty good" but "didn't have anywheres near the stuff I showed them." In "Along Came Ruth," Keefe gripes that Gleason ignored him and picked Williams to pitch against Detroit. Keefe is happy that "before the 1st inning was over ... Lefty was enjoying the shower bath." In "The Busher Pulls a Mays," Keefe complains that Gleason favors Williams and Cicotte and that fellow White Sox players also praise the two. Later, when Gleason tells Keefe that Williams "don't feel good," Keefe, hungover himself, says that if Williams feels "like I do" his relatives should go buy him "1 left handed casket."

Claude Preston ("Lefty") Williams (1893–1959) pitched for the Detroit Tigers (1913–1914) and the Chicago White Sox (1916–1920). George W. Hilton reports that Williams was the White Sox best left-hander, second only to Edward Victor Cicotte on the pitching staff, and that after participating in the 1919 Black Sox Scandal was banned from baseball. Hilton adds that Williams was so moody and inarticulate that Lardner made no attempt to delineate his personality. David L. Fleitz describes Williams's deliberate bad pitching in Game 2 of the scandalous Series (he walked six batters) and how Ray Schalk, his outraged catcher, punched him in suspicion after the Reds' 4–2 victory. (Sources: *Baseball Encyclopedia*, 2479; Fleitz, 182; Hilton, 248)

WILLIAMS (*The Big Town*). He and his brother Palmer Williams, of the Williams Company, have a "flying field" on Long Island near the Decker Hotel, where Finch, Ella, and Katie are summering. The brothers are interested in Bob Codd's experimental "aeroplane" until it crashes and kills Codd.

WILLIAMS ("A Busher's Letters Home"). Keefe boasts that when he pitched for the White Sox against the St. Louis Browns, his hopping fast ball caused Williams to pop "right straight up."

August Williams (1888–1964) played for the St. Louis Browns (1911–1915). (Sources: *Baseball Encyclopedia*, 1742; Hilton, 63)

WILLIAMS ("Horseshoes"). He is a Cub outfielder when Dick Grimes joins the team in a utility capacity.

Fred Williams (1887–1974) played for the Chicago Cubs (1912–1917) and the Philadelphia Phillies (1920–1930). George W. Hilton notes that William made good use of his Notre Dame degree in architecture by later becoming a builder in Wisconsin. (Sources: *Baseball Encyclopedia*, 1740–1741; Hilton, 399)

WILLIAMS, BARNEY ("The Venomous Viper of the Volga"). He is a tough boxer who loses in a vicious fight with Red Burke.

WILLIAMS, BERT (1874–1922). Bahamas-born Egbert Austin Williams was an accomplished stage entertainer. Light-skinned and with black-face makeup, he sang, danced, and clowned effectively, and with his partner George Walker (1873–1911) developed a unique "coon act" and other shows (beginning in the 1890s). Williams composed songs, joined the *Follies* of Florenz Ziegfeld* (1910), and starred in eight subsequent seasons, incorporating African-American folk comedy. The Roaring Twenties had hardly begun when Williams died of pneumonia and heart failure.

As a youth, Lardner often spent his meager savings to see Williams perform in Chicago. *Zanzibar* (1903), Lardner's two-act comic opera, for which he wrote the music and the lyrics, clearly shows Williams's influence. When Lardner became a sports reporter, Lardner continued to admire Williams, and the two drank happily together in obscure saloons. In the 1917 *Follies* Williams sang "Home, Sweet Home, That's Where the Real War Is," music and lyrics by Lardner. In "Insomnia" the sleepless author remembers a song by Williams, in which it is said that "Money is de root of evil" but that nobody objects "to de root." Lardner mentions Williams in "The Busher Abroad" and *The Big Town*, and alludes to him in "The Golden Honeymoon." When Williams died, Lardner's friend Heywood Broun* wrote a partly demeaning obituary column (New York *Morning World*, March 7, 1922). Lardner replied by letter to Broun, who quoted it (*Morning World*, March 9, 1922). In it, Lardner says that Williams was "the greatest comedian and one of the greatest clowns I ever saw," and that he was also "a great natural musician and a masterly singer of 'coon songs,' and when I say singer, I mean singer." Jonathan Yardley strangely says that Williams was Lardner's "lifelong idol" but adds that their "friendship ... could not be called close." (Sources: Elder, 28–32, 244–248; Caruthers [1995], 141; Farnsworth, 38–39; Yardley, 52, 53–54)

WILLIAMS, CHARLIE ("My Roomy"). He evidently works in an administrative capacity with the Chicago baseball team. The St. Louis "hotel people" tell Williams to make Buster Elliott quit singing so loudly. Williams tells John, the manager, about the problem.

George W. Hilton identifies Charlie Williams as Charles W. Williams (c.1870–1938), longtime employee of the Chicago Cubs, and also the Chicago Whales of the Federal League, in various capacities (1885–1917). (Source: Hilton, 346–47)

WILLIAMS, CHARLIE ("Nora"). He is an actor whom Louis Brock suggests for the part of a German in a restaurant scene in Hazlett's play "Nora," revised by Brock, Frank Moon, and Jerry Morris.

WILLIAMS, PALMER (*The Big Town*). He and his brother own an airfield on Long Island and are interested in Bob Codd's experimental airplane until it crashes.

WILMOT (*The Big Town*). The Wilmots are Finch's cousins and live in Bridgeport. When Finch suggests visiting them, Katie, his sister-in-law, pleads a previous date with a dressmaker.

WILSON ("Contract"). He and his wife move from Linden to Chicago. This results in Shelton and his wife, newcomers in Linden, replacing the Wilsons in dinner-bridge parties hosted by Cameron and his wife, Carl Dittmar and his wife, and Robert French and his wife. The Sheltons soon dump the above-named six because they criticize the Sheltons' inept card play.

WILSON, HACK In "One Hit, One Error, One Left," Danny Warner writes that Hack Wilson has become a member of the Brooklyn baseball team after playing for the Cubs and St. Louis. Danny adds that Hack, a fine hitter, is being paid $16,500. In "When the Moon Comes over the Mountain," Danny praises Wilson's determined fielding and vigorous swinging when at bat. In "Lose with a Smile," Danny writes that Wilson and Glenn Wright together "got in a couple of real socks" against the Giants to win for Brooklyn. In "Meet Me in St. Louie," Wilson is mentioned. In "Holycaust," Danny reports that Wilson hit into double plays against Cincinnati, then against

"Chi" fielded badly for a while but hit well. In "The Ides of June," Wilson's hitting is praised.

Lewis Robert ("Hack") Wilson (1900–1948) was an outfielder for the New York Giants (1923–1925), the Chicago Cubs (1926–1931), the Brooklyn Dodgers (1932–1933), and Brooklyn and the Philadelphia Phillies (1934). Wilson became a member of the Baseball Hall of Fame (1979) (Source: *Baseball Encyclopedia*, 1747–1748)

WILSON, MRS. ("Contract"). When she and her husband leave Linden, the Sheltons replace them in neighborhood bridge games. Not for long.

WILTSE, GEORGE In "The Busher Beats It Hence," Keefe says that McGraw wants him to go on the world tour to strengthen his pitching staff, since "Wiltse is a left hander." Keefe also says that while kidding him, Dutch Schaefer said he was "hog fat" compared to Wiltse and Mike Doyle. In "The Busher Abroad," Keefe mentions "geo.Wiltze" as a pitcher who went on the world tour and won a game in Cairo. James E. Elfers describes "Hooks" Wiltze as the Giants "curveball specialist" but also as an "aging veteran."

George LeRoy Wiltse (1880–1959) played for the New York Giants (1904–1914). In *Treat 'Em Rough*, Keefe mentions that McGraw on "Sun. P.M." [October 7, 1917] started another lefty against the White Sox in "the world serious." Sources: *Baseball Encyclopedia*, 2385–2486; Elfers, xx, 188–189; Hilton, 177–178)

WINGO, I. V. ("The Busher Abroad"). Wingo, also spelled "Wingow" by Keene, is a catcher on tour with other baseball players going around the world. He refuses to lend Keefe his catcher's "mast" to help Keefe avoid being pecked by the dangerous Thomas Hawks birds. Keefe renders "Ivy," Wingo's first name, as "I. V."

Ivey Brown Wingo (1890–1941) played for the St. Louis Cardinals (1911–1914) and the Cincinnati Reds (1915–1929), and managed the Reds (1916). James E. Elfers describes Wingo as a "general whiner" who after a double-header (Tokyo, December 7, 1913) wanted "to lie down and rest his aching bones." (Sources: *Baseball Encyclopedia*, 713, 1752; Elfers, xx, 118)

WINSLOW ("Oh, You Bonehead!"). He ran well for Pelham in their football game against the Coach's Leighton team.

WINSLOW, ALICE ("Widow"). She is Ed Winslow's wife and Margaret Winslow's sister-in-law. Alice officiously tries to offer Margaret sympathy following the death of her husband John.

WINSLOW, ED ("Widow"). He is Margaret Winslow's brother-in-law. When his brother John Winslow dies, Ed is mostly concerned about Margaret's financial situation and offers unheeded advice.

WINSLOW, JOHN ("Widow"). He was Margaret's husband. He drank too much coffee and whiskey, smoked too much, minimized the severity of his heart condition, and died.

It is likely that John smoked and drank too much, and avoided answering questions about his health, because he knew of his wife's affair with Dick Randall and wanted to die. On what evidence does Walton R. Patrick suggest that after John Winslow dies, he "suddenly looms up as a very honorable man, now greatly admired by the very pals who joked about him when he was alive"? (Source: Patrick, 130)

WINSLOW, MARGARET ("Widow"). She is John Winslow's widow. She listens indifferently to would-be sympathy and advice from several visitors before, during, and after John's funeral. What she wants is to continue an affair with Dick Randall, who, however, withdraws pusillanimously. So Margaret plans to follow Mrs. Milburn's advice and take a vacation. Mrs. Milburn did so and found a second husband in Miami. Margaret thinks Los Angeles might be better.

WISE, MAX ("Rhythm"). He is a publisher of musical compositions, including Harry Hart's. When Hart, in desperation, asks his advice, Wise says he should team again with Benny Kane.

WITKOWSKY, ETHEL M. She was one of Lardner's girlfriends. She was from Chicago and vacationed with her family at Barron Lake, east of Niles, Michigan. The Lardner family also vacationed there. The Witkowsky family, which was Jewish, and the Lardners disapproved, to Lardner's protracted sorrow. (Sources: Lardner, Jr., 22; Caruthers [1995], 4, 84; Yardley, 57–58)

WOLF ("The Jade Necklace"). He is the vice president serving under L. N. Bauer, head of Colossal Films Incorporated. Wolf tells Bauer to hire a handsome Irish actor to rival Supreme film company's matinée-idol Dennis Byrne. Bauer hires Maurice Kavanaugh, and takes Kavanaugh and Wolf to Hollywood to produce *The Jade Necklace*.

WOLFE ("Ex Parte"). He and his brother are in the furniture business. Bess and Jeff Cooper buy good modern furniture from them.

WOLFE, JAKE "Ex Parte"). He and his brother, furniture dealers, sell good items to the Coopers.

WOLFGANG ("The Battle of Texas"). Kid Gleason has Keefe "work out" with Wolfgang and Red Faber.

Medford John Wolfgang (1890–1947) was a spitball pitcher for the Chicago White Sox (1914–1918) before being released to Milwaukee (1919). (Sources: *Baseball Encyclopedia*, 2490; Hilton, 242–243)

WOLTZ, LARRY ("The Venomous Viper of the Volga"). He is a boxing referee. A racist from the South, Waltz is sure, Luke Lewis says, to see that Jem Cook, an African-American, will lose in a fight against Teddy Walsh in Buffalo.

"WOMEN" (*Liberty*, June 20, 1925; RAB, RU). (Characters: Frank Baker, Bill Boone, Helen Buck, Gephart, Mike Healy, Huggins, Bill Hutton, Young Jake, Jansen, Joe, Johnnie Lambert, Lefty, McDonald, McGraw, Meusel, Baldy Pierce, Jim Preston, Sam, Smitty, Dick Trude.)

Mike Healy, who is a utility baseball player, and Gephart, Lefty, and Young Jake are all on the bench. Jake gripes that it's June and he isn't playing yet. Healy says Jake might not see action by August, September, or next year. Jake and Lefty notice a "damn cute" girl in the stand. Healy warns them that all women are "poison." He says that but for a woman he'd be playing third base instead of Smitty, who'd be warming the bench, and launches into reminiscences that some of his teammates, who have heard before, try but fail to interrupt:

Four years ago he was "bought" by this team after playing well for two years with Toledo. He was to replace Johnnie Lambert, their third baseman, excellent but 35 years old and with a bad knee. During the winter, a specialist mended Lambert's knee and Healy "froze my dogs" hunting in Michigan. Healy warmed the bench. So did Healy, though if "let loose" he would play so well that "Judge [Kenesaw Mountain] Landis[*] himself couldn't keep me on the bench." Lambert played well, on into May and June. Meanwhile, a girl from Ligonier, Indiana, who watched Healy play in Toledo, "got stuck on me." That fall they got engaged, and next June her sister phoned Healy that the girl was sick, "delirious ... and hollerin' for me." Missing a game during "a serious in Chi," he rushed to Ligonier. She instantly recovered, and they planned a wedding date. Lambert's knee went out. Smitty, replacing Lambert at third, still plays that position. Healy wrote his girl that he'd marry her all right but that she resembled spinal meningitis. She never answered.

The manager orders Healy to coach at third. He lets Smitty, after tripling, get caught off base. Lefty complains that Healy at the time was "lookin' up in the stands." Jake sees that same "cute" girl. His praise of her starts Healy again. During his first year, he was playing well for Dayton, would soon have attracted McGraw's attention but for a woman. Baldy Pierce, an ugly but cocky league umpire, attracted the unique attention of pretty Helen Buck during a September game against Springfield. This, despite Healy's obviously better looks. McDonald, McGraw's scout, was watching Healy, who planned to display his talents. He tagged a Springfield player named Bill Boone out at third before Jansen crossed the plate; but Pierce wrongly called him safe. At bat in the ninth, Healy would have brought in the tying run from third, but Pierce called an obvious bean ball a third strike, ending the game. Pierce explained his call: If Springfield won, the series would be tied, a playoff would be needed next day, and he had a picnic date then. McDonald told Healy that he missed tagging Boone and foolishly took that third strike.

Healy enlightens Jake further. He would have been interviewed by Huggins of New York to replace slipping Frank Baker, except that the phone girl in Healy's hotel, "stuck on me," fibbed to Huggins that Healy was out. She wanted no one to interfere with their date. Dick Trude, an usher, suddenly brings Healy "a mash note" from that "cute" girl in the stand they've all been eyeing. Healy reads it, and tells Dick to return and say the answer she requests is "yes."

Donald Elder's perceptive comment that Lardner "always lived close to tears" intrigued Douglas Robinson, who suggests that those tears sometimes "only surfaced ... in displayed form," for example, as a "somatic response" such as "a hostile frustration in ... 'Women.'" (Sources: Elder, 377; Robinson, 137)

WOOD ("The Busher Comes Back"). Keefe boasts that he pitched successfully for the White Sox against Boston, even though he "worked against Wood at that."

Howard Ellsworth Wood (1889–1985) played for the Boston Red Sox (1908–1915) and then the Cleveland Indians (1917, 1919–1920). George W. Hilton reports that Wood coached baseball at Yale University (1923–1942). (Sources: *Baseball Encyclopedia*, 249; Hilton, 83)

"WORDS AND MUSIC" (*Good Housekeeping*, August 1930). (Characters: Bennett, Hilda Harper, Ketter, Linda Languish, Lincke, Margaret, Newman, Miss Claire Richardson, Mrs. Starr, Roman Starr.)

Hilda Harper goes with her roommate Margaret to *Amourette*, Roman Starr's first sound movie. Although his singing "voice did not screen well," his love scenes with beautiful Lydia Languish were heartbreaking for Hilda, and for other girls thrilled by Roman as well. Margaret is aware of her friend's anguish. Hilda collects clippings about Roman, including a recent account in *Wave Lengths* in which he theorizes that "Art thrives on Love," and contends that if he loved his dream girl, then lost her, he would suffer but sing even more captivatingly. Oh, if Hilda could be that beloved one, she "would never detour for his Art's sake." She writes "Dear Mr. Starr" a long, tender, self-effacing letter, calling herself faithful to his every show at the Royal, saying she is a simple stenographer, but hoping he'll reply — even "with just a little note."

After "five weeks of hell," Hilda knows he won't answer. One morning she reads Miss Claire Richardson's interview of Roman, published in the *Bulletin* and so frivolous and uninformative that Hilda would like to slap her. With Margaret's encouragement, Hilda decides to pretend she's a reporter and meet Roman. She identifies herself as the *Gazette*'s Flora Campion to the Royal's doorman and says she's assigned to see Roman. He is given the message and soon appears. He says he's going to do some recording right now but agrees to be interviewed tomorrow morning at 10:30. He tells her his apartment is at "Eight-ten Park" and to have his secretary admit her. Hilda returns to her office, asks Mr. Linke, one of her bosses, for permission to see her dentist in the morning, and gets his "gruff" acquiescence. Sleepless that night, Hilda wishes she could turn on a light and memorize some clippings about Roman Starr to impress him.

Next morning, to avoid getting red-nosed in chilly weather by walking the mile-plus to 810 Park, Hilda takes a taxi, arrives early, walks about anyway, and in due time gives her name — Flora Campion — to a uniformed doorman. He says Mr. Starr's secretary just left, but to go in. The elevator boy gets her to the proper floor. Far beyond his door, left open by the secretary, "Mr. Starr was doing his daily dozen arpeggios." Hilda "ventured" into the living room. His voice is wondrous, "just singing Os." Suddenly his wife, calling him "Gus," berates him for keeping her awake snoring all night, wonders if he's finished breakfast, complains that he shined his shoes with her stockings, and asks where his secretary Bennett is. Sent out, Roman explains, to check on a song involving "Newman's lyric" and "Ketter's ... [redone] bridal melody."

Hilda, retreating "noiselessly," must do something desperately different. Ignorant about where to get poison or alcohol, she buys some cigarettes, lacks matches to light one, and abandons the effort.

The title "Words and Music" is clever. Obviously, Lardner is suggesting that musical-performer Starr's written words are hypocritical. But more subtly, when Starr tells his wife that "Newman's lyric, for the canoe number ... [is] practically the same as 'Pacific Moon,' and Ketter's rewritten the bridal melody," Lardner is implying that creators of musical comedies in general can be word-and-music thieves. The plotting of "Words and Music," however, seems too clumsy to warrant Walton R. Patrick's assertion that its "technique ... is quite deft." (Source: Patrick, 131)

WRIGHT ("Haircut"). He owns a pool room in Whitey's town. Jim Kendall often drank there.

WRIGHT, GLENN In "When the Moon Comes over the Mountain," he is the Brooklyn baseball team captain and "a fine short stop," according to Danny. In "Lose with a Smile," Wright praises Frank Earl for deceptively delivering pitches. Wright got a key hit in a game against the Boston Braves. In "Holycaust," when Danny mentioned "holycaust," Glenn Wright said he thought the reference was to a post–Easter feast. In "The Ides of June," Danny writes Jessie that Glenn Wright praised the home run Danny hit off Bill Hallahan, pitching for St. Louis.

Glenn Wright (1901–1984) played for the Pittsburgh Pirates (1924–1928), the Brooklyn Dodgers (1929–1933), and the Chicago White Sox (1935). (Source: *Baseball Encyclopedia*, 1760)

WURTZ ("There Are Smiles"). He is mentioned as a non-joking traffic policeman, unlike jovial Ben Collins.

WURZ (*The Big Town*). He is the manager of the Decker Hotel, where Finch, Ella, and Katie are vacationing. When Wurz suddenly "showed, with a bag of golf instruments and a trick suit," Finch is not interested in playing with him. Wurz introduces Finch to Herbert Daley, identifying him as "Daley the horseman ... up from the South."

WYETH, JAMES ("Freedom of the Press") *see* **MACOMBER, THE REV. WALLACE**

"THE YELLOW KID" (*Saturday Evening Post*, June 23, 1917; ABS, LOB, RAB). (Characters: Jake Atz, Bill, Cahill, Harry Childs, Lefty Crosby, Gilbert, Mary Lloyd, McGowan, Joe Martin, Buck Means, Patrick.)

I. The narrator, a married man named Bill, is a member of Cahill's team [the White Sox]. Here is his story:

We drafted Lefty Crosby from the Texas League. Gilbert, my teammate, said Crosby was "faster'n Johnson" though not wild enough to be scary, also very handsome, and both illiterate and terrified by women. Buck Means, his former Dallas Club teammate, told us this "out o' spite" and jealous of Crosby's ability. Buck added that McGowan, a Dallas outfielder, enjoyed pretending to read aloud to Crosby from newspapers phony criticism of his pitching and praise of his good looks. This distressed him. McGowan also sent phony love letters to Crosby. Someone would read them to him, and that scared him into hiding, except to emerge to pitch. I warned Gilbert that revealing Crosby's weakness might hurt his pitching. But Gilbert told Harry Childs, who when traveling to an exhibition game in Dallas pretended to be reading from a Chicago paper — Crosby said reading on trains hurt his eyes — to the effect that Crosby, a Francis X. Bushman* lookalike, might "take the female sex by storm" in Chicago and New York if he encouraged them. Childs told the blushing fellow that Cahill would like him "tied down" (by marriage) and therefore able to pitch even better. When Crosby said he preferred being single, Childs accused him to secretly loving a Mexican "peacherita." In Fort Worth, Childs got a girl to terrify Crosby by phoning him; in Oklahoma City, Childs criticized a newspaper photo for not doing Crosby justice.

Crosby's considerate friend Joe Martin read the menus to hungry Crosby and tried to shield him from Childs, with only partial success. The day spring training ended, Childs bought a rule book and read phony restrictions on left-handed rookie pitchers — they can't warm up the day of a game, can't wear a glove, etc. I tried to assure Crosby that Childs was trying to be funny. Regardless, Childs persuaded Crosby that Cahill would order him to pitch the home opener in Chicago; further, that since "Friday is Lady's Day" the stand and boxes would be full of "womenfolks," and "showgirls" in reserved seats behind our bench. Crosby immediately pleaded that his "old souper felt kind of numb," even "rotten."

II. Cahill scheduled Crosby to pitch not Friday but Sunday, against Cleveland. He was scoreless for five innings. Then Childs, angry at being pulled from the outfield after the fifth, told Crosby when both were resting that a gorgeous "peach" sitting behind them wanted to meet him. Crosby proceeded to walk the first four batters in the sixth. Cahill, calling him a "yellow dog," sent him to the showers. Childs told us what he had done, and Martin asked him to lay off. He wouldn't, though. So we proceeded to tell Cahill, who ordered Childs to desist at least during games, or be sent to Texas. While Childs temporarily quit razzing him, Crosby became the fastest and best in "the whole league."

III. But Childs resumed. On the train from Cleveland to St. Louis, we were playing cards while Crosby watched. Childs pretended to be angry at Gilbert and planted his gun, loaded with blanks, on the table threateningly. Crosby turned white, almost fainted, and left. In the train washroom, Childs brandished the gun before Crosby, who fled without his collar. Crosby couldn't pitch against the Browns. Once again Cahill warned Childs.

IV. Childs contented himself with writing letters to Crosby, purportedly from admiring women. I read some of them to him when he complained that their "funny" handwriting was puzzling. Crosby began reminiscing. He said he could talk to his sister but never to girls in school, which he left at age 12 to join "a minin' gang up North." The men there were satisfactory, until in a saloon brawl "the guy that took care of me" was shot dead. Ever since, Crosby feared not only girls but also guns. What else?, I wondered. Bean balls, he answered. So I praised his facing .400 hitters more bravely than "some o' the rest of our beautiful pitchers."

V. The hotel we stayed during games in Detroit had a telegraph operator named Mary Lloyd. She was pretty, loquacious, and decent. We all liked her, including Childs, who "probably fell for her stronger than any o' the rest." I encouraged him, but he said whenever he tried to get friendly she'd say "Back up!" "I and Gilbert" observed Mary when she first laid eyes on Crosby. She asked about "that handsome wretch." We said his pitching outwitted Cobb and Veach. She said she'd ask him to spare her Detroit batters. I told her he was girl-shy, which she thought "hardly fair to our sex," handsome men being rare. She threatened to approach him and thus spoil his pitching, but I said we'd boycott her hotel if she did.

One afternoon Mary wanted to meet Crosby. Figuring it was safe because rain had prevented the game and we'd be leaving Detroit tomorrow, we spotted Crosby, and Martin produced the reluctant fellow. Smiling her "best," she held out her hand, which he touched left-handed, but then spun around and disappeared up the elevator. Outraged, Mary said she'd "like to scratch his handsome face." On the night train, Childs happily revealed that Mary let him take her to supper earlier that evening. We knew why. In July in Detroit again, Childs dated Mary every night. One morning, she confronted Crosby with a level stare. He seemed "mighty glad" she said nothing.

VI. Childs replaced Patrick, our injured outfielder, and boasted of wanting to keep in shape and save money, because he planned when we returned to Detroit to propose to Mary, who'd been writing him. Childs hit phenomenally against the Phillies, was cocky when we were playing Washington, and kidded Crosby further. Childs said that "a Mr. Wilson," his White House friend, told him that we'd be getting into the war, that the newspapers said most American guns were left-handed, and that there'd soon be a "call for ... left-handed men." Crosby left, without "no desert." In New York, Childs told Crosby that the Germans attacked Benton Harbor [Michigan] and "able-bodied guys" would have to enlist. Crosby said he had sore ankles and couldn't march, nor could he drive a motorcycle "acrost the ocean." Childs countered that motorcycle tires could be inflated.

In Boston at breakfast, I read a newspaper report that unmarried 19- and 20-year-olds might be drafted. Childs, hearing this, asked Crosby his age; 20, he said. Later, agitated, Crosby told me he'd drown himself in Lake Michigan before entering the army, and wished he were my age. My answer was "or [be] married." Crosby pitched badly that day.

VII. Martin revealed something later. Crosby had asked him how to get married when he hadn't met any girls since he was 15 or 16. Martin spoke of girls wanting to hold hands and recommended Mary, who — remember? — "ast to meet you." Martin persuaded Crosby to let him send Mary a night letter in Crosby's name apologizing for his rudeness and asking to see her again. Mary wired back that she'd "pay attention to him" if he spoke nicely "to her face."

VIII. Childs' good luck ended when. playing in Cleveland, he should have slid into home but didn't, broke his leg, and couldn't proceed to Detroit. Martin, Gilbert, and I wanted to repay Childs for his mean jokes as well as to benefit Crosby. So, once in Detroit, we put Mary and Crosby at her "lunchtime" into a taxi, closed it, and ordered the driver to keep driving fast a while. The couple returned, all smiles, in an hour. Crosby said she "wasn't half bad." By now he's probably past "the First Reader" with her help.

Walton R. Patrick regards "The Yellow Kid" as "expertly written," and "witty and comic." It may be added that the title of this story seems inept: Crosby isn't "yellow" in the dictionary sense of "contemptible," "cowardly," "mean"; he is simply shy. (Source: Patrick, 122)

YOST, MR. (*The Young Immigrunts*). He is the coach of the Michigan football team. When the narrator is proceeding by car with his parents to "Grenitch Conn.," they stop in Ann Arbor to see Bill, the narrator's uncle. The men telephone Mr. Yost, who comes to the hotel to talk briefly.

YOU KNOW ME AL (1916; ABS, LOB, PRL, RAB, RLR, YKM). Six related stories comprising 94 letters and resembling an epistolary novel. They are "The Busher's Letters Home," "The Busher Comes Back," "The Busher's Honeymoon," "A New Busher Breaks In," "The Busher's Kid," and "The Busher Beats It Hence."

"A BUSHER'S LETTERS HOME" (*Saturday Evening Post*, March 7, 1914). (Characters: Al, Allen, Mrs. Allen, Baker, Bumgardner, Benz, Bodie, Bush, Callahan, Charley, Chase, Cicotte, Cobb, Collins, Comiskey, Crawford, Jack Doyle, Easterly, Flynn, Fournier, Frank, Gainor, Kid Gleason, Jackson, Jennings, Johnson, Walter Johnson, Johnston, Jack Keefe, Kelly, Kuhn, Lajoie, Lord, Moriarty, Pratt, Russell, Schalk, Scott, Shotten, Smith, Stanage, Veach, Violet, Walsh, Weaver, Williams.)

In 17 letters to "Friend Al [Blanchard, Bedford, Indiana]," Jack Keefe begins to relate his experiences as a professional baseball pitcher.

"Terre Haute, Indiana, September 6 [1912]." Keefe says he played for the Terre Haute club of the Central League, was observed by White Sox scout Jack Doyle, and was bought by Sox owner Comiskey. Keefe boasts he'll try to compete with Sox ace pitcher Walsh. If unsuccessful, he'll happily return to Terre Haute, but he plans to "make good."

"Chicago, Illinois, December 14." Keefe went to Comiskey's office. Comiskey was away hunting. Keefe will demand $3,000 as salary, since expenses are high.

"Chicago, December 16." Comiskey kidded Keefe about wanting the office furniture as well as $3,000. Keefe signed for $1,500 and may make extra money in the fall "city serious." He'll "demand" more next year.

"Paso Robles, California, March 2 [1913]." Keefe traveled by "De Lukes" train. On the way, people admired his "hight and shoulders." In the hotel dining room, Kid Gleason told Keefe that they didn't charge extra for using forks and that Keefe was already overweight. Manager Callahan told the players to walk for exercise. Keefe didn't. Next day he pitched at batting practice, scared Lord with a fast ball, and impressed Callahan with his "smoke."

"Paso Robles, March 7." Two teams opposed each other. Keefe pitched well, struck out Collins, and used his spitter, which Walsh told him to learn to cover up. Keefe dined with Gleason, Bodie, and others. Frank tolerated kidding from Gleason, who called fat Bodie "a cow." Gleason warned cocky Frank to improve his fielding. Frank saw a pretty "blonde kid" at the hotel dance last night. She wanted his picture. Pals told him he was sold to a Jackson (Mississippi) team down south. Keefe understood the joke because Jackson's in Michigan.

"Paso Robles, March 9." Keefe leaves tomorrow for "Frisco with the first team." He plans to encourage that blonde, from Detroit, who wants him to write her.

"Oakland, California, March 19." Keefe pitched in four games. Three runs scored on him partly due to teammates' errors. He "whiffed" eight in five innings. Callahan kids him often about his poor fielding. If Callahan reviled him as he did a rookie, Keefe would punch him. Keefe and "some of the boys" visited Frisco and saw painted dames at "the Barbers' Coast." That blonde wrote him.

"Los Angeles, March 26." At poker Keefe got four sevens, took the pot and quit. Kelly objected, and Keefe nearly slugged him. Keefe lost when pitching against Los Angeles and then Venice, and Callahan griped that after three weeks he still wasn't cutting loose.

"Yuma, Arizona, April 1." Heading east, they played "a pick-up team," and Callahan for a change praised Keefe. Scott joked when he called his pitch to Baker, an "Athaetics" hitter, his "fadaway" because Baker makes "it fade ... away over the fence." Yuma's Indians don't resemble theater Indians.

"Oklahoma City, April 4." On the train from Amarillo, "a old lady" admired Keefe's build. So he said she should see him naked. This bothered Lord and Weaver. Callahan warned Keefe to pitch and field better in St. Joe, or it's "back to the sticks." Keefe isn't worried.

"St. Joe, Missouri, April 7." Keefe pitched a three-hitter, picked a runner off first, and fielded bunts well. His job is "cinched." Violet (the blonde) writes from Detroit. The team will open in Cleveland. Reporters travel with his team.

"Cleveland, Ohio, April 10." Keefe can save part of his dollar-per-meal allowance at breakfast. Though Callahan won't pitch him for the opener, Keefe doesn't fear Cleveland sluggers Lajoie and Jackson. The Sox second team joined the first in Chi. Gleason misnamed Keefe a "hog fat."

"Cleveland, April 11." Scott lost pitching against Cleveland. Violet sent a postcard. Keefe hopes Al will come see him pitch against the Detroit Tigers in Chicago.

"St. Louis, Missouri, April 15." Behind 7–1 in the sixth, Callahan replaced Benz with Keefe, who did well but was wrongly pinch-hit for by Easterly, who popped out. Cicotte finished for the Sox, who lost. For criticizing him, Callahan, "bawled me awful." Gleason restrained Keefe. Callahan promised Keefe he could start next against the Tigers, since Al will attend. Keefe will see Violet on the 29th.

"Chicago, April 19." Keefe is glad Al and the others didn't attend the game he pitched against the Tigers. He had a sore arm. Cobb stole four bases. Keefe's catcher Schalk demanded wrong pitches. Keefe's teammates made errors behind him. He almost punched Callahan, who refused to relieve him until they were losing 16–2 in the eighth.

"Chicago, April 25." Keefe says his arm is better. When the team plays in Detroit, he'll see Violet. He'll punch Chicago reporters for criticizing him.

"Chicago, April 29." Callahan didn't take Keefe to Detroit but told him to see Comiskey, who paid him and said he sold him to "Frisco." But he'll work instead for Charley in Bedford's billiard hall. Allen luckily won a two-hitter against Cleveland yesterday.

Howard W. Webb Jr. explains that Lardner from 1908 to 1913 steadily developed his unique sports-writer "idiom" and that in "A Busher's Letters Home" "and in the five others [i.e., stories] which compose *You Know Me Al*, Lardner brought the idiom to maturity." "A Busher's Letters Home" was exceedingly popular. Jonathan Yardley says that when it appeared, "[t]he reaction was immediate and staggering." Donald Elder reports that *Post* editor George Horace Lorimer,* who had paid Lardner $250 for it, wanted more stories featuring Jack Keefe and increased his payment per story "at intervals by $250" to $1,500, his "top price at the time." Keefe's unreliable-narrator's style, combining misspellings and mangled grammar on the one hand, and his unconscious self-revelation on the other, set the pattern of the five remaining *You Know Me Al* episodes and for many later baseball stories by Lardner. He also introduced here and used later a clever combination of fictional and real-life characters. The dramatis personae of "A Busher's Letters Home" are nine fictional characters, 34 real-life persons who figure in baseball history and appear in the action, and three other such persons mentioned without appearing. (Sources: Elder, 114; Yardley, 163; Webb, 489)

"THE BUSHER COMES BACK" (*Saturday Evening Post*, May 23, 1914). (Characters: Al, Allen, Mrs. Allen, Altrock, Baker, Barry, Benz, Berger, Bertha, Bodie, Bush, Callahan, Chapman, Chase, Cheney, Cicotte, Clark, Cobb, Collins, Comiskey, Crawford, Cutting, Donlin, Dubuque, Evans, Florence, Fournier, Kid Gleason, Griffith, Joe Hill, Howard, Jennings, Johnson, Johnson, Johnston, Jack Keefe, Lajoie, Leach, Hazel Levy, Kid Levy, Lord, Milan, McBride, Russell, Schaefer, Schalk, Schulte, Scott, Shanks, Sullivan, Turner, Veach, Oskar Vitt, Violet, Ed Walsh, Weaver, Wood, Zimmerman.)

In 18 letters to Al, Keefe describes more experiences as a baseball pitcher.

"San Francisco, California, May 13 [1913]." Keefe explains that Bill Sullivan, ex–White Sox catcher, encouraged him, as did Comiskey, to get more experience pitching for San Francisco in the Coast League and try to return to the majors, preferably to the Tigers, so he can see Violet and also not pitch against Cobb or Crawford.

"Los Angeles, May 20." Keefe pitched brilliantly against Oakland. He likes Howard, Frisco's unsarcastic manager. Violet, who wrote, called him "a busher" on a postcard, dumped him, is "Good riddance."

"San Francisco, July 20." Keefe excuses his delay in writing by saying "a great big stropping girl" named Hazel Carney attended his games, wrote him, and they enjoyed some nickel shows and some beers. He told her his $200 a month pay when she asked, and he proposed. They'll get married this fall, and he'll "show her to you" in Bedford. Howard warned him that "running round with that skirt" was hurting his game.

"Sacramento, August 16." Keefe says the White Sox used their option and have recalled him. Hazel was "all broke up" because he lacks "enough dough to get married" yet. She asked about his higher pay. He'll send for her in October. He hopes Callahan will pitch him in Detroit; he'll show Violet her "treatment" of him was wrong.

"Chicago, August 27." From the stands, Keefe watched White Sox pitcher Johnson against weak-hitting Washington. He told Gleason, that kidder, he wasn't impressed with Johnson's speed. Keefe won pitching against Bender of the "Athaletics," whose batting efforts "Them reporters" wrongly called hits were Sox errors. He'll pitch against Detroit. Tonight he'll play cards over at Allen's, whose wife's sister likes Keefe. But "she ain't much for looks."

"Detroit, Mich., September 6." Keefe pitched against Detroit. Cobb spoiled his "o hit game" by beating out Weaver's slow throw. Keefe "whiffed" Crawford twice. Keefe pleased Callahan by being sarcastic to both Jennings, Detroit's manager, and Cobb, and by winning. That night at the hotel Violet phoned Keefe, denied ever sending that mean postcard, and would have written him "in Frisco" but lost his address. He told her he's engaged. She screamed. He hung up.

"Boston, Massachusetts, September 12." Hazel wrote from Cleveland, will see him in Chi, needs $100 "for her fare and ... some cloths," since she lent a friend $50. Keefe sent $30. Keefe details his fine pitching against Cleveland and the "rotten support" from his teammates. Keefe disobeyed Callahan's order to walk Lajoie, who lined out to Weaver. Callahan was so furious that Keefe could hardly "keep from wrapping his jaw." Next, Keefe won in Boston, pitching against their Wood and despite Lord's misfielding two Red Sox butts. Visiting Boston's fish wharf, Keefe couldn't count all the fish. Violet asked for Keefe's New York address. He sent it but won't correspond with her since he's engaged to Hazel.

"New York, New York, September 16." Keefe would like to punch the Chicago reporter who called his win over Cleveland "lucky." New York is an even better city than Boston. Its "Garden" is indoors, unlike "gardens at home." He didn't like $1 per drink, the sassy waiter, or a man offering a Follies ticket for $3. Gleason bought Keefe a beer, drank pop himself, and promised to "stear" him around town.

"Philadelphia, Pa., September 19." Gleason took Keefe around New York but prevented him from talking to a "lonesome" pair "of peaches" whose guess that they were ball players Gleason denied. He told one to wash "your disguise from your face." He told Keefe they'd not "even leave you your fast ball." He took Keefe to a movie. Reminded of Violet, Keefe sent her three postcards. Callahan will pitch him in Washington against Johnson. A letter from Violet almost made Keefe cry.

"Washington, D.C., September 22." Keefe says Washington is beautiful, has lots of "colored people." He saw the White House and the Washington Monument. Some White Sox pitchers get sick thinking of opposing "big Walter" Johnson. Keefe doesn't.

"Washington, September 22." After gloating he beat Johnson "one to nothing," Keefe summarizes the action. Johnson pitched a no-hitter through seven, but Keefe did well and Callahan shouted encouragement. Evans, the umpire, couldn't see Keefe's fast pitches and called strikes balls. Keefe's single was the game winner in the eighth. He celebrated with a "pink cocktail" after the game and wrote to "cheer ... up" Violet. Hazel hasn't written.

"Chicago, September 27." Keefe asks Al to rent him Cutting's house in Bedford — if it's only $12 a month — for him and "Mrs. Keefe." Keefe's team will play St. Louis, then end the season in Chicago against Detroit.

"Chicago, October 3." After thanking Al for leasing that house, Keefe says a White Sox busher lost to Detroit today, and Callahan is saving his best pitchers, including Keefe, for the "city serious." Strangely, he's heard nothing from Hazel.

"Chicago, October 7." The "serious" is now 1–1. Keefe lost because of Zimmerman's fluke Cub hit. Happily, "no good" Hazel wrote she has married Kid Levy and not to come near them. The $30 Keefe sent her "is gone." Violet, "classier," beats Hazel "forty ways." Violet never sent that postcard. They'll wed "inside of a week." Al and Bertha (his wife) will love Violet.

"Chicago, October 9." Keefe beat the Cubs yesterday. The Sox lead 3–1 now and could clinch tomorrow, but he's miserable. Violet wrote she's marrying Joe Hill, a lefty Jennings procured from Providence. Keefe wants Al to break the lease with Cuttings, thinks of playing in Australia, since his heart is broken.

"Chicago, October 12." Keefe resents having to honor Cutting's lease. The Cubs "beat us." Today it's raining. He had some highballs before breakfast. He must visit Allen and his wife tonight, reluctantly, because he's "through with girls."

"Chicago, October 13." Keefe says the Sox won the city championship. Saying "I done it," he details his excellent work, earned $814.30, and will demand $5,000 from Comiskey for next year. He's seeing a show tonight with Florence, Allen's sister-in-law, who "ain't as pretty as Violet and Hazel but ... beauty isn't only so deep." Australia would be too expensive.

"Chicago, October 14." Keefe has a "supprise." He is marrying Florence, who knows baseball well "for a girl" and admires his pitching and looks. He's shopping for furniture and new "cloths." He, Florence, Al, and Bertha will have fun in Bedford. Comiskey raised his pay a thousand, to $2,800 for next year. "Oh you little yellow house."

"The Busher Comes Back" continues Lardner's pattern; of its 57 named characters, 13 are fictional and 44 are real.

"THE BUSHER'S HONEYMOON" (*Saturday Evening Post*, July 11, 1914). (Characters: Allen, Marie Allen, Al Blanchard, Bertha Blanchard, Callahan, Hazel Levy, Comiskey, Kid Gleason, Joe Hill, Violet Hill, Florence Keefe, Jack Keefe, Buck Perry, Tinker.)

Keefe sends Al 21 more letters, all from Chicago.

October 17 [1913]. Keefe writes Al that he married Allen's sister-in-law Florence two days ago, in Chicago, where things cost more than in Bedford. Listing expenses, Keefe complains that he gave the "Preist" $3.50 despite Allen's suggesting $5, refused Florrie's wanting a hotel room with bath at $2 a day instead of $1.50 without, disliked Allen's taking them to a "chop-suye resturunt," but "could not say nothing." He and Florrie are off "to the moving pictures" now, at "a dime apeace."

October 22. Keefe criticizes Florrie. She wants to stay a while in Chicago to help her sister Marie and Allen to settle in their furnished flat, even though Keefe is paying $10 a month for Cutting's house in Bedford. Also, Florrie is often "fusing with her face and her hair." Also, she thought he was "writeing" a girl, not Al. Keefe kidded that he "don't know no girls except you and Violet and Hazel." Her demand to explain about them got him mad, "because no girl can't tell me what to do." Florrie left their hotel room to stay with Marie all night. She's bluffing.

October 24. Keefe sought Florrie at Marie's and pleased her by telling her about "them two poor girls" and "sware[ing]" he "never care[d] nothing about them," which "was easy because it was the truth." He must pack because they are occupying Allen and Marie's "spair bedroom" for a while. He'll have a special beer first near his hotel.

October 28. Florrie is shopping with Marie for more "cloths." Allen got a football ticket from a reporter. Keefe won't go see "a lot of scrapping between little slobs that I could lick the whole bunch of them." Marie and Allen tried to persuade Keefe to rent a $40-a-month flat across the hall from them, but "they seen I was in ernest" against $50 "includeing the house down in Bedford."

November 2. Keefe feels lucky to have "gotten the tip" about that $40 flat. They are renting it for $42.50 "till the 1 of May." The extra $2.50 is for the furniture and means he won't have to buy furniture for $100, as he feared. When he and Allen "goes West "the 2 of Febuery" for spring training, Marie will room with Florrie. Keefe and Florrie will visit Al and Bertha "round Xmas." Keefe asks Al to get Cutting to take $10 for next month and "call off that lease."

November 30. Florrie disliked the oak and "mohoggeny" furniture and straw dining chairs in their flat. For $110 they bought some matching "mohoggeny" items, "mission chairs," rose drapes, a lamp Rose fancied, and a $7 couch "somebody can sleep on if we get to much company." From Keefe's season's-end savings of $1,400, he gave Florrie $200 to send her sister in Texas for her divorce from "a bad egg." The remaining $800 will be enough, since Florrie is "a good girl ... that has got some sense."

December 7. Keefe wanted Al and Bertha to come to Chicago for the holidays. Florrie wasn't sure Bertha would enjoy it and thought Al might visit alone. Keefe doesn't blame Al for not getting Cutting to cancel his lease. Keefe, however, might have used a different approach. Keefe and Florrie invited the Allens to their flat for Thanksgiving dinner ($5); then Florrie wanted a second dinner for four at the hotel (another $5). Keefe urges Al to bring Bertha to visit.

December 20. Keefe says Bertha "must of took offense," but "we would not care how she dressed." She could "come up here in a night-gown." She shouldn't "say we was to swell." Cutting is so mean Keefe "will bust his jaw," though Florrie says "a star pitcher like I" shouldn't "scrap about little things." She's jealous that Keefe writes Al so often. Keefe is sorry Al "can't come" visit.

December 27. Keefe calls Allen stupid like most left-handers. The four of them were on "State St." on the 24th. Marie saw a $100 diamond ring and made Allen buy it. Florrie therefore demanded one. Keefe spent $75 for one, kept back the $15 "rist watch" he had bought for her Christmas present, couldn't get a refund, and will give it to her for New Year's. The cut-glass dish he sent Al and Bertha was "high pricet." Keefe is glad about "the pretty pincushions" they received from them, but Florrie says they "makes a even half dozen" she now has.

"Januery 3 [1914]." Keefe "been pretty sick ever since New Year's eve." The four went to "1 of the swell resturunts downtown." Too much wine. He'd rather "a big stine of my kind of beer." The girls said $5 wine was better than $1 wine. When Keefe suggested the sleepy-looking girls should come home, Marie told him to "shut up and don't be no quitter." Keefe threatened to hit her. Allen slapped him. Keefe "give him a good beating." The two got thrown out. Florrie "paid the hole bill" because Allen was broke. Allen "wants to make friends" again, because "I am a bad guy to monkey with."

"Januery 20." The Allens have moved in with Keefe and Florrie. Keefe hired a "girl who does all the work for $7 a week." They dine out often. Keefe now prefers "other stuff" to beer and can outdrink "the girls and Allen." They'll celebrate Marie's birthday tonight.

"Januery 31." Keefe explains that Allen will take Marie to training camp in California with him. Florrie wants to go too, but he can't afford to take her along even though he worries she'll be alone in Chicago. She resented his telling her that Allen and Marie sponged off him. Too bad Florrie can't stay in Bedford because Al and Bertha would watch over her. Getting Keefe's furniture down there would be hard.

"Febuery 4." Keefe thanks Al for "the invatation" to put up Florrie in Bedford. Al must "axcept" $2 a week for her "bord." Florrie can help make Bertha's face and hair look better. Keefe and

Florrie will be down "about the 18." He'll be in California "till April 14."

"Febuery 9." Keefe says Florrie would prefer to visit "her folks in Texas" but really wants Keefe to ask Comiskey to take her to California "as the club's guest." He'll see Comiskey, who will attend the "league skedule meeting here tomorrow." Keefe has $50 left, owes for rent and the hired girl, and he and Florrie need "new cloths."

"Febuery 11." Trouble. Keefe, "Allen and some of the boys" had some drinks. He saw Comiskey, who gave him $100 against his salary, declined to pay Florrie's way to California, and must have been funny about it all because nearby listeners laughed. Keefe can't "pay her fair."

"Febuery 12." Florrie "bawled her head off" on learning the news, then persuaded Keefe to realize he was worth $3,000, not his contracted $2,800, and to demand the extra from Comiskey.

"Febuery 14." Keefe says he's off to baseball's Federal League. He saw Comiskey, demanded a revised contract for $3,000, was told to "live up" to the old one, and threatened to jump to the Federal League. Comiskey warned him, and Keefe left. He plans to get a $4,000 Federal contract, and surprise Florrie. If Tinker won't pay for Florrie, he'll have enough "to take her with me on all the trips."

"Febuery 15." Keefe is desperate. He went to Tinker's office. Outside, he saw Buck Perry, former Boston pitcher, who revealed his $5,000 contract with Tinker, plus a $500 bonus. Tinker "seen me ... and asked what did I want." Keefe said he'd "jump for $4000 and a bonus." Tinker wouldn't deal, because Keefe was under a White Sox contract. Keefe is going nowhere, lacks money to buy a gun to shoot himself, and wishes he were still pitching at Terre Haute.

"Febuery 17." Keefe, "scared to tell Florrie," asked Allen, "grafting and spongeing on me all winter," for $100, but was refused. If Keefe hit him, he'd have to pay his funeral expenses. When he told Florrie, she "bawled" and said she shouldn't have married him. He wished that too, then apologized. He lacked cash to go get drunk. He asks Al to send him $100, which, living in Bedford, Al can spare.

"Febuery 19." Keefe thanks Al for sending the handy $100, which he'll use for rent and grocery bills. The "the hired girl" must wait a while. He plans to ask Comiskey to "make my salery $3000 like I wanted him to," and "$200 advance money." He'll take Florrie along to Paso Robles.

"Febuery 21." Yesterday Comiskey's secretary told Keefe he was "sold to Milwaukee" and offered him "fair" to there. He refused. The players "says they was all broke" and lent him nothing. Back home, Allen "stood there stareing" and the girls cried. He left for some drinks, returned three hours later, and found them gone. Florrie left him a note saying that he "couldn't support no wife," and that Allen gave her money to return to Texas Keefe is alone in his $42.50 Chicago flat. Can Al send him "fair" to get to Bedford? Keefe won't let Milwaukee "make no sucker out of me." He's "sick and tired of Chi." Send the $25 fast, "old pal."

There is more fiction than fact in "The Busher's Honeymoon." Of its 14 characters, only four are real-life figures.

"A NEW BUSHER BREAKS IN" (*Saturday Evening Post*, September 12, 1914). (Characters: Alcock, Allen, Marie Allen, Joe Benz, Blackburne, Al Blanchard, Bertha Blanchard, Bodie, Boehling, Callahan, Chase, Eddie Cicotte, Ty Cobb, Collins, Comiskey, Sam Crawford, Evans, Fournier, Kid Gleason, Higgins, Joe Hill, Violet Hill, Jackson, Jennings, John, Johnson, Johnson, Allen Keefe, Florrie Keefe, Jack Keefe, Lajoie, Hazel Levy, Kid Levy, McInnis, Moriarty, Charlie O'Leary, Schalk, Scott, Stanage, Veach, Weaver.)

Keefe sends Al 15 more letters.

Chicago, March 2 [1914]. Keefe writes that he saw Johnson, the league president, and learned Comiskey couldn't sell him to Milwaukee. Because of "wavers" problems, Detroit could buy him and Jennings there would surely want him as their best pitcher. He'd like to beat the White Sox and also practice-pitch to Cobb and Crawford, gently of course, to avoid embarrassing them. Funny, he'll be pitching in Detroit, where Violet is. He'll outdo Joe Hill, "that left-hander" husband of hers, who'll be "getting splinters ... slideing up and down the bench." Keefe won't sign with the Tigers "for no less than $5000 at most." Keefe wishes Joe had married Florrie, who "would of drove him crazy," except left-handers are already crazy. Keefe wishes Florrie would "sew" him for divorce and drop his name. He'd pay costs, plus up to $100 to her. He is angry that "her and her sister Marie and ... Allen grafted off of me."

Chicago, March 4. Trying to see Comiskey, Keefe was told by his "asst secretary" John he maybe isn't going to Detroit. John got "fresh" and Keefe "blowed out of the office." He'll require Comiskey to send him to Detroit or expose him to Johnson. Keefe asks Al for $25 — make it

$35 — until he pitches somewhere this year for "5 or $6000" and can "settle ... my dedts." He'll leave "this rotten flat" and return to his old room.

Chicago, March 12. Keefe waited so long to see Comiskey that the secretary "got scared" and showed him in. Comiskey reminded Keefe he tried to jump to the Federal League, presumably wanted Milwaukee because he was known to like beer, and could be pitching for the White Sox under the contract he signed. He told Keefe he could do nothing for him, to go drink water, not try "to drink this town dry," or be waived to Milwaukee or stay with the Sox — under a new, three-year contract at $2800 a year. Keefe accepted, took a ticket for Los Angeles, and will tell Johnson not to "fine Comiskey for not paying attention to the rules." Comiskey was kidding. How could anyone drink a town dry? He hid to avoid seeing his landlord. He'll leave the furniture, which "remind[s] me of Florrie."

Los Angeles, California, March 16. It's good to be here with the team. Kid Gleason greeted him with a friendly punch, said he looked like a barrel, but agreed he must be in shape because he has exercised his "stumach mussels" plenty. Keefe wants to "join the 1st club" with Callahan and practice as "a attraction" to spectators. Meanwhile, Gleason would take the "2d team" to Frisco. Keefe feels he and the White Sox "recrut" pitchers are sufficient, and the White Sox should buy Ty Cobb and Sam Crawford from Detroit, not more pitchers.

San Francisco, March 20. Keefe is "in old Frisco with the 2d team." He was sure Callahan would have him "stick here and wait for the 1st team." But after Gleason said that Callahan wired orders to take Keefe to Frisco, he added that he knows Keefe's wife left him and Allen and Marie are "traveling round with the 1st club." Keefe is sure Callahan will order him to come pitch for him. Meanwhile, he has many Frisco friends.

San Francisco, March 25. Keefe spotted Hazel Levy and Kid Levy in "the café where her and I used to go." They signaled him over for a drink. He agreed, since "they was no use being nasty and let bygones be bygones." When Lavy asked what he was drinking, Hazel "butts in" and says Keefe loves to be the spender. Keefe reminds her she never repaid his $30 loan. Levy threatened to "bust" him. Keefe left to avoid embarrassing the boxer. Anyway, "the music was rotten," and Hazel "has grew to be as big as a horse" and now he dislikes "big dolls" and all women. Keefe's fast ball was humming four innings against the San Francisco club. Charlie O'Leary got a lucky hit over first that Chase misplaced and "Fournier would of eat it up." Keefe "allmost come to blows" when Gleason tried to limit his eating, called him "hog fat," and said if he tried fielding a bunt "you would of busted wide open." Callahan must arrive fast, because that "little slob" Gleason is withholding food from "a big man like I."

Salt Lake City, Utah, April 1. Keefe is heading east with the "2d team," probably to inspire "recruts" that management shouldn't have wasted money on. He worked four innings against Oakland. He felt sorry for their hitters, eased up, and they got some runs. His teammates gave him the "rottenest" support. He probably won't pitch here where some players "has got ½ a dozen wives or so," and, really, "1 wife is a misery."

Des Moines, Iowa, April 10. Keefe figures Callahan is saving him to open the season in Chi tomorrow against Cleveland. Gleason watches Keefe so closely at meals that he had to sneak a second breakfast down the street. Gleason punches him in the "stumach" but is too old for Keefe to show resentment.

Chicago, Illinois, April 16. Keefe had to "fix up about my room rent," thus can't repay Al the $75 borrowed yet. Also, Allen showed up, avoided getting busted by being "yellow" and shaking hands, and told Keefe he should write Florrie, at home in Waco, Texas. Keefe threatened to get "a attorney at law" and "sew her for a bill of divorce" for "Dessertion." Allen said she'd get a divorce for "none support." Keefe sent her $10 to avoid looking bad. He won't agree to talk with Marie Allen, though. She caused his getting married and having no money. Joe Benz pitched the opener and shut out Cleveland. Callahan says he won't let Keefe pitch until he loses weight and doesn't "cover more ground than the grand stand." When the other teams figure out the White Sox "other pitchers," Keefe can enter "to stop them."

Detroit, Michigan, April 28. Callahan pitched Keefe when he was wild after no work and "fines me $50.00 for loosing a 1 to o game in 10 innings." He forgot the bases were full and beaned Joe Hill. Here's what happened. While warming up, he saw Violet in the stands and smiled simply so she wouldn't cry. Cobb didn't play, because of sickness or more likely fearing Keefe. Hill's good pitching for Detroit was luck. He even struck Keefe out, because Evans the ump had it in for Keefe for sassing him last year. Hill blurted at Keefe, "I allready got your girl and your goat." So Keefe shouted he would bean Hill. While

Callahan and Gleason argued about relieving Keefe, he beaned Hill, lost the game, got fined and "suspended without pay," and was attacked by his teammates. But for being "½ starved to death" he would've hurt somebody. He may jump to the Federals and not be treated "like no white slave."

Chicago, May 2. Keefe says he can't repay Al, because the managers fined him $50 and even kept back last year's $100 advance they " should of forgot about." Allen can't make him talk with Marie. He sent Florrie $25 from his $80 "2 weeks' pay." Therefore "she can't come no none-support business on me."

Chicago, May 5. Keefe says Callahan "layed" him off briefly so he'd start thinking right. When the Detroit team arrived, he pitched against Hill, who "had won 4 strate." Keefe ended his "winning streek." Keefe was effective against Cobb and Weaver. He scared Hill with a fast pitch "past his nose," then struck him out. Keefe came to bat in the fifth. Hill shouts he'll bean him. Keene says if he did he'd write Violet to complain. Hill tried three times then had to groove one, which Keefe doubled, scoring Bodie and Schalk, and Weaver scored Keefe, the winning run in the 5–4 game. Callahan was so delighted that he might return Keefe's $50 and Keefe will pay Al "the hole $75."

Chicago, May 29. Repaying Al the $75, Keefe says that in their eastern trip he shouldn't have lost to the "Athaletics," did defeat Boston and New York, saved another New York game for Eddie Cicotte, and defeated Boehling, Washington's pitcher. Allen is so "rotten" he may be sent "somewheres." Florrie phoned him and they're together again, living in Allen's "spair room" free. Keefe knows a secret "about I and Florrie and somebody else." He'll mail this letter and have a beer.

Chicago, June 16. Right after Keefe defeated the "Athaletics" by making McInnis "look like a sucker in the pinch," he learned he has a baby. Florrie names it Allen after "his uncle and aunt Allen," but to Keefe he's Al after his old pal. Despite owing for last winter's flat and Cutting for that Bedford house, Keefe is "the happyest man in the world," because "I got a real family."

Chicago, July 2. Florrie was alarmed because the baby was waving his arms. The "Dr." said he was exercising. The baby waved only his left arm at Keefe. There must be a way to "fix ... babys so as they won't be left-handed." He wouldn't want his kid to be like Allen, Hill, and "some of them other nuts." Still, he might "have some of their luck."

Of the 41 characters involved in "A New Busher Breaks In," 13 are fictional and 28 are real-lifers, many recycled. Keefe's self-deception and self-absorption are brilliantly self-dramatized.

"THE BUSHER'S KID" (*Saturday Evening Post*, October 3, 1914). (Characters: Allen, Marie Allen, Benz, Al Blanchard, Bertha Blanchard, Bodie, Callahan, Cheney, Collins, Comiskey, Cutting, Faber, Kid Gleason, Good, Johnson, Allen Keefe, Florrie Keefe, Jack Keefe, Leach, Mathewson, O'Day, Pierce, Russell, Saier, Schalk, Schulte, Scott, Ben Smith, Billy Sullivan, Weaver.)

Keefe inflicts 13 more letters on Al.

Chicago, Illinois, July 31 [1914]. After "a rotten trip," partly salvaged by "me beating Boston once and the Athaletics two times," Keefe is home, "still liveing at Allen's and his wife." He can "tell you what the kid done." Keefe rushed to see him, and he smiled. Florrie said it wasn't a smile, it was "collect" caused by his "stumach." Keefe wasn't allowed to get the doctor. He didn't enjoy breakfast. The baby cried. Keefe may pitch "a poseponed game" today. He did badly against New York some days ago because Schalk dropped a ball. Keefe will intimidate Detroit fast by avoiding a slow game with many strike-outs, so as to rush back to the kid.

Chicago, August 15. Keefe is gleeful: Kid Gleason promised to come see the kid tomorrow. Gleason joked with Keefe, saying he already knew enough about the "out of luck" baby by knowing his father, saying when Florrie meets Gleason she'll be sorry she married Keefe, etc. Gleason is grateful to Keefe, who realizes that "even if he don't say nothing at all I will know he is kidding."

Chicago, August 17. Keefe boasts about his pitching, but adds that he's "satisfied if I give the club the best I got" and that if he loses a game it won't be his fault. Comiskey may raise his pay next year. Florrie and Marie are shopping for shoes, though Florrie could easily stay in the flat "in her bear feet." When they were gone, Gleason visited, saw the kid, said he must have been "boughten" since he looks so human, picked him up dangerously, patted his head despite that "soft spot," said he must have "a toothacke" because he was sucking his finger, and said he should be trained to pitch because "he looks now like he would divellop into a grate spitter." When Florrie and Marie were just across the street, Gleason had to leave because he said his contract denied him the right to speak to women. But he does, and "severel ... players' wifes ... thought he was a regular comeedion though they really is nothing funny about what he says." Keefe hopes to outpitch Washington's Johnson, here soon.

"New York, New York, September 16." Keefe, on the eastern trip, is worried about "little Al." "Florrie has not wrote since" they played in Philadelphia, their "first stop." He resists going out at night with the boys. Anyway, Callahan, sore about their "rotten" playing, hasn't given out show passes. Allen said Marie was in touch but added nothing about the kid "eccept that he was "balling" at night. If he's sick, Keefe will go home with or without Callahan's permission.

Boston, Massachusetts, September 24. Keefe wired Florrie from New York, then Boston, for news, got a letter in Boston saying all's well but "takeing care" of the baby has kept her busy, then a wire answering his wire. He tried to get a refund on his second "$.60" wire but couldn't. Florrie "is trying to send us both to the Poor House" with all these telegrams. It's "impossable" for women to "use a little judgement." He might as well be allowed to go home because, though Cleveland is "licked the minute I put on my glove," one pitcher can't "win no pennant" alone.

Chicago, October 2. Callahan told Keefe to stay home with some other pitchers, practice daily, and be ready for "the city serious" against "them Cubs." Luckily, Allen went to Detroit or Keefe "would of killed him," because he has been "acting and talking nasty." The baby's continued sick "stumach" Florrie calls the "collect" from drinking milk. Florrie's drinking upsets her too. Allen, kept awake, suggested giving "the little X-eyed brat poison" and said that if he could see straight he'd see Keefe and then "would shoot himself." Keefe replied that he's glad the kid isn't left-handed like Allen. Allen requested rent money. Keefe said Allen grafted off him "all last winter," and as for missing sleep because the kid cried he could sleep on the White Sox bench. Marie kept them from fighting. Keefe would like to winter in Bedford with the kid and Florrie, "but she wont listen to that." About that dress for the kid that Bertha made and sent, Florrie was "just kidding" when she said she'd "use it for a dishrag." Callahan wrongly took Keefe out of that game in Cleveland that they lost anyway.

Chicago, October 4. Keefe says tomorrow's game against Detroit will end the season. At home there was an argument because both Florrie and Marie want to attend "the city serious games," but Keefe can't afford a nurse's "salery" for little Al. Keefe watched sick Al while Allen took the girls to a show, and "none of them bonehead nurses would of knew what to do." The baby cried. Keefe covered him with blankets. He kicked and cried more. Keefe phoned "our regular Dr.," who came over, removed the blankets, and "soaked me 2 dollars." Keefe resisted "a nosion to bust his jaw." Al got worse. Keefe rounded up another doctor from the street, who charged nothing. When Al got worse, Keefe fed him Allen's "stumach acke" medicine. Al was worse. Keefe got the second doctor back. He told Keefe he was a fool and charged $2. Al fell asleep. Doctors are untrustworthy, like policemen. When Allen, Florrie, and Marie returned and Keefe explained his actions, there was another argument. Keefe lacks room to welcome Al Blanchard, who can read about him in the papers.

Chicago, October 6. There was trouble when Keefe pitched against the Cubs. They saw him warming up and decided not to waste Cheney, their best pitcher, but to go ahead and lose with Pierce. All went well until "after there ½ of the 7th" Keefe glanced at the press box to check the scoring and saw Florrie and Marie sitting nearby. They had promised to stay home since Keefe would return and describe his easy win. Was little Al home dead or "balling"? Allen was on the bench. Keefe asked Callahan to let him go home to care for his baby. Callahan called him a "yellow dog" and made him continue pitching or be fined. Before he "knowed what come off," the bases were full and he was replaced. Later he learned Scott subbed for him and "we was licked 3 and 2," because he rushed home to find "a girl 14" who never had "no babys of her own" watching Al. When the others returned, he rebuked Florrie, told the Allens to shut up, and was about to go out for "a hole lot of drinks," when Gleason appeared, met Florrie, suggested they hire a nurse for the baby so Florrie can see the games. Keefe refused. Gleason talked privately with Florrie. Keefe figures he "was persuadeing her to stay home" instead of watching Keefe "win the serious." Leaving, Gleason said "all [was] fixed up."

Chicago, October 8. The White Sox are ahead of the Cubs in the "serious" 2 to 1. Keefe shut them out today and will pitch 2 of the next 3 games, if needed. During the game he got a note from the boy at the team's phone; somebody at home phoned that "the baby was asleep and getting along fine." When home himself, Keefe described his success. Florrie was happy, but Marie was probably "a little jellus" because Allen during the game had been "wearing out the wood on the bench." Still, we'll get "$750.00 apeace" when we win, not the $500 for losing. If Keefe "had of jumped to the Federal," the club would be nowhere.

Chicago, October 11. Cicotte pitched a loss for the White Sox two days ago. Yesterday Callahan sent in Allen after "this here Faber," the Sox pitcher, was losing "allready," and Allen was laughable. Keefe, comforted by phone messages indicating self-sacrificial Florrie was home with healthy little Al, won the last game and the "serious." Allen didn't return home but was probably "out somewheres lapping up some beer" with his winner's share. Keefe figures he and his family "won't stay with the Allens no longer." Keefe can't get Florrie to go to Bedford. And since she was nice enough to stay home with little Al, "I ... must leave her have her own way about something."

Chicago, October 13, Keefe is "all threw with Florrie." Allen came back after being "out lushing beer," and he and Keefe argued. Allen told him that the club paid Florrie $50 to stay home with the baby, but Marie called her a sucker and persuaded her to pay a nurse part of that sum, have her phone the team "every so offten ... that the baby was OK," attend the game herself with Marie, then rush home afterwards by taxi. Keefe got mad, disappeared for "some drinks," returned to sleep them off, and when the Allens left "Florrie and I have not spoke ... and ... won't never ... again." He'll take the baby, maybe "hire a train nurse," and maybe move to Bedford.

Chicago, October 17. Keefe and Florrie have "made it up" and "are threw with Marie and Allen" The three Keefes are "staying at ... the same hotel we was in when we got married only of course they was only the 2 of us then." Keefe asks Al Blanchard to get Cutting "to ree-new the lease on that house," where they will live and where Florrie will care for the baby while he's on baseball trips next year. Maybe "you and Bertha can help her round the house." What happened was this: Florrie at breakfast griped to Marie that they shouldn't "kick on the baby crying" when Allen after "a bad night ... was snoreing" worse "than a hole wagonlode of babys"; she also praised Keefe's pitching, which provided $750 to Allen, who was "a sucker the 1 inning he pitched;" and she accused Marie of being "jellous." Marie ordered Florrie to take "your brat" and leave. Keefe told Florrie he wanted to take the baby; she said he needed milk; he said watermelon would do as well since he always has "the collect"; she threatened to "sew" him for "dessertion" and explained she was proud to go watch him "pitch like you can do." Keefe "could not hardly blame her," said he'd think it over, consulted an attorney to find out whether "could I take little Al away," was told "it would probily kill him to be tooken away from her," and was charged "$10.00 the robber." They taxied to the hotel, and "Florrie has gave up and will go to Bedford ... with me now."

Chicago, October 20. Keefe thanks Al Blanchard for his "kindnus" in inviting the three to stay with him and Bertha, who "will be crazy about the baby." Keefe reports the time their train will arrive and wants Ben Smith to "have a hack down to the deepo" to get them to Blanchard's house, preferably not for "$.25" but free. They'll arrive "in time for a late supper," and maybe Bertha can serve "spair ribs and crout.... You know me Al."

"THE BUSHER BEATS IT HENCE" (*Saturday Evening Post*, November 7, 1914). (Characters: Allen, Marie Allen, Al Blanchard, Bertha Blanchard, Callahan, Comiskey, Crawford, Mike Donlin, Doyle, Steve Evans, Faber, Hern, Allen Keefe, Florrie Keefe, Jack Keefe, Mcgraw, Mathewson, Merkle, Schaefer, Jack Sheridan, Speaker, Ted Sullivan, Dummy Taylor, Thorpe, Wiltse.)

Keefe offers 10 letters to "Friend Al."

"Chicago, Ill., Oct. 20 [1914]." The White Sox and "the giants" are going on a world tour. Callahan wanted him to go, but he won't leave Florrie and little Al. It would also be expensive "paying rent and grocerys for them some wheres and me not getting nothing out of it" and also sending "some thing home to the Mrs." Maybe later Keefe will pay half for that "hack at the deepo," if unused by anyone else. Florrie says she doesn't mind avoiding Bedford "for an other week ... [or] if we dont go for 6 years." Callahan tells him "the fans would be sore if they did not get no more chance to look at you." He'll stay and pitch "this here exibishun game" against "the giants." He hopes Al and Bertha can "eat ... up" those spair ribs and crout, and says "I and Florrie [will] accept of coarse" any dinner but "would not want to make no meal off of sardines or something."

Chicago, Oct. 25. Since the Sox are short of men, Keefe was persuaded to go to the coast but won't go farther. In Chicago, Callahan talked him into showing his advertised ability to the fans. He started pitching, but his arm felt lame. Not like "them yellow dogs," however, he continued pitching. Merkle foolishly swung at a pitch Keefe "was trying to waist" and hit a home run. Next, "smart alex Mcgraw" wished Keefe were going around the world for his team to beat, and Keefe told Callahan his arm was sore. Callahan and "some of the other boys coaxed" him to accompany them to the coast. When he discussed it with Florrie, she preferred for him to go west "a bout 3 or 4 weeks" rather than for them to go to Bedford. He lectured her about tending the baby. Those two remaining in the hotel will "cost me $6.00 a week." Florrie can eat light until they get to Bedford. Keefe will "stop off at a hole lot of places" and write Al when he can. He'll wake up little Al to "say good by."

"St. Joe, Miss., Oct. 29." Keefe hasn't pitched yet, which made "the giants" and Mcgraw glad. Crowds "wanted to shake hands with Mathewson and I." They know about "real pitchers" despite "what them reporters says." Mathewson, "a old man" now, still fools batters so easily by "stick[ing] the 1st ball right over with o on it" that Keefe longs to be in the National League too with its weak hitters. Mathewson said he didn't need to pitch his famous "fade a away" at any White Sox batter. When Keefe told Mcgraw that "Mathewson could not learn me nothing" about pitching, Mcgraw agreed. Also he wished Keefe were along for the entire trip because he liked associating with "boys that is funny and dont know nothing a bout it." He also said "them dolls acrost the ocean will be pretty sore" not to see Keefe, who wondered if they "has heard a bout me." Yes, said Mcgraw, adding that if Keefe weren't married he "probily could marry the Queen of europe." He meant it "this time Al because he did not crack a smile." Keefe decided it wouldn't "be fare to Florrie" to take the "hole" trip, although she "leave me and beat it for Texas last winter." But "I am not that kind of a man. You know me Al."

"Abilene, Texas, Nov. 4." Keefe won twice. Mcgraw asked him to "go all the way a round the world," pitching for his team since his Mathewson isn't going, his Hern has "not got no experiense," and his Wiltse is left-handed. Crawford and Speaker complained they wouldn't go if Keefe pitched against them, but Callahan said batting against Keefe would be excellent practice. Today's game being rained out, a bunch of notables, including Keefe, gave speeches to the disappointed crowd. Al, you "did not know I was a speech maker," but "the boys says that I done just as well as Dummy Taylor could of." Keefe is unworried that Florrie hasn't written, because she promised to "let me know was they some thing the matter."

"San Dago, Cal., Nov. 9." But for Florrie and little Al, Keefe would go around the world, make Bedford people "jellus," and pitch so well for Mcgraw that the White Sox wouldn't like it. All this despite Callahan's urging him to go to please people "in Rome and Paris and Africa and them other countrys" because the other pitchers "is not no real stars like you and Mathewson." If Keefe asked Florrie to let him go, "she would make a big holler." Florrie and Marie Allen "has had a quarrle." Callahan wanted Allen to go if he could find him and asked Keefe where he is. Keefe told Callahan he's "threw with him" and doesn't know where he is. He does but won't tell. Why inflict Allen on Callahan or give Allen a "chancet to go a round the world"? Keefe wishes he'd met Florrie next year. Maybe he wouldn't have married her, but "I guess I would on acct. of little Al."

"San Francisco, Nov. 14." Keefe will pitch here today. Callahan alerted reporters to expect a crowd. Marie Allen got Florrie to write that she has reconciled with the Allens and wants all of them to live together again this winter in Chicago. Keefe answered that "I and Florrie is comeing to Bedford." She wrote that Allen wonders if Callahan is short of pitchers and Allen might "change his mind and go a long on the trip." Keefe replied that Callahan's team was full.

"Medford, Organ, Nov. 16." Keefe was relieved during the game. "My arm felt like a wet rag" because of "the change in the clime." Hitters popped up, and the wind took the ball into the crowd of "40000 people" "somewheres and was a 2 bagger." "Doyle hit 3 of them pops." On the train, Mcgraw didn't kid as usual, tried but couldn't get Keefe to go on the trip, and said "the girls over to Paris will be sorry." They all go next to Washington, that is, "the state Washington."

"Portland, Organ, Nov. 17." Keefe is going around the world after all. Mcgraw and Callahan told him that Comiskey got a letter from President Wilson warning that "the king of Japan" would refuse "the White Sox and giants" permission to play in Japan unless stars were brought along. Wilson even feared war. Keefe decided to go, if Florrie could be persuaded. She agreed, if she could stay with the Allens "in Chi all winter and not go to no Bedford." Callahan urged Keefe to agree, saying he "could see all them diffrent countrys and tell Florrie" and maybe go around the world with her and little Al when he was older. He sent Florrie half of his $500.00 savings. Keefe will strengthen White Sox batters by pitching against them. He'll write Al a letter on the boat and "male it" from "either Japan or Yokohama," and send postcards to Bertha, and "her and Florrie will ... get acquainted" later.

"Seattle, Wash., Nov. 18." Keefe decided not "to go on no trip a round the world and back," will tell Callahan or Mcgraw, and plans to take the train "to Chi" and "supprise" Florrie. It wouldn't be right to deprive little Al of him and "to be tooken care of by no train nurse." Schaefer, who's going, explained a lot. He told Keefe people get "ship recked," and "swiming" in the ocean is unlike in rivers because if you move your feet sharks bite them with poison that "gives you the hiderofobeya and ... you start barking like a dog"; also "in the pacific Ocean" you use your hands to "scare the sord fish a way" and can swim only using "your stumach mussles"; Wiltse and Mike Donlin lack such muscles, but "hog fat" Keefe has used his plenty; perhaps Keefe could "flote" if he didn't talk for some days; if wrecked, one could swim to "the sandwich islands" for some food; they might get shot at by "the Swittserland war ships," and "they was as wild as most of them left handers." Jack Sheridan, an umpire, said "Schaefer was kiding me." Keefe didn't "believe ½ of what Schaefer" said. Still, Keefe has "got a $1000.00 insurence policy" just in case, but when dead he wouldn't know "if the insurence co. comes acrost."

"Victoria, Can., Nov. 19." Keefe will go on the trip after all. He's glad he didn't write Florrie he wouldn't because now he'll write he will, although he might not see little Al again because "it is pretty near a cinch that some thing will either happen to I or him." Callahan asked why Keefe wasn't going once Florrie wired permission. Keefe answered about Schaefer's telling him "how dangerus the trip is," but he "didn't beleive none of it," and yet "supose some thing should happen"? Callahan praised "the Umpires of Japan" as their safe ship. Mcgraw said they might cancel going, if Keefe weren't coming, because "president Wilson" feared war with Japan in that case. Callahan suggested getting Allen to join the team. Keefe agreed to go, since "some of the players wifes" were going and "would be dissapointed if they was not no trip." If he "drownded," Keefe wants Al to check on the insurance, send Florrie his banked $250.00, have her live in Bedford, have Bertha help her, and don't let little Al become left handed. Moreover, Florrie won't "have to buy no lot in no cemetary and hire no herse." If Keefe "done to you [anything] that was not OK remember by gones is by gones," and Keefe is Al's "best old pal." If Mcgraw lets Keefe pitch against the White Sox in Japan, "Crawford and Speaker will wisht the boat had of sank. You know me Al."

The publisher George H. Doran (1869–1956) reminisces in his autobiography thus: "I had the good fortune to publish Ring Lardner's first book, *You Know Me,* [sic] *Al.* I was very proud to have it, and looked forward to a long and happy association with Ring. In my absence abroad he wrote once or twice to my office. A careless and stupid editor neglected those letters and quite justifiably Ring took offence and offered his books to Scribner's, who only too gladly snapped them up. My regret was the greater because it separated Ring and myself, for he never quite recovered from the affront, for which I was officially but not personally responsible." The truth, though, is different. Lardner contracted with the Bobbs-Merrill Company to publish eight of his next nine books (1917–1921), had Doran publish his *Say It With Oil* (1923), and did not turn to Scribner's until they published his *How to Write Short Stories* (1924) and reprinted *You Know Me Al* (1925). More reliably, Doran graciously adds that "*You Know Me, Al* is a glorious book. It will long live to mark the spot where a sport-writer became human and not technical. It made sport of sport and gave a lightness and humour to an otherwise dull page in the papers of the days before Ring and Al."

In his history of publisher Charles Scribner's, Roger Burlingame, after praising *Scribner's Magazine,* newly designed in 1928, says that it published "some of the best material in its history. [Ernest] Hemingway [1899–1961], F. Scott Fitzgerald,* Ring Lardner, Don Marquis (1878–1937), Zona Gale (1874–1938), Tom and James Boyd [Thomas Boyd (1898–1935) and James Boyd (1888–1944)] gave it their best stories." The reality is that none of Lardner's stories appeared in that magazine.

Martin Seymour-Smith concludes thus about Jack Keefe's letters to Al: "They are not more vile than human beings can actually be and Lardner's ear for midwest vernacular is masterly." George W. Hilton summarizes the contention of Isaac Edgar Clark, author of an unpublished 1944 University of Texas M.A. thesis on Lardner's handling of language. Clark argues that Keefe's sudden over-dividing of words, for example, "a lone, "a long," "a bout," "an other," "a way," ad nauseam, and his omitting apostrophes are crafted by Lardner to reflect Keefe's exposure in schools to proper English, his imperfect apprehension of it, and his experiments with wording he thinks may be right.

One may conclude that Clark's theory is more interesting than persuasive.

Donald Elder advocates this two-pronged approach to *You Know Me Al* for alert readers: "In the character of Jake Keefe, Ring reduced the baseball hero to purely human dimensions. It may be that people take an unaccountable pleasure in seeing their idols diminished; it brings them closer. But it is probable that most people liked the Keefe stories simply because they were funny. Nevertheless to discerning readers they were a great deal more than that; they exploded the myth of the baseball hero, although they did him no visible damage, to judge by his continued popularity. And Jack Keefe is not merely a baseball player; he is an average American, and there are millions of him outside ball parks." To make Elder's comments a propos now, one should add the following: Not many of today's overpaid major-league baseball players are role models; and, unlike Keefe, too few of them are average Americans.

John Lardner, Jr., concerned with the baseball part of his father's masterpiece, says that "all the essential truth about ball-playing can be found in *You Know Me Al.* Its broader values to one side, there has never been a sounder baseball book. The story flows along with unpretentious smoothness. But if you stop to pick over the accounts of ball games, you see that each detail is correct in relation to place, weather, time of year, and the hitting, pitching, or fielding idiosyncrasies of each of a hundred players. Baseball strategy is set down as accurately as the speech and characters of Keefe, his friends, his girls, and his in-laws. I have never read a piece of baseball fiction, besides this one, in which there was no technical mistake." All true, if the reader makes allowances for fictitious Keefe's inaccurate commentary on real-life baseball figures, of whom there are 79 — from Nicholas Altrock to Henry Zimmerman. Apt here is Matthew J. Bruccoli's critical perception: "Lardner's custom of populating his stories with fictional characters and actual figures buttressed the authenticity of his fiction, which dealt with men working at their trade."

Walton R. Patrick, after analyzing Jack Keefe, concludes thus: "The ironic refrain 'You know me Al' runs through the book as a reminder that Jack holds a false image of himself, but that refrain is counterbalanced by the equally persistent cry for sympathy: 'Al, I am up against it again.'" More often, he laments, "I don't know where I am going to head in at." Patrick continues: "Being what he is, Jack is doomed eternally to be up against it, so that the underdog role he plays evokes both laughter and sighs, as Lardner clearly intended it to."

After much discerning commentary on *You Know Me Al,* George W. Hilton notes this: "The set [of six epistolary stories] ends as Keefe characteristically goes off on a world voyage contrary to his original intentions. Keefe had been drawn so well, and his path so clearly set, that sequels were inevitable." *You Know Me Al* was so popular that Lardner wrote a Bell Syndicate comic strip called "You Know Me, Al" (September 22, 1922–September 26, 1925), appearing in over a hundred newspapers and earning Lardner about $20,000 annually. Keefe as minor-leaguer turned major-leaguer triggers Douglas Robinson's protracted theory about majoritarianism vs. minoritarianism, in baseball and in life. (Sources: Bruccoli, ix; Burlingame, 223; Doran, 252; Elder, 118, 176–177; Hilton, 9, 169; Lardner, Jr., 14; Caruthers [1995], 162; Patrick, 49; Robinson, 118–127; Seymour-Smith, 203)

YOUMANS, VINCENT (1898–1946). New York–born popular composer. Early in life, Youmans was a runner for Wall Street brokers. He served in the U.S. Navy during World War I, at which time he composed and produced musical shows for navy personnel. His hit musicals include *Two Little Girls in Blue* (1921); *No, No, Nanette* (1925, revived 1971), which featured the songs "Tea for Two" and "I Want to Be Happy"; *Hit the Deck* (1927); *Great Day* (1929); *Smiles* (1930); and *Take a Chance* (1932). His most endearing song is "Without a Song" (1929). He also provided music for shows by Florenz Ziegfeld.* Youmans' later creativity was diminished owing to his increasing addiction to alcohol and his abortive decision to live on his life-insurance dividends. At least nine movies (1930–1955) contain music by Youmans.

Lardner knew, liked, and admired Vincent Youmans, who is mentioned in "Poodle" and "Rhythm." In "Second-Act Curtain," Booth, a lyricist, suddenly thinks up a melody, phones "Mr. Youmans," and whistles to learn if he's heard it; Youmans replies that he composed it for *Smiles.* This is an in-joke: Donald Elder notes that Lardner wrote lyrics for six songs in *Smiles,* produced by Ziegfeld. Elder also reports, as does Jonathan Yardley, that arguments between Youmans and Ziegfeld hampered Lardner's efforts to cooperate with the two hotheads (1930). Ring Lardner Jr. mentions Youmans in his biography of the Lardner family. (Sources: Elder, 265–268; Lardner,

Jr., 174, 200; Caruthers [1995], 228; Yardley, 302, 342, 343)

YOUNG ("Back to Baltimore"). He pitches for the Boston Braves. Dixon, then manager, told inept William Baker, Jr., when he joined the team, to take batting practice with Young, who was fast but wild. Dixon wanted a pitch to hit and disable Baker, but no accident ensued.

YOUNG, DENTON TRUE "CY" (1867–1955). He was a legendary major-league baseball pitcher. George W. Hilton reports that Young pitched for "Cleveland of the National League" (1890–1898), the St. Louis Cardinals (1899–1900), the Boston Red Sox (1901–1908), the Cleveland Naps (1909–1911), and the Boston Braves (1911). He amassed incredible records: 511 wins and 313 losses, 816 games started, 753 complete games, 77 shutouts, etc. Young managed the Red Sox (1907). He was elected to the Baseball Hall of Fame (1937). Hilton notes that "[t]he modern award for outstanding pitcher of the year was named in Young's honor in 1956."

In "Sick 'Em," the narrator jokes that when Smitty began to pitch badly against "the Athaletics," "Cy Young could of run to the plate as fast as this bird throwed." In "The Battle of Texas," Keefe jokes that slow railroad trains in Texas "run like old Cy Young was paceing them." Such remarks are owing to Cy Young's obesity and consequent slowness of base running. Young, however, claimed that he had to retire only because he grew too fat to field bunts. (Sources: *Baseball Encyclopedia*, 713, 2499; Hilton, 239)

THE YOUNG IMMIGRUNTS (*Saturday Evening Post,* January 31, 1920; YI). (Characters: Bill, Bill, David, Mr. Duffy, Father, Dr. Heywood, Mrs. Heywood, Artie Hofman, John, Mother, Mr. Yost.)

Preface. "The Father" writes that the author, "Ring W. Lardner, Jr.," born August 19, 1915, was about four when the manuscript was found in November, 1919. The Father mentions that he is more pleasant and wittier than described here, and that he retyped the sloppy manuscript.

Chapter 1. "My Parents." One of my married parents is attractive; the other "tall and skiny," "swarty," with big feet and owl eyes. Father got back from seeing the fight between Jack Dempsey* and "Jessie" Willard* in Toledo. My brothers are John, 7, Jimmie, 4, and David, "almost nothing." I am 4 and named after Father but called "Bill thank God." We kids "razed hell" in Chicago when my parents were gone to Connecticut to buy "a costly home." Our nurse said, "lamely," we behaved fine.

Chapter 2. "Starting Gaily." Father reports "sports of all sorts," wrote up "the worst series," then returned to Indiana, where the family "spent ... the summer on my granmother." He was "rarther cross," having "bet on the wite sox." Father told Mother we'd start east when he was ready. He bought a car. Mother ordered our nurse to take John, Jimmy, and David east by train. She, Father, and I would drive. Our nurse looked "gastly." Leaving Monday from "Goshen Indiana" by car, we planned to stay that night with my uncle in Detroit, go by boat to Buffalo and drive via Middlebury to Connecticut. We stopped past Coldwater by "1 side of the road" to lunch on "costly viands ... fernished by my grate ant"—"frid chicken," milk, and doughnuts. Father pleased me by saying "in calm tones" that we'd stop to eat at Ypsilanti, where the "normal school" is. I hoped to see what "normal people ... are like." We went south to Ann Arbor. Mother mistook its football field for Ypsilanti, and "smirk[ed]" when corrected by Father with "a corse jesture." We "stoped" at my uncle Bill's fraternity house in Ann Arbor and took him to supper at a hotel. Father phoned Mr. Yost, Michigan's football coach. He came and talked football, a "subjeck" Mother interrupted by mentioning the league of nations. We drove past Ypsilanti and were "in frunt" of our "ant and uncles" Detroit house at "nerly midnight." They "set ... since 7" waiting up.

Chapter 3. "Lake Erie." I must "exclaim to my readers" about Buffalo, where "9 oclock ... is only 8 oclock in Goshen ... as Buffalo peaple are qeer." My uncle, who "digs soors or something," found that Father must drive "the car on the board of the boat" by 3. With "nerves of steal," he did so, then waited for us. My uncle got us "to the worf" at "nerly 5." Mother "arsked" what Father had been doing. "Haveing a highball," he said, presenting "a wry smile." A "hub bub" began at "the gangs plank." Many "throwed rice." Father, who "seams to know everything," said "Bride and glum [were] going to Niagara Falls." We "steem[ed] up the river." To my mother's query whether "Canada [is] over there," Father, "explodeing a cough," said it wasn't "the Austrian Tyrol." I overheard bride and glum talking "in the porch" of the ship. Glum: Are you warm enough? Bride: "I am comfertible"; when do we get to Buffalo? Glum: 9; are you warm enough? Bride: "[C]omfertible; when to Buffalo? Glum: 9; it's cold here for you. Bride "replid": Maybe. They left for "the spacious parlers." Mother wondered to Father if the bride will be sufficiently warm 8 years hence. Father: Perhaps the weather will change; are you warm? Mother's "catchy reply": No. Next morning, we had "brekfus" and soon were at the Buffalo "worf."

Chapter 4. "Buffalo to Rochester 76.4." Glum looked at "his costly watch," and bride and glum left "out of my life." A fellow "with a flagrant Adams apple" told Father where to get gas for our "costly moter." We "filled with gas it was 27 cents" and headed for Rochester on what Father said "barshly" were "grate roads." Mother agreed "with a knowing wink." We approached Batavia, with Father "sloughing down." When Mother "coyly" hoped for lunch here, Father "cough[ed]" "in Rochester," where we "stoped ... and shared a costly lunch."

Chapter 5. "My Father's Idear." Father "halled out his map," but his "grate idear" of avoiding Syracuse and heading east through Lyon became "a holycost of the first water." We dead-ended at a stalled train. Father whispered "the 4 Horses of the Apoplex," Mother "mustard ... curage" to suggest a u-turn. Father's answer "I cant spell." We found "a dirty mechanic" who told blushing Father he could go via Geneva to Syracuse and repeated these directions when Father wondered about "a short cut." You could send all our "conversation" by "7 that evening" in a day telegram to Syracuse "for 30 cents."

Chapter 6. "Syracuse to Hudson 183.2." Father "weedle[d]" a room with bath at a Syracuse hotel. While we were in the "dinning room" having "a late and futile supper," a man "reckonized" Father. He was Mr. Duffy and tried to get Father to "boxing matchs ... that night." Father said he was busy. Mother "quaintly" asked where Father met Mr. Duffy. Father: In Boston, where else, since he was named Duffy? Next morning we saved time by walking through "purring rain" to where Father "horded the car." Mother "chuckled" that we'd die of cold. Father: "What of it[?]." He drove us "charming[ly]" past Oneida, which "he pronounced ... like ... a biscuit." On to Utica. Mrs. Heywood drove past us in "a closed car," unlike our wet one. She "stoped," and Mother introduced me as Bill, "the third [son]," and remembered when Dr. Heywood treated me for "that slite attack of obesity." On to Herkimer, where it rained "with renude vigger." Mother suggested lunch there. So Father drove us on to Little Falls. He was soaked not only by rain but also for "5 for that [hotel] room," where we got into dry clothes at Mother's "informal" suggestion. After "a meger lunch," on past Fonda, Amsterdam, and Schenectady. Mother mentioned Albany and asked who was governor. Father: Smith. Mother "sulkily": "Queer name." Father was upset when a talkative policeman gave directions over the river to New York. I won't "repete the conversation" on the way to Hudson.

Chapter 7. "Hudson." We were on Hudon's "main street" when a man aged 12 "hoped on the runing board" and directed us to a hotel. It was full. Across "the st" a "woman agrede to hord us for the night." The 12-year-old took Father to a garage to leave the car. Judging "from the viands," our supper, "finely," was late. Mother asked for us to be "called at ½ past 5." Our "lanlady" while "useing her handkerchief": "[I]f I am awake." Noise and "gulish screaks" made us "more than ready" to leave next morning. We last saw the "lanlady" in her "bear feet" and "sredded night gown."

Chapter 8. "Hudson to Yonkers 106.5." Father took "½ a hour" to get our "costly moter," said the garage was locked, and had to "roust him." Mother "quired ... barshfully": How'd you find him? Father's "posthumous reply": By using "the brains god gave me." At "brekfus" in Rhinebeck, Mother asked what the next town was. Father: "Pokippsie." Mother wanted to buy "a koop for David" there. Father got ill-tempered when "myself and mother" did buy David a koop and me a "kap." When Mother said my "kap" made me look "cute," Father "replid ... tenderly," "What of it[?]" In Peekskill, Father said his cousin "gos to school" there. "What of It[?]," Mother rejoined, "with a loud cough." Father spoke of "steem engines" in Harmon, causing Mother to regard Father "with ill consealed admiration." He commented on prisoners in Ossining and John D. Rockefeller's Tarrytown estate. In Yonkers he said "the ruling class" is represented here by umpire Bill Klem and referee Bill Langford.

Chapter 9. "The Bureau of Manhattan." We went beyond "Spuyten Duyvil" into "the Bureau of Manhattan." Giving "a quaint smirk," Mother asked Father to confide in her his plans. Father: I'll leave you at the 125th Street train station, to wait for the others, and Bill and I will drive to open our house in "Grenitch," then you get the "4 4" train to "Grenitch," and we'll meet you at the station.

Chapter 10. "N. Y. to Grenitch 500.0." Father and I were so confused that we neared Pittsfield. "Are you lost daddy[?]" "Shut up he explained."

A New Rochelle "policeman with falling archs" told us to get to "Grenitch Conn" by taking "the Boston post." Father said he "all ready subscribed to one out of town paper."

Chapter 11. "How It Ended." We met the train and "helped the bulk of the famly off." The nurse had "a slite stager" when asked about their train trip. Mother was mad that Father forgot to buy David some milk. Father "accidently" kicked me when I told "mudder" that "We got lost." I boasted to Jimmie I saw our house first. John said he and David "crid" on the train. My mother coughed saying I was a "good boy." Now "fare well to the characters in this book."

Donald Phelps rightly, though truly neatly verbosely, contends that the lingo of the supposed narrator of *The Young Immigrunts* constitutes "a magically accurate rendering of the polymorphous glamor of language," though admittedly "precocious [in] ... a little boy." Lardner's strained effort is based on a move that he, his wife, their four sons, and the sons' nurse made from Indiana to a rented house in Greenwich, Connecticut. In the story, Lardner parodies *The Young Visiters; or, Mr. Salteena's Plan* (1919), by Daisy Ashford, age nine, with a preface by Sir James Barrie (1860–1937). Donald Elder describes Daisy's book as something Lardner relished and could spoof, with its "misspellings" and "the high-flown language of a Victorian novel." Elder adds that Lardner's work, however, goes beyond parody to become "a wonderful burlesque of ordinary domestic life based on the hilariously trivial details of an auto trip from Goshen to 'Grenitch.'" Ring Lardner Jr. says that his father didn't believe any child wrote *The Young Visiters*. Lardner's son adds that *The Young Immigrunts* "is a skillful parody that ... stands up by itself" with no need for readers to read "the original." Then, however, he compares *The Young Visiters* and *The Young Immigrunts*, arriving at two conclusions. First, Lardner's parody is very thorough. But second, because of "prudishness," Lardner strictly avoids what Miss Ashford's book reveals, which is "unconscious" but "slightly salacious" sexual innuendoes. Jonathan Yardley agrees that *The Young Visiters* was "a sitting duck for a spoof," and says that the humor in that spoof lies in the narrator's "characterization of his father, his eccentric spellings and his child's-eye view." Lisa Chaney, in her biography of Barrie, asserts that he received, read, and enjoyed "a typescript he had from a publisher, who described it as the 'unaided' work of a girl of nine," and further that "Barrie found the little book so amusing he agreed to write a preface for it." Edward A. Martin says that behind the burlesque features of *The Young Immigrunts* "was Lardner's growing, embittered sense of the dissolution, the near-chaos, the incoherence of American life." Maxwell Geismar, after surveying Lardner's oeuvre, sadly suggests that "[p]erhaps the typical climax of Lardnerian courtship occurs in 'The Young Immigrunts.'" (Sources: Chaney, 329, 330; Elder, 165, 165–166; Geismar, 13; Lardner, Jr., 102–104; Martin, 161; Phelps, 93; Yardley, 221)

ZEIDER, ROLLIE (*The Young Immigrunts*). It is mentioned that Rollie Zeider has such a big nose that he shouldn't attract attention to faces by calling the narrator's father "owl eyes."

Rollie Hubert Zeider (1883–1967) played baseball for the Chicago White Sox (1910–1912), the White Sox and the New York Yankees (1913), and the Chicago Cubs (1916–1918). Donald Elder and Jonathan Yardley provide evidence that Lardner knew and admired Zeider. (Sources: *Baseball Encyclopedia*, 1771; Elder, 72, 83, 85; Yardley, 92, 175).

ZIEGFELD, FLORENZ ("FLO," "ZIGGIE") (1867–1932). Chicago-born theatrical manager-producer. When a youth, Ziegfeld produced a show of dancing chickens (1889), which authorities soon closed because he was inspiring his chickens to dance by electrifying their dance grid. He promoted musical attractions at the Chicago Columbian Exposition (1893). He vacationed in Europe (1906), gambled successfully in Monte Carlo, established a stable of racehorses, lost everything, and returned home to work. As a theater manager he made many American and European performers famous, while developing a personal style of extravagances, eccentricities, and sexual dalliances. With *The Follies of 1907*, an early Broadway musical revue, Ziegfeld introduced the first of 20 annual *Ziegfeld Follies*. Eva Tanguay,* whom Lardner mentions in *Treat 'Em Rough*, was featured in the 1907 *Follies*. Eddie Cantor (1892–1964), Lardner's Long Island neighbor and friend, starred in the 1916, 1917, and 1918 *Follies*. Ziegfeld's wives were the publicity-hound French actress Anna Held (1873–1918; married 1897? or 1901?—divorced 1912) and the canny American actress Billie Burke (1885–1970, married 1914). Ziegfeld produced cabaret and dinner-theater revues and traditional musical comedies such as *Sally* (1920), *Show Boat* (1927), *Whoopee* (1928), and *Bitter Sweet* (1929). When sound movies were perfected, Ziegfeld produced *Follies* movies in Hollywood.

Lardner and Ziegfeld had a long, troubled professional relationship. Donald Elder reports that Lardner saw Ziegfeld's *Follies* on tour in Chicago (1907), attended "every annual edition ... thereafter," knew and admired Bert Williams,* a Ziegfeld African-American performer, and wrote music and lyrics for Williams. Elder wonders "if they ever reached the stage." Lardner alludes to Williams in "The Golden Honeymoon." The year Williams died, Lardner began writing for Ziegfeld, and Elder says that in doing so Lardner "was to meet with continued frustrations." In *The Big Town*, the comedian Jimmy Ralston boasts of knowing and being underpaid by Ziggy Ziegfeld for his Follies performances. Marjorie Farnsworth writes that "Florenz vastly underrated the ability of Ring Lardner," failed to make good use of work Lardner prepared for the 1917 *Follies*, and later unsuccessfully sought help from Lardner when Ziegfeld and Vincent Youmans* were having difficulties with their musical comedy *Smiles* (1930). For the 1922 *Follies* Lardner co-wrote the book and wrote five sketches. One was used, one mangled, and three eliminated. In "The Dames" (*Hearst's International*, March 1923), Lardner writes about attending *Follies* rehearsals and associating with the dancers. Also, he and Gene Buck* collaborated on a play starring Fannie Brice (1891–1951), singer and comic whom Ziegfeld first promoted. Buck and Lardner converted his *Gullible's Travels* into an inept play, which Buck said he sold (1925) to Ziegfeld, who wanted to convert it into a musical comedy. Lardner declined. Lardner published "A Day with Conrad Green" later that year. Since villainous Conrad Green is transparently patterned after Ziegfeld, Lardner figured their friendship would be at an end. Not so. Ziegfeld beseeched Buck to resume work with Lardner on the Gullible effort, but frequent and protracted trouble with composer Youmans stymied the project. Lardner remained friends with Youmans. Lardner came close to writing sketches for the redoubtable W. C. Fields (1880–1946), originally another Ziegfeld protegé. Elder provides details about Ziegfeld, Lardner, and *Smiles*, Ziegfeld's final show. Partly because Lardner respected Youmans' accompanying music, he wrote some lyrics for the Boston opening of *Smiles* and more for its New York revision. Stars in *Smiles* included Fred Astaire (1899–1987) and his sister Adele Astaire (1898–1981). Jonathan Yardley says that *Smiles* "ran sixty-three performances [in New York] before dying a well-deserved death. It was the end of Ring's Broadway career." (See also Berlin, Irving; Davies, Marion; "A Day with Conrad Green"; "The Facts"; Green, Conrad; "Liberty Hall"; Sears, Paul; Shearer, Norma; "There Are Smiles.")

Lardner did not live to see *The Great Ziegfeld* (1936), a splendid movie starring William Powell (1892–1984) as Ziegfeld, Luise Rainer (b. 1910) as Anna Held, Myrna Loy (1905–1993) as Billie Burke, and William Demarest (1892–1983) as Gene Buck,* and with Eddie Cantor and Leon Errol (1881–1951) in supporting roles. (Sources: Elder, 246, 247, 262–266, and passim; Farnsworth, 73, 148, 150–151, and passim; Caruthers [1995], 228; Lardner, Jr., 144, 199–200; Leiter, II, 1028–1034; Streissguth, 386; Yardley, 239, 344)

ZIMMERMAN In "The Busher Comes Back," Keefe complains that when in the White Sox game against the Cubs he pitched a ball over Zimmerman's head, "he must of shut his eyes and throwed his bat," because he got a hit. In a later game, Keefe "whiffed Zimmerman three times." In "My Roomy," Zimmerman, called Heinie, is one of several Chicago baseball players rejecting Buster Elliott as a roommate. In "Horseshoes," Zimmerman plays third base for the Cubs. When Zimmerman breaks a leg, Speed Parker gets lucky and replaces him.

Henry ("Heinie") Zimmerman (1887–1969) played for the Chicago Cubs (1907–1915), the Cubs and the New York Giants (1916), and the Giants (1917–1919). Donald Elder notes that Lardner knew Zimmerman well, liked him, and wrote about him in his column "In the Wake of the News." George W. Hilton adds that the broken leg is fictional and that Zimmerman was banned from baseball because of his part in the 1919 Black Sox Scandal. (Sources: *Baseball Encyclopedia*, 1772–1773); Elder, 61–63, 108–109; Hilton, 92, 399)

"ZONE OF QUIET" (*Cosmopolitan*, June 1925; RU). (Characters: Henry J. Belden, B.F., B.F., Peewee Byers, Doctor Cox, Barney Gallant, G.F., Miss Helen Halsey, Doctor Holland, Mrs. Judson, Miss Eleanor Lyons, Marian, George Morse, Charley Pierce, Roy Stewart, Tyler.)

Doctor Cox leaves sleeping medication with nurse Miss Eleanor Lyons, tells her not to talk to her patient, a man, about 40, recovering after surgery. The doctor departs. Miss Lyons immediately tells her patient that she's off at 7 P.M., will see a show with her G.F., and recommends night-nurse Miss Halsey. Miss Lyons adds that she trained in Baltimore, where Doctor Holland (when she asked him) replied that he hoped she wasn't as dumb as she looked. The show she'll see with her G.F. is *What Price Glory?* Roy Stewart, her G.F. Marian's B.F., got the tickets. The patient asks says he's probably "a D.F. not to know" but asks anyway "what a B.F. and G.F. are?" Miss Lyons agrees he's dumb not knowing G.F. means Girl Friend and B. F. means boy friend.

Next morning, Miss Lyons tells her patient that Tyler, an "interne," said her ankles are as pretty as Helen's. Helen? Miss Halsey, of course. Helen was engaged to a Tufts College fellow. Why "mope" about him? He's been dead four years. When asked, the patient says he's reading *Vanity Fair.* Miss Lyons thought *Vanity Fair* was a magazine, hasn't read it, since she's making Christmas presents for her sister, married and old at 29. A former B.F., Charley Pierce, once cleverly said we're "a long time dead." A former G.F. lied to Charley about her, then married Charley. After *What Price Glory?* Miss Lyons partied at Barney Gallant's, where her G.F. Marian's B.F. Roy asked for Miss Lyons's hospital phone number while Marian powdered her nose.

Next morning, Miss Lyons gushes to her patient. She danced all hours last night with — he guessed it — Roy. A B.F. in Washington told her that dancing with her "was just like dancing with nothing" — meaning, get it?, she was "slender," not "stout." Dancing with Marian, whom she likes all right, resembles "moving the piano." Miss Lyons reminisces about Henry J. Belden, a Great Neck case she handled. He died. It's "a scream" that her "last five cases ... has all died." Miss Halsey even expressed worry when "you was operated." Miss Lyons hates when her patients, especially men, die. Mrs. Judson was the only patient whose death she didn't mind. Nephritis. Miss Lyons was sick last night; Roy's B.F. — Roy brought him and another girl — gave her scotch after gin. She tried to phone Marian, to see what she knows, but she's on a case in Hudson, New York.

Next morning, Miss Lyons appears upset.

Next morning, she gloats to her patient about dancing all last night. No, not with Roy. With George Morse. Know him? Marian is engaged to "dumb-bell" Roy. Miss Lyons liked Roy's "great line," but "you don't want to live with a clown." Morse, the new B.F., works for J. P. Morgan. She wonders whether her patient has finished "that book yet."

What Price Glory? (1924) was the popular, influential play by Laurence Stallings (1894–1968) and Maxwell Anderson (1888–1959). Its impressive anti-war bitterness would be lost on Miss Lyons, but not on Jack Spears, whose commentary on the play and the subsequent silent Fox movie classic (1926) is gripping. The film was directed by Raoul Walsh (1887–1980), and starred Dolores Del Rio (1905–1981), Edmund Lowe (1890–1971), and Victor McLaglen 1886–1959). In a letter to F. Scott Fitzgerald* and his wife (January 9, 1925), Lardner reports having seen *What Price Glory?* the play, pronounces it "a bear," and predicts it should "beat a record or come near." Lardner makes "Zone of Quiet" reflect Roaring-Twenties times by also dropping the names of Bugs Baer,* movie stars Richard Barthelmess (1895–1963), Julia Hoyt (1897?–1955), and Norma Talmadge,* band leader Paul Whiteman,* and speakeasy entrepreneur Barney Gallant.* Lardner even mentions "the Algonquin," the celebrated literary club, whose members admired him.

Jonathan Yardley reports that Lardner was hospitalized early in 1925, suffered the gabbling of a dumb nurse who asked him about *Vanity Fair,* which he was reading, and so on — all of which surfaced in "Zone of Quiet." (Sources: Caruthers [1995], 170–171, 172; Langman and Borg, 647–648; Spears, 56; Yardley, 289)

Bibliography

The Baseball Encyclopedia, 10th ed. New York: Macmillan, 1996.

Berg, A. Scott. *Max Perkins: Editor of Genius*. New York: E. P. Dutton, 1978.

Berryman, John. "The Case of Ring Lardner: Art and Entertainment." *Commentary* 22 (November 1956): 416–423.

Bibesco, Elizabeth. "Lament for Lardner." *Living Age* 345 (December 1933): 366–368.

Boyd, Thomas. "Lardner Tells Some New Ones." *Bookman* 59 (July 1924): 601–602.

Bruccoli, Matthew J., ed. "Introduction" to *Ring Around the Bases: The Complete Baseball Stories of Ring Lardner*. Columbia: University of South Carolina Press, 1992.

_____, and Richard Layman. *Ring W. Lardner: A Descriptive Bibliography*. Pittsburgh: University of Pittsburgh Press, 1976.

Burlingham, Roger. *Of Making Many Books: A Hundred Years of Reading, Writing, and Publishing*. 1946. University Park: Pennsylvania State University Press, 1997.

Carpenter, Harry. *Boxing: A Pictorial History*. Chicago: Henry Regnery, 1975.

Caruthers, Clifford M., ed. *Ring Around Max: The Correspondence of Ring Lardner & Max Perkins*. DeKalb: Northern Illinois University Press, 1973.

_____, ed. *Letters of Ring Lardner*. Washington: Orchises, 1995.

Chaney, Lisa. *Hide-and-Seek with Angels: A Life of J. M. Barrie*. London: Hutchinson, 2005.

Cowlishaw, Brian T. "The Reader's Role in Ring Lardner's Rhetoric." *Studies in Short Fiction* 31 (Spring 1994): 207–216.

Cox, James M. "Toward Vernacular Humor." *Virginia Quarterly Review* 46 (Spring 1970): 311–330.

Dardis, Tom. *The Thirsty Muse: Alcohol and the American Writer*. New York: Ticknor & Fields, 1989.

Davies, Peter. *Davies' Dictionary of Golfing Terms*. New York: Simon and Schuster, 1980.

Dawidoff, Nicholas, ed. *Baseball: A Literary Anthology*. New York: Literary Classics of the United States, 2002.

Dickson, Paul. *The New Dickson Baseball Dictionary*. New York: Harcourt Brace, 1999.

Doran, George H. *Chronicles of Barabbas: 1884–1934*. New York: Harcourt, Brace, 1935.

Douglas, Donald. "Ring Lardner as Satirist," *Nation* 122 (May 26, 1926): 584–585.

Elder, Donald. *Ring Lardner: A Biography*. Garden City, NY: Doubleday, 1956.

Elfers, James E. *The Tour to End All Tours: The Story of Major League Baseball's 1913–1914 World Tour*. Lincoln and London: University of Nebraska Press, 2003.

Evans, Elizabeth. *Ring Lardner*. New York: Frederick Ungar, 1979.

Faber, Charles F., and Richard B. Faber. *Spitballers: The Last Legal Hurlers of the Wet One*. Jefferson, NC: McFarland, 2006.

Fadiman, Clifton. "Ring Lardner and the Triangle of Hate." *The Nation* 136 (March 22, 1933): 315–317.

Farnsworth, Marjorie. *The Ziegfeld Follies*. New York: G. P. Putnam's Sons, 1956.

Fleitz, David L. *Shoeless: The Life and Times of Joe Jackson*. Jefferson, NC: McFarland, 2001.

Garland, Brock. *War Movies*. New York: Facts on File, 1987.

Geismar, Maxwell. "Ring Lardner: Like Something Was Going to Happen," pp. 3–36 in *Writers in Crisis: The American Novel, 1925–1940*. Boston: Houghton, Mifflin, 1947.

Goren, Charles. *The Sports Illustrated Book of Bridge*. New York: Time Incorporated, 1961.

Gropman, Donald. *Say It Ain't So, Joe! The Story of Shoeless Jackson*. Boston and Toronto: Little, Brown, 1979.

Hemingway, Ernest. "Defense of Dirty Words: A Cuban Letter." *Esquire* 2 (September 1934): 19, 158B, 158D.

Hensley, Donald M. *Burton Rascoe*. New York: Twayne, 1970.

Herbst, Josephine. "Introduction" to Ring W. Lardner, *Gullible's Travels, Etc.* Chicago & London: University of Chicago Press, 1965.

Higgs, Robert J. *Laurel & Thorn: The Athlete in*

American Literature. Lexington: University Press of Kentucky, 1981.

Hilton, George W., ed. *The Annotated Baseball Stories of Ring W. Lardner, 1914–1919*. Stanford, CA: Stanford University Press, 1995.

The Home Coming of Charles A. Comiskey, James C. Callahan, and John J. McGraw, compiled by R. W. Lardner and Edward G. Heeman. Chicago: Edward G. Heeman, 1914.

Horne, Gerald. *The Final Victim of the Blacklist: John Howard Lawson, Dean of the Hollywood Ten*. Berkeley: University of California Press, 2006.

Katz, Ephraim. *The Film Encyclopedia*. 5th ed., by Fred Klein and Ronald Dean Nolen. New York: Collins, 2005.

Langman, Larry, and Ed Borg. *Encyclopedia of American War Films*. New York: Garland, 1989.

Lardner, John. "Introduction" to Ring W. Lardner, *You Know Me Al*. New York: Macmillan, 1960.

Lardner, Ring, Jr. *The Lardners: My Family Remembered*. New York: Harper & Row, 1976.

Leiter, Samuel L., ed. *The Encyclopedia of the New York Stage, 1920–1930*. 2 vols. Westport, CT: Greenwood Press, 1985.

Lewisohn, Ludwig. *The Story of American Literature*. New York: Modern Library, 1939.

Light, Jonathan Fraser. *The Cultural Encyclopedia of Baseball*. Jefferson, NC: McFarland, 1997.

Martin, Edward A. *H.L. Mencken and the Debunkers*. Athens: University of Georgia Press, 1984.

May, Charles E. "Lardner's HAIRCUT." *Explicator* 31 (May 1973): #69.

McCallum, John D., ed. *The Encyclopedia of World Boxing Champions Since 1882*. Radnor, PA: Chilton, 1975.

McBride, Joseph. *High and Inside: An A-to-Z Guide to the Language of Baseball*. Np: Contemporary Books, 1997.

Mencken, H. L. *The American Language*. New York: Alfred Knopf, 1919.

_____. "The Library." *American Mercury* 2 (July 1924): 376–383; 8 (June 1926): 251–255; 29 (June 1933): 251–255.

Overton, Grant. "Ring W. Lardner's Bell Lettres," *Bookman* 62 (September 1925): 44–49.

Patrick, Walton R. *Ring Lardner*. New York: Twayne, 1963.

Phelps, Donald. "Shut Up, He Explained." *Shenandoah* 29 (1978): 84–100.

Pritchett, V. S. "The Talent of Ring Lardner." *New Statesman* n.s. 57 (April 25, 1959): 580–581.

Quirk, Tom. *Coming to Grips with* Huckleberry Finn*: Essays on a Book, a Boy, and a Man*. Columbia and London: University of Missouri Press, 1993.

Robinson, Douglas. *Ring Lardner and the Other*. New York: Oxford University Press, 1992.

Seldes, Gilbert. "Introduction" to *The Portable Ring Lardner*. New York: Viking Press, 1946.

Seymour-Smith, Martin. *Who's Who in Twentieth Century Literature*. New York: McGraw-Hill, 1977.

Silverman, Jeff, ed. *Lardner on War*. Guilford, CT: Lyons Press, 2003.

Smith, Leverett T., Jr. "The Diameter of Frank Chance's Diamond: Ring Lardner and Professional Sports." *Journal of Popular Culture* 6 (Summer 1972): 133–156.

Sommers, Robert. *The U.S. Open: Golf's Ultimate Challenge*. New York: Atheneum, 1987.

Spears, Jack. *Hollywood: The Golden Era*. South Brunswick and New York: A. S. Barnes, 1971.

Streissguth, Tom. *The Roaring Twenties*. New York: Facts On File, 2001.

Sugar, Bert Randolph, ed. *The Ring: Record Book and Boxing Encyclopedia*. New York: Atheneum, 1981.

Van Doren, Carl. "Beyond Grammar: Ring W. Lardner, Philologist Among the Low-Brows." *Century* 106 (July 1923): 471–475.

Van Natta, Don, Jr. *First Off the Tee: Presidential Hackers, Duffers, and Cheaters from Taft to Bush*. New York: Public Affairs, 2003.

Weaver, John V. A. "Ring W. Lardner — Serious Artist." *Bookman* 54 (February 1922): 586–587.

Webb, Howard W., Jr. "The Development of a Style: The Lardner Idiom." *American Quarterly* 12 (Winter 1960): 482–492.

Wilson, Edmund. "Ring Lardner's American Characters," pp. 37–40 in *A Literary Chronicle: 1920–1950*. Garden City, NY: Doubleday & Company, 1956.

Yardley, Jonathan. *Ring: A Biography of Ring Lardner*. 1997. New York: Rowman & Littlefield, 2001.

Woolf, Virginia. *The Moment and Other Essays*. New York: Harcourt, Brace, 1948.

Index

Page references to main entries and important namings are in **boldface**. The name of each fictional character is followed by the title of the only work or the first work in which the character appears. Real-life athletes, others associated with sports, and other persons not Lardner's extended family are indexed by name without further identification. If a character in a fictional work is based on a real-life person, both character and person are separately indexed. Critics quoted or paraphrased are not indexed, nor are recipients of letters from Lardner.

www.ingramcontent.com/pod-product-compliance
Lightning Source LLC
Chambersburg PA
CBHW081401090726
47908CB00012B/2755

* 9 7 8 0 7 8 6 4 3 6 8 8 0 *